For
DADDY

Jov
Christmas

from
Mark

# HardCore

# HardCore

## 3 NOVELS

## THE KILL-OFF
## THE NOTHING MAN
## BAD BOY

*Jim Thompson*

Introduction by Roderick Thorp

DONALD I. FINE, INC.
*New York*

*Library of Congress Catalogue Card Number: 86-82111*

*ISBN: 1–55611–001–4*

*Manufactured in the United States of America*

*10 9 8 7 6 5 4 3 2 1*

This book is printed on acid free paper. The paper in this book meets the guidelines for permanence and durability of the Committee on Production Guidelines for Book Longevity of the Council on Library Resources.

# Contents

# Introduction

## *by Roderick Thorp*

TWO OF MY father's brothers were writers, and my grandfather before them. They worked for newspapers and magazines, free-lanced, pot-boiled and only did other jobs when they had to make ends meet. They considered themselves professionals. But none of my grandfather's children went to college; one of the two who were writers died leaving his wife a mountain of debt, and the other's only legacy was found on a shelf in a basement, a roll of small bills wadded in a coffee can.

Nothing any of the three men wrote remains available to readers today. Most American writers' lives can be summed up like that.

When Jim Thompson died on April 7, 1977, all of his work was out of print in the United States. But Jim Thompson was remembered by publishers and readers, and now his work is finding its way back into print, and Thompson's twenty-nine novels are getting the attention they deserve.

Twenty-nine novels. In one four-year period beginning in 1952, Jim Thompson produced thirteen novels and entertainments, and co-wrote Stanley Kubrick's first Hollywood feature, a gritty thriller called *The Killing.* Thompson wrote quickly but he was a careful writer, too. His longtime friend and agent, Jerry Bick, says, "Jim was the kind of man who would agree to write a letter for you for nothing, and then take eight days slaving over it."

Thompson occasionally had to do other work—in his young manhood he was a bellboy and an oil-field roustabout—but he wrote all of his life, selling his first short story at the age of fifteen, working on the N. Y. *Daily News* and the L. A. *Mirror* and, during the Roosevelt Era, heading the Oklahoma Writers' Project, when he wrote a pamphlet entitled *Economy of Scarcity.* So he had range as well as the stamina and determination that are absolutely necessary for this craft.

In 1941, thirty-five years old, ten years married and with no evidence in hand that he could write a novel, Thompson traveled to New York and talked a publisher into giving him a typewriter and a subsidy. Eight weeks later he delivered his first novel, *Now and On Earth,* the first of his three novels published in hardcover that didn't sell. With three children to support, Jim Thompson had to keep writing.

Thompson was before his time, which is to say that he had a vision of the world that was unpalatable to the mass-market audience accustomed to the moldy treacle of *Forever Amber, Captain from Castile* and the annual emissions of Frank Yerby, and of no interest to self-styled more "serious" readers who were snapping up the war-is-hell-but-the-army-is-worse malarkey being mass-produced by a gaggle of bright new names.

Thompson's vision makes him like nobody else. His is a world peopled with psychopathic killers, expensive sluts, crooked cops, moronic publishers (talk about literary risks!), filthy-minded doctors, cretins, perverts, obsessives— well, read today's paper. Thompson's novels don't have good guys, just anti- heroes and the women who deserve them. In *The Nothing Man,* Deborah Chasen is so horny for Clinton Brown that she tells him she's glad his wife has died. Clinton Brown doesn't have a penis. Then he kills Deborah Chasen. Or he thinks he does. Thompson is *always* like that. Most of us want to forget that the government tolerates a certain amount of insect parts and rodent feces in our wedding cakes. For Thompson, that information is essential to finding a meaning of life—and some meaning it is. Thompson's characters enjoy picking their noses. Why? Thompson won't buy into the lies we tell ourselves.

If Thompson's vision sentenced him to the low rent district of original paperback publication, that marketplace doomed him to an out-of-hand criti- cal rejection that helped stifle his voice. Yet what was wrong with original paperback publication was right for Thompson, too. It gave him an otherwise unavailable opportunity to keep going, and found him the readers who would later encourage others to read his books: writers like R. V. Cassill, Barry Giffort and Stephen King, and the moviemaker Stanley Kubrick.

Paperback originals brought a writer a top price of two or three thousand dollars. John D. MacDonald, Elmore Leonard and Louis L'Amour were at the top in their genres, but Jim Thompson was the master of the field, not submit- ting to the plot formulas editors were looking for, but very much constrained by the peculiar censorship of the period. The joke in those days was that the sex was all on the lurid covers that were designed to catch a buyer's eye. Inside, it was, "And so I kissed her, and kissed her again," followed by a new paragraph that began, "Later . . ." Thompson's books smolder anyway. He studied humanity, and understood the meaning of a downcast eye or a stam- mer. There is always a second level of experience below the surface action of a Thompson novel, just like life itself.

Most of the time he wrote cleanly, moving his story quickly, sparing us the self-indulgence of the florid prose the second-rater thinks is *style.* And Thomp- son remembers that the best novelists are always good reporters: setting the scene in *The Nothing Man,* he delivers as clear an account of the doings in the small daily newspaper as I have ever read. And finally, he *experiments: The Kill-Off* shifts point of view, which editors regard as dangerous because they think readers want somebody to root for. In *The Kill-Off,* Thompson is not only shifting point of view, he's advancing the story with every shift, a story that revolves fascinatingly around an old woman who refuses to get out of bed. Think about it for a moment: how can *anybody* write a novel like that?

Paperback originals cost a quarter or thirty-five cents, depending on the number of pages. There was no advertising except at the point of sale, where publishers' logos appeared on tin badges affixed to the revolving wire racks that held the books. Reviews were infrequent, confined to short paragraphs in journals the readers of the books didn't know existed. Thighs and cleavage spilling across the covers notwithstanding, the paperback originals of the '40s and '50s were the cleanest of the publishing business. "We shipped to the distributors, they loaded the racks, and that's all there was to it," recalls one veteran editor wistfully. "The great thing about paperback originals was the wonderful democracy of them. The readers could afford to be adventurous, and if they liked a writer, they'd come back to him." Leonard, L'Amour and MacDonald built followings that allowed them to become hardcover stars, but there was never a doubt that Jim Thompson was the king. "He was trying to make art, and he required very little work," one editor recalls. "His copy was very clean, and dealing with him was always easy and professional."

So what happened? What went wrong? Television killed paperback originals, along with pulp magazines, B movies, and 95% of the market for popular short fiction. Not being a genre writer, Jim Thompson had to turn to television itself to make a living. The co-writing credit on *The Killing* had been followed by another on the harrowing Kubrick film *Paths of Glory,* but Thompson's television work bears no such distinction. The Writers' Guild of America credits Jim Thompson for stories and co-writing on a half-dozen television series, only one of which, *Dr. Kildaire,* remains in the public memory at all.

Jim Thompson was a big man, six feet four, weighing 200 pounds. A strong man who had worked a lot of hard jobs in his youth. People who knew him in the last ten years of his life, however, say he aged prematurely. At 68 he looked 78, and you can see for yourself in the 1975 remake of Raymond Chandler's *Farewell, My Lovely,* which starred Robert Mitchum and the sultry English actress, Charlotte Rampling. Jim Thompson plays Judge Grayles, Rampling's husband, a once-powerful man now too old and weak even to protest when he catches Rampling and Mitchum wrapped in each other's arms. As Grayles, Thompson merely drops his eyes and backs out of the room. It's an agonizing moment even if you don't know anything about the performer. One recent viewer of the film who knew Thompson's work saw it as a strangely sad metaphor for Thompson's final relationship to the craft to which he had given his life. Or was it something else—something better? Raymond Chandler is all but sacred in the pantheon of American popular novelists. Was Thompson's only motion picture acting a signal to the knowing that the makers of *Farewell, My Lovely* were really trying? One of the makers was Jerry Bick.

"I got him the job because he needed the money," Bick says. "He was always broke."

*Broke* is relative. In those last years, three of Thompson's books were made into films. *The Getaway*—that's right, with Steve McQueen—*The Killer Inside Me,* and *Pop. 1280,* retitled *Coup de Torchon* (Clean Slate) by Bernard Tavernier, who moved the setting to Africa.

That last film had a ready-made market because French readers had discovered Thompson years before. In France—the French are ga-ga over American gangsterism and violence—Thompson is accepted as the equal of Chandler and Dashiell Hammett, if not their better. Chandler and Hammett wrote about cops and robbers and the husky-voiced dames around them. Like James M. Cain and France's own Louis-Ferdinand Celine, Jim Thompson writes about the violence and insanity in those who think they're regular folks. Nice guys —Republicans, even.

So what kind of a guy was Thompson himself? Jerry Bick says he was a man of "perfect integrity. He was absolutely the most honest, generous, gentle man I have ever known."

There's more, not a hint of a dark side so much as the whisper of how much Jim Thompson believed what he was saying. Bick again: "He was sensitive, even nervous. He was like a child, he couldn't bear the realities of everyday life."

Of course he drank. Writers drink. Five out of six of our dead Nobel laureates were drinkers, and the last didn't deserve the prize. Thompson probably managed himself as well as anyone with a drinking problem. "He fell asleep in the chair sometimes," Alberta Thompson says. "He was disappointed with the way his work was received, but we had our good times, too. We had vacations in New York and Las Vegas. He liked to go out to dinner and parties —you know, cocktail parties."

Was he a man who didn't know what to do with himself when he wasn't writing? Alberta Thompson, who is now 77 and a great-grandmother, was married to Jim Thompson for 46 years. "He *lived* for his writing," she says. "He wrote every day, eight hours a day, even when the words wouldn't come."

A man possessed by a vision the world was only beginning to buy when he died. He was prematurely aged, remember. There were two small strokes from which he mostly recovered—except he was no longer able to write. "The doctor, who was our friend, swore there was no cancer," Alberta Thompson says. "Jim just wasted away. After those two strokes when he found he couldn't write, my guess is that he just starved himself to death."

Jerry Bick believes that. So do I.

# THE
# KILL-OFF

# I

## KOSSMEYER

MOSTLY, SHE WAS a woman who loved scandal—and lived by it.

Luane Devore made a specialty of being impetuous, bold, headstrong and —she thought—sultry.

Mostly, though . . . It was Sunday, only two days after the season had opened, when Luane Devore telephoned. As usual, she sounded a little hysterical. As usual, she was confronted with a dire emergency which only I could handle. Significantly, however—or at least I thought it significant—she did not calm down when I told her to go to hell, and to stop acting like a damned fool.

"Please, Kossy," she burbled. "You must come! It's vitally important, darling. I can't talk about it over the telephone, but—"

"Why the hell can't you?" I cut in. "You talk about everything and everyone else over the phone. Now, lay off, Luane. I'm a lawyer, not a baby-sitter. I'm here on a vacation, and I'm not going to spend all my time listening to you moan and whine about a lot of imaginary problems."

She wept audibly I felt a very small twinge of conscience. The Devore estate didn't amount to anything any more. It had been years since I'd gotten a nickel out of her. So . . . well, you see what I mean. When people don't have anything —when they can't do anything for you—you kind of have to go a little easy on 'em.

"Now, take it easy, honey," I said. "Be a big girl for Kossy. The world ain't going to come to an end if I don't dash up there right now. It ain't going to kill you, is it?"

"Yes," she said. "Yes, it is!" And then she hung up with a wild sob.

I hung up also. I came out of the bedroom, crossed the living room and returned to the kitchen. Rosa was at the stove, her back turned to me. She was talking, ostensibly mumbling to herself but actually addressing me. It is a habit of hers, one she has resorted to more and more frequently during the twenty-odd years of our marriage. I listened to the familiar words . . . *hum* . . . *loafer* . . . *time-waster* . . . *thinks-nothing-of-his-wife-but* . . . and for the first time in a long time I was affected by them. I began to get sore—angry and sad. And a little sick on the inside.

"So I'm sorry," I said. "She's a client. She's in trouble. I've got no choice but to see her."

"A client, he says," Rosa said. "So, of course, everything else he must drop. She is his only client, is she not? His first case?"

"With a good lawyer," I said, "it is always the first case. Don't make such a production out of it, dammit. I'll be back in a little while."

3

"In a little while, he says," Rosa said. "In a little while, he was going to help with the unpacking. He was going to help clean up the cottage, and take his wife bathing and—"

"I will," I said. "Goddammit, you want me to put it in writing?"

"Listen to him," she said. "Listen to the great attorney curse at his wife. See how he acts, the great attorney, when it is his wife he deals with."

"Listen to yourself," I said. "See how you act."

She turned around unwillingly. I stood up and put on a performance, watching her face slowly turn red then white. I am pretty good at such mimicry. Painfully good, you might say. I have a talent for it; and when a man is only five feet tall, when he has had no formal law education—damned little formal education of any kind—he leaves no talent undeveloped.

"This is you," I said. "Mrs. Abie. Why don't you go on TV? Go into vaudeville? They love those characters."

"N-now—" she smiled weakly. "I guess I'm not that bad, Mister Smarty."

"Mister Smarty," I said. "Now, there's a good line. You just keep it up, keep building on that stuff, and we'll be all fixed up. We'll be getting a nice offer for our property."

"Maybe," she snapped, "we'd better not wait for an offer. If you're ashamed of your own wife, if you're so worried about what your friends may think of me—"

"What I'm ashamed of is someone that isn't my wife. This character you've slipped into. Goddammit, you're supposed to amount to something, and yet half the time you—"

I stopped myself short.

She said, "Listen to him, listen to the great attorney . . ." And then she caught herself.

We stood staring at each other. After a long moment, I started to break the silence; and the first word was a swear word and the second one was an ain't. I broke off again. "Look at who's talking," I said. "Me, telling you how to behave!"

She laughed and put her arms around me, and I put mine around her. "But you're right, darling," she murmured. "I don't know how I ever got into the habit of carrying on that way. You stop me if I do it any more."

"And you stop me," I said.

She warmed up the breakfast coffee, and we both had a cup. Chatting and smoking a cigarette while we drank it. Then, I got the car out of the garage, and headed up the beach road toward town.

Manduwoc is a seacoast town, a few hours train-ride from New York City. It is too far from the city for commuting; there are no local industries. According to the last census, the population was 1,280 and I doubt that it has increased since then.

It used to be quite a resort town, back before the war, but the number of summer visitors has declined steadily in recent years. The natives got a little too independent; they leaned a little too heavily on the gypping. So, what with so many places closer to the population centers, Manduwoc began to go downhill.

The largest hotel here has been boarded up for the past two summers. Some business establishments have closed down permanently; and at least a third of the beach cottages are never rented. There is still a considerable influx of vacationers, but nothing like there used to be. Practically the only people who come here now are those who own property here. People who, generally speaking, are out to save money rather than spend it.

The town proper sits a few hundred yards back from the ocean. Built around a courthouse square, it is adjoined, on the land side, by an area of summer estates, and, on the sea side, by the usual resort installations. These last include the aforementioned hotels and cottages, a couple of seafood restaurants, a boat-and-bait concession, a dance pavilion and so on.

Our cottage, which we own, is about three miles out. The others—the rent-cottages, I should say—are all close-in. I was approaching them, row upon row of identical clapboard structures, when a man stepped out onto the road and began to trudge toward the village. He was tall, stoop-shouldered, very thin. He had a mop of gray-black hair, and his angular, intelligent face was almost a dead white.

I pulled the car even with him and stopped. He went on walking, looking straight ahead. I called to him, "Rags! Rags McGuire!" And, finally, after another hail or two, he turned around.

He was frowning, in a kind of fiercely absent way. He came toward me slowly, his features twisted in that vacant scowl. And, then, suddenly, his face lit up with a smile of friendliness and recognition.

"Kossy! How are you, boy?" He climbed into the seat with me. "Where you been hiding yourself?"

I said that Rosa and I were just getting settled down; we'd be dropping by the pavilion as soon as we were finished. He beamed and slapped me on the back, and said that was the Kossy kid. And then he went completely silent. It wasn't an awkward silence. Not seemingly, that is, on his part. But there was something about it, something about his smile—and his eyes—that made me more ill at ease than I have ever been in my life.

"I don't suppose—" I hesitated. "I mean, is Janie with the band this summer?"

He didn't say anything for several seconds. Then, he said no, she wasn't with him. He had a new vocalist. Janie was staying in the city with the kids.

"I figure that gives her enough to do," he added. "Just bringing the kids up right, y'know. After all, you take a couple of boys that age, and a woman don't have time to—Yeah? You were saying, Kossy?"

"Nothing," I said. "I mean—well, the boys are all right, then?"

"All right?" He looked bewildered for a moment. Then, he laughed amiably. "Oh, I guess you saw that little story in the papers, huh? Well, that wasn't Janie. That wasn't my family."

"I see," I said. "I'm certainly glad to hear it, Rags."

"Ain't it hell, though?" he said musingly. "A guy wants some publicity—he knocks himself out to get some—and he just can't swing it. But let something phony come along, something that won't do him no good, y'know, and he'll make the papers every time."

"Yeah," I said. "That's the way it seems to go, all right."

"I thought about suing them," he said. "But then I thought, what the hell? After all, it was a natural mistake. It was the same name—names—see? And Janie does have a rep for tipping the bottle."

I was almost convinced. In fact, I'm not at all sure that I wasn't. There were probably any number of small-time band leaders named McGuire. It would be easy to confuse one with another, particularly in a case where a story had to be written largely from newspaper files. And that had been the case in this instance. The two boys had died in the crash. Janie—if it *was* Janie—had lived, but she had been in a coma for days.

Rags had me drop him off in front of a bar. I drove on through town, wondering, worrying, then mentally shrugging. He wasn't a close friend—not a friend at all, really. Just a guy I'd got to know during the summers I'd come here. I liked him, like I like a lot of people. But he wasn't my business. Luane Devore was; and straightening her out would be headache enough for one day.

She lived in a two-story, brick box of a house on the land-side outskirts of Manduwoc. It sat a few hundred feet back from the road, at the apex of a wooded slope. The driveway curved up through an expanse of meticulously clipped, lushly green lawn; in the rear of the house, there was more lawn, stretching out fan-wise to the whitewashed gates and fences of the orchard, barnyard and pasture. I parked my car beneath the portecochere and took a quick glance around the place.

A sleek Jersey grazed in the pasture. Several dozen Leghorns scratched and pecked industriously in the barnyard. A sow and half a dozen piglets wandered through the orchard, grunting and squealing contentedly as they gobbled the fallen fruit. Everything was as I remembered it from last season. Over all there was an air of peace and contentment, the evidence of loving care, of quiet pride in homely accomplishments.

You don't find that much any more—that kind of pride, I mean. People who will give everything they have to a humble, run-of-the-mill job. All the office boys want to be company presidents. All the store clerks want to be department heads. All the waitresses and waiters want to be any damned thing but what they are. And they all let you know it—the whole lazy, shiftless, indifferent, insolent lot. They can't do their own jobs well; rather, they won't do them. But, by God, they're going to have something better—the best! They're going to have it or else, and meanwhile it's a case of do as little as you can and grab as much as you can get.

So I stood there in the drive, looking around and feeling better the longer I looked. And, then, from an upstairs window, Luane Devore called down to me petulantly.

"Kossy? *Kossy!* What are you doing down there?"

"I'll be right up," I said. "Is the door unlocked?"

"Of course it's unlocked! It's always unlocked! You know that! How in the world could I—"

"Save it," I said. "Keep your pants on. I'll be right with you."

I went in through the front door, crossed a foyer floor that was waxed and polished to a mirror-like finish. I started up the stairs. They were polished to the same gleaming perfection as the floors, and I slipped perilously once when I stepped off of the carpet runner. For perhaps the thousandth time, I wondered how Ralph Devore found the time to maintain the house and grounds as he did. For he did do it all, everything that was done here and a hundred other things besides. Luane hadn't lifted a hand in years. It had been years since she had contributed a penny to maintaining the place.

There was a picture of them, Ralph and Luane, on the wall at the turn in the stairs. One of those enlarged, retouched photographs hung in an oval gilt frame. It had been taken twenty-two years before at the time of their marriage. In those days, Luane had resembled Theda Bara—if you remember your silent-motion-picture stars—and Ralph looked a lot like that Spanish lad, Ramon Navarro.

Ralph still looked pretty much as he had then, but Luane did not. She was sixty-two now. He was forty.

Her bedroom extended across the front of the house, facing the town. Through its huge picture window, she could see just about everything that went on in Manduwoc. And judging by the gossip I'd heard (and she'd started), she not only saw everything that happened but a hell of a lot that didn't.

Her door was open. I went in and sat down, trying not to wrinkle my nose against that bedfast smell—the smell of stale sweat, stale food, rubbing alcohol, talcum and disinfectant. This was one room that Ralph could do nothing about. Luane hadn't left it since God knows when, and it was so cluttered you could hardly turn around it.

There was a huge television set on one side of the room. On the other side was a massive radio, and next to it an elaborate hi-fi phonograph. They were operated from a remote control panel on a bedside table. Almost completely circling the bed were other tables and benches, loaded down variously with

magazines, books, candy boxes, cigarettes, carafes, an electric toaster, coffee
pot, chafing dish, and cartons and cans of food. Thus surrounded, with everything imaginable at her fingertips, Luane could make-do for herself during the long hours that Ralph was away. For that matter, she could have
done so, anyhow. Because there was not a damned thing wrong with her.
The local doctor said there wasn't. So did a diagnostician I'd once brought
down from the city. The local man "treated" her, since she insisted on it.
But there was nothing at all wrong with her. Nothing but self-pity and
selfishness, viciousness and fear: the urge to lash out at others from the sanctuary of the invalid's bed.

I sat down near the window, and lighted a cigar. She sniffed distastefully,
and I sniffed right back at her. "All right," I said. "Let's get it over with.
What's the matter now?"

Her mouth worked. She took a grayish handkerchief from beneath her
pillow, and blew into it. "It—it's R-Ralph, Kossy. He's planning to kill me!"

"Yeah?" I said. "So what's wrong with that?"

"He is, Kossy! I know you don't believe me, but he is!"

"Swell," I said. "You tell him if he needs any help just to give me a ring."

She looked at me helplessly, big fat tears filling her eyes. I grinned and gave
her a wink.

"You see?" I said. "You talk stupid to me, and I'll talk stupid to you. And
where the hell will that get us?"

"But it's not—I mean, it's true, Kossy! Why would I say so if it wasn't?"

"Because you want attention. Excitement. And you're too damned no-
account to go after it like other people do." I hadn't meant to get rough with
her. But she needed it—she had to be brought to her senses. And, I admit, I
just couldn't help it. I very seldom lose my temper. I may act like it, but I very
seldom do. But this time it was no act. "How the hell can you do it?" I said.
"Ain't you done enough to the poor guy already? You marry him when
he's eighteen. You talk his father, your caretaker, into getting him to marry
you—"

"I did not! I—I—"

"The hell you didn't! The old man was ignorant; he thought he was doing
the right thing by his son. Setting him up so that he could get a good education
and amount to something. But how did it turn out? Why—"

"I gave Ralph a good home! Every advantage! It's not my fault that—"

"You didn't give him anything," I said. "Ralph worked for everything he
got, and he helped support you besides. And he's still working anywhere from
ten to twenty-four hours a day. Oh, sure, you've tossed the dough around.
You've thrown away the whole damned estate. But Ralph never got any of it.
It all went for Luane Devore, and to hell with Ralph."

She cried some more. Then she pouted. Then she pulled the injured dignity stunt. She *believed,* she said, that Ralph was *quite* satisfied with the way she had treated him. He'd married her because he loved her. He hadn't wanted to go away to school. He was never happier than when he was working. Under the circumstances, then . . .

Her voice trailed away, a look of foolish embarrassment spreading over her flabby, talcum-caked face. I nodded slowly.

"That just about wraps it up, doesn't it, Luane? You've said it all yourself."

"Well . . ." She hesitated. "Perhaps I do worry, brood too much. But—"

"Let's pin it down tight. Wrap it up once and for all. Just what reason would Ralph have to kill you? This place—all that's left of the estate? Huh-uh. He has it now, practically speaking. He'll have it legally when you die. After all the years he's slaved here, worked to improve it, you couldn't will it to someone else. You could, of course, but it wouldn't hold up in court. I— Yeah?"

"I—nothing." She hesitated again. "I'm pretty sure she couldn't be the reason. After all, he's only known her a couple of days."

"Who?" I said.

"A girl at the dance pavillion. The vocalist with the band this year. I'd heard that Ralph was driving her around a lot, but, of course—"

"So who doesn't he drive around when he gets a chance?" I said. "It's a way of picking up a few bucks."

She nodded that that was so. She agreed that most of Ralph's haul-and-carry customers were women, since women were less inclined to walk than men.

"Anyway," she added thoughtfully, "if it was just another woman—well, that couldn't be the reason, could it? He could just run away with her. He could get a divorce. He wouldn't have to—to—"

"Of course, he wouldn't," I said. "And he doesn't want to, and he doesn't intend to. Where did you ever get the notion that he did, anyhow? Has he said anything, done anything, out of the way?"

She shook her head. She'd *thought* he'd been behaving rather oddly, and then she'd heard this gossip about the girl. And then she'd been feeling so poorly lately, sick to her stomach and unable to sleep nights, and—

The telephone rang. She broke off the recital of her various ailments, and snatched it up. She didn't talk long—not as long as she obviously wanted to. And what she did say was phrased obliquely. Still, with what I'd already heard in town, I was able to get the drift of the conversation.

She hung up the receiver. Keeping her eyes averted from mine, she thanked me for coming to see her. "I'm sorry to have bothered you, Kossy. I get so worried, you know, and then I get excited—"

"But you're all squared away now?" I said. "You know now that Ralph has no intention of killing you, that he never did have and never will have?"

"Yes, Kossy. And I can't tell you how much I—"

"Don't try," I said. "Don't tell me anything. Don't call me again. Because I'm not representing you any longer. You've gone too damned far this time."

"Why—why, Kossy." Her hand went to her mouth. "You're not angry with me j-just because . . ."

"I'm disgusted with you," I said. "You make me want to puke."

"But why? What did I do?" Her lower lip pulled down, piteously. "I lie here all day long, with nothing to do and no one to talk to . . . a sick, lonely old woman . . ."

She saw it wasn't going to work, that nothing she could say would square things between us. Her eyes glinted with sudden venom, and her whine shifted abruptly to a vicious snarl.

"All right, get out! Get out and stay out, and good riddance, you—*you hook-nosed little shyster!*"

"I'll give you a piece of advice first," I said. "You'd better stop telling those rotten lies about people before one of them stops you. Permanently, know what I mean?"

"Let them try!" she screamed. "I'd just like to see them try! I'll make things a lot hotter for 'em than they are now!"

I left. Her screeches and screams followed me down the stairs and out of the house.

I drove back to the cottage, and told Rosa the outcome of my visit. She listened to me, frowning.

"But, dear—do you think you should have done that? If she's that far gone, at the point where someone may kill her—"

"No one's going to, dammit," I said. "I was just trying to throw a scare into her. If anyone was going to kill her, they wouldn't have waited this long."

"But she's never gone this far before, has she?" Rosa shook her head. "I wish you hadn't done it. It—now, don't get angry—but it just isn't like you. She needs you, and when someone needs you . . ."

She smiled at me nervously. With a kind of nervous firmness. The cords in my throat began to tighten. I said what Luane Devore needed was a padded cell. She needed her tail kicked. She needed a psychiatrist, not a lawyer.

"What the hell?" I said. "Ain't I entitled to a vacation? I got to spend the whole goddamned summer with a poisoned-tongue maniac banging my ear? I don't get this." I said. "I thought you'd be pleased. First you raise hell because I'm going to see her, and now you raise hell because I'm not."

"So I talk a little," Rosa shrugged. "I'm a woman. That don't mean you should let me run your business."

I jumped up and danced around her. I puffed out my cheeks and rolled my eyes and fluttered my hands. "This is you," I said. "Mrs. Nutty Nonsense. You know so damned much, why ain't you a lawyer?"

"The great man," said Rosa. "Listen how the great attorney talks to his wife . . . I'm sorry, dear. You do whatever you think is right."

"And I'm sorry," I said. "I guess maybe I'm getting old. I guess things get on my nerves more than they used to. I guess—"

I guessed I might possibly have been a little hasty with Luane Devore.

"Don't let me influence you," Rosa said. "Don't do what you think I want you to. That way there is always trouble."

# II

## RALPH DEVORE

THE DAY I began thinking about killing Luane was the day the season opened. Which was also the day the dance pavilion opened, which was the day I met Danny Lee, who was the vocalist with Rags McGuire's orchestra. She was a she-vocalist even if her name was Danny. A lot of girl vocalists have boys' names. Take Janie, Rags' wife, who was always with the band until she had that bad accident—I mean, until this year, because there wasn't really any accident, Rags says. It was another party by the same name, and she is staying at home now to look after their boys who did not actually get killed after all. Well, Janie always sang under the name of Jan McGuire. I don't know why those girls do that, because everyone knows that they're girls—they do, anyway, as soon as they see them. And with Janie, you didn't even need to see her to know it. You could just feel it, I mean. You could just be in the same building with her, with your eyes closed maybe, and you'd know Janie was there. And, no, it wasn't because of her voice, because she had more kind of a man's voice than a woman's. What they call a contralto, or what they would call a contralto if she wasn't a pop singer. Because they don't seem to classify pop vocalists like they do the other kind. Rags was kidding when he said it —he used to kid around a lot—but he told me that Janie was the only girl singer in the country who wasn't a coloratura. Or, at least, a lyric soprano. He didn't know where the hell they all came from, he said, since there didn't used to be a coloratura come along more than once every ten years. Well, anyway, he can't say that any more; I mean, about Janie being the only girl who isn't a coloratura. Because Danny Lee isn't one either. She's got the same kind of voice that Janie had—only, well, kind of different—and she even kind of looks like Janie; only Rags gets sore when you say so, so I've never done it but once. Rags is awfully funny in some ways. Nice, you know, but funny. Now, me, when you like a person, when you think a lot of 'em, I think you ought to show it. I mean if you're me, you have to. You can't do anything else, and you wouldn't think of saying or doing anything to hurt them. But a lot of people are different, and Rags is one of them. Take with Janie. I know he thought the world of Janie, but he was all the time jumping on her. Always accusing her of something dirty. She couldn't look at anyone cross-eyed, just being pleasant, you know, without him saying she was running after the guy or something like that. And it just wasn't so. You wouldn't find a nicer girl than Janie in a month of Sundays. Oh, she drank a little, I guess. These last few years, she drank *quite* a bit. But—well, we'll leave that go a while.

12

Now, I was saying that I'd thought about killing Luane that first day of the
season. But that isn't really the way it was. I mean, I didn't actually think
about killing her. What I thought about was how it would be maybe if she
wasn't there. I didn't want her not to be there exactly—to be dead—but still,
well, you know. I started off wondering how it would be if she was, and then
after a while I began kind of half-wishing that she was. And then, finally, I
thought about different ways that she might be. Because if she wasn't—dead,
I mean—I didn't know what I was going to do. And you put yourself in my
place, and I don't think you'd have known either.

Usually—during the winter, anyway—I lay around in bed until five-thirty
or six in the morning. But that day was the first of the season, so I was up at
four. I dressed in the dark, and slipped out into the starlight. I did the chores,
sort of humming and grinning to myself, feeling as tickled as a kid on Christmas morning. I felt good, I'll tell you. It was dark and the air was pretty nippy
at that hour of the morning, but still everything seemed bright to me and I
had that nice warm feeling inside. It was like I'd been buried in a cave, and
I'd finally managed to get out. And that was kind of the way it was, too, in
a way. Because this last winter had really been a bad one. Take the engineer's
job at the courthouse, firing the boilers; now that's always been my job—an
hour morning and evening and an hour on Saturday morning—but last winter
it wasn't mine. And the school custodian job—four hours a day and two days
once a month—that had always been mine, too, and now it wasn't. I talked
to the head of the county commissioners, and he sent me to the county
attorney. And the way he explained it—about the boilers—was that the commissioners could be held liable for any money they spent in excess of what was
necessary. So automatic boilers were being installed, and that was that. I tried
to argue with him, but it didn't do any good. It didn't do any good when I
talked to the president of the school board, Doctor Ashton. They were dividing
my job up among some of the vocational students. I wouldn't be needed now
or at any time in the future, Doc said. And he gave me one of those straight,
hard-eyed looks like the county attorney had.

So there I was. A hundred and fifty dollars a month gone down the drain.
Practically every bit of my winter income, except for a little wood-cutting and
stuff like that. Well, sure, I'd always kept a pretty big garden, canned and dried
a lot of stuff. And, of course, there were the pigs, and we had our own eggs
and milk and so on. And, naturally, I had some money put by. But, you know,
you just can't figure that way; I mean, you can't count on standing on rock
bottom. You do that, say, and what happens if things get worse? If a rainy day
comes along, and that water that's only been up to your chin goes over your
nose? Money can go mighty fast when you don't have any coming in. Say you
run in the hole five dollars a day, why in a year's time that's almost two
thousand dollars. And say you're forty like I am, and you've got maybe

twenty-five years to live unless you starve to death . . . ! I tell you I was almost crazy with worry. Anyone would have been. But now it was the first day of the season, and all my worries were over—I thought. I'd just work a little harder, make enough to make up for what I didn't make during the winter, and everything would be fine. I mean, I thought it would be.

I finished my chores. Then, I spread a big tarp in the back of the Mercedes-Benz, and put my mower and tools inside. You're probably wondering what a man like me is doing with a Mercedes, them being worth so much money. But the point is they're only worth a lot when you're buying; you go to sell one it's a different story. I did get a pretty good offer or two for it, back when I first got it—two seasons ago—but I kind of held on, thinking I might get a better one. And, of course, I liked it a lot, too, and I did need a car to get around in, to haul myself and my tools and passengers during the season. So, maybe it was the wrong thing, but it looked to me like I couldn't really lose since I'd gotten it for nothing. So, well, I've still got it.

The man who did own it was a writer, a motion-picture writer, who used to come up here for the season. He began having trouble with it right after I went to work for him, and he had me tinker on it for him; and it would run pretty good for a time and then it would go blooey again. He got pretty sore about it. I mean, he got sore at the car. One morning he got so mad he started to take an ax to it, and I guess he would have if I hadn't stopped him. Well, back then, there was a summer Rolls agency over at Atlantic Center—that's a pretty big place, probably ten times as big as Manduwoc. So I suggested to this writer that as long as he needed a car and he didn't like the Mercedes, why not let me tow him over there and see what kind of a trade-in he could get.

Well, you know how it is. Those dealers can stick just about any price tag on a car they want to. So this one said he could allow six thousand on the Mercedes (he just boosted the Rolls price that much), and the writer snapped him up on it. And as soon as he'd driven off, the dealer signed the Mercedes over to me. I tinkered with the motor a little. I've never had to touch it since.

Yes, this writer was pretty sore when he found out what had happened. He claimed I'd deliberately put the Mercedes on the blink, and he threatened to have both me and that dealer arrested. But he couldn't prove anything, so it didn't bother me that much. I mean, after all, a man that's got twenty-five or thirty thousand dollars to throw away on a car, has got blamed little to fuss about. And if he can't protect an investment like that, he shouldn't have it in the first place.

After I'd finished loading the Mercedes, I went in and did a quick job on the house. Which didn't take long since I'd slicked everything up good the night before. I ate breakfast, and then I fixed more breakfast and carried it up to Luane. We had a real nice talk while she ate. When she was through, I gave her a sponge bath, tickling her and teasing her until she was almost crying she laughed so hard. As a matter of fact, she did cry a little but not sad like she sometimes does. It was more kind of wondering, you know—like when you know something's true but you can't quite believe it.

"You like me, don't you?" she said. "You really do like me, don't you?"

"Well, sure," I said. "Of course. I don't need to tell you that."

"You've never regretted anything? Wished things had been different?"

"Regret what?" I said. "What would I want different?"

"Well—" She gestured. "To travel. See the world. Do something besides just work and eat and sleep."

"Why, I do a lot besides that," I said. "Anyway, what would I want to travel for when I've got everything I want right here?"

"Have you, darling?" She patted my cheek. "Do you have everything you want?"

I nodded. Maybe I didn't have everything I wanted right there in the house, her being pretty well along in years. But working like I do, I didn't have to hunt very hard to get it. Most of the time it was the other way around.

Well, anyway. I got her fixed up for the day with everything she might need, and then I left. Feeling good, like I said. Feeling like all my troubles were over. I drove up to Mr. J. B. Brockton's place, and started to work on the lawn. And in just about five minutes—just about the time it took him to get out of the house—all the good feeling was gone, and I knew I hadn't seen any trouble compared with what I was liable to.

"I'm sorry, Ralph," he said, sort of kicking at the grass with his toe. "I tried any number of times to reach you yesterday, but your phone was always tied up."

I shook my head. I just couldn't think of anything to say for a minute. He wasn't like some of the summer people I worked for—people who just order you around like you didn't have any feelings, and maybe make jokes about you —about the "natives"—in front of their company. He was more like a friend, you know. I liked him, and he went out of his way to show that he liked me. Why, just last season he'd given me a couple suits. Two hundred and fifty dollar suits, he said they were. And, of course, he was probably exaggerating a little. Because how could just a suit of clothes cost two hundred and fifty? But even if they only cost fifty or seventy-five, it was a mighty handsome gift. Not something you'd give to people unless you thought an awful lot of them.

"Mr. Brockton," I said. And that was as far as I could go for a minute. "Mr. Brockton, what's the matter?"

"Well, I'll tell you, Ralph," he said, not looking at me, still kicking at the grass. "Doctor Ashton's son got in touch with me by mail a week or so ago. I've decided to give the work to him."

Well. You could have pushed me over with a dew drop. I didn't know whether to laugh or cry.

"Bobbie Ashton?" I said. "Why—what would Bobbie be doing doing yard work? Why, he must have been joking you, Mr. Brockton! Doc Ashton, why, he always hires his own yard work done, so why would Bobbie—"

"I've already engaged him," Mr. Brockton said. "It's all settled. I'm sorry, Ralph." He hesitated a second; then he said, "I think Doctor Ashton is a good man. I think Bob is a fine boy."

"Well, so do I," I said. "You never heard me say anything else, Mr. Brockton."

"I like them," he said. "And I come here to rest, to enjoy myself. And I do not like—in fact, I refuse, Ralph—to be drawn into community quarrels."

I knew what the trouble was then. I knew there was nothing I could do about it. All I could do now was to get to some other place as fast as I could. So . . . so I made myself smile. I said I could see how he might feel, and that he shouldn't feel bad about it on my account. Then I started reloading the Mercedes.

"Ralph," he said. "Wait a minute."

"Yes, sir?" I turned back around.

"I can give you a job with my company. In one of our factories. Something that you could do, and that would pay quite well."

"Oh?" I said. "You mean in New York City, Mr. Brockton?"

"Or New Jersey. Newark. I think you'd like it, Ralph. I think it would be the best thing that ever happened to you."

"Yes, sir," I said. "I guess you're probably right, Mr. Brockton, and I sure do appreciate the offer. But I guess not."

"You guess not?" he said. "Why not?"

"Well, I—I just guess I hadn't better," I said. "You see, I never lived anywhere but here. I've never been any further away than Atlantic Center, and that was just for a couple of hours. And just being away that far, that little time, I was so rattled and mixed up it was two-three days before I could calm down."

"Oh, well," he shrugged. "You'd get over that."

"I guess not," I said. "I mean, I *can't,* Mr. Brockton. It's kind of like I was rooted here, like I was one of them—those—shrubs. You try to put me down somewhere else, and—"

"Oh, I'm not trying to! Far be it from me to persuade a man against his will."

He nodded, kind of huffy-like, and headed for the house. I drove away. I knew he was probably right. I kind of wished I could leave Manduwoc—just kind of, you know. And before that day was much older I was really wishing it, with hardly any kind-of at all. But there just wasn't any way that I could.

Luane would never leave here. Even if she would, what good would it do?

Any place we went, people would laugh and talk about us like they'd always done here. There'd be the same stories. Well, not exactly the same, I guess, because outsiders wouldn't know about Pa. So they wouldn't be apt to say that Pa and Luane, well—that I was really her son instead of her husband. Or, her son as well as her husband. But however it was, it would be bad. And Luane would start striking back twice as hard, like she'd struck back here. Probably she'd do it anyhow, even if people did have the good manners and kindness to keep their mouths shut. Because she'd been the way she was now for so long, she'd lost the knack for being any other way.

I felt awful sorry for Luane. She'd sure given up a lot on my account. She was a lady, and she came from a proud old family. She'd been a good church-goer and a charity-worker, and everything like that. And then just because she wanted someone to love before she got too old for it, why there was all that dirtiness. Stuff that took the starch right out of you, and filled you up with something else. No, it didn't bother me too much; I guess I just didn't have enough sense to be bothered, and, of course, I never amounted to anything to begin with. But it did something pretty terrible to Luane. She didn't show it for a long time, except maybe a little around me. She had too much pride. But the hurt was there inside, festering and spreading, and finally breaking out. And then really getting bad. Getting a little worse the older she got.

I sure wished Luane could go away with me. I figured I could make out pretty fine with Luane. With someone like that, you know, someone who knew her way around and could tell you what to do—someone that really loved you and you could talk to, and—and . . .

Well, I guess I just hadn't wanted to face the facts there at Mr. J. B. Brockton's place. I mean, it was such an awful setback, I didn't feel like I could bear any more; I just couldn't admit that it would be the same way wherever else I went. Because what was I going to do if it was? How was I going to live? What would I do if I couldn't make out here, and I couldn't go any place else?

You can see how I'd be kind of stunned. So scared that I couldn't look at the truth even with my nose rubbed in it.

So, anyway, I went on to all the other estates. I made them all, just taking "no" for an answer at first, and then arguing and finally begging. And, of course, it was the same story everywhere. I was just wasting my breath and my time. They were sorry, sure; most of 'em said they were, anyhow. But Bobbie Ashton had asked for the work, and Doc Ashton was an influential man—and he treated most of them—so Bobbie was going to get it.

It was noon by the time I'd gone to the last place I could go to. I drove down to the beach and ate the lunch I'd packed that morning. Gulping it down, not really tasting it.

Twenty-five years, I thought. Twenty-five years, but no, a man like me would probably live a lot longer than that. Thirty-five or forty, probably.

Maybe even fifty or sixty. Fifty or sixty years with everything going out and nothing coming in!

Yes, there was a little work around town, for the local residents, you know. But it wasn't worth bothering with. Just fifty cents here and a dollar there. Anyway, the kids had it all sewed up.

I wondered if it would do any good for me to talk to Bobbie, but I didn't wonder long. He'd made up his mind to run me out of town—to get back at Luane through me.

Doc Ashton settled here a little short of seventeen years ago. His wife had died in childbirth, so he had this Negro wet nurse for Bobbie, the woman who still works for them as housekeeper. Doc was quite a young man then. The woman was young, too—in fact, she's still fairly young—and pretty good-looking, besides.

Well, Bobbie was sick when he got here, the colic or something. And he no sooner got over that than he was hit by something else. Every disease you ever heard of practically, why Bobbie had it. One right after another. Year after year. He couldn't play with other kids, couldn't go to school; he was hardly out of the house for almost twelve years. Then, finally, I guess because he'd had every blamed sickness there was to get, he didn't get any more. He began to shoot up and broaden out. All at once, he was just about the healthiest, huskiest—and handsomest—kid you ever saw in your life. And smart! You couldn't believe a kid could be that smart, and probably you won't find many that are.

I suppose he got a lot of it from all those books he'd read when he couldn't do anything else. But there was plenty more to Bobbie's smartness than book-learning. He just seemed to have been born with a head on him, a head with all the answers. He could do things without being told how or reading about 'em, or maybe even hearing of 'em before. Not just lessons, you know, but *anything!*

He went through eight grades of grammar school in a year. He went through high school in a year and a half. At least he could have gone through, if he hadn't dropped out the last semester. Now, it didn't look like he'd be going to college; he wouldn't be studying to be a doctor. And how Doc Ashton would be feeling about that, I hated to think.

I wadded up my lunch sack, and put it in a trash basket. Then, I got a drink of water from one of the picnicker fountains, and drove up to the dance pavilion.

The big front doors were swung open. I went inside, circled around in front of the bandstand, and stopped in the doorway of Pete Pavlov's office. He was at his desk, bent over some papers. He glanced up, squirted a stream of tobacco into a spittoon and bent back over the papers again.

He's one of those round-faced, square-built men. About fifty, I guess. He wore khaki pants with both a belt and suspenders, and a blue work shirt with a black bow tie. His hair was parted on the side, and there was a blob of shaving soap up around one of the temples.

I waited. I began to get a little uneasy, even though I was practically sure that I had a job with him for the summer. Because any time Pete Pavlov could do anything to annoy people in Manduwoc, he was just about certain to do it. I mean, he'd go out of his way to get under their hides. And giving me work would get under 'em bad.

He didn't need to care what they thought of him; his business was all with the summer trade. He owned most of the rent cottages, and the pavilion, and two of the hotels, and oh, probably, two-thirds of the concession buildings. So to heck with Manduwoc, was the way he felt. The town people hadn't ever done anything for him. In fact, they'd always been kind of down on him, sort of resentful. Because even back when he was a day laborer, cleaning out cesspools or anything he could get to do, he was as independent as a hog on ice. He'd do a good day's work, but he wouldn't say thank-you for his pay. If anyone called him by his first name or just Pavlov, he'd do exactly the same thing with them. No matter who they were or how much money they had.

He straightened up from his desk, and looked at me. I smiled and said hello, and remarked that it was a nice day. I said, "I guess I better be getting to work, hadn't I, Pete?"

He waited for me to say something else. I didn't, because I was just too worried. Here was maybe another twenty-five dollars a week going down the hole. The only chance I had left for any income.

Pete kind of squirmed around in his chair, kind of scratching his rear, I guess. He leaned back and picked something out of his nose, and held it up and looked at it. And then he pushed his lips out, moved them in and out, while he stared down at his desk.

"Well, hell," he said. "I tell you how it is, Ralph. The way this goddamned summer business is going, I figure on hiring out myself."

I didn't say anything. I guessed things weren't as good for him as they used to be, but I knew he was still setting pretty. He had plenty, all right, Pete Pavlov did. It would take more than a few slack seasons to hurt him much.

"What are you looking like that for?" he said. "You think I'm a goddamned liar?" Then, his eyes flickered and shifted, and he let out a whoop of laughter, and slapped his hand down on his desk. "Well, you're right, by God! I wish you could have seen your face! Really had you going, didn't I?"

"Aw, no, you didn't," I said. "I knew you were joking all the time."

"You know what a broom looks like?" He waved me toward the door. "Well, see if you can find one that'll fit your hands."

I got out. I got busy on the restrooms, and after a while, as he was leaving for downtown, he looked in on me. Stood around talking and joking for a few minutes. He asked about Luane, and said he was pretty goddamned hurt the way she never told any dirty stories about him. I laughed, kind of uncomfortable, and said I guessed that was his fault, not hers. Which was mainly the way it was, of course. Because how can you mud a man up when he's already covered himself with it? To annoy people, you know. What's the point in saying that a man does such and such or so and so when he lets 'em all know it himself?

He had a family, a wife and daughter, but Luane couldn't do much to dirty them, either. There just wasn't enough to them, you know, to hold dirt. They were dowdy and drab. They went around with their shoulders slumped and their heads bowed—like they might cut and run if you looked their way. No one was interested in them. There wasn't anything to be interested in. And if the time ever came when there was, well, I figured Luane would do some tall thinking before she gossiped about it.

You see, years ago—before Luane and I were married—her father gave Pete an awful raw deal. Cheated him out of a pile of money, and then placed it in Luane's name, so that Pete couldn't sue. Luane's always felt kind of guilty about it. She'd think a long time before she did anything else to hurt Pete or his family

"Well," Pete said. "I got a feeling that this may be a good season after all. The best damned season yet."

"I think it will, too," I said. "I think you're right, Pete."

He left. I finished with the washrooms, and went back to his office.

I pulled a chair up to the air-vent, took off the grate and crawled up inside the duct. I crawled through it slowly, squirming along on my stomach, brushing all the dust and cobwebs and dead bugs in front of me. It was so hot and stuffy I could hardly breathe, and I kept sneezing and bumping my head; and I was just about one big muddy smear of sweat and dust. I crawled through all the duct, the branches and the main, and came out at the rear of the building.

I dropped down to the roof of the blower shed. I started up the big four-horse motor, tightened the belt to the fan, and went in the back door of the men's room.

I looked at myself in the mirror, and, man, was I a mess! Dirt and cobwebs from head to foot. I started to turn on the water at one of the sinks, and then I stopped with my hand a couple of inches away—kind of frozen in the air. I stood that way for a few seconds, listening to the piano, to Rags, listening to *her.* Then I turned toward the door, picking up my broom sort of automatically, and went out into the ballroom.

It was pretty shadowed in there, and there was just the swivel-necked light on over the piano. So, for a second, I thought it was Janie up there singing.

Then I started across the floor, and pretty soon I saw it was another girl. She had the same kind of voice as Janie, and the same kind of candy-colored hair. But she was quite a bit bigger. I don't mean she was any taller or that she probably weighed any more, but still she was bigger. In certain places, you know. You could see that she was without even half-way studying the matter. Because it was still pretty warm there in the ballroom, and Rags was stripped to the waist. And all she had on was a bra and a little skimpy pair of shorts.

I thought she was a mighty good singer, but I knew Rags wasn't pleased with her. I knew because he was putting her through *Stardust,* having her rehearse it when he'd always told me that no singer needed to. "That's one they can't bitch up, see?" he'd told me. "They can do it with all the others. But *Stardust,* huh-uh."

He brought his hands down on the keys suddenly. With just a big crash. She stopped singing and turned toward him, her face hard and sullen-looking.

"All right," Rags said. "You win, baby. I'll send for Liberace. Me, I'm too old to run races."

"I'm sorry," she mumbled, not looking a darned bit sorry.

"Never mind that sorry stuff," he said. "Your name's Lee, ain't it? Danny Lee, ain't it?"

"You know what it is," she said.

"I'm asking you," he said. "It's not Carmichael or Porter or Mercer, is it? This ain't your music, is it? You've got no right to bitch it up, have you? You're goddamned right, you haven't! It's theirs—they made it, and the way they made it is the way it should be. So cut out the embroidery. Cut out that bar-ahead stuff. Just get with it, and stay with it!"

He picked up his cigarette from the piano, and tucked it into the corner of his mouth. He brought his hands down on the keys. He seemed to kind of stroke them—the keys, I mean. But yet there was no running together. Every note came through, clear and firm, soft but sharp. So smooth and easy and sweet.

Danny Lee took a deep breath. She held it, the bra swelled full and tight. She was nodding her head with the music, tapping one toe. Listening, and then opening her mouth and letting her breath out in the *Stardust* words. Soft-husky. Pushing them out from down deep inside. Letting them float out with that husky softness, still warm and sweet from the place they'd been.

I looked at Rags. His eyes were closed, and there was a smile on his lips. I looked back at the girl, and I kind of frowned.

She didn't hardly have to move at all, to look like she was moving a lot. And she was moving a lot now. And if there was one thing that burned Rags McGuire up, it was that. He said it was cheap. He said singers who did that were acrobats.

Rags opened his eyes. His smile went away, and he lifted his hands from the keys and laid them in his lap. He didn't curse. He didn't yell. For a minute he hardly seemed to move, and the silence was so thick you could cut it with a knife. Then he motioned for her to come over to the piano. She hesitated, then went over, kind of dragging her feet, sullen and hard-faced, and watchful-looking.

And then Rags reamed her out—real hard. It was pretty rough.

She took her place again. Rags brought his hands down on the keys, and she began to sing. I moved in close. Rags gave me a little nod. I stood up close, drinking her voice in, drinking her in.

She finished the song. Without thinking how it might seem to Rags—like I might be butting in, you know—I busted out clapping. It had been so nice, I just had to.

Rags' eyes narrowed. Then he grinned and made a gesture toward me. "Okay, baby, take off," he said. "You've passed the acid test."

I guess he meant it as kind of an insult. Just to her, of course, because he and I are good friends, and always kidding around a lot. Anyway, she started down at me—and gosh, I'd forgot all about what a mess I was. And then she whirled around, bent over and stuck out her bottom at me. Kind of wiggled at me.

Rags let out a whoop. He whooped with laughter, banging his fists down on the top of the piano. Making so much noise that you couldn't hear what she was yelling, although I guess it was mostly cuss words.

He was still whooping and pounding as she marched back across the bandstand, and down the steps to the dressing room.

I grinned, or tried to. Feeling a little funny naturally, but not at all mad.

# III

## Rags McGuire

I SAW HER for the first time about four months ago. It was in a place in Fort Worth, far out on West Seventh Street. I wasn't looking for her or it, or anything. I'd just started walking that night, and when I'd walked as far as I could I was in front of this place. So I went inside.

There was a small bar up front. In the rear was a latticed-off, open roof area, with a lot of tables and a crowd of beer drinkers. I sat down and ordered a stein.

The waitress came with it. Another woman came right behind her, and helped herself to a chair. She was a pretty wretched-looking bag; not that it would have meant anything to me if she hadn't been. I gave her a couple bucks, and said no, thanks. She went away, and the three-piece group on the bandstand—sax, piano and drums—went back to work.

They weren't good, of course, but they were Dixieland. They played the music, and that's something. They played the music—or tried to—and these days that's really something.

They did *Sugar Blues* and *Wang Wang,* and *Goofus.* There was a kitty on the bandstand, a replica of a cat's hat with a PLEASE FEED TIIE sign. So, at intermission, I sent the waitress up with a twenty-dollar bill.

I didn't notice that it was a twenty until it was in her hand. I'd meant to make it a five—which was a hell of a lot more than I could afford. Anything was a lot more than I could afford. But she already had it, and you don't hear the music much any more. So I let it go.

The waitress pointed me out to them. They all stood up and smiled and bowed to me, and for a moment I was stupid enough to think that they knew who I was. For, naturally, they didn't. They don't know you any more if you play the music. Only the players of crap, the atonal clashbang off-key stuff that Saint Vitus himself couldn't dance to. To these lads I was just a big spender. That's all I was to anyone in the place.

I saw the waitress go over to a table in the corner. There was a man seated at it, facing me, a guy with a beer-bleared face and a suit that must have cost all of eighteen dollars. There was also a girl, her back turned my way. The waitress whispered to her, and the girl got up. Her companion made noises of protest, and a burly, shirt-sleeved character who had been lurking in the vicinity, grabbed him by the collar and hustled him out.

The girl started toward the bandstand. There was a small burst of hand-clapping and stein-thumping. And my eyes snapped open and my heart pounded, and I half rose out of my chair. And then I settled back down again. Because, of course, it wasn't Janie. Janie wouldn't be in a joint like this, she wouldn't be hanging around with bar-flies. Anyway, I knew where Janie was, at home looking after the boys, whoring and guzzling and . . .

Janie was back in New York. I'd talked to her long-distance that night—had her sing to me over the telephone. It was *Melancholy Baby,* one of our all-time hit recordings, one of the dozen-odd which still sell considerably—and thank God they do. Although I don't know who the hell buys them. Probably they all go to insane asylums, the patients there. It must be that way, the poor devils must all be locked up, since there seems to be nothing on the outside any more but tone-deaf morons.

Why, goddammit, I talked to a man a while back, one of those pseudo-erudite bastards who is mopping up with articles about modern "music," the so-called up-beat, "cool" crap. I said, let me ask you something. Suppose the printer started "interpreting" your articles. Suppose he started leaving out lines and putting in his own, suppose he threw away your punctuation and put in his own. How would you feel if he did that, an "interpretation" of your stuff?

I shouldn't have wasted my time on him, of course. I shouldn't even have spit on him. He called himself a music critic—a critic, by God!—and he'd never heard of Blue Steele!

The girl didn't look like Janie. Not the slightest. I'd only thought she did at the time.

She sang. It was *Don't Get Around Much Any More,* another old hit of Janie's and mine. And she bitched it up. Brother, did she bitch it! But when I closed my eyes . . .

She had a voice. She had what it took, raw and undeveloped as it was. And she hit you. That's the only way I can say it—she hit you. She brought out the goosebumps, like that first blast of air when you step into an air-conditioned room.

And God knows I don't expect much. I work for something good, I do my best to get it. But I don't really expect it.

I began to get a little excited. I did some fast mental calculations. I was working single at the moment, doing a series of club dates. And I was just squeaking by. But the resort season wasn't too far off, and I had some recording checks due; and it would be easy enough to whip together another band. I could just about swing it, I thought. A five man combo, including myself, and this girl. I couldn't make any money with it, not playing the music. I'd be very lucky, in fact, if I could break even. But I *could* do it—do something, by God, that needed to be done. Give this mixed-up world something that it ought to have, regardless of whether it knew it or wanted it.

She finished the song. She was at my table before I could motion to her. I was still wrapped up in my calculations. I heard her pitch, but it was a minute or two before it sank in on me. And perhaps I should have expected it; and perhaps, by God, I should not have. From some girls, yes. From any other girl. But not her, not someone with the music in them.

I wanted to spit on her. I wanted to break my stein, slash her throat with it so that she would never sing another word. Instead, I said, fine: I hated sleeping by myself.

I suppose my expression had startled her. At any rate, she drew back a little. She didn't mean *that,* she said. All she meant was that maybe I could buy her dinner some place and we could have a nice visit, since she was alone, too, and maybe I could help her buy a new dress because a drunk had spilt some beer on this one, and—

She was really a nice girl. She told me so herself. She was just doing this (temporarily, of course!) because her mother was awfully sick—a sick mother, no less!—and she had a couple of younger brothers to support, and her father was dead and crops had been awfully bad on this farm she came from. And so on, ad infinitum, ad nauseam. The only thing she spared me was the fine-old-Southern-family routine. If she'd pulled that I think I *would* have killed her.

I took a couple of twenties out of my wallet and riffled them.

She simpered around a little more, and then she went back to my hotel with me.

I looked at her, and suddenly I turned and ducked into the bathroom. I hunched over, hugging my stomach, feeling my guts twist and knot themselves, wanting to scream with the pain. I puked, and wept silently. And it was better, then. I washed my face, and went back into the bedroom.

I told her to get her clothes on. I told her what I could and would do for her.

All the clothes she'd need; good clothes. A year's contract at two hundred dollars a week. Yes, two hundred dollars a week. And a chance to make something of herself, a chance eventually to make two thousand, five thousand, ten thousand. More than a chance, an absolute certainty. Because I *would* make something of her; I would not let her fail.

She believed me. People usually do believe me if I care to make the effort. Still, she hung back, apparently too shocked by the break I was offering her to immediately accept it. I gave her twenty dollars, promised her another twenty to meet me at the club in the morning. She did so—we had the place to ourselves except for the cleaning people—and I gave her a sample of what I could do for her.

A good sample, because I wanted her firmly hooked. With what I had in mind, the two hundred a week might not be enough to hold her. That invalid mother and two brothers et cetera, not withstanding. I wanted to give her a glimpse of the mint, boost her high enough up the wall so that even a whoring moron such as she could see it.

And I did.

I worked with her a couple hours. At the end of that time, she was no longer terrible, but merely bad. Which to her, of course, seemed nothing less than wonderful.

She was beaming and bubbling, and the sun seemed to have risen behind her eyes.

"I can hardly believe it!" she said. "It seems kind of like magic—like a beautiful dream!"

"The dream will get better," I said. "It will come true. Assuming, that is, that you want to accept my offer."

"Oh, I do! You know I do," she said. "I don't know how to thank you, Mr. McGuire."

I told her not to bother; she didn't owe me any thanks. We went back to my room, and I closed and locked the door.

She seemed to crumple a little, grow smaller, and the sun went out of her eyes. She stammered, that she wouldn't do it, then that she didn't want to. Finally, as I waited, she asked if she had to.

"I've never done anything like that before. Honestly, I haven't, Mr. McGuire! Only once, anyway, and it wasn't for money. I was in love with him, this boy back in my home town, and we were suppose to be married. And then he went away, and I thought I was pregnant so I left, and—"

"Never mind," I said. "If you don't want to . . ."

"And it'll be all right?" She looked at me anxiously. "You'll still—s-still—?"

I didn't say anything.

"W-Will it? Will it, Mr. McGuire? Please, please! If you only knew . . ."

If I only knew, believed, that she was really a good girl. If I only knew how much she wanted to sing, how much this meant to her. You know.

I shrugged, remained silent. But inside I was praying. And what I was praying was that she would tell me to go to hell. I could have got down and kissed her feet for that, if she had insisted on being what the good Lord had meant her to be or being nothing; keeping the music undefiled or keeping it silent where it was. If only it had meant that much to her, as much as it meant to me—

And it didn't. It never means as much, even a fraction as much, as it means to me. Not to Janie. Not to anyone.

No one cares about the music.

Except for me it would vanish, and there would be no more.

Slowly, she unbuttoned her dress. Slowly, she pulled it down off one shoulder. I stared at her, grinning—wanting to yell and wanting to weep. And blackness swam up on me from the floor, dropped down over me from above.

I came out of it.

She was kneeling in front of me. My head was against her, and she was wet with my tears. And she was crying, and holding me.

"Mister McGuire . . . W-what's the matter, M-Mist—Oh, darling, baby, honey-lamb! What can I—"

She brushed her lips against my forehead, stroked my hair, whispering:

"Better now, sweetheart? Is Danny's dearest honey-pie bet—"

"You rotten, low-down little whore," I said.

Pete Pavlov was waiting at the station when we came in late Thursday night. The boys and Danny went on down to their cottages, and I went to his office with him.

I like Pete. I like his bluntness, his going straight to the point of a matter. There is no compromise about him. He knows what he wants and he will take nothing else, and whether it suits anyone else makes not the damnedest bit of difference to him.

He did not ask about Janie, nor the why of the new band. That was my business, and Pete minds his own business. He simply poured us a couple whopping drinks, tossed me a cigar and asked me if I knew where he could lay his hands on a fast ten or twenty thousand.

I said I wished I did. He shrugged and said he didn't really suppose I would, and just to forget he'd said anything. Then he said, "Excuse me, Mac"—Pete has always called me Mac—"Know I didn't need to tell *you* to keep quiet."

"That's okay," I said. "Things pretty bad, Pete?"

He said they were goddamned bad. So bad that he'd fire his hotels if he could collect on them. "Those goddamned insurance companies," he said. "Y'know, I figure that's why so many people get burned to death. Because the companies won't pay off on empty buildings. Guess I should have fired mine while they were open, but I kind of hated to take a chance on roasting someone."

I laughed, and shook my head. I hardly knew what to say. I knew what I should say, but I wasn't quite up to saying it, hard-pressed as I was.

He went on to explain his situation. He'd never borrowed any money locally. He'd always done business on a cash basis. Then, when things began to tighten up, he'd gone to some New York factors; and now the interest was murdering him.

"No usury laws when it comes to business loans, y'know. Did you know that? Well, that's the way she stands. I don't get up ten, twenty thousand, I'm just about going to be wiped out." He took a chew of tobacco, grunted sardonically. "Own damned fault, I guess. Too goddamned stubborn. Should have unloaded when things first started slipping."

"You couldn't have done it, Pete," I said. "If you knew how to give up, you'd never have got to where you are."

He said he guessed that was so. Guessed he didn't know how to lay down, and didn't want to learn.

"Pete," I said. "Look. Your contract is with the agency, and I can't cut the price. But I can rebate on it."

"Hell with you," he said. "You ugly, ornery over-grown, bastard."

He walked around the room, grunting that there were too damned many throats in need of cutting, without bleeding some dull-witted son-of-a-bitch like me who ought to have a guardian looking after him.

"Nope," he said, turning back around. "I ain't that bad off. If I was, I just wouldn't have signed up for you this year."

"Maybe you shouldn't have," I said. "And look, Pete. You can't break that contract, but if I should refuse to play—"

"Nope. No, now listen to me," he said. "I wouldn't do it, even if I didn't like to listen to that damned pounding of yours. I got to keep the pavilion open. Once I closed it, it'd be kind of a signal. I might as well paint a bullseye on my butt, and tell 'em all to start kicking."

We went on drinking and talking. Talking of things in general, and nothing much in particular. He said that when Kossmeyer came down the three of us ought to get together some night and have us a bull session. I said I'd like that —some time when I was feeling good and didn't have anything on my mind.

"I like him," I said. "He's a hell of an interesting little guy, and a nice one. But sometimes, y'know, Pete, I get a feeling that he ain't where I'm seeing him. I mean, he's right in front of me, but it seems like he's walking all around me. Looking me over. Staring through the back of my head."

Pete laughed. "He gives you that feeling too, huh? Ain't it funny, Mac? All the people there are in the world, and how many there are you can just sit down and cut loose and be yourself with."

I said it certainly was funny. Or tragic.

"Well, hell," he said, finally, "and three is seven. Daddy's gone and went to heaven. Guess you and me ought to be getting some sleep, Mac."

We said good-night, and he went off toward town, his chunky body moving in a straight line. I went to my cottage, feeling conscience-stricken and depressed by my failure to help him. By my failures period. Bitch and botch, that was me. In common honesty I ought to start billing myself that way: Bitch And Botch And His Band And Bitch. I could work up a theme song out of it, set it to the melody of—well, *Goodie Goodie.* Let's see, now. Tatuh ta ta tum, tatuh . . . I worked on that for a minute, and then swore softly to myself. I couldn't do anything right any more. Not the simplest, damnedest ordinary thing.

Take tonight, for example. My people were new here; there are rows and rows of cottages, all exactly alike. Yet I hadn't bothered to see that they got to the right ones, to see that they were comfortably settled. I'd just gone my own merry way—thinking only of myself—and to hell with them.

It didn't matter, of course, about Danny Lee. She could sleep on the beach for all I cared. But my men, poor bastards, were a different matter. They had enough to bear as it was—those sad, sad bastards. Just barely squeaking by, year after year. Working for the minimum, and tickled to death to get it. Big-talking and bragging, when they know—for certainly they must know—that they were unfitted to wipe a real musician's tail.

It must be very hard to maintain a masquerade like that. I felt very sorry for them, my men, and I was very gentle with them. They had no talent, nothing to build on, nothing to give. There can be nothing more terrible, it seems to me, than having nothing to give.

I unpacked my suitcases, and climbed into bed.

I fell asleep, slipping almost immediately into that old familiar dream where everyone in the band was me. I was on the trumpet, the sax-and-clarinet. I was on the trombone, at the drums, and, of course, the piano. All of us were me —the whole combo. And Danny Lee-Janie was the vocalist, but she-they were also me. And it was not perfect, the music was not quite perfect. But it was close, so close, by God! All we-I needed was a little more time—time is all it takes if you have it to work with—and . . .

I woke up.

It was a little after twelve, noon. The smell of coffee drifted through my window, along with snatches of conversation.

It came from the boys' cabin—they were batching together to save money. They were keeping their voices low, and our cottages, like the others, were thirty feet apart. ("Don't like to be crowded," Pete told me, "and don't figure anyone else does.") But sound carries farther around water:

*"Did you hear what he said to me, claimin' I had a lip? Why, goddammit, I been playin' trumpet . . ."*

*"Hell, you got off easy! What about him asking me if I had rheumatism, and I needed a hammer to close the valves . . .?"*

*"The wildeyed bastard is crazy, that's all! I leave it to you, Charlie. You ever hear me slide in or off a note? I ever have to feel for 'em? Why . . ."*

They were all chiming in, trying to top one another. But the drummer finally got and held the floor. I listened to his complaints—the bitter low-pitched voice. And I was both startled and hurt.

Possibly I had seemed a little sharp to the others, but I certainly hadn't meant to. I had only been joking, trying to make light of something that could not be helped. With the drummer, however, I had been especially gentle— exceedingly careful to do or say nothing that might hurt his pride. He had nothing at all to feel bitter about that I could see.

It was true that I had joked with him, but in the mildest of ways. I had not so much corrected him as tried to get him to correct himself.

I had tossed him a bag of peanuts on one occasion. On a couple of others I had suddenly held a mirror in front of him, at the height of his idiotic, orgiastic contortions. I had had him look at himself, that was all. I had said nothing. It was pointless to say anything, since English was even more than a mystery to him than music, and I saw no necessity to. It seemed best simply to let him look at himself—at the man become monkey. And how that could possibly have made him sore, why he should blame me for the way he looked . . .

Well, the hell with it. He wasn't worth worrying about or bothering with. None of them were. Only Danny Lee—Danny Lee's voice. I wished to God I could have gotten hold of her a couple of years sooner. By now, she'd have been at the top, so good that she wouldn't have been caught dead in a place like this.

I shaved and bathed and dressed. I walked over to her cottage, and told her to show at the pavilion at two o'clock sharp.

Then I dropped in on the boys.

They saw or heard me coming, for their voices rose suddenly in awkward self-conscious conversation. I went in, and there was a stilted exchange of greetings, and a heavy silence. And then two of them offered me coffee at the same time.

I declined, said I was eating in town. "By the way," I added. "Can I do anything for you guys in town? Mail some letters to the local for you?"

They knew I'd heard them then. I looked at them smiling, one eyebrow cocked; glancing from one sheepish, reddening, silly face to another.

No one said a word. No one made a move. They almost seemed to have stopped breathing. And I stared at them, and suddenly I was sick with shame.

I mumbled that everything was Jake. I told them they'd better get out and have some fun; to rent a boat, buy some swim trunks—anything they needed —and to charge it to me.

"No rehearsal today," I said. "None any day."

I got out of there.

I ate and went to the pavilion, and went to work with Danny Lee.

After a while, Ralph Devore showed up.

Ralph's the handyman-janitor here. Also the floorman—the guy who moves around among the dancers, and maintains order and so on. He's a hell of a handsome guy, vaguely reminiscent of someone I seem to have seen in pictures. He has a convertible Mercedes, which, I understand, he got through some elaborate chiseling. And dressed up in those fancy duds he has (given to him by wealthy summer people) he looks like a matinee idol. But he wasn't dressed up now. Now, when Danny Lee was seeing him for the first time, he looked like Bowery Bill from Trashcan Hill.

She was so burned up when he gave her a hand—and I kidded her about it—that she flounced her butt at him.

She stomped off to the dressing room. Ralph and I chewed the fat a little. And I began to get a very sweet idea, a plan for giving Miss Danny her comeuppance. I could see that Ralph had fallen for her. He wanted her so bad he could taste it. So with him looking as he did—or could—and Danny being what she was . . .

I put it up to Ralph, giving him slightly less than the facts about Danny. I said that she not only looked like a nice girl, but she *was* one. Very nice. The sole support of her family, in fact. So how did that cut any ice? He wasn't going to rape her. He could just take her out, and leave the rest up to her. If she wanted to cut loose okay, and if not the same.

"Well . . ." He hesitated nervously. "It just don't somehow seem right, Rags; I mean, fooling a nice little girl like that. I don't like people foolin' me, and—"

"So where's the harm?" I said. "If she really wants to hang on to it, money won't make any difference to her. If it does make a difference—all the dough you're supposed to have—there's still no harm done. What she loses can't be worth much."

"Well, yeah," he said. "Yeah, but . . ."

I was afraid he was going to ask why my enthusiasm for the enterprise. But I needn't have worried. He was too absorbed in Danny, so hard hit that he was in kind of a trance. And vaguely, with part of my mind, I wondered about that.

Ralph had seen sexy babes before. Seen them and had them. They were invariably kitchen maids or shop-girls on an outing, but still they had what it took. All that Ralph, being married, was interested in.

"She looks kind of tough," he murmured absently. "Awful sweet, kind of, but tough. Like she could be plenty hard-boiled if she took the notion."

"Oh, well," I said. "Think what a hard time, she's had. Supporting an invalid mother and—"

"I bet she knows her way around, don't she?"

"And you'd win," I said. "She can take care of herself, Ralph. You won't be taking advantage of her at all."

"Well . . ." He squirmed indecisively. "I—I—What you want me to do?"

He had some good clothes in his car. I told him to get washed and change into them, while I fixed things up with Danny. "And hurry," I said, as he hesitated. "Get back here as fast as you can. You can't keep a high class girl like her waiting."

He snapped out of it, and hurried away.

I went down to the dressing room.

She was waiting there, sullen and defiant and a little afraid. I hadn't told her she could go to her cottage, so she waited. I looked at her sorrowfully, slowly shaking my head.

"Well, you really tore it that time, sister," I said. "You know who that guy was? Just about the richest man in this county. Owns most of the beach property around here. Has a big piece of this pavilion, as a matter of fact."

"I'll bet!" she said—but a trifle uncertainly. "Oh, sure."

"How did Pete Pavlov stack up to you?" I said. "Hardly a fashion-plate, huh? You just can't figure these local people that way, baby. They keep right on working after they get it. They don't go in for show while they're working."

She studied my face uncertainly, trying to read it. I took her by the elbow and lead her to the window. "Who does that guy look like down there?" I said; for Ralph was just taking his clothes out of the Mercedes. "What do you think a buggy like that costs? You think an ordinary janitor would be driving it?"

She stiffened slightly; hell, that Mercedes even bowls me over. Then she shrugged with attempted indifference. So what, she asked. What did it mean to her if he was loaded.

"Just thought you'd like to know," I said. "Just thought you might like to meet him. He could do a lot for a gal if he took the notion to."

"Uh-huh," she said. "You just want to help me, I suppose! You're doing *me* favors!"

"Suit yourself." I picked up my shirt and began putting it on. "It's entirely up to you, baby. You do a little thinking, though, and maybe you'll remember me doing you a favor or two before. It maybe'll occur to you that I can't be any harder on you than I am on myself, and it ain't making me a penny."

"All right!" she snapped. "What do you want me to do about it? I've tried to thank you! I've—I've—"

"Never mind," I said. "I'm satisfied just to see you get ahead. That's all I've ever wanted."

I finished buttoning my shirt. I tucked the tails in, studying her out of the corner of my eye.

She was wavering—teetering one way, then the other. Wavering and then convinced, like the stupid moronic tramp she was. There was nothing in her head. Only in her throat.

And you could dump a thousand gallons of vinegar down it, and she'd still expect the next cup to be lemonade.

"Well," she said. "He did seem awfully nice. I mean, I couldn't tell what he looked like much, but he acted nice and respectful. And—and he clapped for me."

"He's a wonderful guy," I said. "One of the best."

"Well . . . well, I guess I ought to apologize, anyway," she said. "I ought to do that, even if he was only a janitor."

She preceded me up the steps. She started to open the door that leads out to the bandstand, and suddenly I put out my hand.

"Danny. Wait . . . baby."

It was the way I said it, the last word. A way I'd never thought I could say it. To her. She froze in her tracks, one foot on one step, the other, the shorts drawn high and tight upon her thighs. Then, her head moved and she looked slowly over her shoulder.

"W-what?" she stammered. "What did you cal—say?"

"Nothing," I said. "I guess I . . . nothing."

"Tell me," she said. "Tell me what you want, Rags."

"I want," I said. "I want . . ."

The unobtainable, that was all. The nonexistent. The that which never-would-be. I wanted it and I did not want it, for once achieved there would be nothing left to live for.

"I want you to get your butt out of my face," I said. "Fast. Before I kick it off of you."

# IV

## Bobbie Ashton

I FINISHED AT the Thorncastle estate about four-thirty in the afternoon, and Mr. Thorncastle—that fine, democratic fat-bottomed man—paid me off personally.

My bill came to twelve dollars. I looked at him from under my lashes as he paid it, and he added an extra five. Managing to stroke my hand in the process. He is a very juicy-looking character, this Thorncastle. I had some difficulty in getting away from him without kicking him in the groin.

Father was already at the table when I reached home. I washed hastily and joined him, begging his pardon for keeping him waiting. He snatched up his fork. Then he slammed it down, and asked me just how long I intended to keep up this nonsense.

"The yard work?" I said. "Why, permanently, perhaps. It would seem well suited to my station in life—you know, with so much racial discrimination—and—"

"Stop it!" His face whitened. "Don't ever let me hear you—"

"—and there's the money," I said. "A chance to advance myself financially."

"Like Ralph Devore, I suppose! Like the town oddjobs man!"

I shrugged. The facts of the matter were under his nose even if he, like the rest of the town, was too dullwitted to see them. Ralph had earned approximately twenty-eight hundred dollars a year for the past twenty-two years. He had spent practically nothing. Ergo, he now had a minimum of fifty thousand dollars, and probably a great deal more.

He had it. He would have to. And now that his income was cut off, he would be worried frantic. For fifty thousand would not represent enough security to Ralph. Not fifty thousand or a hundred thousand. He would visualize its disappearing, vanishing into nothingness before his life span had run. He would be terrified, and his terror must certainly react terrifyingly upon Luane.

I wondered where he had hidden the money, since, naturally, he had hidden it—how else could he keep its possession a secret?—as, in his insecurity, he would feel that he had to.

Well, no matter where it was now. There was still this first stage of the game to play. When it was played out, I would concentrate on the money—locate and appropriate it. And watch what happened to Luane, then.

She had behaved very badly, Luane. She had made the serious mistake of telling the truth.

That was unfair; it was theft. The truth was mine—I had earned it painfully and it belonged to me. And now, after years of waiting and planning, it was worthless. A heap of rust, instead of the stout, sharp-pronged lever I was entitled to.

What good was the truth, now? How could I use it on *him,* now?

Not much. Not enough. Not nearly enough.

He was talking again, bumbling on with his nonsense about my returning to school whether I thought I was or not.

"You're going, understand? You're going to complete your education. You can finish up your high school here, or you can go away. And then you're going on to—"

"Am I?" I said.

"You certainly are! Why—what kind of a boy are you? Letting some gossips, some fool woman spoil your life! No one believes anything she says."

"Oh, yes, they do," I said. "Yes, they do, father. I could name at least three who do, right here in our own household."

He stared at me, his mouth trembling, the mist of fear and frustration in his eyes. I winked at him, hoping he would start blubbering. But of course he didn't. He has too much pride for that—too much dignity. Ah, what a proud, upright man my father is!

"You have to leave," he said slowly. "You must see that you have to leave this town. With your mind—with no outlet for your intelligence . . ."

"I'll think about it," I said. "I'll let you know what I decide."

"I said you'd leave! You'll do what I say!"

"I'll tell you what I'll do," I said. "Exactly, dear father, as I damned please. And if what pleases me doesn't please you, you know what you can do about it."

He stood up, abruptly, flinging his napkin to the table. He said, yes, he confounded well *did* know what he could do; and he'd just about reached the point where he was ready to do it.

"You mean you'd call in the authorities?" I said. "I'd hate to see you do that, father. I'd feel forced to go into the background of my supposed incorrigibility, and the result might be embarrassing for you."

I gave him a sunny smile. He whirled, and stamped away to his office.

He was back a moment later, his hat on, his medicine kit in one hand.

"Do one thing, at least," he said. "For your own good. Stay away from that Pavlov girl."

"Myra? Why should I stay away from her?" I said.

"Stay away from her," he repeated. "You know what Pete Pavlov's like. If —if you—he—"

"Yes?" I said. "I'm afraid I don't understand. What possible objection could

Pavlov have to his daughter's going about with Doctor Ashton's well-bred, brilliant and, I might add, handsome son?"

"Please, Bob—" His voice sagged tiredly. "Please do it. Leave her alone."

I hesitated thoughtfully. After a long moment, I shrugged.

"Well, all right," I said. "If it means that much to you."

"Thank you. I—"

"I'll leave her alone," I said, "whenever I get ready to. Not before."

He didn't flinch or explode, much to my disappointment. Apparently he'd been partially prepared for the trick. He simply stared at me, hard-eyed, and when he spoke his voice was very, very quiet.

"I have one more thing to say," he said. "A considerable quantity of narcotics is missing from my stock. If I discover any further shortages, I'll see to it that you're punished—imprisoned or institutionalized. I'll do it regardless of what it does to me."

He turned and left.

I scraped up the dishes and carried them out into the kitchen.

Hattie was at the stove, her back turned to me. She stiffened as I went in, then turned part way around, trying to keep an eye on me while appearing occupied with her work.

Hattie is probably thirty-nine or forty now. She isn't as pretty as I remember her as a child—I thought she was the loveliest woman in the world then—but she is still something to take a second look at.

I put the dishes in the sink. I moved along the edge of the baseboard, smiling to myself, watching her neck muscles tighten as I moved out of her range of vision.

I was right behind her before fear forced her to whirl around. She pressed back against the stove, putting her hands out in a pushing-away gesture.

"Why, mother," I said. "What's the matter? You're not afraid of your own darling son, are you?"

"Go 'way!" Her eyes rolled whitely. "Lea' me alone, you hear?"

"But I just wanted a kiss," I said. "Just a kiss from my dear, sweet mother. After all, I haven't had one now, since—well, I was about three, wasn't I? A very long time for a child to go without a kiss from his own mother. I remember being rather heartbroken when—"

"D-don't!" she moaned. "You don't know nothin' about—Get outta here! I tell doctor on you, an' he—"

"You mean you're not my mother?" I said. "You're truly not?"

"N-no! I tol' you, ain't I? Ain't nothin', nobody! I—I—"

"Well, all right." I shrugged. "In that case . . ."

I grabbed her suddenly, clamped her against me, pinning her arms to her sides. She gasped, moaned, struggled futilely. She didn't, of course, cry out for help.

"How about it," I said, "as long as you're not my mother. Keep it all in the family, huh? What do you say we—"

I let go of her, laughing.

I stepped back, wiping her spittle from my face.

"Why, Hattie," I said. "Why on earth did you do a thing like that? All I wanted was—What?" My heart did a painful skip-jump, and there was a choking lump in my throat. "What? I don't believe I understood you, Hattie."

She looked at me, lips curled back from her teeth. Eyes narrowed, steady, with contempt. With something beyond contempt, beyond disgust and hatred.

"You hear' me right," she said. "You couldn' do nothin'. Couldn' an' never will."

"Yes?" I said. "Are you very sure of that, my dearest mother?"

"Huh! Me, I tell *you.*" She grinned a skull's grin. "Yeah, I ver' sure, aw right, my deares' son."

"And it amuses you," I said. "Well, I'll tell you, mother. Doubtless it is very funny, but I don't believe we'd better have any further displays of amusement. Not that I'd mind killing you, you understand. In fact, I'll probably get around to that eventually. But I have other projects afoot at the moment—more important projects, if I may say so without hurting your feelings—"

She moved suddenly, made a dash for her room. I followed her— it adjoins the kitchen—and leaned absently against the door. The locked door to my mother's room.

The door that had been locked for . . .

Yes, my recollection was right; it is always right. I had been about three the last time she had kissed me, the last time she had cuddled, babied, mother-and-babied me. I would have remembered it, even if I did not have almost total recall. For how could one forget such a fierce outpouring of love, the balm-like, soul-satisfying warmth of it?

Or forget its abrupt, never-to-be-again withdrawal?

Or the stupid, selfish, cruel, bewildering insistence that it had never been?

I was a very silly little boy. I was a very foolish, bad little boy, and I had better pray God to forgive me. I was not sweets or hon or darlin' or even Bobbie. I was Mister Bobbie—Master Robert. Mistah—Mastah Bobbie, a reborn stranger among strangers.

My continuing illnesses? Psychosomatic. The manifold masques of frustration.

My intelligence? Compensatory. For certainly I inherited none from either of them.

I listened at night, when they thought I was asleep. I asked a few questions, strategically spacing them months apart.

She'd had a child; she'd had to wet-nurse me. Where was that child? Dead? Well, where and when had he died? When and where had my mother died?

It was ridiculously simple. Only a matter of putting a few questions to a fatuous imbecile—my father—and an oversexed docile moron, my mother. And listening to them at night. Listening and wanting to shriek with laughter.

He'd be ruined if anyone found out. It would ruin my life, wreck all my chances.

It would be that way *if.* And what way did the blind, stupid, silly son-of-a-bitch think it was now? What worse way could it be than as it was now?

And, no, it did not need to be that way. Needn't and wouldn't have been for a man with courage and honesty and decency.

I had deduced the truth by the time I was five. Several years later, when I was able to be up and around—to post and receive letters secretly—I proved my deductions.

He, my father, had practiced in only one other state before coming to this one. It had no record of a birth to Mrs. James Ashton, or of the death of said Mrs. Ashton. There was, however, a record of the birth of a son to one Hattie Marie Smith (colored; unmarried; initial birth). And the attending physician was Dr. James Ashton.

Well?

Or perhaps I should say *well!*

As a matter of fact, I said goddammit, since the cigarette was scorching my fingers.

I dropped it to the floor, ground it out with my shoe and rapped on my mother's door.

"Mother," I said. "Mammy—" I knocked harder. "You heah me talkin' to you, mammy? Well, you sho bettah answer then, or your lul ol' boy gonna come in theah an' peel that soft putty hide right offen you. He do it, mammy. You knows all about him—doncha?—an' you knows he will. He gonna wait just five seconds, and then he's gonna bus' this heah ol' doah down an' . . ."

I looked at my wristwatch, began counting off the seconds aloud.

The bed creaked, and I heard a muffled croak. A dull, weary sound that was part sigh, part sob.

"Now, that's better," I said. "Listen closely, because this concerns you. It's my plan for finishing you off, you and my dearly beloved father . . . I am going to take you out to some deserted place, and bind you with chains. I shall so chain you that you will be apart from each other, and yet together. Inseparable yet touching. And you shall be stripped to your lustful hides. And in winter I shall douse you with ice-water, and in summer I shall smother you with blankets. And you shall shriek and shiver with the cold, and you shall scream and scorch with the heat. Yet you shall be voiceless and unheard.

"That will go on for seventeen years, mother. No, I'll be fair—deduct a couple of years. Then I'll bring you back here, pile you into bed together, and give you a sample of the hell that could never be hot enough for you. Set you on fire. Set the house on fire. Set the whole goddamned town on fire. Think of it, mammy! The whole population. Whole families, infants, children, mothers and fathers, grandparents and great-grandparents—all burning, all stacked together in lewd juxtaposition. And it shall come to pass, mammy. Yeah, verily. For to each thing there is a season, mammy, and a time—"

She was moaning peculiarly. Keening, I suppose you would say.

I listened absently, deciding that Pete Pavlov should be spared from my prospective holocaust.

No one else. At least, I could think of no one else at the moment. But certainly Pete Pavlov.

It was early, around eight o'clock, when I arrived at the dance pavilion. The bandstand was dark. The ticket booth—where Myra Pavlov serves as cashier —was closed. Only one of the ballroom chandeliers was burning. There was, however, a light in Pete's office. So I vaulted the turnstile, and started across the dance floor.

He was at his desk, counting a stack of bills. I was almost to the doorway when he looked up, startled, his hand darting toward an open desk drawer.

Then he saw it was I and he let out a disgusted grunt.

"Damn you, Bobbie. Better watch that sneakin' up on people. Might get your tail shot off."

I laughed and apologized. I said I hoped that if anyone ever did try to hold him up, he wouldn't try to stop them.

"You do, huh?" he said. "How come you hope that?"

"Why—why, because." I frowned innocently. "You have robbery insurance, haven't you? Well, why risk your life for some insurance company?"

I suspect, from the brief flicker in his eyes, the very slight change in facial expression, that he had entertained some such notion himself—that is, I should say, a fake robbery to collect on his insurance. He needed money, popular opinion notwithstanding. A robbery would be the simplest, most straightforward means of getting it. And he was a simple (I use the term flatteringly) straightforward man.

I would have been glad to help him perpetrate such a robbery. Broadly speaking, I would have done anything I could to help him. Unfortunately, however—although I respected him for it—he distrusted me instinctively.

So he treated me to a long, unblinking gaze. Then he grunted, spat in the spittoon and leaned back in his chair. He rocked back and forth in it, hands locked behind his head, looking down at the desk and then slowly raising his eyes to mine.

"I tell you," he said. "Used to be a hound dog around these parts. Fastfootedest goddamned dog you ever saw in your life. You know what happened to him?"

"I imagine he ran over himself," I said.

"Yup. Bashed his brains out with his own butt. Hell of a nice-looking dog, too, and he seemed smart as turpentine. Always wondered why he didn't know better'n to do a thing like that."

I smiled. Pete would not have wondered at all about the why of his allegorical dog. Nor the why of anything. Like myself, Pete's concern was with what things were, not how or why they had become that way.

He finished counting the money. He put it in a tin cash box, locked it up in his safe and came back to the desk. Sat down on a corner of it in front of me, one thick leg swung over the other.

"Well—" His hard, hazel-colored eyes rolled over on my face. "Figure on sleepin' in here tonight? Want me to move you in a bed?"

"I'm sorry." I got up reluctantly. "I was just—uh—"

"Yeah? Something on your mind?"

"N-no. No, I guess not," I said. "I just dropped by to say hello. I didn't have anything to do for a while, so I—"

He looked at me steadily. He spat at the spittoon without shifting his eyes. I cleared my throat, feeling a hot, embarrassing flush spread over my face.

He stood up suddenly, and started for the door. Spoke over his shoulder, his voice gruff.

"Ain't got nothing to do myself for a few minutes. Come on and I'll buy you a sody."

I followed him to a far corner of the ballroom; followed, since he kept a half-pace in front of me. I wanted to pay for the drinks, but he brushed my hand aside, dropped two dimes into the Coke machine himself.

He handed me a bottle. I thanked him and he grunted, jerking the cap on his own.

We stood facing the distant bandstand where the musicians were arriving. We stood side by side, almost touching each other. Separated by no more than a few inches—and silence.

He finished his drink, smacked his lips and dropped the bottle into the empty case. I finished mine reluctantly, disposed of the bottle as he had.

"Well . . ." He spoke as I straightened from the case; spoke, still looking out across the ballroom. "You and Myra steppin' out again tonight?"

I said, why, yes, we were. As soon as she got off work, that is. And after a moment, I added, "If that's all right with you, Mr. Pavlov."

"Know any reason why it shouldn't be?"

"Why—well, no," I said, "I guess not. I mean—"

"I'll tell you," he said. He hesitated, and belched. "I ain't got a goddamned bit of use for you. Never have had, far back as I can remember. But I guess you already know that?"

"Yes," I said. "And I can't tell you how sorry I am, Mr. Pavlov."

"Can't say I'm not sorry myself. Always rather like someone than dislike 'em." He belched again, mumbling something about the gas. "On the other hand, I got no real reason not to have no use for you. Nothing I can put my finger on. You've always been friendly and polite around me. I don't know of no dirty deals you've pulled, unless'n it's this stuff with Ralph, and I can't really call that dirty, considering. Might've gone off sideways like that myself when I was your age."

"I knew you'd understand," I said. "Mr. Pavlov, I—"

"I was sayin'—" He cut me off curtly. "I got no reason to feel like I do, and reasons are all I go by. People don't give me no trouble, I don't give them any. I rock along with 'em as long as they rock with me. And whether I like 'em or not don't figure in the matter. All right. I guess we understand each other. Now, I got to get busy."

He nodded curtly, and headed back toward his office.

I moved toward the exit.

Myra had come in while Pete and I were talking, and she called to me from the ticket booth. I looked her way blindly, my eyes stinging, misting. Not really hearing or seeing her. I went out without answering her, and sat down in my car.

I got a cigarette lighted. I took a few deep puffs, forcing away my disgusting self-pity. Recovering some of my normal objectiveness.

Pete detested me. It was fitting that he should—things being as they were. And I would not have had it any other way—things being as they were.

But what a pity, what a goddamned pity that they were that way! And why couldn't they have been another, the right and logical way?

Why couldn't my own dear father and mother, those encephalitic cretans, those gutless Jukesters, those lubricous lusus naturae—why couldn't they have had Myra inflicted upon them? Why should Pete have to suffer such a drab, spiritless wretch as she? Why couldn't they have had her, and why couldn't he have had—

Myra. A feeling of fury came over me every time I looked at her. I'd had some plans for her—vague but decidedly unpleasant—long before she came to the office that day a couple of months ago.

Father was away on some calls. I glanced at the notes on her file card.

This was her second trip. She was having menstrual difficulties—something that a good kick in the stomach or a dose of salts would have jarred her out of. But father, that wise and philanthropic Aesculapian, had set her up for a series of hormone shots.

She said she was in a hurry, so I prepared to administer the medication.

Yes, I do that: take care of routine patients. Rather, I did do it, until father became wary. I know a hell a lot more about medicine than he does. A hell of a lot more about everything than he does. In this case, for example, I knew that what Myra needed—deserved—was not hormone.

I gave her a hypodermic. She "flashed"—to use the slang expression; barely made it to the sink before she started vomiting. I told her it was perfectly all right, and gave her another shot.

Well, someone like that, someone with only part of a character, is made for the stuff. The stuff is made for them. She was hooked in less than a week. She doesn't go to father any more, but she does come to me.

I "treat" her now. I give her what she needs—and deserves. When I am ready to. And after certain ceremonies.

Ten-thirty came. Not more than five minutes later, which was as fast as she could make it, she was running toward the car. Begging before she had the door open.

I told her to shut up. I said that if she said one more word until I gave her permission, she would get nothing.

I had her well trained. She subsided, mouth twisting, gulping down the whimpers that rose in her throat.

I drove to a place about six miles up the beach—Happy Hollow, it is called, for reasons which you may guess. I suppose there is some such place in every community, dubbed with the same sly euphemism or a similar one.

It—this place—was not a hollow; not wholly, at least. Most of its area was hill, wooded and brushy, marked with innumerable trails and side-trails which terminated in tire-marked, beach-like patches of sand.

I stopped at one of these patches. The only tire-marks were those of my own car.

I made her take her clothes off. I grabbed her. I shook her and slapped her and pinched her. I called her every name I could think of.

She didn't speak or cry out. But suddenly I stopped short, and gave her the shot. I was tired. There seemed no point in going on. Action and words, words and action—leading to nothing, arriving nowhere. It wasn't enough. There can be no real satisfaction without an objective.

Myra lay back in the seat, breathing in long deep breaths, eyes half shut. She didn't have a bad shape. In fact, without clothes on—she simply couldn't wear clothes—she shaped up quite beautifully. But only aesthetically, as far as I was concerned. I felt no desire for her.

I wanted to. My mind shrieked that I should. But the flesh could not hear it.

She dozed. I may have dozed myself, or perhaps I merely became lost in thought. At any rate, I snapped back to awareness suddenly, aroused by the dull lacing of light through the trees, the throb of a familiar motor.

Myra sat up abruptly. Stared at me, eyes wide with fright. I told her to sit still and be quiet. Just do what I told her to, and she'd be all right.

I listened to the motor, following the progress of the car. It stopped, with a final purring *throb-throb,* and I knew exactly where it had stopped.

I hesitated. I opened the door of the car.

"B-Bobbie . . ." A frightened whisper from Myra. "Where you going? I'm afraid to stay—"

I told her to shut up; I'd only be gone for a few minutes.

"B-but why? What're you going to—?"

"Nothing. I don't know. I mean—hell, just shut up!" I said.

I went down the trail a few yards. I branched off into another, and then another. I came to the end of it—near the end of it, and hunkered down in the shadows of the trees.

They weren't more than twenty feet away, Ralph Devore and that what's-her-name—the girl with the orchestra. I could see them clearly in the filtered moonlight. I could hear every word they said, every sound. And the way it looked and sounded . . .

I could hardly believe it, particularly of a guy like Ralph. Because when Ralph stepped out with 'em, it was for just one thing and he lost no time about getting it. Yet now with this girl—and, no, she certainly didn't hate him. She obviously felt the same way about him that he did her, and that way—

I didn't know what it was for a moment. Then, when I finally knew—remembered—realized—I refused to admit it. I grinned to myself, silently jeering them, jeering myself. Ralph was really making time, I thought. Here it was only the sixth week of the season, he'd only known this babe six weeks, and they were cutting up like a couple of newlyweds. Newlyweds, sans the sex angle. Which, of course, they'd soon be getting around to.

Maybe—I thought—I ought to do the silly jerk a favor. Go up to his house some night and bump off Luane. It could be made to look like an accident. And believe me, it would need to look damned little like one to leave Ralph in the clear. Father was the coroner, the county medical officer. As for the county attorney, Henry Clay Williams . . . I shook my head, choking back a laugh. You had to hand it to that goddamned Luane. She had a positively fiendish talent for tossing the knife, for plunging it into exactly the right spot to send the crap flying. Henry Clay Williams was a bachelor. Henry Clay Williams lived with his maiden sister. And Henry Clay Williams' sister had an abdominal tumor . . . which created a bulge normally created by a different kind of growth.

At any rate, and unless the job was done in front of witnesses, it would be ridiculously easy to get away with killing Luane. Just make it look like an accident, enough like one to give Brother Williams an out, and—

I leaned forward, straining to hear them, Ralph and the girl, for they were clinging even closer to each other than they had been, and their voices were consequently muffled:

"*Don't you worry one bit, honey*"—her. "*I don't know how, but—but, gosh, there's got to be some way! I just love you so much, and you're so wonderful and—*"

*"Not wonderful 'nough for you"*—him. Old love-'em-and-scram Ralph, for God's sake! Why, he sounded practically articulate. *"Ain't it funny, sweetheart? Here I am an old man—"*

*"You are not! You're the sweetest, darlingest, kindest, handsomest . . ."*

*"Anyways, I mean I lived all these years, and I reckon I never knew there was such a thing. Like love I mean. I guess I . . ."*

I found that I was smiling. I scrubbed it away with my fist, scrubbed my eyes with my fist. But it kept coming back. That word, the one he'd spoken, the one I'd been ducking—it kept coming back. And I knew that there was no other word for what this was.

He wasn't going to pitch it to her. She wasn't going to hit him up for dough. They were in love—*ah, simply, simply in love!* Only—*only!*—in love. And, ah, the sweetness of it, the almost unbearable beauty and wonderment of it.

To be loved like that! More important, to love like that!

I smiled upon them, at them. Smiled like a loving god, happy in their happiness. Probably, I thought, I should kill them now. It would be such a wonderful way—time—to die.

I glanced around absently. I ran a hand back under the bushes, searching for a suitable club or rock. I could find none—nothing that would do the job with the instantaneousness necessary, nothing that was sufficiently sturdy or heavy.

I did locate a pointed, dagger-like stick, and I considered it for a moment. But a very little mental calculation established that it would never do. It wasn't long enough. It would never pass through that barrel-chest of Ralph's and go on into her bosom. And if I did not get them both at the same time, if I left one to live without the other—!

I almost wept at the thought.

A strange warmth spread over me. Spread down from my head and up from my feet. It increased, intensified, and I did not know what it was. How could I, never having experienced it before? And then at last I knew, and I knew what had brought it about.

I straightened up. I backed down the trail quietly, and then I turned and strode toward my car excitedly, my mind racing.

There could be nothing now, of course. Dope inhibits the sexual impulses, so she would have to be tapered off first. But that should be relatively easy; she should unhook almost as easily as she had been hooked. If I could just get the stuff to work with—and I *would* get it, by God! I'd kill that stupid son-of-a-bitch, my father, if he gave me any trouble . . .

I cut off the thought. Somehow the thought of parricide, entirely justifiable though it was, interfered with the other.

I would get what I needed in some way. That was all that mattered. And meanwhile I could be preparing her, laying the necessary groundwork. And meanwhile I *knew.*

I KNEW!

I reached the car. I climbed in, smiling.

She had her coat draped over her, but she was still undressed. I told her, lovingly, to get dressed. Lovingly, with tender pats and caresses, I started to help her.

"D-don't . . . !" She shivered. "What d-do you want?"

"Nothing," I said. "Only what you want, darling. Whatever you want, that's what I want."

She stared at me like a snake-charmed bird. Her teeth chattered. I took her in my arms, gently pressed my mouth against hers. I smiled softly, dreamily, stroking her hair.

"That's all I want, honey," I said. "Now, you tell me what you want."

"I w-want to go home. P-please, Bobbie. Just—"

"Look," I said. "I love you. I'd do anything in the world for you. I—"

I kissed her. I crushed her body against mine. And her lips were stiff and lifeless, and her body was like ice. And the glow was leaving me. The life and the resurrection were leaving me.

"D-don't," I said. "I mean, please. I only want to love you, only to love you and have you love me. That's all. Only sweetness and tenderness and—"

Suddenly I dug my fingers into her arms. I shook her until her silly stupid head almost flopped off.

I told her she'd better do what I said or I'd kill her.

"I'll do it, by God!" I slapped her in the face. "I'll beat your goddamned head off! You be nice to me, you moronic bitch! Be sweet, you slut! Y-you be gentle and tender and loving—you love me, DAMN YOU, YOU LOVE ME! Or I'll . . . I'll . . ."

# V

## DR. JAMES ASHTON

IT MAY RING false when I say so, but I did love her. Back in the beginning and for several years afterward. It became impossible later on, will it as I would and despite anything I could do. For we could share nothing but a bed, and that less and less frequently. We could not share the most important thing we had. It *was* impossible—you see that, do you not? So the love went away.

But once long ago . . .

She was twenty-two or -three when she came to me. She was practically illiterate—a shabby, life-beaten slum-dweller. There was a great deal of race prejudice in that state—there is still, unfortunately, so much everywhere—and Negroes got little if any schooling; they had no place to live but slums.

I hired her as my housekeeper. I paid her twice the pittance, the prevailing and starvation wage for Negro houseworkers. I gave her decent quarters, a clean attic room with a lavatory, there in my own house.

She was thin, undernourished. I saw to it that she got plenty of good wholesome food. She needed medical attention. I gave it to her—taking time from paying patients to do so.

I shall never forget the day I examined her. I had suspected the beauty of her body, even in the shabby ill-fitting clothes I had first seen her in. But the revelation of it was almost more than the eyes could bear. Of all the nude women I had seen—professionally, of course—I had seen none to compare with her. She was like a statue, sculpted of ivory by one of the great masters. Even frail and half-starved, she—

But I digress.

She was very grateful for all I had done for her. Overflowing with gratitude. Her eyes followed me wherever I went, and in them there was that burning worship you see in a dog's eyes. I think that if I had ordered her to take poison she would have done so instantly.

I did not want her to feel that way. At least, I made it very clear to her that she owed me nothing. I had done no more than was decent, I explained. No more than one decent person should do for another—circumstances permitting. All I wanted of her, I said, was that she be happy and well, as such a fine young woman should be.

She would not have it so. I wanted—was more than willing to, at any rate —but not she. There was an immutable quality about her gratitude. Wherever I was, there was it: quietly omnipotent, passively resistant, a constant proffering. Impossible to dispose of; beyond, at least, my powers.

I did not wish to hurt her feelings. I could see no real harm in accepting what she was so anxious to give. It was all she had to give. And the gift of one's all is not lightly rejected.

Finally, around the middle of her second month of service with me, I accepted it.

There was no love in it that first time. None on my side, that is. It was merely a matter of saving her pride, and, of course—to a degree, at least—physical gratification. But after that, very quickly after that, the love came.

And it was only natural, I suppose, that it should.

I came from a very poor family; migrant sharecroppers. My parents had twelve children—three stillborn, five who died in early childhood. The largest house we ever lived in was two rooms. I was six or seven years old before I tasted cow's milk, or knew that there was such a thing as red meat. I was almost a grown man before I owned a complete set of clothes.

If it had not been for a plantation overseer's taking an interest in me, if he had not induced my father to let me remain with his family when my own moved on, I should probably have wound up like the rest of the brood. Like my living brothers and sisters . . . if they are living. Hoe-hands. Cotton-pickers. White trash.

Or, no, I do myself an injustice. I could never have been like them. I would have found some way to push myself up, overseer or no (and life with him, believe you me, was no bed of roses).

Through grade school, high school, college and medical school—in all that time, I cannot remember having a complete day of rest.

I worked my way every step of the way. I did nothing but work and study. I had no time for recreation, for girls. When I did have the time, when I was at last practicing and reasonably free from financial worry, I had no, well, knack with them. I was ill at ease around girls. I was incapable of the flippery-dippery and chitchat which they seemed to expect. I learned that one young lady I liked—and who, I thought, reciprocated my feeling—had referred to me as a "terrible stick."

So, there you have it. Hattie loved me. A woman more beautiful than any I had ever seen loved me. And I could be with her in the most intimate way —talk to her of the most intimate things (although she could not always answer intelligently)—and feel not a whit of awkwardness.

I fell in love with her deeply. It was inevitable that I should.

I was, of course, quite alarmed when I learned that she was pregnant. Alarmed and not a little angry. For she had failed to take the precautions I had prescribed and entrusted her to take. As I saw it, there was nothing for it but an abortion, even though she was three months along. But much to my chagrin, for she had always done as I wanted before, Hattie refused.

She was virtually tigerish in her refusal, threatening me with what she would do if I attempted to take the foetus from her. Then as I became firm—considerably shocked by her conduct—she turned to pleading. And I could not help feeling touched, nor the feeling that I had been taken sore advantage of.

The boy (she always spoke of him as a boy) would be able to "pass." After perhaps two hundred years of outrace-breeding, after eight generations, there would be a child of her blood who could pass for white . . . Couldn' I understand? Didn' I see why she jus' *had* to have it?

I relented. I could have insisted on the abortion, and she would have had to submit. But I did not insist. Except for me, the child would not have been born.

When the pregnancy began to show, I moved her out of the house. From that day on, until she gave birth, I called on her at least twice a week.

I could not go through such an experience now. There were times, even then, when I thought I could stand no more. A white man—*a white doctor!*—visiting in the Negro slums! Treating a Negro woman! It was unheard of, unprecedented—a soul-shaking, pride-trampling experience. White doctors did not treat Negroes. Generally speaking, no one did. They simply did without medical attention, administering to themselves, when it was necessary, with home remedies and patent nostrums; delivering their own babies or depending on midwives.

All in all, they seemed to get by fairly well in that manner—although, Negro vital statistics being what they are, or were, one cannot be sure. And in the good health she was enjoying, I think that Hattie could have gotten by quite well without me. But it apparently didn't occur to her to suggest it. She *didn't* suggest it, anyway; and I hardly felt able to.

For that matter, I don't know that I would have been willing to leave her untended. In fact, and on reflection, I am quite sure that I would not. I was deeply in love with her, deeply concerned for her and our child. Otherwise, I would not have done what I did when the birth became imminent.

Negroes were not treated by white doctors, as I have said. This meant that they were not admitted to white hospitals—and there were nothing but white hospitals. There was a ramshackle, poorly staffed county institution which admitted Negroes, but not unless it was absolutely impelled to. If a Negro was dying he might get in. If he did, he would probably never live to regret it.

Well. I was on the staff of one of the white hospitals. I had only recently obtained the appointment. I got Hattie admitted to it as a white woman, of Spanish-Indian descent.

I did that, knowing almost certainly that the fraud would be discovered. I loved her that much, thought that much of her—and, needless to say, the child.

They were giving her narrow-eyed looks from the moment she stepped through the door. They suspected her from the beginning; me and her. I could see that they did, see it and feel it. Then, when she was coming out of the anaesthesia, when she began to talk . . .

I shall never forget how they looked at me.

Or what the chief of staff said to me.

I was forced to remove her and the child the following day. I did not put it to an issue—how could I?—but if I had refused to remove them, I believe they would have been thrown out.

That was the end of my staff job, of course. The end of my practice, of everything in that state. Probably I can consider myself lucky that I wasn't lynched.

It was several days before I could nerve myself even to leave the house.

There was only one thing to do: relocate. Move to some place so remote and far away that no word of my secret would ever reach to it. Some place, yes —now that the die was cast—where Hattie could be accepted as my wife.

Down here where we were, they were always on the lookout for colored blood, expert at detecting it. But in a new location—the kind I had in mind —and with a little intensive coaching for Hattie, as to her speech and mannerisms . . . well, my plan seemed entirely feasible.

I believe it would have been, too, if circumstances had not turned out as they did.

I saw a practice advertised here at Manduwoc. I left Hattie and the boy behind, and came here to look at it.

It seemed to fit my needs to a *t*; in remoteness, in distance from that other state. It was not too big a thing financially, the town being as small as it was. But there was a large farm-trade area to draw from, and I was confident that a live-wire could double or even triple the present practice.

I decided to buy it. I went to Henry Clay Williams to have the papers drawn up.

Hank, I should say, was not then the county attorney. He was, in fact, only a few years out of law school. But he was a very shrewd man, very knowing; and he took an immediate liking to me. He looked upon me as a friend, as I did him. He was determined that I should get off on the right foot, and he knew how to go about it.

I owe a lot to Hank. More than any man I know of.

He was very adroit with his advice; he came out with it in a rather backhanded way. He'd lead with a feeler as to my notion on things; then, on the next time around, he'd move in with something a little stronger.

I mustn't think he was nosy, he said. Far be it from him to give a whoop what a man's politics or his religion or his race was. But there were still a hell of a lot of hidebound mossbacks around. People with foolish prejudices— shameful prejudices, in his opinion—although, of course, they had the same right to their ideas that he had to his. And the center of population for those people, by God—Hank gets pretty salty at times—seemed to be right here in Manduwoc!

I laughed. I said it was certainly unfortunate that people had to be that way.

"But what's a man going to do, Jim?" he said. "A man's got a living to make and wants to get somewhere, what can he do about 'em?"

"I guess there's nothing much he can do," I said. "It's a problem of education, evolution. Something that only time can take care of."

"I don't see how he can go around with a chip on his shoulder, do you, Jim?" he said. "Why, look, now. Some of my very best friends are—well, let's say, people that aren't exactly popular around here. My *very* best friends, Jim. But a man can't live off his friends, can he? That wouldn't be fair to them, would it? He has to live with the community as a whole, doesn't he?"

"That's the way it is," I said. "It's too bad, but—"

"It's outrageous," he said. "Absolutely outrageous, Jim. Why, my blood actually boils sometimes at some of the carryings-on in this town. I don't mean that they're not good people, understand? The salt of the earth in many respects. They're just narrow-minded, and they don't want to broaden. And if you try to buck 'em, give 'em the slightest reason to get their claws into you —hell, they don't actually need a real reason, if you know what I mean—why, they'll rip you apart. I've seen it happen, Jim. There's a man here in town, now, a Bohunk contractor name of Pete Pavlov. He . . ."

"I see," I said. "I understand what you mean, Hank."

"And you think I've got the right slant, Jim? You agree with me?"

"Oh, absolutely," I said. "There's no question about it. Now, there is one thing—in view of what you've told me. As I've mentioned, my wife died recently, and—"

"A great loss, I'm sure. My deepest sympathies to you, Jim."

"—and I have our infant son to take care of," I said. "Or, I should say, I have a Ne—nigger woman taking care of him. A wet nurse. I suppose I could get another one for him, but—"

"Oh, well," Hank shrugged. "She's a southern nigger, isn't she? Knows her place? Well, that'll be all right. After all, no one could expect you to take a baby away from its nurse."

"Well, I certainly wouldn't want to," I said.

"And you don't have to. As long as she stays in her place—and I guess you'll see to that, won't you? ha-ha—she'll get along fine."

. . . . I don't see how I could have done anything else.

I certainly had no easy row to hoe myself.

It is only in recent years that I have been able to take things a little easy. Before that it was work, work, work, until all hours of the day and night. Fighting to hold onto the old practice, to build it into something really worthwhile. Fighting to be someone, to build something . . . for nothing.

I had no time for them, the boy and her. No time, at least, on many days. Perhaps—to be entirely truthful—I did not want time for them. And if I did not, I hardly see how I can be faulted for it.

It was awkward being with her, even in intimacy. She made me feel uncomfortable, guilty, hypocritical. I had become something here, and I was rapidly becoming more. I was a big frog in a little puddle. A deacon in the church. A director of the bank. A pillar in the community. Yet here I was, sleeping with a Negro wench!

I would have stopped it even if it had not become dangerous. My conscience would not have allowed me to continue.

As for the boy, I did—and do, I am afraid—love him . . . as I did her, so long ago. He was my own flesh and blood, my only son. And I loved him, as I loved her. But like her, although in a different way, he made me uncomfortable. It distressed me to be around him.

I cannot say why, exactly, but I am confident of one thing. It was not a matter of resentment.

I did not blame him, an innocent child, for my own tragic and irremediable error.

If I could lay the whole truth before him, I might be able to make him understand. But naturally I cannot do that. It is impossible for him to be absolutely sure of the truth. He may guess and suspect and think, but he cannot *know*. He can only know if I admit it, so of course I never will.

Probably, he wouldn't understand, anyway. He wouldn't allow himself to. He is too selfish, too filled with self-pity—yes, despite his arrogant manner. If he understood, he could not play the martyr. He would have no justification for his vileness and viciousness—assuming, that is, that it could be justified. For certainly, whatever I may or may not have done, such conduct could never be justified.

I don't know how such a—a *creature* could be my son.

I don't know what to do about him.

I have no control over him whatsoever. I can't—and he knows I can't—appeal to the authorities for help. And, no, it isn't because of the scandalous, fiendish lies he would tell. I can be hurt by scandal, of course; in fact, I have been hurt. But not greatly. I am too thoroughly entrenched here. Everyone knows too well where Dr. James Ashton stands, and what he stands for.

I have not taken the stringent measures (which I doubtless should have) because I love him. I can't cause him hurt, regardless of how much he deserves it. Also, as you may have surmised, I am afraid of him.

It is a hideous thing to live in terror of one's own son, but I do. I try to keep it concealed, to carry on, to maintain some semblance of father-and-son relationship, but it is becoming increasingly difficult. I am terrified of him, more and more every day. And he is very well aware of the fact. I have the frightful feeling at times that he can read my mind. At times, I am almost sure that he can. He seems to know what I am going to do even before I know it myself.

Nonsensical as it sounds, he *does* know. So, I have not taken the steps which I doubtless should have. I have avoided seriously contemplating such steps. He would kill me before I could carry them out.

He is capable of it. He has threatened to—to kill both Hattie and me.

To be fair to him, if that is the right word, he has made no such threats recently. There were occasions recently when I was hopeful that he might be coming to his senses. But . . .

About three weeks ago, I thought I saw signs that he was losing interest in that degrading yard work. He was leaving later in the mornings, returning earlier at night. He apparently felt—I thought—that he had cheapened me all he could by doing such work, and was now on the point of dropping it.

I asked him to do so. "Not on my account," I said. "I know it's useless to appeal to you on those grounds. Just do it for yourself. Just think of what it looks like for a boy of your background, and intelligence to—"

"I'm considering it," he said. "I may possibly do it, if you don't urge me to it."

"Well, that's fine," I said. For, God pity me, there was some comfort—a relative lot—in even such an insolent, heartless reply as that. "You don't have to do that kind of work, or any work. I'll be delighted to give you any money that you need."

"Don't be offensive," he said. "Don't bother me."

He said it quite mildly. I felt considerably encouraged.

Then, I came home the following night to find every drawer, every cabinet, in my office had been opened and rummaged through. No, he hadn't broken them open. He had simply picked all the locks.

Now, he was seated in my chair, his feet up on my desk, absently smoking a cigarette.

I was so angry that for a moment I forgot my terror. I told him that he had better explain himself, and promptly, or he would have serious cause to regret it.

"Where is the stuff?" he said. "In your safety-deposit box?"

"It's where you'll never—what stuff?" I said. "I've warned you, Bobbie, you—"

"I had an idea it was," he nodded. "Well, it looks like I'll just have to buy some."

He got up and started to leave. I grabbed him and whirled him around. "You rotten, filthy scum!" I said. "I'll tell you what you'll do, and what will happen to you if you don't! You'll—"

"Let go of me," he said.

"I'll let go of you! I'll drag you straight down to the courthouse! I'll—"

I let go of him of him suddenly. The fiendish sadistic whelp had crushed his cigarette into my wrist.

"Don't ever do anything like that again," he said calmly. "Do you understand me, father?"

"Bobbie . . . son," I said. "For God's sake, what do you want? What are you trying to do? That—that girl—"

"Don't interfere with me," he said.

He drove into the city the next day. He has made one other trip in since then. For what purpose, I needn't explain.

How he manages it I don't know. How a seventeen-year-old boy in a strange city can promptly locate a narcotics peddler and make a purchase, I don't know.

Perhaps he doesn't buy it. God—and I know I'm being ridiculous—he may make it! I have an insane notion that he could, if he wanted to. Anything that is mean and vicious, rotten, cruel, filthy, senseless . . . !

He is still doing the yard work, of course. Degrading himself, playing the flunkey, to buy dope for her.

If I could discover his motive, I might be able to do something. But what possible motive could he have? The girl is completely undesirable. As intelligent and handsome as he is, he could have his way with virtually any girl in town, without the deadly risk he is running. For it is a deadly one. It would be so, even without the complication of narcotics. Pete has only to find them together in a certain way—and that will be the end.

Pete will kill him. Pete might even kill me.

I have almost driven myself crazy wondering what to do, but I can think of nothing. I can only wait, go on as I always have and wait—watch helplessly while doom approaches.

And Luane is responsible. Bobbie was always somewhat peculiar, withdrawn, but except for that sluttish old hypochondriac it would never have happened.

I broke with her last week. I may have to tolerate him, but I do not have to put up with her.

I told her there was nothing at all wrong with her, that I would not under any circumstances visit her again, that if she wanted a doctor she would have to call another (the nearest is twenty miles away). Then I walked out, leaving her to whine and complain to her own filthy self.

I should have done that long ago. I forebore only because it might seem that I was bothered by her slander, and thus lend weight to it.

Bobbie seemed pleased when I mentioned the matter casually at the dinner table.

"That was very wise of you," he said. "I'd expected you to do it sooner."

"Well," I said, "as a matter of fact, I had been con—"

"But, no, I can see that this way is better," he said. "It eliminates you pretty conclusively from the potential list of suspects. Now, if you'd cut her off sooner, let it be known that you were no longer going near her place *before* you established that you held no grudge against her . . ."

"Stop it!" I said. "What are you talking about, anyway? I refuse to listen to any more such nonsense!"

"Why, of course." He winked at me, grinning. "It isn't very discreet, is it? And we don't need to talk, do we, dear father?"

I have been wondering lately if he is really my son. Wondering idly, wishfully perhaps, but still speculating on the matter. After all, if she would hop into bed with me so quickly, why not with another? How do I know what she was doing during the hours when I was away from the house? Obviously, she was of not much account. A woman who would behave as shamelessly as she did, tempting me until I could withstand it no longer, playing upon my kindness and sense of honor . . .

Well, never mind. He is my son. I know it. And I would be the last man in the world to attempt to evade my responsibilities. But that changes nothing, as far as she is concerned.

She had better not complain to me any more about Bobbie's abuse. Not one word. Or I personally will give her something to complain about. I would send her packing if I dared to, which regrettably I don't. It would look bad, as though the scandal had hit home. It would look like I was afraid—on the run.

So things stand; to this sorry, unbearable state I have come. Chained to a Negro woman—and I am *not* responsible to her. Inflicted with a son who—who—well, at least he isn't a Negro. Not really. If a Negro was only one-sixteenth white, would you call him a white man? Well, it's the same proposition. It's—

It's unbearable. Maddening. Completely unjust.

I don't know what I would do without the comfort of Hank Williams' friendship. I spend much of my free time with him, and he spends much of his with me. We understand each other. He admires and respects me. He is glad that I have gotten ahead, even though his own success has been somewhat modest. True, he seems unaware that he hasn't gotten on—he seems to have forgotten that he ever talked of being senator or governor. But, no matter. He is my friend, and he has proved it in many ways. If he wishes to be a little smug, boastful, I can bear with it easily. Never in any way do I let on that his "success" wears a striking resemblance to failure.

We were talking the other night about our early days here. And he, as he is wont to do, passed some remark as to his progress since then. I said that his was a career to be proud of, that very few lawyers had risen so high in so brief a time. He beamed and smirked; and then with that earnest warmth which only he is capable of, he said that he owed his success to me.

"Well," I said. "I've certainly boosted you whenever I could, but I'm afraid I—"

"Remember our first talk together? The day I was drawing up those papers for you?"

"Why, yes," I said. "Of course I remember. You set me straight here, saw that—"

"Sure! Uh-hah. You sly old rascal you!" He threw back his head, and laughed. "I set *you* straight. A country bumpkin, a small town lawyer, set a big city doctor straight. He told *him* how to get on in the world!"

I didn't say anything. I was too bewildered. For I had told him nothing that day. Nothing until I had pretty well ascertained his own feelings.

"Oh, I understood you, all right!" he laughed. "Naturally, you couldn't come straight out with it; you had to spar around a little, make sure of how I felt first. But . . ."

He winked at me, grinning. I stared at him, feeling my hands tighten on the arms of my chair; then, as the murderous hatred drained out of me, feeling them slowly relax and grow limp.

He had done me no injury. His intelligence, his moral stamina, that vaguely concrete thing called character—all had been stunted at the outset. Perhaps they would have amounted to little, regardless; perhaps environment and heredity would have dwarfed them, without the withering assistance of our long-ago, initial conversation.

At any rate, he had not harmed me; he had not changed me one whit from what I essentially was. Others, doubtless, many others, but not me.

If anything, it was the other way around.

He was frowning slightly, looking a little uncomfortable and puzzled. He repeated his phrase about my having had to spar around with him, until I was sure of how he felt.

"And how did you feel, Hank?" I said. "Basically—deep down in your heart?"

"Oh, well," he shrugged. "You don't need to ask that, Jim. You know how I stand on those things."

"But back then," I insisted, "right back in the beginning. Tell me, Hank. I really want to know."

"We-el—" He hesitated, and spread his hands. "You know, Jim. About like most people, I guess. A lot of people, anyway. Kind of on the fence, and wishing I could stay there. But knowing I had to jump one way or the other, and knowing I was pretty well stuck on the side I jumped to. I—well, you know what I mean, Jim. It's kind of hard to put into words."

"I see," I said. "I hoped . . . I mean, I thought that was probably the way you felt."

"Well," he said; and, after a moment, again, "Well."

He studied me a trifle nervously; then, unable to read my expression, he gave out with that bluffly amiable, give-me-approval laugh of his.

It was a hearty laugh, but one that he was ready to immediately modulate. His face was flushed with high good humor: a mask of good-fellowish hilarity which could, at the wink of an eye, with practiced effortlessness, become the essence of gravity, sobriety, seriousness.

I laughed along with him. With him, and at myself. Our laughter filled the room, flowed out through the windows into the night; echoing and reechoing, sending endless ripples on and on through the darkness. It remained with us, the laughter, and it departed from us. Floating out across the town, across hill and dale, across field and stream, across mountain and prairie, across the night-lost farm houses, the hamlets and villages and towns, the bustling, tower-twinkling cities. Across—around—the world, and back again.

We laughed, and the whole world laughed.

Or should I say jeered?

Suddenly I got up and went to the window. Stood there unseeing, though my eyes were wider than they had ever been, my back turned to him.

And where there had been uproar, there was now silence. Almost absolute silence.

He could not stand that, of course. After almost twenty years, it dawned on me that he could not. Whenever there is silence, he must fill it. With something. With anything. So, after he had regained his guffaw-drained breath, after he had achieved a self-satisfactory evaluation of my mood, he spoke again. Went back to the subject of our conversation.

"Well, anyway, Jim. As I was saying, I'm eternally grateful to you. I hate to think what might have happened if we hadn't had that talk."

I winced, unable to answer him for a moment. Immediately his voice tightened, notched upward with anxiety.

"Jim . . . Jim? Don't you look at it that way, too, Jim? Don't you kind of hate to think—"

"Oh, yes—" I found my voice. "Yes, indeed, Hank. On the other hand . . ."

"Yeah? What were you going to say, Jim?"

"Nothing," I said. "Just that I doubt that it would have changed anything. Not with men like us."

# VI

## MARMADUKE "GOOFY" GANNDER (INCOMPETENT)

WHEN I AWAKENED it was morning, and I was lying on the green pavement of The City of Wonderful People, and a hideous hangover held me in its thrall.

I sat up by degrees, shaking and shuddering. I massaged my eyes, wondering, yea, even marveling, over the complete non-wonderment of the situation. For lo! I invariably have a hangover in the morning, even as it is invariably morning when I awaken: and likewise, to complete the sequence of non-marvelousness, I invariably awaken in The City of Wonderful People.

"Hell," I thought (fervently); "the same today, yesterday and—*Ouch!*"

I said the last aloud, adding a prayerful expletive, For the sunlight had stabbed into my eyes, speared fierily into my head like a crown of thorns. In my agony, I rocked back and forth for a moment; and then I staggered to my feet and stumbled over to Grandma's bed.

It was not a very nice bed, compared to those of the City's other inhabitants. Untended, except for my inept ministrations, it was protected only by an oblong border of wine bottles, which seemed constantly to be getting broken. And it was sunken in uncomfortably: and the grass was withered and brown —yeah, generously fertilized as it obviously was by untold numbers of dogs, cats and rodents. The headboard of the bedstead was of weathered, worm-eaten wood, a dwarfed phallus-like object bearing only her name and the word "Spinster": painfully, or perhaps, painlessly, free of eulogy.

I studied the bleak inscription, thinking, as I often do when not occupied with other matters, that I should do something about it. I had considered substituting the words "Human Being," with possibly a suffixed "Believe It Or Not." But Grandma had not liked that: she had considered it no compliment. And she had made no bones—no pun intended—about letting me know it.

I sat facing her bed, my head bowed against the sun, staring down into the sunken hummock. The grass rustled restlessly, whispering in the wind; and after a time there was a dry, snorting chuckle.

"Well?" Grandma said. "Penny for your thoughts."

"Now, that—" I forced a smile. "Now, that is the sort of thing that brings on inflation."

Grandma snickered. She asked me how I was getting along with my book.

I said fine, that, in fact, I had finished it.

"Well, let's hear some of it," Grandma said. "Start right with the beginning."

"Certainly, Grandma," I said. "Certainly . . . 'Once upon a time, there were two billion and a half bastards who lived in a jungle, which weighed approximately six sextillion, four hundred and fifty quintillion short tons. Though they were all brothers, these bastards, their sole occupation was fratricide. Though the jungle abounded in wondrous fruits, their sole food was dirt. Though their potential for knowledge was unlimited, they knew but one thing. And what they knew was only what they did not know. And what they did not know was what was enough.' "

I stopped speaking.

Grandma stirred impatiently. "Well, go on."

"That's all there is," I said.

"But I thought you said you'd finished. That's no more than you had before."

"It's all there is," I repeated. "As I see it, there is nothing more to say."

We were silent for a time. Without talk to divert me, my hangover began to return, crept slowly up through my body and over my head. Shaking me, sickening me, gnawing at me inside and out like some hateful and invisible reptile.

Grandma snickered sympathetically. "Pretty sick, aren't you?"

"A little," I said. "Something I took internally seems to have disagreed with me. Or, I should say—in all fairness—I disagreed with it. It was entirely friendly and tractable until I removed it from the bottle."

"You know what to do about it," Grandma said. "You know what you've got to do."

"I don't know whether I can make it," I said. "Rather, I have a strong suspicion that I can't make it."

"You've got to," Grandma said, "so stop wasting good breath. Stop talking and start moving."

I groaned piteously, making futile motions of arising. The flesh was willing, but also weak. And as for spirit, I had none whatsoever.

"Verily, Grandma," I moaned. "Verily, verily. I would swap my soul to Satan for one good drink."

"Cheapskate," said Grandma. "Now, cut out the gab and get on your way."

I nodded miserably. Somehow, I managed to get to my feet. "I shall do as you say, Grandma," I said.

Grandma made no reply. Presumably she had returned to her well-earned sleep.

I turned and tried to tiptoe away from her. I lost my balance and fell flat on my face, and minutes passed before I could pick myself up again. Finally, after several similar fallings and pickings-up, I reached the road to town.

A truck was coming from the opposite direction. It looked like Joe Henderson's, and it was. I swung an arm, limply, thumb upraised, in the gesture as old as hitchhiking. Joe slowed down, and came to a stop. Then, as I reached for the door, he jabbed one finger into the air, and roared away.

I walked on, more strengthened, more firm in my purpose than otherwise. I wondered what loss Joe could suffer that could not be recouped by insurance, and I decided that the tires of his truck would be a very good bet.

Another farm truck drove up behind me—Dutch Eaton's. Dutch stopped and leaned out, asked me solicitously if I was tired of walking.

"Yes," I said, "but please spare me the suggestion that I run a while. It was not very amusing even when I first heard it, back during my cradle days."

His fat face reddened with anger. He sputtered, "Why, you crazy, low-down—!"

"Listen," I said. "Listen, listen, Mr. Eaton. What is it that is gutless, brainless and moves around on wheels? A swine, Mr. Eaton. A pig in overalls."

He had been easing the door open. Now, he sprang out with a furious roar, and, whirling, I also sprang. I am almost always equal to such emergencies. Weak though I may have been a moment before, the strength and the agility to save myself invariably come to me. And they did now.

So I leaped the ditch, and vaulted easily over the fence. I walked on up into the orchard in the rear of the Devore estate, listening to Dutch curse me, and, finally, drive away.

Temporarily, I was so absorbed in thought that I almost forgot my hang-over. In a sense, I had reason to be grateful to Dutch Eaton and Joe Henderson. Yet I must confess that the emotion I felt for them was very far from gratitude.

Joe and Dutch, I thought. They had been on bad terms with one another for years. What would be the result, say, if Joe's tires should be slashed on the same night that Dutch's barn burned down?

"Lord World forgive me," I murmured, "for their minds are even as those of a Paleolithic foetus, and I know all too damned well what I do."

I had passed through the orchard by now, and arrived at the barnyard. Moving boldly but quietly, I went through the gate, crossed the barnyard and backyard, and entered the back door of the house.

No, there was no danger. I knew that, having visited the place several times before. Ralph would be away. Luane would be in bed, and her bedroom was on the front. As long as I was quiet, and no one can be more quiet than I, I could prowl the downstairs at will.

I stopped inside the door a moment, listening. Faintly, from upstairs, Luane's voice drifted down to me as she talked over the telephone:

". . . . course, I hate to say anything either. Far be it from me to say a word about anyone, and you know it, Mabel. But a thing like that—a young girl lifting her skirts for a nigger—and that father of hers, always acting so high and mighty . . ."

I hesitated, feeling vaguely impelled to do something. Knowing that if anything could ever have been done, it was too late now. Pete Pavlov would soon hear the gossip. As soon as he ascertained its truth, he would act. And there could be no doubt about how he would act—what he would do.

I frowned, shrugged, and pushed the matter out of my mind; mentally disconnecting the vicious whine of Luane's voice. I could not help the inevitable. On the other hand, I hoped, I could help myself to a drink; and my need for one was growing.

I opened the cupboard, a familiar section of it. I studied the several bottles of flavoring extract, my mouth watering. And then miserably, having noted the labels, I turned away. There was no end, apparently, to Ralph's skimping. Since my last visit, he had substituted cheap, nonalcoholic extracts for the fine, invigorating brands he had previously stocked.

I looked through the other cupboards. I hesitated over a large bottle of floor polish: then, insufficiently intrigued by its five per cent alcoholic content, I turned away again. Finally, I lifted a trap door in the floor, and went down into the cellar.

I had no luck there, either. Ralph's cider was freshly made—still sweet; and he had done his canning as expertly as he did everything else. Out of all the endless jars of fruit and vegetables, there was not a one that was beginning to ferment.

I went back up into the kitchen. Sweat pouring off of me, my nerves screaming for the balm of drink. I went through the connecting door to the front hall, and stood at the foot of the stairs.

There would be plenty to drink up there. Rubbing alcohol. Female tonic. Liniment. Perhaps even something that was made to be drunk. And if Luane would only go to sleep, if she would cease her poisonous spewing for only a few minutes . . .

But, obviously, she would not. Already she had another party on the wire, and when she had finished with that one she would immediately ring up another. And so on throughout the day. She would never stop—unless she was stopped. As well she deserved to be, aside from my crying need. But I could not envision myself now in the role of stopper, and being unable to I could not act as such.

Another day, perhaps. Some other day, or night, when thirst and hopelessness brought me here again.

I left the house. I retraced my steps through the orchard, and walked toward town, turning eventually into the alley that ran behind Doctor Ashton's house.

Doctor Ashton would not be at home at this hour, nor would he assist me if he was. As for his son, Bobbie, who doubtless was also away, I had accepted his help but once, and that once was more than enough. I still shuddered when I recalled the experience. What he gave me, that angel-faced phlegmatic fiend, I do not know. But it practically removed my bowels, and nausea shook me like a terrier-shaken rat for the ensuing three days.

I could look for nothing, then, from Ashton or his son. But the Negro woman, Hattie, would be at home; she never went anywhere. And doubtless out of superstition—a kind of awe of the so-called insane—she had given me drink several times in the past.

I knocked on the back door. There was a *sluff-sluff* of house slippers, and then she was standing at the screen, looking out at me dully.

"Go 'way," she said, before I could speak. "Go 'way and stay 'way. Don't want no more truck with you."

I read the tone of her voice, the reason behind her attitude. At least, I believe I did. I told her she was completely mistaken if she believed I was bad luck.

"Listen, listen, Miss Hattie," I said. "You see this caul in my left eye? Now, I'm sure you know that a man with a caul in his eye—"

"I knows you an' 'at eye bettah be moving," she said. "You an' it want to go on keepin' company. Get now, you heah me? Get along, crazy man!"

"Please," I said. "Please do not refer to me as crazy. I have a document in my pocket, signed by the state's chief psychiatrist, certifying to my sanity. Now, surely, and even though our mental hospitals are crowded to twice their capacity, he wouldn't have declared me sane if—"

"Okay," she cut in flatly. "Okay. You stays right there, an' I gives you a drink, awright."

She turned away from the screen. I could not see what she was doing, but I heard water gushing into what apparently was a large flat pan.

Hastily, I got off the steps and moved back into the yard. "Listen, listen," I said. "You don't need to do that. I'm leaving right now."

She came to the door again, eyes sparkling in malicious triumph. She said that I had *better* leave, and stay left.

"But you had better not," I said. "Listen, listen, Miss Hattie. Leave the house at no time. Particularly do not leave it at night. Great evil will befall you if you do."

A trace of fear tightened the contours of her off-ivory face. "Huh! What make you think I goin' anywhere?"

"Listen, listen," I said. "Because it is so written that you may, and that great and dreadful evil will result. So it is written. But listen, listen. If I had a drink —a very large one—I could doubtless change the writing."

I had been too eager. She let out a grunt of relief and unbelief, and returned to the kitchen.

I continued on my dreary, drinkless way.

Frequently, or I should say occasionally, I have had some success at the courthouse. There are always a number of loafers around; also, needless to say —and if you will excuse the redundancy—the county office-holders. So I went there today, hoping to amuse them as I sometimes had in the past. To titillate and entertain them with my wisdom, and thus obtain a few coins. Alas, however! Alas, and verily, and lo. Seldom have I been appreciated less than on this day, the day when my need was greatest.

I was chased out of office after office. I was brushed aside, cursed out, elbowed and shoved along by one loafer after another.

. . . I had been unwilling to call on Pete Pavlov, except as a last resort, for a couple of reasons. For one thing, it was quite a long walk across town to the beach area; an almost intolerable walk for one in my condition. For another, I had called upon him so often in the past that further appeals would not only be embarrassing, but were apt to prove fruitless.

There was nothing else to do now, however; and when there is nothing else to do I do what there is nothing else to do.

Shaking and wobbling, I walked the several blocks through town, entered the dance pavilion and crossed the wide, waxed floor to the door of his office. He was bent over an account ledger, cursing and mumbling to himself now and then as he turned its pages. I waited, nervously, my hands twitching and trembling even as the leaves of an aspen.

Not many people will agree with me, but Mr. Pavlov is a very kindly, soft-hearted man. On the other hand—and everyone *will* agree with me on this —he is no fool. And the merest hint, intentional or no, that he might be will send him into an icy rage.

He looked up at last, took the tobacco cud from his mouth, and dropped it into a convenient gaboon. "What the hell you want?" he said, wiping his hand on his pants. "As if I didn't know."

"Listen, listen, Mr. Pavlov," I said. "Humiliated and embarrassed though I am, I find myself impelled to—"

He yanked open a desk drawer, took out a bottle and glass and poured me a drink. I gulped it, and extended the glass. He returned it and the bottle to the drawer.

"Tell you what I'll do with you," he said. "I'll—no, you listen—listen for a change! You go back there in the john and wash up—and use some soap, by God, get me?—and I'll stake you to a square meal."

I said, certainly, certainly, yessir: I could certainly use a good meal. "You can give me the price of the meal now, Mr. Pavlov. That will save time and time is money, and—"

"And the farmer hauled another load away," said Mr. Pavlov. "Just keep on standing there, arguing with me, and you won't get nothing but a kick in the butt."

He meant it; Mr. Pavlov always means what he says. I departed hastily for the washroom. After all, this was the best offer I had had all day—the meal, I mean, not the kick—and I had a notion that it might be improved upon.

I washed thoroughly: my hands, wrists and those portions of my face that were not covered by beard. It was probably as clean as I have been during the thirty years of my existence.

I returned to the office, where Mr. Pavlov complimented me reservedly.

"Looks like you got a few coats of rust off. Why don't you chop that damned

hair and them whiskers off, too? Ought to, by God, or else buy yourself a
bedsheet and sandals."

"Listen, Mr. Pavlov," I said. "I will do whatever you say. If you would like
to give me the money for a barber—or a bedsheet and sandals—along with the
price of a meal, I will—"

"I ain't giving you a nickel," said Mr. Pavlov. "I'll take you to a restaurant
and pay your check myself."

I protested that he was being unfair: it was implicit in our agreement that
I should spend the money on liquor. He grunted, studying me with thoughtfully narrowed eyes.

"Shut up a minute," he said. "Goddammit, if I give you another drink, will
you shut up and let me think?"

"Listen, Mr. Pavlov," I said. "For another drink, I would—would—"

I broke off helplessly. What wouldn't one do when he is slowly being
crucified?

I snatched the drink from his hand. I took it at a gulp, noting that he had
left the bottle on the desk in front of him.

"Huh-uh," he said, as I extended my glass. "Not now, anyways. I got
something to say to you, and I want to be damned sure you understand."

"Listen," I said. "I understand much better when I'm drinking. The more
I drink the more my understanding increases."

"Shut up!" There was a whip-like crack to his voice. "Now, here's what I
was going to say, and you'd better not repeat it, see? Don't ever peep a word
about it to anyone. Suppose I was to give you something of mine. Kind of let
you take it away from me. I mean, nobody would know that it was you that
took it, but—Goddammit, are you listening to me?"

"Certainly, certainly, yessir," I said. "If you were thinking about pouring
a drink for yourself, Mr. Pavlov, I will take one, too."

"Dammit, this is important to you," he said. "There'd be a nice piece of
change in it for you, and all you'd have to do is—" He broke off with a
disgusted grunt. "Hell! I must be going out of my mind to even think about
it."

"You appear very depressed, Mr. Pavlov," I said. "Allow me to pour a drink
for you."

"Pour one for yourself," he snarled, with unaccustomed naivete. "Then
you're gettin' the hell out of here to a restaurant."

It was a quart bottle, and it was practically full.

I picked it up, and ran.

I hated to do it, naturally. It was not only ungrateful, but also shortsighted;
in eating the golden egg, figuratively speaking, I was destroying a future hen.
I did it because I could not help myself. Because it was another nothing-else-to-
do.

When a man is drowning, he snatches at bottles.

I ran, making a wild leap toward the door. And I tripped over the doorsill, the bottle shot from my hands, and it and I crashed resoundingly against the ballroom floor.

I scrambled forward on my stomach, began to lap at one of the precious puddles of liquor.

Mr. Pavlov suddenly kicked me in the tail, sent me scooting across the polished boards. He yanked me to my feet, eyes raging, and jerked me around facing him.

"A fine son-of-a-bitch you turned out to be! Now, get to hell out of here! Get out fast, and take plenty of time about showing up again."

"Certainly," I said. "But listen, listen, Mr. Pavlov. I—"

"Listen, hell! I said to clear out!"

"I will, I am," I said, backing out of his reach. "But please listen, Mr. Pavlov. I will be glad to assist you in a fake holdup. More than glad. You have been very good to me, and I will welcome the opportunity to do something for you."

He had been moving toward me, threateningly. Now he stopped dead in his tracks, his face flushing, eyes wavering away from mine.

"What the hell you talkin' about?" he said, with attempted roughness. "You better not go talkin' that way to anyone else!"

"You know I won't," I said. "I don't blame you for distrusting me after the exhibition I just put on, but—"

He snorted half-heartedly. He said, "You're crazy. Crazy and drunk. You don't know what you're sayin'."

"Yes, sir," I said. "And I don't know what you said. I didn't hear you. I wasn't listening."

I turned and left. I went out onto the boardwalk, wondering if this after all was not the original sin, the one we all suffer for: the failure to attribute to others the motives which we claim for ourselves. The inexcusable failure to do so.

True, I was not very prepossessing, either in appearance or actions. I was not, but neither was he. He was every bit as unreassuring in his way as I was in mine. And as you are in yours. We were both disguised. The materials were different, but they had all come from the same loom. My eccentricity and drunkenness. His roughness, rudeness and outright brutality.

We had to be disguised. Both of us, all of us. Yet obvious as the fact was, he would not see it. He would not look through my guise, as I had looked through his, to the man beneath. He would not look through his own, which would have done practically as well.

It was too bad, and he would be punished for it—as who is not?

And I was in need of more—much, much more—to drink.

Down at the end of the walk, a girl was standing at the rail, looking idly out to sea. I squinted my eyes, shaded them with my hand. After a moment, she turned her head a little, and I recognized her as the vocalist with the band.

She was clad in bathing garb, but a robe was draped over the rail at her side. It seemed reasonable to assume that the robe would have a pocket in it, and that the pocket would have something in it also.

I walked down to where she stood. I harrumphed for her attention and executed a low bow, toppling momentarily to one knee in the process.

"Listen, listen," I said. " 'How beautiful are thy feet with shoes, O, my princess. Thy—' "

I broke off abruptly, noting that her feet were bare. I glanced at her midriff, and began anew:

" 'Thy navel is like—' "

"You get away from me, you nasty thing, you!" she said. "Go on, now! I don't give money to beggars."

"But who else would you give money to?" I said. "Not, surely, to people with money."

"You leave me alone!" Her voice rose. "I'll scream if you don't!"

"Very well," I said, and I moved back up the boardwalk. "Oh, verily, very well. But beware the night, madam. Lo, and a ho-ho-ho, beware the night."

The warning seemed justified. Molded as she was, the night could hold quite as much danger for her as it did delight.

Ahead of me, I saw Mr. Pavlov come out of the pavilion and swagger away toward town. Studying him, his high-held head, the proud set of his shoulders, the hurt I had felt over his caution in talking to me was suddenly no more.

He had behaved thusly I knew—I *knew*—because he actually did not intend to perpetrate a fake holdup. He neither intended to nor would. He might think the contrary, go so far as to plan the deed. But he would never actually go through with it.

He was as incapable of dishonesty, of anything but absolute uprightness, as I was of sobriety.

He turned and entered the post-office building. I crossed to the other side of the street, continued on for another block and suddenly lurched, and remained lurched, against a corner lamppost.

People passed by, grinning and laughing at me. I closed my eyes, and murmured alternate threats and pleadings to the Lord World.

Halfway down the block, there was a grocery store. Mr. Kossmeyer, the lawyer who comes here every summer, was parked in front of it, loading some groceries into the back seat of his car.

I pushed myself away from the lamppost, and stepped down into the gutter. I walked down to where Mr. Kossmeyer was, and tapped him on the shoulder.

He jumped, cursed and banged his head. Then, he turned around and saw that it was I.

"Oh, hello, Ganny," he said. "I mean—uh—Judas."

"Oh, that's all right, Mr. Kossmeyer," I laughed. "I know I'm not really Judas. That was just a crazy notion I had."

"Well, that's fine. Glad you've snapped out of it," Mr. Kossmeyer said.

"I'm really Noah," I said. "That's who I really am, Mr. Kossmeyer."

"I see," he said. "Well, you shouldn't have to travel very far to round up your animals."

He sounded rather wary. Disinterested. His hand moved toward the front door of his car.

"Listen, Mr. Kossmeyer," I said. "Listen. I'm accepting contributions for an ark, materials or their monetary equivalent. Planks are a dollar each, Mr. Kossmeyer."

"They ain't the only thing," said Mr. Kossmeyer. "So is a quart of wine."

He seemed a lot smarter than he used to be. Summer a year ago, I sold him a reservation to the Last Supper.

"Listen, Mr. Kossmeyer, listen," I said. "All the world's a stage, and all the actors, audience; and the wise man casteth no stink bombs. Doesn't that stir you, Mr. Kossmeyer?" I said.

"Only to a limited degree," said Mr. Kossmeyer. "Only to a limited degree, Noah. I feel nothing at all in the area of my hip pocket."

"Listen, Mr. Kossmeyer, listen," I said. "They've got a new resident out in The City of Wonderful People. They've got a man that's TRULY HUMBLE. He's TRULY HUMBLE, but he always acted like the snootiest, most stuck-up man in town. You know why he acted that way? You know why, Mr. Kossmeyer? Because he was so lonesome for company. The planks are really only ninety-eight cents, Mr. Kossmeyer, and I can bring back the change from a dollar."

"A little more finesse," said Mr. Kossmeyer. "A little more english on the cue ball."

"Listen," I said. "Listen, Mr. Kossmeyer. I'm thinking about digging him up, and putting him on television. There ought to be millions in it, don't you think so? A TRULY HUMBLE man, just think of it, Mr. Kossmeyer!"

"I think I'll drive you down to the library," said Mr. Kossmeyer, "and lead you to the history section."

"I could put falsies on him, Mr. Kossmeyer," I said. "I could teach him to sing and dance. I could—listen, Mr. Kossmeyer, listen, listen. There's a couple of other new residents out in The City of Wonderful People. They're MOTHER AND FATHER, and they're the most wonderful of all. Listen, Mr. Kossmeyer, listen. They're DUTIFUL AND LOVING PARENTS, they're GODFEARING AND LOYAL, they're HONEST and KINDLY and STEADFAST and GENEROUS and MERCIFUL and TOLERANT and WISE and—"

"What the hell they got, for God's sake?" said Mr. Kossmeyer. "A tombstone or a billboard?"

"Listen, Mr. Kossmeyer," I said. "Listen. It's the teensiest stone you ever saw. Not much bigger than a cigarette package. I figure that fellow who writes on the heads of pins must have done the inscription. It's practically impossible to read it, Mr. Kossmeyer. Virtually impossible. They've got all those virtues, yet no one can see them. You know why it's that way? You know why, Mr. Kossmeyer? Listen, listen, listen. It's supposed to be symbolic. It's symbolic, Mr. Kossmeyer, and I just remembered you can get a pretty good grade of plank for—"

"Listen, Noah, listen, listen," said Mr. Kossmeyer. "Which is the shortest way to that building-supply store?"

# VII

## HATTIE

I GUESS I just don't think no more. Not no real thinking, only little old keyhole kind.

Reckon you know what I mean. Reckon you know what it does to a body. May be a mighty big room, but you sure ain't going to see much of it. And you keep looking through that keyhole long enough, nothing ain't never going to look big to you.

Get to where that eye of yours just won't spread out.

Used to think pretty tolerable, way back when, long long time ago. Back when Mr. Doctor was talking to me and teaching me, and telling me stuff. Seemed like I was just thinking all the time, and thinking more all the time. Big thinking. Almost could feel my brain getting bigger. Then, we comes here and that was the end of that and the beginning of the other.

Mr. Doctor stopped; stopped himself from pushing me on, and stopped me from pushing. Just wouldn't do, he said. Got to be in a certain place, so I got to fit in that place. Don't do nothing that would maybe look like I don't belong in that place. Just sink down in it, and don't never raise my head above it.

Too bad and he sure hates it, Mr. Doctor said. But that's the way it's got to be. And what good's it going to do me, he said, filling my head full of a lot of stuff I wasn't never going to use?

Guess he right, all right. Anyways, he stop with me. Me, I didn't put up no fuss about it. Catch me arguing with Mr. Doctor. Never did it but the once, long long time ago, and maybe that used all my arguing up. Took all my fighting for the one battle, maybe. And maybe I just didn't see no call to fight.

Don't work up no sweat going down hill. Awful easy thing to do, and that little old keyhole at the bottom, it don't bother you at all.

Can't think no more. Ain't got the words for it. Mr. Doctor, he tell me one time back when he was telling me things, he tell me the mind can't go no farther than a person's 'cabulary. You got to have the words or you can't talk, and you got to have 'em or you can't think. No words, no thinking. Just kind of feeling.

Me, I get hungry. I get cold and hot. I get scared, and sick. Mostly, I get scared and sick. Scared-sick, kind of together. And not doing no real thinking about it. Just feeling it and wishing it wasn't, and knowing it's going to go right on being. A lot worse maybe.

Because he, that boy, he acting nice now. He trying to pretend being friendly. And that boy, he act that way, you sure better watch out for him. He sure about to get you then.

He come out in the kitchen other night after supper. Right there with me before I know it. And he smile and sweet-talk, and say he going to help me with the dishes.

"Go 'way," I said. "You lea' me alone, hear?"

"Well, we'll let the dishes go," he said. "Let's go in your bedroom, mother. I have something I want to talk to you about."

"Huh-uh. No, suh," I said. "You ain't gettin' me in no bedroom."

"I'm sure you don't mean that," he said. "You're my mother. Every mother is interested in her son's problems."

I go in the bedroom with him. Scared not to. He got his mind made up, and that boy make up his mind, you sure better not get in his way.

Meanest boy in the world, that boy. Just plain lowdown rattlesnake mean.

I get on bed. Get way back against the wall with my legs drawn up under me. He sit down on chair at side of bed. He takes out a cigarette, and then he looks at me, and asks if it's all right he could smoke.

I don't say nothing. Just keep my eyes on him, just watching and waiting.

"Oh, excuse me, mother," he said. "Allow me."

He stick a cigarette at me. He strike a match and hold it out, and me I put that cigarette in my mouth and puff it lit. Had to. Scared to death if I don't, and scared if I do.

I take a puff or two, so's he won't go for me. Then, he start talking, ain't watching me close, I squeeze it down in my fingers and let it go out.

"Now, it's a money problem I wanted to discuss with you, mother," he said. "Largely one of money. I don't suppose you have a considerable sum you might lend me?"

"Huh," I said. "Where I get any money?"

"I'd probably need several thousand dollars," he said. "There'd be some traveling to do. I'd need enough to get reestablished, for two people to live on, for an extended period."

"Why'n't you go away?" I said. "How I get any money, I don't draw no wages? You want money you knows who to go to."

He look at me a little while. He look right on through my head it seem like, and I figure he's really about to come after me. Figure I really make one big mistake in kind of talking back to him. But what else I do, anyhow? Can't be nothing much but back-talk when you talk to him.

Can't think no more.

Can't do nothing, and can't do something.

Scared if I do and scared if I don't.

He go on looking at me, and I know my time really come. Then, he say, that's perfectly all right, mother. Say he really didn't expect me to have any money, but he thought he should ask. Say it might've hurt my feelings, him needing money and not giving his mother the 'tunity to help.

Crazy-mean, that boy. He nice and polite that way, he crazy-meaner than ever.

"But you're quite right, mother," he said. "I do know where to get it. Or, more accurately, I know where I could lay my hands on a large amount of money. The difficulty is that there is another person who needs it—who will need it, I should say. His situation is quite similar to my own, and it would place him in a position practically as difficult as mine if he didn't have it. So under the circumstances—what do you think I should do, mother?"

"Huh?" I said. "What? What you talkin' about, boy?"

"I'm sorry," he said. "Please don't feel I don't trust you, mother; it isn't that at all. It's just that you might be placed in a very compromising situation if I gave you any details, spoke in anything but the most general terms. And I believe you can advise me quite as well on that basis. What's your best opinion, mother? If you were in my place, would you feel justified in extricating yourself from an untenable position at this other man's expense?"

What I think? Me—what *I* think? What I got to think with? Or listen with, or talk with?

That mean boy, I see him too well'n too close—plenty too close, a mean-crazy boy like him—but I sure don't hear him. Might as well be talking a zillion miles away.

"Lea' me alone," I said. "Why you all the time devilin' me? I ain't done nothin' to you."

"Relatively," he nodded. "Yes, I see. Relatively, you have done nothing. And, of course, you meant that as an answer to my question. You did mean it so, didn't you, mother?"

"Fo' God's sake," I said. "Fo' God's sake, jus'—"

"I suppose it's always that way, don't you, mother? It's inevitable. There are certain rigid requirements for being one's self, a tenable self. They may not be violated, despite any exigencies, regardless of the temptation and the nominal ease with which violations could be accomplished. Otherwise, he becomes another. And how, if he cannot cope with the problems of his own self— live in pride and contentment within its framework—can he dwell in that other? Obviously, he can't. He loses identity. He may have been little, but now he is nothing. He doesn't know what he is. Yes, you're absolutely right, mother. I'm so glad you could advise me out of the background of your experience."

Don't know what he talking about.

Don't want to know.

"Now, there's another thing I wanted to ask you about, mother," he said. "Since I can't help myself—am past the point of help, let's say—should I help this other man? Should I remove an obstacle in the path to the solution of his problem? I have nothing to lose. It would help him immensely. In fact, he might not be able to bring himself to do it. Or if he did, he might suffer from regrets. It might cast a pall over the goal he achieves by so doing. How do you feel about it, mother? Do you think I should help him or not?"

How do I feel? What he care? What do I think? Think nothing. Just think nothing.

Can't.

Him, he might be talkin' about killing someone, and I wouldn't know it.

He look at me, one of them pretty-smooth eyebrows cocked up, them even pretty-white teeth showing; kind of smiling and kind of frowning. And I know he as mean-crazy as they come—you just look at that boy and you see he is. But for maybe a second or two I don't see it. What I see is sort of a picture that all at once just popped up out of nowhere, that kinda seemed to wooze out of my eyes and spread itself over him. And me—I—I almost laugh out loud.

I think—thought, *"Why, my heavens, Hattie, what in the world has come over you? How can you be afraid of this fine young man, your son? What . . . ?"*

The picture go away, back wherever crazy place it come from. Me, she, the me that'd thought them words go back to the same place. Nothing but the regular me, now, and it don't do no thinking. Don't see nothing but through that bitty old keyhole. Just sees meanest boy that ever lived.

He been that way for years. I watch it coming on him. Oh, sure, he don't do nothing with it for a long time. He wait until he big and strong. But I see it all right, he *let* you see it. He nice and polite all the time, but he let you see it; make you know what you can 'spect. Poke it right at you.

"Yes, mother?" he said. "Can you answer my question?"

"Go 'way?" I said. "How I know? I—me—"

"Why, of course," he said. "Naturally, you wouldn't know. It's not something a person can advise another about, is it? The individual concerned has to make his own decision. Thank you, very much, mother. I can't tell you what a comfort it's been to talk over my problems with you. Now, I see you're looking a little tired, so perhaps I'd better . . ."

He stand up. He put one knee on the bed, and start to lean over toward me. Smiling that pretty white-teeth smile, fastening on to me with them soft brown eyes. An' . . .

Knew I was going to get it then. He had been playing around, all politey and smiley, and now he going to do it. Something mean. Something bad. Had to be, because there couldn't be no other be. Couldn't think of no other. Couldn't think no more but little old keyhole stuff.

Don't know what I going to do. House almost in a block by itself, and I yell my lungs out and no one hear me. No good yelling. Couldn't do it nohow, scaredysick as I was. Couldn't do nothing nohow. Just ain't nothing to do but wait, and hope he won't be too mean. No meaner than I can stand.

Can't move. Feel like I frozen, I that stiff and cold. Can't hardly see nothing. Just kind of a white blur moving toward me, pushing right against my face. Then, I can't really see nothing. Just feel something, sort of soft and warm, pressing me on the forehead.

It go away. I get my eyes open somehow, and he standing back on the floor again.

"Good-night, mother," he said. "I hope you sleep well, and please don't worry about anything. After all, there's no longer anything to worry about, is there?"

He stand there and smile, and I figure he really going to get me now. He just been playing around so far, but now he through. Can't scare me no worse, so now he going to get me.

He turn around and leave. He close the door real gentle-like. But, me, I ain't being fooled. Ain't going to get me out there where he probably hiding, all set and waiting for me. Just about bound to be.

Why he act like he do if he ain't up to something? Why he make all that talk at me? Why he keep calling me mother and be so nicey-nice, and—an' kiss me goodnight?

Huh! Me, I know that boy. Seen that meanness coming on him a long, long time. He up to something all right. Fixing to get me.

I hear front door open. Hear it close.

I hear his car starting up, going away.

And all at once, I just flop over on my face and cry. Because he *ain't* got me, and he *ain't* going to. Him or nobody else.

Can't.

Just ain't nothing to get.

# VIII

## LUANE DEVORE

IT WAS MONDAY night. The dance pavilion is closed for business that night, but of course Ralph still has things to do there. Or things to do somewhere.

It was a little after eight, a little after dark. I heard the front door open quietly.

I hadn't heard Ralph's car, but I naturally assumed it was Ralph. The house is well-insulated. If he had driven up the old lane from the rear—as he sometimes does—I wouldn't have heard the car.

I turned around slightly in the bed. I waited a second, listening, and then I called, "Ralph?"

There wasn't any answer. I called again, and there still wasn't any. I made myself smile, forced a laugh into my voice.

Ralph is such a tease, you know. He's always playing funny little jokes, doing things to make you laugh. I suppose he seems pretty dull and stodgy to most people, but he's really worlds of fun. And it's always that sweet, silly puppyish kind. Even while you're laughing, you get a lump in your throat and you want to take him in your arms and pet him.

Oh, I can understand his attraction for women. His looks and youthfulness are only part of it. Mostly, it's because you enjoy being around him. Because he's so funny and sweet and simple and . . .

"Ralph!" I called. "You answer me now, you bad, bad boy. Luane will be terribly angry with you, if you don't."

He didn't answer. He—whoever it was—didn't. But I heard the floor creak. I heard more creaks, coming nearer, moving slowly up the stairs.

Just the creaks, sounds; not footsteps. Nothing I could identify.

I called one more time. Then, I swung my feet out of bed and . . . and sat there motionless. Half paralyzed with fear, helpless even if I was not so badly frightened.

The phone was out of order. *As he—this person—doubtless knew.* It was useless to yell. And if I locked the door, well, it could be forced. And then I would be trapped in here, in this one crowded, cluttered room, with even less chance of saving myself than I had now.

I got up, took an uncertain step toward the door. I hesitated, stared slowly around the room. And suddenly I was almost calm.

*Save myself! I thought. Save myself!*

Now, surely I should know how to do that.

\* \* \*

73

Kossy came to see me the first Sunday of the season. I had called him, indicating that there was something I wanted to talk to him about when he had the time—strictly at his own convenience. And he raced right over. He didn't hurry on my account, of course. Catch one of *those* people doing anything for you unless there's a dollar in it. Probably he thought Ralph would be here, and he could load up on a lot of free eggs and fruit and vegetables.

Oh, well. I suppose I am exaggerating a little. Kossy really doesn't seem to care about money; he'll treat you just about the same way, whether he's getting a fat fee or nothing. And I suppose my call may have sounded rather urgent. But—

But why should he care about money? I wouldn't either if I had all he's got. Why should he blame me, a poor, helpless sick old woman for sounding a little excited?

He was very mean and insulting. Not that he usually isn't. As soon as I was convinced that there was nothing to worry about, I ordered him out of the house. I should have done it long before, because I'd heard some pretty unpleasant stories about that man. How he'd cheated and swindled people right out of their eyeteeth. I can't say just who I heard them from, but they're all over town. And where there's so much smoke, there must be some fire.

At any rate, he not only insulted me, but he gave me some very bad advice. Because I most certainly did have something to worry about! He convinced me temporarily—and against my will—that I hadn't. But I knew better. The season was only two days old, and I'd already seen it in Ralph—seen it in the way he talked and acted and looked. And that was only the beginning.

He came home late that night, very late, I should say, since he is always out working as long as he can find work to do. I sleep a lot during the day, however, so I was awake.

He fixed a snack for me; he was too tired to eat, himself, he said. He was going to go straight to bed—in fact, he got a little stubborn about it. But I cried a little and pointed out how lonesome it was for me all day by myself, so we talked a while.

I studied him, listening to what he said, noticing what he didn't. I began to worry again. I began to get frightened.

I hardly slept a wink all night. I hardly slept a wink any night, because Ralph didn't change back to what he had been—he kept going farther and farther the other way.

I was practically out of my mind by the end of the week. I was going to call Kossy, but I didn't have to. He came to see me. As of course, I should have known he would. Catch *him* letting go of a good thing! He's probably building up his bill, so that he can attach this property.

Anyway, he was afraid not to come. He knew what I could do if I took the notion. I've never said anything about him yet, mind you—hardly anything

—but if he wanted to be mean and ugly, I certainly had a right to defend myself!

I cried a little, and told him about Ralph. He sat and stared at me like I was some strange kind of animal, instead of a poor, sick, helpless old woman who needed comfort and sympathy. And then he said that he'd be goddamned.

"Kossy, darling," I said. "I've asked you so many times please not to use—"

"I tell you what I won't use," he said. "I won't use any words you ain't used ten thousand times yourself. I hadn't ought to bother with you at all, but as long as I am I'll—"

"All right, Kossy, dear," I said. "I'm just an old woman. I can't stop you if you insist."

"Luane," he said. "For God's sake—Aaah, nuts—" he said, and threw up his hands. "Never mind. Let me see if I got this straight. Ralph is seeing this girl every night; you're sure of that. But he *isn't* sleeping with her. And you're bothered because he *isn't!*"

I said, no, Ralph wasn't. "He always has before," I said. "He's a-always been honest before—c-come home and told me about it afterwards."

"But—but—" He waved his hands again. "You mean you want it that way? You want him to make these babes?"

"W-well. I don't really want him to," I said. "But it wouldn't be fair to stop him, since I—well, you know. And as long as he tells me about it . . ."

He gave me an odd look, as if he was a little sick at his stomach. He said something about, yes, he could see how I might enjoy that.

"Well, never mind," he went on. "It kind of knocked me over for a minute, but I guess I get the picture. Ralph is playing it clean with this gal. In your book, that makes him in love with her. Suppose he does a switch, goes after what he always has, what does that make him?"

"Please," I said. "Please don't joke about it, Kossy."

"Okay," he shrugged. "Say he's in love with her. Say he's going to stay in love. And you don't like it, naturally. But it don't add up to his planning to kill you."

"But it does! I mean, it could," I said. "I—well—"

"Yeah?" He waited, frowning at me. "How does it? I seem to remember that we were all over that the other day. Ralph could get a divorce. He could just up and leave. We agreed that he could."

"Well," I said. "I guess he could—I mean, I know he could. But—but—"

"Yeah?"

He stared at me. He—and that shows what a crook he is! Honest people move their eyes around. They don't have a guilty conscience, so they don't feel they have to brazen someone down. It's only crooks who do that.

"Okay," he said. "You want to hold out something, go ahead. It ain't my neck."

"But I'm not," I said. "I—it's just that when I talked to you the other day, I didn't know he was so serious about this girl. I—"

"So now you know. And he can still walk away or get a divorce, so it still don't shape up to a murder."

"I—well, here's what I was thinking," I said. "The season will end in a couple months, and of course the girl will be leaving. So whatever . . . if Ralph is going to do anything, he'll have to do it by then. And—and—"

Kossy waited a moment. Then he grimaced and reached for his hat.

"Don't!" I said. "I'm trying to tell you, Kossy. After all, it isn't easy for me to discuss Ralph this way, to think of some reason why my own husband would w-want t-to—to—"

"Well, sure." He cleared his throat uncomfortably. "I don't suppose it is. But—"

"But there is a reason why he might, Kossy. This property isn't worth nearly what it used to be, but it would still bring five or six thousand dollars—maybe as much as ten. And if Ralph needed money, if he was so mean and selfish that he couldn't wait until I died . . ."

Kossy's eyes narrowed. Blinked. He nodded slowly.

"Yeah," he said. "Could be. That would seem like a world of dough to Ralph, particularly now that he's been so hard hit in the job department. I don't suppose there's any use pointing out to you that if Ralph is planning something, you're at least partly at fault."

"I am not!" I said. "I haven't said a single solitary word about anyone! Anyway, Ralph doesn't blame me in the least, he knows I haven't said half as much as I could have, and—"

"Okay. Okay," Kossy sighed. "Forget it. Ralph wants to kill you, maybe. He's got a double motive, maybe: to clear his way for the girl, and to cash in on what's left of the estate. Say that that's the situation. What do you want me to do about it?"

"Well, I . . ."

I didn't know. How should I know what to do? That what his job. And he'd been plenty well paid for it! I hadn't ever actually caught him stealing from me, but there'd been a great deal of talk about—

"You think it over," he said. "See what develops, and we'll talk again in a few days. Meanwhile, I want to say something about these lies of yours—*shut up! don't interrupt me!*—and I want you to take it to heart. If—"

"But I haven't said a word!" I said. "Honestly, Kossy. I—And I just hope someone does try to start something! I'll—"

"You'll damned probably get killed," he said. "I mean it, Luane. It's the law of averages. You get enough people sore enough to kill you—and you've got just about the whole damned town—one of them is almost certain to do the job. So cut it out, get me? Better still, see if you can't undo some of the damage.

Try to do it. Admit you've been lying, apologize to the people you've harmed. Use that phone for something decent for a change."

Well, of course, I wasn't going to do anything like that! I'd die before—I just wasn't going to do it! In the first place, I hadn't said anything. He was just irritated by the few harmless little jokes I'd told about him. In the second place, it was all true what I'd said; and I guessed that if anyone was cowardly enough to harm someone for telling the truth, they'd have done so by now. And just what was I supposed to do all day, pray tell? Just lie here all day like a bump on a log, and never have a little harmless chat with anyone?

I tried to explain to Kossy how absolutely ridiculous it all was. But just try to tell *that* man anything! He looked at me, not really listening to what I was saying, and then he sighed and shook his head.

"Okay, maybe you can't help it," he said. "Take it easy, and I'll see you in a few days."

I was just a little worried after he'd gone; I mean, about someone wanting to kill me besides Ralph. Then, I just shoved it out of my mind—almost—because a person can only worry about so much and that's all, and I had more than my limit with Ralph.

Because I hadn't told Kossy everything. I hadn't told him the most important thing.

He came back the latter part of that week. He kept coming back, week after week—he was here the last time this morning—but it didn't help any. I certainly couldn't do any of the silly things he suggested.

Ralph hadn't said or done anything out of the way. He was different, but it wasn't something you could put your finger on. Outwardly he was just as nice and considerate as ever, so how could I have put him under peace bond? Obviously, I couldn't. I wouldn't have even if I had a concrete reason to, because that *would* have fixed things up. It would have brought everything to a showdown—killed the last bit of hope I had. And the same thing would happen if I let Kossy speak to him. Or if I had one of the county authorities do it.

Ralph wouldn't feel sorry for me any more. He wouldn't pity me. He'd just go ahead and do what he wanted to do—what he wasn't yet nerved-up to doing.

As you can see, Kossy has been absolutely no help to me. None whatsoever. Here I am, a sick old woman whom nobody loves, and I can get no help from my own attorney, a man who has stolen thousands of dollars from me.

The foolish little squirt even brought a gun here, a revolver, and wanted me to keep it! I refused even to touch it.

"Oh, no, you don't!" I said. "No, siree! People have accidents with guns. Accidentally-on-purpose accidents. As soon as Ralph or anyone found out I had that thing, they'd fix up a little accident for me."

"But, dammit, Luane," he said. "What the hell else can you do? What can I do for you? Now, you keep it—keep it where you can get to it fast. And if anyone goes for you, use it."

"*Wh-aat?*" I said. "You're suggesting that I should *shoot* someone? W-why —why, how dare you, Kossy! What kind of woman do you think I am?"

"God!" he almost shouted. "I don't know why the hell I don't kill you myself!"

He said some other very mean, nasty things, and then he slammed out of the house.

He came back for the last time this morning.

He said that he still thought I was in much more danger from others than I was from Ralph. Then, when I said he simply didn't know what he was talking about, he began to get ugly. And nosy.

"Y'know, Luane," he said, "the more I think about it, the less I can see Ralph committing murder for the few thousand bucks this estate would bring. It's hard for me to see him as a murderer, anyway, and for that kind of dough it just don't seem to figure at all."

"Well, you're absolutely wrong," I said. "For a man like Ralph, who's never really had anything—"

"Uh-huh. Because he's cautious, ultra-conservative. Ralph wouldn't bet that the sun comes up in the east unless he got a thousand-to-one odds. He'd take no chance except for something big. He—no, now, wait a minute! Let's take a good look at Ralph. He's been odd-jobbing around this town for more than twenty years. Working around people who are hip-deep in dough—who are almost disappointed if they don't get chiseled. But did Ralph ever clip one of 'em? Did he ever pad a bill, or walk off with a few tools or steal gasoline and oil, or pull any of the stunts that a guy in his place ordinarily would? Huh-uh. Never. In all those years, he—"

"Oh, yes, he did!" I said. "He most certainly did! How do you think he got that car, pray tell?"

"Not by killing anyone. Not by running any real risk at all. In all those years, he pulls just one perfectly safe bit of chiseling—and he collects a high-priced car!" Kossy shook his head slowly, giving me that mean, narrow-eyed grin. "Who are you kidding, sister? You know goddamned well Ralph wouldn't kill you for this estate. If you really thought he would, you'd just sign it over to him."

"Why, I would not!" I said. "There'd be nothing to stop him then. It would be just like throwing him in that girl's arms!"

"Well?" he shrugged. "What choice you got? What choice has Ralph got? How you going to get by if he stays here?"

"Why, we'll get by just fine!" I said. "We'll—uh—"

"Yeah? How will you? Out with it, goddammit!"

"Well, we'll—You leave me alone!" I said. "You stop it! You're j-just as mean and hateful as—as—" And I broke down and began to cry. Undignified as it was, and as much as I despise weepy women.

That's probably how that girl holds onto Ralph—by crying all over him. Making him feel sorry for her. Ralph is so good-hearted, you know. He hates to see anyone unhappy, and he just won't let them be. And they just about can't be when he's around. He's so much fun, so sweet and funny at the same time, and—

At least, he was—the mean, selfish thing! Why, even this morning, he was carrying on pretty much as he used to. And it was just pretense, of course, but I almost forgot that it was, and . . . and it was nice.

"Come on, Luane," Kossy said. "Let's have it."

"I c-can't!" I said. "I don't know what you're talking about. You leave me alone, you mean hateful thing, you!"

"Look, Luane—" He put his hand on my shoulder, and I shook it off. "Don't you see it, honey? Don't you see that you can't hold Ralph in a trap without being in it yourself? Of course, you do. That's why you're so frightened, as you have every right to be. Let him go, Luane. Let him out of that corner you've got him in. If you don't . . ."

"K-Kossy," I said. "Kossy, d-darling . . . you don't really think he would, do you? Y-you said you didn't—couldn't see him k-killing—"

"God!" He slapped his forehead. "Oh, God! I—Look. Tell me what it is, what you're squeezing Ralph with. I have to know, don't you understand that?"

"I k-know . . . I mean, I *can't!*" I said. "There isn't anything, and—don't you dare say there is! Don't you dare tell anyone there's something—that I'm—"

He sighed and stood up. He said something about my being his client, God help him, whatever that meant: probably that it wouldn't be ethical for him to say anything. Not that that would stop him, of course. He's always talking, saying mean things about me. I haven't said anything half as mean about him as he has about me. Every time he leaves here, he goes around laughing and telling people how old and ugly I look.

Anyway, he certainly doesn't know anything. He's always contradicting himself, saying one thing one minute and something else the next.

First he tells me that Ralph won't kill me, and then he says he will. He says that Ralph won't, but that there's plenty of others who might. And if *that* doesn't prove he's crazy, what would? Kill me—a bunch of cowardly, lying, lowdown sneaks like they are! They don't have the nerve. They have no reason to. I've never done anything to harm them.

I've never harmed anyone, Ralph least of all, but now . . .

*NOW!*

. . . Ralph? Is it Ralph on the stairs?

But why won't he answer me? What can he gain by not answering? Why is he doing it—if it is he, if he is going to—this way?

To lure me out there? Maybe I shouldn't go. But if I don't . . .

It must be someone else. It simply wouldn't make sense for Ralph to do it this way. As for someone else, why would they—he—she . . . ?

They're afraid, unsure? They haven't made up their mind? They're waiting to see what I do? They're trying to lure me out of the room—like Ralph would, is, might?

If I only knew, I might save myself. If I knew who it was—before the person becomes sure—I might save myself.

If . . . If I go out. If I don't go out.

*Save me, I prayed. Just let me save myself. That's all I want. It's all I've ever wanted. And that's certainly not very much to ask, is it?*

I went out.

I saw who it was.

# IX

## Danny Lee

ALTHOUGH I AM but of a humble station in life, I come from a proud old southern family, which was directly descended from that proud old southern warrior, Robert E. Lee, and we lived in a proud southern village which shall here be Nameless. Then, when I was but a slip of a girl, I loved unwisely and not too well, and my proud old father drove me out into the storm one bitter night. So, I went to a large city where I stumbled anew into a new pitfall. I mean, I didn't do anything wrong, really. Never again did I repeat my first and only fatal mistake. But there was this place I worked in where you could hustle drinks and where if you could sing a little or dance or something like that, you could keep whatever the customers gave you. And one night an orchestra leader entered its portals, and I innocently agreed to accompany him to his room. I didn't have the slightest idea of what evil designs he wanted. I simply went because I felt sorry for him, and I had to send some money back to my invalid mother and my two brothers, and—

Oh, I did not! I'm making all of this up.

I don't have any mother or brothers or any family except my father, and if he has anything to be proud of I don't know what it is. The last time I heard he was in jail again for bootlegging back in our home town.

He had a little two-by-four restaurant. I used to serve drinks to the customers, and two or three times when it was someone I liked real well and I simply had to have something to wear or go naked, I let them you-know. I finally picked up a dose from one of them. Pa said that as long as I got it, I could figure out how to get rid of it. So I stole ten dollars he had hidden, and went to a place near Fort Worth.

I couldn't get a restaurant job, which was the only kind of work I knew, since I couldn't get a health certificate. And I couldn't get that, of course, until I got over the dose. So practically flat broke as I was—without even money enough for a room— it looked like I was really in a pickle.

I said it *looked* that way. Because actually, I guess, it was lucky I didn't have room money. Otherwise, I wouldn't have gone into that cheap little burlesque house just to rest a while and try to think.

There were four chorus girls in the line. Pretty old girls, it looked like. I didn't think they could sing half as good as I could, and the dancing they did was mostly just wiggling and shaking. I watched and listened to them a while. Finally, I got up enough nerve to go to the manager and ask him for a job.

He took me into his office. I sang and wiggled for him, and he said I was

81

okay, but he didn't have a job open right then. Then, he winked and asked me how about it—you know—and said there was a fast ten bucks in it for me. I told him, I couldn't. He offered me twenty, and I told him no again. And I told him why, because it would be a dirty trick on him. He was awfully appreciative. He said most girls in my position would have taken the money, and not given a damn whether they dosed some poor son-of-a-bitch. (Those are his own words and I'm only repeating them because I want to tell the whole truth and not leave out anything. Not a bit more than I have to. I don't use that kind of language myself.)

He appreciated my telling him so much that he gave me a job after all. He had to fire another girl to do it, and naturally I was sorry for that. But she was really too old to be working, anyway. I told her so, when she started cursing me out. And she didn't have much to say after that.

I started seeing a doctor right away—as soon as I got a paycheck. He got me cleared up fast, and things were pretty nice from then on. For quite a while. All the men who came to the show—you hardly ever saw a woman—liked me. They'd start clapping and whistling and calling for me, even while the other girls were doing their numbers. Then, when I went on stage they wouldn't let me go. They were really crazy about me, even if it doesn't sound nice for me to say so, and I couldn't begin to tell you how many of them tried to date me up. If I'd been willing to you-know for money like some of the other girls did, I could have made all kinds. I wouldn't have had to just barely skimp by like I was doing, because that manager could really squeeze a quarter until the eagle screamed. But, anyway, I didn't do it. Not even once, as much as I was tempted.

I remember one time when I just about had to have a new pair of shoes, and I saw an absolutely darling pair in a window, marked down from twenty-three ninety-nine to fourteen ninety-eight. It was such a wonderful bargain, I just didn't see how I could pass it up. I felt like I'd die if I didn't have those shoes! And while I was standing there a man who came to the show all the time came along, and offered to buy them for me. But I turned him down. I hesitated a moment first, but I did.

My real name is Agnes Tuttle, but I changed it when I went to work at the show. I was going to make it something kind of unusual, like Dolores du Bois. But the other girls had given themselves fancy names—Fanchon Rose, and Charlotte Montclair and so on—so I decided to make mine simple. It seemed best to, you know. It stood out more. And if I'd had the same sort of name as those other girls, people might have thought I was cheap and shoddy, too.

I'd been at the show about six months when the police raided it and closed it down. The manager got a big fine, and had to leave town. The girls went back to doing what they had been doing, which was you know what. I hardly knew what to do.

I felt it would be kind of a step down to take a waitress job. There's nothing wrong with being a waitress, of course. But it doesn't pay much, and it's darned hard work. And in view of my experience, I felt that I simply ought to and had to have something better. I was like that then; awfully ambitious, I mean. Willing to do almost anything to be a big-name singer or something like that. Now, I feel just about the opposite. In the first place, I know I'm not much good as a singer and never will be, like Rags McGuire says. In the second place, I just don't care. All I want now is just to be with Ralph, forever and always —and by golly, I *will* be!—and . . .

But I'll tell you about that later.

I didn't have money to travel on, and there weren't any jobs like I wanted in Fort Worth. Oh, there were a few, of course, but I couldn't get them. All the talent for them was hired through New York agencies, so I didn't stand a chance, even if I'd had the training and the presence and the clothes. I guess I was pretty awful, then. And I don't just mean my voice. I tried to wear nice things without being flashy, and I tried to be careful about makeup and using good English. But trying isn't enough when you don't have money to work with, and you're not sure of what you're trying for.

I guess I couldn't really blame Rags for thinking I was something that I wasn't.

I was working in a beer garden at the time I met him. It wasn't a very nice place, and it wasn't a real job. I just hung out there, like several other girls did. I got to keep any money a customer gave me for drinking with him, and I also got a commission on what he bought. Then, a few times a night I'd sing a number. And the orchestra and I divided the change that the customers tossed up on the bandstand.

Well, Rags dropped into the place one night, and a waitress tipped me off that he was a big spender. So, after I'd done a number, I went over to his table. I didn't know who he was—just about the greatest jazz musician of all time. I just thought, you know, that if he was going to throw money around, he might as well throw some my way. And I thought he looked awfully interesting, too.

Well. I guess I did just about everything wrong that I could. I just botched everything up, not only that night but the next day when he gave me a singing try-out, and offered me a contract. I—I just don't know! I still squirm inside when I think about it. But I know I didn't act that way just because of the money. I wanted to get ahead, of course, but mostly I wanted to please him. I thought I was doing what he wanted me to do, and he seemed so terribly unhappy I felt that I should. But . . .

He had no use for me from then on. From then on, I was just dirt to him. He wouldn't let me explain or try to straighten things out. I was just dirt, and he was going to keep it that way.

I tried to excuse him. I told myself that if I'd had a family like his, and the same terrible thing happened to mine that happened to his—though he won't admit it did—why, I might be pretty hard to get along with, too. But, well, you can't keep excusing people forever. If they're simply determined to despise you, you just have to let them. And all you can do about it is to despise them back.

Rags has just done one nice thing for me in all the months I've worked for him. That was when we came here, and he introduced me to Ralph. He didn't mean to be nice, of course. He meant it as a mean joke on me—telling me that Ralph was a very wealthy man and so on. But that was one time Mr. Rags got fooled. Ralph told me the truth about himself that very first night, and I told him the truth about myself. And instead of being mad and disappointed with each other, like Rags thought we would, we fell in love.

Ralph was so cute when he told me about himself. Just like a darling little boy. All the time he was talking I could hardly keep from taking him in my arms and squeezing him. He couldn't make a living any more in this town, it seemed, because everyone was mad at his wife. On the other hand, he'd lived here all his life, and he wouldn't know what to do anywhere else. Not by himself, I mean. And the idea he kind of had in mind in meeting me was— well, he got pretty mixed up at that point. But I understood him, the poor darling. He didn't need to put it into words for me to understand, any more than he's had to put certain other things into words.

While he was hesitating, not knowing quite how to go on, I patted him on the hand and told him to never mind. I said I was awfully glad he seemed to think so much of me because I liked him a lot, too. But maybe if he knew the truth, he'd change his opinion of me.

Well, he didn't try to shut me up like most men would have. You know, just say to forget it and that it didn't matter. He just nodded kind of grave and fatherly-like, and said, "Is that a fact? Well, maybe you better tell me about it, then."

I told him. Everything there was to tell, although I may possibly have forgotten a few little things. When I finally stopped, he waited a minute, and then he told me to go on.

"G-go on?" I said. "But that's all there is."

"But I thought you were supposed to have done something bad," he said. "Something that might change my mind about you."

Well . . .

My eyes misted over. I could feel my face puckering up like some big old baby's. I sat there, looking and feeling that way and not knowing what to do. And Ralph reached out and pulled my head against his chest.

"You go right ahead, honey," he said. "You just cry all you want to."

Well, I cried and I cried and I cried. It just seemed like I could never stop, and Ralph told me not to try. So I cried and I cried. And everything that was in me that wasn't really me—that didn't really belong there—was kind of washed away. And I felt all clean and nice and peaceful. And I was never as happy in my life.

Ralph . . .

I know I get pretty silly whenever I start talking about him, but I just can't help it. And I just don't care. Because however much I rave, I still don't do him justice. He's the handsomest thing you ever saw in your life, for one thing. A lot handsomer than most anyone in pictures—and don't think I won't make him try out for pictures when we get away from here! But that's only one thing. Along with it, he's just the nicest, kindest, understandingest—well, everything. He's mature, and yet he's awfully boyish. The most wonderful sweetheart a girl ever had, but kind of fatherly, too.

We saw each other every night after that. We talked about what we were going to do—kind of talking around the subject. Because it looked like there was just about only one thing we could do. And things like that, they're not something you can very well talk about.

Yes, that mean old hen he was married to would give him a divorce, all right. Or he could just leave, like I'd suggested, and to hell with the divorce. She'd let him know that—those things—although she hadn't said so in so many words. The trouble was she wouldn't let him take the money that belonged to him, money he'd worked for and saved dollar by dollar. She wouldn't even let him take half of it. She kept it under the mattress of her bed, and she made it clear to him that anyone who got it would have to kill her first.

Ralph was afraid to sue her. He had a record book of his savings, showing when and how much he put away. But that wouldn't necessarily prove that the money was his, would it? She might have told him to keep the record for her. And, anyway, those lawsuits drag on forever, and the only ones that get anything out of 'em are the lawyers.

At first, I told Ralph to let her keep the money, the old bag! But Ralph didn't want to do that; we'd need it ourselves to get a decent start in life. And after I thought about it a while, I wouldn't have let him if he had wanted to.

It was his money, wasn't it? His and mine. When something belongs to a person, they ought to have it and if someone tries to stop them *they* ought to have something.

I told Ralph that he ought to speak up to her, instead of just beating around the bush. I said that I'd be glad to talk to her myself, and if that didn't do any good I'd slap some sense into her. But Ralph didn't think that would be a very good idea. And I guess it wasn't.

She'd probably put the money in the bank, and tell the police she'd been threatened. Then, if anything happened, why you know where we'd be.

I was sorry afterwards that I'd said anything like that to Ralph. Because I was perfectly willing to do what I said I would and heck of a lot more. But it might have sounded a little shocking to say so. I mean, even if I wasn't a woman, if I was Ralph, say, and I said something like that to me, why I'd—oh, well, you know what I mean.

It was best to keep things the way they'd been, except for that once. Talking about what had to be done, but not *really* talking about it. Not actually admitting that we were talking about it.

By doing that, you see, we'd never really know. There'd never be anything to make us uncomfortable about each other. After all, she was a pretty old woman. Her health was bad, and everyone in town hated her guts. And, well, all sorts of things could happen to her, without us having a thing to do with them.

And neither of us would need to know that we had unless . . .

The weeks raced by. They went by like days, and before we knew it the season was almost over. And we were still talking, and nothing had happened.

Then, that Monday night came.

The dance hall was closed that night. Ralph was working there—not any regular hours, but just until he got through. We weren't seeing each other afterwards, because I had a sore throat.

I don't know how I got it exactly. Maybe from sleeping in a draft. Anyway, it wasn't really bad, and if I'd been anything but a singer I wouldn't have bothered to call a doctor.

I was sitting out on the stoop when he came. He painted my throat, looking kind of nervous and haggard, and then he asked me why I hadn't been in the first time he called.

"I spend thirty minutes finding the right cottage," he said, "and then when I finally locate it—"

"I'm so sorry about that, doctor," I said. "You see, I was taking a shower, and it was some time before I heard you calling and pounding at the cottage next door. I came right out as soon as I did, but—"

"W-what?" he said. "The cottage next . . . ?"

"Uh-huh. It's unoccupied; so many of them are . . . But I thought you saw me, doctor. I ran out on the stoop and called to you, just as you were driving away, and I thought you called and motioned to me. I supposed you meant you had no more time right then, and you'd have to come back later."

He looked at me blankly for a moment. Then, his eyes flickered in a kind of funny way, and he snapped his fingers.

"Why, of course," he said. "Now, that I see you in the light, I can . . . You had a robe on, didn't you, and a—uh—did you have a bathing cap?"

"That's right," I said. "A robe and a bathing cap, because I'd just come out of the shower. I suppose I looked quite a bit different than—"

"Not a bit," he said firmly. "Not a particle. I'd have recognized you instantly, if it hadn't been so fixed in my mind that you were in the other cottage. Let's see, now—about what time was that?"

I told him I guessed it was a little after eight. Somewhere along in there. Just about the time it was getting dark.

"You're right," he said. "You're absolutely right, Miss Lee. Let me compliment you on your memory."

"Now, that's real sweet of you, doctor," I said. "But, after all, why shouldn't I remember? I mean, a girl just about *couldn't* forget anything connected with a distinguished looking gentleman like you."

I smiled at him, looking up from under the lids of my eyes. He beamed and harrumphed his throat, and said I was a very fine young lady.

He repeated that several times while he was repacking his medicine kit. He said he wanted me to take very good care of myself, and any time I needed him, regardless of the hour, I was to let him know.

I thought he was awfully sweet and nice. Kind of distinguished and mature, like Ralph. He asked if he might use my phone, and I said, why certainly, and he called a number.

"Hank?" he said. "Jim . . . Just wanted to tell you that it's—you know—all right . . . I remembered where—I mean, I can account positively for the time. There's a young lady who saw me, recognized my car and my voice, and . . . Who? Well, that one. The one we were discussing. She—What? Why—yes, I suppose that's true. I hadn't thought about it that way, but . . ."

I'd gone over by the door to be polite; so that it wouldn't look like I was snooping, you know. He turned around and looked at me, kind of frowning as he went on talking.

"Yes. Yes, I see. Naturally, unless I was sure that she—unless there was an observer I could hardly be observed. But . . . Yes, Hank. That's the way I feel. On the one hand . . . Absolutely. Had to be. No reason to consider it anything else . . . Exactly, Hank! And as long as that's the case    Fine, ha, ha, fine. See you, Hank . . ."

He hung up the receiver. He picked up his medicine kit, gave me a funny little nod, and started out the door. On the stoop he paused for a moment and turned around, facing me.

"Allow me to compliment you again," he said. "You're a very smart young woman, Miss Lee."

"Now, that is *sweet,*" I said. "That's a *real* compliment . . . coming from a smart man like you."

I gave him another under-the-eyelids smile. He turned suddenly, and left.

I thought he seemed a little cranky. I wondered if he thought I hadn't really seen him that first time—because actually, I hadn't. I said I had because he'd started off being so cross, and I was afraid he might think I hadn't been at home when he called. But all I'd really seen was his car driving away. Or a car that looked like his.

Oh, well. Probably I was just imagining things. After all, he remembered seeing me perfectly, so why should he think I hadn't seen him?

I put on some make-up and went out on the beach. I sat down with my back to the ocean. After a while, I saw a light come on in Rags McGuire's cottage. I walked down to it, and knocked on the door.

He was sitting on the side of the bed, drinking out of a bottle. He's been drinking a lot lately, but on Mondays he drinks more than usual.

"Well!" he said. "If it isn't little Miss Bosoms, the girl with the tinplated tonsils! How come they let you out, baby, or ain't you been in yet?"

"I don't know what you're talking about and I don't care," I said, "and all I've got to say to you is I'm quitting, you mean hateful, dirty old—old—"

"Bastard, son-of-a-bitch, whoremonger," he said. "Now, you sit right down there, honey, and I'll think up some more for you. I'll do that, an' you tell me where you were around eight o'clock tonight."

"If it's any of your business," I said, "I was in my cottage at eight o'clock and for all the rest of the evening. I had a sore throat, and the doctor saw me about eight and again just a little while ago, if it's any possible concern of yours."

His eyes widened. He broke out laughing suddenly, slapping his knee. "Doc Ashton? Oh, brother! You two—you *and* Doc Ashton! Will this burn a certain little lawyer I know! Who dreamed it up, baby, you or Doc?"

"I haven't the faintest notion of what you're talking about," I said. "But since you seem to be so curious as to my whereabouts at certain times, perhaps I might inquire about yours."

His laugh went away. He put the bottle on the floor, sat staring into the neck of it as if there was something there besides the whiskey.

"I don't know," he said. "I don't know where I was. But I was all alone, Danny. I was all alone."

It seemed awful silent then. The only sound was the waves, lap-lapping, whispering against the sand.

I began to get sort of a funny feeling in my throat. I was just about to say I'd work out the rest of the season—these last two weeks—but he spoke first.

"So you're quitting, huh? Well, that's something. That's at least one break you've given me."

Then he got up and came over to me, and took my face between his hands. "You didn't mean it, Danny, and I didn't mean it. Besides, I don't want you to leave, Danny. Besides, I love you, Danny."

He stooped and kissed me on the forehead.

I said, "Rags . . . Oh, g-gosh, Rags. I—"

"I couldn't keep you any longer," he said. "I couldn't pay you, understand? But I think you're one of the finest girls I've ever known, and I think you have one of the very finest voices I've ever heard. I wished you'd go on with it; I did wish that. But now . . . now, I know you mustn't. It would never do. Because the one thing is all you can have, Danny—the music is all you can have, Danny—and if it isn't enough . . ."

He took his hands away from my face, let them slide down my arms. Then he scowled suddenly, and gave me a shake. "Posture!" he said. "Goddammit, how many times do I have to tell you? You've got two feet, haven't you? You're not an obstetrical case, are you? Well, stand on them then, by God."

I said I was sorry. I stood like he'd told me to, like he'd taught me to.

"All right," he said. "Let's have it. Make it *Stardust*. Even you can't bitch that one . . . Well, what are you waiting for?"

"I—I c-can't!" I said. "Oh, R-Rags, I—"

He ran his hands through his hair. "Okay, go on! Get the hell—no, wait a minute. Sit down over there, right there, dammit. I'll let you hear *Stardust* like it ought to be sung . . . almost."

I sat down by his desk. He sat down in the other chair, and put in a long-distance call to his wife.

The call went through, and he held the receiver a little away from his ear.

"Hi, Janie," he said. "How's it going? How are the boys . . . ?"

I couldn't understand what she said, because it was just kind of sounds instead of words. A sort of quack-quacking like a duck would make.

"They're asleep, eh? Well, that's fine. Don't bother to wake them up . . ."

The boys couldn't be waked up. Never, ever.

"Listen, Janie. I've got a kid here I want you to sing for. I—*Janie!* I said I wanted you to sing, understand? . . . Well, get with it, then. Give me *Stardust*, and give it loud. This kid here is pretty tone-deaf . . ."

She couldn't sing, of course. How can you sing when you don't have a nose and only part of a tongue, and no teeth . . . and hardly any place to put teeth? But there was a click and a scratch; and her voice came over the wire.

It was pretty wonderful, her singing *Stardust*. A platter has to be pretty wonderful to sell three million copies. But Rags had started frowning. He squirmed in his chair, and the cigarette in the corner of his mouth began a kind of nervous up-and-down moving.

He held the receiver away from him. He looked at it, frowning, and then he lowered it slowly toward the hook. And the farther down it went, the farther it was away from him, the more his frown faded. And when it was completely down, when the connection was broken, he wasn't frowning any more. He was smiling.

It was a kind of smile I'd never seen before. A dreamy, far-off smile. One of his hands moved slowly back and forth, up and down, and one of his feet tap-tapped silently against the floor.

"Do you hear it, Danny?" he said softly. "Do you hear the music?"

"Yes," I said. "Yes, I hear the music, Rags."

"The music," he said. "The music never goes away, Danny. The music never goes away . . ."

# X

## Henry Clay Williams

I KNEW FROM the moment I sat down at the table that morning that I was in for trouble. I knew it before Lily had said a word. Probably most men wouldn't have, even if they had lived in the same house with a sister as long as I have with Lily, but I'm an unusually close observer. I notice little things. No matter how small it is, I'll see it and interpret it. And nine times out of ten my interpretation will be correct. I've trained myself to do it. A man has to, as I see it, if he wants to get ahead. Of course, if he doesn't, if he wants to remain a small-town lawyer all his life instead of becoming the chief legal officer of the sixteenth-largest county in the state, why that's his privilege.

I began to eat, knowing that Lily was going to land on me, and why, and trying to prepare myself for it. Finally, when she still held back, I gave her a little prod.

"I notice you're running low on pepper," I said. "Remind me to bring some home tonight."

"What? Pepper?" she said. "What makes you think I'm running low?"

"Why, I just supposed you were," I said. "You have plenty? There's still plenty in your kitchen shaker?"

She sighed, and pursed her lips together. She sat looking at me silently, her glasses twinkling and flashing in the morning sunlight.

"I just wondered," I said. "I noticed that you only peppered one of my eggs when you cooked them, so . . ."

"Is there a pepper-shaker in front of you?" she said. "Well, is there or isn't there, or hadn't you noticed?"

She sounded unusually irritable for some reason. I said, why, of course, I'd noticed the shaker, and it didn't matter at all about the eggs.

"I was simply curious about them," I said. "You always pepper them, each one the same amount, so naturally I wondered why you hadn't—"

"I see," she said. "Yes, I can see how you might get pretty excited about it. It would be a pretty big thing to a big man like you."

"Now, I didn't say I was excited," I said. "I said nothing of the kind, Lily. If my memory serves me correctly—and I think you'll agree that it usually does—the words I used were 'curious' and 'wonder.' "

I nodded to her, and put a bite of egg in my mouth. Her lips tightened, then she spoke shaky-voiced. "So you were curious, were you? You were wondering? You were curious and wondering about why I hadn't peppered an egg! Well, I'll tell you something I'm curious and wondering about, and that's what

91

you intend to do when you are no longer the chief legal officer of the sixteenth largest county in the state. For after the elections this fall, Mr. Henry Clay Williams, *you're going to be out of a job!*"

She deliberately timed that last with the moment when I was taking a swallow of coffee to wash the egg down. I coughed and choked, feeling my face turn red. The egg tried to go one way and the coffee another, and for a long moment I was certain I'd strangle.

"Now, goddammit," I said, when I was able to speak. "Why—what the hell—"

"Henry! *Henry!* Don't you use that language in this house!" Lily said.

"But—it's—it's crazy! Outrageous! Why, I've always been—I mean I've been county attorney since—"

"Very well," she said. "Very well, Henry. But don't forget that I warned you."

She got up and started to clear off the table. I hadn't finished breakfast yet —although I certainly didn't feel like eating any more—but she went right ahead, regardless.

The bulge under her apron seemed larger today. I glanced quickly away from it, as her eyes shifted toward me. It was very annoying, that tumor. Having to live with it constantly, and yet never daring to look at it, let alone to discuss it. Perhaps it wouldn't have been for most men, but when you have trained yourself as I have—when you are used to observing and . . .

I observed that her glasses had an unusually high sparkle this morning. Obviously, then—I was immediately aware—there must be some dust on them. She couldn't keep her glasses clean, and yet she was trying to pass herself off as a prophet!

I was about to make some pointed reference to these facts. But she left for the kitchen at that moment with a load of dishes, and when she returned I decided it wasn't wise. After all, you don't cure a trouble by adding to it. That's always been my policy, at least, and it's worked out very well. If—

*Out of a job! Lose the election!*

She was seated at the table again. She looked at me, nodded slowly, as if I had spoken out loud.

"Yes, Henry. Yes. And if you had any brains at all, you wouldn't need me to tell you so."

"Now, see here, Lily," I said. "I—"

"Any brains at all, Henry. Or if you were even capable of listening. Hearing anything besides the sound of your own voice or your own thoughts, anything that might deflate the largest ego in the sixteenth largest county in the state. You're a fool, Henry. You're a—"

"I am, am I?" I said. "Well, I guess I know how to keep my glasses clean, anyway!"

The glasses flickered and flashed. Her eyes squeezed shut behind them for a moment. Then, she opened them again, keeping them narrowed; and her nostrils twitched and flared. And I knew the explosion was coming.

"Listen to me, Henry. What I'm saying is not for myself. I don't expect *you* to have any consideration for me, your own sister who has practically given up her life for you, taken care of you since you were wet behind the ears. I don't expect you to care if I'm so slandered and gossiped about that I'm almost ashamed to go out in public. I'm only concerned about you, as I've always been, and that's why I'm saying you are going to lose the election unless you get up a little spunk, and act like a man for a change instead of a fat, blind, stupid, egotistical *jellyfish!*"

She paused, breathing heavily, her bosom heaving up and down. I was going to say something back to her, but I decided it wasn't worthwhile. I couldn't lose the election. I—why, I just *couldn't*. And when a person can't do something . . .

"Yes," she said. "Yes, you can, Henry. You know I'm right. You know you don't have good sense. You—shut up when I'm speaking to you, Henry! *Henry!*"

"I'm not saying anything," I said. "All I was going to say was—"

"Nothing that would make any sense, that's what you were going to say. You were going to say that no one in this town pays any attention to Luane Devore, but they do, all right. Perhaps they don't believe what she says, but they remember it—and they wonder about it—and when a man is a spineless incompetent to begin with, it doesn't take a deal of wondering to dump him out of his sinecure. At any rate, you seem to have forgotten that it takes more than the town vote to elect you. You have to have the farm people, and they don't know that when Luane Devore says you—we—that she's lying!"

"Well, they will," I said. "After all, you've had that tumor quite a while now, and when you don't have a—I mean, when nothing happens, why—"

I swallowed back the words. I looked down at my plate, tried to keep my eyes there, but something seemed to pull them back up.

She stared at me, silently. She sat there, staring and waiting. Waiting. Waiting. Waiting and waiting.

I threw my napkin on the table, and jumped up.

I marched to the telephone, and asked for the Devore residence. There was a lot of clicking and clattering; then the operator said that the Devore line was out of order.

"Out of order, eh?" I said. "Well—"

Lily took the phone out of my hands. She said, "Did you say the Devore line was out of order, operator? Thank you, very much."

She hung up and put the phone back on its stand. It seemed to me that she owed me an apology for doubting my word, but naturally I didn't get one.

Instead she asked me what I was going to do about the line being out of order.

"Why, I'm going to fix it, of course!" I said. "I'm a telephone repair man, ain't I?"

"Please—" She put her fingers to her forehead. "Please spare me your attempts at humor, Henry."

"Well, I'll wait until it's in order. Naturally," I said. "I'll call her later on from the office."

"But suppose it isn't repaired today?" She shook her head. "I think it would be best to go and see her, Henry. Lay down the law to her in person. Tell her that if she doesn't stop her lies, and if she doesn't issue a public retraction immediately, you'll have her indicted for criminal slander."

"But—but, look," I said. "I can't do that. I mean, going out and jumping all over a sick old woman, and—and it wouldn't look right! No matter what she's done, why she's a woman, a sick old woman, and I'm a man—"

"Are you?" Lily said. "Then, why don't you act like one?"

"Anyway, it's—it's probably illegal," I said. "Might get into a lot of trouble. I'm a public official. If I use my public office in a personal matter, why—All right!" I said. "Go ahead and shake your head! You're doggone good at telling someone else what to do, but when it comes to doing it yourself that's something else again, ain't it?"

"Very well, Henry." She turned away from me. "Could I impose on you to the extent of driving me out there?"

"Why, certainly," I said. "I'm always gl—*what?*"

"I'll see her myself. I'll guarantee that by the time I'm through, she'll have told her last lie. And if you don't want to drive me out, I'll walk. I'll—"

Suddenly, she was crying, weeping wildly. Suddenly, all the coldness and calmness were gone, and she was a different woman.

It was like that time years ago, when we were kids out on the farm. She'd taken me down in the meadow that day to search out some hens' nests. We came to one, half-filled with eggs, and just as she reached for it, a rattlesnake reared up on the opposite side. And what happened then—my God!

She busted out bawling, but it wasn't the usual kind. Not the way people cry when they're frightened or hurt or something like that. It was, well, wild —crazy. More like real mean cussing than bawling. It scared hell out of me, a six-year-old kid, and I guess it did the same to the snake, because he tried to whip away. But she wouldn't let him. She grabbed up that deadly rattler in her bare hands, and yanked him in two! Then she threw the pieces down, and began to jump on them. Bawling in that wild, crazy way. And she didn't stop until there wasn't enough left of that snake to make a grease spot.

I've never forgotten how she acted that day. I don't think I ever will. If I'd had any idea that my harmless little remark at breakfast would have started anything like this . . .

*"I'll take care of her! I'll fix that filthy slut! I'll t-teach her how t-to—"*

"Lily!" I said. "Listen to me, Lily! I'm going to—"

*"You! You don't c-care! You don't know what it means to a woman t-to— I'LL CLAW HER EYES OUT! I'LL PULL HER FILTHY TONGUE OUT OF HER THROAT! I'LL—LET GO OF ME! Y-YOU LET—"*

I didn't let go. I held on tight, shaking her as hard as I could. And I didn't like doing it, you know, but I was more afraid not to.

As soon as she was quieted enough to listen, I began to talk. To tell her and keep telling her that I'd see Luane Devore myself. That I definitely and positively promised I would. I kept repeating it until it finally sank in on her, and she snapped out of her fit.

"All r-right, Henry." She shuddered and blew her nose. "I certainly hope I can depend on you. If I thought for a moment that—"

"I told you I would," I said. "I'll do it this evening. Right after I close the office."

"After? But why can't you—?"

"Because," I said, "it's a personal matter; you can't get around that. Even seeing her after office hours could put me in a pretty awkward position if someone chose to make anything out of it. But I certainly can't do it on the county's time."

She hesitated, studying me. At last, she sighed and turned away again.

"All right," she said. "But if you don't really intend to, I wish you'd say so. In fact, the more I think about it, the less I care whether you do talk to her. I'm perfectly willing to do it myself—I'd *like* doing it—"

"I said I'd do it," I said. "Immediately after five tonight. Now, it's all settled, so forget it."

I left before she could say anything more. I drove down to the courthouse, and went up to my office.

It was a pretty busy morning, all in all. I had a long talk with Judge Shively about the coming election. Then, Sheriff Jameson dropped in with a legal matter, and I had another long conference with him. As you may or may not know, a sheriff gets part of his income from feeding prisoners. This county pays Jameson fifty cents per meal fed, and what he wanted to know was, could he feed them one double meal a day instead of two, and still collect a dollar.

Well, it was a pretty fine legal point, you know. Something you might say was this way or that, and you could make a case out either way. I finally decided, however, that there might be just a leetle danger in the double-meal proposition. But I pointed out that the word meal could mean just about whatever he wanted to. A bowl of beans could be a meal or a plate of fried potatoes, or even a hunk of bread.

It was eleven o'clock before I got Jameson straightened out. I was hoping I'd have time to take a deep breath—maybe get out and see a few voters—but it just wasn't in the cards. Because now that I'd gotten all those other things cleared up, why Nellie Otis, my secretary, needed me.

Oh, I didn't really mind. Nellie is an attractive young woman, as well as an excellent secretary and there are twelve votes in the Otis family—and she's always so appreciative of everything I do for her.

She stood by watching, all the time I was untangling the ribbon on her typewriter. She said she just didn't know how I did it; she'd tried and tried herself, and she'd just made it worse. I said there was nothing to it, really. It was just a matter of going straight to the *source* of the trouble, like it would be in any other problem.

I passed it off lightly that way, but it *was* a pretty bad snarl. Just about the worst I'd ever untangled for her, and that's really saying something. By the time I'd finished with it, and gotten washed up, it was five minutes after twelve. The whole morning was gone, and I was already into my lunch hour.

I was turning away from the washroom sink when I happened to glance out the window. And I just stood there for a moment, staring, wondering well, what the hell next.

Now, there, I thought, that's really something. Kossmeyer and Goofy Gannder! One great man talking to another great man. Yes, sir, I thought, water really finds its level.

Mind you, I have nothing against Kossmeyer. I've never said a word against him to anyone. But I do feel—yes, and I'm justified—that if he's what's supposed to be smart, why I don't want to be.

The way I look at it, if he's so damned smart, why isn't he rich? Where's the proof that he's smart? Why, half the time he don't even use good English!

I had him figured right from the beginning. He's one of those jury jaybirds, one of those howlers and pleaders. All the law he knows you could put in your right eye. And he's just been lucky, so far. If he ever came up against a man who dealt in *facts* and *details,* I guess you know how long he would last.

I went to lunch.

The afternoon was even busier than the morning.

The way the work was piling up, it began to look like I might be so tied up I couldn't get out to see Luane Devore tonight. But, then, I thought about the way sis had acted, and I decided I'd better, work or no work.

I was on my way out of the courthouse when Sheriff Jameson called to me and asked me to step into his office. He'd confiscated a batch of evidence, and he wanted my opinion of it before he went into court on it. I tested it. I told him I wouldn't hesitate to go before the Supreme Court with evidence like that. So he laughed, and gave me a bottle to take with me.

It was a little after five when I got in my car and headed out of town. Just before I got to the Devore place, I took a right fork in the road and drove up toward the hills. The land up there isn't much good any more. Either worn out, or eroded and gullied of its topsoil. All the farms have been abandoned, including the one where I was born and raised.

I turned into the lane that led up to our house. I stopped in the yard, all grown up to weeds now, and looked around. One side of the barn-loft was caved in. All the windows of the house were broken, and the kitchen door creaked back and forth on one hinge. And the chimneys had toppled, scattering brick across the rotting and broken shingles of the roof.

It was kind of sad. Somehow it made me think of that poem, *The Deserted Village,* I used to give at Friday afternoon school recitals. It was sad—but it was nice. Because everything had gone to hell now, but in my mind it hadn't. In my mind, nothing had changed; everything was as it used to be. And the way it used to be . . . nothing was ever nicer or finer than that.

No worries. No one fussing at you. Always knowing just what to do and what not to do, and knowing that it would be all right if you made a mistake. Not like it is now, when you mean well but you ain't real sure of yourself, and there's no one to come straight out and set you straight.

Not like it is now, when people can't understand that you're truly sorry about something—and being sorry is about all you can do—and they wouldn't give a damn if they did understand.

I took a big drink of the whiskey, I guessed I ought to be seeing Luane Devore, but it was so nice and peaceful here, and I had all evening to do it. So I got out, and went up the back walk to the kitchen.

The big old range was still there. Lily had said what was the sense of moving an old wood-burner into town, for pity sake. So we'd left it behind, and consequently, fine stove that it was, it was rusting into junk. It looked like junk. But in my mind I could see it like it had been. Like I'd used to keep it when I was a kid, and Mama and Papa were still alive.

That was my job, keeping the stove blacked and polished. I did it every Saturday morning, as soon as it was cooled off from breakfast, and no one was allowed in the kitchen while I was doing it. First, I'd take a wire brush and dry-scrub it all over. Then, I'd get busy with the blacking rags and polish. I'd rub it in good, get it wiped so clean you couldn't raise a smudge on your finger. After that, I'd take a little kindling splinter and tip it with the blacking, and get down in all the little cracks and curleycues.

We didn't do any farm work on Saturdays, except for just the milking and feeding, of course. So when I was through, I'd roll back the doors to the living room, and Mama and Papa and Lily would come in.

Mama would take a look, and kind of throw up her hands. She'd say, why, I just can't believe my eyes; if I didn't know better I'd think it was a new stove! And Papa would shake his head and say, I couldn't fool him, it *was* a new stove. I'd gone out and snuck one in from somewhere, and no one could tell him different. So, well, I'd have to take and show him that it was really just the same old stove, and . . .

Lily hardly ever said anything.

I used to wonder about it, wanting to ask her why but somehow kind of shy about doing it. And one time when I'd saved up a lot of nickels—I got a nickel every time I polished the stove—I took them all and bought her a big red hair-ribbon. I brought it home from town inside my blouse, not telling anyone about it. That night, when she was out in the kitchen alone doing dishes, I gave it to her. She looked at it, and then she looked at me smiling at her. Then she doused it down in the dishwater, and threw it into the slop pail. I watched it sink down under the scummy surface, and I didn't know quite what to do. What to say. I didn't feel much like smiling any more, but I was kind of afraid to stop. I was kind of, well, just afraid. Mama and Papa always said if you were nice to others, why they would be nice to you. But I'd done the nicest thing I knew how, I thought. So all I could think of was that Mama and Papa must be wrong, or maybe I didn't know what was nice and what wasn't. What was bad and what was good. And for a minute I felt all scared and bewildered and lost. Well, though, Lily grabbed me up in her arms suddenly, and hugged me and kissed me. She said she'd just been joking, and she was just mixed-up and absent-minded and not thinking what she was doing. So . . . everything turned out all right.

I never said anything to Mama or Papa about it. I even lied to Mama and said I'd lost all my nickels when she asked me what had happened to them. That was about the only time I can ever remember her scolding me, or Papa saying anything real sharp to me—because she felt he had to be told about it. But I still didn't tell about the ribbon. I knew they'd be terribly upset and sad if they knew what Lily had done, and I'd've cut off my tongue before I told them. It's funny how—

Dammit, it's not funny! There's nothing funny about it. And why the hell does it have to be that way?

Why is it when you feel so much one way, you have to act just the opposite? So much the opposite?

Why can't people leave you alone, why can't you leave them alone, why can't you just all live together and be the way you are? Knowing that it's all right with the others however you are, because however they are is all right with you.

I wandered through the house, drinking and thinking. Feeling happy and sad. I went up the stairs, and into my little room under the eaves. Dusk was coming on, filling the room with shadows. I could see things like they had been, almost without closing my eyes. It all came back to me . . .

The checked calico curtains at the windows. The circular rag rug. The bookcase made out of a fruitbox. The high, quilted bed. The picture above it

—a picture of a boy and his mother, titled *His Best Girl.* The little rocking chair . . .

The chair was still there. Lily hadn't mentioned moving it, and I kind of didn't like to. I hesitated, and then I tried to sit down in it.

I was a lot too big for it, of course, because San—because Mama and Papa had given it to me the Christmas I was seven. I kept squeezing and pushing, though, and finally the arms cracked and split off, and I went down on the seat. That was pretty small for me too, but I could sit on it all right. I could even rock a little if I was careful. So I sat there, rocking back and forth, my knees almost touching my chin. And for a while I was back to the days that had been, and I was what I had been in those days.

Then some rats scurried across the attic, and I started and sighed and stood up. I stood staring blankly out the window, wondering what the hell I'd better do.

Dammit all, what was I going to say to Luane? She'd just start screaming and crying the minute I opened my mouth, and I'd wind up making a fool of myself like Lily says I always do. It wouldn't do any good to ask her for a retraction, because I wouldn't be able to make myself heard in the first place and in the second place she'd know there wasn't a damned thing I could do. She'd know I wouldn't take her into court. Trials cost money, and voters don't want money spent unless it has to be. And they sure wouldn't see it as having to be in this case. They might be sore at her. They might want her to catch it in the neck. But using county money to do it just wouldn't go down with them. Besides that—besides, dammit, I *couldn't* bring her to trial. I didn't dare do it.

She was Kossmeyer's client. He'd fight for her to the last ditch, regardless of what he thought of her personally. He'd fight one of the best trial lawyers in the country would be fighting *me*—he'd put me on the witness stand and mimic me and get everyone to laughing, and shoot questions faster than I could think. And—

I took a drink. I took a couple more right behind it. My shoulders sort of braced up, and I thought, well who the hell is Kossmeyer, anyway? He ain't so goddamned much.

I took another drink, and another one. I let out a belch.

He—Kossmeyer—he didn't really know anything. He was just a fast talker. More of an actor, a clown, than he was a lawyer. No good outside of a courtroom where he couldn't pull any of his tricks.

Outside of a courtroom, where he had to deal strictly in *facts,* he'd be no good at all. I could make a fool out of him—with the right kind of facts. It would be all over the county, all over the state, how Hank Williams had shown Kossmeyer what was what.

Maybe . . .

Oh, hell. I just couldn't talk to Luane. She wouldn't listen to me, and—damn her, she ought to be made to! To listen or else. And what, by God, could she do about it if she was? What could Kossmeyer do about it? You'd have your facts all ready, you know. So you'd just smile very sweetly, and say, why there must be some mistake. The poor woman must have gone *completely* out of her mind. Why, I've been right here at home with my sister all evening. And Lily would swear that I had been, and—

God Almighty! What was I thinking about? I couldn't do anything like— like *that!* I wouldn't any more think of—of—hurting anyone than I would of flying. So . . .

*But they kept hurting me, didn't they? They wouldn't leave me alone, would they?*

And if I didn't do something, what would I tell Lily?

Could I get away with lying to her again? If I could—give her a real good story and make it sound convincing—why, that would give me some time, and maybe I could think of something to do. Or maybe I wouldn't have to do anything at all. You know how it is. Lots of times if you can put something off long enough, it just kind of takes care of itself.

But I sure hated to try lying to Lily. Remembering the way she acted this morning, it almost made me shiver to think about lying to her.

And why should I have to, anyway? Why not do the other as long as it was perfectly safe?

God, I didn't know what to do! I knew what I ought and wanted to do, but actually doing it was something else.

I looked at the whiskey bottle. It was only a third full. I lifted it to my mouth, and started gulping. I took three long gulps, stopped a second for breath, and took three more gulps. I coughed, swayed a little on my feet, and let the bottle drop from my fingers.

It was empty. My eyelids fluttered and popped open, and I shuddered all over. Then, my shoulders reared way back, and I seemed to have a ramrod where my spine had been.

I gave the bottle a hard kick. I laughed and made a pass in the air with my fist.

I went down the stairs, and drove away.

It was about a quarter of nine when I got home. Lily met me in the hall—all ready, it looked like, to open up on me, so I opened up first.

"Now, just one minute, please!" I said. "You listen for a change, and then if you've got any questions you can ask 'em. Now, you'll recall that—"

"H-Henry. Henry!" she said. "I—I'm—"

"You'll recall—" I raised my voice. "You'll recall that I was against seeing

Luane. I told you it was highly inadvisable, occupying the position that I do, but you insisted. So—"

"H-Henry . . ." she said shakily. "You—you did see her?"

"Naturally. Where do you think I've been all evening?" I said. "Now, it didn't turn out at all well—much worse even than I expected. So whatever you do, don't let on to anyone that I— What's the matter with you?"

She took a step back from me. Her hand fluttered to her mouth.

"Y-you've been drinking," she said. "You d-don't—didn't know what you were—"

"I've had a drink," I said. "Just a swallow or two, and I don't want to hear anything about it. I—"

"Shut up!" Her voice cracked out suddenly like a whip. "Listen to me, Henry! The sheriff called here a few minutes ago. I was positive you were up to something foolish, staying away like this, so I didn't tell him you weren't here. I said you were taking a bath, and you'd have to call him back. Now—"

"B-but why?" My stomach was sinking; it was oozing right down into my shoes. "W-what d-does—"

"You know why, what! Going out there so drunk you—you— You killed her, understand! Luane's dead!"

Doctor Jim Ashton arrived at the Devore place right behind me, and we went in the house together. Jim looked pretty drawn, sickish. Surprisingly— or maybe it wasn't surprising—I'd never felt better or more self confident in my life. I'd been kind of set back on my heels for a second, but I snapped right out of it. The fogginess washed out of my mind, taking all of the old foggy unsureness with it. I had a keyed-up, coiled-tight feeling, and yet I was perfectly at ease.

Sheriff Jameson and a couple of his deputies were inside. I talked to Jameson, and then I went into the living-room and talked to Ralph Devore. He appeared a little stunned, but not greatly upset. He answered all my questions promptly and lucidly. And—I should add—most satisfactorily. I clapped him on the back, offered him my condolences and told him not to worry about a thing. Then, I went back out into the hall.

Luane Devore lay at the foot of the stairs in her nightgown. Although she was sprawled on her stomach, her legs back up on the steps, her head was twisted completely around so that her face was turned upward. Her lips were bruised and swollen, smeared with drying blood. There were several other bad bruises on her face and, of course, her neck was broken.

Jim finished his examination, and we stepped into the dining room to confer. I told him about Ralph, why Ralph had to be completely above any suspicion. He was pretty startled, naturally—I had been myself when I saw the proof of Ralph's innocence. But, then, he shrugged and nodded.

"I'd call it an accident myself," he said. "That's a long fall from the top of those stairs. A fall like that could easily have bruised her up much more than she is. Of course, when someone has lived in hot water all her life, you hardly expect her to die of chilblains, but . . . ."

I laughed. I said it was odd that an accident should get her when so many people had motives for doing so. But there it was, wasn't it? He said it was an accident. I said it was. So did the sheriff. That made it an accident, and anyone would have a hell of a time proving that it wasn't.

I laughed again. He gave me an odd, searching look. I hesitated—my laugh had sounded pretty loud, I guess—and then I asked him what was on his mind.

"Well—uh—nothing." He frowned uncomfortably. "You were . . . the sheriff reached you at home tonight?"

"Why, yes," I said. "What of it?"

"Nothing. Lily was there with you, I suppose? Well—" He shook his head. "That's good. I'm glad to hear it. And Bobbie's out with the Pavlov girl—and I'm glad of that, for once. But . . . ."

"Oh," I said slowly, as if I was just beginning to see what he meant. "Look, Jim. Don't take this the wrong way, but where were you—"

"Quiet!" he said sharply. "I don't want to talk about it here."

"But, look," I said. "The time of death can't be fixed absolutely. So whether you—"

"I said I didn't want to talk about it here!" he snapped. "Can you meet me down in front of the courthouse in about fifteen minutes?"

"Why, sure," I said. "Even sooner. But—"

"Good! Do it, then."

He left. I went back out into the hall.

The nearest undertaking service was thirty miles away, so it would be some time before Luane's body could be removed. Sheriff Jameson agreed to stick around until the job was over; also to see that Ralph was taken care of comfortably for the night. He had one of his deputies put a couple of things of Ralph's into my car—things I was taking custody of temporarily—and then I left for town.

Jim Ashton was parked in front of the courthouse. He got out of his car as I drove up, started talking while I was still climbing out of mine.

"You asked me a question about fixing the time of death, Hank. Here's the answer. When a fatality is discovered as quickly as this one was, you can come damned close to fixing the time it occurred. Oh, you can't pin it down to a matter of minutes and seconds, but you can place it within a very narrow period. And, Hank, I can't account for my time during that period in this case!"

"But it was an accident," I said. "Anyway, you're not the only one who—"

"Who else is there? My son is in the clear. You and Lily are. Ralph is.

There's that girl he's been chasing around with, of course, but if he's out of the picture she just about has to be, too. Anyway, she's in a lot better spot than I am. And, damn her, it's her fault that I'm—but, let it go. The time of Luane's death can be placed within a certain period, and everyone but me can—"

"Just a minute." I put a hand on his arm. "Calm down, Jim. You were the one who examined Luane. What's to stop you from saying she died during a period that you can account for?"

He looked at me blankly. Jim's supposed to be a very intelligent man—and I'm sure he is—but he certainly couldn't keep up with me tonight. No one could have.

"Oh," he said, at last. "Why, yes, I guess I could, couldn't I?"

"Why not?" I winked and nudged him. "What's to stop you?"

A relieved smile spread over his face. Then he glanced over my shoulder, and the smile went away.

"There," he nodded grimly, and I turned around and looked. "That's what's to stop me!"

I'd expected Kossmeyer to be tipped off, and I knew he'd move fast as soon as he was. But I hadn't thought he would move this fast. And I hadn't planned on his doing what he had done—or, rather, what he was preparing to do.

His convertible was just about in the middle of the block, opposite us. Just passing under a streetlight. We could see him plain as day, and the man he had with him. The doctor who sometimes came here from out of town.

They passed on by, took the road that led toward the Devore place. Jim sighed and said, well, that was that, he guessed.

I told him I was sure everything would work out all right, but it didn't seem to help much. He drove away, still looking mighty sickish, and I took the stuff out of my car and carried it up to my office.

I was feeling a mite let-down myself. Kind of, you know, like someone had given me a little punch in the stomach. And it wasn't because I was worried about Jim. Jim hadn't killed Luane, I was positive of it. So unless he confessed —and I doubted if even Kossmeyer could break Jim Ashton down—he couldn't be convicted. He could be put to plenty of grief, of course; so much that he might just about as well be guilty as innocent. But—

Dammit, he almost deserved to be. If he hadn't been so careless or unlucky or dumb or something, I'd have had Kossmeyer against a stone wall. I could have put that little louse in his place, and made him like it.

I cussed, and took a kick at my wastebasket. I got busy on the telephone, trying to make the best of the situation. About thirty minutes passed. I'd just hung up after a call when the phone rang.

It was Jim. He had an alibi for the time of Luane's death, after all. Not only that, but the Lee girl also had one! They were each other's alibi!

I almost let out a war whoop when he told me the news. I think I would have if I hadn't glanced out the window and seen Kossmeyer coming up the walk.

I hung up the phone, thinking by God that this made everything perfect—hell, better than perfect!

I listened, grinning, as Kossmeyer came up the steps and down the hall. As he neared the door, I wiped off my grin and stood up.

I was very polite to him. Oh, extremely. I said it was a great honor to have such a distinguished visitor, and that I would feel privileged to assist him in any poor way that I could.

He looked a little startled, then embarrassed. Then, as he sat down across from me, he laughed sort of shyly. "I'm sorry," he said. "I just supposed that since we knew each other so well, and since it's pretty common practice to call in an outside doctor—"

"I'm delighted that you did," I said. "Nothing could have pleased me more. Now, as long as you're taking such an extraordinary interest in the case—"

"Extraordinary? It's extraordinary to be interested in the death of a client?"

"If you please," I said. "Perhaps if you will not interrupt we can conclude our business quickly. Now, I have here a canvas sack containing approximately fifty-seven thousand dollars. It belongs to Ralph Devore, and here is conclusive proof in the form of a ledger. I think you'll agree with me that—"

"Sure, I will," he nodded. "I'd sure as hell agree anyway that the guy could never be convicted. Luane couldn't have kept him from leaving her. He had no monetary motive for killing her. He was on the scene right about the time of her death, but—Yeah, counsellor? Go right ahead."

Go right ahead? Hell, there was hardly anything to go ahead with! I'd been all set to surprise him; I'd had it all planned. Just how he'd look and what he'd say, and what I'd say and—and everything. And then that damned stupid Jameson or one of his deputies had had to spoil it all.

"Well," I said, "as long as you've already been told . . ."

"Ought to have known without being told." He shook his head. "Ought to have been able to guess how things stood. On the other hand, who'd've ever thought that a guy like Devore would have that kind of dough? Or any considerable sum?"

"What's the difference?" I said. "It was his money. He certainly wouldn't have had to kill her to get his own money, would he?"

"You're quite right," he said gravely. "He would not have had to. I have no grounds for thinking that he did kill her—or, for that matter, that anyone did."

"You—" I paused. "You don't think that anyone did? You mean, you think it was an accident?"

"Well," he shrugged, "why not? There's that broken telephone line, of course, but you can't make anything out of that. Yeah, I'd be willing to let it go as an accident."

He looked at me, frowning a little. I looked down at my desk, feeling my face turn red, hardly knowing what to do or say next. He'd spoiled everything. Everything I'd planned to say, why—why, now I couldn't. All I could do was just sit there, like a bump on a log. Looking like a damned fool, and knowing that he thought I was one.

He cleared his throat. He murmured something about not envying me my job, and a prosecutor's really having a hard row to hoe.

"Used to be on that side of the desk myself, y'know," he added. "Guess a lot of trial lawyers start off as prosecutors. Gives 'em all around experience, and the longer they stick to it the better they get. You know what I always say, Mr. County Attorney? I say, you show me an experienced prosecutor, and I'll show you a topflight lawyer!"

I didn't say anything. I couldn't even make myself look up at him. He cleared his throat again.

"I'm afraid I've interrupted you so much that I've broken your chain of thought. Were you going to—uh—May I see that list?"

I shoved it toward him, the list of people who had a good reason for wanting Luane dead and who they had been with at the time of her death. He went down the double-column of names, murmuring aloud, kind of talking to himself but also speaking to me:

"Bobbie Ashton and Myra Pavlov . . . Lily and Henry C. Will—Oh, now, really. I hope you don't think that was necessary on my account . . . Doctor Ashton and Danny Lee. Hmm, hmm. Well, what the hell, though?"

He laid the list back on my desk. He murmured that I had certainly done a first-rate job of investigation; then, after a long awkward pause, he suddenly laughed.

My head came up. It was such a warm-sounding, friendly laugh that it was hard for me to keep from joining in.

"Y'know, Mr. County Attorney," he chuckled, "sometimes I feel like one of those characters in a Western movie. The guy that gets such an exaggerated reputation for toughness that he can't hardly tip his hat without someone thinking he's going for a gun. Sure, I try to take care of my clients, and maybe I'm overly conscientious about it. But I certainly don't go hunting for trouble. I don't like trouble, y'know? There's too damned much of it already without creating any."

He laughed again, giving me a sidewise glance, trying to draw me into his laughter. I looked back at him coldly—letting *him* squirm for a change, letting him feel as foolish as I had.

"Well—" He stood up awkwardly. "I guess—uh—I guess I'd better be going. See you around, huh? And my compliments on your thoroughness in handling this investigation."

He nodded, and started for the door. I let him get halfway there before I spoke.

"Just a moment, Mr. Kossmeyer . . ."

"Yeah?" He turned around.

"Come back here," I said. "I haven't told you you could leave yet."

"Wh-aat?" He laughed, kind of frowning. "What the hell is this?"

I stared at him silently. He came slowly back and again sat down across from me.

"You complimented me on my thoroughness," I said. "It suddenly occurred to me that I haven't been thorough enough. Where were you at the time of Luane Devore's death?"

"Where was—? Aw, now—"

"Luane said a great many ugly things about you. Whether they were true or not I don't know, but—"

"Then maybe we'd better stick to your question," he said quietly. "I was with my wife at the time."

"Oh? Your wife, eh?" I shook my head, kind of grinning down my nose. "Just your wife? You have no one else to support your story?"

"No one. There's only the one person. I'm in the same boat with those other people on your list—with you, for example."

"Well," I shrugged. "I suppose I'll have to accept that, then. I can't say that I'm completely satisfied, but—uh—"

His face had gone white. The pale had pushed up, spread over the summer's tan; and all his color seemed concentrated in his burning black eyes.

"Why ain't you satisfied?" he said. "What's there about me or my wife that makes our word less reliable than that of these other people?"

His voice was kind of a low, quivering purr. A kind of wound-up, coiled-tight undertone. He spoke again, repeating his question, and the quiver became stronger. The tenseness, the coiling seemed to extend to his body.

I began to get a little nervous, but I couldn't stop now. Not the way he was looking at me, the way he sounded: the way, in so many words, he was threatening me. If he'd just laughed again or even smiled a little; given me an opening to say, oh, hell, of course I was just joking . . .

"You've been kicking me in the teeth all evening," he said, "and I took it. But I ain't taking that last. When you tell me that my wife's word is no good —that she and I ain't as decent and upright as other people—then you throw the door wide open. You got a hell of a lot more tellin' to do then, buster, and by God you'd better not clown around when you do it. Because if you do—"

"Now, w-wait a minute," I said. "I—I—"

"What are you trying to cover up, Williams? Why did you go to such lengths to *prove* that this was an accident? You felt you had to, right? You had a guilty conscience, right? You knew—you sit there now, knowing that it was not an accident but murder. And knowing full well who the murderer is. That's right, isn't it, Williams? Answer me! You know who killed Luane Devore, and by God, I think I do, too! You've as good as admitted it. You've put the finger right on yourself! You've—"

"N-no! *NO!*" I said. "I w-was with my sister! I—"

"Suppose I told you I'd talked with your sister? Suppose I told you she's admitted that you weren't with her? Suppose I told you I've only been playing with you all evening—getting you out on a limb with this one-person alibi deal? Suppose . . ."

His voice had uncoiled; he had uncoiled. He was in front of me, leaning toward me, pounding on the desk. He was there, but he was also behind me, to the side of me, above me. He seemed to surround me like his voice, closing in, shutting out everything else. Chasing me further and further into a black, bewildering labyrinth where only he and the voice could follow. I couldn't think. I—I—

I thought, *Isn't it funny? How, when you feel so much one way, you act just the opposite?*

I thought, *She never said nothin'. Mama and Papa said I did real good and she hated it. She hated me. All her life she's—*

"She did it!" It was me, screaming. "S-she said she was going to! S-she—she—she says I wasn't to home, why she wasn't either! S-she—she—"

"Then she can't alibi for you, can she? You can't prove you were at home. And you weren't, were you, Williams? You were at the Devore house, weren't you, Williams? You were killing Luane, weren't you, Williams? Killing her and then faking—"

"*N-N-NO! NO!* Don't you s-see? I couldn't I—I couldn't hurt no one! H-honest, Mr. Kossmeyer! I—I ain't that way. I k-know it l-looks like—like —but that ain't me! I couldn't do it. I didn't, d-didn't, didn't, didn't . . ."

He was making little motions with his hands, motioning for me to stop. The whiteness was gone from his face, giving way to a deep flush. He looked ashamed and embarrassed, and kind of sick.

"I'm sorry," he said. "I didn't really think you killed Luane. I just got sore, and—"

"He didn't kill her," said a voice from the doorway. "I did."

# XI

## MYRA PAVLOV

PAPA JUST ABOUT scared me to death when he came home for lunch. He didn't act much different or say anything much more out of the way than he usually does—I guess he really didn't actually. But I kept feeling like he knew about Bobbie and me, and that that was why he was acting and talking the way he was. And finally I just got so nervous and scared that I jumped up from the table, and ran up to my room.

Afterwards, sitting up on the edge of my bed, I was scared even more. I thought, Oh, golly, now I *have* done it. Now, he *will* know there's something wrong, if he doesn't already. I shivered and shook. I began to get sick to my stomach; kind of a morning sickness like I've had a lot lately. But I didn't dare go to the bathroom. He might hear me, and come upstairs. He might start asking Mama questions, and that would be just as bad, because she's even scareder of him than I am.

It's funny how we feel about him; I mean, the way we're always so scared of him. Because there's actually no real reason to be. He's never hit Mama or me. He's never threatened us or cussed us out. He's never done anything of the things that mean men are supposed to do to their families, and yet we've always been scared of him. Almost as far back as I can remember, anyway.

Well, after a moment or so, Mama left the table too, and came upstairs, stopped in the doorway of my room. I held my hand over my mouth and pointed. She pointed to my shoes. I slipped them off, and followed her down the hall to the bathroom. And, golly, was it a relief to get in there.

I used the sink to vomit in, and Mama kept running the water to cover up the noise. It was sure a relief.

We went back to my room, she in her shoes and me in my stocking feet. We sat down on my bed, and she put her arms around me and held me. She was kind of stiff and awkward about it, since we've never done much kissing and hugging or anything like that in our family. But it was nice, just the same.

It wasn't much later, but it seemed like hours before Papa left. Mama's arms slid away from me, and we both heaved a big sigh. And then we laughed, kind of weakly, because it was sort of funny, you know.

"How are you feeling, girl?" Mama said. "Girl" is about as close as she ever comes to calling me a pet name. I said I was feeling pretty good now.

"Stand up and let me take a look at you," Mama said.

I stood up. I pulled my dress up above my waist, and Mama looked at me. Then, she motioned for me to sit down again.

"It doesn't show none at all," she said. "You couldn't tell there's a thing wrong by looking at you. Of course, it wouldn't need to show if he's—he's—"

"Do you think he has, Mama?" I started to tremble a little. "Y-you don't think he has heard anything, do you, Mama?"

"Well, sure, now," Mama said quickly. "Of course, he hasn't. I reckon he'd sure let us know if he had."

"But—but what makes him act so funny then?"

"Mean, you mean," Mama said. "When did he ever act any other way?"

She sat, turning her hands in her lap, looking down at the big blue veins in the rough red flesh. Her legs were bare, and they were red and rough, too; bruised-looking where the varicose veins were broken. She was just kind of a mass of redness and roughness, from her face to her feet. And all at once I began to cry.

"There, there, girl," she said, giving me an awkward pat. "Want me to get you something to eat?"

"N-no." I shook my head.

She said I'd better eat; I'd hardly touched my lunch. She said she could bake me up something real quick—some puff bread or something else real tasty.

"Oh, Mama." I wiped my eyes, suddenly smiling a little. "That's all you ever think of! I'll bet if a person had a broken leg you'd try to feed them!"

"Well . . ." She smiled, kind of embarrassed. "I guess I would probably, at that."

"Well," I said. "I guess I could probably eat a couple of those fresh crullers you made this morning. Maybe a couple of cups of good strong coffee, too. All at once, I'm actually really pretty hungry, Mama."

"You know, I kind of am myself, girl," Mama said. "You just stay here and rest, and I'll bring us up a bite."

She brought up some coffee and a half-dozen crullers, and a couple of big thick potroast sandwiches. We were both pretty full when we finished—at least, I couldn't have eaten anything more. And I felt kind of peaceful, dull peaceful, you know, like you do when you're full.

A fly buzzed against the screen. A nice little breeze drifted through the window, bringing the smell of alfalfa blossoms. I guess nothing smells quite as good as alfalfa, unless it's fresh-baked bread. I wondered why Mama wasn't baking today, because she almost always puts dough to set on Sunday night, and bakes bread on Monday.

"Guess I just didn't have the will for it," she said, when I asked her about it. "You bake all day in this weather, and it takes the house a week to cool off."

"It wouldn't if you cooked with gas," I said. "You ought to make him put in gas, Mama!"

Mama made a sort of sour-funny face. She asked me if I'd ever known of anyone to make Papa do anything. "Anyway," she added, slowly. "I don't think he could do it now, even if he wanted to. I don't think he's burning coal any more just to bother the neighbors."

I said that, well, I thought so. I *knew* so. "Why did you ever marry him anyway, Mama? You must have known what he was like. There certainly must have been some signs of it."

"Well . . ." She brushed a wisp of hair back from her forehead. "I told you the why of it about a hundred times already, girl. He was older than me, so he got out of the orphanage first. And then he started dropping back to visit, after he was making money, so . . ."

"But you just didn't marry him to get away from the place?" I said. "That wasn't the only reason, was it?"

"No, of course not," Mama said.

"He was different then, Mama? You were in love with him?"

She looked down in her lap again, twisting her hands. Words like "love" always embarrass Mama, and her face was a little flushed.

"It wasn't the only reason I married him," she said. "Just to get away from the orphanage. But maybe . . . I kind of think maybe he thought it was. We shouldn't talk about him like we do, girl. Shouldn't even think things like we do. He's pretty sensitive, you know, quick to catch on to what someone else is thinkin', and—"

"Well, it's his own fault," I said. "What else can he expect, anyway?"

Mama shook her head. She didn't say anything.

"Mama," I said. "What did you mean a minute ago when you said Papa probably couldn't have the house piped for gas, even if he wanted to? You didn't mean he didn't have the money, did you?"

"No, of course, not. I didn't mean anything—just thinking nonsense and I said it out loud," Mama said quickly. "Don't you ever breathe a word around about your Papa not having money, girl."

I said I wouldn't. In the first place it would be silly and a lie; and then it would make Papa awfully mad. "He's got all kinds of money," I said, "and, Mama, I just g-got to—"

I started crying again. Right out of a clear blue sky without any warning.

"I can't stand it any longer!" I said. "I'm getting so scared, and—could you get some money from him, Mama? Make him give you enough for me and Bobbie to—"

I didn't finish the question. It was too foolish. I wouldn't even have started to ask it if I hadn't been half-scared to death.

"I don't know why he has to be so hateful!" I said. "If he wants to—to— Why doesn't he do something to that dirty old Luane Devore? She's the one that's causing all the trouble!"

"There, there, girl," Mama mumbled. "No use in getting yourself—"

"Well, why doesn't he?" I said. "Why doesn't he do something to her?"

"He wouldn't see no call to," Mama said. "As long as it was the truth, why Papa wouldn't . . ."

She frowned, her voice trailing off into silence. I spoke to her a couple times, saying that it wasn't fair and that I just couldn't go on any longer. But she didn't say anything back to me.

Finally, when I was about ready to yell, I was getting so nervous, she sighed and shook her head.

"I . . . I guess not, girl. I thought I had a notion about some place I might get some money for you, but I guess I can't."

"But maybe I could!" I said. 'Bobbie and me! Who—"

"You keep out of it," Mama said sharply. "You couldn't get it, even if it could be got. I thought for a moment I might get it, part of it anyway, because I'm your Papa's wife. But—"

"But I could try!" I said. "Please, Mama! Just tell me who it is, and—"

"I told you you couldn't get it," Mama said, "and trying wouldn't get you anything but trouble. This party would tell Papa about it, and you know what would happen then."

"Well . . ." I hesitated. "I guess you're probably right, Mama. If you couldn't get it, why, I don't see how I could. Is it an old debt someone owes Papa?"

Mama said it was kind of a debt. It was and it wasn't. And there was no way that the party could be forced to pay it.

"For one thing," she added, "the party's got no money to pay with that I know of. Papa thinks different—I kind of got the notion he does from some things he's let slip—but you know him. Someone says something is white, why he'll say it's black, just to be contrary."

"I just can't imagine," I said. "I just can't see Papa letting someone get away without paying him what they owe."

"I told you," Mama said. "They—this party don't really owe it. I mean, they do and they ought to pay, but—"

"Tell me who it is, Mama," I said. "Please, please, Mama. I—I've got to do something. I c-can't be any worse off than I am now. If you won't see the party, do anything to help me, at least—"

"I can't girl." Mama bit her lip. "You know I would if—"

"Can't what?" I said. "You can't help me, or you can't let me help myself?"

"I—I just . . ." She pushed herself to her feet, started loading dishes back onto the tray. "I'll tell you how you can help yourself," she said, looking hurt and sullen. "You can just stay away from that Bobbie Ashton until he's ready to marry you."

I started crying again, burying my face in my hands. I said, what good would that do, for heaven's sake. Bobbie might get mad or interested in someone else.

Anyway, even if I did stop seeing him, it wouldn't change anything when Papa found out about us.

"You k-know I'm right, Mama," I sobbed. "H-he'd still—he'll kill us, Mama! H-he's going to kill me, and—and I've got no one to turn to. You won't h-help me, a-and you w-won't let me do anything. All you can do is just fuss around and mumble, a-and ask m-me if I want something to eat, a-and—"

The dishes rattled on the tray. One of the cups toppled over into its saucer. Then, I heard her turn and shuffle toward the door.

"All right, girl," she said, dully. "I'll do it tonight."

"M-Mama—" I took my hands away from my face. "You know I didn't mean what I said, Mama."

"It's all right," Mama said. "You didn't say anything that wasn't true."

"But I didn't—you'll do what, Mama?"

"I'll see that party tonight. It won't do no good, I'm pretty sure, but I'll do it."

She went on out of the room, and down the stairs. I sat forward on the bed, studying myself in the dresser mirror. I certainly looked a fright. My eyes were all red and my face blotched, and my nose swollen up like a sweet potato. I hadn't put up my hair last night either. And now, what with the heat and my nervous sweating, it was as limp and drab-looking as a dishrag.

I went to the bathroom, soaked my face in cold water and dabbed it with astringent. Then, I took a nice long lukewarm bath, putting up my hair as I sat in the tub.

I tried to tell myself that I hadn't said anything out of the way to Mama, that she'd certainly never done much of anything else for me, and that it was no more than right that she should do this. I told myself that—those things —and I guess there was a lot of truth to it. But still I began to feel awful bad —awful ashamed of myself. She'd always done as much for me as she could, I guessed. It wasn't her fault that Papa had just about taken everything out of her that she had to do with.

There was last spring, for example, when I graduated from high school; she'd gone way out on a limb to help me then. To try to help me, I should say. I'd told her that she simply couldn't let Papa come to the graduation exercises. I'd simply *die* if he did, I told her, because none of the other kids had any use for me now, and if he came it would be ten times worse.

"You know how it'll be, Mama," I said, kind of crying and storming. "He won't be dressed right, and he'll go around snorting and sneering and being sarcastic to the other parents, and—and just acting as awful as he knows how! I just won't go if he goes, Mama! I'd be so embarrassed I'd sink right through the floor!"

Well, Mama mumbled and massaged her hands together and looked bewildered. She said it really wasn't right for me to feel that way about Papa; and maybe she could drop him a few hints so that he'd look nice and behave himself.

"I don't hardly know what else I can do," she said. "He means to go, and I don't see how—"

"I told you how, Mama!" I said. "You can pretend like you're sick, and you don't want to be left alone. You can do it just as well as not, and you know it!"

Mama mumbled and massaged her hands some more. She said she guessed she could do what I was asking, but she'd sure hate to. "He'd be awfully disappointed, girl. He'd try to cover it up, but he would be."

"I just bet he would!" I said. "Naturally, he'd be disappointed missing a chance to make me feel nervous and cheap. I just can't stand it if he goes, Mama!"

"But it means so much to him, girl," Mama said. "You see, he hardly had any education himself, not even as much as I did. Now, to have his own daughter graduating from high school, why—"

"Oh, pooh!" I said. "I won't go if he goes, Mama! I'll run away from home! I'll—I'll k-kill myself! I'll . . ."

I really ranted and raved on. I'd been feeling awfully upset and nervous anyway, because I'd just started going with Bobbie Ashton at the time, and he wasn't nice to me like he is now, and—but never mind that. That was a long time ago, and I don't like to think it ever even happened. Anyway, to get back to the subject, I kept insisting that Papa just couldn't go to the graduation exercises. I ranted and raved and cried until finally Mama gave in.

She agreed to play sick, and keep Papa at home.

She was upstairs in bed that evening when he came in. I was out in the kitchen, getting dinner ready. I heard him come through the living room and dining room. I could feel those eyes of his boring into the back of my neck as he stood in the kitchen doorway. He didn't say anything. Just stood there staring at me. I dropped a spoon to the floor, I was so nervous and scared, and when I picked it up I had to turn away from the stove. Facing him.

I really didn't recognize him for a second, actually. I really didn't. He'd changed clothes down at the pavilion, and the way he was dressed now, well, I just didn't think he *could* be. I'd never seen him look like this before . . . and I never did again.

He was wearing a brand new blue suit, a real stylish one. He had on a new hat, too—a gray Homburg—and new black dress shoes—the first he'd ever worn, I guess—and a new white shirt, and a tie that matched his suit. He looked so smart and kind of distinguished that I actually didn't know him for a second. I was so surprised that I almost forgot to be scared.

"W-why—why, Papa," I stammered. "Why—where—"

He grinned, looking embarrassed. "Stopped by a rummage sale," he said gruffly. "Picked this up while I was there, too."

He pushed a little package at me. I fumbled it open, and there was a velvet box inside. And inside the box was a wristwatch. A platinum wristwatch with diamonds in it.

I stared at it; I told him thank you, I guess. But if I'd had the nerve I'd've told him something else. I might have even thrown the watch at him.

You see, I'd been hinting for a watch for months—hinting as much as a person dares to with Papa. And all he'd ever do was just laugh or grunt and laugh at me. He'd say things like, well, what the hell do you want a watch for? Or, what you need is a good alarm clock. Or, them damned wristwatches ain't nothing but junk.

That's the way he talked, acted, and all the time he was planning to buy me a watch.

All the time he was planning on buying these new clothes, dressing himself up so people would hardly know him.

"Here's something else," he said, tossing a glassine-topped box on the table. A box with an orchid in it. "Stole it out at the graveyard."

I said thank you again—I guess. I was so mixed up, mad and not mad—kind of ashamed—and nervous and scared, that I don't know what I said. Or whether I actually said anything, really.

"Where's your mother?" he said. "Didn't throw herself out with the trash, did she?"

"S-she's upstairs," I said. "She-she's l-lying—"

"Lyin' about what?" He laughed; broke off suddenly. "What's the matter? Spit it out! She ain't sick, is she?"

I nodded, said, yes, that she was sick. I'd been working myself up to saying it all day, and now it just popped out before I could stop it.

Anyway, what else could I have said? Mama wouldn't know that I didn't want her to play sick now—that I'd just as soon she didn't. If I tried to change our story, it might get her into trouble with Papa. Get us both in trouble.

Well, naturally I looked awfully pale and dragged-out. And, of course, he thought I looked that way on account of Mama. He cursed, turning a little pale himself.

"What's the matter with her?" he said. "When'd she take sick? Why didn't you call me? What'd the Doc say about her?"

"N-nothing," I stammered. "I—I d-don't think she's very sick, Papa."

"Think?" he said. "You mean you ain't called the doctor? Your mother's sick in bed, and—For God's sake!"

He ran to the hall telephone, and called Doctor Ashton. Told him to get over to the house as fast as he could. Then he started upstairs, hurrying but kind of dragging his feet, too.

The doctor arrived. Papa came back downstairs, and out into the kitchen where I was. He paced back and forth, nervously, cursing and grumbling and asking questions.

"Goddammit," he said, "you ought to have called me. You ought to've called the doctor right away. I don't know why the hell you—"

"P-papa," I said. "I d-don't think—I mean, I'm sure she's not very sick."

"How the hell would you know?" He cursed again. Then he said, "What the hell does she have to go and get sick for? She ain't had a sick day in twenty years, so why does she got to do it now?"

"Papa . . ."

"She better cut it out, by God," he said. "She gets sick on me, I'll put her in a hospital. Make her stay there until I say she can leave. Get some real doctors to look after her, and—Yeah? Dammit, if you got something to say, say it!"

I tried to say it, to tell him the truth. But I didn't get very far. He broke in, cursing, when I said Mama wasn't really sick; then he stopped scolding and cursing and said, well, maybe I was right: sure, she wasn't really sick.

"Probably just over-et," he said. "Probably just been workin' too hard . . . That's about the size of it, don't you think so, Myra? Couldn't be nothing' serious, could it?"

"No, Papa," I said. "P-papa, I keep trying to tell you—"

"Why, sure, sure," he said. "We're—you're getting all upset over nothing. You just calm down now, and everything will be fine. There's not a thing in the world to worry about. Doc will get Mama up on her feet, and we'll all go to the graduation together, and—Now cut out that goddamn bawling, will you? You sound like a calf in a hailstorm."

"P-papa," I sobbed. "Oh, Papa, I j-just feel so bad that—"

"Well, you just cut it out," he said, "because there ain't a damned lick of sense to it. Mama's going to be just dandy, and—an'—"

Doctor Ashton was coming down the stairs. Papa kind of swallowed, and then went out to the foot of the staircase to meet him.

"How—how is she, Doc?" I heard him say. "Is she—?"

"Your wife," Doctor Ashton said, "is in excellent physical condition for a woman her age. She is as healthy as the proverbial horse."

Papa let out a grunt. I could almost see his eyes clouding over like they do when he's angry. "What the hell you talkin' about, anyway? What kind of a doctor are you? My wife's—"

"Your wife is not sick. She has not been sick," said Doctor Ashton, and, ooh, did he sound mean! He had everything pretty well figured out, I guess, and the way he dislikes Papa it tickled him to death. "That's a very handsome outfit you're wearing, Pavlov. I take it that you planned on attending the graduation exercises tonight."

"Well, sure. Naturally," Papa said. "Now, what do you mean—"

"It must have come as quite a surprise to your family." The screen door opened, and Doctor Ashton stepped out on the porch. "Yes, quite a surprise. The apparel, that is, not your plans for attending the exercises."

Papa said, "Now, listen, goddammit. What—" Then he said, "Oh." Just the one word, slowly, dully.

"Yes," the doctor said. "Well, there's no reason at all why you can't attend, Pavlov. None at all. That is, of course, if you still want to."

He laughed softly. He went on out to his car, and drove away. And minutes later, it seemed like I could still hear that laugh of his.

I waited in the kitchen, stood right where I had been standing. Not moving, except for the trembling. Hardly even breathing.

And Papa stayed out in the hallway. Not moving either, it seemed. Just standing and waiting, like I was standing and waiting.

I was sure he was just working up to an explosion. Putting all the mean ugly things together in his mind, so he could cloud up and rain all over me and Mama. That was what he was going to do, I was sure, because he'd done the same thing before. Made us wait, you know. Wait and wait, knowing that he was going to do something and getting so jumpy we were about to fall apart. And then suddenly cutting loose on us.

I wished that he'd cut loose now, and get it over with. I wished he'd just do it, you know; not because it was so hard to go on waiting, but because it would kind of even things up. And maybe he'd stop feeling the way he must be feeling now.

It sounds funny—or, no, I guess it doesn't—but I'd never really cared about how he felt before. I mean, I'd never actually thought about his having any feelings—about being able to hurt his feelings. Because you'd never have thought it from the way he'd always acted. He'd always gone out of his way to show that he didn't care how anyone felt about him or acted toward him, so . . .

Maybe Mama is right. She was an awfully pretty girl back when she married Papa, and Papa was kind of short and stocky like he is now, and about as homely as a mud fence. So, since she never could express herself very well and she's always been so kind of frozen-faced and shy—just embarrassed all to pieces just by the mention of love or anything like that—why, maybe Papa did think she married him just to get away from the orphanage. And maybe that's the reason, partly the reason, anyway—

Oh, I don't know. And the way things are now, I couldn't care less. Because he certainly doesn't care anything about me, even if he might have at one time.

How could he—a father that would actually kill his own daughter if he found out a certain thing about her?

Bobbie says I have things all wrong; Papa would do it because he cares so much. But that just doesn't make any sense, does it, and as sweet and smart as Bobbie is, he can say some awfully foolish things.

Well, anyway, getting back to that night:

Papa didn't do what I expected him to. He started for the kitchen once, but he stopped after a step or two. Then he took a couple of steps toward the stairs, and stopped again. Finally, he went to the screen door and pushed it open, paused with one foot inside the house and the other on the porch.

"Got to go back to the office," he called. "Won't want any supper. Won't be able to go to the graduation. You and Mama have a good—you two watch out for the squirrels."

I called, "P-papa—wait!" But the screen door slammed, drowning out the words.

By the time I got to the door, he was a block up the street.

He never wore those clothes again. I saw Goofy Gannder in the Homburg one day, so I guess Papa probably gave him the whole outfit, and Goofy traded the other things for booze.

Well, as I was saying, Mama really had tried to help me that one time, at least, and it wasn't fair to say that she hadn't. Also, as I was about to say, it wasn't very nice of me to get her to try anything again. She'd have to face Papa afterwards. He'd take out on her what he couldn't take out on me, and an old woman like that—she was forty-six her last birthday—she just wouldn't be able to take it.

Aside from that, it probably wouldn't do any good; I mean, she probably wouldn't get away with whatever she was thinking about doing. She'd be so scared and unsure of herself that she'd make a botch of it, get herself into a lot of trouble without making me any better off than I was now.

So . . . so I finished putting up my hair, and went back to my bedroom. I put on a robe, went downstairs and told Mama I was sorry about the way I talked to her.

She didn't answer me; just turned away looking hurt, sullen-hurt. I put my arms around her and kissed her, and tried to pet her a little. That got her all red-faced and embarrassed, and kind of broke the ice.

"It's all right, girl," she said. "I don't blame you for being upset, and I'll do what I said I would."

"No, Mama," I said. "I don't want you to. Honestly, I don't. After all, you said you were sure it wouldn't do any good, so why take chances for nothing?"

"Well, I'm pretty sure that it wouldn't—that I couldn't get any money from this party. But . . ." She paused, relieved that I was letting her off, but a little suspicious along with it. "Look, girl. You're not planning on—on—"

"On what?" I laughed. "Now, what in the world could I do, Mama? Hold up a bank?"

Actually, I wasn't planning on doing anything. The idea didn't come to me until later, when I went back upstairs. It seems kind of funny that I hadn't thought of it before—under the circumstances, I mean—but I guess it actually really wasn't so strange. I just hadn't been desperate enough until now.

"So you just forget all about it, Mama," I said. "Don't do anything tonight, anyway. If something else doesn't turn up in a few days, why—"

"But I'll have to do it tonight, girl! Have to if I'm goin' to at all."

"Why do you?" I said. "If it's waited all these years, why can't it wait a little longer?"

"Because it can't! This party's telephone will—will—"

She broke off abruptly, turning to stir something on the stove. "My heavens, girl! I get to jabbering with you, and I'll burn up everything in the house."

"What about the telephone, Mama?" I said. "What were you going to say?"

"Nothing. How do I know, anyway?" Mama said. "Lord, what a day! I'm getting so rattled I don't know what I'm saying."

I laughed, and said I wouldn't worry again. I told her I really didn't want her to see the party she'd mentioned—that I'd really be very angry if she did. And she nodded and mumbled, so that took care of that.

I went back up to my room. I took off my robe, put on some fresh underthings and stretched out on the bed. It was nice and cool. I'd left the bedroom door open, and the draft sucked the alfalfa-smelling breeze through the window.

I closed my eyes, really relaxing for about the first time all day. My mind seemed to go completely empty for a moment—just cleared out of everything. And then all sorts of things, images, began to drift through it:

Mama . . . Papa . . . Bobbie . . . the pavilion . . . Me . . . Me going into the pavilion. Unlocking the ticket booth. Going into Daddy's office, and opening the safe. Taking out the change box, and—

My eyes popped open, and I sat up suddenly. Then, I remembered that this was Monday, that there wouldn't be any dance tonight so I wouldn't have to work.

I sighed, and started to lay back down again.

I sat back up, slowly, feeling my eyes get wider and wider. Feeling my stomach sort of squeeze together inside, then gradually unsqueeze.

I got my purse off the dresser. I took out my key ring, stared at it for a moment and dropped it back in the purse.

It was almost four o'clock. I undid my hair, even though it had only been up a little while, and then I began to dress.

Mama came upstairs while I was putting my face on. She started to go on by to her own room, but she saw me dressed and fixing my face, so she turned back and came in. She asked me where in the world I thought I was going at this time of day.

"Oh, I thought I'd meet Bobbie in town tonight," I said. "I think it might be better than having him come here to the house, if people are doing any talking."

"But it ain't tonight yet," Mama said. "You haven't even had your supper yet. What—"

"I don't want any supper, Mama," I said. "Heavens, I just got through stuffing myself just a little while ago, didn't I? Anyway, the real reason I want to leave early is so I won't have to see Papa. I just can't face him again so soon, after the way he acted at lunch."

Mama started getting nervous. She said Papa would be sure to wonder about my being away at supper time, and what was she going to tell him?

I turned around from the mirror, looking pretty exasperated, I guess, because I certainly felt that way.

"Why, for heavens sake, just tell him the truth, Mama," I said. "I mean, tell him I ate late and I didn't want any supper—dinner—so I just went on into town. I'll just walk around or drink a malted or something until it's time to meet Bobbie. Good grief, there's nothing wrong with that, is there? Can't I even go down town without explaining and arguing and arguing and explaining until—"

"What you getting so excited about, girl?" Mama looked at me suspiciously. "You up to something?"

I drew in my breath real deep, giving her a good hard stare. And then I turned back to the mirror again.

"Look, girl," Mama mumbled, apologetically. "I'm just worried about you. If you've got some notion of—well, I don't know what you might be thinking about doing. But—"

"Mama," I said. "I'm going to get awfully mad in a minute."

"But, girl. You just can't—"

"All right, Mama," I said. "All right! I've argued and explained just as much as I'm going to, and now I'm not going to say another word. Not another word, Mama! I told you why I was leaving early. I told you I couldn't bear to face Papa tonight, and I can't. I simply *can't,* Mama, and there's no reason why I should, and I haven't the slightest intention of making the slightest effort to do so, and—and I'm not going to say another word about it, and I don't want to hear another word about it!"

She twitched, and rubbed her hands together. I'll bet they wouldn't be so red and big-veined if she wasn't always rubbing them together. She started to argue again, but I told her I'd cry if she did. So that stopped her right at the start.

"Well," she mumbled, "you're going to drink a cup of coffee first, anyway. I'm not going to let you leave this house without at least something hot on your stomach."

"Oh, Mama," I sighed. "Well, hurry up and get it, if you're going to! I can't drink it after I put my lipstick on."

She hurried downstairs, and brought me up some coffee. I drank it, and started fixing my mouth.

She watched me, twitching and massaging her hands. I caught her eye in the mirror, gave her a good hard look, believe me, and she shifted her eyes quickly. She didn't look at me again until I was all through.

"Well," I said, "I guess I'd better run along, now, if I want to miss Papa."

"All right, girl." She got up from the bed where she'd been sitting. "Take care of yourself, now, and don't stay out too late."

She started to kiss me good-bye; and that was kind of funny, you know, because she doesn't go in much for kissing. I pretended I didn't know what she meant to do, turning my head so as not to get my face smeared.

After all, I didn't have time to fix it again, did I? And if she wanted to kiss someone, why did she have to wait until they were in a hurry and all ready to go somewhere?

"Girl," she said, nervously. "I don't want you getting upset again, but— promise me, girl! Promise you won't—"

"Now, Mama, I *have* promised," I said. "I've told you and told you, and I'm not going to tell you again. Now, will you please stop harping on the subject?"

"You don't have to do anything, girl! I'll go—I'll think of something. Something's bound to turn up."

"Well, *all right!*" I said. "All right, for heaven's sake!"

And I snatched up my purse, and left.

She called after me, but I kept right on going, down the stairs and out the door. Then, as I was going out the gate, she called to me again—waved to me from the bedroom window. So, well, I gave her a smile and waved back.

I honestly wasn't mad, you know, and naturally I didn't mean to do anything that would make her feel bad. It was just that I had so much on my mind, that I simply couldn't stand any more.

It was a little after five when I got downtown, about five-fifteen. I wanted Papa to get clear home before I went to his office, so that meant I had almost forty-five minutes to kill. Well, thirty-five minutes, anyway, figuring that it would take ten minutes to walk down to the pavilion.

I sauntered around the courthouse square a couple of times, looking in the store windows. I stopped in front of the jewelry store, pretending like I was interested in the jewelry display, but actually looking at myself in the big panel-mirrors behind it.

I thought I looked pretty good tonight, considering all I'd been through. I honestly looked especially good in spite of everything.

I had on a white Cashmere sweater I'd bought two weeks before—I guessed it wasn't rushing the season too much to wear it. I had on a new blue flannel skirt, and extra-sheer stockings and my practically new handmade suede shoes.

I studied myself in the mirror, thinking that whatever else you could say about him, you certainly couldn't say he was stingy. Mama and I could buy just about anything we wanted to, and he'd never say a word. All he ever insisted on was that we pay cash.

Mama always kept a hundred dollars cash on hand. As far back as I could remember, she did. Whenever she or I bought anything, why, she'd tell him, and he'd give her enough to bring her back up to a hundred dollars.

Actually, she—or I should say, I—hadn't spent much until this summer. I was actually scared to death of going in a store; afraid, you know, that the clerks might be laughing at me or talking about me behind my back. And Mama was even worse than I was. We never bought anything until we just had to. When we couldn't put it off any longer, we'd just take the first thing that was showed to us and practically run out of the place.

Papa just talked awful about us. I never will forget some of the mean things he said. He said he'd rent Mama out as a scarecrow, if it wouldn't've been so hard on the crows. And he said I looked like a leaky sack of bran that was about to fall over.

Well, he certainly hasn't had any cause to talk that way since I started going with Bobbie. Not about me, anyhow. I simply couldn't look dowdy around Bobbie, so I just *made* myself shop like a person should. And after I'd done it a few times, I didn't mind it at all. I mean, I actually really liked it, and I really *did* do some shopping from then on.

Nowadays, I hardly ever go into town without buying something.

Why not, anyway? Papa has plenty of money. If he can't treat me decent, why at least he can let me *look* decent.

I glanced at my wristwatch, saw that it was getting close to six. I started for the pavilion, walking fast. Wondering how much money there'd be in his strongbox

I never touched the strongbox ordinarily. I had no reason to, in my ticket-selling job, so I didn't know how much was in it. But I knew there'd be a lot. Papa didn't do any business with the banks that he didn't absolutely have to. He'd always paid "cash on the barrelhead," as he says, for practically everything. And when you have as many interests as Papa, that takes a lot of cash.

Of course, the dance business had fallen off quite a bit, and some of his other things weren't doing so well. But, goodness, what of it? Look at all the property he owned! Look at all the money he'd made when business was good! Papa could lose money for years, and he'd still be rich. Everyone in town said so. Maybe there wouldn't be as much in the strongbox as there used to be, but there'd still be plenty. Two or three thousand dollars, at least.

I was about a half block from the pavilion when I saw Ralph Devore come out of the rear exit, and climb up into the air-conditioner shed.

I stopped dead in my tracks. I thought, Oh, golly, how *could* I have forgot about him? Why does he have to be working all the time? I was actually sick for a moment, I was so disappointed. Then, I just tossed my head and kept right on going. Because it suddenly dawned on me that it didn't make a bit of difference whether Ralph was there or not. Even if he saw me, which wasn't likely, it wouldn't matter.

Ralph wouldn't think anything of my going into Papa's office. After all, I was the owner's daughter, and it just wouldn't occur to him to try to stop me or ask me what I was doing. Of course, he'd talk later when Papa missed the money, but I didn't care about that. Bobbie and I would be gone by that time, and we'd never come back.

I went through the door of the pavilion. I started across the floor, my knees just a little shaky. Ralph was pounding on something back in the air-conditioner shed—hammering on something. The noise came out through the ballroom air-vents, *thud-bang, thud-bang,* and I kind of walked—marched—in time to it.

My feet began to drag. That crazy pounding, it was just awful; it made me feel like I was in a funeral procession or something. And it kept right on going on, after it *wasn't* going on. I mean, I realized suddenly that Ralph wasn't pounding any more, and all that noise was coming from my heart.

I took a deep breath. I told myself to stop acting so silly, because there just wasn't any sense to it.

Bobbie and I would be a long way from here in another hour. Papa would know I'd taken his money—I wanted him to know it! But he wouldn't be able to catch up with us himself, and he'd never call on the police. He'd have too much pride to let anyone know that his own daughter had stolen from him.

I was at the door of his office. I opened my purse and took out my keys, fumbled through them until I found the right one.

I unlocked the door. I stepped inside, closed it behind me, and flicked on the light. And screamed.

Because Papa was there.

He was sitting at his desk, his face buried in his arms. There was a half-full bottle of whiskey in front of him.

He sat up with a start when I screamed. He jumped up, cursing, asking me what the hell was the idea, and so on. And then when I just stood staring at him, my mouth hanging open, he slowly sat down again. And stared at me.

Ralph came running across the ballroom floor. He stopped in the doorway of the office, and asked if something was wrong. Papa didn't say anything, even look at him. Ralph said, "Oh, uh, excuse me," and went away again.

Papa and I went on staring at each other.

He didn't need to ask why I was here. He knew. I'd've bet a million dollars that he did. He'd been scheming and planning all along, figuring out ways to get me so scared and desperate that I'd finally try this. And then, when I did try, when he'd let me get my hopes all up, thinking that I'd found a way out . . .

Oh, he knew all right! He'd planned it this way. What else would he be doing there if he hadn't? Why hadn't he gone on home to supper like he always did?

I backed toward the door. I thought, *Oh, how I hate you! HOW I HATE YOU! I hate you so much that—that—! I hate you, hate you, hate you!*

Papa nodded. "Figured you probably did," he said. "Well, you got a lot of company."

I turned and ran.

It didn't occur to me until later that I must have said what I was thinking. That I'd actually yelled it at him.

# XII

## Pete Pavlov

I'D GOTTEN THE letter from Doc Ashton the week before. I didn't answer it, so that Monday he phoned me. I told him to go to hell and hung up.

Only thing to do, as I saw it. And wrong or right, a man's got to go by what he sees. He's got a chance that way. It's a lot handier for him. Any time a butt needs kicking, he knows whose it is.

I punched out a few letters on my old three-row typewriter. I carried them down to the post-office, thinking that they didn't make typewriters like they used to. Thinking that they didn't make nothing like they used to, from bread to chewing tobacco. Then, kind of snorting to myself and thinking, Well, by God, look who's talking! Maybe they don't make nothing like they used to because there's no one to do the making. Nothing but a lot of whining old guys with weep-bags in place of guts.

I guessed I must be slipping. If I'd been like this back at the time I built the post-office building . . . *Well, maybe it would've been a hell of a lot better, I thought. I wouldn't be in the spot I'm in now, and there'd be quite a few less bastards around town to give me trouble.*

Yeah, the post-office job was mine. Built it under contract for old Commodore Stuyvesant, Luane Devore's father. It's still the biggest building in town —four stories—and it was a pretty fancy one for those days. The upper three floors were offices, each with its own toilet and lavatory. All the plumbing, the water and drain pipes, was concealed.

Well, we were about through with the job, except for the interior decorating, when I discovered a hell of a thing. I'll never forget the day that it happened. I was up on the fourth floor at the time. I'd taken the chaw out of my mouth and tossed it in the toilet. Then I'd flushed it down and drawn myself a drink from the lavatory. And I was just about to toss it down when I noticed something in the water. A few little brown specks, so tiny you could hardly see them.

I cussed, and dumped out the water. I got myself a can of stain, and went through the building from top to bottom, flushing toilets and turning on faucets. They all turned out the same as the first. They were all cross-connected, to use the plumbing term. You had to be looking for the stain in the water, and looking damned hard, but it was there. Some of the waste water was coming out through the lavatory taps.

You see . . . Well, you know what the inside of a toilet bowl looks like. It has a water inlet built into it; it has to have to flush; and it also has a sewage

124

outlet. It has the two right together, flowing together. If the plumbing ain't exactly right, some of the sewage can get into the water inlet. Into the water you drink and wash with.

Well, the first thing I did was to cut off the water at the main. Shut off every drop in the building. I told the workmen they'd been screwing around too much on the job, that they could do their washing and drinking on their own time from now on. And they didn't exactly love me for that, naturally. But it was the way it had to be. I couldn't tell them the truth. If I had, it would have got all over town. People would always have been leery of the building. You could fix the trouble, and take an oath on it, but they'd never really believe that you had.

I spent the rest of the day checking the blueprints on the job, tracing out the miles of piping foot by foot. Finally, I spotted what was wrong. It was in the blueprints, the drawings, themselves. Not something that was my fault.

I took the drawings, and went to see the Commodore. Luane was right in the living room with him. And they sure were two damned sick people. I told 'em I didn't see what they had to feel bad about.

"It's the architects' fault," I said. "You've got something pretty new here, in this concealed plumbing, but you ain't got a new-style building to put it in. The architects should have known that with all this angling and turning the water pipes were just about bound to get a vacuum in 'em—Yeah, Commodore?"

"I said," he said, kind of dead-voiced, "that the architects aren't responsible. The blueprints were drawn up from a rough design I made myself. I insisted on having my own way, despite their objections, and they've got a waiver in writing."

I asked him why the hell he'd done it—why pay for expert advice and then not listen to it?

He grimaced, almost crying. "I thought they were trying to run up their bill on me, Pete," he said. "The architect gets six percent of the cost of a job, you know, and since I'm not exactly a trusting person . . ." He broke off, grimacing again. "Not that I've had much reason to trust people. Offhand, I'd say that you were the only completely honest man I've ever met, Pete."

"Well—well, thanks, Commodore," I said. "I—"

"Have you told anyone about this difficulty, Pete? None of the workmen know? Well, do you suppose that if it wasn't corrected—uh—do you suppose the result might be, uh, very serious?"

"I don't know," I said. "Maybe some of the tenants wouldn't be hurt at all. Maybe it might be quite a while before the others came down with anything. I don't know how many might get sick or how many might die, but there's one thing I do know, Commodore. I know I ain't drinking no sewer water myself, and I ain't letting anyone else do it. So—"

I broke off. He was looking so shocked and hurt that I apologized for what I said. Yeah, by God, *I* apologized to *him!*

"Quite all right, Pete," he said. "Your concern for the public welfare is wholly commendable. Now, getting back to our problem, just what if anything can be done about it?"

I told him. The whole building would have to be repiped. Of course, we could use the same piping but it would have to come out of the walls and be put on the outside. What it actually added up to was ripping out the interior of the building, and doing it over again.

"I see." He bit his lip. "What about your men, Pete? How will you explain to them?"

"Well—" I shrugged. "I'll tell 'em I pulled a boner, and I'm making good on it. That won't hurt me none, and they'll be glad to believe it."

"I see," he said again. "Pete—Pete, I have no right to ask it, but everything I have is tied up in that building. Everything! I've exhausted my credit. If I attempt to get any more the building will be plastered with liens from basement to roof. Once it's finished, I'll be in fine shape. The government will lease the ground floor, and I have tenants signed up for most of the offices. But I can't finish it, Pete, unless—and I have no right at all to ask you—"

Luane was sniffling. He put his arm around her, looking at me apologetically, and after a moment she turned and put her arms around him. It seemed pretty pitiful, you know. I took out my notebook and did some figuring.

I didn't have hardly any ready cash, myself, but my credit was first-class. By stretching it right to the limit, I could finance the rework that had to be done, which would probably tot up to about eight thousand dollars.

Well, the Commodore practically wrung my hand off when I told him I'd do it. And I thought for a minute that Luane was going to kiss me. Then the Commodore gave me his note for ten thousand—ten thousand instead of eight. Because I'd literally saved his and Luane's lives, he said, and even with the two thousand bonus they'd still be eternally in my debt.

Well, I guess I probably don't need to tell you the rest of it, but I'll do it anyway. Just in case you're as dumb as I was.

The Commodore denied that he owed me a red cent for the rework. He said it was due to my own errors, as I'd publicly stated, and that he was contemplating suit against me for failing to follow the architects' specifications.

"Naturally, I'd hate to do it," he said smoothly, sort of smiling down his nose. "I imagine you have quite enough problems, as it is."

I told him that wasn't the only thing I had. I had his note for ten thousand, and I'd collect every penny of it. He shook his head, chuckling.

"I'm afraid not, Pavlov. You see I have no assets; I've transferred everything I owned to my daughter, Luane."

Luane didn't seem too happy about the deal. I looked at her, and she dropped her eyes; and then she turned suddenly to the Commodore.

"Let's not do this, father," she said. "I know you mean it for my benefit, but—"

"Yes," the Commodore nodded. "So the choice is yours. My feeling is that a woman untrained for any work—an unemployable, unmarriageable spinster, to state the case succinctly—is going to need every dollar she can get. But if you feel differently . . ."

He spread his hands, giving her that down-the-nose smile.

Luane got up and left the room.

I left, too, and I never went back. Because what the hell was the use? I couldn't get anything from her. He didn't have anything to get. He even had me staved off on giving him a beating, him being as old as he was.

So that was that. That was how I made out dealing with an "old-school gentleman," and a "true aristocrat" and the town's "first citizen" and so on.

It took me five years, working night and day, to get out of debt.

Ralph was sweeping up the dance floor when I got back to the pavilion. I kidded around with him a few minutes, and then I went for a walk down the beach. It was a good walk, sort of—looking at all the things I'd built, and knowing that no one had ever built better. In another way, it wasn't so good: the looking gave me a royal pain. Because I could have collected just as much on cheaper buildings. And if I'd built cheaper, I wouldn't have been in the spot I was in.

I wondered what the hell I'd been thinking about to sink so much dough into seasonal structures. I guessed I hadn't been thinking at all. I'd just done it automatically—building in the only way I knew how to build.

I ran into Mac's singer, Danny Lee, on the beach. She was in a bathing suit, sunning herself, and I sat down by her and talked a while. But not as long as I wanted to. It couldn't do me any good, you know; not just chatting about things in general. And I was afraid if I hung around very long, I might do more than that. Because that little girl, she was the kind that comes few and far between. She was my kind of woman.

That Danny—if she went for you, she'd go all the way. She'd kill for you, even if she knew it might get her killed. You could see it in her. Anyways, I could see it. And it was all wrapped up in such a pretty package.

Well, though, maybe she was my kind of woman, but I wasn't her kind of man. She wouldn't have wanted no part of an old pot-bellied bastard like me, even if she hadn't had Ralph Devore on the string. So I shoved off before I said or did something to make a damned fool of myself.

I circled back toward the pavilion. Rags called to me from his cottage, so I went in and had coffee with him.

He asked me how the money situation was with me, and I said that it was

just about like it had been. He said he was in just about the worst shape he'd
ever been in himself.

"Don't know what the hell I'm going to do, Pete. I won't have no band after
we close here, and I don't feel like going out single any more. I would, if there
was a decent living in it. But it's hard to break even with me on the road and
Janie and the boys in New York."

"Yeah," I said, looking down at the floor. Feeling kind of awkward like I
always did when he mentioned those boys. "Yeah—uh—I mean, what about
recordings, Rags? Can't you get some of them to do?"

He snorted and let out a string of cuss words. He said he wasn't making any
more recordings until he was allowed to do the job right. Which would be just
about never, unless he owned his own record company.

"I wished you did," I said. "If I was in a little bit better shape, I'd—"

"Yeah, yeah—" He cut me off. "Forget it, Pete. It's really the only damned
thing I want to do, but I know it's impossible."

He drained the coffee from his cup, and filled it up with whiskey. He took
a sip, smacked his lips and shuddered. After a minute or two, he asked me what
I thought about the setup between Danny and Ralph Devore.

"I mean, what can come of it, Pete? How do you think it will wind up?"

I shrugged. I said I guessed I hadn't done much thinking about it.

"I've been wondering," he frowned. "It looks like the real thing between
'em. But that pair—Ralph, in particular—well, they ain't just a couple of
lovesick kids. They wouldn't go way out on a limb unless they saw some way
off of it."

"No," I said. "I don't figure they would."

"I wonder," he said. "I've been thinking. Y'know, when I first introduced
them, I told her he was a rich man. And lately I've been thinking, wouldn't
it be a hell of a joke if . . ."

"Yeah?"

"Nothing. What the hell?" he laughed. "Just a crazy notion I had."

"Well, I guess I better be going," I said. "Getting to be about my lunch
time."

I headed back into town, and across to the far side. I started to pass by the
neighborhood church, and then I slowed down and went back a few steps. I
stopped in front of the vacant lot, between the church and the parsonage.

I stood there and stared at it, making myself look thoughtful and interested.
Finally, I took a rule out of my pocket, and did a little measuring.

The curtain moved at one of the parsonage windows. I took out a notebook
and jotted a few figures into it. Pretended to make some calculations.

I've had a lot of sport with that vacant lot. Once I made out like I'd found
some marijuana growing on it, and another time I pretended I was going to
buy it for a shooting gallery. What with one stunt and another, I've kept the

preacher of that church worried for years. I knew he was peeking through the curtains at me now. Watching and wondering, and working up to another worry-spell.

He came out of the parsonage, finally. He didn't want to, but he just couldn't help it.

I went on with my measuring and figuring, acting like I didn't see him. He hesitated in the yard, and then he came over to the corner of the fence.

"Yes?" he said. "Yes, Mr. Pavlov?"

"Yes," I said. "Yes, sir, I think this will do just fine."

"Fine?" He looked at me water-eyed, his lips starting to tremble. "Mr. Pavlov, what—what do you want of me? I'm an old man, and—"

"Remember when you wasn't," I said. "Remember real well. But talking about this lot here, I was just wondering if it wouldn't be a good spot for a laundry. Thought maybe you could throw some business my way."

He knew what I was driving at, all right. No wonder either, after all these years. He looked at me, his eyes watering, his mouth opening and closing. And I told him what I had in mind was the bedsheet business.

"Tell you what I'll do," I said. "You tip off your pals to send their sheets to me, and any patching they need—like buckshot holes, you know—I'll do it for nothing. Probably no more than fair, anyways, since I maybe put 'em there."

"Mr. P-Pavlov," he said. "Can't you ever—?"

"Guess you didn't need many seats in your church for a while, did you?" I said. "Guess most of the fellows didn't feel like settin' down. Not much more like it, maybe, than some of the folks they visited with bullwhips."

I grinned and winked at him. He stood leaning against the fence, his mouth quivering, his hands gripping and ungripping the pickets.

"Mr. Pavlov," he said. "It—that was such a long time ago, Mr. Pavlov."

"Don't seem long to me," I said. "But me, I got a long memory."

"If you know how sorry I was, how often I've begged God's forgiveness . . ."

"Yeah?" I said. "Well, I guess I better be going. I stand around here much longer, I might lose my appetite."

My house was in the next block, a big two-story job with plenty of yard space. It was probably the best-built house in town, but it sure didn't look like much. What it looked like was hell.

I'd been pretty busy at the time I finished it, fifteen years ago. Had four or five contract jobs running—jobs I'd taken money on. Figured I had to take care of them, and do it right, before I prettied up my own place.

So I did that. And while I was doing it, my neighbors hit me with a petition. I tore it up, and threw it at 'em. They took me into court, and I fought 'em to a standstill. If they'd just left me alone, stopped to consider that they didn't have no monopoly on wanting things nice—but they just wouldn't do that.

They tried to make me do something. No one makes me do anything.

The house has never been painted. The yard has never been cleaned up. It's littered with odds and ends of lumber, sawhorses, left-over brick and so on. There's a couple of old wheelbarrows, almost rusted and rotted to bits, and a big mixing trough, caked with cement. There's—

But I already said it.

It looks like hell. It ain't ever going to look any other way—at least, it ain't going to look any better—as long as I'm alive.

It was a couple of minutes after twelve when I went in. So lunch was already on the table, and Myra and my wife, Gretchen, were standing by their chairs waiting for me.

I said hello. They mumbled and ducked their heads. I said, well, let's sit; and we all sat down.

I filled their plates and mine. I took a couple bites—it was beef and potato dumplings—and then I mentioned the matter of Doc Ashton.

"Dug up a big building job for me over in Atlantic Center," I said. "How'd you feel about us all going there to live for four or five months?"

Gretchen didn't look up, but I saw her eyes slant toward Myra. A kind of red flush spread over Myra's face, and her hand shook as she raised her fork.

Half way to her mouth, the fork slipped out of her fingers, landed with a clatter on her plate. She and Gretchen jumped. I laughed.

"Don't worry," I said. "We ain't going. I never had no notion of going. Just thought I'd tell you about it."

I took a big bite of grub, staring at them while I chewed it. Myra's face got redder and redder. And then she jumped up suddenly, and ran out of the room.

I laughed. I didn't feel much like it, but I did. Gretchen looked up at last.

"Why don't you leave her alone?" she said, not mumbling or whining like she usually does. "Ain't you done enough, taking all the spirit out of her? Beatin' her down until she goes around like a whipped dog? Do you have to go on and on, seeing how miserable—"

"Huh-uh," I said. "That's something I ain't going to do. I sure ain't going on and on."

"What—" She hesitated. "What do you mean by that?"

I shrugged. After a moment or so, she turned and left, headed up the stairs toward Myra's room.

I finished eating, wiping my plate clean with a piece of bread. Afterwards, I dug my teeth a little with a toothpick, and after that I took a big chaw of tobacco. I looked at my watch, then—saw that it was two minutes to one o'clock. I went on looking until the hands pointed to one sharp. Then, I got my hat off the hallrack and started back toward town.

I did everything just like always, you know. Seemed like I hadn't ought to, but I'd never had but one way of doing things, and I stuck to it now. Right or wrong, it was my way. And to me, it seemed right.

Take the spirit out of 'em? Why, hell, I tried to put spirit into 'em! I gave 'em something to be proud of—something to hold their heads high about. I built something out of nothing, just my head and my two bare hands. And I never bent my back to no man while I was doing it. I never let no one take the spirit out of me. And believe me, there was plenty of them that tried. Why, those two—Gretchen and Myra—if they'd taken just half of what I took—

I got back to my office. I finished my chaw, and took a big drink of whiskey. And I kind of laughed to myself and thought, Well, hell. What you got to show for it all, Pieter Pavlovski? A wife? Gretchen's a *wife?* A daughter? Myra— that sheep-eyed slut—is *your* daughter? Well, what then, besides the buildings? *Aside* from your buildings. Because them buildings ain't yours no more. You've held onto them as long as you can, and . . .

I took another big drink. I tried to laugh again, because it was a hell of a joke on me, you know. But I just wasn't up to laughing. Not when it was about losing this pavilion and the hotels and the restaurants and the cottages and— and everything I had. All the things that took the place of what I didn't have.

I couldn't hardly think about it, let alone laugh.

I took the gun out of my desk. I checked it over, and put it back in the drawer again.

I thought, her fault, his fault, theirs, mine, the whole goddamned world's —what the hell's the difference? It's a bad job. It's got your name on it. So there's just one thing to do about it.

It was about nine-thirty when Bobbie Ashton showed up at my office. I'd been drinking quite a bit, and it gave me a pretty bad jar when I looked up and saw him in the doorway. I didn't cuss him out, though—just grunted a "How are you, Bobbie?" and he smiled and sat down.

I said I thought him and Myra were out on a date tonight.

"We were," he nodded. "I mean, we still are. I just drove by to see you for a minute."

"Yeah?" I said. "Wasn't going to ask me if it was all right for you to go with her, was you?"

"No," he said. "I was going to ask if—had you heard that Mrs. Devore was dead?"

"Well, yeah." I sat up a little in my chair. "Ralph called and told me. What about it, anyway?"

"Perhaps nothing," he said. "On the other hand . . ."

He took a long white envelope out of his pocket, and laid it on my desk. He stood up again, smiling a cool, funny little smile.

"I want you to read that," he said. "If it becomes necessary—that is, to protect an innocent person—and you may interpret the word liberally—I want you to use it."

"Use it? What the hell is it?" I said. "Why not use it yourself?"

His smile widened. He shook his head gently. And then, before I could say anything more, he was gone.

I opened the envelope, and began to read.

It was a confession, written in his own handwriting, to the murder of Luane Devore. It told how he'd figured out that Ralph must have had a pile of money saved, and how he needed a pile himself. And it went on to say just how the murder had come about.

He'd had a handkerchief tied over his face. He'd kept quiet—not saying anything, I mean—so she couldn't recognize his voice. He'd slipped upstairs, not intending to really hurt her; just to give her a shove or maybe a sock, so's he could grab the money. And it wasn't his intention to steal it outright. He was going to send it back anonymously as soon as he could. But—well, everything went wrong, and nothing worked out like he'd planned.

Luane was waiting for him at the head of the stairs. She piled into him, and he tried to fight her off. And the next thing he knew, she was lying at the foot of the stairs, dead.

He forgot all about the money, and beat it. He was too scared to do anything else. . . .

I finished reading the confession. I glanced back over it again, kind of marveling over it—wondering how the thing could sound so true unless it was. There was just one hole in it that I could see. That part about him being scared. If it was possible to scare that kid, I didn't know how the hell it would be.

I took another drink. I struck a match to the confession, and tossed it into the spittoon. Because nothing had changed. Killing Luane was one crime he'd never be punished for. And probably he knew it, too.

That was why he'd written the confession—probably. He knew he was going to die anyway, so the confession couldn't hurt him and it might help someone else a lot.

I got my gun out, and slid it into my hip pocket. I turned off the lights and went out to my car.

It was no trouble finding them, Bobbie and Myra. Just a matter of driving a while, and then getting out and walking a while, creeping along a winding trail. All I had to do was think of where I'd go if I was in his place. And the place I'd've gone to was the place he'd taken her.

They were stretched out on a patch of sand in a little clearing, and they were locked together. I couldn't really see her, just him. And that made it pretty hard, because him—he—was all I really cared about.

I didn't know how he'd got to her. Or why. I was afraid to even think about it, for fear I might try to excuse him. And it couldn't be that way. I was pretty sure he wouldn't want it that way. But it was damned hard, just the same.

Me and him—we were so much alike. We thought so much alike. That was how he'd been able to confess to a killing I'd done—yeah, I killed Luane—and have his facts almost completely straight.

I had planned on sticking Luane up for the money. I had worn a handkerchief over my face, and I hadn't answered when she called downstairs, so that she couldn't recognize my voice.

Then, right at the last minute, I changed my mind; I couldn't go through with the stunt. I'd never pulled anything sneaky in my life, and I couldn't do it now. And, by God, there was no reason why I should.

She owed me money. Ten thousand dollars with almost twenty-five years' interest. I jerked the handkerchief down off my face and put the gun in my pocket, and told her I was there to collect.

"And don't tell me you ain't got it," I said, when she started jabbering and squawking ninety to the minute. "Ralph's made it, and he ain't spent it—and he ain't got it either. You're keeping it to keep him. If Ralph had it, he'd've jumped town with that singer long ago."

I went on up the stairs, walking slowly and keeping a sharp eye on her. She begged, and then she began yelling threats. I'd never get away with it, she yelled. She'd have me arrested. I wouldn't get to keep the money, and I'd go to prison besides.

"Maybe," I said, "but I figure not. Everyone thinks I got plenty of money, and even my worst enemy wouldn't never accuse me of stealing. So I figure I'll get away with it. It'll be as easy as it was for you and your Pa to cheat me."

Well, I thought for a minute that she was going to give up. Because she stopped yelling and stood back against the wall, as if to let me pass. Then, just as I took the last step, she screamed and lunged at me.

I flung my arm out, trying to ward her off. It caught her a sweeping blow, and being off balance like she was, she went down the stairs head-first.

I went down and took a quick look at her. I got out of there. I didn't need money no more.

. . . I kind of sighed. I took the gun out of my pocket, staring across to the patch of sand where Bobbie and Myra were.

I hesitated, wondering if I ought to toss a rock at them. Give 'em a chance, you know, like you do when you're out hunting and you see a setting rabbit.

But they weren't rabbits. He wasn't, anyway. And if I didn't get them now, I'd just have to do the job later. And there wasn't going to be any later for me. I wouldn't be roaming around after tonight. So I raised the gun and took aim.

I waited a second. Two or three seconds. He turned his head suddenly, and kissed her. And, then, right at that moment, I started shooting.

I figure they died happy.

I blew the smoke out of my gun, went back to my car and headed for town. I drove to the courthouse and turned myself in for the three killings.

Kossy was my lawyer at the trial. But there wasn't nothing a lawyer could do for me. There wasn't nothing I'd've let him do. So now it's all over—or it damned soon will be—and now that it is, I kind of wonder.

I wonder if I really did kill Luane Devore.

She was a pretty tough old bag. Could be that the fall downstairs just knocked her out, and someone else came along and finished the job. Could be that someone was hiding in the house right at the time I was there.

It would be just about a perfect murder, you know. They, this party, could do the killing and I'd take the blame for it. Anyone who knew me knew that I would.

Who do I think did it—that is, if I didn't?

Well, I don't figure it was anyone you might ordinarily suspect, the people who seemed to have the best motives. The very fact that they had good reasons for wanting Luane dead—and that everyone knew it—would be the thing that would keep them from killing her. They'd be too afraid, you know, that the job might be pinned on them.

Aside from that, and maybe excepting Danny Lee, all the prime suspects were too fond of living to commit murder. They'd proved it over and over, through the years; proved it by the way they lived. They'd give up their principles, their good name—everything they had; just as long as they could go on living. Living any damned old way. And people like that, they ain't going to take the risk of killing.

Me, now, I'm not that way—just in case you haven't discovered it. I have to live a certain way or I'd rather be dead, which I'm just about to be. Putting it in a nutshell, I never had but one thing to live for. And if I thought I was going to lose that, like I did lose it, why . . .

I guess you see what I'm driving at. Whoever killed Luane was a one-reason-for-living person. Whoever killed Luane was someone who didn't seem to have a motive—who could do it with a good chance of never being suspected. And there's only one person I can think of who fits that description.

She was smart and efficient, but she'd stuck to the same cheap dull job for years. She was pretty as a picture and a damned nice girl to boot, but she'd never gotten married.

She stuck to her job and she'd never gotten married for the same reason—because she was in love with her boss. She never showed it in any of the usual ways. She never made any passes at him—she wasn't that kind. And she never stepped out with him. There wasn't a thing she did that could cause gossip about her. But, hell, it was plain as day how she felt. It was clear to me, anyway. I'd seen the way she kowtowed to him, and made over him, and it kind of made me squirm. I'd think: Now, why the hell does she do it—a gal that could have her pick of jobs and men? And of course there couldn't be but one reason why she did it.

She must have known that he was nothing but a fat-mouthed dunce. She must have known he wasn't ever going to marry her—that he was too self-centered to marry anyone, and that his sister probably wouldn't let him if he wanted to. But that didn't change anything. Maybe, women being like they are, it might have made her love him all the more. Anyway, she was crazy about him—she *had* to be, you know—crazy enough to kill anyone who hurt him. And someone was hurting him. It was getting to the point where he might lose his job—the only one he could hold—and if he did they'd be separated, and—

Yeah, that's right. I'm talking about Nellie Otis, the county attorney's secretary.

I figure that Nellie killed Luane—if I didn't do it. I guess I ain't ever likely to know for sure, and I don't know as I give a damn.

I was just wondering, you know, thinking. And now that I've thought it through, to hell with it.

# THE
# NOTHING
# MAN

# I

---

WELL, THEY ARE all gone now, all but me: all those clear-eyed, clear-thinking people—people with their heads in the clouds and their feet firmly on the ground—who comprise the editorial staff of the Pacific City *Courier*. Warmed with the knowledge of a day's work well done, they have retired to their homes. They have fled to the sweet refuge of their families, to the welcoming arms of brave little women and the joyous embrace of laughing kiddies. And with them has gone the clearest-eyed, clearest-thinking of them all, Dave Randall, none other than the *Courier*'s city editor.

He stopped by my desk on his way out, his feet firmly on the ground—or, I should say, the city room floor—but I did not look up immediately. I was too shaken with emotion. As you have doubtless suspected, I have a poet's heart; I think in allegories. And in my mind was an image of countless father birds, flapping their weary wings to the nests where the patient mother birds and the wee little birdies awaited them. And—and I say this unashamed—I could not look up. All the papa birds flapping toward their nests, while I—

Ah, well. I forced a cheery smile. I had my family; I was a member of the happy *Courier* family—clear-eyed, clear-thinking. And what bride could be finer than my own, what better than to be wed to one's work?

Dave cleared his throat, waiting for me to speak; then he reached over my shoulder and picked up an overnight galley on my column, *Around the Town With Clinton Brown*. The *Courier* is generous in such matters, I should say. The *Courier* believes in giving its employees an opportunity to "grow." Thus, desk men may do reporting; reporters may work the desk; and rewrite men such as myself may give the fullest play to the talents which, on so many newspapers, are restricted and stunted by the harsh mandates of the Newspaper Guild.

We take no dictation from labor bosses. Our protector, our unfailing friend and counselor, is Austin Lovelace, publisher of the *Courier*. The door to his office is always open, figuratively speaking. One may always take one's problems to Mr. Lovelace with the assurance that they will be promptly settled. And without "outside interference."

But I shall touch on these things later. I shall have to touch upon them since they all figure, to an extent, in what the head-writers term the Sneering Slayer murders, and this is the story of those murders. For the nonce, however, let us get back to Dave Randall.

He laid the column galley back on my desk, clearing his throat again. He has always—well, almost always—had trouble in talking to me; and yet he insists on talking. One almost feels at times that he has a guilty conscience.

"Uh, working pretty late, aren't you, Brownie?"

"Late, Colonel?" I said. I had gained control of myself at last, and I gave him a brave, clear-eyed smile. "Well, yes and no. Yes, for a papa bird with a nest. No, for a nestless, non-papa bird. My work is my bride and I am consummating our wedding."

"Uh . . . I notice your picture is pretty badly smudged. I'll order a new cut for the column."

"I'd rather you didn't, Colonel," I said. "I think of the lady birds, drawn irresistibly by my chiseled, unsmudged profile, their tail feathers spread in delicious anticipation. I think of their disappointment in the end . . . you should excuse the pun, Colonel. As a matter of fact, I believe we should dispense with my picture entirely, replace it with something more appropriate, a coat of arms say—"

"Brownie—" He was wincing. I had barely raised the harpoon, yet already he was wincing. And there was no longer any satisfaction in it for me—if there had ever been any—but I went on.

"Something symbolic," I said. "A jackass, say, rampant against two thirds of a pawnbroker's sign, a smug, all-wise-looking jackass. As for the device, the slogan—how is your Latin, Colonel? Can you give me a translation of the phrase, 'I regret that I had only his penis to give to my country'?"

He bit his lip, his thin face sick and worried. I took the bottle from my desk and drank long and thirstily.

"Brownie, for God's sake! Won't you ever give it up?"

"Yes," I nodded. "Word of honor, Colonel. Once this bottle is finished I shall not drink another drop."

"I'm not talking about that. Not just that. It's—everything else! You're getting too raw. Mr. Lovelace is bound to—"

"Mr. Lovelace and I," I said, "are spiritual brothers. We are as close as two wee ones in the nest. Mr. Lovelace would think my motives lofty, even should I turn into a pigeon and void on his snowy locks."

"You'll probably do it," said Dave, bitterly.

I hate to see a man bitter. How can you have that calm objectivity so necessary to literary pursuits if you are bitter?

"Yes, you'll do it," he repeated. "You won't stop until you're fired. You'll keep on until you're thrown out, and I have to—"

"Yes?" I said. "You mean you'd feel it necessary to leave also? How touching, Colonel. My cup runneth over with love—of, need I say, a strictly platonic nature."

I offered him a drink, jerking the bottle back as he tried to knock it from my hands. I took a drink myself and advised him to flee to the bosom of his family. "That is what you need, Colonel," I said. "The cool hand of the little

woman, soothing away the day's cares. The light of love and trust that shines
from a kiddie's—"

"Goddam you, shut up!"

He yelled it at the top of his lungs. Then he was bending over my desk,
bracing himself with his hands, and his eyes and his voice were tortured with
pleading and helplessness and fury. And the words were pouring from his
mouth in a half-coherent babble.

Goddamit, hadn't he said it was a mistake? Hadn't he admitted it was a
boner a thousand times? Did I think he'd deliberately send a man into a field
of anti-personnel mines? . . . It was a tragedy. It was a hell of a thing to happen
to any man, and it must be ten times as hard when the guy was young and
good-looking, and—and it was his fault. But what more could he do than he'd
already done? What did I want him to do?

He choked up suddenly. Then he straightened and headed for the door. I
called after him. "A moment, Colonel. You didn't let me finish."

"You're finished!" He whirled, glaring at me. "That's one thing you're
finished with. I warn you, Brownie, if you ever again call me Colonel, I'll—
I'll—Well, take my tip and don't do it!"

"I won't," I said. "That's what I wanted to tell you. I'm cutting it all out.
Everything. After all, it was just one mistake in a war full of mistakes. You'll
never have any more trouble with me, Dave."

He snorted and reached for the door. He paused and looked at me, frowning
uncertainly. "You—you almost sound like you meant that."

"I do. Every word of it, Dave."

"Well"—he studied me carefully—"I don't suppose you do, but—"

He grinned tentatively, still studying me. Slowly the suspicion went out of
his eyes and the grin stretched into a broad, face-lighting smile. "That's great,
Brownie! I'm sorry I blew my top a moment ago, because I do know how you
feel, but—"

"Sure," I said. "Sure you do. It's all right, Dave."

"Why don't you knock off for the night? Come out to the house with me?
I'll open a bottle, have Kay cook us up some steaks. She's been after me to
bring you home to dinner."

"Thanks," I said. "I guess not tonight. Got a story I want to finish."

"Something of your own?"

"We-ell, yes," I said. "Yes, it's something of my own. A kind of melodrama
I'm building around the Sneering Slayer murders. I suppose it'll baffle hell out
of the average whodunit reader, but perhaps he needs to be baffled. Perhaps
his thirst for entertainment will impel him to the dread chore of thinking."

"Great!" Dave nodded earnestly. He hadn't of course, heard anything I'd
said. "Great stuff!"

He was looking happier than I'd seen him for a long time. I think he'd have looked happy even if I'd taken him up on the dinner invitation.

"Well—ha, ha—don't work all night," he said.

"Ha, ha," I said. "I'll try not to."

He clapped me on the back, clumsily. He said good night and I said good night, and he left.

I studied the page in my typewriter, ripped it out and put in another one.

I had got off on the wrong foot. I had begun the story with Deborah Chasen when, naturally, it had to begin with me. Me—sitting alone in the city room, with a dead cigarette butt in my lips and an almost full quart of whisky on my desk.

The two Teletype machines began to click and clatter—first the A.P.'s, then the U.P.'s. I strolled over and took a look at them.

Pacific City, in the words of our publisher, is a "city of homes, churches, and people"—which translated from its chamber-of-commerce *lingua franca* means that it is a small city, a nonindustrial city, and a city where little goes on, ordinarily, of much interest to the outside world. The *Courier* is the only newspaper. The wire services do not maintain correspondents here but are covered, when coverage is necessary, by our staffers.

I ripped the yellow flimsies from the teletypes and read:

LOS ANG 601PM SPL AP TO COURIER
PACITY CHF DET LEM STUKEY REPTD MISSING OVER TWENTYFOUR
HOURS. TRUE? UNUSUAL? POSSIBLE CONNECTION SNEERING SLAYER
CASE? LETS HEAR FROM YOU COURIER. THATCHER AP LA

LA CAL 603 PM UP TO COUR
RADIO REPTS DETEC CHF LEM STUKEY MISSING. HOW ABOUT THIS
COURIER?WHY NOT MENTIONED ANY YOUR EDITIONS?
UNIMPORTANT? OFTEN MISSING? ANSWER DALE (SIG) LOS ANG UP.

I tossed the flimsies into a wastebasket and strolled over to a window. . . . True? Yes, the report was true enough. Pacific City's Chief of Detectives Lem Stukey *had* been missing for more than a day. . . . Unusual? We-ell, hardly. The police department wasn't alarmed about it. They hadn't been able to locate him in any of the blind pigs or whorehouses where he usually holed up, but he could have found a new place. Or, perhaps, someone had found a place for him. . . .

Anyway, the wire services couldn't expect us to follow up on a query at this hour. We were an afternoon paper. Our "noon" edition hit the streets at ten in the morning, our "home" at noon, and our "late final"—a re-plate job—

at three in the afternoon. That was more than three hours ago, so to hell with
A.P. and U.P. To hell with them, anyway.

I stared out the window—out and down to the street, ten stories below. And
I was sad, more than sad, even bitter. And all over nothing, nothing at all,
really. Merely the fact that the last line of this story will have to be written
by someone else.

I turned from the window and marched back to my desk. 1 successfully
matched myself for two drinks and received another on the house.

I looked back through what I had written. Then, I lowered my hands to the
keys and began to type:

*The day I met Deborah Chasen was the same day I got the letter from the
Veterans' Administration. It was around nine of a morning a couple of months
ago, and Dave Randall . . .*

DAVE HAD, ON that morning, brought it over to my desk. He stood lingering a moment afterward, trying to look friendly and interested. He mumbled something about "Good news, I hope," and I opened the letter.

It was, as I've said, from the Veterans' Administration. It announced that my disability compensation was being increased to approximately eighty dollars a month.

I shoved back my chair. I stood up, clicked my heels together, and gave Dave a snappy salute.

"Official communication, sir! Sergeant Brown respectfully requests the colonel's instructions!"

"Carry on." He looked nervously around the office, that sickly smile on his face. "Brownie, I wish—"

"Thank you, Colonel. The hour for the morning patrol approaches. Do I have the colonel's permission to—?"

"Do any goddamned thing you want to," he said, and he strode back to his desk.

I sat down again. I winked at Tom Judge, who worked the rewrite desk opposite me. I gave him a smile, a very cheery smile considering that I hadn't had a drink since breakfast.

Tom didn't smile back. "Why do you keep riding him?" He scowled. "Why make things tough on a good guy?"

"Why, Tom," I said. "You mean you and the colonel are—like *that?*"

"I mean I like him. I mean if I were in his place I'd straighten you out or kick your ass out of here. Boy"—he shook his head disgustedly—"talk about justice! Where the hell do you get off drawing a pension anyway?"

"It is puzzling," I said, "isn't it? Obviously I am not disabled for employment. Obviously I have suffered no disfigurement. I am even more handsome than on the day I was born, and my mother boasted—with considerable veracity, I believe—that I was the prettiest baby in town."

His eyes narrowed. "I get it. You're a fairy, huh?"

"Is that an assertion," I said, "or merely a surmise?"

"Don't think I'm afraid of you, Brown!"

"Aren't you?" I said. "Then perhaps you'd like to do something about my statement, made herewith, that you are a nosy, dull-witted son-of-a-bitch and a goddamned lousy newspaperman."

His face went white and he made motions at getting up from his chair. I got up and walked into the john.

A moment later he followed me in.

I could see that he was still sore, but he was trying to cover up. He would wait for a better time to pay me off.

"Look, Brown. I didn't mean t-to—"

"And I," I said, "apologize for calling you a son-of-a-bitch."

"About the pension, Brownie. Not that it's any of my business but—well, I guess it must have something to do with your nerves, huh?"

"That's it." I nodded soberly. "That's it exactly, Tom. A considerable portion of the nerves—kind of a nerve center—was completely destroyed."

I watched him carefully, afraid for a moment that I might have said too much, wondering, what he would do—and what I would do—if the truth did dawn on him. Because there is something hideously funny about a thing of that kind. People laugh about it, privately perhaps, but they laugh. They give you sympathetic smiles and glances, their faces tight with laughter restrained. And even when they do not laugh you can hear them . . . *Poor guy! What a hell of a—ha, ha, ha—I wonder what he does when he has to . . . ?*

You can't work. You can't live. You can't die. You are afraid to die, afraid of the complete defenselessness to laughter that death will bring.

But I needn't have worried about Tom Judge. He lacked the inquiring mind, the ability to follow up on a lead. He was, to mention a statement I had not retracted, a goddamned lousy newspaperman.

"Gosh, I'm sorry, Brownie. I guess that would make you pretty edgy. I still think you're pretty tough on Dave, but—"

I told him I didn't mean anything by it. "Not only is he my friend," I said, "but I respect him professionally. I wouldn't want you to embarrass him by repeating the compliment, but Dave strikes me as typifying the genus *Courier*. Clear-eyed, clear-thinking, his feet firmly on the ground and his head—"

Tom laughed halfheartedly. "Okay," he said, "you win."

He returned to the rewrite bank.

I, because the *Courier*'s first deadline was past, went out on my morning patrol.

It was one of my better patrols. The officer of the day was at his post, and the heavy artillery stood waiting and ready.

"All secured?" I said.

"All secured," said Jake, the Press Club bartender.

"Proceed with maneuvers," I said.

He bent his wrist smartly. Bottle tilted over glass in a beautifully executed movement.

"Excellent," I said. "Now, I think we shall have close-order drill."

"Beggin' your pardon, sir, but—"

"Yes?"

"You only had—I mean you ain't completed the barrage."

"A new tactic," I said. "The remainder of the barrage will follow the drill."

"Okay. But if you fall on your face, don't—"

"Forward, *harch!*" I said.

He lined three one-ounce shot glasses up on the bar, placed a two-ounce glass at the end of the line, and filled all four.

I disposed of them with dispatch and dipped into the bowl of cloves. "Reports or inquiries?" I said.

"I don't know how you do it," he said. "I swear, Mr. Brown, if I tried that I'd—"

"Ah," I said, "but I have youth on my side. Wondrous youth, with the whole great canvas of life stretching out before me."

"You always drink like that?"

"What's it to you?" I said, and I went back to the office.

I was experiencing that peculiar two-way pull that had manifested itself with increasing frequency and intensity in recent months. It was a mixture of calm and disquiet, of resignation and frantically furious rejection. Simultaneously I wanted to lash out at everything and do nothing about anything. The logical result of the conflict should have been stalemate, yet somehow it was not working out that way. The positive emotions, the impulse to act, were outgrowing the others. The negative ones, the calm and resignation, were exercising their restraining force not directly but at a tangent. They were not so much restrictive as cautionary.

They were pulling me off to one side, moving me down a course that was completely out of the world, yet of it.

I wondered if I was drinking too much.

I wondered how it would be—how I would manage to eat and sleep and talk and work: how to live—if I drank less.

I decided that I wasn't drinking enough, and that henceforth I should be more careful in that regard.

Dave Randall looked at me nervously as I sat down. Tom Judge jerked his head over his shoulder in a way that meant that Mr. Lovelace had arrived.

"And, Brownie," he leaned forward, whispering, "you should've seen the babe he had with him!"

"How, now," I said. "Much as it pains me, I shall have to report the matter to Mrs. Lovelace. The marriage vows are not to be trifled with."

"Boy, for some of that you could report me to my wife!"

"Let me catch you," I said, sternly, "and I shall."

It was an average morning, newswise. I did a story on the Annual Flower Show and another on the County Dairymen's convention. I rewrote a couple of wire stories with a local twist and picked up a few items for my column. So it went. That was the sort of thing—and about the only sort of thing—that got into the *Courier*.

Mr. Lovelace frowned on what he termed the "negative type" of story. He was fond of asserting that Pacific City was the "cleanest community in America," and he was very apt to suspect the credibility of reporters who produced evidence to the contrary. I could have done it and got away with it. For reasons that will become obvious, I held a preferred place in the "happy *Courier* family." But I was temporarily content with the *status quo,* and there was no one else. It had been years since any topflight reporter had applied for a job on the Pacific City *Courier.*

With my last story out of the way, I began to feel those twinges of mental nausea that always herald the arrival of my muse. I felt the urge to add to my unfinished manuscript, *Puke and Other Poems.*

I rolled paper into my typewriter. After some preliminary fumblings-around, I began to write:

> *Lives of great men, lives en masse*
> *Seem a stench and cosmic ruse.*
> *Take my share, I'll take a glass*
> *(no demi-tasse—it has to knock me on my ass)*
> *Of booze.*

Not good. Definitely not up to Omar, or, perhaps I should say, Fitzgerald. I tried another verse:

> *Sentience, my sober roomer,*
> *Steals my warming cloak of bunk*
> *(I'm sunk, sunk, sunk.)*
> *Leaves me an impotent assumer*
> *Of things that I can take when drunk.*

Very bad. Far worse than the first stanza. *Assumer*—what kind of word was that? And when was I ever actually drunk? And the wretched, sniveling self-pity in that *sunk, sunk, sunk. . . .*

I ripped the paper out of the typewriter and threw it into the wastebasket. I didn't do it a bit too soon, either.

Mr. Lovelace wasn't a dozen feet away. He was heading straight toward me, and the "babe" Tom Judge had mentioned was with him.

I don't know. I never will know whether she was a little slow on the uptake, a little dumb, as, at first blush, I suspected her of being, or whether she was merely tactless, unusually straightforward, careless of what she said and did. I just don't know.

I gave Mr. Lovelace a big smile, including her in the corner of it. I complimented him on his previous day's editorial and asked him if he hadn't been losing weight and admired the new necktie he was wearing.

"I wish I had your taste, sir," I said. "I guess it's something you have to be born with."

No, I'm not overdrawing it. It doubtless seems that I am, but I'm not. He couldn't be kidded. However good you said he was, it wasn't ever quite so good as he *thought* he was.

I poured it on, and he stood beaming and rocking on the balls of his feet, nodding at the woman as if to say, "Now, here's a man who knows the score." Even when she burst out laughing, he didn't catch on.

He looked at her a little startled. Then the beam came back to his face and he chuckled. "Uh—just finished telling Mrs. Chasen a little story. Kind of a delayed punch, eh, Mrs. Chasen?"

She nodded, holding a handkerchief over her mouth. "I'm s-sorry, but—"

"Nothing to be sorry about. Often affect people that way. . . . Uh, by the way, Mrs. Chasen, this is the Mr. Brown I spoke to you about. Come along with us, eh, Brown?"

I followed them out into the reception room. "Mrs. Chasen," he explained, "is a very dear friend of ours—uh—of Mrs. Lovelace and myself. Unfortunately—uh—we did not expect Mrs. Chasen's visit and Mrs. Lovelace is out of town, and—uh—well, you know my situation, Brown."

"Tied up every second of the day," I said promptly. "Not a moment to call your own. Perhaps it's not my place to say it, Mrs. Chasen, but there isn't a busier man in Pacific City than Mr. Lovelace. The whole town leans on him. Because he is strong and wise, they—"

She started laughing again, staring at him with narrowed, unblinking eyes. And it was a nice laugh to hear, despite the undertone of contempt. And the way it made her tremble—*what* it trembled—was pleasant to watch.

Mr. Lovelace waited, smiling, of course, but with a nervous glance at the foyer clock. "So if you'll—uh—take over, Brown," he resumed. "You know. Show Mrs. Chasen our local points of interest, and—uh—play the host, eh?"

I knew what he meant. I knew exactly where Mrs. Chasen stood. She was an acquaintance of his and his wife's, a friend, perhaps, of a friend of theirs. And as such, she could not be given the fast brush-off. But she was certainly not their very dear friend. She wasn't because Mrs. Lovelace was *not* out of town, and he, Mr. Lovelace, was about as busy as the zipper on an old maid's drawers.

The Grade-C Tour. That was what Mrs. Chasen was supposed to get. A drive around the city, a highball or two, a meal in a not-too-expensive place, and a firm shove onto her train.

"I understand, sir," I said. "I'll show Mrs. Chasen what we mean when we call this the Friendly City! Just leave everything to me, Mr. Lovelace, and don't worry about a thing. You have far too many cares as it is."

"Uh—ha, ha,—excellent, Brown. Oh, don't bother to come back today. Make a holiday of it. You can make the time up some other day."

"Do you see?" I turned to Mrs. Chasen, spreading my hands. "Is it any wonder we all love Mr. Lovelace?"

"Let's go," she said. "I need some fresh air."

If she'd been balancing a glass of water on her head, she wouldn't have spilled a drop with the nod she gave him. She turned abruptly and stepped onto the elevator.

I studied her, as best I could, on the way down to the street. And I liked what I saw, but I couldn't say why I liked it.

She wasn't any youngster—around thirty-five, I'd say. Added up feature by feature, she was anything but pretty. Corn-colored, almost-coarse hair, pulled back from her head in a horse's tail; green eyes that were just a shade off center; mouth a little too big. Assessed individually, the parts were all wrong, but when you put them all together you had a knockout. There was something inside of her, some quality of, well, fullness, of liveness, that reached out and took hold of you.

When she stepped from the elevator, I saw that she toed-in a little, her ankles were over-thin, the calves of her legs larger than the norm. But it was all all right on her. On her it looked good. She preceded me to the street, the outsize hips swinging on the too-slender waist—or was it the slenderness of the waist that made her hips seem outsize?

One thing was certain, there was nothing at all wrong with Mrs. Chasen's bank balance. Not, that is, unless she'd given Saks Fifth Avenue and I. Magnin a hell of a kidding.

We reached the sidewalk and I started to take her by the elbow. She turned and looked up into my face.

"Have you," she said, "been drinking, Mr. Brown?"

"Why," I said, drawing away a little, "what makes you think I—why do you ask that?"

I didn't know what to say. The question had caught me completely off guard, and I still couldn't make up my mind whether she was stupid or only appeared to be.

As I say, I never could make it up.

"It's pretty early in the day to be drinking," I hedged.

"Not for me," she said, "under the circumstances. I'm going to have a drink, Mr. Brown. Several drinks, in fact. And you can come along or not come along, just as you please. As far as I'm concerned, you and your dear Mr. Lovelace—"

"Tut," I said. "Tish and pish, Mrs. Chasen. You have just said a naughty word, and there is only one thing to be done. We shall have to wash out your mouth."

"What"—she laughed a little nervously—"what do you—?"

"Come, Mrs. Chasen," I said. "Come with me to the Press Club."

I made a Charles Boyer face, and she laughed again. Not nervously, now. Rather, I thought, hungrily.

"Well, come *on!*" she said.

## III

SHE LEANED BACK in the booth, her green eyes crinkled and shiny with laughter, her breasts under the sheer white blouse shivering and shaking. I'd used to visualize breasts like those, but I never thought I'd live to see any. I'd considered them—well, you know—physically impractical. Something that looked very good in the blueprint stage, but impossible of achievement.

It just went to show—as Mr. Lovelace often remarked. Yes, sir, here was the proof; there was no problem too big for American genius and know-how.

". . . You crazy thing, Brownie! Do you always talk so crazy?"

"Only with people I love, Deborah. Only with you and Mr. Lovelace."

"You said it, Brownie! You said it that time!"

"So I did," I said, "and I shall take my punishment with my elbows firmly on the table. . . . Close-order drill?"

"With a barrage, Brownie! A *big* barrage!"

"Jake," I called, "advance with artillery."

Perhaps she hadn't been too tactful about it, but she'd had a right to be sore at Mr. Lovelace. Her late husband, late and elderly *("but he was a fine man, Brownie; I liked him a lot")*, had been an oil man. The Lovelaces had often visited them at their place in Oklahoma. Then, six months ago, her husband had died, and she had found herself with a great deal of money and even more time than she knew what to do with. . . . Money and time and a growing suspicion that she was not highly regarded in the circles she had formerly moved in. *("And why not, Brownie? I was good to him. I waited on him hand and foot for ten years.")*

She had fought back; she had delivered two snubs for every one she received. But you lose at that game, even when you win. There is no satisfaction in it. Finally, she had begun to travel—she was on her way to the Riviera now—and today she had stopped off here. And Lovelace, of course, had given her the firmest brush-off of all. *("But I'm glad I stopped, Brownie. You know?")* She was lonely as hell, though not the kind to admit it. The chances were that she would always be lonely. Because that manner of hers—whatever its motivation—was not something that would ordinarily win friends and influence people.

I had a hunch that she had even got under the Lovelace hide.

I stole a glance at my wrist watch and looked back at her. Thus far, she was holding her drinks very well. But train time was four hours away—she was catching the four-fifteen into Los Angeles. So it seemed to me that some food was indicated.

I picked up a menu, turned it right side up, and started to pass it across the table.

"I'll," she said, "have the hot turkey sandwich with mashed potatoes and buttered asparagus."

I nodded. "That sounds—Say, how did you know that was on the menu?"

"I read it." She smiled, pleased as a child with herself.

"Upside down? And sitting way over there?"

"Uh-huh. My eyes are wond—I mean, I have very good eyesight."

"In that case," I said, "you had better order the steak. You will be the only person in history ever able to see a Press Club steak."

We had the turkey sandwiches. I bought a bottle from Jake, and we got my car off the parking lot.

"Where are we going, Brownie?" she said. Then, before I could answer: "I know something about you."

"I was afraid of that," I said. "Yes, officer, you have the right person. I am actually Tinka Tin Nose, girl insect exterminator."

"You're sad."

"Why wouldn't I be with a name like that?"

"I know. You want to know how I know?"

"I've already told you."

"Crazy!" She gave it up. "Where did you say we were going?"

"Well, we have several points of interest. Ensconced in the basement of the public library is the largest collection of Indian artifacts in southeast Pacific County. Why, they have a *metate* there that actually makes your hands itch for a pot, and—"

"Pooh!"

"Check! You're a thousand per cent on the ball, D.C., and let me be the first to congratulate the new manager of our Pooh division. . . . How about a son-of-a-bitch? Would you like to see the world's biggest son-of-a-bitch, Deborah?"

"I thought I'd met him this morning."

"Sharp!" *Or was she?* "But this guy is in another class. He's our Chief of Detectives here, and—No sale?"

It wasn't Obviously, and I say this in all modesty, she was quite content with the company present.

"Well," I said, "I'll have to take you some place. I may be asked to account for my time. What about a visit to our city animal shelter?"

"Animal shelter!" She wrinkled her nose. "Double pooh!"

"It's a nice long ride," I said carelessly. "Way out in the country, you know. I think you might enjoy it."

"Oh?" She sidled a glance at me, then nodded firmly. "I think I might, too."

That, then, was the way it happened. And, as you can see, there was nothing sinister about it, nothing premeditated. That trick she'd pulled in the Press Club—reading upside down and backward—had made no real impression on me. I hadn't been even mildly interested in why she thought I was sad.

We drove out to the shelter—well, call it dog pound, if you like—stopping at intervals for drills, bombardments, and barrages. By the time we reached our destination the bottle was empty, and Saks, Magnin, et al. knew little about the anatomy of Mrs. Chasen that I didn't know.

She was a little mussed. She was happy as all hell. I'd brought her back into the human race again, and her heart was right in her eyes. She could carry on by herself from now on. The ice was broken, and she'd be all right—as right, at any rate, as she could be. Much righter than she had been.

. . . The shelter was—and is—supported by donations; rather, I should say, it was supposed to be supported by them. Because the cash that came in wasn't half enough to operate the place decently. If Mr. and Mrs. Peablossom, the old couple who superintended the shelter, hadn't donated most of their wages, the dogs would have been completely starved instead of the two thirds starved that they usually were.

Mrs. Peablossom insisted on fixing tea for us, and afterward the old gentleman walked us out to the gate of the compound.

"I just don't know what we're going to do, Mr. Brown," he fretted. "The kennels have fallen to pieces. We have to let them run loose there in the court —and they keep coming in, more and more of them, and I can't bear to have them put to sleep—poor homeless fellows—but hardly anyone adopts a dog any more, and . . ."

He rambled on worriedly, while Deborah and I stood looking through the wire-mesh gate. There must have been two hundred dogs in there, closed in by the six-foot-high wall. They lay panting on the hot, shadeless pavement or milled around listlessly, pawing and sniffing hopelessly at the twigs that had blown over the wall.

I fumbled at my wallet, then shoved it back into my pocket. "I'm a little short of funds today, Mr. Peablossom, but—"

"That's quite all right, Mr. Brown. You've done far too much already."

"But *I* haven't done anything," said Deborah, and she opened her purse. She took out a fifty-dollar bill and handed it to him.

"Bless you!" The old man almost wept. "Thank you so much, Mrs. Chasen. Do you have dogs of your own?"

"No," she said. "I don't like dogs." She saw my frown. "I mean I'm afraid of them. A big dog knocked me down when I was a little girl and I never got over it. I've been terrified by them ever since."

I reached up to lift the hasp of the gate, but Mr. Peablossom caught my arm. "I don't believe you'd better go in today, Mr. Brown. The dogs are so hungry, and—"

"You think they're *that* hungry?"

"Well," he hesitated, looking apologetically at Deborah, "you know how it is with dogs, Mr. Brown. They can smell fear. It makes them worse than they might be ordinarily."

"I know," I said. "Well, we've got to be going, anyway. Mrs. Chasen has less than an hour to catch her train."

The old man saw us out to the car and stood waving until we were out of sight. Deborah leaned back in the seat, looking at me out of the corner of her eyes. "Brownie—"

"Yes?" I said.

"Do you—do you think I'm pretty?"

"No," I said. "You're too big, too little, too something every way I look at you, so you can't be pretty. What you are is just the damnedest, delightfulest chunk of woman I ever laid eyes on."

She sighed comfortably. "You really mean that, don't you?"

"Every word."

"And you like me? You know, Brownie? *Like?*"

"Like isn't quite the word," I said. "I'm crazy about you. Almost any man would be if you didn't scare him off. Which reminds me, Deborah . . ."

I suggested several ways by which she could do herself a favor: thinking before she spoke; aiming her laugh in some direction other than a person's face.

"Would you like me better that way, Brownie?"

"I like you just as you are," I said. "But I'm out of the picture. You're leaving and—"

"Leave with me, Brownie."

"Wha-at?" I jerked the car back onto the road in the nick of time. "Why, Mrs. Chasen, are you suggesting—?"

"Anything! Any way you want it, darling. I'd like to have you marry me, but—"

"But—but, honey!" I shook my head. "That's crazy! You don't know anything about me."

"Yes, I do. All I need to know."

I laughed shakily. The whisky was wearing off. My nerves were rising on edge, slicing up saw-toothed through the skin. . . . *All you need to know, eh? What do you know, anyway? That I can spiel the crap until your head spins? Why not? That I'm hot as a two-dollar pistol? Why not? I spiel it out to keep from drowning in it, and I was only emasculated—only!—not castrated. . . .*

"You'll feel different tomorrow," I said. "Let's face it, Deborah, we've had quite a bit to drink today."

"I want you to come with me, Brownie."

"No," I said. "Now drop it, will you? It's too damned idiotic to talk about."

"Then I'll stay here. I won't take my train."

"I said to drop it!" I snapped. "Of course you'll take your train. You've got a drawing-room bought and paid for. You've got your steamship passage. You're going to get on that train and—"

"Not without you," she said calmly. "Either you go, or I stay."

"I tell you, you can't! I can't! We hardly know each other. I haven't got anything but my job, and you—"

"Uh-huh," she nodded pleasantly. "I have plenty for both of us."

"B-But—dammit, people just don't do those things!"

"Pooh on people," she said.

It was like fighting something that wasn't there, something you couldn't believe in fighting—fighting yourself. She'd seemed as lost as I was, and it had been so long, so very long since I'd let myself touch a woman. I'd wanted to help her, shove her back into the mainstream of life that I could never be part of. And . . .

We were entering the edge of town. I slowed the car slightly. I made my voice harsh.

"All right, Mrs. Chasen. You won't let me do it the nice way, so we'll have to make it the other. I don't like you. I don't like your looks. You're stupid. You're cockeyed. I haven't seen hair like yours since I stopped riding horses. You've got a can on you like a whale, and I wouldn't get near that topside of yours in a high wind for all the—"

"B-Brownie! S-Stop!"

I stopped.

"I'm sorry," I said. "I don't enjoy talking to you this way. You were just a job with me—an assignment—and I tried to—Goddam you!" I said.

For she was laughing. Her head was thrown back and the green eyes were crinkled and flashing, and that topside I'd mentioned was trembling and shivering. She was laughing all over. I could almost see the naked, rippling flesh, feel it shivering against mine, while the green eyes looked up into mine. Hot, then curious. And at last pitying and disgusted.

My hands on the steering wheel were wet with sweat.

"You're so funny, Brownie!"

"Yeah," I said. "Very funny. I even keep myself in stitches."

She put her hand on my knee, gave it a quick, firm squeeze. "Funny and sad," she said. "But you won't be sad with me. I'll make you the happiest man in the world."

"There's just one way you can do that," I said. "Get on your goddamned train and get out of town, and don't come back."

"Huh-uh," she said. "Now, you park right here and we'll go in and get my bags."

We parked. I took her by the shoulders and turned her around facing me.

"No, Brownie"—she tried to squirm away—"there's not a bit of use in telling me that my—my—"

"I'm not," I said. "I'm telling you I'm nuts about you. I think perhaps I even love you. But—well, call me any name you like. Think what you want to. I thought we'd just have a high old time together, and then you'd go your way and I'd go mine. So—I didn't see how it would make any difference. But—"

I didn't have to say it. All the laughter went out of her eyes, and she turned slowly away from me. "That's—?" She changed the question into a statement. "That's true, Brownie."

"It's true. We're separated, but we're still married. She'd never give me a divorce."

"Well . . ." She fumbled for the door handle.

"I'm sorry, Deborah."

She shrugged, and the horsetail of corn-colored hair brushed against her shoulders. "D-Don't be," she said. "Don't be sad, Brownie. That's the way it is, so . . . t-that's the way it . . ."

She got out and walked toward the station, and she didn't look back.

# IV

I MAY BE WRONG—I have been wrong about so many things—but I can't recall ever hearing or knowing of a son-of-a-bitch who did not do all right for himself. I'm talking about *real* sons-of-bitches, understand. The Grade-A, double-distilled, steam-heated variety. You take a man like that, a son-of-a-bitch who doesn't fight it—who knows what he is and gives his all to it—and you've really got something. Rather, *he's* got something. He's got all the things that are held out to you as a reward for being a non-son-of-a-bitch. For being unlike Lem Stukey, Chief of Detectives of the Pacific City police department.

He poured himself another drink, shoved the bottle across his desk toward me, and gestured with his glass. He was a good-looking guy—gigolo-ish good-looking. With a little less beef on his belly and a lot less larceny in his heart, he might have been an instructor in a dollar-a-lesson dance academy.

"I don't make you, Brownie," he said. "I just don't dig you at all, keed. Ain't I always treated you right? You ever ask me for anything you didn't get? Hell, I try to be a pal to you, and—"

"Stuke," I said. "Will you shut up for a minute?"

"But—well, sure, Brownie. Go right ahead."

"It's this way, Stuke. I'm immune, know what I mean? I've developed a tolerance for sons-of-bitches. I can drink with you and enjoy it. I can let you do me a little favor without having the slightest desire to puke. In a sort of hideous way, I actually like you. But—"

"I like you, too, Brownie. You're my kind of people."

"Now, let's not carry this too far," I said. "But speaking of favors, Stuke, I do you one every day. Every time I sit down at my typewriter without writing that Lem Stukey is the chief pimp, gambler, all-around and overall racketeer of Pacific City I'm doing you a favor. And any time you think I'm not—"

"Brownie!" He spread his hands. "Did I say no? I know you could blast me. You're the only guy that could. From what I hear, you could maybe write a story that old lovey drawers was beating his own wife, and he'd see that it went on the front page. . . . I *know*, see? I got the highest appreciation for your friendship. I know what you can do, or I wouldn't be asking—"

"Don't," I said. "Don't ask. I'm too tired even to tell you to go to hell."

"Hard day, huh?" He shook his head sympathetically. "I'll give you a couple bottles when you leave. Anything I can do, keed, anything at all. Just put a name to it."

I sighed and picked up my glass. He was a hard man to say no to, but no was all you could say. Once you said yes, you'd keep right on saying it the rest of your life.

157

"All right, Stuke," I said. "Let's get back to the beginning. I said I was immune. I can drink your whisky, talk with you, spend an evening with you now and then. I can do you the negative favor of doing nothing. But that's all I can do. That's all I will do. I will not, as you put it, give you the smallest boost. I will not, either by word or deed, do anything which might even remotely assist in making you county judge."

"Aw, Brownie. Why—?"

"I've told you. You're a menace, a plague, a son-of-a-bitch. You do enough damage where you are, but at least you're bracketed within fairly narrow boundaries. I shudder to think of you operating in the almost unlimited periphery of the judiciary."

"Okay. Throw the big words at me. Show me up. I ain't had no education. I'm just a poor boy who worked hard and—"

"Broth-er!" I said. "When you say that, smile!"

"Well"—he smiled a little sheepishly—"I got an idea how you feel, Brownie. You think a man ought to be a lawyer to—"

"Not necessarily," I said. "The job doesn't require it, and I've known some pretty good judges who weren't lawyers. It could work out, although it violates general precedent, if—*if,* my dear Lem—a man was sincere, honest, and devoted to the public's interest. Which you are not. . . . No, Stuke, you stay where you are and there'll be no trouble from me. Mr. Lovelace wants the *Courier* all sweetness and light. No scandal, no exposés, nothing that would reflect on the fair name of Pacific City. That's the way he wants it, and that's the way he shall have it—up to a point. You won't be knocked; you won't be blasted out of your present job. But neither will you be boosted upstairs."

He was silent a moment, his black, beady eyes fixed on me in an unblinking stare. Then he shrugged with pretended indifference.

"Suit yourself, Brownie. I was just trying to be a pal to you. The band-wagon's already rolling, and I thought maybe you'd want to hop on."

I choked and coughed. I laughed so hard I almost fell out of my chair. "Stuke. Please!"

"You think I'm lyin', huh?"

"Of course you're lying. When did you ever do anything else?"

"I got plenty of influential friends. How you think I climbed into this job?"

"Like you say," I said, "by working hard. You brought your little red-handled shovel to work with you, and you dug twenty-four hours a day. Before the alarums and excursions were sounded, you had uncovered any number of figurative but exceedingly smelly bodies. Now? Huh-uh. Alas, poor Stuke, they know you well. No more bodies. No county judgeship. No—and I'm probably offending etiquette in mentioning it—whisky in this bottle."

He laughed and popped the cork on another quart. "The whiz don't do anything at all to you, does it, keed? Just makes you spout a little smoother."

"That," I said, "is because I am a *Courier* man. I have my head in the clouds and my feet firmly on the ground."

"Yeah." He grinned. "Ain't it the truth?"

He stopped arguing about the county judge deal. We sat drinking and kidding, listening to the slash of the rain against the windows.

It was only a little after five. Less than an hour ago I'd taken Deborah to the station. But it was almost pitch dark outside with the sudden and violent storm that had struck the city. Stuke shook his black, oily head, cocking a hand to his ear.

"Dig them waves, will you? Almost three blocks away, and you'd think the ocean was coming right through the door."

I nodded absently, thinking of Deborah, wishing I could stop thinking of her. I wondered why she'd said—how she'd known—I was sad, right when I was kidding the hardest.

"What you doing tonight, keed? What you say we step out and play some babes?"

I shook my head. That was an easy one to duck. "Go over to Rose Island tonight? In this storm?"

"Yeah," he sighed, "that's right. No ferries runnin' tonight, and no one would take a charter boat out even if you was crazy enough to ride with 'em. . . . Maybe I could—"

"Now, Stuke, you should know better than that. No loose women in Pacific City . . . not in the respectable mainland sections of Pacific City."

"Well—" He broke off abruptly, frowning. He cursed and snapped his fingers. "Christ, pal, I almost forgot to tell you. I ought to have my ass kicked!"

"I'll go along with the last statement," I said. "What about the first one?"

"I'm sorry as hell, keed. I meant to call you at the time, but it was almost three o'clock, see, and I figured you'd already be gone from the office." He swallowed and his eyes shifted away from mine. "She came in on the two-thirty bus, Brownie. One of the boys spotted her."

It was too well done, too carelessly done. Mrs. Clinton Brown's arrival wasn't something that Stuke would forget. By pretending that he had, he was proving the opposite. It meant plenty to him.

"My wife's over on the island?" I said. "I don't suppose you know the address?"

"Well, let's see, now," he frowned. "It's—oh, yeah, it's The Golden Eagle, cottage seven. It ain't so bad as most of 'em, keed. Little tourist camp on the south shore."

"I know what it is," I said. "You can bring your own whore instead of renting theirs."

He clucked his tongue sympathetically. I set my glass down and raised a hand to my temples. I had to do it; I had to cover my face. Sick and stunned as I was, I was choking with laughter.

"It's a damned shame, Brownie. I thought she'd given up bothering you."

"Y-Yeah," I said, shakily. "It's certainly strange."

"How come you put up with her, anyhow? A man's got to support his wife but he don't have to live with her."

"One of those things," I mumbled. I lowered my hand and stood up.

He jumped to his feet also. "Where you going, Brownie? You can't go over to the island tonight. I ain't gonna let you even try it!"

The hell he said! He'd have given his eyeteeth to have me try it.

"Don't worry," I said. "There's no way I could get over there tonight. I just want to go home."

"I'll go with you. I can see this has hit you pretty hard, keed. A time like this, a man needs someone to talk to. I'll take us along a couple bottles, and—"

"I'll take the bottles," I said, "and go by myself."

He looked at me, trying to appear concerned and worried while he sized me up. But there wasn't anything for him to see. The two-way pull had taken hold and he wasn't looking at the real me—the me-in-charge-of-me. I'd moved off to one side, and I was moving faster every second. I was miles away and ahead of him.

"Okay, Brownie," he shrugged, "if that's the way you want it."

He took two quarts of whisky from a filing cabinet and twisted a newspaper around them. We said good night, and I left.

I walked out to my car, walked not ran, and I was soaked to the skin before I'd gone twenty feet. I slid into the seat, shivering yet not really conscious of the cold. I uncorked one of the bottles and raised it, staring blankly through the streaming windshield.

Until the last time—her last hell-raising visit to Pacific City—I'd been as easy on her as a man could be who was through with his wife. I'd put it to her as I had in the hospital: that it was just simply a case of not loving her any more. But it hadn't worked, and I'd seen it wasn't going to work. In a way, I was actually holding out hope to her. So, the last time, I'd got tough, tough and nasty. And it seemed to have done the job.

She hadn't been in Pacific City for three months. I'd have sworn that in another three months or so she'd be filing for divorce, that she'd make the break final and marry someone else. That was what she should have done. That, I was sure, was what she would have done. Except for Lem Stukey.

Lem wanted something that only I could deliver. He'd been looking for a way to force me to deliver. So I figure he'd started wondering about her, and he'd got in touch with her and started her to wondering: *Think it over, keed.*

*There ain't no other woman; you can't get him to go out with a babe. And the guy's drinkin' himself to death. Something's botherin' him, see? Maybe he done somethin' wrong while he was in the army, and he split with you to keep from mixing you up in it. . . .*

Well, Ellen would know that I hadn't done anything "wrong." She'd know that her Brownie wasn't the kind to commit bigamy or get himself an incurable dose or engage in espionage, or involve himself in any similarly shameful situation or activity. Still, I'd seemed quite contented with our marriage before I entered the army, yet afterward—as soon as I was shipped back to the states —I'd insisted on splitting up. And since there wasn't another woman, since I wasn't in love with someone else, why . . . ?

Stukey had prodded her. He'd kept her mind on the puzzle. And the truth must have finally dawned on her or she wouldn't be here.

It was rather strange, of course, that he'd told me she was back, but—

I shook my head. It wasn't strange. Very little went on in Pacific City that Lem didn't know about. I'd know that he knew she was back, and his failure to tell me would have seemed suspicious. As it was, he hadn't carried the matter off too well. He'd overacted—been a little too offhand. I hadn't thought him capable of embarrassment but obviously he had been.

I held the bottle to my mouth, swallowing steadily. Swallowing and swallowing. A hammer seemed to swing against my heart, numbing it, and another hammer swung against my back, driving through from my back to the heart. And it seemed to push forward, numb and lifeless, and press out through the skin.

Then it slid back into place. The numbness went away. It beat slowly but firmly.

I lowered the bottle. It was more than a third empty. I'd just killed myself, but I wasn't dead. There wasn't, I thought, listening to the roar of the ocean, anything that would kill me. I was going to go right on living, forever and ever, and. . . . How could I? How could I live in a world of snickers and whisperings and amused pity?

I corked the bottle and started the car.

I drove up to the center of town, circled the Civic Center (WPA 1938), and turned back in the direction I'd come from but on another street. It was probably unnecessary, this maneuvering, but you could never be sure with the Lem Stukeys of the world. They operated with a peculiar shrewdness that transcended intelligence. They had climbed to their pinnacles by doing the unexpected. At any rate, I had plenty of time. Time, with me, was endless.

There was no tail on me; I made sure of the fact. I drove through the wind-hurled downpour to the piers, wound the car through the dark chaos of sheds and warehouses, and parked in the shadows—if shadows there were in this blackness—of a sheet-iron storage building.

I uncorked the bottle and dug some dry cigarettes out of the pocket of the car. I sat drinking and smoking, thinking how strange it was that the thing that had to be done was always the hardest to do.

She wasn't bad, you see. She was weak, spiteful, stubborn; she'd made her own life a hell as a means of making mine one. But, except for what had happened to me, she wouldn't have done what she had. The flaws of character and spirit would never have appeared.

I think the truest maxim ever coined is the one to the effect that untried virtue doesn't count.

Years before, when I was a kid, I owned a little Ford runabout, a Model T. And I took care of that car as a man takes care of his love—for I did love it. I was and remain a Model T guy, more comfortable with imperfection than its opposite, cherishing the ability to discern and shore up a latent weakness. I knew the car wasn't a Cadillac. Hell, what would a guy like me do with a Cad? It was a Model T, and I treated it good and it treated me good. When I sold it, after two years of trouble-free driving, it was actually in better shape than the day I bought it.

Two months later it was on the junk heap.

*Less* than two months after I split with Ellen, she was whoring.

I belched and kicked open the door of the car. . . . It was too bad but that's the way it was. If I had to live, I had to work. And if I had to work, I had to be around people. And if I had to be around people, I had—I had to be around people. They mustn't know.

Mr. Clinton Brown regrets the necessity of murdering Ellen Tanner Brown.

I stuffed the full bottle into my pocket and carried the other under my arm. I staggered down the pier to the community dock and climbed down the ladder. Somewhere near the foot of it, I paused and peered around in the darkness. Then I said eenie-meenie-miney-moo-toodle-de-doo, and let go.

Everything was a little confused for a moment. My head was planted firmly in a boat, but my feet were in the clouds.

Having great faith in the wisdom of providence, particularly that section dealing with the laws of gravity, I remained unperturbed. *I am a* Courier *man,* I thought, *and a* Courier *man does not miss the boat.*

My feet came down and my head came up, and my ass end was planted firmly in the water. Clear-eyed, I let it remain there while I got the bottle from under my arm and bought myself a drink. Then I pulled it over the side, untied the mooring rope, and picked up the oars.

# V

I HAVE NEVER been able to understand the high regard that leaders of dangerous missions have for sobriety. Sober, one challenges the fates; unsober, the
fates cannot be bothered with you. While the drunk wanders unharmed amid
six-lane traffic, a car swerves up on the sidewalk to pick off the sober man.
While the drunk walks away from an eight-story fall, the sober man stumbles
from the curb and breaks his neck. It never fails. That's the way it is, so that's
the way it is.

Take me, which you are doomed to do for some two hundred pages. Take
me. I know nothing about boats. I had never been in a rowboat before. And
while I wasn't drunk, naturally, since I cannot get drunk, I was very far from
sober. A sober man would never have got fifty feet from the dock. Not being
sober, I got a mile and a half, all the way to Rose Island.

Due to my falling or being thrown out of the boat a couple of times, and
subsequent willy-nilly driftings while the boat found me again, my trip was
something less than speedy. But I got there. I pulled the boat up on the beach
and finished the opened bottle. Then, having got my bearings, I headed for the
Golden Eagle cottages.

They were only about a block away. I couldn't have debarked much nearer
to them if I'd ridden the ferry and taken a taxi. There were twelve of them,
laid out in a triangle with its base to the ocean. Number seven was at the end.
Its shades were drawn, but I could detect a little light inside. I seemed to hear
a faint stirring and splashing.

I tapped softly on the door. There was silence for a moment, then a splash
and a muted, "Yes?"

"Brownie," I said.

"Brownie! What in the—?"

The door flew open. She pulled me inside, stood against me naked, her arms
around my neck, her thick black hair buried against my chest.

"Gosh, honey! Gee, it's good to see you! I—but you're soaked! Let me
take—"

"I'm all right," I said, and I pushed her away. "I'm going to keep on being
all right."

I walked on into the room and sat down in a chair. For a moment she stood
where I had pushed her; then she came and sat down on the bed opposite
me.

She smiled at me, timidly, swinging her bare legs to and fro, holding her
knees together while she swung her legs out from each other. "You're—you're
not mad at me, Brownie?"

163

"I wish you hadn't come back, Ellen," I said. "It's going to make things very hard for both of us."

"No, it won't, honey! I—Did you know I only called the office one time today? Just once! They said you were gone for the day, so I said, thank you, I'll call again tomorrow and—and—that's all I did. Honest!" She nodded her head vigorously, her eyes fixed anxiously on my face.

I said, "So you called one time. Why did you call at all?"

"H-Haven't you any idea, Brownie?"

"Sure. You had a dime."

The smile faded and a sullen look edged into its place. Then the look faded, without disappearing, and the smile—a semblance of it—returned. "Maybe . . . I guess maybe you've got a right to talk that way. But—but think of me, honey! I h-hadn't done anything, and—"

"Hadn't done anything!" I jeered. "You didn't need to do anything. I didn't know my way around when I married you. I'd never been anywhere or seen anything. After I did, I wised up. I saw I was married to a goddamned flabby-tailed dumbbell with a fried egg for a brain."

"You dirty bas—! Oh, Brownie, *don't!* Don't, honey. You don't mean—"

"The hell I don't I've seen better tail on a mule."

She stuttered and spluttered, trying to curse and beg me at the same time. Trying to fight down her temper. I'd touched her on her sore spots. She *didn't* have much in the way of an education. Her rear end *was* a little on the wriggly side.

"Y-You burn me up! You—"

"Not me," I said, "that hot little business of yours. Remember that poem I dedicated to you?"

"You're goddamned right, I remember! Of all the dirty—"

"By the way, what did you do with the rest of those sonnets? I was thinking, perhaps, you'd like to have them autographed."

She told me what she'd done with them. Something indelicate but completely practical.

"They didn't catch fire?"

"You burn me— That's right! Sit there and laugh! You done—you did all this! Why shouldn't you laugh about it?"

"Jesus," I said. "What a freak you turned out to be! Do the boys make you put a sack over your head?"

It was going swell. She was getting angrier and angrier. I had her sold, and if I could just keep her that way . . . she'd live.

I—

She began to cry.

She'd very seldom done that, really cried. She'd grown up in pretty rugged circumstances, and she'd never got the crying habit. But on those rare occasions when she did break down, she pulled all the stops. She cried like the child she'd never been.

She didn't cover her face with her hands, and all of it was puckered and reddened. Her eyes were tight shut. Her nose ran. Her mouth, with the ludicrously drawn-down corners, opened so wide you could see her tonsils.

I tried to laugh, and I couldn't. I jerked the cork on the second quart and took a big slug, and it didn't do any good. It had always got me to see her cry. It did now.

*You do not have your head in the clouds, Brown,* I thought. *Your feet are of clay and the arches are falling.*

I took another drink. I gripped the arms of the chair. I said, "Look, now. Now see here, dammit. There's no sense in—in—"

And she shuddered and sobbed, "Y-You—you h-hurt my f-feelings. . . ."

And suddenly I was on the bed with her, dabbing at her eyes with my handkerchief, telling her to blow her nose, dammit. And she shuddered and choked back the tears.

"Aw r-right, Brownie. I—I—w-will."

She clung to me, shivering with my wetness but clinging tighter when I tried to draw away. She curled up on the bed, drawing me down with her, burrowing and snuggling her head against my shoulder.

After a while, she said, "H-Honey . . . ?"

"Yes," I said.

Another silence. Then: "I know what—what happened. I don't know why I didn't guess in the beginning, because you couldn't be mean to anyone and—"

"All right," I said. "You know."

"Why didn't you tell me, honey? It wouldn't have made any difference. There's more to marriage than—than *that.*"

"A great deal more," I said. "There's more to a house than a roof, but you'd find it impractical to live without one. You'd move from one room to another and they'd all be fine—and not worth a damn. Finally, you'd have to move out."

"You don't know! You can't be sure! It—you think this is better?"

"It doesn't need to be like this. I hoped you'd remarry."

"I can't! H-How can I when I still love you?"

My hands trembled on her bare back. I had to keep on, but I knew it was no use. She was a child, weeping for a broken doll, stubbornly refusing any other.

"Look," I said. "Listen to me, Ellen. A lot of people have thought I was a pretty smart guy. You always thought so. Have you changed your mind?"

"No, Brownie, but—"

"Wasn't I always good to you? Didn't I always do what was best for you? Now, answer me. Isn't that so?"

"Yes."

"Why do you think I did it this way? Do you think it was easy for me, ridiculing you, breaking every bond between us so that you could form new ones with someone else? Do you think it's something that popped into my mind on the spur of the moment?"

"Of course not, honey. But—"

"I thought it over for weeks. I studied the record of what had happened in similar cases. I talked it over with two damned good psychiatrists. I told them what you—we—were like, and—"

Her head jerked back. "Like? What *am* I supposed to be like?"

"Don't," I said. "Let's not get started on another row. I told them the truth, that you were anything but a nympho but also very far from frigid. I told them that you'd always—Well, skip it. There wasn't any real best thing to do, but I did the best there was."

"And look how it turned out!"

"It would have turned out this way, anyhow, if you can't face facts. My telling you the truth wouldn't have made any difference. Don't you—"

"We could have tried, couldn't we? How do you know how it would have turned out when we didn't even try? You don't know everything! You.... Oh"—she hesitated and I heard her swallow heavily—"it's—it's t-too late Brownie? You don't want to come back to me now, after what I've—I've—?"

I kissed her on the forehead, wondering abstractedly why the weakest of us seem always subjected to the greatest stress. Good and evil: were there such things or were there only weakness and strength? Was a car bad because it became junk? Was a woman bad who became a whore?

"Brownie . . . is t-that the reason w-why—?"

I kissed her again. "You haven't done anything," I said. "Not a single thing."

"Let's try it, Brownie! Why, honestly, I won't mind a bit! Really, I won't. We'll have all those nice funny talks together, and you can read to me in the evenings and—and maybe we can get Skipper back from those people! Or we can get another dog. Why, we could even adopt a baby, honey, and it would be just like—"

"Don't," I said. "For Christ's sake, DON'T!"

But she wouldn't stop. She went on and on, over and over that one refrain, earnest, tearful, laughable, maddening: *It wouldn't, honey! It wouldn't make a bit of difference!* My heart began to beat time to it. The blood roared and raced through my brain, beating time.

"Brownie!" she said. "Brownie!"

I drifted back from a faraway place. A place where all the straight paths were blocked off and everything moved at a tangent.

Her voice had become firm. "You understand, Brownie! We're stopping this foolishness right now! We need each other, and we're going to have each other. I've tried your way. Now you're going to try mine. I'm going to—I'm going to make you, Brownie!"

"Spread it all out," I said. "Lay the cards down."

"I—cards?"

"Card, then. Lem Stukey. Either I do as you say, or you get tough. You get me or you have a little talk with Lem."

She drew her head back, looked into my face frowning. "I d-don't understand. What would I—?"

"He's been in touch with you, hasn't he? He sent you the dough to come back here on?"

"We-ell, he—he—" She blushed. "Well, he was just being nice. Just because he liked me."

I laughed.

"Well, he was—he does!" she snapped. "What's so funny about it?"

"Nothing," I said. "But that's the deal, isn't it, El? You have to tell me, you know. You can't make threats without showing what you're threatening."

"But I haven't—" She paused; she was silent for several seconds. "What if I—how could I threaten you with *that*?" she said, in a half-shamed voice. "It isn't any crime. You couldn't help—"

"You know what I mean," I said. "You know what I'm like. You know what newspaper business is like. It's a closed world; there's no place you can go where you're not known. Put it in plain language. Put yourself in my place. How long could you live in a world where everyone knew you didn't have a pecker?"

"Brownie! That's dir—"

"You mean it's funny," I said. "Sure it is. You could even catch the doctors and nurses in the hospital grinning about it. You know I couldn't take it, El. You may not know that I might not get the chance to take it. Because there are a hell of a lot of places that wouldn't hire me. That's right; that's straight from the case histories. They're afraid of you. They figure you're not normal."

"But—listen to me, Brownie! I—"

"That's what you're threatening me with," I said. "You'd do that to me, or you'd let Lem do it. Put me under his thumb for keeps. You'd take away the only thing I have left, the little pride and integrity that gives me an excuse to go on living. You love me—you can't love anyone else, you say—and you'd do that to me?"

"*No!*" She gripped me fiercely. "No, I won't, Brownie I won't have to because—No, I won't do it, honey! I don't know what I was thinking about! I've just been kind of crazy and lonely and hopeless-feeling, and—" Her voice trailed off.

After a moment she said reproachfully, a trifle angrily, "After all, I *could* get a divorce on those grounds. That would be a lot worse, wouldn't it?"

You see? She didn't know what she was going to do. How, then, could I?

"Yes," I said. "That would be worse. You wouldn't get the nice chunk of change you can get out of Lem."

"I—You've got a lot of right to talk about him," she said, "after the way you've acted. You're the one that's always running people down. Even if I did tell him, what makes you think he'd—"

"For God's sake!" I said. "What are you saying, Ellen? First, you don't have anything to threaten me with. Next, you have something but you're not going to use it. Then, you're going to use it—you're going to pass it on to Lem—but he isn't going to. You don't make sense from one minute to—"

"Oh, sure!" she said sullenly. "You're a genius, and I'm a dumbbell. Well, maybe I'm not as dumb as you think."

"Let it go. It's no use," I said.

"Whatever I got out of Stukey it wouldn't be enough! After all I've been through!"

"No," I said. "It wouldn't be enough."

I sat up and uncorked the bottle. I took a drink, replaced the cork, and fumbled for a cigarette. I didn't have any with me, of course, any dry ones. They were back in the car. I reached out to the reading stand, took a cigarette from her package, and lighted it.

"Brownie—" She sat up, too, half sat up, with her legs folded under her.

"Yes?" I said.

"You know I wouldn't do that, don't you?" She smiled at me brightly. "It's like you say. How could I when I love you so much? And—but, oh, Brownie! Let's go back together! Please, darling. It won't make any difference, and even if it does a little it'll still be better than this. I just can't go on like—"

"No," I said. "You can't, and you won't."

And I brought the bottle down on her head.

I stood looking down at her, and my head swam and I weaved slowly on my feet. The wetness and the exertion and the long talk were sobering me, and when I sobered I became drunk. Far drunker than any amount of whisky could make me. All my sureness was gone, and the ten thousand parts of an insane puzzle were scattered to the winds.

She lay, twitching a bit and moaning, with her head and shoulders slumping toward her knees, her thighs in a tangent curve to her legs. A question mark. She was a question, and she had to be answered.

Had it been necessary?

Or had I done it because I wanted to?

Was every move I made, as Dave Randall had once angrily declared, designed to extract payment from the world for the hell I dwelt in? Had I tried to destroy slowly and, failing that, killed wantonly?

It was a nice question. It was something to think about on these long rainy evenings.

I took another stiff drink.

The terrible sobriety-drunkenness, with its terrible questions, began to fade. I slid back into the sideways world. This was the way it was, and the way it was was this.

Yet it was hard to leave her like this. Something seemed to need doing, some small thing. Something she'd always wanted, perhaps, without conscious awareness of the want.

I could think of only one thing.

I pulled the sheet over her now semi-conscious body. I upended the bottle of whisky and sprinkled it over the sheet. I jerked several matches from a pad and struck them.

"You said to," I said. "Remember, Ellen? You always said to burn you up. . . ."

And I let the matches fall.

# VI

It was still pitch dark outside, still raining a downpour, but the wind was dying and the worst of the storm seemed to be over. I pushed the boat into the bay and hopped in. I started to row. And then, slowly, I let the oars slide out of my hands and drift away into the darkness. . . . Let the boat decide, I thought. Leave it to the ocean. They brought me here; now, they can return me. Or not return me. I wash my hands of all responsibility.

I leaned back across the thwarts, letting my fingers trail in the water. I closed my eyes, feeling the boat rock and roll, feeling it turn round and round gently as it moved out into the bay. It was very peaceful for a time. Very restful. I had had nothing to do with anything, and now I had nothing to do with this. I was a man following orders, clear-eyed, clear-thinking, and if those orders had led me—led me . . .

*She had looked very beautiful. She had glowed, oh, but definitely she had glowed. She had been all lit up, burning with a clear-blue flame, and then the mattress had started to smolder and . . .*

I screamed but there was no sound. I was throwing up.

The boat had begun to spin. It was caught in the trough between two tall shore-bound rollers, pulled by one and pushed by the other, and it spun faster and faster. Suddenly it reared up on end and shot to the crest of the first wave. It hung poised there for a moment, then it dropped down, spinning, to the other side.

Tons of water plunged into it. It went down, vanished as completely as though it had never existed, and I went on. There was a thunderous roar, an incessant crashing. And then I was gripping something hard and slimy . . . one of the piles of the pier.

That's the way it was to be, then. The decision had been made. I pulled myself from pile to pile until I found the ladder. I climbed up to the pier and returned to my car. I drove away.

My house—to use the noun loosely—is some six miles north of Pacific City. Years ago it was occupied by a railroad section gang—in the days when section hands were largely itinerant Mexicans. When I discovered it, it was a lopsided ruin, headquarters seemingly for the county's population of creeping and crawling things.

The railroad gladly rented it to me for five dollars a month. A hundred dollars and a few hundred hours work has made it reasonably habitable. It is a little noisy, perhaps, since it sits on railroad right-of-way, and it is more than a little sooty. But as rental properties go in Pacific City—properties within the financial reach of the modest-salaried man—it is still very much a bargain. We

170

do not believe in "government handouts" here, you see. We scorn socialistic housing programs. We hold to the American way of life, the good old laws of supply and demand. That is, the landlords supply what they care to in the way of housing and demand what they feel like. And the tenant, bless him, oh, hail his rugged independence, is perfectly free to pay it and like it. Or sleep in the streets. Where, of course, he will be promptly arrested by Lem Stukey for vagrancy.

I will say this for Stukey: he is absolutely fearless and relentless where vagrants are concerned. Let Lem and his minions apprehend some penniless wanderer, preferably colored and over sixty-five, and the machinery of the law goes into swift and remorseless action. Sixty days on the road gang, six months on the county farm—so it goes. Nor is that always as far as it goes. In an amazing number of instances, the vagrant appears to be the very person responsible for a long series of hitherto unsolved crimes. . . .

Good old Lem and his rubber hose! Unless I missed my guess, I'd be seeing him shortly.

I parked my car at the side of the house and went inside. I filled a water glass with whisky and put it down at a gulp. Fire blazed through me. My heart did frantic setting-up exercises for a moment, then steadied off into a slow, steady pounding. All at once I felt almost happy. For the first time in a long time, life seemed really interesting. There was a rift—and a widening one— in the dead-gray monotony of existence.

I went into the bedroom and shucked out of my clothes. The phone rang and I trotted back into the living-room to answer it, pulling a robe around me.

"Brownie—Clint?" It was Dave Randall.

"Why, Colonel," I said. "How nice of you to call! How are all the wee ones and—"

"Brownie, for God's sake! Have you seen Lem Stukey?"

"Frequently," I said. "As a devoted *Courier* man, I am brought into contact with many strange—"

"Please, Brownie! He hasn't been in touch with you in the last hour or so?"

"No"—I put a frown into my voice—"what's up, Dave?"

"It's about—Where have you been all evening, Clint? Lem's been tearing up the town to find you. He called me. He even called Mr. Lovelace."

"But why? What about?"

I smiled to myself. It was wonderful to be interested again.

"I—I think I'd better come out there, Brownie. I think perhaps, I'd better bring Mr. Lovelace with me."

"Oh?" I said, and I made the voice-frown a little stronger. "What's the trouble, Dave?"

"I can't—I think I'd better tell you in person. Brownie—"

"Yes?"

"Where have you been tonight?"

"Drinking. Riding and drinking. Walking and drinking. Sitting by the road-side and drinking."

"Were you with anyone? Is there any way you could establish your where-abouts?"

"No," I said, "to both questions. . . . Look, Dave, I didn't run over anyone, did I? I was pretty woozy, but—"

"I'll see you," he said. "I'll be right out."

We hung up. I sat down on the lounge and went to work on the bottle. I was feeling better and better. There was nothing in my stomach but this clean, fresh whisky, and there was nothing in my mind but a problem. No Ellen. No oblong of bright-blue flame. Only an interesting problem.

About ten minutes had passed when a car roared up the lane from the highway and skidded to a stop in the yard. It was Lem Stukey, and he was by himself. naturally, on anything as good as this, he would be by himself. I looked up as he walked in. I blinked my eyes, frowned, and took another drink from the bottle.

He stood in the doorway, his hands on his hips, his hat thrust back on his oily head. And there was an expression of sad reproach on his sleek, round face.

He waited for me to speak. I let him go right on waiting. Finally he crossed the room and pulled up a chair in front of me.

"Keed," he said, sorrowfully, "you shouldn't've done it. You should have knowed you couldn't get away with it."

"Well," I shrugged, "nothing ventured, nothing gained."

"She wasn't worth it, Brownie."

"No," I said, "I don't suppose she was. But, then, who is?"

"I don't see no way out for you, keed. Not unless I was to kind of take a hand personally. If I was to do that, now, call it an accident—"

"Why don't you?" I said. "After all, a pal's a pal, I always say."

"You mean that, Brownie? You'll play ball with me like I been askin' you to?"

"Well"—I hesitated—"isn't it pretty muddy outside?"

"Muddy? I don't dig you, keed."

"To play ball."

"Look!" he snarled, and his hand closed over my arm. "What the hell are you talking about?"

"I don't know," I said. "What are you talking about?"

He jumped up and stood over me. I started to rise and he shoved me back hard.

"I'm talking about murder, you smart bastard! You were over to the island tonight. You killed her. You coldcocked her and set fire to her. Left her to burn up in the bed. Only she didn't burn up, see. She didn't die right away. I figure her hair probably cushioned the blow, and she came to when she felt herself burning'. Anyway, she got up and got to the dresser. She got something out of her purse. She had it balled up in her hand when the island cops found her."

I looked at him, blinking a little owlishly, sifting through the situation one fact at a time. It wasn't particularly startling, although I suspect that I was guilty of at least a small start. I'd been pretty wobbly on my pins when I swung the bottle, and she did have a thick head of hair. And the whisky would have tended to burn away before the bedclothes themselves caught fire.

Now, as to this "something" she'd taken from her purse . . .

"To borrow an expression," I said, "I don't dig you, keed. Just who am I supposed to have killed?"

"Don't pull that innocent crap on me! Who the hell else would have killed your wife? She wasn't robbed. It's a cinch it wasn't a rape murder. Anyone that wanted any of that could have had it for—"

I came up then, and I came up swinging. I hit him an open-palmed slap across the jaw, hit him so hard his hat sailed from his head. His hand darted to his hip, but he didn't draw the gun. I sat back down again and buried my face in my hands.

After a while I said, "Are you sure it was murder? It couldn't have been an accident?"

"Who you kidding?" he said. "You goin' to tell me that she fell on *top* of her head? That she wiped the place clean of fingerprints herself?"

"Wi—!" I caught myself, choked the word into a meaningless grunt. "This object she had in her hand. What was it?"

"A poem, kind of a poem. She put the finger right on you, keed. She'd had it a long time; it was practically worn out with all the folding and refolding it had gone through. You wrote it for her, and she'd been carrying it around all this time. Ever since you split up. Yessir, she knew that when we saw it, we'd—"

"It had my name on it?"

"It didn't need no name on it. She never really went for no one but you. Anyway, she sure wasn't going for anyone three-four years ago when this must've been written. When you an' her were still tied up."

"Maybe she wrote it herself."

"Huh-uh. She wasn't up to anything that sharp. And what the hell? A dame's dying, and she goes for a poem she's written? You know better than that, keed. You wrote it. It sounds like you to a *t,* and she knew I'd see that—"

"What was it?" I said. "Have you got it with you?"

"It figures, Brownie. It all adds up to just one guy. No one else had any motive. No one else would have written a thing like this. It had to be someone that lives here—someone I'd know—and, palsy, that ain't no one but—"

"I'd like to hear it," I said. "Do you mind?"

"I don't mind a bit, keed." He took a notebook from his pocket and opened it. "Catch a load. I don't know that I can pronounce all the words just right, but—"

"Go ahead. I'll try to interpret."

"Sure," he said, and he read:

> *Lady of the endless lust,*
> *Itching lips and heaving bust,*
> *Lady save it, lady scram, lady hang it on a nail*
> *Get thee hence nor leave behind you*
> *Any vestige of your tail.*

He finished reading and looked at me sharply. I looked back at him indifferently. I'd written it, of course, it and some fifty or sixty similar bits of doggerel. But that had been long ago, and they'd been done on various odds and ends of paper and on a variety of typewriters. On the Red Cross machines in hospitals. In newspaper offices. In dollar-an-hour, type-your-own-letter places. They couldn't be traced to me. I'd written them out of bitterness and brooding —at a time when I was still bitter and brooding—out of hate and resentment and restlessness. And, finally, I had presented them to Ellen. I had dedicated them to her.

I'd shown them to no one but her. No one but she knew that I had written them. I wondered what masochistic urge had led her to save this one after destroying the others.

"Well, keed?" Stukey grinned at me. "What you say?"

"I gather that that's a copy," I said. "Where's the original?"

"The cops over on the island have it. They read it off to me over the telephone."

"You haven't seen it yourself, then? You don't actually know that it's as they described it? Old and creased and—"

"What the hell you gettin' at?"

"I've already arrived. But you, my dear Stukey, are very far behind. You didn't see the poem. You didn't see her. You don't know—"

"They're kidding me, huh?; He let out a snort. "They made it all up just to cause some excitement."

"You're chief of detectives. You seem to regard this as a pretty important case. So important that you had to bother my publisher and editor about it. Yet you've got your evidence by telephone. Why? Why didn't you go over there?"

"Well—uh—" He licked his lips. "You know, keed. The bay's been kinda choppy. Ain't no real reason why I couldn't have gone, if I'd figured it was necessary, but—uh—"

"A little choppy, eh? The ferries and charter boats aren't running, and it's just a little choppy. Cut it out, Stuke. You didn't go because you couldn't No one could have."

"That's what you say! I—"

"So did you, earlier this evening. Remember our conversation at your office? No one could have crossed that bay tonight. *No one.* Certainly he couldn't have crossed it twice. If you don't know that, you ought to be back walking a beat, which, now that I think of it, might be an excellent idea."

His face reddened; his round, overbright little eyes shifted nervously. "Now, look, Brownie. It's just as plain as day—"

"—or the nose on your face." I nodded. "But you can't see it. You were so red hot to get something on me that you overlooked the plain facts of the matter. You say that she got up and got that poem out of her purse. How do you know she did? How do you know it wasn't simply made to look that way by the person who killed her?"

"Well—" His tongue moved over his lips again. "But why would—?"

"The poem belonged to him, the murderer, not her. Obviously he was a man with a perverted sense of humor, a maniac in the broad sense of the term. He visited her, doubtless as a client. He murdered her. Then he arranged for her to be found in such a way as to throw you off his trail yet satisfy his ego. And, stupid man that you are, he was entirely successful."

I smiled at him pleasantly and took another drink. I lighted a cigarette, coughing slightly on the smoke as I choked back a laugh. This was far better than I had thought it would be. There were truly wonderful possibilities in it.

"That's what happened, Lem," I said. "It had to be a maniac. You can't make sense out of it in any other way."

"You call that sense?" he growled.

"For a maniac, a sadistic killer, yes. By the way, I assume the ferries have resumed service? Well, then, you've let him get completely away from you. He's not even on the island any more."

There was something very close to fear in the too-bright eyes. Fear and wonder and awe. "You're"—he cleared his throat hoarsely—"you're takin' it pretty calm, keed. Your wife gets killed in just about the most God-awful way a woman could, and you sit there grinning and—"

"She wasn't my wife," I said. "She hadn't been my wife in a long, long time. As for my reaction to the—the—well, I don't wear my emotions on my sleeve, Stuke. My actions don't necessarily reflect my feelings."

"Yeah," he grunted. "I'll buy that. I'll go right on down the line on that one. I sit listenin' to you sometimes, chewin' the fat with you, and I get to wonderin' what the hell—"

I held up a hand, interrupting him. "I'll tell you what you'd better do, Stuke. What you'd better start wondering about. You've botched this thing from beginning to end. My wife has been brutally murdered by a maniac, and you've let him get away. You'd better start wondering about how you're going to keep your job."

"I had, huh?" He laughed nervously. "Now, look, Brownie, like I said a moment ago, she just wasn't worth any bad trouble."

"I disagree with you. . . . What did you say when you talked to Dave Randall and Mr. Lovelace tonight? Something rather suggestive, eh, laden with nasty implications?"

"Me? Me knock a pal?" He made a gesture of hurt denial. "You know I wouldn't do a thing like that. All I done was mention that your wife had been killed, an' that I—well, I was trying to get ahold of you to break the bad news. That's all I said, Brownie. So help me."

I shrugged. I didn't particularly care what he'd said. I still wasn't letting him off the hook. Mr. Lem Stukey was going to go to work, at long last. He was going to give the city a long-delayed cleaning up. Not strictly because of the entertainment it would provide me, not entirely. Through him I could make atonement. I could offset with good the evil of Ellen's death.

"I'm telling you, Brownie," he said, "I didn't knock you. There ain't nothin' for either of us to get in an uproar about. Now, I been thinkin', and the way I see it we're both off base. It was an accident."

"It couldn't have been. You said so yourself."

"I can't change my mind? An accident's got to be logical? She was drinking. She spilled booze all over herself. She catches herself on fire, lighting a cigarette. She falls down and knocks herself out. She—"

"Before or after igniting herself? And what about the poem?"

"Look, Brownie"—he leaned forward, pleading—"we get cases like this all the time. Just about like this. Someone gets stiff in his hotel room. He bangs himself up an' flops down on the bed smoking, and he wakes up burning an' the room's so full of smoke he can't see. An'—well, you know how it is. He tried to get out of the place, but he wants to take his money with him, so—"

"I see," I nodded slowly. "You think that's what she intended to do, huh? She tried to get her money, but got the poem instead. Mmm, I suppose it might have been that way. But that still doesn't explain the poem."

"What's there to explain? Lots of people carry poems around. We got a fellow down at the office—you know him, Stengel, works over in identification —and he does it. He clips 'em out of newspapers, or maybe he hears 'em over the radio and copies 'em down. Never seen him yet when he didn't have some verse in his wallet, ready to spring it on you."

"But this particular little item—"

"Look, Brownie, pal"—his eyes flickered with annoyance—"you're fighting me. It was pretty cute, wasn't it? Something a dame like—something she might have got a big bang out of. Maybe she copied it off a privy wall. Maybe some place where she was working, slingin' hash, say, and one of the waitresses passed it around and she got hold of a copy. The point is it don't mean nothing, so we don't even have to consider it. I ain't even going to mention it in my report."

"Well—" I stared at him absently.

"Well?" he said. "It was an accident, huh? We let it go at that. I don't give you no trouble; you don't give me none."

I hesitated. I was trying to remember something. Everything was reasonably clear up to a certain point: I could remember swinging the bottle, spilling the whisky over her, dropping the matches. But after that . . .

After that, from that time until I reached the boat, nothing. Only the long blue oblong of flame, and then nothing. If Stukey hadn't been so sure of himself, if he hadn't gone off half-cocked, he might have tripped me up in a dozen places.

"You were very sure," I said, "that she'd been slugged. There wasn't any doubt in your mind. What made you so certain, Stuke? Just the fact that she couldn't have easily struck the top of her head against something?"

"That was a big part of it, sure, but there was this quart whisky bottle layin' in the bed an'—"

"I see. You thought she'd been hit with that. What brand of whisky was it?"

"Couldn't say. It was all charred, see, the label burned off and—"

"And the fingerprints? Did you dust the place?"

"Uh-huh. The boys went over it from top to bottom, and the only prints they found was hers an' a few of the maid's. I figure she must've cleaned the place up good before she started her party. Nice clean little lady, huh?" He drooped a lid over one eye. "Looks like she even wiped off the doorknob."

"I suppose the boys also looked for tracks around the outside?"

"Tracks? Why, keed, there could have been a herd of elephants around that place and their tracks wouldn't have lasted five minutes in that rain."

"Now, that poem—"

"Forget it. Put it out of your mind, pal. Typewritten—God knows when or where. The paper, it might have come from any place. A dime store or a drugstore or—"

"You were completely wrong then in your initial suspicions? There is absolutely nothing to connect me with this murder?"

"Absitively and possolutely, Brownie. I was all wet up to here. But don't use that word, huh? Don't say murder. It was an accident and—"

A car was pulling into the yard. He paused, shooting me a look of inquiry.

"That would be my publisher," I said, "and my editor. They have come to condole with me. Also, I suspect—at least on the part of Mr. Randall—to lend me moral support."

"Yeah? Well, that's nice." He stood up, brushing at his pants. "I guess I'll just trot along, then, an'—"

"You," I said, "will stay right here."

"But, pal . . . Oh, well, sure. You want me to square you up with 'em, huh? I don't remember saying anything out of the way, but—"

"You will square yourself up," I said. "You will explain just what you intend to do about apprehending my wife's murderer."

# VII

MR. LOVELACE WAS patently not in the most pleasant of humors. A man of regular habits was Mr. Lovelace, a man who, like so many of the lower lower-animals, liked his full ten hours' sleep each night. Now that sleep had been disturbed; he, Austin Lovelace, had been disturbed twice in *one* night! And without, as he saw it, any very adequate cause.

It was the old, old story. Because he was strong and wise—a tower of strength among pygmies—he was constantly overburdened. Everyone loaded his trifling troubles upon him.

He was sleepy, puzzled, fretful. Very, very fretful. For me, the loyal, hard-working—and appreciative—servant, he managed a mumbled word of sympathy and a semi-fatherly handclasp. But it was obviously an effort.

"Very sad. Tragic. . . . Insist you take the remainder of the week off, understand? Take as much time as you need—uh—within reason."

"Thank you, sir," I said. "I believe two or three days will be sufficient. I own a burial plot in Los Angeles, and I thought—"

"By all means. Certainly. Much better than a local burial. Incidentally, Mr. Brown"—his lips pursed pettishly—"I was rather shocked to learn that—uh —that a man of your caliber was married to—to—"

"I understand, sir," I said. "But I was very young at the time. It was long before I came to the *Courier*. I hadn't yet had the chance to profit from my association with you."

"Well—ahem—I, uh, certainly wouldn't want to chide you in your hour of bereavement. Am I correct in understanding that you had not lived together as man and wife for some time?"

"Not for several years, sir. Not since I entered the army."

"Ummm. I see." The stare he gave me was considerably less peevish. "A marriage in name only, eh? A youthful mistake from which you were unable to extricate yourself?"

"Yes, sir," I said. "You might call it that."

It was bad, shameful, to speak of her in this way. But, you see, there no longer was a her. Now there was merely a problem, and out of the bad much good could come.

He gave me a forgiving clap on the back. Then, after a look of puzzled distaste at Lem Stukey, he turned annoyed to Dave Randall.

"Well, Randall? I believe there's nothing more to be said or done, eh?"

"N-No, sir." Dave started nervously. "I—I guess it wasn't really necessary for you to—I guess I shouldn't have bothered you to come out here, sir."

179

"My own thought. Why did you, Randall? I seem to recall that you mentioned that you would later explain the need for my presence."

"Well, I—I—"

"Yes? Speak up, man!"

Lovelace fed on nervousness, even as he did on flattery. Let him catch you jumpy, uneasy, and he would be after you like a hungry hound. And Dave couldn't explain, of course. He couldn't say what he'd thought—that he was sure I was in a bad hole and was apt to need plenty of help to climb out.

He'd been positively pale with fear when he arrived, and he'd been almost pitifully relieved when it dawned on him that I was very far from the shadows of the gas chamber. That was all he could think of: that I wasn't guilty; that what he had done to me, through a serious error in judgment when he was my commanding officer, had not resulted in murder.

Now he had to think of something else. The old man was demanding an explanation. And Dave could only stand and squirm, stammer helplessly.

"Mr. Randall! Are you keeping something from me?"

"N-No, sir. I—I guess I was just a little excited, sir."

"Yes? I would not have said that you were an excitable type, Mr. Randall. Are you—uh—are the duties of your position too much for you? Would you like to step down for a time?"

I decided to intervene. Not, you understand, that I greatly minded Dave's squirming. The good colonel—he who had been so cocksure, so peremptory with his orders—would do much more squirming before I was finished with him. I intervened because it suited me. It was time to start taking the good from the bad.

"I believe I can explain, sir," I said. "We'll want the story for our first edition. I imagine Dave thought we'd better discuss the handling of it."

"Oh? Well, why didn't he say so, then? No reason to—*Story!*" He gulped, his eyes widening in a horrified double-take. "Did you say story, Mr. Brown? Surely, you don't plan on—"

"We'll have to, sir. This is one we won't be able to bury. It's another Black Dahlia case. The Los Angeles papers will give it a whopping play. It'll be a front-page story in every paper between here and L.A. We couldn't pass it up, even if we wanted to."

"*If* we wanted to? *If*, Mr. Brown? You know the policy of the *Courier*. A family paper for family people."

"If," I repeated, and Lem Stukey cleared his throat.

"Them other papers," he said. "They won't play up the story if there ain't one. We keep quiet about it here—call it an accident—and what are they gonna—"

"But it wasn't an accident," I said. "It was murder. And knowing Mr. Lovelace as I do, I feel certain that he will not blink at it. He will not hush it up, and thus leave unchanged the conditions that gave rise to the crime."

Lovelace's jaw sagged. Slowly he sank down on the lounge.

"I'm sorry, sir," I said. "I'm sure you must see that I am right."

"B-But the *Courier* . . . Pacific City! I just—Uh, what did you mean, Brown? About the conditions which gave rise to it?"

I didn't answer immediately. I poured a drink and pressed the glass into his hand, and he took it like a child taking candy. He swigged it, shuddered, and swigged again. I sat down and began talking.

Stukey scowled down at the floor. Dave listened, watching me curiously, but nodding occasionally at what I said.

". . . a very unhealthy situation here for some time, Mr. Lovelace. The sort of situation that breeds murder. Riff-raff drifting in from everywhere because of the climate. Thieves, pickpockets, prostitutes, confidence workers. Keep that—them—in mind, and then bear in mind that we have a large floating, tourist population, people with money and—"

"But—but I don't understand!" Lovelace frowned querulously at Lem. "Why have you allowed this, sir? Weren't you aware of these undesirables in our midst? What kind of chief of detectives do you call yourself?"

"As a matter of fact," I said, carefully, "Mr. Stukey has kept them under quite good control. But he's only one man, not the entire department. And I think we've made his job seem a pretty thankless one. There's been little or no recognition for work well done. There's been no incentive to give the city the wholesale housecleaning it needs."

"Incentive? Recognition?" He continued to frown at Stukey. "He draws a very handsome salary, as I recall. Why should he—?"

"Don't we all, sir? Don't we all need more than mere money? For that matter, we've had something worse here than a lack of incentive. There's not only been no encouragement to do something about local crime, there's been every encouragement to do nothing. I think you know what I mean, sir. You're sensitive about the good name of Pacific City. The police department knows it, as do we all. Naturally, the tendency has been to keep the lid on crime rather than to expose it and cast it out."

He didn't like that. Mr. Lovelace, need it be said, liked no criticism, either implied or direct. So, after letting him hang for a moment, I lifted him off the hook.

"Of course, I'm not excusing Mr. Stukey. In the final analysis, the fault is largely if not completely his. He chose the easy way out, the course of least resistance. After all, sir, it hasn't been exactly pleasant for me to lay these facts before you. But I felt that it was my duty to do it—I did not see how I could delay longer in view of tonight's happenings—and I knew that you, sir, regardless of your personal feelings, have nothing but respect and admiration for the man who does his duty."

He puffed up a little. Some of the sag went out of his shoulders. "Quite right, Mr. Brown. And—uh—thank you for the compliment. I hope, naturally, that the situation is not as bad as you believe. . . . What do you recommend?"

"Solving this murder," I said, "should be the first item on our agenda. At least, we should leave no stone unturned in trying to solve it. We want to serve notice to the world at large that murder is not taken lightly in Pacific City."

He sighed, hesitated, nodded firmly. "Yes, yes. By all means. . . . You, sir —Stukey, is it? What are you doing about this murder?"

"What murder?" Lem grunted, sullenly. "He says it's murder. I don't."

"How's that? Mr. Brown—?"

"Mr. Stukey is a conservative," I said. "He's jumped to the wrong conclusions a time or two and it's made him ultra cautious. I wish it were an accident, sir, but I'm sure you'll agree with me that it couldn't have been. . . ."

I explained the circumstances under which the body had been found, bearing down heavily on the wiped-away fingerprints. He nodded grimly, scowling at Stukey.

"Certainly it was murder, some mentally deranged person. . . . You don't agree, sir? You intend to persist in your quaint theory that—"

"I ain't overlooking any bets," said Lem, hastily. "I got the island boys workin' on the murder angle. I thought maybe—maybe I might have a line on the killer myself, but . . . but I'll keep 'em on it, Mr. Lovelace. We'll turn that place upside down."

"Well, I should think so!" snapped Lovelace. "An accident! What ever led you to think for a moment that—?"

"I was just tryin' to keep an open mind, Mr. Lovelace." Stukey was almost whining. "Like I said, I ain't passing up any bets."

Lovelace harrumphed angrily and glanced at me. I said I had complete confidence in Mr. Stukey's ability to handle the case. "I'm not sure that he needs or wants any suggestions from me, but—"

"Certainly he does! Why shouldn't he?"

"Well," I went on, "it seems to me that the two things tie in together—that is, the solving of the murder and the city-wide cleanup. I believe that every known or suspected criminal, every person who has no legitimate reason for his presence here, should be brought in and questioned. Probably the murderer will be among them. If not—well, we will have done our best. At any rate, as rapidly as the suspects are eliminated, they should be ordered out of the city and kept out."

"Excellent," said Lovelace firmly. "Is that all clear to you, Chief?"

Stukey hesitated, but only for a fraction of a second. Mr. Lovelace might be a fathead but you didn't say no to him in Pacific City when he asked for a yes.

"I got it," he said. "Me and Clint understand each other real well."

Mr. Lovelace stood up. He shook my hand again, then sauntered toward the door with his arm around my shoulder.

"I—uh—" He paused. "I—it has occurred to me that we have been rather inconsiderate here tonight. You have lost your—she was your wife, after all —and under such tragic circumstances. Yet we have allowed you to—we have called upon you to—"

"I am a *Courier* man," I said simply. "I have tried to act as I know you would have acted."

"I—uh—ahem—I am afraid you do me too much credit. In your case, I . . . Are you feeling entirely well? I was thinking that—uh—well, shock, you know. I would be happy to refer you to my own physician if—"

"Thank you, sir," I said, "but I believe the worst is now over. Now it is largely a matter of prayer, of consulting the spirit, of rising above personal tragedy into a newer and finer life."

"Well—uh—"

"Onward and upward," I said. "That is the answer, sir. My head in the clouds, my feet firmly on the ground."

I helped him into the car and closed the door. Dave took me by the arm, drew me away a few feet. "I'm sorry as hell, Brownie. I know how much— how you felt about her."

"A woman that wasn't my wife?" I said. "A youthful mistake? A floozy? A—"

"Brownie!"

"Yes, Colonel?"

"Is there anything at all—? Would you like to have me come back and stay tonight?"

"Why don't you?" I said. "We can talk over old times, our joyous carefree days in the army when—"

He let go my arm. He almost threw it away from him. Then he got a grip on himself and made one more try. "You did a swell job on Stukey, fellow. What you're doing—Ellen would have been proud of you."

"I wonder," I said. "I'll have to ask her the next time I see her."

"We'll get the guy who did it, Brownie! By God, we'll pour the coal on Stuke until—"

"Yes," I said, "we'll get him. Someone will get him."

"Well. . . . Think you'll make it all right? You wouldn't like to have me send out a doctor?"

"Send out a surgeon," I said. "I am heavily burdened and wouldst shed my balls."

He whirled and walked away.

I went back into the house. Lem Stukey had moved over to the lounge and was taking a drink from the bottle.

"Well, keed." He didn't seem particularly discomfited now. If anything, he appeared pleased, and I was confident I knew why. "It looks like we got to find ourselves a murderer, don't it?"

"Not necessarily," I said. "We, or rather you, have to look for one. You have to round up our local riffraff and eliminate them as suspects, also eliminating them from Pacific City."

"For nothin', huh? I drive all the easy dough out of town and I don't get nothin' out of it. That ain't reasonable, Brownie. I'm willing to play along with you—hell, don't I always go along with a pal? But you got to—"

"I don't got to," I said. "I've played along with you too long, Lem. Now I'm through."

"But why? You're sore about tonight? Jesus, pal, you can't blame me for—"

"I don't blame you. I'm not sore," I said. "Not in the way you mean. Something very bad has happened; that bad has to be offset. That's as close as I can come to explaining what I mean."

"And where do I come in? What do I get out of it?"

"Nothing more than you deserve. To put it succinctly, you do not get a murderer who is not one. You do not get some half-witted odd-job man and sap him into making a confession. It wouldn't work, Stuke, even if I were willing to let you do it. We know the murderer is someone of fairly high intelligence. You'd be laughed out of town if you tried to pin the job on one of your typical fall guys."

"Yeah?" His eyes glinted. "So suppose I hang it on some smart baby. Someone like you."

"You do that," I said, "and we'll discuss the matter again."

He stood up, slamming on his hat. He walked toward me slowly and I crossed my legs, bringing one foot up in line with his crotch. I hoped he would try something, but I was sure that he wouldn't.

He didn't.

"Look, Brownie. Don't you see what you're doin' to me, pal? It ain't just a matter of gettin' no credit—of knockin' myself out and losin' out on all the easy dough and not getting no credit for solving the murder. That's bad enough, but it ain't just that."

"No," I said, "it isn't just that."

"You see it, huh? If I don't get the murderer—"

"If you don't get the murderer, or, let us say, until you do get the murderer, you have to keep on looking for him. You won't be able to let things get back in the shape they've been in. Yes, I see that, Lem, and now that you see it I think you'd better leave."

He left, cursing. I waited until I heard him drive away, and then I got up and stood in the doorway a few minutes.

It had stopped raining about an hour before, and now the moon had come out and a few stars, and the air was clean and balmy. I stood drinking it in in long deep breaths. I turned and craned my neck, looking in at the kitchen clock. It was only one, a few minutes after one. It seemed like years had passed since—

And it was only a little after one.

I closed and locked the door. I went into the bedroom and turned on the light. I came back and turned off the living-room light. I started back into the bedroom. I went a few steps and then I dropped down on the lounge and began to cry.

About nothing, really; I suppose you would call it nothing. Certainly not over a problem. How can one cry over a problem? Or an answer—if there was an answer? I cried because—Just because, as kids cry, as she had used to cry. . . .

Because things were a certain way, and that's the way they were.

# VIII

AFTER A WHILE I got up and went into the kitchen. I cracked four eggs into a glass, filled the glass with whisky, and tossed them down. I stood very still for a moment, swallowing fast, letting them get anchored. When I was sure they were going to stick, I took another drink and lighted a cigarette.

Another long time had passed, at least ten years. But the clock said twenty minutes of two. I refilled my glass with whisky and began cleaning the kitchen.

There was not a great deal to be done since the soot is more or less ineradicable and my meals at home are confined largely to eggs, milk, and coffee. But I did what little there was to do: scrubbing the sink, wiping off the drainboard and stove, sweeping the floor, and so on. I put the egg shells into the garbage pail and carried it out to the incinerator. I lingered a minute or two after dumping it, looking down at the railroad tracks. I often stand there at night, on the bluff overlooking the tracks, watching the trains go by, wondering if it wouldn't be better to . . .

But the last train for the night had passed more than two hours ago. The last one was the "milk" train—a combination freight and passenger that left Pacific City at eleven-thirty and loafed into Los Angeles some seven hours later. There wouldn't be another train until six forty-five.

I went back into the house and returned the garbage pail to its container. I filled my glass again and went to work on the living-room.

I cleaned it up—two-fifteen.

I cleaned up the bedroom—two thirty-five.

I made a stab at cleaning the bathroom (that part of the house that I have made into a bathroom)—two forty-three.

I had put a big pan of water on the kitchen stove and lighted a couple of burners under it. When it had heated, I carried it into the bathroom, climbed upon the ancient cast-iron stool, and, reaching upward and outward, dumped it into a five-gallon can that rested on a shelf near the ceiling.

I undressed and stepped under the can. I pulled a rope and the water rained down from a nozzle in the bottom of the can.

I put some clothes back on and mopped up the bathroom.

I finished at seven minutes after three. And I had never been more wide awake in my life.

Obviously it was time for stern measures. I took them—two full glasses, one behind the other.

I went to sleep then. Or, I should say, I lost consciousness. I didn't come out of it until a little after seven when the phone started ringing.

I sat up and looked at it. I mumbled what the hell and cut it out, for God's sake, and it went right on ringing. I rubbed my eyes and reached for the whisky. The bottle was empty, so I went out into the kitchen and opened another one. I came back into the living-room and sat down on the floor in front of the phone. I slugged down a few drinks, lighted a cigarette, and eased the receiver off the hook.

I shouted "HELLO" at the top of my lungs.

I heard a clatter at the other end of the line, then someone breathing heavily. The someone was Dave Randall.

"Brownie . . . hello, hello, Brownie!"

"Don't yell so loud," I said. "It hurts my ears, Colonel."

"I hated like hell to bother you, Clint, but—can you come down for a while?"

"Come down? You mean to work?"

"Don't do it if you don't feel up to it, but I'm shorthanded as hell. I've got three people working out of the police station—our friend Stukey is really bearing down on this clean-up campaign—and what with Tom Judge off sick I—"

"*He's* sick," I said. "I hope it's something serious?"

"It will be," Dave promised, "when I get hold of him. His wife called in to the switchboard this morning before I got down. I've been trying to call him back, but I haven't been able to raise anyone at their place. . . . How about it, Brownie? If you could just lend a hand for a couple of hours, just until some of the people in society and sports show up. . . ."

I let him wait while I took a drink. Then I said, "Well, I'll tell you, Colonel. I am a true-blue *Courier* man; I flinch from neither rain nor sleet nor Chamber of Commerce luncheons, but—"

"Never mind. Sorry to have bothered you," he said, "Take it easy and—Oh, yes. Brownie? Are you still there?"

"Yours to command, Colonel. Up to a point."

"I thought you'd want to know. They've got a red-hot clue to the murderer."

"So soon?" I said. "I think I'd better have a little talk with Mr. Stukey."

"He isn't pulling anything this time, Clint. It's the real thing. You know how those Golden Eagle cottages sit up on posts? Don't have any real foundation under them?"

"Y-No. I've never been around the island much."

"Well, some guy was crawling around under them last night. The cops figure that he may have been hurt when he—when he was struggling with her and crawled under there to pull himself together. Or perhaps he was just too scared or drunk to know what he was doing. Anyway, it looks like he must have been there not too long after the murder."

"Why does it look like that?"

"Why? Well, because of the imprint of his body, his hands and knees. They picked up several almost perfect handprints."

"How do they know they were made last night?"

"Because there wouldn't be any imprints, otherwise. Last night was the first time it's rained in weeks. There's a little seepage under the cottages and— Look, Brownie, I can't talk any longer now. I'll call you back the first chance I get."

"Don't bother," I said. "On second thought, I think I'll come down."

I hung up the phone. I sat there cross-legged on the floor, staring blankly into the black perforations of the mouthpiece as I reached for the bottle.

I tried to remember and, as I had last night, I drew a blank. I was bending over her. Then I was at the boat. And in between there was nothing.

My clothes . . . ? No, all that water would have washed them clean in seconds. I couldn't remember, and there was no way I could find out. The finding out would have to be done by someone else.

Thinking, or rather, trying to think, I put coffee on the stove and went into the bathroom to shave.

I didn't believe I had crawled around under there. Surely, or so it seemed to me, I would not have wiped away my fingerprints only to leave a much broader clue. Then there was the matter of time. I had no recollection of events between my setting the fire and my arrival at the boat, but I did have a very strong impression that they were but briefly separated.

I hadn't done it. I was sure—almost—that I hadn't. It had been someone else. *But why would anyone else?* Probably some drunk had wandered out of a bar, or been tossed out, and he had holed up under the cottages for a snooze. He'd awakened when the cops arrived; he'd heard the ruckus and decided it would be a damned good idea to take a powder. And—

That was what had happened. I hoped.

I got cleaned up, and went into the kitchen. I poured whisky into an outsize cup and filled it with coffee.

I leaned against the sink, sipping it, taking an occasional long look at my hands. What I don't know about criminology would fill a five-hundred-foot bookshelf, but I'd learned at least one thing in my police-beat years: leaving or picking up a recognizable set of fingerprints is not as simple or easy as it is reputed to be. I talked to a detective one time who, on one of his off days, dusted and picked up prints throughout his five-room house. He didn't get one of himself or his wife or their two kids that would have served to identify them. This under so-called favorable conditions.

In mud, now, in anything as coarse as earth . . . Well, there might be handprints, but fingerprints—huh-uh. I didn't think so. . . . I hoped not.

If Stukey had picked up a decent set of prints, even one good fingerprint, I'd have heard about it. By now, he'd have been printing me. Unless, of course, he was afraid of what I would do if he was wrong and he intended to do it casually. That would be Stukey's way, no doubt. To build the thing up big, and himself with it, then, say, to invite me to have a drink from a nice clean glass.

It was strange the way I felt. I hadn't given a damn for years, not a good goddamn whether I lived or not. And last night I had sort of tried to get the whole meaningless mess over with. I had taken a hands-off attitude in a gone-to-hell situation, and I had gone to hell and come right out again. And now I cared. Now I wanted to live. I wanted to badly enough to be afraid.

I turned the matter over in my mind, examining my emotions, probing their perverse strangeness, and, need it be said, consulting frequently with the whisky bottle. And so, gradually, I became clear-eyed and keen, and I could see my feelings for what they were—not abnormal but normal. Normal to a degree which, where I was concerned, would never do.

But there was no cause for alarm. I had known such feelings in the past, and down through the years their duration had become increasingly brief. They were in the wrong soil. They bloomed and withered almost simultaneously. I cared, yes, but only about a game, only about a problem, not about living or dying. It was an interesting game—the one interest without which there would be emptiness. And I wanted to win; I wanted to make *them* lose. But it was nothing to become fear-sick about.

Let them worry. With me it was only a game.

The old two-way pull began to assert itself. I headed for town, sitting very straight and circumspectly in the car seat but moving sidewise, mentally. Moving off to one side, off into a world known only to me, where I could see *them* without being seen.

Just a game. That was all I could win or lose. That was all *I* could do.

I parked the car in front of the Press Club and went upstairs. Jake, the officer of the day, was at his post. We went through maneuvers. We held close order drill ending with a barrage. I stood back from the bar and we saluted.

"All secured, officer?"

"All secured, sir!"

"An excellent patrol," I said. "Everything is shipshape, jim-dandy, and crackerjack, and I hereby decorate you with the highest order of the land, the most coveted of awards, the—"

"On the house," he said, and he shoved my money back. "Look, Mr. Brown, maybe it ain't none of my business but shouldn't you be—"

I brought him to attention with a crisp command. I marched out and proceeded to the *Courier.*

Dave Randall hadn't exaggerated his need for help. He had taken a typewriter over to the city desk and was trying to do rewrite and his own job. The only regular rewrite man he had was Pop Landis. And Pop, nice guy that he was, was slow as all hell, and he was more than swamped with the running story of the murder and the crime clean-up.

I took his carbons off the hook and sat down at my desk. I began to read, briefing myself to take over, stopping now and then to write some minor but "must" story.

They had handled Ellen as delicately as they could without distorting the facts. Our relationship was barely mentioned. The dirt would fly in the out-of-town papers, but here the emphasis was all on the murderer and the consequent criminal roundup.

I skimmed through the dupes . . . *long-estranged wife of Courier reporter, Clinton Brown . . . burial to be in Los Angeles . . . death attributed to asphyxiation . . .*

Asphyxiation? I read back through that part again, somehow glad that it had been that way.

*. . . painfully but by no means critically burned, according to the coroner's office. The relatively minor nature of the burns, coupled with the fact that the mattress was almost completely consumed, indicates that Mrs. Brown must have revived soon after the maniac's departure. Panic-stricken and dazed, she was unable to find her way out of the smoke-filled cottage before succumbing to . . .*

It was surmised that the murderer (for reasons best known to himself) had crawled about beneath the cottages. There were handprints, kneeprints, elbowprints (no mention of fingerprints). There was the imprint of his body, where he had apparently lain prone . . .

I paused. My heart did a small flip-flop—strictly, of course, because of the excitement of the game. I looked down at the typewritten page again. I read . . . and sighed with relief. *About five feet seven inches tall and rather heavy-set . . . shoes, approximately size eight. . . .*

It wasn't me, then. Not by more than five inches and two and a half sizes. There was no way it could be twisted into being me. And whoever it was— some stumblebum, doubtless—he was safe; he wouldn't suffer for what I had done. Stukey would never find him. He didn't know enough about the guy, and what he did know fitted too many people.

I'd been working less than an hour when Mr. Lovelace came in. He gave me a startled look, then passed on by. He said something indistinguishable but obviously sharp to Dave Randall, and Dave followed him into his office.

He came out after about five minutes and scuttled over to my desk. Red-faced, almost cringing, he told me to beat it. "Right now, Brownie. The old man gnawed me out to a fare-thee-well. I knew it was a hell of a bad thing to have you come in to work right after—to handle a story about it. But I didn't know who the hell else to—"

"I would have been grieved," I said, "if you had not called me. I am wed to my work and stand ready at all times to do my husbandly duty, and I shall so inform—"

"Don't! For God's sake, Clint, just get out of here. If you want to do something, go out and see if you can get hold of Tom Judge. Tell him I said by God to get in here, and do it fast."

"Suppose he is locked in nuptial bliss with his wife? Do I have the colonel's permission to—"

"Brownie! Please!"

I stood up and slid my coat off the back of my chair, put it on, and picked up my hat. I—

I don't know what prompted me to say it; perhaps something in Pop's stories jogged my memory. Or, perhaps, it was the constant jangling of the telephones. I don't know why, but I said, "By the way, Colonel, did you talk to—did Ellen call in here yesterday?"

"Not that I know of. Why?"

"No reason." I shrugged. "She usually did call as soon as she hit town."

"Well, she didn't call yesterday to my knowledge. No one said anything about it. Why don't you ask Bessie?"

"I'll do that," I said, but I didn't do it.

I left the city room, walking right on past the cubicle where Bessie and her switchboard sat. I didn't want Bessie's memory jogged. I wanted her to forget that Ellen had called and that the call had been answered.

It was evidence, you see. Or, rather, it would be evidence if the person who had talked to Ellen could not satisfactorily explain his whereabouts on the night before. And little as I liked Tom Judge . . .

# IX

LEM STUKEY'S OFFICE was so crowded that I could hardly get in the door. He had two secretaries answering telephones; he was surrounded by reporters, our boys and those who had flown in from out of town; a dozen-odd cops and detectives milled around his desk. Being Lem, of course, with an eye ever to the main angle, he spotted me at once. And he pushed his way through the crowd and grabbed me by the hand.

"Jesus, keed, I'm glad to see you. Been thinkin' about giving you a ring, but. . . . Let's get out of here, huh?"

He propelled me across the hall into an unoccupied jury room. He closed the door and leaned against it, mopping his brow with exaggerated dismay. "You ever see anything like that in there, pal? I ask you now, ain't that something?"

"Let me ask you," I said.

"You mean you ain't heard the news yet? I figured the boys at the *Courier* would be keepin' you—"

"I've heard, but it doesn't look like something yet. It looks like the old giant economy-size frammis. The old hoop-tee-do with a full year's supply of hot air. Any minute now you'll be announcing that you expect to make an arrest within twenty-four hours."

"Uh-uh. It's going to take me a little longer than that."

"Why should it? I can spot you fifty medium-sized, heavy-set guys of no specific age or coloring in five minutes."

"Pally"—he gave me a placating tap on the arm—"you sit right down there, huh? That's the keed. Now, you're still sore, ain't you? I jumped you last night. I tried to push you around, and—"

"And you got pushed around," I said. "And I'm not sore."

"I'm apologizin', Brownie. Let a guy apologize, won't you? I was all wrong, and whatever you handed me I had comin'. Jesus, I'd have been sore myself. A guy's wife gets killed, and the first he hears about it someone's tryin' to pin it on him."

"All right." I sighed. "I was sore. You've apologized. Now, all is forgiven and we love one another like brothers."

"You ain't just a-woofin', keed!" He nodded firmly. "Jesus, it almost makes me shiver when I think how I almost missed out on this. And I would have missed out on it if it hadn't been for you. If you hadn't've thrown the old hooks into me, I—"

"What have you got?" I said. "Just, by God, what have you got, anyway? Nothing. A bum crawls under those cottages to get out of the rain and—"

"Huh-uh. A bum with good shoes and a full suit of clothes? Huh-uh. Anyway, you don't find no bums over on the island. It takes a buck to get over and back on the ferry, and there ain't nothin' over there for them without dough."

"So it wasn't a bum, then. Just some guy who'd had too much to drink."

"That I'll buy. He—Now, wait a minute, keed." He held up a hand. "Let me give you the whole picture. You got a right to know and I'm goin' to give it to you. But under the hat, get me? I don't want to tip the guy off."

"You mean you picked up some fingerprints?"

"Fingerprints? What gave you that idea?"

"Nothing. Go on," I said.

"First of all—well, we done it last but I'll give it to you first—we raked the island from one end to the other. We went over that place with a—uh—"

"Fine-tooth comb?"

"Yeah, a fine-tooth comb, and we didn't turn the guy up, so we know he came over on this side. Okay. Now, get this. The ferry didn't begin running until ten-thirty last night; it didn't start back here with a load until ten-thirty. Then it didn't make another run until one in the morning, when it made its last trip of the day. Well, that last trip—"

"Let's skip the last one," I said. "The roundup was on by that time. The passengers were all checked and cleared before they were allowed to get on board."

"Right. Right on the nose. So that put our boy on the ten-thirty ferry. . . . Now, wait a minute, keed. I know what you're going to say: There was plenty of people waitin' to get back to this side, two hundred and four of 'em according to the ferry receipts, and you're going to say that stops us. But it don't, Brownie. It don't make it nearly as tough as it sounds. First you rule the women out. Then you rule out the couples. That cuts the total down to maybe sixty or seventy, just the stags."

"Which is still," I said, "no small number of people."

"Did I say no? But it don't look so tough no more, does it? Let me give you the rest of it. . . . We checked the hotels. The guy didn't show at any of 'em. We checked the buses and trains. He didn't leave town. We checked the bay-side parking lots. He didn't pick up a car—"

"He could still have had one. He could have parked on the street."

"Not near the ferry, not unless he wanted to walk three blocks. And a guy on a party wouldn't do that to save four bits. . . . That leaves us the streetcars and taxicabs. The streetcars—well, that's kind of a toughie. We got to work from the fare zones, maybe check out whole neighborhoods. I say we got to, but I don't think we actually will. The guy's soaking wet. Everyone on the ferry was. He wouldn't want to screw around with no streetcars. I figure—"

"What about walking?"

"Well"—Stukey frowned grudgingly—"maybe. But it ain't very likely. It was pouring down rain. He'd be afraid of being picked up. . . . No, I think the taxis is where we'll get him. O' course, he probably didn't get out right at his house. And maybe he didn't go home right away. But—"

"In other words," I said, "if you check everyone in Pacific City, you may find him."

"Now, it ain't that bad," he protested. "It's going to take some time, sure, but we can do it."

"And after you do, then what? What have you got?"

"I got a killer. I got a guy that's got some goddamned tall explaining to do if he ain't a killer."

"And you'll have some to do. You're asking for it, Stukey. You're setting yourself up for the town's number one horse's ass."

He looked at me, puzzled. Still looking at me, he took out a cigar and lighted it, took a slow, thoughtful puff.

"I guess I don't dig you, keed. We been knockin' ourselves out on this. I thought you'd be tickled pink."

"Well"—I forced a laugh—"I appreciate it, of course, but if it doesn't lead to anything. . . . You said yourself the guy was probably some drunk."

"He probably had a load on. It's pretty hard to hang around the island without taking on a load. But being' drunk don't make him innocent; it's a hell of a lot more likely to make it the other way. A crazy killing like this, it's just the kind of a thing—"

"But there's so damned many loose ends, Stuke. The poem and—well—"

"So what? We just forget him because we can't dope it all out?"

"No, of course not. But—"

"Yeah?" His head was cocked to one side; his voice was a little too smooth. "Is that what you're sayin', pal? You want us to lay off the only hot lead we got?"

I laughed again, making it sound fretful and tired and jibing. "I guess I'm just not my usual cheery self today, Stuke. I'm not thinking like a *Courier* man. My ass is dragging, and the compass is pointing south."

"Well, sure. I can understand that. But—"

"Frankly," I said, "I think that seeing you engaged in honest work has thrown me into a state of shock. You have stunned me, Stuke. Such industry, such brilliance in one whose chief activity heretofore has been—"

He grinned, chuckled, and the puzzled look went out of his eyes. "That's the old keed. That's the old Brownie boy. . . . All foolin' aside, though, pal, I'm doin' all right, huh? You got any suggestions, you just say so."

"I wouldn't think of giving you any," I said. "You're doing too well by yourself." I meant every word of it. I didn't have the slightest doubt that he would catch the guy.

He hooked his thumbs in his vest, trying to suppress a smirk of pleasure.

"I got a hunch on this one, keed. I'd lay a case against a cork that he's our killer."

"Maybe. You may be right. But I imagine you'll have a hard time proving it."

"Huh-uh. A guy like that wouldn't be a pro. He wouldn't make you prove it. All we got to do is grab him and sweat him, and he'll cave in like a whore's mattress."

"That sweating," I said. "I would be very, very careful about that, Stuke."

"Am I crazy?" He leaned forward earnestly. "I got a plateful of gravy, and I spit in it? Not me, pal. Strictly legit, that's me. You put me on the right track, and I'm ridin' it clean to the end of the line. Incidentally, Brownie—"

"Yes?"

"I'll see that you get the story first. You personally. I'll keep the guy under wraps until—"

"You don't need to do that," I said.

"Don't need to? Hell, ain't we pals? Didn't you—" He broke off abruptly, blinking at me. Then his lips stretched in a slow, surprised grin. "Well, say, now! I—"

"That's right. If you get this man and if he is the killer, you can write your own ticket, right on up to and including county judge. I couldn't stand in your way if I wanted to."

He was in a generous mood. Moreover, I suspect, he was not at all sure that I wouldn't be of use to him. So he declared that purely out of friendship he would still see that I got first crack at the story. "Just because I love you, keed. But don't let out nothin' I told you this morning. If the killer got wind of it, it might blow the whole deal."

"I won't tell a soul," I promised. "In fact, it has suddenly dawned on me that I don't know any souls."

He snickered and said that was the keed, the old Brownie boy.

"Do you know any souls, Stuke? They don't have to be anything fancy. Just a good old-fashioned soul who would like to go steady with a badly frazzled id."

"The keed," he said, a trifle impatiently. "The ol' Brownie boy. Be seein' you, pal."

I left the police station and bought a fifth of whisky. Then I headed my car toward Tom Judge's house.

He lived in the corner house of a block-long double row of identical structures, all four rooms, all painted brown, all tar-paper-roofed with a little tin chimney near the back and another up front. Back when I was a youngster, and not a very young youngster, we called these affairs shotgun houses, and they rented for about twelve dollars a month. Tom's rent was ninety-five, which was just a little less than half his take-home pay.

The phone was ringing as I stepped upon the porch, and dimly, apparently in the rear of the house, a baby was crying. I knocked and the crying stopped abruptly. Then, after a moment or two, the ringing stopped also.

I knocked again, long and loudly. I tried to open the screen. It was locked. The shades at the window and door were drawn. I leaned back against the porch rail, opened the bottle, and slugged down a stiff one.

It was the first drink I'd had since my morning patrol and it refreshed me wonderfully. I bought two more and then, of course, accepted one on the house. I left the porch, walked around to the rear, and pounded on the back door.

The baby cried again. For a split second. Otherwise silence.

I took a drink. I drew back my foot and kicked the door as hard as I could. It flew open and I walked in.

# X

MRS. JUDGE WAS standing in a corner near the stove, holding the baby to her breast. She wasn't twenty-five, I knew, but she looked ten years older. Flat-chested, unhealthily fat through the hips, thin-necked. You don't live very high on the hog when you're married to a semi-incompetent reporter on a small-city newspaper. You age fast.

Her face was made up, her hair was in curlers, and both jobs had obviously been done in a hurry. She looked at me trembling, wide-eyed. I gave her a reassuring smile and looked at Tom.

An open trunk stood on the kitchen floor. He had been packing it, and he was still holding an armful of clothing. Slowly he let it drop, and his mouth opened and closed silently.

"Going somewhere?" I said.

"N-No. N-No, Brownie." He gulped and shook his head. "J-Just s-storing a f-few—"

He wanted to act sore; he knew he should. But he just wasn't up to it. He looked haunted, as gray-pale as a sheet of copy paper.

"I—I—" He gulped again. "I heard about your wife, Brownie. M-Midge and I h-heard it over the radio, and I'm s-sure s-sor—"

"Easy," I said. "Just take it real easy. You've not been particularly fond of me. The feeling has been reciprocated. But this is a friendly visit. Now, how about a drink?"

"I—I d-don't—"

I uncapped the bottle and pushed it at him. "Take it," I said. "Take a big one."

"You take it, Tom." Mrs. Judge spoke for the first time, giving me a half-defiant look. "Tom doesn't drink much. He's not used to drinking. He—he-he—"

"I know," I said. "Your drink, Tom."

He almost snatched the bottle from my hands. He tilted it thirstily, gagged and shivered, and thrust it back at me. A little—a very little—of his usual belligerent assertiveness returned.

"Well, Brownie"—he hiccuped—"I know you're probably upset about your wife, but that's no reason to—"

"Friendly," I said. "I said it, and I meant it. I'm here to ask you some questions and give you some answers."

"Yeah? You are, huh? What makes you think—?"

"Maybe you don't want to. But I think you'd better listen before you make up your mind."

He hesitated, looked at his wife. Her eyes moved to my face and her lips began to tremble. "He's good," she said. "Y-You—he's told me about you! He t-tries so hard, h-he works twice as hard as you do, a-and—all you can do is make fun of him! H-He—I—it's your fault! Y-You can p-play around and everything is s-so easy for you, and h-he—"

"No," I said. "No, it isn't easy for me, Mrs. Judge."

"It is! He told me how it is! You make fun of him because it's easy for you and—And you can blow in all your money on yourself, and all he can do is —is—" Her voice broke and she began to sob.

Tom said, "Midge, honey. You shouldn't—"

I said, "It's all right. I understand how Mrs. Judge feels; I think I understand how you've felt. But I'm trying to be your friend now."

She brushed her nose against her arm and gave the baby a little pat. She looked from me to him and nodded. "You talk to him, Tom. You take another drink."

Then she shuffled out of the room and elbowed the door shut behind her. I sat down at the table and he sank down across from me. I had a drink. I waited until he had taken one.

"All right," I said. "Here's the first question. My wife called the office yesterday afternoon. You talked to her. What was the substance of your conversation?"

"W-What—what makes you think—?"

"She always called as soon as she got in town. She didn't talk to anyone else or they'd have told me about it. Your desk is right across from mine. You'd have answered my phone."

"B-But—but I'm not always there!"

"She'd have kept ringing until she got an answer. And if she hadn't got one she'd have called the city desk."

He stared down at the cracked oilcloth of the table, his fingers fumbling at the pocket of his shirt. I took out my cigarettes, put one in his mouth, and held a match for him.

"I'm not sore, Tom," I said. "If I were sore I wouldn't be sitting here. And you wouldn't be either—very long."

"W-What?" His head snapped up. "What do you mean?"

"You know what I mean. But let's take it from the beginning. You talked to her. You got her to give you the number of her cottage. Then you told her I was gone for the day, and you suggested something to the effect that you would be happy to take my place."

His dull, chubby face reddened and he spread his hands. "Brownie, I—I— Christ, what can I say?"

"It's all right. You behaved quite normally. You haven't had much of what passes for good times. No later than yesterday morning I'd called you a lousy newspaperman and a son-of-a-bitch. Why not put one over on me through the pleasant medium of laying my wife?"

He shook his head miserably. "Brownie, it—that's not quite—"

"It's close enough. What did she say to the proposition?"

"Well . . . she didn't really say anything. She just sort of laughed."

"And you construed that as an invitation? Go on."

"Go—go on?"

"Spill it. Tell me all. Go and on. A phrase meaning to proceed."

I felt sorry for him, responsible for him. But he didn't need to make it twice as tough as it was by acting like a Piltdown moron.

"You went over to the island," I said. "Take it from there and keep going."

"I . . . well, I went over around four. A little after four, I guess it was. A little while before the storm started. It was still light then, of course, and I didn't want to—to go down there yet, so I stopped in a bar. I had a couple of drinks and—"

"Did you see anyone you knew?"

"Huh-uh. I mean, I don't think there was anyone there that knew me. I didn't talk to anyone or. . . . Well, it started raining, pouring down, but drinks were awfully high in there and someone said the ferry had stopped running and I didn't know quite what to do. I'd been kind of nerving myself up. I'd got to thinking about how crazy this was—me with a wife and kid, and you, a guy I worked with—how it might get me in all kinds of trouble. And—and I'd just about decided to drop it. I mean it, Brownie! If the ferry had been running or if I'd had enough dough to hang around there in the bar, I—Jesus, Jesus! Why couldn't it have been that way? Why—"

"I wonder," I said. "Go on, Tom."

"There wasn't anything else to do, so I did it. I bought a fifth at the bar—tequila, the cheapest thing they had. Then I went down to her cottage. I figured we'd—well, we'd just drink and talk and as soon as the storm was over. . . . All right, all right"—he paused and sighed—"go ahead and laugh."

"That was a grimace," I said, "of unadulterated pain."

"Yeah? Well, anyway, I guess you know what happened. She wouldn't let me in. She bawled hell out of me, said I'd taken a hell of a lot for granted, and slammed the door in my face. I—God, Brownie, it wasn't right! If she hadn't wanted me to come, she ought to have said so. She shouldn't have laughed and acted like, well, it would be all right."

"Very few of us," I said, "behave as well as we should. Perhaps you've noticed that. . . . I take it that, having no other refuge, you retired beneath the cottages?"

"Yeah, hell. What a mess. Soaking wet and damned near broke, and I had to lay under there like a goddamned rat or something. Couldn't even sit up straight, and it wasn't a hell of a lot dryer under there than it was outside.

I kept crawling around, trying to find a dry spot. I guess most of those places were empty but there was one—well, you could hear the bed going up and down, and then the people getting up and going to the bathroom and—and —And me under there like a rat. Like a goddamned drowned rat. You—I guess it wouldn't have meant anything to you, Brownie. But—hell, what difference does it make? I opened up the tequila and started hitting it. I kept pouring it down, I was so damned miserable and wet and.. . . . All at once I went out like a light. It was just like something had hit me over the head.

"I don't know how long I was out. I came to all of a sudden and I couldn't figure out where I was. I was scared as hell, and I heard someone pounding and a bunch of guys calling back and forth. And I could see flashlights shooting around on the ground. I remembered where I was then and that really chilled me. All I could think of was that the place was being raided and what the hell I was going to say if they found me. I crawled up to the end where the street was, and then I ran across into that little park and—I don't know where all I did go. It was still so damned dark and raining so hard. I think I passed out a couple of times. Then—I don't know how long it was, but finally I heard the ferry whistle and I cut down to the landing. There was a big crowd there, and they were all wet, too—I mean they'd got pretty wet in the rain and most of 'em were stiff or half stiff from hanging around the bars all evening. I squeezed onto the ferry with 'em and went straight down to the john. I was down there in one of the stalls, having a few drinks when—"

"You'd kept the tequila with you then? That's good."

"Yeah, I'd held onto it somehow. So I thought I'd got out of the mess without any real trouble, and I was trying to pull myself together when these two guys came in. Boat hands, they were. They were talking about a woman being killed over in the cottages, and—and I didn't think about it being her b-but, God, I'd been there and I'd been crawling all around and—and—And then I got home and Midge and I turned on the radio, and—"

"How did you get home?"

"I took a taxi—all but the last five blocks. I only had sixty cents, see, so I rode out fifty cents' worth and gave the driver a dime tip and walked the rest of the way."

"You didn't give him your address?"

"No. I just had him head up Main and down Laurel until the meter showed four bits, and then I got out."

That was good in a way and bad in a way. The driver didn't know where he'd gone, but he'd remember him. And a neighborhood like this, particularly a neighborhood like this, would receive a thorough going-over by Stukey's boys.

"Y-You—" Two big tears were in the corners of his eyes. "I've t-told you the God's truth, Brownie. I d-don't need to—You know I didn't kill her, don't you?"

"Yes, Tom," I said. "I know you didn't kill her."

"B-But they think I did! They've got evidence! They know I was there. They know what I look like. They—"

"They don't," I said. "Get me? They don't. They know a guy of about your build and size was there, but that's all they know."

"That's all they need! That cab driver and knowing what I look like and—! I've got to get away, Brownie! It's the only thing I can do!"

"It's the one thing you can't do," I said. "They'll be watching the trains and buses. If you did manage to get out of town, they'd trail you down. You'd be hanging a sign on yourself."

"B-But—"

"The cab driver will be mistaken, if and when they turn you up. It'll be your word against his. Yours and. . . . What about your wife? She knows about this? She'd swear that you were at home all evening?"

"S-She—" His voice dropped to a whisper. "She knows. S-She'd swear to it. But—"

"Good. That'll be good enough. You both stick to that story and there's not a damned thing they can do. They'll try to, of course, if they find you. . . ." If, hell! They'd find him, all right, but I didn't want him any more frightened than he was. "Just deny everything and keep denying, and they'll have to let you go."

He lifted the bottle, slowly set it down untasted.

"I—I d-don't think I can do it, Brownie. They get to questioning me and—"

"You've got to. Once they place you on that island at the time of the murder, once they get you to admit you saw her, that she refused to let you in and you laid around under those cottages drinking—"

"I know. Jesus!" He shivered. "It's all I've been thinking about. They'll think I was sore at her. They'll think I hung around to—to—"

"Right. So you do what I told you to do. Don't admit a damned thing."

"B-But—but they'll get me all tangled up! I . . . I don't think I can take it!"

"How about the gas chamber? Can you take that?"

He buried his face in his arms and began to sob. I watched him for a minute and then I reached across the table, grabbed him by the hair, and jerked his head up.

"Now, listen to me," I said. "You didn't kill her and you're not going to let anyone talk you into thinking you did. You're absolutely safe. A rough seventy-two hours is the worst they can give you. That's all, and then it's over. You can take it. I know you can. *Know* it, Tom; get me? If I didn't think so, I wouldn't say it!"

He tried to work up a smile, not much of one, but it was a large improvement on blubbering. "Y-You're swell, Brownie. You really think I can—?"

"Didn't I say so? Now, get yourself shaved and whatever else you have to do, and come on with me. I'll drop you off at the office."

"Office? Oh, God, no, Brownie. Not to—"

"Yes, to the office. They need you. It looks bad to lay off." I stood up and pulled him up. "Get moving. You can tell the colonel your phone's been out of order if he gives you any guff. He'll probably be so glad to have some help he won't say anything."

It was like pulling teeth to get him started, and even after we were in the car and on our way downtown he kept on arguing and pleading, begging to be let off. He "just couldn't do it" and "everyone would know" and "I'm s-sick, Brownie" and so on, until I almost decided to take him home and let come what might. Not because I was irritated by him—although I was—but because I was afraid my efforts were being wasted. For if he had no more stamina than this, if he behaved this way now, he wouldn't hold out five minutes against Stukey. He'd cave in right away, and since that was the case . . .

But perhaps he would stiffen up; perhaps, given a day or so, he would become his usual resentful self, a man dedicated to the proposition that what was demanded of him should automatically be withheld. Perhaps the very arrogance and in-turned sullenness that had got him into this mess would get him out of it. It seemed logical that it would. Fate would have to be very cruel indeed to reform his dully dogged spirit now.

So I resisted his begging. I gave him drink for his stomach and steady pep talk for his nerves, and if the bottle was exhausted—and it was—by the time we arrived at the *Courier* building, it had nothing at all on me.

Sighing heavily, Tom opened the door and slowly eased one foot out to the curb. He hesitated, then suddenly turned around again.

"Brownie. I—"

"No," I said. "No, no, no, no! Think of the brave little woman. Think of the wee kiddie. And drag yourself to hell upstairs!"

"I'm going, Brownie. But I may not see you again and you've been so swell—"

I groaned. I removed my hat and slapped myself on the forehead.

He frowned slightly, but he didn't budge. "It's about Dave. He's always been nice enough to me, and you—well, you know how you've been. But things are different now. Maybe Dave's never done anything against me, but you've done plenty for me. We're on the same side, and anyone that's got it in for you—"

"Got it in for me?" I said. "Not that there is anything serious in my sniping at the colonel—the colonel understands my playful nature—but aren't you just a little confused?"

"I know." He nodded. "You're all the time riding him, and maybe you've been asking for it. But that doesn't cut any ice with me. You start noticing him, Brownie. Notice how he'll load you up—try to swamp you with work—when he's got other guys doing nothing. And he's always getting you out of the office, shooting you out on assignments. He doesn't want you around where you can shine up to the old man. He's jealous and—"

I stopped him. Strangely, or perhaps not so strangely, I was angered by what he said.

Dave was my own particular little target, and I wasn't going to have anyone else tossing darts at him. They had no reason to; there was such a thing as being fair. If Dave kept me loaded with work, it was because of the high percentage of incompetent staffers such as Tom Judge. If he tried to keep me out of Mr. Lovelace's way, it was because of a well-warranted fear that I might do or say something irreparably embarrassing.

I said as much, in a properly oblique way.

"I want to set you straight on this, Tom," I said firmly. "Dave would be the last person in the world to do anything to harm me. He's so constructed that he'd feel strongly responsible for any misfortune I suffered. I know; he's proved it. Every time I've lost a job he's quit also and hired me on at his next paper."

"Maybe he was afraid not to. You might have hung around drinking and needling him, giving him so much trouble he'd get fired himself."

I wouldn't have done that. Dave wouldn't have had to put up with it if I had done it. All he would have had to do was reveal a certain secret, and I would never have shown my face in another newspaper office. . . . Of course, if he did reveal it—

It was as though Tom were reading my mind, reading a thought that had never been there until now.

"It's none of my business, Brownie—but you got something on him? I mean, did he pull a bad boner somewhere or—"

I shook my head, to myself as well as him. A boner, yes, but there'd been hundreds and thousands of boners, and the war was a long time over. It was simply a mistake. No culpability had attached to it then, and certainly none could now.

Dave had nothing to fear from me. He put up with me only because of his own stricken conscience. Naturally, he didn't want—

"Dave's all on edge, Brownie. It wouldn't take much to throw him completely. He's got a lot of dough tied up in a house here, and he's not a kid any more, and newspapers are folding all over the country. If he thought he might lose out here—"

"He won't. There's no reason why he should," I said. "You're utterly and completely wrong, Tom. Dave and I are actually pretty good friends. If we weren't, he'd have fired me long ago."

"No, he wouldn't. The old man wouldn't let him. Why, I'll bet if you took a notion to knock him to Lovelace he'd—"

"Go on," I said. "Just get the hell up there and get to work. You're the boy with the troubles, remember? Well, don't forget it. Just forget about me, and remember what you have to do."

He nodded grudgingly, climbed out, then leaned back inside again.

"You watch him," he said. "Sneak a look at him sometime when he thinks your back is turned. You'll see. That guy could kill you and enjoy doing it."

# XI

I HELD MIDDAY maneuvers at the Press Club; early in the afternoon I stopped by the coroner's office. He was a stuffy, conceited bastard. He wasn't at all sure when he could release Ellen's body, but he "thought" he might be able to do it by Friday.

I pointed out that this posed a difficult situation. It would mean that the burial couldn't take place before Sunday, which might be impractical for the undertaker and undoubtedly would increase his charges. Moreover, it would crowd me seriously for time, if I was to be back at work on Monday morning.

He shrugged. My troubles, he indicated, were no concern of his.

I have never got along with coroners. They are either laymen of the lower orders who must pretend to be much, or they are fatheaded medical failures who are sore at the whole world for that which only they have wrought.

Our discussion continued on an increasingly less amiable plane. I finally suggested that if he simply had to have a body around I would buy him one from the local rendering plant, a cow, horse, or anything he named, and when he tired of playing with it he could stuff it—he, personally, and not a taxidermist.

That did it. Ellen's body would be released Saturday, he said, and not a goddamned day before. Meanwhile, I was to get out of his office and stay out.

I got out and called Dave. As I saw it, the funeral couldn't be held before late Monday, or more than likely, Tuesday; in other words, I would probably be off until the following Wednesday.

Dave hesitated, studying the calendar, I imagine. He said it would be all right, he guessed. He'd have to get Lovelace's okay, but he was sure it would be all right.

"How about coming out to the house for dinner before you leave?" he added. "Do you good to get some homecooked food. Kay told me to ask you."

"Good, sweet Kay," I said. "Dear, kind Kay. Tell me, Colonel, wouldn't you say she has a truly wonderful soul?"

"Good-by," he said shortly. "I'll talk to you when you're not half stiff."

"You misunderstood me," I said. "I said *soul,* not—"

"Look, Brownie," he snapped. "I'm trying as hard as I know how to—"

"You're fed up with me, aren't you?" I said. "You've had it up to here. It would suit you fine if I dropped dead."

It slipped out involuntarily.

Dave made a sound that was midway between a grunt and a gasp. I didn't blame him for being startled. I was myself.

He was silent for a long moment; then his voice came back over the wire, worried, warm with concern. "Look, boy. Where are you calling from? I'll come and get you and take you home."

"I'm sorry, Colonel," I said. "Sergeant Brown presents his apologies. I have become patrol happy; the maneuvers have got me clobbered."

"They must have when you talk like that. Where are you calling from?"

"I'm all right," I said. "Forget it, forgive it, and God bless you. "Twas a slip of the tongue and nothing more."

"But . . . I just don't understand. Of course, I get a little annoyed with you at times, but I thought you knew how I felt about you. Entirely aside from friendship, you're the best man I've got. I couldn't run the place without you."

"Thanks," I said. "Thanks a lot, Dave. I said a damned foolish thing, and I'm sorry, and let's leave it at that."

"Well . . . look." He was still troubled. "I was thinking about that dinner invitation. Naturally, you don't feel up to social occasions so soon after— afterward. Why don't we make it next week, sometime after you get back from Los Angeles?"

I didn't want to make it any time. My idea of an agonizingly misspent evening was one in the company of Kay Randall. I was afraid to refuse, now, however, in view of what I had said to Dave. He would think I had meant it. And somehow—whatever I felt about him and however I acted—I did not want him to think that.

So I accepted with thanks, and a mental note to kick Tom Judge's tail. I went home, knocked myself out with booze, and fell asleep.

The next day, Thursday, I had another talk with Lem Stukey. He hadn't turned up anything with the streetcar company, and he'd had the same result with the taxi operators. But he was by no means discouraged.

"We didn't expect nothing on the streetcars." He shrugged. "Just checked them out as a matter of form. The bastard took a cab, and don't think hell ain't going to pop when I turn it up."

"But you've already—"

"We've checked the trip sheets, we've talked to all the drivers who worked that night. Now we pull 'em in one at a time and find out which one's lyin'. Don't you worry none, keed. He's makin' it tough for us—and he'll sure as hell regret it—but he ain't making it impossible."

"I don't get you," I said. "Why would he lie about it?"

"Probably got a criminal record. Afraid of getting mixed up with cops. Or maybe his license has run out. Hell, there's all kinds of reasons. Maybe he knocked the fare down. Maybe he did a hit-and-run and doctored his trip sheet to put him in another neighborhood."

"You amaze me, Stuke," I said. "I had thought you cunning but never intelligent." And I realized, with further amazement, that Stukey was constantly coming up with little things like that, things that maybe didn't stamp him a genius but that sure as hell proved he was no slob.

"We'll get him," he promised. "We're just gettin' warmed up."

I left Lem and paid a visit to the express company and an undertaker. I made a long-distance call to a Los Angeles undertaker and repaired to the Press Club. Dave had been trying to reach me. I called him, immediately following maneuvers.

He had talked to Lovelace, and it was all right for me to lay off the extra time. Perfectly all right. However—

"Oh-oh," I said. "Pray proceed, Colonel, while I hoist my pack and rifle."

"I wouldn't ask you myself, Clint. The old man wants you to handle it if you possibly can. It's a pretty big thing, and . . ."

He gave me the essential details. The president of one of the Mexican Federal banks, immediately across the border, had embezzled several million pesos. The fraud hadn't been made public yet, and the president, who was en route from New York after a vacation, was unaware of its discovery. But he was due to be arrested as soon as he stepped off the plane in the morning. I was to be on hand to get the story.

I should point out here, perhaps, that the yarn wouldn't have been a big one in New York or Chicago. For that matter it wouldn't have got a very big play in Los Angeles. But because of our geographical location—because it concerned a neighboring city, although a Mexican one—it would be of prime interest to our readers.

I agreed to handle it.

I got up at six the next morning. At seven I was at the border city's airport, where I met the plane.

The president was on it, but so also were two Federalistas. They had got on at Los Angeles, and they took charge of Señor Presidente as soon as the plane touched in Mexico. They hustled him into a waiting limousine and sped away. I learned that they intended taking him fifty miles down the coast to another city, but that was all I learned.

I called Dave. He talked with Lovelace while I waited. The decision was for me to continue to the second city.

I did. The president had been put aboard a government plane and was on his way to Mexico City.

So there went my story, for the local authorities could give me no information on the case. The chief of police, a surprisingly young, friendly guy, sympathized volubly and insisted on drinking his lunch with me.

We drank and drank *and* drank, tequila mainly with an occasional mescal and chasers of that wonderful creamy cerveza—beer such as I have seldom tasted outside of Mexico. The chief became very gay. It was too bad, he said, that I was driving a car. Otherwise he would take his car and we would go to the island together—"your Rose Island, Cleent"—and then I could cross over to Pacific City on the ferry.

I blinked, rather owlishly, according to the mirror in the back bar. I said, "Now, wait a minute, *amigo caro.* Just how in the—?"

"You do not know, yes? You think I keed, no?" He grinned delightedly. "Come. I show you."

He led me over to the wall, stabbed a shaky finger at a framed map of Baja California. The finger weaved, slid, and came to a stop at a point near the Mexico-California border.

"Here is—*hic*—is how you say, pen—pen-in—?"

"Peninsula."

"Yes. Pen-in—well, you see eet, yes? How way out here eet come? Yes. And here is teep of island. And here . . . what you say is here, Cleent?"

"Something never to be taken internally," I said. "An insipid beverage, somewhat salty in this instance—"

"Ha, ha. Is water, you say, yes? You be wrong, Cleent. *Poquita, si.* Two, three inches, yes, but no more. Underneath is beeg—how you say?—reef. Rock. Like pavement."

"You're joking," I said. "You mean to tell me you can drive a car from here to here?"

"*Si.* Many time I have. Many peoples they do. Like I say, is rock. *Muy bueno camino*—ver' fine road."

Many peoples they do, but I never had. In fact, I had never heard of the reef. It wasn't so surprising, I guess; I seldom got over to the island. I could do all the drinking I wanted to at home or in the Pacific City bars. And as far as the cat-houses went—

So you see, I had no reason to know much about the island, and how you got there other than by ferry or charter boat.

But still, the information disturbed me. It was an extra little item in a story I thought I knew pretty well letter-perfect. Now I saw I didn't know it all. It was another piece of a jigsaw puzzle that I thought I had all locked together.

The information shouldn't *really* have disturbed me. Since Stukey knew everything else that might possibly be of use to him, he doubtless knew of this land route to the island. And he had quite properly ignored it as a factor in shaking my alibi. I couldn't have made this roundabout round trip on the night of the murder; I wouldn't have had time. For that matter no one could have done it during the storm. To have driven across almost four miles of reef— almost three times the width of the bay—to have done that on a pitch-black rainy night with a heavy sea running, well, it was simply out of the question. It was many times as fantastically dangerous and impossible as what I had done.

It had no bearing, then; otherwise, Stukey would have mentioned it and have looked into it. It didn't affect me. It didn't affect Tom Judge. It didn't—it was meaningless. But somehow it bothered me.

It lingered in my mind, nagging me, long after I had shaken hands with the Mexican police chief and headed back toward the border. I reached the U.S. customs station early in the afternoon. I knew several of the guards there, and I asked them about the reef. They knew about it, of course. It wasn't worth while to keep a customs officer there, but it was kept under observation by the border patrol.

I wondered about that—whether any very close watch had been kept on the night of the storm. I doubted it like hell.

We talked a minute or two more, and I mentioned casually that they had probably had an easy time of it during the storm. They admitted as much. "Sat around on our cans all evening, Brownie. Didn't a thing cross over but one taxi."

"Do you re—?"

I cut off the question abruptly. I didn't want them curious, and anyway, they couldn't have told me anything. A dark stormy night outside and a snug, comfortable guardhouse. And cabs always got a very fast check. They weren't searched as private passenger cars were. There would have been a quick glance through the window, and fast, "Birthplace? U.S. Citizen?" and then a wave onward—dismissal.

I drove on, still vaguely disquieted. I stopped in Pacific City for a few groceries and some bottles and went on out to the house. I mixed eggs and whisky. I drank them, took a bottle into the living-room, and sat down on the lounge. I got up and sat down on the floor. I stared at the telephone.

Tom Judge was on a very bad spot. Stukey was certain to find him soon unless he was diverted from him. An element of doubt should be introduced; another person should be brought into the case. Why not push that reef business at Lem? Talk it up to him? Why not sic him on that lone taxicab that had crossed the border? Point out that a man might have gone down in a cab, and *walked* across on the reef?

No, no. No! That was stupid. Lem would already have thought about it. Crossing on foot would have been even more hazardous than by car. And what would have been the purpose in it, anyway? What could he—Dave Randall —have hoped to accomplish by it? To catch me there, perhaps? To go in after I had left and—and—?

And nothing. It was reasonless. It was impossible. Absolutely without basis. How in the hell had I started thinking about this? Why did I persist in so thinking?

A taxicab had crossed the border. There was a submerged reef connecting with the mainland. And that fathead Tom Judge had said Dave had it in for me. . . . That was all I had to go on. The reef, the cab, and the twisted imaginings of Tom, a guy who was always trying to stir things up, dividing the world into enemy and friendly camps, and attaching to first one side, then the other. And out of that—and despite the fact that I *knew* who had killed Ellen—

But did I know? She'd got up after I left. Somebody had wiped away fingerprints. She'd died of asphyxiation, not—

Suddenly I laughed out loud. I laughed so hard that the whisky slopped out of my glass. For at last I'd remembered, and I was almost foolish with relief.

Dave had been at home that night. Stukey had called him there and then Dave had called me. Everything had been happening at once, and I guess I'd been halfway off my rocker, but now I remembered. Dave had been at home. The colonel had been in the bosom of his family, tossing the wee ones on his knee perhaps while the little woman hummed a happy roundelay. . . .

I sat drinking and thinking, musing idly, trying to sort out my feelings about Dave. They were pretty confused.

In a way, I liked him; I felt sorry for him. Yet there was another side of me that hated him, that was determined to make him go on suffering for what he had done to me. I wanted him to steer clear of trouble for two reasons. Because I liked him—because I hated him. He was a nice guy—and I wanted him to stay right where he was. Where I could get at him, dig at him day after day until . . .

I don't know. It is hard to be specific about one's emotions. It is difficult to stop a story at a certain point and give a clear-cut analysis of your feelings, explain just why they are such and such and why they are not something else. Personally I am a strong believer in the exposition technique as opposed to the declarative. It is not particularly useful, of course, when employed on an of-the-moment basis, but given enough time it invariably works. Study a man's actions, at length, and his motivations become clear.

# XII

I DROVE UP to Los Angeles on Sunday and took a room at the Press Club. The Pacific City undertaker got the lead out of his can and the one in L.A. did likewise, and the funeral was held late Monday.

It was a nice funeral, I thought. Stukey and the Randalls sent flowers, also Mr. Lovelace and the *Courier* staff. Too, the newspaper lads I knew in Los Angeles had bought a couple of big bouquets, and there was one giant-sized wreath without a card on it. I didn't think much about it. I supposed that it had been bought by the city hall crowd in Pacific City and that the card had been lost.

There were four press cars in the funeral procession. They were there on business, the boys were, since the story was still news. They had to shoot pictures and get me to do some surmising about the killer and so on, enough to pad out into a few paragraphs. But I was acquainted with most of them, and having them there was good. It made the thing seem more like a real funeral.

They were on overtime at the end of the ceremony. So the reporters phoned in their stories and the photogs sent in their plates by motorcycle courier, and we all went to the Press Club. We bumped a couple of tables together and started drinking. We had dinner and continued drinking.

Luckily, they wouldn't let me pay for anything. I had to borrow on my car to bury Ellen, and I was very, very short of money.

A waiter came up with a telephone call slip. I looked at it, casually, and shoved it into my pocket. I didn't recognize the number. I couldn't recall knowing anyone by the name of D. Chase. It was probably some friend of Ellen's, I thought. Someone who wished to offer condolences.

The party broke up about nine, and I bought a bottle and went up to my room. As a tried and true *Courier* man—one who did not need to be watched to do his duty—I suppose I should have driven back to Pacific City that night and gone to work Tuesday morning. But I was tired, and there was much heavy thinking to be done. And something told me it could not be done amid the hustle and bustle of Pacific City's greatest and only daily.

I stood at the window of my room, gazing out and downward. A fog had settled over the city, and the lights bloomed up out of it, blurred and hazy. Now and then there was the muted scream of a siren as an ambulance weaved northward through the traffic to Georgia Street Receiving.

Los Angeles. Sprawling, noisy, ugly, dirty—and completely wonderful. It would always be home to me, this place and no other. It would never be home to me.

211

I turned out the lights and dragged a chair up to the window. I cocked my feet up on the radiator and leaned back.

Tom Judge: at the outside, Stukey would have him in a day or two. Logically, he should have run him down before this. And exactly what was I going to do about it?

Tom might be able to hold out. He might be able to take a seventy-two-hour sweat—the three-day "investigation" period in which his sole hope and defense would rest on his own personal guts.

As I say, he might. But there was at least a fifty-fifty chance that he wouldn't. And once he broke down, it would be too late for me to do anything.

If only the murderer could have been tied in more closely with the poem. That is, if it could be established that the poet and the murderer were the same man. So far the poem had drawn very little attention. It had been mentioned by the police, paraphrased in various papers, and that was all. Ellen had had it, for reasons known only to herself. Dazed and dying she had grabbed it up —doubtless accidentally. That was the official attitude, and it was too bad that it was that.

Anyone who knew Tom would know him incapable of the poem. A few paragraphs of plodding prose were Tom's literary limit.

So it was unfortunate that the poem had been brushed off so lightly. It was unfortunate that there was not some way of proving that the murderer and the poet were one and the same man.

The phone rang. Softly, in actuality, yet it seemed loud and ominous, as phones do at night in dark hotel rooms.

I frowned at it. Then, I stretched an arm out and lifted it from the writing-desk. A husky, feminine voice said, "Mr. Brown—Brownie?"

"Who is this?" I said.

"I'll bet you can't guess. I'll bet you've forgotten me already."

I sighed. I said nothing. There is nothing much to say to people who ask you to guess their names while betting that you have forgotten them.

"It's Deborah, Brownie." She laughed a little uncomfortably. "You know, Deborah Chasen."

I remembered. I said something then, but I don't recall what. Something like: "Well, how are you?" or "What are you doing here?"

"I'm fine," she said. "I've been here all the time, Brownie. I was—I heard about your wife."

"I see," I said.

"Yes," she said. "I heard about it, so I didn't go. I've been waiting here for you. Did you get the flowers I sent?"

"Flowers? Oh, the wreath," I said. "I wondered who it was from."

"I sent them for you," she said. "Just on your account, Brownie, not hers. I'm not sorry about her. I'm glad."

"Well, that's very nice of you, Deborah," I said. "I see you're still your subtle, tactful self. Now, if you'll give me that horse laugh of yours my evening will be complete, and I'll go to bed."

She did laugh; then her voice went soft and throaty. It was as though she were breathing the words rather than speaking them.

"Brownie, darling—isn't it wonderful? I was just sick when I left Pacific City that afternoon. I wanted to die; I would have, too; I didn't care about anything any more. And then the next morning I read that—about her! It was like being born again, Brownie. Honestly, I was just so happy I cr—"

"Jesus, God," I said. "What kind of a woman are you? Do you realize that you're talking about my—"

"I don't care. You love me; I know you do. We love each other, and she was in the way. Now—well, now she isn't. . . . I want to see you, darling. Shall I come over there, or do you want to come over here to my hotel?"

I cursed her silently. It was on the tip of my tongue to say that I was leaving immediately for Pacific City, but I caught myself in time. As surely as hell was full of sulphur, she'd follow me there.

"Deborah," I said, wearily, "you are a goddamned pest. I don't want any part of you, or any other woman. I've tried the double harness once and I damned well got a belly full of it, and I'm playing it alone from now on. I—"

"Pooh. I'll change your mind."

"Nothing will change my mind," I said. "Now, I suggest you take a nice cold shower and eat a couple of pounds of saltpeter and—"

"Oh, Brownie!" She laughed delightedly. "You sweet crazy thing you! I'll come over there, darling."

"No!" I said. "No, wait a minute, Deborah. I do want to see you, naturally, but I've had a pretty rugged week and I. . . . Well, why don't we let it ride until tomorrow, baby? I'll give you a ring, and perhaps we can have lunch and a few drinks."

Silence. Then the sound—sounds—of a cigarette lighter clicking, and a long, slow exhalation. I could imagine the green eyes narrowing, hardening.

"Brownie," she said, quietly.

"Try to understand, Deborah. Put yourself in my place. My wife was killed less than a week ago. I buried her today. Now you expect me to—"

"Brownie."

"Well?" I said.

"I was doing all right before I met you. I didn't have anything, but I didn't expect anything. Then y-you—you know what you did, Brownie. You didn't tell me you were married. You held me and kissed me, and y-you . . . you did a lot of things I wouldn't have let you do if I'd known. And then you—now you—"

"Deborah," I said. "Just put it this way. Just say that I was a heel and I still am, and let it go at that."

"No! You're not, Brownie. You couldn't be if you tried. . . . Boy!" She sniffled. "I'm an expert on heels! I know all about 'em, and I know. . . . So what is it, darling? Is it the money? Are you afraid I'll embarrass you? Are—"

"Wait," I said. "Wait a minute, Deborah."

"I'll do anything you say, Brownie. Anything! Just d-don't—don't drive me away from you."

"Wait," I repeated. "I've got to think."

She waited. I thought. And, of course, I didn't need to, I already knew what I would have to tell her, prove to her if necessary. That I simply couldn't provide what she above all women would want.

She would be sorry, doubtless, perhaps even angry, but there would be no further argument; she would have no illusions about its importance. Deborah might have a very beautiful soul, but it was no good at all in bed. She would be stunned at the idea of substituting a fireside chat for a good hard roll in the hay.

So . . . I would have to tell her. But I couldn't do it over the phone. I couldn't —I didn't think I could make it stick—and I didn't want to.

I wanted to see her one more time.

"There's a little bar near here," I said. "A couple of blocks south on Main. It's called the Gladioli. If—"

"I'll find it. I'll be there. Right away, Brownie?"

"Right away," I said.

I put on a clean shirt and a fresh tie. I combed my hair in front of the dresser mirror, and suddenly I drew my arm back and hurled the comb against the glass.

My reflection tossed it back at me. His lips moved, and he cursed, and he asked why the hell it had to be this way. Why, if he didn't have the other, did he have to have all this? He said oh, you're a pretty bastard, you are. A knock-'em-dead son-of-a-bitch. They turn around to look at you, they stretch their goddamned sweet necks to get a peek. And . . . and that's all there is. Only what they can see. I don't get it, by God! Why, when there's nothing to do with, do you have to look like . . .?

The reflection shrugged. He said, that's the way it was, so that's the way it was.

Then he reached for his coat and turned wearily away. And I turned off the light, and left.

She was there ahead of me, standing up near the glazed front of the place, peering anxiously up and down the street. I came up while she was look-ing the other way, and she whirled around, startled, taking a swift step for-ward so that for a moment we were pressed against each other. I gave her a little hug, and she said, "Brownie! Oh, *Brownie!*" and gave me a harder one.

We entered the dimly lit bar. She let go of my arm and led the way to a rear booth, rounded hips swinging, slim-ankled, full-calved legs stretching and pressing impatiently against her skirt, horsetail of corn-colored hair brushing the small, square shoulders. She had a mink stole draped over her arm. She was wearing a thin white blouse and a tailored fawn-colored suit. They made her look bigger in all the big places and smaller in all the small ones.

We sat down on the same bench of the leather-upholstered booth; she pulled me down beside her. A sleepy-looking waiter brought drinks and went away again.

"Brownie," she whispered. "Brownie, darling. . . ." And her breast shivered against my arm.

She pulled my face down to hers and we kissed. And then gently she pushed me away again.

"I'm terribly sorry, Brownie. I must have sounded awful. It was just that I love you so much, and I know how mean she must have been and—"

"She wasn't," I said. "Foolish perhaps, but not mean."

"Well, anyway, I'm sorry. I'm—you won't have to be ashamed of me, Brownie. You just tell me how you want me to be, and whenever I get—"

"Deborah," I said, "listen to me."

"Yes, darling."

"I'm—there's something I have to tell you. I should have told you in the beginning, but it's not an easy thing to talk about and—well, I didn't think it was necessary. You were leaving. I never expected to see you again."

"Yes?" She lighted a cigarette. "What is it, Brownie?"

"I can't marry you. I can't sleep with you."

"Oh?"

"No! That was the trouble between me and my wife, why we were separated. I couldn't be a husband to her."

"Oh . . . I see. And all the time I thought . . ." The green eyes flashed happily and her face broke into a smile. "That doesn't mean a thing, darling! Not a thing."

"It—it doesn't *mean* anything?" I said.

"Why, of course, it doesn't! It was the same way with me and my husband. You just . . . a certain person simply isn't the right one, and you get to where you not only can't—"

"Listen," I said. "You just don't understand, Deborah. What I'm—"

"I know. I know exactly what you mean. I—No, let me tell you, Brownie. You've got a right to know, anyway. Even after he died, I couldn't. I tried— I'm human and I—I—well, I tried; just like you have, probably. And I couldn't do it. It was like there just wasn't any such thing as far as I was concerned. I'd lost all desire for it, and I was sure it was gone for good. I was sure until that day in Pacific City when I—"

"Deborah," I said. "You don't know what you're talking about. What I'm talking about."

"You think I don't." She laughed. "You just think I don't, Brownie! That's why I was so completely broken up when I found out you were married. I knew it had to be you or no one; that if it weren't you then there simply wouldn't be anyone. . . . You'll see, darling." Her voice sank to a throaty, caressing whisper and her eyes burned like green fires. "It'll be all right for both of us. It'll be like nothing ever was before. . . ."

You see, you do see, don't you, how very hard it was? How even I, with stalwart purpose in my heart and lofty motives in my mind, might hesitate? She had to be told, yes, and certainly I intended to tell her. But she was making it so hard and she was so sure of herself, so positive that everything was now all right, so happy. . . . And in a way I loved her.

Her small hard hand moved under the table and came to rest on my thigh. It moved down, up, down, up. It stayed up, pressed there firm yet trembling. She shivered and leaned against me.

Then, that sleepy-soft whisper again: "You've made me so happy, darling, and I'll make you so happy. You'll see, Brownie. You'll never be sad again."

"Sad?" I said, and I pressed the buzzer for the waiter. I needed one more drink. I would tell her after the second drink. "You are speaking in paradoxes, Deborah. I am a jolly *Courier* man, a member of the happy *Courier* family. We know no sadness, only joy in a job well done."

"You're sad," she said. "That's why you write those terribly sad poems."

# XIII

THE WAITER CAME and went, came back with drinks and went away again. In the interim, while we were waiting for him to get out of the way, we made meaningless small talk.

He left for the second time. She sipped her drink, her fingers toying with the cardboard menu, a faintly teasing smile on her lips.

"Surprised you, didn't I? You thought it was a secret."

"A very rare type of secret," I said. "One dealing with the non-existent. Newspapermen don't write poetry, Deborah, never, never, ever. That's traditional."

"Oh, ye-es?" she drawled, smiling. "I know one that does. He was writing one the first time I saw him. In the office. He got rid of it very fast, but not quite fast enough. . . . Not for someone who could read a menu upside down and across the table."

I lifted my glass. I took a very long swallow and set it down again. "Poetry," I said. "It places me in a pretty bad company, doesn't it? I mean, that poem she had. They think there's a possibility that the killer may have written it."

"Do they?" She shrugged. "Oh, well. . . ." Just, oh, well. Meaning nothing; meaning a great deal.

"Yes," I said. "That's what they think, and I have a strong hunch they may be right. I think they may have even more reason to think so in the not-too-distant future."

Here was my answer. Just a matter of minutes before—in my hotel room I had been wondering how I could draw Stukey's attention away from Tom Judge, how I could prove once and for all that the murderer and the poet were the same person.

Now I knew how I could prove it.

Through Deborah.

If, say, there was another murder, and if a poem similar to the first one was found on the victim . . .

"Let's not talk about . . . it." She frowned. "But you won't write any more of those poems, will you? I think they're bad for you."

"I think they could be, myself," I said. "I certainly wouldn't care to have them become a matter of public knowledge, Deborah."

"Don't you worry, darling." She patted my thigh. "I'd never tell anyone. Now you just stop being said, hmmmm? Because there's nothing to be said about, now."

"Perhaps not," I said. "How can one be sad when he has the sky and the stars to gaze upon and God's own green carpet to rest his aching arches?

Morning's at seven, Deborah. Morning's at seven, the hillside's dew-pearled, God's in his heaven, all's right with the world."

"That's awfully pretty, Brownie. Did you write that?"

"Yes," I said. "I did it under my pen name, Elizabeth Khayyam. I wrote it one eventide on a windswept hill while watching a father bird wing home to his wee ones. There was a long caterpillar in his beak and he had it swung over his shoulders, muffler fashion, as a shield against the wintry cold. I . . . Listen to me, Deborah! For God's sake, listen!"

She had been laughing, looking at me fondly. Now she went serious and she said, "No, Brownie. Whatever it is, I don't want to hear it. Not tonight, anyway."

"But you just don't—"

"You don't know everything about me either. What's the difference? I just don't care, Brownie! We're together and we're going to stay together, and that's all that matters. Oh, it's so wonderful, darling. Just think! Me, finding you, getting you back after I thought I'd lost you. The only man in the world I could—"

"Please," I said. "I—The world's a hell of a big place, and—please, please—"

"No. No," she said. "I won't listen. I only know I'd die without you. I don't want to hear anything that might—I don't want to hear anything. I don't need to. It wouldn't matter. Nothing about her or you and her or. . . . It wouldn't matter, Brownie. I—I—I wouldn't care if you'd killed her!"

She nodded firmly, her eyes somehow cold yet burning. Up near the bar, the juke box suddenly began to blare, shaking the walls with its clamor before someone turned down the control.

I took a cigarette from my package. I lighted it and inhaled, slowly, stalling for time.

Had the poetry meant anything to her? Had she been hinting, giving me a warning, when she said that it was bad for me? Did she know that I *had* killed Ellen, and . . .?

Probably she wouldn't care now—that is, if she did know. She could rationalize that. Ellen was no good. Ellen would have had it coming to her. Ellen was nothing to her, and I was everything. *But—*

But what about later when she discovered that I was not everything, that I was nothing? That I was merely another blank page in her book of life. How would blunt, straight-to-the-mark Deborah Chasen behave then? She would have no use for me—would she? And I knew what her attitude was toward people for whom she had no use. "She was dead, and I was so happy. . . ."

Wasn't that what she had said?

Perhaps I could tell her the truth and it would be all right. But if it wasn't all right—if she turned spiteful and vengeful—I'd be sunk. It would be too late

to draw back, too late to try to silence her. I'd have lost the game, and there
wouldn't be another one.

So . . .?

I tamped out my cigarette and swallowed the rest of my drink. "Your
fabulous fanny," I said. "Is it quite comfortable, Deborah? Then keep it where
it is while I procure my car and carpetbag, and we shall then head south into
the dawn."

She let out a delighted squeal.

"Brownie! You sweet, funny. . . . But hadn't I better—?"

"We will send for it," I said. "Whatever you need we will send for, Deborah.
Meanwhile, with me providing a toothbrush and you providing yourself we
shall want for nothing. We shall have paradise enow."

She smiled, looking a little puzzled through the tenderness, but she didn't
argue. She was right up on top of the load after a hard climb, and she was going
to do nothing to upset the applecart.

"Do you believe in a personal paradise?" I said. "A personal hell?" Do you
have a soul, Deborah?"

"Hurry," she said. "Hurry as fast as you can, darling. We get in your car,
I'm going to take this girdle off."

I hurried, but I was quite a little while at that. Because I had something more
to do than get my car and check out at the club.

There was a hotel up the block and on the opposite side of the street. I
remembered its arrangements well from the days when I was working in Los
Angeles and covered conventions there.

Immediately inside the lobby entrance, a staircase led to the mezzanine. A
little beyond the head of the stairs was the public stenographer's desk. She
wasn't there at this hour, naturally, but her typewriter, a silent machine, was,
and her wastebasket hadn't been emptied.

I sat down, dipped into the basket, and selected a discarded second-sheet
with only a few lines at the top. I creased it and tore them off.

I turned the paper into the typewriter.

The poem went very fast; I suspect that I was lifting it, at least in part, from
my original manuscript. When I had finished, I laid it on the desk and scrubbed
both sides of the page with my handkerchief. I folded it, using the handkerchief, picked it up with same, and stuffed it into my pocket. . . .

I am somewhat hazy in spots about the ride to Pacific City, but my general
recollection is that she enjoyed it immensely. Not that I didn't—although my
mind was not exactly pleasure-bent—but I didn't matter. I meant it to be her
party, and I believe it was a dilly.

The highway was practically barren of traffic. I had had the foresight to lay
in a plentiful supply of beverages, and I saw to it that she sampled them
generously. We rode southward into the fog, her laughter growing louder and

louder. She braced her feet against the dashboard and raised her hips off the seat, trying to remove the girdle. She tried it a half dozen times, and each time she'd barely get started when laughter overpowered her. She flopped back in the seat, snickering and sputtering and guffawing. She hugged me around the hips, giggling and choking, shivering against me.

"B-Brownie, you—you s-st. . . . Ha, ha, ha, ha—y-you s-stop n-now, B-Brownie . . . !"

"You bray like a goddamned jackass, Deborah," I said. "Like a bitch baying at the moon."

"B-Brownie! Now, that's not in . . . ha, ha, ha, ha. . . ."

"Shall I breed you, Deborah? Is your tail tingling, my prize bitch?"

"Ha, ha. . . . D-Don't talk about d-dogs, Brownie. I—I—Oh, d-darling . . . ha, ha, ha, ha. . . ."

She was so wonderfully earthy and human. Eve before the apple, Circe with the giggles, Pompadour on a night off.

About thirty miles out of Los Angles, I turned the car onto the beach and got out. I opened the door on her side, and she lay back with her legs stuck out and her skirts up, and I got a good two-handed grip on the girdle.

I gave a hell of a yank.

Well, I got rid of the thing, the girdle, and I found out something. About her size. However big she looked in certain places, she wasn't actually; it was simply the way she was built. There just wasn't enough of her to be big. As a man with some experience in such things, I'd say that she couldn't have weighed much more than a hundred and ten pounds.

So I yanked, thinking there was much more ballast than there was, and the girdle skidded off of her. My hands shot upward and backward, flinging the girdle into the ocean. I stumbled and fell flat on my back. Then she was out of the car and beside me.

She sat back, looking down at me almost gravely. And the sand felt peaceful and soft and warm, and so did she.

"You're very soft," I said. "Very soft and warm, Deborah."

"I don't have any pants on," she said. "I guess that's why I feel that way."

"I'll tell you something," I said. "You'll never die, Deborah. There is no death in you, only life. So long as there is laughter, so long as there is warmth and light, so long as there is soft flesh, fresh and sweet-smelling like no perfume ever made, so long as there is a breast to cup and a thigh to caress . . . you'll live, Deborah. You'll never die."

"That's awfully pretty," she said. "Want me to tell you something?"

"Please do," I said.

"I don't care if I do die. Not now, Brownie. Not after tonight."

We drove on to Pacific City.

We got to my shack just before dawn.

And I killed her.

# XIV

I DIDN'T KILL her right away. As a matter of fact it was that night, more than sixteen hours later. Just as I was about to decide that I wasn't going to do it.

You see, the two-way pull wasn't working as it should. It was pulling on me, trying to jerk me out into that other world, but she was pulling, too, pulling me in the opposite direction. And she was stronger than it was.

It was strange, very, how strong she was, how one so small could be so strong. I didn't believe that I could kill her. I was afraid to do it. I wasn't afraid of being caught, you understand. I was quite sure that I wouldn't be, and, since I am writing this some weeks later, you are aware that I was not. It was a fear away from and beyond the purely personal. It was as though she were life itself, the root of all life, and when I killed it, that, her, all life would vanish.

*And I had visions of a parched and withering earth, a vast and empty desert where a dead man walked through eternity.*

I didn't think I could kill her.

It is hard to believe that I did.

Even now, now more than ever, as I sit here alone in the *Courier* city room, and I am above self delusion and below reproach—now when my one task is to set the record straight—it is hard to believe that I did it.

I find myself thinking that there must have been someone else, someone who knew about her and—

But, of course, I did do it. The act of murder is not to be forgotten quickly, and I remember the facts of this one well. I did it . . . but not then. More than two thirds of a day passed, in the meantime, and I think you should be told about that.

I think we should keep her alive as long as we can. . . .

I parked the car at the side of the house, and we went inside. She went to the bathroom while I drew the shades, and then she came out and I went.

She'd slept for about the last hour of the ride, and she was fairly wide awake now. She stood in the center of the living-room, smiling at me a little timidly as I came in, and she said she bet she looked a sight, didn't she?

"Awful," I agreed, and I gave her a kiss on the mouth and a small swat on the rear. "A hung-over hussy if I ever saw one. You must have a drink and pull yourself together."

"Oh—uh—" She hesitated. "Do you want a drink, Brownie?"

"It gags me to think of it," I said. "But I shall force it down. I will not let you drink alone."

I fixed us two whopping drinks and brought them in to the lounge. She curled up at my side, pulling my arm around her, and we sat there drinking and talking. And saying very little. A train thundered by, leaving the house a-tremble. She pulled my arm tighter, pressing my hand against her breast.

"Brownie. You're . . . you're not still afraid? I mean, you don't think it might not be all right?"

"I am sure it will be," I said. "In such a package only quality could prevail."

"No, really, darling. If you're—"

"Really," I said. "Honest and truly. And you have your whole life to prove it to me."

"Mmmm," she said, and she wriggled. "Promise me something, Brownie? Don't die before I do. I wouldn't want to live without you, darling! Without your love."

"I promise," I said. And after a moment I added, "We will die together, Deborah. That is the way it will be. When you die, I will die."

"Will you, Brownie? Would you really want to?"

"I don't think," I said, "it will be a matter of wanting."

We drank. I kept filling our glasses. She asked me if my legs didn't get awfully stiff from driving, and wasn't I awfully tired. I said that they did indeed, and that I didn't get so much tired as tense. As soon as I got limbered up and relaxed a little . . .

"Brownie," she said.

"Yes?"

"I—nothing."

Several minutes passes; five or it might have been ten.

"Brownie—"

"Yes?"

"Nothing."

We went on drinking. I began to have a hard time keeping up with her. Finally she mumbled something about getting a sleeping pill, and she started to get up. Then she fell back, letting her head slide down into my lap.

She stared up at me squinting, drowsy and dizzy. One of her fingers wobbled and wavered, pointing at me. "Y-You know what? Y-You j-jus' got one eye. P-Poor Brownie o'ny got one eye. . . ."

"The other one is turned inward," I said. "It is examining my soul."

"Mmmm?" she mumbled. "Jus'—just got—"

Her eyelids closed, and her lips parted and stayed parted. She slept.

I carried her into the bedroom and put her on the bed. I loosened her brassiere, took off her shoes, and pulled the spread over her. Then I went back to the lounge.

I poured another drink, but I didn't take it. Exhaustion suddenly overpowered me, and in a split second I was sound asleep. . . .

When I awakened the phone was ringing and she was kneeling at the side of the lounge, shaking me.

I started to sit up. I flopped back down again, yawning and rubbing my eyes.

I looked at her, dully, wondering who she was and how she had got here.

"The phone, darling," she said. "Hadn't you better answer it?"

"Phone?"

"It's been ringing a long time, Brownie. Shall I answer it for you?"

That brought me awake, or much more awake than I was. It brought back my memory. I asked her the time, and she said it was a quarter of three.

"Probably the paper." I sat up, yawning. "Let 'em ring. If they knew I was back, they'd wonder why I hadn't come in. Might want me for something even this late."

"All right, Brownie. Want to go back to sleep again?"

"Yes—no," I said. "How about some coffee?"

"I've got some made, darling. I'll get it right away."

She went out into the kitchen. The phone stopped ringing. I sat looking down at the floor, at the blanket which must have been covering me.

It didn't necessarily mean anything. Neither it nor the fact that my shoes were off and the buckle of my belt unfastened. When you have drunk as long and as much as I have, you do a great many things without remembering or thinking about them. Just automatically. Frequently I have undressed and put myself to bed without ever knowing that I had done it.

So this, the condition I had awakened in, was doubtless more of the same. But so long as she was awake, it seemed like a good idea for me to be. She might be getting curious. She might become actively curious if she had the opportunity. *Maybe she already had.*

I washed while the coffee was heating and held brief and silent confab with that strange guy in the mirror. He looked a little haggard this morning—I suspected an incipient case of cirrhosis of the soul—but withal he seemed reasonably at peace. He was strongly of the opinion that Deborah should not be killed.

"Unnecessary, my dear man," he advised me. "I suspect, as you did originally, that she is not greatly endowed with sharpness. She is not stupid, of course; she can be not-sharp and not-stupid, also. She is just a very natural, very lovely, very simple and straightforward woman."

"Yeah, sure. But she said—"

"A manner of speaking; we all say things like that. But—assume that it was not. Let us say that she saw the connection between the poetry and Ellen's death. It didn't change her love for you. She went right on loving and trusting you. Would she, then, feeling about you as she does, suddenly turn on you because of something you cannot help? And—to make another far-fetched assumption—suppose she did? You have an airtight alibi, haven't you? You couldn't have crossed the bay that night. So, what if she should—?"

"I don't know," I said. "I don't know to all the questions. The deal's so goddamned screwed up, and—and I can't take chances—and there's

Tom Judge. I don't know why the hell they haven't nabbed him already."

"What about Tom Judge, anyway? The fact that there's another murder and another poem while he's in custody won't necessarily establish his innocence of the first one."

"It will throw considerable doubt upon the matter of his guilt. I'll do the rest. After I talk with Mr. Lovelace and Mr. Lovelace talks with Mr. Stukey, Mr. Judge will be released. And promptly."

"We-ell . . . I suppose so. But—want to make a small bet? I'll bet you don't kill her. You can't."

"You think not, huh?"

"I *know* not. You can't kill her, Brownie. If she gets killed, it won't be by you."

She'd whipped up some toast and scrambled eggs along with the coffee, and it tasted better than any food I'd eaten in a long time. She'd already had a bite, she said, but she had coffee with me. We sat at the table, smoking and drinking coffee, making quite a bit of conversation but saying very little. She hadn't slept a great deal, she said. She'd had a hard time sleeping in recent years and had come to depend heavily on sleeping pills. Having taken none before retiring, she'd been pretty wakeful despite the booze.

We moved in to the lounge after a while, and she sat with her legs drawn up, her head resting against my shoulder.

"Brownie," she said. "Am I keeping you from anything? If there's anything at all you have to do—"

"I'm doing it," I said. "This is what most needs doing right now."

"I thought you might get me that toothbrush . . . if you're going out. I could use one."

"I may have to go out later on," I said. "I'll get whatever you need then."

It occurred to me suddenly that it might have been Stukey calling a while before. He might already have Tom Judge. But . . . no, it wasn't likely; it must have been the paper checking on me. Stukey wouldn't have stopped with a call. Knowing me as he did, he would have come out to see if I was there.

We drank, or rather, I did. Deborah barely sipped at her glass. The afternoon—what there was left of it—slipped away and darkness came. And she never asked that we—that we go—

Deborah stirred lazily. She stretched, arching her breasts, and stood up. She asked me if I wouldn't like her to fix something to eat, and I said, well, I would have to give the matter some thought. We were discussing it when the phone rang.

I glanced at the clock: seven straight up. There wouldn't have been anyone at the paper for hours.

I picked up the receiver. It was Stukey.

"We got him, keed. It'll knock you flat when you hear who it is."

He told me who it was. Tom Judge. It did not surprise me in the least.

"Good God!" I said, putting a good heavy exclamation mark behind the phrase. "It's incredible. I never liked the stupid jerk, but I wouldn't have thought—Has he confessed yet, Stuke?"

"There ain't hardly been time yet. We just pulled him in. But he's our boy, all right, pal. He fits all the specifications, and he's got that old guilty look written all over him."

"And he's been identified, of course? By the cab driver."

"We-ell, no." He hesitated. "The taxi angle didn't pan out. We picked him up on an anonymous tip. Came in on the switchboard, and that dumb ox we got workin' there didn't trace—"

"What about his wife?" I said. "She admits he wasn't at home that night?"

"We-ell,"—again a pause—"no. But, o' course, she's lyin'. . . . He's it, Clint; I'd swear to it on a stack of Bibles. How soon'll you be down?"

It was my turn to hesitate, and I did, lengthily. Then I let him hear an uncomfortable laugh.

"This one kind of throws me, Stuke," I said. "If it was anyone else but him —another *Courier* employee—I. You see what I mean? There's no real evidence against him. Suppose you had to turn him loose, and I had to go on working with the guy?"

"Well, yeah. But, keed, I *know* this baby is—"

"You knew the same thing about me. Remember?"

"Naw! No, I didn't," he protested. "I couldn't find you anywhere and I figured you was the only one with a motive, and—and I was sore. But I knew you hadn't done it as soon as I cooled off. I didn't have that ol' hunch like I got about this guy. Why, hell, Clint, I—"

"I'm not throwing it up to you," I said. "I'm just pointing up the possibility that you might be wrong about Judge. . . . I think I'd better steer clear of this for the moment, Stuke. Anyway—unless Judge cracks before then—I want to talk with Mr. Lovelace before I get personally involved."

"Well, yeah," he said grudgingly. "I see what you mean."

"He'd be damned sore, you know, if Judge wasn't guilty. He'll probably be damned sore, in any case. The idea of a *Courier* man being a murderer won't sit at all well with the old boy."

"No. . . ." There was a thoughtful silence. "I guess he won't like it much. But, looky, keed, I ain't playing hotsy-totsy with no murderer just because—"

"You're damned right you're not," I said. "If you did, you'd have me on your tail. All I'm saying is that I'd better keep out of the frammis until I talk to Lovelace, unless Judge spills in the meantime. You can hold him seventy-two hours, can't you?"

"Well, sure. But—"

"I'll let it ride, then," I said. "I'll talk to Lovelace in the morning and get in touch with you afterward. I'd do it tonight, but we can't break the story before morning, anyway, and Lovey gets pretty hot if he's bothered at night."

Stukey grunted, cursed under his breath. He said, "Well, I sure as hell hate to. . . . What you think, keed? I ought to go pretty easy on this character until you get the word? Just kind of leave him alone and let him stew?"

"I wouldn't want to advise you," I said. "I don't have much use for Judge, and—well, you know, my own wife and all. I might give you the wrong dope."

"Uh-huh. Sure. Well"—he sighed—"you'll buzz me in the morning, then?"

"As soon as I talk to Lovelace."

We said good night and hung up. I was reasonably confident that he would give Tom little trouble tonight. And by morning. . . .

By morning?

She knelt down in front of me, resting her elbows on my knees. "Brownie. Is it—is there something wrong?"

"They think they've got the man who killed Ellen," I said. "One of the boys from the paper. I—it's hard to believe that he's guilty."

"Poor Brownie. It's just one thing after another, isn't it? Want another drink, darling? Something to eat."

"No," I said. "I don't think I do."

"Why don't you get out for a while, darling? Ride around and get a little fresh air. You must be getting awfully restless."

"Well, I—"

"You do that, Brownie." She cocked her head to one side, smiling at me. "Pretty please? I'll lie down while you're gone."

I grabbed her in my arms. I hugged her, burying my face in her hair. "God," I said. "Jesus, God, Deborah. If you only knew—"

"I do know," she said. "You love me. I love you. I know that, and—that's enough."

"I wish it was as simple as that," I said. "I wish—"

"It is, Brownie. It *is* that simple."

I kissed her.

I left the house and drove away.

I drove up on the hill first, up into the Italian section of town, where I had a few drinks at a bar. Then I bought a bottle in a liquor store, pulled the car onto a side street, and sat there drinking alone in the dark.

I drank for a while. I wondered . . . about her, about Ellen. About myself.

Why? I asked. Why had I done what I had to Ellen? That was a mere by-phrase with her—the "you burn me up." An imbecile would have known that, and I was not, by the most exaggerated estimate, an imbecile. I had had to kill her—*perhaps*—and perhaps I would have to kill Deborah. But the other . . .

Was it because . . . well, hadn't she always been hysterically afraid of fires? And Deborah—wasn't she morbidly afraid of dogs?

I tried to look at myself squarely, to think the thing through. I couldn't do it. Something kept getting in the way, bending my vision around into a circle; and while I was in that circle I was not of it. It did not touch me. Between the man who wanted to look and the man to be looked at, was a heavy curtain. Drawn, of course, by the inner man.

It was now after nine o'clock. I gave up the searching and started home. I wasn't going to kill her; I knew that much, at least. There was no need to—no real reason—and I wasn't. And . . .

And suddenly there was a reason, many of them, and I was going to do it. The two-way pull had me to itself. All resistance had ended abruptly, and I was swung far out into that other world. There was nothing to hold me back. It was as though she had suddenly ceased to exist.

I let the car coast into the yard quietly, the motor stilled. I eased the door of the house open. Silently, I went in.

The kitchen had been cleaned up and the dishes put away. The living-room had been swept and put in order. I hesitated, looking around, and it was ridiculous to feel that way, in view of what I intended doing, but I was troubled, worried about her.

To have left her alone, in this isolated railroad-side shack. . . . She'd have been helpless, although she'd have doubtless tried to fight. And if there'd been a scuffle, the house might be like this. Put to rights, and . . .

I went into the bedroom.

I heaved a sigh of relief.

She was all ri—she was there. Stretched out on the bed on her stomach. She was lying with her face in the pillow, her arms akimbo on it, the horsetail of corn colored hair hanging down to one side.

So quiet. So peaceful and calm and trusting. So . . . quiet.

Actually, she must have been one of those nervous sleepers. You could see how she had been balled up tight; you could see it by the way the sheets were wrinkled and the mattress depressed. Now, finally, she had straightened out, her body stretched out full length. But she was still tense, her fingers sticking out rigidly, her whole body stiff, unbending, motionless.

That's how she lay there, and I heaved a sigh of relief, and I killed her.

I stood over her, staring down, studying her position: the way her neck formed an unsupported bridge between the pillow and her shoulders.

I stooped down at her side, balling my hand into a fist. I raised it, brought it down hard.

There was a dull pop, and her neck sagged and her head bent backward.

I picked up her purse, put the poem in it, lifted her in my arms and carried her out to the car.

It was all right. It was a game again. I had been forced to play and with an inordinately heavy handicap. And I had won, and she perforce had lost. But . . .

But already I was feeling the emptiness, the lifelessness.

And off in the not-too-distant distance, it began to move toward me . . . *The withered and dying world, the vast and empty desert where a dead man walked through eternity.*

I reached the dog pound.

I threw her over the wall.

# XV

I . . . I AM going to get through this part very quickly. About the next morning, that is, the discovery of the body—what was left of it—and . . . and so on. I got through it rather well at the time. I had the crutch of work—pressure—and Tom Judge's situation. And I had to do it. And it was a game. Now, however—

Now, I shall have to get it over with quickly.

I must do so. . . .

The story broke about five minutes before deadline, and I handled it. It was short, thank God. The paper was already made up, and there was only one brief yarn that the news editor could yank. So this one had to be short also. There wasn't a whole lot to say, for that matter, since the body had only been discovered a few minutes before.

Those half-starved dogs were always fighting and raising hell, and the Peablossoms—the old couple—hadn't investigated the racket until morning. By that time, of course, there wasn't much left of. . . . Well, they'd identified her by the contents of her purse: by, among other things, a nearly empty box of sleeping pills with her name on it.

I say *they'd* done it, meaning the cops, not the Peablossoms. They'd also found the poem in her purse.

There was no way of knowing how long she'd been dead, whether she'd been killed there and tossed into the stockade or whether she'd been brought there after being killed. The only clue to the murderer was the poem.

The Peablossoms hadn't heard a car during the night, but then, they wouldn't have heard one with the dogs carrying on. There were a great many footprints and tire tracks around the place. Far too many to be of value as clues.

Well, I wrote the story. Then Dave and I were called into Lovelace's office for a conference.

He was in a very bad humor, and he took it out on Dave. This "Judge fellow." He'd always known he was no good, should've been fired long before. Dave should've fired him. Now he was a murder suspect—a *Courier* man under arrest for murder! Shocking. Inexcusable.

And Deborah Chasen—*that* woman! She, it appeared, was also Dave's fault. An editor was supposed to know what was going on, wasn't he? He was supposed to have news sources, people who kept him informed? Well, why, then, hadn't Dave kept track of her, a woman "posing" as a friend of the Lovelaces? Should've known she was back in town. Should've known she'd get into trouble. Now, she'd been killed, a woman identified with the proud name of Lovelace, and . . .

"Shocking. Inexcusable. Very bad management, Randall."

Dave took it, squirming and sweating and trying to protest. Finally he escaped—rather he was called out to the desk—and I had a chance to work.

"Obviously" (and let us put that *obviously* in quotes) the two murders—Ellen's and Deborah's—had been committed by the same person. The poems "established" that fact. Certainly two such poems in the possession of two mysteriously murdered women could not be mere coincidence. The man hated them—the hard murderous hate shone through the lines—so . . .

I bore down on the poems so heavily that I almost believed what I said.

"But I don't need to explain all this to you, sir," I said. "You felt that the colonel needed a good jacking up and you took this opportunity of delivering it—of making him sweat a little, if you'll excuse the expression. But you can see that Judge couldn't be guilty. He was in jail at the time of the second murder; therefore he couldn't possibly be guilty of either one. . . . That's your opinion, isn't it, sir? I've stated your own thoughts correctly? You feel that Judge—the *Courier*—is in no way involved in this scandal?"

It was, it appeared, exactly the way he felt. I had stated his own thoughts perfectly, and he complimented me on my astuteness.

"Very—uh—shrewd of you, Brown. Couldn't have put the matter more clearly myself. But this—this Chasen woman—"

"I was coming to that, sir. When you call Detective Stukey about Judge—You were going to do that right away, I suppose? After all, a *Courier* man shouldn't—"

"Certainly!" he snapped. "Demand his immediate release! Can't think what the police department is coming to to make such a ghastly error."

"Well," I went on, "I was thinking you might clarify Mrs. Chasen's position while you were talking to Stukey. We have our duty to the public, sir. We can't allow baseless rumors to get into circulation. As I see it—regardless of her claims—Mrs. Chasen was *not* a friend. She was not even an acquaintance, in the accepted sense of the term. It seems to me, sir, that she was merely another visitor to the building, one of the many sight-seers who come here yearly to—"

"Exactly! That's exactly the case, Mr. Brown. Don't know why I—uh—I'll call Stukey immediately."

He called, and Stukey was far from pleased, from what I could gather. But he didn't have any evidence against Tom, and he hadn't been able to make him talk. And there was no small amount of logic in "Lovelace's" opinion about the connection between the two murders. Moreover—most important, of course, was the fact that Lovelace was Lovelace. You didn't say no to him if you could avoid it.

Stukey had no grounds for avoiding it.

So Tom was promptly released . . . and fired almost as promptly. Just as soon as he could be reached by phone. He'd not been a very good worker to begin with, and now he'd had the bad judgment to get himself arrested. And—

But we don't need to go this fast. We can slow down a little now.

I talked a while longer, "restating" Mr. Lovelace's thoughts for him. He frowned a trifle, but he was forced to admit that I had voiced them perfectly.

"Uh—yes. Must be done, I suppose. Public duty and all. Of course, the murderer may have left the city—"

"I'm positive he hasn't," I said. "As sure as I'm sitting here, sir, he's still in town."

"Yes—uh—probably. Doubtless. Have to get him, eh? See that this Stukey fellow—uh—keeps out the—uh—dragnet. Continues the clean-up. Right?"

I told him his mind worked like a steel trap. "I don't know how you do it, sir. I mean, see right through to the point of things."

"You think—*ahem*—you really think I do, Mr. Brown?"

"Like a steel trap," I repeated firmly. . . .

Dave was just heading for Lovelace's office as I came out, and I thought he appeared somewhat chagrined when he learned that everything had been settled without him. Along with the chagrin, however, was considerable relief at getting the old man off his neck. And he seemed pleased at the latter's instructions to fire Tom Judge.

"I should have done it long ago." He nodded. "Just didn't have the heart. Now it's out of my hands."

I started toward my desk. He touched me on the arm. "By the way, Brownie. You spent the better part of a day with Mrs Chasen. . . ."

"You're right," I said. "It all comes back to me now that you mention it."

"I'm not trying to pry, but—you thought quite a bit of her, didn't you? I got the impression that you were pretty annoyed with Lovelace's references to her."

"I loved her, Colonel," I said. "Her image is permanently graven on my heart. I could have gone for her in a large way—if, unfortunately, I had not lacked certain essential equipment."

He winced, managed a sympathetic smile. "Well, we'll put someone else on this one. You keep out of the office today—go out to the Fort. They're having maneuvers with a lot of VIP's present. You phone in the story—maybe an interview or two if it's convenient—and don't show back here until tomorrow."

I was startled almost to the point of speechlessness. My absence would leave the office seriously undermanned, and Stukey would certainly want to talk to me. To send me off for the day on a relatively unimportant story was virtually idiocy. Or something.

"You go on," Dave repeated firmly, in answer to my puzzled mumblings.

"I've got a guy coming in—used to work on the labor rag here before it folded —and Stukey can wait. He won't know what the hell to do, anyway, and I can probably give him about as much dope on Mrs. Chasen as you can."

"But, Colonel—" I stared at him frowning, still too stunned for proper speech. "I—I don't believe—"

"I don't want Stukey bothering you. That's one reason I'm getting you out of here. Now, go on and take it easy and—and, look. How about that dinner tonight? Come on out to the house about six, huh?"

I said I would. I wanted to talk to the colonel, outside of the office with its many interruptions. There was a terrible price attached to the privilege, but I believed it would be worth it. Broadly speaking, of course. In actuality, there was no proper compensation for the torture of an evening with Kay Randall.

I drove out to the Fort, leisurely, wondering how, if I ever found the opportunity, I should polish Kay off. The most appropriate way, I felt, would be to hit her with a father. She always called Dave "father" and I think that any wife under sixty who does that should be hit with one.

Again—and this would be especially fitting—she might be drowned in mayonnaise. Kay cooked with mayonnaise; it was her rod and her staff, kitchen-wise. Mayonnaise was to Kay as can opener is to Newlywed. I felt reasonably sure that she had whole hogsheads of the stuff concealed in the cellar. If one could surprise her at just the right moment—catch her while she was dipping out a couple of ten-gallon pails for the evening meal—well . . .

But probably she had become immune to it; probably she could breathe in it as a fish breathes in water. In any event there were other ways, and all very pleasant to contemplate.

One might ash tray her to death, for example. You could place her at the end of a vast room while you sat at the other end. And you would be equipped with unlimited cigarettes and a thimble-size ash tray, and she with a pair of binoculars. Then . . . well, perhaps your own experience will allow you to imagine the rest. Driven by an insane urge, Kay would have to empty the tray each time you dropped a speck of ash in it. And each time, before returning to her post, she would have to give you a bright little smile and say, "My! You *do* smoke a lot, don't you?" As soon as she returned to her post, of course, you would drop ashes again and Kay would . . .

No. No, it was nice to think about, but it would never work. Kay had been in training too long. There might be ways of running her to death, but you could never do it with the ash-tray routine.

Probably no one method would be adequate to dispose of her, for that matter. You would have to use a combination of all available means. You might, say, join the several hundred doilies and antimacassars in the living- room into a sack, fill it with mayonnaise, and tie it over Kay's head. Then you could remove her shoes and start dropping ashes on her feet, and Kay—

Hell.

To hell with Kay. How could I think of Kay when Deborah—

But I couldn't think about Deborah either. I was afraid to think about her. . . .

I arrived at the Fort and repaired to the public-relations office. Except for brief intervals, I stayed there until quitting time, sprawled out on a lounge within reaching distance of the bar.

The story wasn't worth my time. The p.r. men could cover it better than I could, and I felt that they should. P.r. men don't work enough. They are always pushing you to take a story, and when you agree they let it slide and come at you with something else. They will give you pictures, yes, possibly some you can use if you are real hard up. They will set up interviews, yes, possibly with someone quite well known in his own neighborhood. But stories, no. They can talk story, but they can never give you one. Some strange psychological quirk keeps them from carrying through.

However, I got them to work, and they produced a fairly good story on the maneuvers as well as two interviews with the VIP's.

"You can do it, men," I said as I swung open the doors of the bar. "You have lingered in the nest too long, and now you must fly. Begone, and do not return without you-know-what. Otherwise, no word anent this occasion shall creep into the *Courier,* and your asses shall be ashes."

It was what they needed—firm words and a steely eye. They tottered away, nervous but determined, and they returned triumphant. I called their stuff in to the desk.

At three o'clock I sent in some pictures for overnight and knocked off. I went home and cleaned up, taking no more time about it than I had to. Then I went to a bar and stayed until a quarter of six when I started for Dave's house.

Until the last six months or so, they had been living in a comfortable apartment at a surprisingly reasonable rental. But Kay had wanted "a little place of their very own," so they had got this thing. It was little, all right, all bright new paint and shiny doorknobs—and rooms approximately the size of packing crates. But it was a very long way from being theirs. By the time Dave paid off the mortgage, his two "kiddies"—four and six—would be well past the voting age.

Kay *knew* that I wanted to see the "little ones," so I was taken in for a look immediately. And that I could have done without.

The little boy, the oldest, had said a naughty word, it seemed, and the little girl had repeated it after him. Kay beamed down at them primly, commanding them to confess their evil to me.

They confessed, sniffling and rubbing their eyes.

"And Mother had to punish you, didn't she? She had to wash your mouths out with soap."

They admitted it. Also that poor mother had been hurt by the punishment much worse than they.

Well, the poor little devils had got one break anyway. They'd been put to bed without any dinner.

We left, and Kay led me up the hall to the bathroom where she was *sure* I wanted to wash my hands.

"Just my mind," I said. "I've been thinking some naughty thoughts."

"Oh, you! You're so funny, Clint!" She laughed. And her eyes said, *The hell you are, bud!*

We went into the living-room. Kay produced two hand-cut glasses and a bottle of sixty-cent sherry, and gave Dave and me a drink. She waited, standing, poised to snatch the glasses from our hands the moment we were finished.

We did and she did, and dinner was served.

It was mayonnaise and something else, something I couldn't immediately identify. It was served on individual plates of Haviland china.

"Well, Father?" Kay smiled at Dave, firmly. "How do you like it?"

Dave mumbled that it was very good, slanting an apologetic glance at me. "Afraid we should have given you something else, Brownie. You'd probably have preferred a steak."

"Oh, of course, he wouldn't!" Kay laughed. "Clinton can eat steak any time. . . . How do *you* like it, Clint?"

"I'd like to have the recipe," I said. "I don't believe I've ever eaten rubber gloves prepared in quite this way."

Her eyes flashed, but she went right on laughing. She was a laughing little woman, this Kay. A joyous little mother.

"Silly! You can't tease me, Clinton Brown. It's iced frankfurters in hot mayonnaise-parsnip ring."

"No!" I said. "I don't believe it."

"Mmmm-hmmm. That's what it is."

"Clint—" Dave frowned. "If you don't—"

"Now you just leave Clinton alone, Father. He can speak for himself."

"It's wonderful," I said. "I don't know how you do it, Kay."

She wasn't kidding me any. Not a goddamned bit. There couldn't be such a thing as iced frankfurters in hot mayonnaise-parsnip ring. This was just what I'd thought: rubber gloves in hand lotion with chopped sponge dressing.

I ate quite a bit of the stuff. I'd had almost nothing to eat since Deborah —since the day before, and I was hungry. It was going to make me sick—I could feel the sickness coming on—but I went ahead and ate.

Kay brought coffee (an unreasonable facsimile thereof, I should say) and something called Marshmallow Grape Surprise. I wasn't up to any further surprise, nor was Dave apparently, so she ate her dessert alone.

"Oh, Clinton!" she said, lapping up the last bite of the mess. "You didn't get our flowers, did you? I mean, the ones we sent to the funeral."

"Kay—" Dave squirmed.

"Now, Father. I just asked Clinton a simple question. I know he couldn't have got them. We didn't get any card of acknowledgment."

She smiled at me, wide-eyed. I said I couldn't understand why she hadn't got the card. "I sent it registered mail," I said. "Registered with return receipt requested."

"Y-You"—she stammered—"you did?"

"Are you sure the kiddies didn't get hold of it?" I said. "They might have mistaken it for a naughty picture."

"Clint—" said Dave.

I was getting tired. Tired and damned sick.

"I got the flowers," I said, "and thank you very, very much. Thank you for all your kindness, Kay. Incidentally, I hope you weren't disturbed when the police called here that night. I could never forgive myself if you were."

"The police?" Kay looked blank. "The police didn't call here."

"A man named Stukey. He called here trying to locate me."

"Not here, he didn't. I was home all—Oh!" Her face cleared. "Father was at the Chamber of Commerce banquet that night. The answering service must have referred the call there."

"Answering service?" I looked at Dave. "I thought—"

"Mmmm-hmmm," said Kay. "It's awfully convenient for Father when he has to be away from home at night. He just gives them the number of the place where he'll be and they call there direct. Just as though it were his own number. I mean, when this number is dialed they automatically call the other—"

"Very interesting. But suppose it was someone who wanted to talk to you?"

"Oh, I never take any calls in the evening! All my acquaintances know that. I keep my evenings free for Father and the kiddies."

That figured, all right. She could give her undivided attention to making them miserable.

"Of course, it's one more expense and I—well—" She sighed bravely. "Goodness knows we don't have a penny to spare. It seems we're always having company, and. . . . Well, anyway, I feel that it just can't be avoided with Father away so much. Let's see, where did you have to go last night, Father? The Rotary Club, wasn't it?"

"Uh—yes," Dave muttered, and he lifted his coffee cup.

His hand trembled. His eyes wouldn't meet mine.

There'd been no Rotary Club meeting last night. There'd been no Chamber of Commerce banquet on the night that Ellen was killed.

I pushed back my chair and stood up.

"I'm going to have to go," I said. "I'm—I don't feel very well."

"Oh, no, you're not!" Kay cried gaily. "We're going to keep him right here, aren't we, Father? We're going to keep this big, bad ol' Clinty right here where we can—"

"Sorry," I said, "and thanks for the dinner. I have to go."

I started to turn away from the table. She jumped up and flung her arms around me from the rear, hugging me around the waist.

"Help me, Father! You know what he wants to do. He's going off to some dirty ol' bar, and—"

I brought an elbow back suddenly. She grunted and reeled backward, batting her fat little head against the wall.

"F-Father," she whimpered. "H-He—he!"

"I saw it." Dave was looking at me at last, very white around the mouth. "Get out, Clint. I've put up with. . . . I've tried to—to—*Get out!*"

"Out of your house, Father?" I said. "Out of your life? Out of your journalistic sphere? Could you possibly mean that I am fired, Colonel?"

"Clint! I'm asking you to—"

"I thought you were telling me," I said. "Am I fired, Colonel?"

"Yes!" he yelled. "Yes! Now—get—out!"

I got out. I couldn't have stayed another minute if I'd been paid to.

I headed for the car, half-doubled over, a thousand hot knives twisting in my stomach. I started vomiting, and I am an old hand at that game, a charter member of the Heave-It League, but this was in a class by itself.

I drove homeward, my head necessarily out the window all the way, and I was going as strong when I got there as when I had started. There wasn't anything in me, but the heaving went right on.

I uncorked a bottle and upended it into my mouth. The stuff wasn't halfway down before it started bouncing. I choked and made another try. The same thing happened—and more.

A great hand seemed to grab me in the guts and squeeze. The bottle fell from my hands. I fell to the floor, writhing.

That one passed, that convulsion. But there were indications that others were on the way. I staggered into the bedroom, jerked open the bureau drawers. I knew what I had to do, but there was something else I had to do first. Get into some pajamas. A pair with all the buttons and no holes. Even then there was a chance that they might see, but—

But I had to risk it. I knew I'd die if I didn't.

I was struggling to get my pants over the pajamas when Stukey arrived. He gave me one startled glance. Then, with none of the questions asked which he had doubtless come to ask, he started helping me with the pants.

"Jesus, keed!" he panted. "Come on! Let the screwin' clothes go. I'll take you in my car, open up the siren. You got any particular place in mind?"

"Any of them," I said. "Any hospital."

"Jesus!" He pulled my arm around his shoulders, lugged me toward the door. "When'd it hit you, pal? What done it?"

"I—rubber gloves," I said. "An original recipe."

" 'At's the ol' keed, the Brownie boy," he said. "Pile it in, pal."

# XVI

As you have probably guessed, it was a case of acute food poisoning, one of the more painful and dangerous kinds since it was the result of spoiled meat. The franks had had pork in them, and bad pork can be deadly. Fortunately, I'd expelled the stuff quickly, and I'd wasted no time in getting to the hospital where my stomach was washed and penicillin administered. Such crisis as may have existed was over within an hour or so. My insides were sore as a blister and I hardly had the strength to raise a hand, but I was out of danger.

I was in the hospital two days—very dreary ones, since the authorities made drinking difficult for me and sometimes impossible. There was little to do except lie there and think, endlessly, unproductively, unpleasantly. To chase myself around and around in that unbroken, seamless circle.

Kay . . . well, of course, she'd done it deliberately. I'd had a standing dinner invitation for weeks, and she'd known that I'd come eventually. So a few franks —just enough for me—had been allowed to spoil, and, their rottenness disguised with more slop, I'd eaten them. Yes, she must have done it deliberately, or so I believed—and I will admit to some slight prejudice where Kay is concerned. But just what her motivation had been, I was not sure. Was it merely some more of her sheer orneriness, a typical Kay Randall stunt? Had the little woman only been demonstrating that regardless of poor ol' softie-Father's feelings, *she* had no use for me and I'd better behave if I didn't want to catch what-for?

That was probably the case. And to be fair to her—a painful necessity—she probably had had no intention of killing me. Dave told her everything, practically, or, rather, she wormed everything out of him in long jolly evenings beside the mayonnaise bowl. She would sit him down amid the antimacassars and pull his sweet ol' funny head into the environs of her cute little old belly button, and then Father would simply have to tell her what was on his mind. She would be very hurt if he did not; she would be afraid he didn't love her any more. And when Kay felt that way—as Father well knew—the aforesaid environs went out of bounds. There were no larksome expeditions thereto, nor invasions thereof, nor maneuvers thereon. So Father, who was already yearning for a brisk patrol with a barrage at the end, would tell all (approximately). He would say, *"Well, it's Brownie, dammit. I don't mind, personally, but I'm afraid Mr. Lovelace will . . ."* And Kay's eyes would grow moist and her mind murderous, and she would say, *"Oh, how awful. Perhaps if we showed more interest in Clinton, invited him out for a good home-cooked meal. . . ."*

Exit Father and Mother to bedroom. Enter frankfurters, parsnips, mayonnaise, and Clinton Brown.

That must have been the deal. Kay had given Clint a lesson, and Clint would know that he had had one. He—I—would know that the poisoning had been intentional, and take the hint. I was to lay off of Father or else.

So . . .

But there was Tom Judge, what he had told me. And there was the fact that Dave had been away from home on those two nights, that he had lied about his whereabouts and let me think, at least in the instance of Ellen, that he *had* been at home. Then there was that reef connecting the mainland and the island, and a lone taxicab crossing the border. And . . . and most of all there was Deborah, that strange feeling I'd had about her, that I could never have . . .

Did I say yes? Did I say that it did make sense? I did not. I didn't pretend to know what it all meant—if it meant anything. Nevertheless it existed, so much to be explained, and I *had* been poisoned. I had almost been killed.

I went round and round the circle, thinking, trying to look into myself where the clue to the mystery probably lay. What had I overlooked, what small factor, that kept me from seeing what I should see?

I didn't know. I don't know now—now, when this manuscript is approximately two-thirds finished and its pages flow higgledy-piggledy over my desk. *(And has someone crept into the room? Is someone lurking in the shadows behind me, trying to read what I have written?)*

But I can tell you this, my good friends—oh, yes, and you sorry ignominious foes—I have a strong hunch that I *will* know before it comes time to type # # # or—30—. And my hunch tells me that I will be quite as much surprised as you are.

Now, perhaps a few words about the doctor are in order.

I had slept almost none at all the first night, but promptly at seven o'clock a nurse came in and induced me to wash and presented me with a breakfast tray. She was a grimly prim little person, unpleasantly reminiscent of Kay Randall. She crisply advised me that I was to partake of the food at once and that it would do me a lot of good (an obvious and preposterous falsehood). I replied that it was just such victuals as these that had put me where I was and that the burned child shuns the fire.

We were discussing the matter, i.e., the digestibility of cold oatmeal, skim milk, and stale toast when the doctor came in. He told the nurse to leave the tray; I could eat or go hungry, just as I pleased. She left, and without preliminary he asked me how much whisky I drank a day. I replied that I never kept track of it.

"You'd better start in," he said curtly. "The amount of alcohol in your bloodstream now would be lethal for the average person. I can't answer for the results if you keep on going as you've been doing."

"That's fair enough," I said. "After all, I don't believe I consulted you in the matter. May I ask a question, Doctor?"

He nodded, flushing, an angry glint in his eye. "If you make it snappy."

"It's a question that's frequently arisen in my mind when coming in contact with the medical profession. Briefly, if treating the sick annoys you so much, why don't you get into another racket?"

"All right"—he turned on his heel—"I've warned you. And I'm telling you this, too. You'll do no drinking while you're here. You can crack up and go into d.t.'s, that's up to you. But you won't do it in this hospital."

He stalked out righteously, a true-blue man of mercy, a man who took no nonsense from the people who paid him. Around nine o'clock in the morning, Stukey arrived.

I thanked him for his help the night before. I demanded the pint which I felt sure was responsible for the bulge in his coat.

"Well, look, keed." He hesitated. "They told me downstairs that—"

"They are insane," I said. "Feeble-minded. A few of the worst mental cases, allowed to play hospital as occupational therapy. My word on it, Stuke, also my hand. Place the pint in it."

"Yeah, but—pal. If it's going to—"

"Did it ever? Have I ever been noticeably affected by it? Give, my friend."

He gave it to me, watching the door anxiously as I drank. I had a small one —no more than a third, at most—and tucked the bottle under my pillow.

"Now," I said. "Now, you will have some questions."

"Yeah," he nodded tiredly, "I guess. Goddammit to hell, anyway."

He didn't get down to the questions immediately. He was sore about having had to let Tom Judge go, and the dragnet wasn't producing anything, and he knew it wasn't going to (nothing but a reduction in his graft). And he was completely baffled as to how to proceed.

I told him to keep a high heart; honest effort was never lost. If nothing else resulted from the investigation, we would at least have a clean city.

"Yeah." He looked at me oddly. "A lot of fun, ain't it?"

"We-ell," I said, "I do believe there are slight overtones of humor."

"Uh-huh, sure. Real funny, all right. I try to be a pal to you, an'—"

"Perhaps I can be one to you," I said. "I was down to Mexico the other day, and I learned about a reef—"

"I know all about it. Hell, there was waves running ten feet high over the damned thing. A guy tried to cross on that, and he'd've wound up in Key West."

"Still, it's within the realm of possibility," I said.

"That realm I don't know nothing about. Maybe they got a bay up there, too, and a guy who could've swum across it in the storm."

"Is that an innuendo, Stuke? Are you returning to your original evil suspicions?"

He grinned sheepishly and shook his head. "Lay off, will you? How many times I got to apologize? I was sore and I wasn't thinkin' straight and—well, to hell with it. What d'you know about this Mrs. Chasen?"

"Something special," I said. "Something extra special, Stuke. I wanted to bring her down to the police station that day, but she wouldn't go. Afraid you'd want to fingerprint her, I believe—very broadly speaking—and her rear end was tender from previous attempts."

"No foolin', keed. Where—"

"I drove her around for the better part of a day. I fed her lunch, booze, and put her on the train."

"You took her out to the dog pound."

"And back. With many a pleasant way stop along the lonely route. As I say, Stuke, she was quite a dish. A wonderful partner in the ancient and honorable pastime of parking."

He sat staring at me steadily for a second. He frowned and said, "Yeah, but, keed—" Then he shrugged and went on: "You know she was supposed to take a boat to Europe? Well, how come she didn't instead of hangin' around L.A.?"

"Doubtless she was in love with me," I said. "She couldn't leave California as long as I was in it. Of course, we'd only known one another for less than a day, but—"

"Cut it out, Brownie. What'd she say when you saw her in L.A.?"

"Now, now, Stuke. Puh-lease!"

"Okay, so you didn't see her. Didn't talk to her either, I suppose?"

"I did not," I said. "The record of her call to the Press Club is an outrageous forgery, one more link in a Communist plan to do me in."

Stukey grinned reluctantly. "No offense, keed. Just habit. I even try to trip myself up. What'd she call you about?"

"About Ellen. You know, to say that she was sorry and so on."

"Yeah? What else?"

"Oh, just to say that she loved me and there could never be another man in her life and—"

"Always clownin'." He sighed. "She didn't mention any other guy? Someone that could have brought her back here, or she might've come back here to see?"

"No, she didn't. As I mentioned a moment ago, there could be no other man where she was concerned."

"Keed," he said, "I'm beggin' you. Be serious, huh? This thing has got me runnin' in circles. The autopsy—well, maybe it wouldn't have told us nothin', anyway, but even that nothin' would have been some help. We could've found out what *didn't* happen to her, if we'd had anything halfway like a corpus, an' —An' it's all like that, keed! Just nothin' to work on. There's fifty buses into here a day and six trains and four airplane flights, an' how the hell you goin' to know when she got here or whether she came alone or . . . or what? I'm telling you. Let me tell you how it stands. I got a couple of pretty good pictures of her from her home-town paper, and we duped a batch and showed 'em around. Well. Up to date we got her placed on eight buses and one train and there's a truck driver that swears she tried to thumb a ride out of Long Beach with him."

I opened the bottle and had another drink. I offered him my deepest sympathy. "Just keep striving, Stuke," I said. "Your head in the clouds and your feet on the ground."

"I'm laughin'," he said. "It's funny as hell, this is. On top of everything else I got those bollixing poems. All the something I got is something to screw me up."

"You don't think they're a clue?" I said.

"Clues, schmooz. Sure, they're a clue and what the hell you goin' to do with it? The guy's got a head on him, he's sharp like tacks, he ain't a money killer. That's your clue, an' you can buy it cheap. It ain't givin' me nothing but ulcers."

"Terrible," I said. "Now, wait a minute, Stuke. I'm not laugh—"

"Well"—he shrugged and stood up—"I wish I could. Why'n't you kill that jug, so's I can take it with me."

I took the last drink and handed him the bottle. He trudged out drearily, his snappy hat pulled low over his eyes, a pronounced sag in the shoulders of his suit.

I was a little ashamed for having laughed at him, and I'd honestly tried not to. But I hadn't been able to help it. Poor Stuke, lord of the pimps and bookies, terror of the panhandlers—Stukey, stripped of his last penny of graft and with no prospects but hard work. No graft, no glory. Nothing but having to earn his salary if he hoped to keep drawing it.

Poor Lem. I couldn't help laughing, pathetic as he was.

He returned that night with another pint, and the next morning, ditto. Not officially. It wasn't business, keed, he said. He just happened to be out this way and figured I could use a little company.

He came out Saturday morning and drove me home, and he remained to visit there, with rather startling, even alarming, results. You see, I was getting just a little weary of him. I had had several hours of his moaning and groaning in a mere forty-eight, and—

But let's move back a bit. Back to the hospital and Thursday.

Stukey didn't know about my trouble with Dave, so, as a friendly act, he'd left word of my illness at the office. He hadn't talked with Dave, just the switchboard operator. But I knew that Dave would be informed as soon as he arrived at work, and I was frankly worried when he didn't call.

It was just possible that he *had* fired me, that he intended to make it stick, or try to. And I knew what would happen if he did. Lovelace was already a little down on Dave just as he was very much up on me. He'd never let Dave fire me. He'd insist that I be taken back. Moreover, he'd credit Dave with one more error in judgment, one more than Dave could comfortably stand.

And if Dave got stubborn, he'd be fired himself.

I didn't want that. I didn't want his position made so shaky that he might fall out of it. Not yet, anyway. *Status quo*—with, naturally, reasonable deviations: that would do me for the present.

It was almost noon before he did call. But the delay was not, it developed, due to stubbornness or a last-ditch struggle with Lovelace. It was just that he had difficult and embarrassing things to say, and he had put off saying them as long as possible.

"Brownie," he began, "I—are you all right? I m-meant to call you earlier, but I thought you might be asleep, and the nurse said you were fine."

"A true conservative," I said. "I hope her noncommittal prognosis didn't upset you?"

"Brownie. Look, fellow—"

"As a matter of fact, Colonel, I am doing as well as could be expected. A little light in the abdominal area, but then I have been for several years. One of those things, you know, or rather the absence of one of those things. I—yes, Colonel?"

"About last night, Brownie. I—that was all my fault. You were deathly sick, and she—we tried to prevent you from leaving. I'm sorry, and I'm sure you're sorry. Why don't we just say the whole thing never happened?"

"All of it? The climactic scene where we faced one another across the Marshmallow Grape Surprise, our stomachs growling in agony and bitter frankfurter-flavored burps on our lips?"

"Brownie"—he laughed nervously—"I . . . well, of course, you know you aren't fired. I'd never have said it if—if you hadn't practically forced me to. I'm not saying that I wasn't at fault, too, but—"

"Let's just lay it to mayonnaise nerves," I said. "I'll be ready to return to work Monday, Colonel, according to the latest dispatch. So if you're positive you didn't mean it—"

"Of course I didn't mean it! My God, Brownie, how could we break up after all the years we've been together? I"—he hesitated and cleared his throat—"I *have* tried to be a friend, Brownie. I—I know how you feel about that— the accident, and I've tried to make up for it the best I could. I. . . . Look. Will you do me a very great favor?"

"Such as eating a nice home-cooked meal? Practically anything but that, Colonel."

"It's about Lovelace. What I want you to tell him about . . . about why you're off work."

"Yes?" I said. And suddenly I was frowning. "Just what am I supposed to tell him?"

"I had to do it, Brownie! I"—his voice broke, and picked up again, shamed, embarrassed—"I . . . maybe it wasn't necessary, but I was afraid to take the chance. You know how he's been toward me lately. And he—he and his wife have been down on Kay ever since—well, you can guess. They spent an evening with us, too. I just couldn't risk it, Clint. I'm head over heels in debt and—"

"Let's have it, Colonel," I said. "I didn't damned near die of rotten meat served up by the Mayonnaise Queen, so what is the ailment that keeps me from work at a time when I'm badly needed? Creeping clap? Too much marijuana? A slight case of—"

"Please, Clint! Don't make me feel any cheaper than I do already."

"Tell me," I said. "And tell me what I do if Lovelace decides to check up."

"He won't. I told him it was nothing serious, but you were supposed to have absolute rest for a few days. That's not too far from the truth, is it, Brownie? You do need a rest. You've been under a terrific emotional strain."

"Old Reporters' Home," I said, "roll wide your doors and trundle out the straight jacket. Here comes Brownie."

"All right, Clint. Have your own way about it. If you don't know me well enough by this time to—"

"Oh, I do, Colonel," I said. "I don't doubt your motives in the slightest. Until Monday, then, eh, when I shall stagger wan and wild-eyed into the *Courier* city room."

"Clint. I wish you didn't feel—"

"So do I," I said. "And a very good morning to you, Colonel."

I hung up. I dug under the pillow for the bottle before I remembered that it wasn't there.

Well, I didn't have to have a drink. I could use one, but I didn't have to have it. My hand wandered under the pillow again, and I jerked it back with a suddenness that set the fingers to tingling.

Damn the bottle. Damn Dave. Yes, and a double-damn for Clinton Brown. Dave couldn't hurt me with Lovelace. He hadn't tried to get me in trouble, only to keep himself out of it. But still, I wished he hadn't done this.

It didn't mean anything. That answering-service deal didn't mean anything. Nor the reef, nor the cab across the border, nor—None of them meant a thing, by itself.

But when you put them all together . . . ?

Meaningless even then. They still added up to nothing that I could see.

But I wished he hadn't done this.

# XVII

I WAS HALF-STARVED by Saturday morning, and I made the mistake of saying so as Lem Stukey drove me home.

He knew exactly what I needed, Stuke did. It seemed that his middle name was Grub, he was a chow hound from way back. His old lady, his mother, had taught him how to cook—when she wasn't busy droppin' another kid—and he was kinda hungry himself. He'd been screwing around on this case for goddamned near twenty-four hours straight, and some chow would fit right into the old spot.

It was no trouble at all, keed. Honest. We was pals, wasn't we, and he wanted to eat himself. Anyway, he didn't have a thing to do. He was already half nuts from this screwy deal, and he was going to have to pull out a while. Jesus, a guy couldn't keep goin' night and day, could he? A guy was entitled to eat, wasn't he?

And he wasn't gettin' nowhere nohow. Just puttin' out, and not gettin' a goddamned thing back.

We got to the house, and he lugged the stuff he'd bought into the kitchen. I wasn't to do a thing, he insisted. I was to park it and let it rest, and he'd take care of everything.

He hung his coat over the back of a chair, tucked an apron into the belt of his high-waisted pants, and rolled up the sleeves of his striped silk shirt. I lingered a moment, watching him. He studied the various packages, his hands absently stroking his oily black hair. Then he nodded, deciding to begin with the steaks. He unwrapped them, and his polished nails trailed over them lovingly.

"Ain't that something, keed? You ever—What's the matter, pal? You don't like 'em?"

"They look wonderful," I said. "I was just reminded suddenly that I was out of salad oil."

"Not now you ain't. I got some. I got everything we need, keed, so you just park it and leave the chow to me."

I went into the living-room, taking a bottle with me. I parked it.

I was being needlessly finicky, I supposed. That was probably salad oil on Lem's hair, entirely edible and harmless. As for the nail polish, well, it would cook off. The fire would take care of it.

I called that I was going to take a bath, and Lem called back to go right ahead. There was plenty of time. You tried to hurry good chow and you'd screw it up sure as hell.

I wished he wouldn't use that word—at least in connection with food. More

245

than that, I wished he'd clear out. I wondered why he was hanging around.

I took a quick cold shower, necessarily having to dress and undress in the bathroom. I got the cuffs of my pants wet, and they clung irritatingly around my ankles. I began to feel a little toward Stuke as I felt toward Kay Randall.

I went back to the living-room and picked up the bottle.

We ate in there, the living-room, my food on the coffee table, Stuke's on one of the kitchen chairs with another chair pulled up in front of it.

It was very good. I forgot all about the hair oil and the nail polish. Almost all about it. I ate, stealing a glance now and then at Stukey. He was tackling the food with both hands, stuffing it down. Eating as though it might be snatched away from him. It made me wince a little to watch him. I felt a faint twinge of sickness that was not entirely of the stomach.

"You mentioned your mother a while ago," I said. "Something about your family. You came from a large one?"

"Well"—he gulped, swallowed, and stabbed another piece of steak—"kind of. Six boys and three girls. Yeah"—gulp—"they was nine of us, one right behind the other. They used to call us the stairsteps over at the ol' sixth-ward school."

"You mean . . . you mean this is your home, where you were born?" I don't know why I was startled by the idea. "Somehow, I—"

"Yeah? Yeah, we was all born and raised here. Not the old folks, y'know, but all us kids was. All livin' here right now."

"No," I said. "No, they are not, Stukey. And I say that as a close student of the city payroll."

He choked on a mouthful of salad. Chuckled. "You—Off the record, keed?"

"Off the record."

"Well, you look for Stowe sometime. Or Sutton. Or Sutke or—le's see. I guess that's about the crop, countin' the two Stowes. The girls is married and don't hold jobs." He forked more steak and stacked salad on top of it. He nodded to me seriously. "There's nothing' crooked about it, you understand. O' course, I got 'em all in with the city, but there ain't nothin' funny about the names. We just couldn't use the other, see, and we kind of switched it around to suit ourselves. You ever hear of a goddamned name with two *z*'s and an *x* in it?"

I said I had been spared that. "Your parents. Are they still living?"

"Yeah, they're still around. I—You didn't know that? I thought you knew I lived with 'em. . . . Kind of funny, ain't it? I mean, you see a guy day in and day out, and it comes up you don't know hardly nothin' about him."

"Yes," I said. "Yes, that is strange, Stuke."

"Yeah, I got a couple acres out on West Road. Gives the old man some place to screw around. He never had no trade, y'see. He was a farmer in the old country, and about all he could do over here was yard work. Spading up

gardens an' mowing lawns an' trimming hedges and stuff like that. He—"
Stukey swallowed and laughed suddenly. "Jesus, I just remembered something."

"Yes?" I said. "Share it with me, Stuke."

"Sure." His eyes brimmed with laughter. "I wonder what in the hell made
me think of it. Why, Christ, it must've been almost thirty years ago. I was—
yeah—I was just about seven, an'—or was it eight? Well, anyway. The old man
was working on a place out in Hacienda Hills, an' this dame—the lady of the
house—finds herself short a diamond brooch. She'd just misplaced the damn
thing, you know, and she found it the same day. But meanwhile she just knows
the old man hooked it, and she calls the cops on him. An'—*ha, ha*—Jesus,
keed—*ha, ha, ha, ha* . . ."

He paused and brushed the tears from his eyes. He went on: "He couldn't
talk English, see? Just maybe a few words. He didn't know what it was all
about an' he was scared as hell, naturally, and all he could think of to do was
keep his mouth shut. Well—*ha, ha*—you know how that would sit with the
cops. They dragged him out in the garage of this place, and they took turns
workin' on him. Hit him with everything they could lay hands on. Hoehandles,
rakes, spades, every goddamned thing. If that dame hadn't found her brooch
an hour later, they'd've broken every hand tool on the place. . . . You never
seen nothin' like it, Clint; the old man was black and blue for the next three
months."

"And that's funny?" I said. "You can laugh about that?"

"Cryin's better? What the hell, the old man thought it was a good joke, too.
But I ain't told you all of it. . . . The cops was kind of worried an' sorry about
makin' the mistake, so they brought him out to the house and helped the old
lady put him to bed. They were pretty good guys, it turned out. Kind of tough
and stupid maybe, but they wasn't makin' no one trouble just for the hell of
it. They turned out their pockets before they left, gave the old man every nickel
they had. Came to almost four bucks in all."

I set my coffee cup down and leaned forward on the lounge. "Stuke," I said.
"Lem. How in the name of God, just how, with an example like that before
you, can you be like you are?"

"I don't dig you, keed." A puzzled frown wrinkled his forehead. "How you
mean? What example?"

"Let it go," I said. "What could I mean? They gave your father four bucks,
and that was that. That fixed up everything."

"Yeah, it kind of did." Stukey nodded. "The old man took the dough and
started to night school. Learned to talk English real good."

I couldn't say why I was annoyed by the story. I couldn't say, for that
matter, that the story was the source of my annoyance. Probably it was Stukey.
I was tired and drowsy. I had much on my mind. I wanted to be alone, and

there seemed to be no immediate prospect of that. He showed no signs of leaving.

He sat with his chair tilted back against the wall, the pointed toes of his shoes hooked through the rungs. He was looking down at the food plates, frowning thoughtfully, and picking at his teeth, with a match.

He raised his eyes slowly, letting them come to rest on me. He stared at me, frowning, so deep in thought, apparently, that he was unaware of his stare.

He must have studied me for several minutes, the small bright eyes never shifting from my face. I coughed and cleared my throat, and he gave a little start. But he continued to look at me, and his frown deepened.

"Look, Brownie, what's it all about, anyhow?"

"A very good question," I said, "but I'm afraid I can't give you the answer, offhand. I suggest that you consult an encyclopedia—the A to Z section."

"Why, keed? Why you doin' it to me? We ain't goin' to pull this guy in in no dragnet. You know we ain't. All this—all it's gettin' is me."

"Not solely," I said.

"So? So we're gettin' rid of the hustlers and fast boys. We're cleanin' things up. What does that mean to you?"

"That," I said, "would probably be impossible for you to understand, my friend. I'm not implying, of course, that you are not a highly sentient and understanding soul. I wouldn't think of doing that, old pals that we are."

He grinned feebly, letting the chair legs down to the floor. "Always clownin'," he grumbled. "All the time clownin'. . . . Just the same, keed, why'n't you give it a rest? It ain't doin' you no good, if you ask me. It's gettin' to where you don't seem to feel right no more unless you're—"

"Yes?" I said, for he had abruptly cut off the sentence, and there was a trace of furtiveness about him. "You were about to say?"

"Nothin'." He shrugged. "What's the difference? I got two murders on my hands. I couldn't lay off of 'em even if you wasn't pokin' at me."

"But you'd much sooner I wouldn't poke, wouldn't you?" I said. "You could be much more leisurely about your investigation. And you could drop it at your own convenience."

"Well—" He began another shrug, then looked at me in sudden alarm. "Now, wait a *min*-ute, keed. That ain't very nice, is it? You make it sound like —like—"

The tiredness and drowsiness had dropped from me like a robe. I was still irritated with him, but I was no longer in any hurry to have him leave. "I was just thinking," I said, "about Ellen. Wondering about her. Do you suppose someone had her come back here—sent her the money to come on?"

"I—how you mean? Who'd want to do that?"

"Who, indeed? But it should be easy to find out, don't you think? The person wouldn't have sent her cash; at least, I don't believe he would. And I doubt very much if he'd've sent anything as potentially incriminating as a check. So that leaves us money orders, records of which, naturally, should be readily available to us. . . . Why don't you look into them? Or would you like to have me do it?"

"That"—he hesitated—"that wouldn't prove nothin'. Just because he sent her some dough."

"We-ell," I said, "I think it might, Stuke. Particularly if he didn't have a satisfactory explanation for his whereabouts at the time of the murder or murders."

"Maybe he couldn't give no good alibi without foulin' himself up. Maybe he was bedded down with a doll or something like that. Maybe"—his tongue flicked over his lips—"maybe the people who could alibi for him are sore at him now. He might've had to push 'em around since then, and they'd like to see him stuck."

I leaned back against the wall, folding my hands behind my head. "But you agree that she might have been sent some money by one of our local residents? Why do you suppose he did it, Stuke?"

"What's the difference? What if I told—could tell you? You wouldn't believe me."

"Oh, come, now," I said. "You mean one old pal wouldn't believe another old pal? Why don't you  "

"I'll tell you," he said. "I'll tell you this, Brownie. You're going to forget all about anyone sendin' her a money order. You ain't going to nose around them money-orders records a goddamned bit. You been pushin' me all over the map, keed, and I been takin' it an' it kind of looks like I got to keep on takin' it for a while. But this way—huh-uh. We don't go no farther in this direction."

He had moved over in front of me, as he talked, and now he was looking straight down into my face. He didn't appear threatening, only intensely, deadly serious.

"I'm going to drop it, eh?" I said. "Just what makes you so sure of that, Stuke?"

"I got a couple of reasons. For one thing, you know damned well I didn't kill her, her or the other dame. I didn't have no cause to. It wouldn't have made me nothin'. Huh-uh, Brownie. I ain't killed anyone, and you know I ain't. You can dig into this deal an' make me look pretty bad. You can turn on the heat until I start stinkin' and they toss me on the dump. But you won't be doin' it because you think I'm the killer."

"And your second reason? The remaining half of the why I am not going to nose around those money-order records a goddamned bit?"

"Why don't we let it lay, keed? Let's skip that one."

"Let's not," I said.

"Okay. I'm tellin' you. You start pushin' me on this frammis an' I'll make you the saddest, sorriest son-of-a-bitch on the West Coast. I wouldn't want to, understand. I'd maybe screw myself by doin' it. But I'd be gettin' it anyway, so that wouldn't matter. Lay off of it, Brownie; don't do no more pushin' on it. Because the old crap will fly and most of it'll be yours."

Well . . .

He sounded like he meant it. It was just possible that, sufficiently aroused, he could carry the threat out. He was a resourceful man when he chose to be, and he had connections in various shady places.

Of prime consideration, of course, was my knowledge that he hadn't committed the murders. Not only because I had, but because they would have got him nothing. Stukey did not do things which got him nothing.

There was no point, then, at least for the present, in pursuing the matter. There was no point in forcing him out of his job. I didn't want him to lose it. As with Dave, the *status quo* suited me fine.

"Lem," I said, "this has been a very nice morning. Good whisky, inspired food, and intriguing conversation. Two old pals, eating and drinking together, baring their souls in long significant silences and occasional muted bursts of profanity. I think I shall let you ride a while, Lem. 'Twere obscene to do otherwise. Amid such beatitude, the smallest flaw would loom as hideously large as a shotgun at a wedding."

"The keed." He grinned. "You want I should wash up these dishes, Brownie?"

# XVIII

THE STATUS QUO continued—with almost indiscernible deviations. Dave was his usual jumpy, worried-sick self. Or more so. Lovelace was his normal, dim-witted self—or more so. And Stukey, of course, remained Stukey. I was still his old pal, the keed, and this goddamned clean-up was killin' him and he was gettin' nowhere fast on them goddamned murders. . . . There was just nothin' to go on, keed. Nothin' but nothin'.

Stories about the murders and the consequent man hunt became fewer and shorter. Even the big Los Angeles papers, with unlimited space to fill, began making it a second-section item.

The emptiness . . . that continued, too. Only broadening now, widening, spreading its deadening atmosphere farther and farther, until as far as one could see there was nothing but desert, parched and withered and lifeless, where a dead man walked through eternity.

The two-way pull . . . that did not continue. It lay dormant within me, of course, awaiting summons. But there was no urgency for the present, and so for all practical purposes it did not exist. Somehow that made the emptiness worse. There was no relief from it, no excursions into that strange outer world where all things moved at a tangent. I was tied to this world . . . and the emptiness. The shack represented something absolutely essential to me, though completely undefinable. I had to stay there, and . . . And she had been there. I couldn't leave the place where she had been. I couldn't disturb it. The lounge where she had sat, the stove where she had cooked, the bed where she had lain.

Nothing could be changed. Everything must remain as it was.

It was strange how much she had meant to me, and still meant to me. So much, much more than Ellen had, although I had known Deborah for a total of hardly two days. I don't mean that I hadn't loved Ellen or that I wasn't sorry about her. But I had loved Deborah in a different way, and I was sorry about her in a different way.

I suppose . . . Well, it may have been because of Deborah's admitted and undebatable need for me. She needed me, and no one but me could fill that need. I did not feel that Ellen had needed me. She insisted that she did, childishly and stubbornly, but I was confident that she didn't. I had always felt that I bored Ellen a little, that she resented my modest mental attributes. I was certain that, if she chose to, she could have been much happier with someone else.

Deborah . . .

How could I have done it, merely to—to—win a game?

. . . I ran into Tom Judge a couple of times.

251

The first instance was about a week after his release from jail. He advised me that he was "chief rewrite man" on the Pacific City *Neighborhood News.* He was doing all right, by God. He was pulling down a hell of a lot more than he'd ever got on that lousy *Courier,* and I could tell that to Lovelace the first time I saw him.

I congratulated him and promised to deliver the message. I walked on, considerably depressed. The *Neighborhood News* was printed in a job shop. It was circulated free once-a-week, providing the publisher sold enough advertising to make its issuance worth while.

The second time I saw him was something more than two weeks later, the same day I heard from Constance Wakefield (of whom much more and soon).

The *News* publisher, it appeared, had tried to get smart with Tom, and Tom had told him where to get off. Tom didn't take any guff from anyone, a fact which—as he pointed out—I knew as well as he did. He didn't *have* to take any guff; maybe some guys did, but he sure as hell didn't. He was now working as an ACCOUNT EXECUTIVE (capitals, please) for a radio station . . . and could I let him have a ten-spot? Just until the ol' commissions started rolling in?

I gave him twenty.

I returned to the office and went to work on the copy for *Around the Town With Clinton Brown.* Thinking about Tom. Feeling that I should do something to help him.

I can't honestly say that I wanted to help him. I had never liked him—and I still didn't—and I had missed few opportunities to give him the needle. Tom and the needle were made for each other. One could not, at least I could not, see the first without seeking the second. Apart, their situation seemed abnormal, and there was an irresistible urge to set it aright. They were natural inseparables, like lead and zinc or Kay and mayonnaise.

Still, despite my dislike for him, I wished there was some way of getting him back on the *Courier.* I was at least indirectly responsible for his discharge, and, strange as it may seem, I rather missed him.

But there was no way I could think of. And if I did manage to get him reinstated he probably wouldn't last long. It was too bad, but it was that way, so that's the way it was.

My phone rang. A straight call from the outside, since there was no accompanying "Hey, Brownie," from the city desk.

I picked up a pencil, lifted the headset from the receiver hook, and said, "Brown, *Courier.* "

"How do you do, Mr. Brown," said a reedy but somehow resonant voice. "This is Constance Wakefield."

"Miss? . . . Yes, Miss Wakefield."

"You may have heard of my—our books, Mr. Brown. I am the owner-editor of Wakefield House, the Los Angeles publishers. I have—"

"I'll tell you, Miss Wakefield," I said. "I believe the Brown you want is in our advertising department. If you'll just hold on a—"

"I wanted Mr. Clinton Brown. That's you, isn't it?"

"Yes, but I'm afraid—"

"It's concerning a manuscript of yours. A collection of poems."

The pencil slid from my fingers. I picked it up again, slowly turning it end over end.

"Miss Wakefield," I said. "Did you say—?"

"Your wife left it with me, Mr. Brown. That is to say, your late wife."

# XIX

CONSTANCE WAKEFIELD. . . .

Age about forty. Height about five feet eight. Weight about one hundred and five.

She was all long, bony legs and long, thin, bony wrists and hands. One of those straight-up-and-down women, reminiscent of a stovepipe in almost every detail but warmth. Erect. Aloof. Sallow. Nearsighted and asthmatic.

Constance Wakefield.

I don't have her catalogued yet, and I doubt that I ever will. I can't say, positively, whether she was merely greedy and naïve or an outright blackmailer. Probably . . . but, no, I don't think I shall make even a qualified declaration on this point. Our talk was hedged about so much that any conclusion would be largely surmise.

I can say that whatever her intentions were, they boded very serious danger for me. Also that the subsidy publishing business—wherein hopeful amateurs are induced to pay for the publication of their work—is riddled with racketeers.

There was a convention in Pacific City that week—some fraternal order, I believe—and the lobby of her hotel was packed. I pushed my way through it to the stairs, mounted them to the fourth floor, and was admitted to her room.

I didn't think I'd attracted any attention, nor would it matter greatly if I had. I look in on all conventions in the interests of the *Courier.* I could have been doing that.

So that was one risk taken care of. As for her telephone call to the *Courier,* well, that, I was very glad to hear, had not been made from her room. She'd been looking forward so much to meeting me—she said. (And she said it almost as soon as I stepped through the door.) So she'd called me from the lobby, from a booth, immediately after registering; she simply couldn't wait until she got upstairs. And—a pale smirk—wasn't that terrible of her?

We sat down, and she fumbled a cigarette into a long imitation-ivory holder. I leaned forward with a match and she jerked away, startled. Then she accepted the light quickly and drew away again.

She wore two pair of glasses, one over the other. She peered at me through them, her eyes bulging behind the lenses like watery oysters. "I—I've had your manuscript for some time, Mr. Brown." She coughed and wiped her lips with a yellowish handkerchief. "It's not something that one could publish without a great deal of thought."

"No," I said. "I don't imagine it would be."

"My first decision was to return it to your wife. In fact, I called her and asked that she come in and pick it up. But she never came, and when I called again she'd moved from that address, so"—another smirk, rather nervous— "I held onto it."

"That was very considerate of you," I said. "You'd have been justified in throwing it away."

The oysters squirmed slightly. I gave them a pleasant smile.

"Well—uh—of course, I couldn't have done that, Mr. Brown. Manuscripts are precious things. Always entitled to respect and conscientious treatment, regardless of one's approval or disapproval."

"I see," I said. "Am I correct in assuming, Miss Wakefield, that you wish to publish those poems?"

"Well, uh, naturally they would have to have a great deal of editing."

"Yes," I said. "I should think they would."

"Much more than Mrs. Brown gave them—that is, I assume that it was she. The meter is rather—uh—unsteady and there are a number of misspellings and —uh—so on."

"I see." I nodded; and that was one mystery cleared up.

I'd wondered about that, how she could have brought herself to show those "nasty, filthy poems" to anyone. Now I knew.

Poor Ellen. She'd probably slaved all of a couple of hours over the things, her child's face puckered in concentration, lips moving with the scratching of her pencil. She'd show Mister Brownie she wasn't so dumb. Yes, and he wouldn't get a single penny of her imminent riches.

Miss Wakefield wheezed suddenly and coughed with a strangled, rasping sound. Her handkerchief moved quickly to her lips.

"Excuse me, Mr. Brown. This low coastal area—*ahummm*—I—*hmmm— aah*—find breathing very difficult. Now, returning to your manuscript—"

"I was about to ask," I said, "whether you'd shown it around any."

"Shown—shown it around?"

"To your editorial staff, say. Or do you do all your own reading?"

"Yes," she said firmly. "Yes, I do all my own reading, Mr. Brown. To be perfectly frank, I have no staff, editorial or otherwise. My business is such that I can handle everything nicely by myself."

I was quite sure that it was, but I was glad to hear her say so. The "vanity" publisher is generally not so much publisher as printing salesman. All he needs to start in business is an office and a printing-house connection.

"No," Miss Wakefield went on, "no one has read the poems but me, Mr. Brown. No one whatsoever. I . . . . I—uh—it might be, of course, that I shall want to seek an outside opinion as to their merit, but—"

"Yes?"

"But only in the event I contemplated publishing them on a straight royalty basis as opposed to our co-operative plan. You see my position, Mr. Brown?

I naturally couldn't assume the entire financial cost of the enterprise without making reasonably sure of the book's salability."

"You shouldn't do it, anyway, Miss Wakefield," I said. "In all fairness to you, I couldn't let you take such a gamble on an unknown author. Just what would my share of the co-operation come to under your co-operative plan?"

"Well"—she had the grace to blush a little—"that would be governed by, uh, various factors."

"Just for the printing, say. And, of course, your own time and expenses."

"Well . . . two thous—eighteen hundred? Fifteen hundred, Mr. Brown?"

The fifteen hundred was it, apparently. She wasn't going any lower. And while I didn't propose to give her anything, I felt a show of reluctance was in order.

"Isn't that rather high, Miss Wakefield?"

"I don't think so." Her voice had firmed. "I think it is quite reasonable. Under the circumstances."

"The circumstances?"

"The circumstances. I have had the manuscript under study for several months. I have laid tentative plans for its publication and promotion. I have made this trip to Pacific City to see you. In short, Mr. Brown, I have already made a substantial investment in the book."

She nodded righteously, emphasizing the gesture with a phlegmish wheeze. The handkerchief went up and down again, and she went on: "Yes, Mr. Brown, I believe fifteen hundred dollars is extremely reasonable. For that modest sum you retain the undivided rights to the book and all profits accruing therefrom."

"Providing," I said, "there are any."

"Naturally. No publisher can guarantee that a book will be successful. I do believe, however, that this one stands a very good chance, Mr. Brown. I am so strongly of that opinion that I am almost of a mind to publish it on a straight royalty basis, without the customary subsidy. After all, there has been a great deal of publicity about these—*hummm*—so-called Sneering Slayer murders, and a manuscript by the husband of one of the victims—"

"Just a minute," I said. "Let's make a supposition, Miss Wakefield. Let's suppose that I demand the immediate return of that manuscript."

"Do you?"

"Not at all. A mere hypothesis."

"We-ell . . . I look on it this way, Mr. Brown. Your name is not on the manuscript, but Mrs. Brown said it was yours and in the absence of any contrary proof—any, uh, dispute—I would feel justified in assuming that you were the author. On the other hand—"

"Yes," I said. "On the other hand, Miss Wakefield?"

"I have an investment in the manuscript, made in good faith. If I should find myself threatened with the loss of that investment—if, that is, you should demand the return of the poems—I think I should insist upon proof that they were yours."

Very neat, no? Despite my personal involvement in the situation, I felt a sneaky admiration for the old girl.

"Do you have the manuscript with you, Miss Wakefield?"

"It is in the hotel safe, Mr. Brown. Manuscripts are such precious things. I live in dread that one may be burned up or lost or—uh—"

"I'd like to go through it with you," I said. "Why don't I pick you up in my car this evening, and we can drive out some place for dinner? I—"

"Please!" The oysters did vigorous sit-ups. "Thank you so much, Mr. Brown, but I'm afraid it would be impossible. I'm not at all a well woman. I require a great deal of rest even after the light sedentary duties of a quiet day. And in the damp—*ahhh-hummm*—night air. . . . Unthinkable, Mr. Brown. Now, I *could* have the manuscript brought up here, or we might examine it in the lobby."

"It's not important," I said, "and I imagine you'd rather not, wouldn't you? As long as any doubt remains about our future relations?"

"Well, yes, Mr. Brown. I think I would like to have a definite commitment before"—wheeze, cough, and handkerchief—"before turning the manuscript over to you for—uh—study and revision."

"I understand. Now I don't know —it's just possible that I might not be able to do the revisions to my own satisfaction. I might prefer to leave the book unpublished rather than have it be a discredit to me."

"Oh, I'm sure it wouldn't be! I'm confident you can do a wonderful job, Mr. Brown."

"But the other possibility exists, Miss Wakefield. What would be your attitude if it materialized?"

"We-ell—" She hesitated quite a bit over that one. "Of course, I already have an investment in the project. My time and—uh—expenses. And, of course, the typesetting and the time on the printing presses must be contracted for in advance. . . ."

Very good again, no? If it was blackmail—and I was by no means sure that it was—it would be very hard to prove.

"I—uh—I believe I would have to declare your money forfeit, Mr. Brown. I would be compelled to."

"Naturally. Certainly," I said. "Well . . . fifteen hundred dollars, eh?"

"I'm sure you can obtain it, Mr. Brown. I—uh—due to the nature of this business, I am forced to inquire into a prospective author's financial situation, and your wife was quite helpful. I understand that you draw a comfortable salary—one which might be borrowed against substantially—and you have a pension and a car and a quantity of furniture. And, doubtless, there are friends who would—"

"Yes," I said, "I think I can probably—How long were you going to be in town, Miss Wakefield? I suppose you want to conclude the transactions before you leave?"

She said that was exactly what she wanted to do. Travel was expensive and a serious drain on her energies, and there was really nothing to be gained— was there?—by delay. "Today is Monday. I would have to leave here no later than Friday night. I—uh—I wouldn't care to go to greater expense, and I have an appointment with my doctor in Los Angeles on Saturday morning."

"I'm sure I can get it by Friday," I said. "It may be rather late in the day, since I have to work. But—"

"Oh?" She frowned. "I hope it wouldn't be very late. If I don't check out of my room by five, I have to pay for another day."

"I'll keep in touch with you," I said. "If it should happen that I couldn't meet you until after five, you could check out and wait for me in the lobby. Or you could have your dinner here while you're waiting."

"Ye-es, I could do that. But is there a train—?"

"There's one at six-thirty, nine, and eleven-thirty. Of course, you'd be on your way long before eleven-thirty."

I wasn't just woofing, as Stukey would say. Constance Wakefield didn't know it, but she was on her way already.

"Well"—she peered at me carefully, nodded—"that should be all right. Of course, if I could get away sooner—"

"Possibly you can," I said. "I'll do my very best, Miss Wakefield, and possibly I can get you away before Friday."

I promised to keep in touch and went back to the office. At the first opportunity, I dipped into a volume supplied us by the U.S. Weather Bureau. The weather and meteorological conditions in general are must news items in places like Pacific City. I used the volume regularly, and, to the best of my recollection, there would be no moon—

I was wrong. I stared down at the page, weighing the importance, if any, of my error.

Thursday—not Friday—was the moonless night. On Friday there would be a crescent moon. Perhaps, then—? I shook my head, and closed the book.

The light wasn't sufficient to be a factor. It would be dark enough on Friday. Absolute darkness would have been preferable, of course, but Constance might not cooperate on Thursday. She wouldn't be anxious enough. She'd still have a day to spare, and she might decide to use it.

So Friday it would be. I'd send Constance along to her Maker then, and she'd need some repairs when she arrived. It would be a pleasure. There was no alternative—as I saw it.

Perhaps she didn't see the connection between the manuscript poems and the poems found in possession of Ellen and Deborah. But it was there to be seen, and sooner or later—probably sooner—it would be. Certainly Stukey would spot it. He'd know how to follow it up, expand it into evidence.

Two poems were useless to him. He might back-trail me for years without ever identifying them with a typewriter that I had had access to. Or if he did manage to do so, what of it? Other people had used the same typewriters. They could have written the poems as well as I.

With the manuscript, however, his job would be simplicity itself. He'd have more than fifty poems to work on. He'd turn up one typewriter I'd used after another. He'd follow me back and back, tracing me through the years, checking the typewriters in every place I'd lived or worked. No one else, of course, would have duplicated my trail. They wouldn't have been in all or even a great many of the places I had been in. By sheer weight, if nothing else, the evidence would prove me the author of the Sneering Slayer poems.

It was unfortunate that the author of the poems was so definitely associated with the author of the murders. Unfortunate, that is, for Constance. I'd convinced Lovelace that the two were the same man, and he'd forced Stukey to adopt that theory—at least, Stukey voiced no other in his public pronouncements. And he and we were the chief information sources of the out-of-town newspapers.

The poet was the killer. The point was indisputable—thanks to me. And it was too bad for Constance, but Constance had put herself on the spot. Constance should have stood in Los Angeles

I called her the following afternoon. I told her I'd been turned down by the bank but that a friend had promised to help, and I'd probably have the money in a day or two.

I let the next day, Wednesday, slide without calling. Around four, on Thursday, I gave her another ring.

The friend would let me have only half the money, and only on condition that I was able to raise the other half. But, I went on, there was absolutely no reason to worry. I knew exactly where I could get the remaining seven hundred and fifty—from an old army pal who would be in town on Friday. Late Friday morning or possibly in the afternoon. He'd been away on vacation and —

She was just a little perturbed. She wheezed and coughed, and said she *did* hope I didn't fail her.

I said I wouldn't.

Friday came. I called her shortly before noon and again at four o'clock. The second call, I told her, was being made from the home of my vacationing friend. He was due to drive up at any moment. As soon as he did, we'd go to the other friend's house and assemble the money. All this would take a little time, of course; they'd probably have to scurry around and get some checks cashed. Perhaps, if she didn't hear from me within the next couple hours, she'd better go on to the station. I'd meet her there with the money—in plenty of time to catch the nine-o'clock train.

Well. She really wheezed and sneezed on that one. This was extremely aggravating, Mr. Brown. All this uncertainty and delay and—and sitting around a drafty depot in the night air! Unless I was absolutely sure . . .

I was sure.

At two minutes of nine, just as she was heading with angry determination toward the Los Angeles train, I had a redcap page her. She hesitated (I was watching her from a bar across the street). Then she trudged after the redcap to the telephone, and I returned to the booth in the bar.

She was boiling angry—wheezing like a teakettle. I cooled her off fast.

I told her I was tired and disgusted myself. I'd been on the move all day, not waiting around for someone else to do something. I'd finally got my two friends together, and they expected to turn up the money within the next couple hours. If that was unsatisfactory to her, all she had to do was say so and—

No, I wasn't going to traipse way down there with part of the money. There was no reason why I should. I'd bring it all when I came—a couple of hours at the outside—but if she didn't care to wait it was perfectly all right with me.

She decided to wait.

I called her at eleven-fifteen.

I simply couldn't make it tonight, I said. There wasn't the slightest doubt about being able to get the money; it wasn't a question of money but time. So, inasmuch as she'd checked out of her hotel and already bought her ticket, I suggested that she go on back to Los Angeles. I'd drive up with the money tomorrow afternoon.

She wheezed and sighed. "Very well, Mr. Brown. I understand that this is a perfectly hideous train, and—But, very well. Tomorrow afternoon, then, without fail."

"Or sooner," I said.

I left the bar and hurried up to the corner of the block. I crossed the intersection and went on across the tracks, pausing at the end of a string of freight cars.

The "milk train"—two freight cars and a mail car, with an antiquated coach hooked on at the rear—was drawn up in front of the station. The engineer and the conductor-brakeman were leaning against a baggage truck, gossiping while they waited for the time to pull out.

Miss Wakefield came out of the station. Weaving with the weight of her suitcase, she had almost reached the coach when the conductor-brakeman saw her. He called, "Hey, lady"—and motioned. She came toward him and he sauntered toward her, letting her do most of the walking. He relieved her of her ticket, shrugged indifferently at some comment or question, and walked back to the engineer.

Miss Wakefield struggled up the steps of the coach and disappeared into the dimly lit interior.

I waited, studying the hands of my watch. Eleven twenty-five, eleven twenty-six, eleven twenty-eight, eleven. . . . The engineer climbed into his cab. The conductor boosted himself into the mail car and began waving his lantern. It was as I'd been sure it would be. She was the only passenger. The railroad loses —or claims it loses—money on its milk-train passengers and does everything possible to discourage them.

There was a cry of "Bo-o-ard," followed by a crisp *choo-toot!* The train jerked and began to move.

I ran down the line of freight cars, swung crouching into the open vestibule of the coach. I hung there for a few hundred yards, until we were well past the last of the station sheds and platforms. Then I stood up and went inside the car.

Only the lights at each end were burning. She was about midway of the car, sitting with her back toward me and her legs up on another seat. She'd taken her glasses off and laid them on the window sill. As I bent over her, the oysterish eyes blinked in the darkness, staring up at me blankly.

She didn't recognize me. I doubt that she even recognized me as another person. I was only a shadow among shadows—a Something which suddenly shoved her down in the seat and flipped the back rest over on her, pinning her helpless against the worn plush.

She coughed and wheezed. Her mouth dropped open.

I poured a handful of coins into it, and she choked and strangled, rattling them dully.

She'd wanted money. Ellen had wanted to be burned up and Deborah had wanted—wanted something else—and Constance Wakefield had wanted money. So I'd given it to her, and in such a way as to give her the utmost pleasure from it.

Most people never get a chance to enjoy their money, you know. They strive for it, they get it, and then they are dead. Constance, now—well, Constance would get some satisfaction from hers. It would probably take her an hour or more to strangle. She'd have the money all to herself, with no worries about losing it or someone's taking it away from her.

Possibly she could even take it with her when she died. Part of it, at least. No undertaker would look at her any more than he had to. Any money within her would stand a good chance of remaining there.

Yes, I had done all right by Constance. I had given her money and the opportunity to enjoy it. All that remained now was to relieve her of the manuscript.

It was in her suitcase. I took it out, re-shut the suitcase, and selected a poem at random with handkerchief-covered fingers.

I stuffed the poem into her purse. I gave her a pat on the head and ran back to the vestibule.

The train was still loafing along at approximately twenty miles an hour. I climbed down to the bottom step of the car and dropped off, within a hundred yards of my shack.

Constance Wakefield. . . . I scrambled up the embankment to my yard, thinking about her.

How could I have done this so calmly, as though it were a relatively unimportant act in a crowded day? Had I actually reached a point where murder meant nothing to me?

The problem disturbed me but only in a remote well-I-should-be-ashamed way. Actually, I could feel no guilt. Ellen, yes. I was honestly sorry about Ellen. And certainly I was something more than sorry about Deborah. But I entertained no remorse over Constance. She had not been alive, as they had. She would not have gone on living as they would have, except for my intervention. There had been no life in her, only phlegm and avarice, and how can one take life where none is present?

No, I couldn't feel sorry for Constance. I had done the decent thing, put an end to her poor counterfeit of life in the most suitable way possible.

I reached the top of the embankment. I dropped the manuscript into the incinerator and continued on across the yard.

I was very tired. Tired and just a little sick at my stomach. I wanted to get into the house and undress and slug down a few stiff ones.

I'd done the only thing I could do. I'd had to kill her, so, since it had to be done, I'd tried to make the best of it. But still . . .

"Where have you been?" said Kay Randall. "You answer me, Clinton Brown! *Where have you been?*"

# XX

I WAS TAKEN completely by surprise. I didn't know why or how she had come here, and for the moment I was too startled to ask. I could only think of one thing: that I was in a spot and that I'd have to kill her to get out of it.

"Where have you been?" she repeated. "Where is he? What are you up to?"

"Why—why, Kay!" I said. "What do you mean, where is—?"

"You're up to something! You've got him mixed up in it! That's where he's been all these nights when he was supposed to—"

"Kay," I said, "I don't know what you're talking about. I just stepped out in the back yard a few minutes for a breath of air, and—"

"You did not! I've been parked out in the road for almost a half hour, j-just waiting and wondering what to do and—you didn't come out of the house! You've been somewhere! You've—"

"Now, that's nonsense," I said. "Where would I go without my car? It's a dark night, and you just didn't see me when I—"

"You're lying!" She shrieked it out. "You haven't been in the back yard. Y-You—I don't know what you're up to, but I'll find out! You'll see! You're not going to get away with—"

I'd been edging toward her, and she'd been backing away, and now we were at the side of the house. I reached for her, and she struck at me. Wildly, hysterically. She screamed again that I was lying and that she intended to find out why.

"You'll see! You can't mix Dave up in your dirty—"

The door of the house opened abruptly. Tom Judge peered out.

"Hey, Brownie," he said. "Haven't you had enough air yet? Your drink's getting all warm."

I didn't know what he was doing here either, but obviously he hadn't come with Kay. It appeared, rather, that he had heard her accusations—as anyone within a hundred yards would have—and was lending me his support.

"I'll be right with you," I said, more or less automatically. "Fix me another drink, huh?"

"Sure," he said, giving Kay a superbly insolent stare. "Be careful you don't catch cold—or something."

He slammed the door on that, so hard that her head rocked back. She turned slowly back to me, lifted and dropped her hands helplessly.

"I—I'm s-sorry," she said. "I've j-just been so worried, and—and frightened. I k-know there must be a good reason why he's lied to me, b-but—"

"Why haven't you asked him?" I said. "You indicated that he's been misrepresenting his whereabouts at night for some time."

"I—well, I—"

"That would be a little too direct, wouldn't it? A little too straightforward and honest? You'd rather sneak around and raise hell with—"

"Well!" She flared up. "You *are* trying to get him into trouble, aren't you? You've been doing your best to drive him crazy, haven't you? You're mean and rotten and hateful, and you're trying to make him the same way!"

"Well," I said, "at least I haven't tried to poison him."

She gave me a puzzled look, then turned and took a step toward the road. "Clint"—she hesitated—"I'm sorry. Don't pay any attention to me, hmmm?"

"You can depend on it," I said. "Now and upon all other occasions."

"And—a-and please don't tell Dave I was here."

"Why not?" I said. "The wife of my best friend visits me late at night. Why shouldn't I, as an honorable and upright man, inform him of the fact?"

"Please, Clint. I'm—I'm a-afraid. He isn't himself any more. . . . Like tonight, now. I'd checked with the Civic League and I knew there wasn't any meeting, so—"

So she'd told him he was going to stay at home. Oh, she didn't call him a liar or anything like that. She'd been very sweet and tactful about the matter. Father had simply been killing himself with work, and she was going to put a stop to it. Meeting or no meeting, Father was going to go to bed and get a good night's rest. And, then, playfully but firmly, she'd taken his car keys.

"He wouldn't talk to me, Clint. He just sat and stared, looking at me something—something awful! I went back to the bedroom for a minute, and when I came out he was gone. I guess he must have slipped out and hailed a taxicab."

"Well—" I said.

"Of course, I'm not sure he didn't have to go to some of those other meetings. But if he lied about this one—"

"I see," I said. "Very interesting."

I could have named her two nights when Dave had attended nonexistent meetings, but I could see nothing to be gained by it. I had a hunch that the affair was one to proceed on with great caution.

"Clint. What do you s-suppose—?"

"I don't," I said. "There's probably some very simple explanation for the whole thing, Kay. One that will doubtless surprise you with its simplicity when it finally dawns on you."

"Well"—she shrugged tiredly—"I hope so. I'll—I suppose I'd better go on back home. Good night, Clint."

"Are you going to ask Dave where he's been? When he shows up, that is?"

"N-No," she said, and it seemed to me that she shivered. "I—I don't think I'd better. I'd rather not know if—if—Good night, Clint."

"Good night," I said.

I walked with her to the road and watched as she got into the car and drove off. Then I went into the house.

Tom had a drink waiting for me. Judging by his appearance, I suspected that he had several in his stomach in addition to the one in his hand.

"Hope you don't mind my busting in on you this way," he said, his chin jutting with a trace of belligerence. "Your car was here, and I figured you must be around. Thought you'd just gone for a little walk or something."

"Quite all right," I said. "I hope I didn't keep you waiting long?"

"Huh-uh." He dumped more whisky into his glass. "Don't think it was—couldn't have been more than a few minutes. Seems like I'd just got here when I heard Miss Beauty Bitch yelling at you."

I nodded. Time does indeed fly by when one is stowing away free drinks.

"Boy," he went on, "would I like to give that bitch a good sock in the mush! She was at the Christmas party last year, y'know, the one all the wives came to. Playing up to Lovelace and his old lady, and giving everyone else the snoot. Midge—well, Midge was wearing a dress she'd made over and I thought it looked pretty nice, but Miss Bitch poked fun at it all evening. You know, pretending like she admired it and asking how much it had cost new, and so on, and all the time laughing about it. Boy, I could have murdered her!"

I said that Kay was like the weather: everyone talked about her but no one did anything. He scowled surlily, rocking the ice in his glass.

"She screws around with me, there'll be something done," he promised. "And that goes for Dave, too. Y'know, I always kind of liked the guy, Brownie. You know I did. An' then he turns around and sics that goddamned Stukey on me. Gets me arrested for murder."

"I didn't know that," I said. And I hadn't known—only suspected—that Randall had phoned in the tip to Stukey. "I supposed that the cab driver had—"

"Huh-uh. They didn't have any driver in to identify me like they would have, so I figured it had to be someone else. And the way I figured, it couldn't have been anyone but Dave. We were the only ones in the office at the time she called, see? Maybe he didn't know it was her, but he knew about what time she got into town and he saw me taking a straight-line call over your phone. And that was enough for him. Oh, he did it, all right. I was going to let it slide, but after I heard about this job in L.A. I decided to tell him off before I left town. The bastard admitted he'd done it. Said he hadn't meant to be underhanded; just hadn't felt free to give his name to the cops because the paper was involved."

I shook my head sympathetically. "I'm sure he didn't think you were really guilty," I said. "Dave's just overly conscientious. He saw you take the call and—"

"So what? I saw him take some, too, but I didn't go running to the cops about it. We were alone in the office. He could have talked to her through the desk phone. I'm not saying he did, understand. Just that he could have. If I'd wanted to be a bastard, I could've got him in a jam like he did me."

"Yes," I said. "Very forbearing of you. . . . But what's this about Los Angeles?"

"I'm pulling out, me and the family. We've sold our furniture, and we're heading for L.A. in the morning. I—Oh, yeah. Let me give you this before I forget."

He pulled a roll of bills from his pocket and flipped me a twenty. I hesitated, wanting to give it back to him, then nodded and thanked him. He was very much on edge, more resentfully watchful than usual. He might consider the gift of the twenty an insult.

"You said you had a job in Los Angeles? What paper?"

"Well—uh—it's not definite. They want a top rewrite man, see, and I said I was entirely willing to come in and show 'em what I could do, so—well, I can handle it, all right. They tell me it's actually a hell of a lot easier to work on those big-city dailies. They've got plenty of help, you know. They don't expect you to knock yourself out like you have to on the *Courier.*"

I wanted to say, *You won't last a shift, boy. There'll be a deadline every hour, and all hell will pop if you miss one. There's no time to work your stuff over. You have to hit it on the nose the first shot. And you can't let everything else slide while you're doing it. You'll have to keep answering your phones, two of them, taking down notes on other stories. You'll have a half-dozen stories going at the same time. Sure, they've got plenty of help; they need it. And whether you knock yourself out or not is up to you. That's strictly your own problem, and they're not concerned with it. You . . .*

But why tell him something that he probably already knew? The truth, which fear and false pride kept him from admitting?

"Tom," I said, "that's swell. I know you'll make out fine, boy."

"Yeah," he said, frowning down vaguely at the floor. "I've got to, so I guess I will. I—I've got to get out of this burg. I can't. . . . There's nothing around here for me."

He took another outsize drink, gulped it, shuddered, and stood up. "Well, I guess I better shove off. Guess I ought to have gone home long ago. I've been out wandering around since about six, kind of giving the old town a last once-over, and Midge might be getting worried."

I offered to drive him home, but he declined. He'd just take a taxi, he guessed. He'd just remembered that there was a fellow in town he wanted to see, and . . .

I called a cab for him. We shook hands and he left.

I had an idea that I was acquainted with the fellow he wanted to see, that one and all the other bartenders in town. And I could understand his unease and restlessness. He couldn't have got more than a couple of hundred bucks for his furniture. With that and a wife and baby—and almost no ability—he was tackling one of the toughest towns and toughest jobs in the world.

What would he do when his money ran out? What does a man do when he can accept nothing less than the unachievable?

It was difficult to say, I thought. There was no telling what Tom Judge would do. Something desperate, of course, something foolish. But exactly what . . . ?

# XXI

SUBCONSCIOUSLY, I THINK I must have been prepared for an unusual aftermath to my strangling of Constance Wakefield. I must have been—for I was not particularly startled when that aftermath came—and it seems only logical that I should have been so prepared. This was my third murder, the third time I had gone through the motions of murder. Yet in each of the first two cases . . .

I couldn't be positive that I'd killed Ellen. I'd slugged her and set fire to her, but she hadn't died of the blow or the flames. Asphyxiation had been the cause of death, and it did seem strange that, once on her feet, she couldn't have escaped from that small cabin.

I couldn't be positive that I'd killed Deborah. I'd left her alone in the shack and she'd been lying so very still when I returned. And in my haste to get the hateful deed over—Well? How could I be sure? How could I know that she wasn't already dead when I broke her neck?

So with Constance Wakefield—my "murder" number three. Murder in quotes, yes, for here again there was a strong element of doubt. Again I couldn't be sure that I had actually killed. In fact, it seemed quite certain that I hadn't.

Her body was found late the following morning. It was lying beside the railroad tracks about thirty miles outside of Pacific City.

There was a handful of dimes in her purse and, of course, the poem.

Her death was attributed to heart failure, with concussion a contributory factor.

It was believed that she had fallen or been pushed from the train, with the emphasis very heavily on the *fallen.*

After all, there'd been no other passengers in the coach—the train crew swore to that. And the train hadn't stopped until it was almost seventy miles up the line. True, there was the poem, but that had been penciled over and marked up so much as to be almost indecipherable. It could not be definitely stated that it was another of the Sneering Slayer rhymes. There was at least as good a chance that, intrigued by the other poems, she had tried her hand at one herself.

She was a publisher, wasn't she? She'd be interested in such things, wouldn't she?

Of course, the police were "investigating thoroughly" and "leaving no stone unturned" but what they expected to find under those stones was obviously nothing.

The old girl was half blind. The coach was dark. She'd gone out to the rear platform for some fresh air—a rarity on the milk train—and taken a tumble.

Yes, I am aware of the holes in this line of reasoning. But since this is fact, not fiction, there is nothing I can do about them. If they irritate you sufficiently, you might take them up with the police of the next county, where Miss Wakefield's body was discovered.

I wouldn't say they were stupid. I am reasonably confident, say, that they are capable of tracking an elephant through a snow drift. They could do it, but they wouldn't—unless the elephant was traveling more than thirty miles an hour or sneaking fruit from the orange groves. They would see no occasion to. It would be a "needless expense." And the cops in the next county, like the cops in so many other counties, are under firm edict not to waste the taxpayers' money.

So that was the way things stood with Constance Wakefield. The cops *believed* it was an accident. They finished their thorough investigation with its incident upturning of stones in some forty-eight hours, and they were *convinced* it was an accident.

The Los Angeles papers tried to build the case up as murder. They whooped it up, mixing its meager facts in with rewrites of the previous two cases. And they even sent their own "special investigators" into the county. That went on for three or four days, and then there was a nice juicy murder right in Los Angeles a B-girl carved up and hidden in, of all places, an ice cream cart— and you can guess what happened to the Wakefield story. To hell with that. *This* was something hot.

Although I had seen evidence of great shrewdness in Lem Stukey, I was still surprised at his positive conviction that Constance Wakefield had been murdered. Or, I should say, I was surprised at the insight that brought him to that conviction.

"Maybe I wouldn't feel that way if she'd died in this county." He grinned. "I'd probably let it slide just like those guys are doing. But I figure they got to see it, even if they ain't doing anything about it. Look, now, just looky here. The first one he sets on fire. The next one he tosses to the dogs. The third one he pushes off a train. He—"

"Hold it," I said. "How did he know it was going to kill her when he pushed her off the train?"

"You ain't listening, keed. You're stealing my stanzas. He don't know it's going to kill her. That's what I'm talking about. He couldn't be sure, and he couldn't be sure that what he did to Ellen was going to finish her, and this Mrs. Chasen—he couldn't be—"

"Hold it again," I said. "He could have finished her off before he put her in the—"

"I tell you it's a pattern," Stukey insisted. "I can't lay it out for you like wallpaper, but it's got to be the same guy. He don't carry through, see? He leaves too much to chance. He ain't—well, he don't seem serious about it."

"Murder isn't serious?"

"So maybe he don't really mean to murder 'em. He thinks he does, maybe, but all he's really up to is a rough sort of kidding. You watch a bunch of youngsters sometime, keed. They'll start off talking, razzing each other, and pretty soon they've used up all the dirty cracks they got and they start punching. They're fed up with the talk, see, so they start making with the fists. . . . It figures, pal. You really want to kill someone, you don't play around at it like this guy. You get you a knife or a gun, and you do the job fast and permanent."

I found myself staring at him. I wondered if . . .

". . . Take them dimes in her purse now." He was talking about Constance again. "There was thirty-three of them, wasn't there? And what would a dame be doin' with more than two or three dimes in her purse? I'd say that that was all she did have, Brownie. The guy that bumped her put the other thirty there. He was razzing her, see? Thirty pieces of silver, like Judas got paid off with."

I lighted a cigarette. I said I would like to offer him my theory.

"I'm convinced," I said, "that she was killed by an enraged redcap. Driven mad by dime tips, he followed her onto the train and poured the dimes down her throat with the intent to strangle her. Then, driven by the wild strength born of fear, she disgorged the dimes—frugally stowing them away in her purse—and—"

"Yeah?" He waited a moment for me to continue, then shrugged. "So go on and laugh about it. For all you know he maybe did exactly that. Not any redcap, dammit. The guy that did the other two jobs would fit his pattern."

I asked him how some of his other theories fitted into the pattern, as, for example, his one-time belief that Tom Judge had killed Ellen.

"You say that the same man killed all three. But he was in jail at the time Mrs. Chasen was killed, and he was with me on the night of Miss Wakefield's demise."

"Yeah, I know." He frowned doggedly. "So I can't lay it all out for you. I don't know all the answers. All I'm saying is that every killing's got the same earmarks, and it ain't got 'em accidentally. The same guy's mixed up in—in—"

"Yes?"

"Nothing. What the hell? I was just going to say that it looks almost like two guys. One of 'em, this joker, he half-asses the job up and the second one makes it stick. Now, wait a minute!" He held up a hand. "I said it *looked* that way. I didn't say, it was that way."

"You know," I said, "that's a very interesting idea, Stuke. Why don't you work on it?"

"Me? Now that the guy's finally pulled out of the county?" He shook his head firmly. "Not me, keed. He ain't no skin off my nose from now on." . . .

The *Courier* carried the Wakefield story one day and gave it a back-page squib in one edition the next. And that was the last Pacific City residents heard of her, unless they read the out-of-town papers.

Mr. Lovelace felt that the story lacked local interest. He felt that it was "negative"—the sort of news we'd been printing far too much of lately. We'd have to have less of it from now on, much, much less. It was "unconstructive." It was "depressing." It took up space needed for "worthwhile" items.

He was very firm during our discussion, and I made no very large effort to soften him up. The clean-up campaign *was* getting a little tiresome. At least, I was getting very tired of writing about it. It was the same thing day after day, dry, repetitious—completely lacking in any possibilities for humor. And with the murderer supposedly gone from Pacific City, the basis for keeping it alive was gone.

So I didn't argue with Lovelace at any length or with any great insistence. Perhaps you "couldn't legislate public morals." Perhaps "these things worked themselves out if you gave them time." And perhaps I knew damned well that it would do me no good to argue.

There was that in his manner which said as much.

The discussion was embarrassing to him, for some reason. He seemed prepared to be angry if forced to continue it.

All things considered, it seemed a poor time to test my influence with him. The clean-up story had been getting a daily play in every edition. We dropped it to one edition a day, then to one every other day, then one every three days. And very soon we had dropped it completely.

There was no further mention of it after that. No further mention of the murders. The paper resumed its puerile emptiness, a newspaper in name only as I was a man in name only. There was nothing in either of us. We were façades for emptiness.

Broadly speaking, things became as they were before the murders. Yet the outlines of those things were becoming dimmer to me. It was hard to reach out to them any more—lash out at them any more. It was difficult to remember why I had ever wanted to.

Dave Randall was as he had always been. A little more nervous and jumpy, perhaps, but generally unchanged. So, likewise, with Lovelace and Stukey and everyone else. All the same, as I was the same. And still a change had taken place.

They were receding from me, growing hazier and wobblier of outline. It was increasingly hard to bring them back into focus.

I wondered if the booze could be responsible, and I swore off for twelve of the longest hours in my existence. It was not enough, of course; months would be required to desaturate me. But further abstinence was unthinkable. Perhaps

I could not go on as I had without serious consequences, but neither could I stop. It made me too ill physically. The clarity it brought me was not the kind I desired.

Without whisky, that circle in my mind began to dissolve. I ceased to move around it endlessly, and my vision turned inward. And while I caught only a glimpse of what lay there, that little was so bewildering and maddening—and frightful—that I could look no more.

I tried cutting down gradually on the whisky, and I have continued to try. But these attempts like the other have not been successful. When I reach a certain stage in the cutting down, the circle begins to dissolve, and I must quickly reverse the cutting-down process. I—

I am not like that; that which I caught a glimpse of is not me. I will not accept it nor look at it.

But I am getting ahead of myself again. I am rushing toward the end, and the end will come soon enough.

The emptiness, the meaninglessness went on. Pushing the others farther away from me. Pushing them out of my reach.

It was unbearable. I could not let them go. They were the life I did not have, my one handhold on existence. I had to do something. And I did.

We have a Republican postmaster in Pacific City, and he owes a considerable political debt to the *Courier.* He was glad to let me look into the records of money orders issued. I went back through them. I found what I was looking for within an hour.

Except that I had some idle time to pass, I had no reason to look farther. Nevertheless, I did look, and what I found was definitely not what I had expected to find.

I was puzzled, startled, at first. Then the puzzledness gave way to excitement, and a curious kind of relief.

So this was it. This was why, and possibly how . . .

Well, it was the day before yesterday when I made the discovery; and as I entered the house the phone rang. It was Stukey. He was up on the Hill, he said, up in Italian town. He'd been kind of takin' it easy this afternoon—just sorta screwing around and cutting up touches with the boys. If I wasn't doing nothing, maybe he'd pick up some grub and saunter on down to the shack.

I said that would be fine, I'd been hoping he would call. He said, swell, he'd be right down then. He was on foot, yeah; he'd sent his car back to the station. But it was a nice day, and he kind of felt like walkin' and . . .

"Fine," I said. "That's perfect, Stuke."

# XXII

HE BROUGHT STEAKS, et cetera, and prepared them as before.

We ate as we had before, myself at the coffee table, he from a tray placed upon a chair.

We finished eating and I reached for the whisky bottle. He tilted his chair back against the wall, sipping a bottle of the beer he had brought.

He was giving the beer a play for a while, he said. He'd been hittin' the old whiz too hard, and a guy could only do that so long before it got him. It sneaked up on him before he knew it. Maybe it didn't show on him, but—well, what was the sense in waitin' until you was knocked out? Ain't that the way you see it, keed?

I shook my head. Nodded. Shrugged. I wasn't thinking about what he was saying. I was wondering how I could bring the subject up, how best to mention my discovery.

It should be done obliquely, I thought. I should come in at an angle, letting him see the approach but leaving its terminus in temporary doubt. First a small hint, then a stronger one—watching him, smiling at him. Turning the heat on gradually and—

And letting him sweat.

He rambled on aimlessly, pausing now and then for some comment from me. I nodded and shrugged and shook my head, and finally he lapsed into silence.

That lasted for several minutes, or what I believe on reflection was several minutes. Then he let the legs of his chair down to the floor and announced that maybe he'd better go. I looked kind of tired, like I didn't feel too good, so—

I came out of my reverie. I said that I wouldn't think of letting him go. "We haven't been seeing nearly enough of each other," I said. "Tell me, what great deeds are afoot with Pacific City's finest? How goes the fearless pursuit of panhandlers and unlicensed peddlers?"

"Aaaah." He raised and dropped his shoulders uncomfortably. "Lookit here, keed. You're talkin' to the wrong boy about that. You really want to do something' about it, which I don't figure you do, I'll tell you who to see."

"Yes?"

"Yeah. You talk to the merchants' association, see how they feel about peddlers. You see how the tourist bureau an' the chamber of commerce feels about panhandlers. They'll say I'm too easy on 'em, keed. I don't treat 'em rough enough."

"But you can't be swayed by outside influences," I said. "I am confident of

273

it. The clean-up campaign is a case in point. . . . You are proceeding with it, are you not? The mere absence of publicity has not deterred you?"

"No," he said, "it ain't."

"I was sure of it. I knew that with one such as you there—"

"Listen to me, keed. I want to tell you somethin'."

I tilted the whisky bottle again. I raised my glass and gestured. "By all means," I said. "You tell me something, and then perhaps I shall tell you something."

"The clean-up's over an' done with, and I ain't sorry. But there ain't a damned thing I could do if I was. . . . You really don't see it, Brownie? I didn't expect old Lovey to know straight up, but I didn't figure I'd have to draw a map for you. Who do you think owns all these whorehouses and policy joints? Who do you think owns the horse parlors and deadfalls and mitt mills? Well, it ain't the grifters, keed. They just work 'em. And they pay goddamned fancy rents for the privilege. And the people that get them rents swing plenty of weight around town. Sure, I graft. Why not? If the dirty money ain't too dirty for our best people, like they call them, it's plenty clean for me. But I tell you this, pal. If the stuff wasn't there, I couldn't take it."

I looked down at my glass, slowly added more whisky. I shook my head firmly. "That's an old story, Stuke. Every crooked cop I've ever talked to has the same alibi. He'd like to go straight, but—"

"I ain't said I'd like to. I ain't no hero. I'm just telling you why it's this way, and why it's going to keep on being this way. Yeah, it's an old story, all right, but I don't figure you know it very well so I'll give you the rest. There's the fines we take in from those places. We pull the grifters in once a week, they pay their fines, an' then we let 'em go back to work. It's like taxes, keed, and it comes to enough to pay the overhead for the whole damned department. More than a hundred grand a year that them best people—the regular taxpayers—can keep in their pockets. And that's—"

"Stuke. Please," I said. "You don't have to defend yourself to me. I know your conscience is spotless, your soul pure as driven snow, and—"

"You asked for it," he said stubbornly. "I'm telling you. You claim I'm always layin' into the colored folks—blaming everything that happens on them. Well, maybe I do, kind of, but I got a damned good reason to. Not one out of a hundred can get a decent job, a job where he can get as much as you do, say, or even half as much. They don't make no dough, but they got to keep laying it on the line. They get stuck every time they turn around. Their rents cost 'em plenty, because there's just one section of town they can live in. If they don't want to walk two-three miles to a store in a white neighborhood —where they'll probably get a good hard snooting—they have to buy from the little joints in their own section, places where there ain't much of a selection and the prices are high. It takes every nickel they can get just to keep goin', just to live like a bunch of animals. They're always about half sore, an' it don't take much to make 'em more than half. They make trouble; they start playin' rough. And all me and my boys can do is play a little rougher. Flatten 'em out or get 'em sent up for a stretch. We can't get to the bottom of the trouble, try to fix it so there won't be any more. All we can do is. . . . All right," Stukey sighed, "go on and laugh at me. But just the same, I'm giving it to you straight."

"I wasn't laughing at the remarks," I said, "only at their author. I was wondering what irresistible sociological forces moved you to offer to hush up a murder that you thought I had committed, providing I would play ball?"

He hesitated, frowning. I really think he had forgotten all about it. "All right," he said. "I play along. I got just so much to work with, and I try to get all I can out of it. What about you?"

"About me?"

"Sure. You're smart. You got a good education and a good trade. If things don't go to suit you, you can move on to another job. You don't have to play with anyone."

"I don't understand you," I said.

"Why don't *you* do something? You've got influence with Lovelace. You can swing your weight with him, and if he swings back you ain't really lost anything. Me, I'm nothin' to him. If he gets sore at me, I'm sunk. So how's about it, keed? If you really want somethin' done about Pacific City, why don't you go to work on it?"

"It seems to me," I said, "that I've already—"

"Huh-uh. You ain't done nothin', and you ain't goin' to. This clean-up wasn't nothin' to you but a way to swing the old needle. You could make Lovelace squirm. You could turn the heat on me. You could shake everything to hell up, and it gave you a bang. That's all it meant to you. That's all anything means to you. Just a chance to make someone sweat. From what I hear, you've driven this Randall guy halfway off his rocker. You've got him sweatin' blood, afraid he's going to lose his job. But I could tell him he ain't going to lose it. You won't carry things that far; you don't want him to get away from you."

I poured another drink, and for some reason my hand shook.

"Anything else?" I said.

"Uh-huh. The county judge thing is out. I've been studyin' it over, an' I can see it was just a pipe dream. Maybe I could make it, but I wouldn't last much longer than it would take me to open my mouth. That's the way you figured, huh, keed? That's why you wouldn't give me a boost? You knew I'd lose out all the way around, and you couldn't ride me any more."

"That's all?" I said. "You've nothing more to say?"

"I guess that's about it, Brownie." He shrugged good-naturedly. "No hard feelings?"

"I'd like to say something, then. About Ellen. Now, I believe the evidence indicated that she revived after the murderer's attack. She was up on her feet in an enclosure less than fifteen feet square, and yet she couldn't make it to the door or a window. She died of asphyxiation."

"Yeah," Stukey nodded. "Like I was sayin', keed, the guy acted like—"

"I know. Like he wasn't serious. Like he must have had some help from a second guy. Someone, say, who was being blackmailed by her."

He stared at me silently. There was a peculiar hardness in his small round eyes.

"Which raises this question, Stuke," I said. "Why did you send her almost three thousand dollars in a little more than two years' time?"

# XXIII

His face went completely blank. Then, slowly, a strange look spread over it—not of fear, as I had expected, but rather a compound of regret and annoyance and, mayhap, embarrassment.

He stood up and went out into the kitchen. I heard the ice box door open and close.

He came back and sat down, a freshly opened bottle of beer in his hand.

"A blackmailer," he said thoughtfully. "Not just a one-shot, not just a gal squeezing a little dough when she was in a pinch, but a steady worker. That's the way you saw your wife, Brownie?"

"I—" I paused. "I asked you a question, Stuke."

"And you got an answer. An' here's one to the next question. Why does a guy give a woman dough? Why would he keep sendin' it to her month after month when he ain't even seein' her?"

I heard a laugh. One that was not mine, although it came from me. "Oh, *no*," I said. "No, Stuke. That I can't believe."

"I know you can't. I knew you wouldn't. But that don't change nothin'. I liked her—just liked to talk and visit with her, and she seemed to like it, too. She never asked me for no dough; she never tried to make me for a penny. So . . . so maybe that was part of it. Maybe that meant a lot to a guy who never saw a dame without her hand out. I liked her, and when you like someone you try to help 'em."

I laughed again, the laugh that was not my laugh. So he just liked to talk to her, visit with her; *he* was content with that. And I—

Somehow—I believed him.

"That was all, keed. I can buy the other for a hell of a lot less than three grand, and I can get it a lot handier. I don't have to cover up and sneak around. That wasn't easy for me to do, Brownie. Talkin' about her like I did, pretendin' like I thought—"

"Why did you?"

"Why?" He shot me a puzzled glance. "You mean I should show how I felt in front of you? I shouldn't cover up about a guy's own wife? I guess you and me went to different schools, keed."

I reached for my drink, and the glass slipped from my fingers. It bounced from the coffee table and rolled splashing to the floor. I picked up the bottle and drank from it.

"I believe you threatened me," I said. "I was to lay off of this deal or you'd make me wish I had."

"Let's skip it, huh, pal? I wouldn't do it even if you was to try to make

277

somethin' out of this. Maybe it would give you some trouble, but it would hurt me more. If it got around that I was spreadin' a story like—like—"

"Go on," I said.

"Ah, hell, Brownie." He tilted his chair back against the wall. "I was just sore. It—it ain't really nothin'. It didn't make no difference with me, did it? Why, Jesus, I had it doped out right from the beginning almost: that pension, with nothin' wrong showin' on you, an' breaking up with your wife when there wasn't another babe, an' your drinkin' and ridin' everyone, an'—And this place. You wantin' a home—not just a room—and doing your best to have one. It wasn't hard to figure out for a guy that was really interested. So I did, and what the hell? If it didn't mean nothin' to a lowdown jerk like me, why would—"

"You've known all along," I said. "You've let me think—You let me go ahead and—"

He mumbled apologetically. He raised the beer bottle and drank, his head thrown back to avoid my eyes.

He'd let me go ahead and . . .

It had all started because I was afraid that he . . .

"Let's talk about somethin' else, huh, keed?" He gave me a pleading look. "About this doll, now, that your friend Randall's been playin'. She's no good in trumps, an' you can tell him I said so. He'd better pull out while he's still able to."

"Doll?" I said. "Doll?"

It didn't register on me. There was no room for it in my mind.

"You didn't know about her? Well, damned near everyone else seems to. The guy's practically been livin' with her at night, and she's the kind that talks." He started to raise the beer bottle again, paused. "Come to think of it, maybe you better not tell him nothin'. Just leave her to me. I'll run the little bitch out of town."

The bottle went up. He threw his head back to receive the beer.

Then . . .

I doubt if he knew what happened then.

I hurled the whisky bottle and it crashed sickeningly against the bottle he was holding. His tilted chair shot from under him. He went over backward in a tinkling shower of glass, and his head hit the floor with a thud.

He lay there crumpled and groaning, his face bleeding from a dozen cuts.

I got a length of clothesline rope from the kitchen, swung an end over one of the living-room rafters, and gave him a boost. After all, he'd always wanted me to boost him, hadn't he?

And then I fled the place. I took a room at a hotel. And I have not been back since. And now I am back at the newspaper. The others have all gone, but I think someone has come in, has been sitting in the darkness at the other side of the room. . . .

Of course, I didn't kill him. I know now that I am incapable of killing anyone. He has been missing for more than a day, but not because he is dead. I don't know what—why—

I don't as yet have the answer to certain other questions, I only know that I have not killed and cannot kill, and. . . .

*He is stirring at last, the man who has been sitting there behind me. He has come forward and his hand has dropped down on my shoulder. It is a well-manicured hand. I can smell the odor of hair oil and talcum powder and freshly shined shoes. The hand moves from my shoulder to the stack of manuscript. It rakes it off the desk and into the wastebasket.*

"Jesus, keed. You hadn't ought to write things like that. People might think you're crazy."

HE GRINNED DOWN at me through slightly puffed lips. There was a wide strip of adhesive tape across his nose. His talcumed face was a network of red scratches and cuts.

"I look like hell, huh, keed? Jesus, what'd you run out on me for? That wasn't no way to treat a pal. A guy's chair slips out from under him, and he smashes his face on a bottle an'—"

"What—what are you trying to pull?" I said. "You know I tried to kill you. I botched the job the first time, and you've been waiting for me to try again. You've had the shack staked out. You had them give out the report that you were missing, and—"

"Why, keed"—he widened his eyes in exaggerated amazement—"I don't dig you, a-tall. Like I said, my chair slipped. I'd swear to it, Brownie, get me? I'd *swear* it happened that way."

I got him, all right. I was beginning to get him.

I saw what he intended to do, and a shiver of sickness ran through me. "Why?" I said. "Why did you drop the stake-out? What made you see that I wasn't—that I couldn't—"

His grin widened. His eyes shifted a little, and he jerked his head toward the Teletypes. "Looks like you got a lot of news there, keed."

"Why?" I repeated.

"Maybe you ought to take a look: Maybe it's the same news we got at the station a couple hours ago."

I turned slowly. I walked over to the Teletypes. A long streamer of yellow paper drooped from each. I picked up the one from the A.P. machine.

And I read:

> LOS ANG 101 AM SPL TO COURIER
> THOMAS J. JUDGE, UNTIL RECENTLY A REWRITE MAN ON THE
> PACIFIC CITY COURIER, CONFESSED TO DAY TO THE MYSTERIOUS
> MURDER OF ELLEN TANNER BROWN, ESTRANGED WIFE OF
> ANOTHER COURIER EMPLOYEE. BROKE AND OUT OF WORK, THE
> SULLEN STOCKY NEWSMAN TOLD POLICE THAT HE 'JUST WANTED
> TO GET EVERYTHING OVER WITH.' 'I'M NOT SORRY ABOUT HER,' HE
> DECLARED. 'SHE HAD IT COMING TO HER.' JUDGE'S EARLY
> MORNING CONFESSION TO LOS ANGELES AUTHORITIES EXPLODED A
> WIDELY HELD THEORY THAT MRS. BROWN'S DEATH WAS ONE OF
> THREE SOCALLED SNEERING SLAYER MURDERS. WHILE UNABLE TO
> EXPLAIN CERTAIN SIMILARITIES
> MORE MORE MORE

I swallowed heavily, and my head swam for a moment. Then I read on down the yellow stream into the additional dispatches.

Tom had been lying under the cottages (while I was there) and had returned to consciousness from his drunken stupor (just after I left). He was miserable and thoroughly angry. He had been sorely mistreated, as he saw it; she had lured him there and then laughed at him.

He crawled out from beneath one of the cottages and re-entered hers. She, half hysterical and painfully burned—and engaged in trying to beat out the fire in the bed—had hurled herself at him. He had brutally knocked her to the floor. Then, frightened by what he had done, he had hastily wiped up the room with his coat and fled. There was no actual intent to kill, of course, but still he *had* brought about her death. He had—and I hadn't. And I knew it was the truth.

"Well, Brownie?" Stukey said. "I guess that cleans it up, don't it?"

I stared at him blankly, thinking about Tom Judge, thinking of how much alike Tom and I were. Doubtless that was why I had always detested him so much, because he was so accurate a mirror of my own faults. Tom demanded the benefit of all doubts, but he could give no one the benefit of any. A frown was suspicious, but so also was a smile. . . . Tom Judge, plowing stubbornly down one rocky path when he could have moved over into an easier and friendlier one. He wouldn't try to reorient himself. He wouldn't try to adapt himself to another way of life which, while it would not have been wholly satisfactory, could have been far better than the one he had. Not Tom. Not me. We preferred being miserable, martyring ourselves. Living not as men but human gadflies.

"You see, keed? I figured like everyone else that the three deaths were all tied together. That's what had me thrown. But when this Judge character confessed, I seen right away that you hadn't—"

Stukey had been right about me. I hadn't wanted any change. All I had wanted was to keep everyone under my thumb, to gouge and nibble away at them while I watched them squirm. . . . Dave Randall. He hadn't always let Kay wear the pants in the family. It was I, not Kay, who had stripped him of all his self-confidence. She had merely taken over where I left off. . . . So that was the way it was. That was all I had wanted: to make everyone suffer as I insisted on suffering. Then, when I wearied of the game, when I could no longer continue it, I would kill myself. Or, no—No! I would make *Them* kill *me*. I would do something so blatantly criminal— so botched—that They would know I was guilty, and They would have to . . .

They *would* have to, wouldn't they?

They couldn't leave me to go on . . . into nothingness.

Stukey was watching me, narrow-eyed. He said, "Get it through your noggin, keed. You—"

"You're wrong," I said. "Tom's lying. I went over to the island that night. We argued, and she threatened me, and—and—"

"Huh-uh." He wagged his head. "He ain't lying. Anyway, you couldn't have been over on the island that night. You couldn't have got across the bay. Everyone knows that."

"I tell you I did! I hit her with the bottle. I—"

"Yeah? How you goin' to prove it—and what if you did? You want to be sent up for a couple of years on an assault charge, Brownie? You want to lay around in a cell with no booze and nothin' to do but think?"

He chuckled softly. But his round little eyes were like brown chunks of ice.

"I killed Mrs. Chasen," I said. "I met her in Los Angeles when I went up for the funeral, and—"

"You didn't kill her. She killed herself."

"I tell you I *did* kill her!" My voice rose. "I can tell you just how I did it. I'd been out drinking, and when I came back she was lying on the bed asleep and . . ."

I told him.

He listened thoughtfully, but his head wagged again. "So that was how—" He hesitated. "But you didn't kill her, keed. She was already dead."

"I tell you. . . . What makes you think—?"

"You remember them sleeping pills she had? Five-grain amytals? Well, we checked back on the prescription and she'd had it filled the day before. She'd got thirty of those goofballs and there was only five left in her purse."

"But that doesn't prove she took—"

"I'm tellin' you, keed. We didn't have much in the way of a body to work on, but there was plenty of blood. And that blood was loaded with the goofer dust. More than enough to kill her. Sure, I kept it quiet. The deal was futzed up enough as it was, and it didn't make sense. How in the hell if she'd killed herself could she have wound up in the dog pound? I figured maybe the coroner had called his shots wrong. But—well, it makes sense now. She was already dead when you hit her. And by the way, keed, you didn't break her neck. The coroner would've spotted that. Huh-uh, you hit her, I guess, but you didn't kill her."

He nodded firmly. I reached for a cigarette, then dropped it to the floor unlit. And I was back there in the room with her, looking down on her body—her tense, stretched-out straight body—even her fingers stiff as dead wood. Dead, all right, that's what she was—and somehow I must have known it. Half of me, anyway, half of me must have known it. But the two-way pull had been working, and the other half had to keep at it, pushing and plunging and needling. So I hit her and picked her up and tossed her into the dog pound, *even though I knew she was dead.*

Christ.

His eyes softened a little. "She was a pretty lonely little lady, wasn't she, keed? From what I hear, she didn't get along with most people. So she was kind of nuts about you, and you didn't know how to stave her off and—well, maybe you'd better tell me what happened. Your guess would be better than mine. I figure she must have found out what was wrong with you. She must've seen that things weren't going to be like she'd thought. And I guess a little lady like that . . . I guess she couldn't take it. She didn't want to take it."

*No one but you, Brownie. If I couldn't have you . . .*

"You see, keed? Once I got that first murder out of the way, the real one, the others fell right into line. I could take 'em for what they were, a suicide and an accident."

"You don't know," I said. "You can't be sure. If I confessed to—"

"They'd put you in a nuthouse, Brownie. They wouldn't give you the gas chamber."

"Constance Wakefield was trying to blackmail me. I stalled her and got her to take that late train, and then I got on with her—"

"Save it, keed." He held up his hand. "I got a pretty good idea of what you did, and it don't make no difference, see? You didn't kill her. You didn't ride over into the next county and shove her off the train. It was just what it looked like—an accident."

"But I—I—"

"Okay," he shrugged. "Have it your own way. A couple years for assault and battery, six months for maiming a dead body, a couple of years more on this Wakefield deal—whatever they'd call that. About five years in the pen, say, if they believe you. That or the nuthouse. Is that what you want, keed?"

My throat was dry. I shook my head silently.

He sighed, and the sound was weary and a little sad. "It ain't much fun, is it, keed? You've been slidin' down the rope and havin' a hell of a time for yourself. And now you're at the bottom, and all you can do is hang there. You can't let go and you can't get anyone to give you a shove. It wouldn't make 'em nothing. They can't do your job for you. It—it ain't much fun, is it, keed?"

The Teletypes were clicking again. I turned and stared at them blankly, at the words marching across the yellow paper—across a vast and empty desert where a dead man walked through:

. . . TODAY'S WEATHER IN SOUTHERN AND LOWER CALIFORNIA. CLOUDY WITH THUNDER SHOWERS THIS MORNING, FOLLOWED BY . . .

"You know what I figured on doin', Brownie? Why I came up here? Well, I was goin' to give you the old horse laugh, keed. You were at the end of the line, I figured, and you'd be sittin' here waiting for someone to pick you off. Maybe you'd kidded yourself you was going to do a brodie, but I knew you wouldn't. You couldn't, any more'n you could have killed those other people. You'd make a pass at doin' it, but that'd be as far as it would go. You couldn't carry through with it. And like I been tellin' you, no one else is goin' to do it. There ain't going to be no pinch—no gas chamber. No easy way out. So I was going to lay it on the line for you, and watch you squirm. Make you beg like you've made me beg. Laugh at you like you've laughed at me. But—well, I'll tell you something keed . . ."

. . . FOLLOWED BY CLEARING SKIES, STRONG TO MODERATE WINDS AND . . .

". . . There's one thing about bein' a louse, keed. A no-good like maybe I am. When you're that way—"

"You're not that way," I said. "You're a long way from being a louse, Stuke. I don't know why I ever thought—"

"I'm telling you. When you're a louse yourself, keed, when you know you're a long way from being perfect yourself, the other lice don't look so bad to you. You're all in the same family, and you don't hurt 'em unless you have to. You don't make things no tougher on 'em than you have to. Look at me, Brownie." He gripped me by the shoulders. "I ain't laughin', am I? I didn't stay here to laugh. I'm here to help you."

He gave me a little shake, a brisk puffed-lipped nod of his head.

I said, "There's just one way you can help, Stuke. I—"

"Huh-uh," he said, firmly. "That's out, keed. I couldn't do it. I ain't goin' to. So forget it. You're goin' to snap out of it, Brownie. You're goin' to get your mind off of that—off of yourself, and start thinkin' about something else. That—it ain't everything. It—"

"Isn't it?" I said. "Isn't it rather easy for you to talk, Stuke?"

"It'd be easier not to, keed. A hell of a lot easier."

"But you don't know! You don't know what it's like to—"

"Keed"—he tapped me on the chest—"don't tell me what I don't know. You'd be talking for the next forty years and we ain't got much time. You've got to get cleaned up, get yourself something to eat and a little sleep. You've got to be in here on the job in the morning, and you've got to work harder than you ever worked before. You're going to go on swinging your weight against the rats and the cheaters in this town, but this time you're going to swing it the right way. It ain't going to be a needle job. It's going to mean something. . . . Remember what I told you the other night? Well, I meant it. If the graft wasn't here to take, I wouldn't be taking it."

"But you don't know—I can't! God, how can I?"

"You ain't got no choice," he said.

His eyes were soft, sympathetic, friendly. They were firm and unwavering.

I looked away from him to the Teletype machines and the last lines of the weather forecast:

. . .THUNDER SHOWERS IN THE AFTERNOON. POSSIBLY CLEARING BY EVENING.

# BAD
# BOY

I

MY EARLIEST RECOLLECTIONS are of being pinched. Not in the figurative sense, but actually. I was an awkward, large-headed tot, much prone to stuttering and stumbling over my own feet. My sister Maxine, though somewhat my junior, was quick-moving, quick-thinking, glib and extremely agile. When my actions and appearance irritated her—and they seemed to almost constantly —she pinched me. When I failed to respond quickly enough to her commands, she pinched me. The metaphor, "as smooth as a baby's skin," has always been meaningless to me. My infant hide appeared to have been stippled with a set of coal tongs.

One day, shortly after the Thompson family fortunes had undergone an unusually terrifying nosedive and we had moved into a particularly execrable section of Oklahoma City, Maxine spotted two Negro children returning home from the grocery. They had a large bottle of milk with them. Bringing me up from the steps with a quick pinch, Maxine dragged me out to the sidewalk and accosted the two youngsters.

Would they like to be white? she inquired. Well, in return for their milk, she would perform the transfiguration. She had done the trick for me, and I had been blacker than they were. Much, much blacker. . . and now just look at me.

The tots were a little dubious, but, being pinched, I loudly swore to Maxine's tale. And, being pinched again, I hurried into the kitchen and got the implements—a bar of soap and a scrubbing brush—with which the transformation was to be effected. At Maxine's instigation, I took the patients out to the back-yard water hydrant, and began scrubbing them. Maxine took their milk into the privy (it was that kind of neighborhood), drank all she could hold, then dropped the bottle down the hole.

Emerging, she entered the house, beginning to scream with horror as soon as she had got through the door. Mom came running out, Maxine in the vanguard. Pretending to pull me away from the puzzled Negroes, she got in several energetic pinches, making me howlingly incoherent by the time Mom reached the scene. She gave the tots the price of a fresh quart of milk, wiped them off and dragged me into the house, declaring that she didn't know what she was going to do with me. Snickering hideously, Maxine remained in the yard, free to go about her devilish designs.

Being very young, I was unable to explain the affair within the time that it would have done any good to explain. I got an impression from it, however, very nebulous, then, but one that expanded and jelled later.

I was going to catch hell no matter what I did. I might as well try to enjoy myself.

---

## II

I WAS ALWAYS a sucker for friendship. Anyone who spoke a friendly word to me could have the Buster Brown blouse which I customarily wore. In my earlier years, my father traveled considerably about Oklahoma, seldom staying in any town more than a month—not long enough for me to become accustomed to a strange school, yet too long for me to lay out. Just about the time I began to get acquainted, we would pull up stakes.

So I hungered for friendliness, and no matter how many times I was duped I never ceased to bite on the bait that was put in front of me. There was a game called "push-over" in those days. A boy would come up to you, put his arm around your shoulder and engage you in kindly conversation. Then, just when you were beginning to warm up to him, another boy would kneel behind you, the first would give you a push, and you would fall backwards on your head.

I don't know how many times I fell for this game, and similar ones, before I began to get the idea that what appeared to be friendship might be something else entirely. I never liked the idea, and I fought against it. In later life, more or less as a duty, I would draw back from a proffered kindliness and coldly demand the reason for it.

In time, my father settled more or less permanently in Oklahoma City where he became the law partner of Logan Billingsley, brother of Sherman, the Stork Club proprietor. In the early days of Oklahoma, Pop had been a peace officer, and had saved Logan from being lynched. I know nothing about the merits of the case, but I do know that they became close friends and later partners.

Logan had a son named Glenn, a more mischievous brat than which never lived. I understand that he is now running a swank restaurant in Hollywood, but that has nothing to do with this story.

Glenn led a charmed life. One Saturday afternoon when he was leaning out the office window, he fell out. But he survived the four-story fall with no more than a scratch. He landed on the awning of the street-level drug store, went on through it, and dropped into a baby carriage. The vehicle was empty of its occupant, fortunately, for he made a wreck of it. But, as I say, he wasn't hurt a bit.

We lived over in the west end of town, in the vicinity of the Willard school, and a very tough section it was in those days. I came home nightly with large chunks missing from my person and attire. Glenn came in always whole and happy, and usually bearing a quantity of valuables which had had other owners that morning.

One morning a bunch of older boys dropped him down a manhole and sealed the lid back on. Most lads in such a situation would have perished of fright, but not Glenn. He wandered around through the various arteries of the sewer, picking up a sizeable quantity of small change from the silt along his way. After a few profitable hours of this, he made his way out through another manhole. He then phoned the police, quoting that a friend of his had been thrown into a sewer by a certain group of boys—he gave their names. Then, without giving his own name, he hung up and went into town.

The cops collared the youths at school and readily wrung a confession from them. The victim was identified as Glenn. A search of the sewer was begun for his body and the young criminals were taken to the police station, facing a long stretch in the reformatory.

Late in the afternoon, Glenn put in his appearance and was hailed by the admiring and relieved police as a hero. They brought him home where he was tucked into bed, apparently too shocked by his experience to eat. Actually, there was nothing wrong with him but a stomach-ache and, perhaps, eye strain. He had visited four picture shows and eaten several dollars' worth of candy, ice cream and other delicacies.

After that experience the worst toughs at school shied away from Glenn. He was pure poison.

I always admired him.

## III

LOGAN MOVED ON to New York and greener pastures, and Pop became associated with another attorney, Tom Connors. Tom had been quite a famous man, and he still was a topnotch lawyer when he was sober. He was a good shot and never without a pair of ivory-handled forty-fives given him by the bandit, Pancho Villa.

With two children and another on the way, Pop was becoming a little worried about the future. So, as a backlog against the uncertainties of the law business, he bought a small neighborhood grocery store in the east side of Oklahoma City. He was out of town much of the time, so it was up to Mom and us kids to look after the store.

There was a large garden in the back yard, and also a pear orchard. Our living quarters were in the rear of the store. With free rent and free vegetables and fruit and a small steady business, it looked like we had the financial problem licked.

In this, we figured without Tom Connors.

He came out from the office one summer afternoon when Pop was away, drinking but not in bad shape. We gave him the spare bedroom and left him alone. After a brief nap he went out the back door and came back with a couple of quarts of booze. Then he began to prowl around the back yard.

We had finished eating by the time he returned, and he had finished the bottle, and there was an expression of deepest consternation upon his face.

"My dear Mrs. Thompson," he said, in his best courtroom manner, "what means have you taken to protect that very valuable pear harvest? Do you have a night watchman or a watch dog?"

"No." Mom smiled hesitantly.

Tom shook his head grimly.

He was, he said, my father's friend. As such, he did not propose to see him stripped of his chattels without a protest. He would take care of the pear orchard himself. When Pop returned there would not be so much as a single pear missing.

Procuring a ball of wrapping twine from the store, he went into the back yard and climbed up a tree. He laced the twine back and forth through the twigs and branches, forming a sort of giant cobweb among them before he fell to the ground on his back. Nothing daunted, he climbed into another tree and treated it as he had the first. And so on to the next, and the next.

There were twenty trees in the orchard. I think Tom must have strung well over a mile of string through them. Then, with the cooperation of Maxine and me, he filled a number of tin cans with pebbles, placed a few cans in each room of the house, and tied the end of a string to each of them.

Well, there weren't any pear thieves around that night (although we could never convince Tom of the fact), but there was a high wind. The trees began to sway and dip. The pebble-filled cans started leaping. A barrage of rocks whistled through the rooms, smashing windows, light fixtures and china. Tin cans crawled in and out of the beds. Wrapping cord—miles of it, seemingly —sought grimly to truss us up.

Struck and snagged in some very tender spots, I started squawling for Mom. Maxine miraculously found me in the dark and pinched me. Mom tried to smack both of us and almost broke her wrist on the bed rail. Then, Tom waked up.

He leaped to the floor, a forty-five in each hand, and cried out that we were being raided. Shouting wild instructions in Mexican, he sprang for the back door. Immediately his feet were entangled in a score of cords, and his flailing arms were likewise caught and made helpless. He struggled onward manfully, dragging the cans with him, along with debris, bedclothes and lighter bits of furniture. At last, however, he stumbled, struck his head against the door-casing with the sound of a bursting pumpkin, and fell down.

He began to snore peacefully.

Mom lit a candle, and came in and looked at him. Her face was pretty grim. She was swinging a catsup bottle in one hand. Finally, after an obvious struggle between her better nature and her natural impulses, she threw a blanket over him and we all went back to bed.

Tom got up ahead of us in the morning to go after more whiskey, and by the time we arose he was anything but contrite. Fortified with several stiff slugs, he led us out into the back yard and commanded us to look upon the wreckage there. Would we now tell him (he asked) pointing at the fruit-littered ground, that thieves had not been out during the night. He denied that there had been any wind.

With Mom protesting angrily, Tom went around and posted himself at the front door of the store. Fingering his forty-fives, he questioned and harangued and threatened every patron who sought to enter. He called them by fearful "aliases" and recited their "records" to them. Some of them fled, and some, of sterner stuff, merely stamped away in high dudgeon.

Around noon a tall heavy-set man bearing a brief case turned in at the walk: Pop. He got Tom to go to bed and, later, to a "cure." A week or so after that we disposed of the store.

In that time, as I remember, we didn't have a single customer.

# IV

POP WAS PRACTICALLY self-educated, his financial position was more often than not insecure, and he was careless about dress and the social niceties. But few men had as many friends among the great, the would-be and the near. Few men had their advice so sought after.

Pop had a horror of ignorance—I'll tell you why, shortly—and had made himself an expert on almost everything. Politicians, from presidents to ward heelers, prized his opinion on political matters. Grain speculators consulted him on the crop outlook. Wire services quoted his predictions on the outcome of prize fights and horse races. He knew more about law, accounting, agriculture and a dozen other professions and pursuits than many men who made them their life work.

In the early twenties when we were living in Fort Worth, Texas, Dr. Frederick A. Cook, the Polar explorer, was our dinner guest one night. Doc had entered the oil business a short time before and was riding high. He was renting three floors of a downtown office building, he employed close to a thousand people, and his postage bill alone ran twenty-five hundred dollars a week.

He had brought a batch of advertising literature out for Pop to look at. Pop did.

"Don't send this out, Doc," he advised. "It'll put you in the pen."

"Aw, now, Jim," Doc laughed, annoyed. "My copy-writers have worked on that for weeks. I've got thousands of dollars tied up in printing. What's wrong with it?"

"It violates the blue-sky laws. Your attorneys can show you where."

"But my attorneys say it's all right!"

Pop shrugged and changed the subject. Or tried to. Cook insisted on arguing about the literature. He finally got a little angry about it.

"The trouble with you, Jim," he declared, "is that you're afraid every club is going to fly up and hit you. You're wrong about this deal and I'll prove it to you. I'm going into the mail with this stuff tomorrow!"

He got a twelve-year stretch in Leavenworth.

Pop was a wizard in large affairs, but in mundane matters he was a flop. You couldn't convince him of the latter. Periodically, he went on family-management sprees, and he either refused to admit the horriferous results or attributed them to our failure to cooperate.

As an eight-year-old, I can remember his asking Mom about my tastes in literature. He expressed his dissatisfaction with her reply by going out and buying a twelve-volume set of American history and another set of the letters of the presidents. And he pooh-poohed her angry opinion that the stuff was too old for me.

"You're bringing these children up in ignorance," he declared. "Now, when I was four years old, I could name all the presidents and . . ."

There followed a long list of accomplishments, of which I was no more capable than I was of flying. (I suppose the comparison shamed me all my life.) But for months afterward, I was required to read the books aloud to him every night. I read them at home, while at school I read the adventures of Bow-wow and Mew-mew, and Tom and Jane at grandmother's farm.

In the same fashion, I was drilled in higher accountancy before I had mastered long division; I was coached in political science before I ever saw a civics class; I learned the dimensions of Betelgeuse before I knew my own hat size. I was always a puzzle and a plague to my teachers. I often knew things that they didn't but seldom anything that I should.

I don't mean to give the impression that Pop was harsh. He was anything but. He seldom raised his voice. Never once did he so much as paddle one of us kids. It was simply that he couldn't be content to manage his own sphere and let Mom manage hers.

Every once in a while he would get the notion that we weren't eating properly, and he would undertake to "put a little meat on our bones." These undertakings usually manifested themselves as great messes of what he called "succotash"—beans, tomatoes, corn, peas, and perhaps a bottle of catsup, all cooked together in the largest kettle he could find. Mom would sternly forbid us to eat any of it, so Pop, after disposing of a quart or two, would take the receptacle under his arm and go around and make gifts of it to the neighbors.

It was Pop's greatest fault that he could seldom see bad in anyone. He did not want it pointed out to him, and he refused to admit it when it was. After we sold our grocery store, we moved over on West Main Street in Oklahoma City. There was a family across the street whose little girl was always fighting with Maxine (or vice versa) and Mom, after a few words with her mother, decided that they were trash. Pop said that she shouldn't make statements of that kind. We weren't really acquainted with the people and shouldn't form judgments until we were.

Pop had served us "succotash" that evening, and Mom was not in the best of humor.

"If you think so much of them," she suggested, sweetly, "why don't you call on them? Take them some of that stuff. They look to me like they'd eat anything."

There were a few more words, and, finally, Pop got up and put on his hat. Taking the kettle under his arm, he marched stiffly out of the house and across the street.

Some thirty minutes later he returned—and with him he brought the detested neighbors: the man and woman and their little girl. The man was a small wiry fellow, with the bluest eyes I have ever seen. The woman was a gaudy, gushy type. At Pop's instigation, they were paying us a social call.

Mom sat with her lips compressed, emitting monosyllables when she was forced to. Pop, of course, became more and more hospitable.

It developed that the man was the local agent for a St. Louis automobile dealer, and Pop promptly announced that he was interested in buying a car. Before the visit was over he made an appointment for a demonstration.

When our visitors had finally departed Mom began to laugh rather wildly.

"You buy a car! Are you crazy, Jim Thompson? We've got another baby coming, and we owe everyone in the country now. And you talk about buying a car! I'll just bet you that fellow is a criminal! I'll bet he steals those fine cars he drives around!"

Pop said this was preposterous. "I refuse to discuss the matter further."

"Well, you won't catch me riding with you! Me or any of the kids . . ." And we didn't go, either.

So Pop went for the ride alone, and several others. The price of the car was surprisingly cheap—so much so that Pop, who was usually agile in such situations, found it difficult to avoid buying, and Mom, who loved a bargain, wavered somewhat. But having stated so often that the man was a criminal, she would not back down.

It was just as well. I cannot remember the guy's last name now, although I should, as many crime stories as I have written. But his spry mannerisms and his bright blue eyes had earned him the sobriquet, among the police of six states, of "Monkey Joe." He was the southwestern outlet for a gang of Missouri car thieves who had hundreds of thefts, and, I believe, thirteen murders to their credit.

At the time the pinch was made Freddie, my other sister, had just been born, and we had other things than crime to talk about. But the magazine sections of the Sunday papers kept the case alive until we were less preoccupied. For weeks they were filled with the pictures and exploits of "Joe, the man with the monkey-blue eyes"—which may or may not explain why there was a sudden dearth of Sunday papers around our house.

Pop said there was no connection.

# V

ONE DAY AROUND the turn of the century, a large young man with the profile of President McKinley wandered into Territorial Oklahoma from Illinois. He had a certain ponderosity of manner which set none too well with his background. For, while he could be considered unusually well-read for his day, he had little formal education, and his working experience was confined to a few months as a railroad fireman and a year or so as a country schoolteacher.

He conferred with a highly placed Republican relative—Territorial Oklahoma was governed by Republicans—and this man got him an appointment as a deputy United States marshal. He did not ask for help after that, nor did he need it. For the young man's chief talent was something he had been born with, the ability to make friends. And, I may as well say now, it was to prove no unmixed blessing.

When statehood came, he ran for sheriff in a solidly Democratic county and won by a landslide. He was re-elected for two successive terms, and, except for larger plans, could have held the office indefinitely. The ultimate objective of those plans was the presidency of the United States—for the man believed, and did until the day he died, that any man could be president. As a long step toward that goal, he won the Republican nomination for Congress from his district.

Here, at last, the man's talent for friendship became a curse. A man's best friends, once they turn upon him, become his worst enemies. It was so in the young man's—I may as well say—my father's case.

Pop's honesty was something painful to behold. In the relatively minor office of sheriff, he had seen no occasion to discuss his early history and antecedents, nor to promulgate any but the most general of platforms. As a congressman, however, he felt that his constituents had a right to know all about him and what to expect of him as a legislator. Though it damned near killed him—and I mean that literally—he told them.

The great body of voters—men who had moved into Oklahoma from the deep south, men who had told each other fondly that "Ol' Jim ain't like the rest of them No'thuhnuhs"—heard him in shocked silence, then with purple-faced fury. They learned that the S in his middle name stood for Sherman, after General Sherman with whom his father had marched to the sea. They learned that the South, whether it liked it or not, was part of the United States, and the quicker it accepted the fact the better. They were told that, as a Republican, he stood for the absolute equality of all races, and that he would fight to obtain and maintain that equality.

Needless to say, Pop's honesty cost him the most smashing political defeat in Oklahoma history.

Not only that, but it also made him a fugitive from justice for more than two years.

Like many other frontier peace officers. Pop had been decidedly careless in his official bookkeeping. He knew very little about such work, and he was too busy, or so he thought, running down outlaws. He knew that neither he nor his deputies had ever pocketed a penny of public funds. That being the case, what did it matter if, at the end of his third term, his books showed a technical shortage of some $30,000.

As a matter of fact, it wouldn't have mattered at all except for the debacle of his congressional campaign. Everyone knew he was honest. No one was going to make even an implied assault on a man with thousands of voters in his pocket. He planned, as soon as he had the time and money, to hire a corps of expert accountants and get the sheriff's office mess straightened out. But the end of the congressional race found him without money, virtually without friends, and with an overwhelming host of enemies who intended to see that he was given no time to adjust his accounts.

Overnight, he was faced with criminal charges and the almost certain prospect of a long stretch in prison. Knowing of nothing else to do, he fled to Mexico.

What had been an unusually promising career was now, obviously, at an end. Since he could barely support himself, he was to all purposes permanently estranged from his wife and two small children. He had no money and no way of earning any except by competing on even terms with peon labor. Rather, I should say, uneven terms. The Mexican government had no love for Americans who took jobs from its own starving nationals.

I don't know what other men would have done under such circumstances, but I can speak for myself: I'd have walked into the Rio Grande and kept on walking until my hat floated.

That wasn't, of course, Pop's way of doing things.

All man's troubles, he decided, sprang from ignorance—in this particular case ignorance of law and accounting. He did not know enough, but he would henceforth. He would acquire the knowledge to solve this immediate difficulty, then go on to improve and expand his learning in every possible field.

Somehow, he managed to acquire the funds necessary for correspondence courses in law and accounting. During every minute he had free from drudgery, he studied. After some two years, he received an LL.B. degree by mail, as well as a certificate as an expert accountant. Meanwhile, he had got in touch with former intimates in Oklahoma. Feeling toward him had died down. If he wanted to come back, they'd stake him to expenses and also go his bond while he was fighting the case.

Pop went back. He audited his own accounts and then argued his own case in court. He proved that not only did he owe the county nothing but that the county actually owed him several thousand dollars.

Eventually, he became attorney and official accountant for the Oklahoma Peace Officers Association and developed a large private practice. But even when he was well on the road to success, his open-handedness and his reluctance to dun a client brought on long periods of financial destitution. During such times, Mom, Maxine and I resumed a practice we had begun when he fled to Mexico.

We went to live with Mom's folks in a Nebraska country town.

# VI

I COULD SAY a great deal about the unpleasant features of living with relatives, of living in a gossipy small town where everyone knows your circumstances and has little else to talk about. But I have brooded overlong about these matters in other books (and out of them); so let us dismiss them with the statement that they did exist. Along with everything else, I often managed to have a wonderfully amusing time.

For this, for the attitude which enabled me to have it, I am largely indebted to my Grandfather Myers, the most profane, acid-tongued, harsh, kind, delightful man I ever knew.

I recall an evening when my ultra-pious grandmother had dragged me to a country revival meeting, and I lay shivering in my dark bedroom afterwards. I was too terrified to sleep. I was certain that my six-odd years of life—all spent in sinning from the preacher's standpoint—had earned me one of the hotter spots in hell, and that I would certainly be snatched there before morning.

Then, though I had made no sound—I knew damned well what my grandmother would do if I waked her up—my grandfather crept in in his undershirt and trousers. "Can't sleep, huh?" he jeered, in a harsh, mocking whisper. "Let some goddam fool scare the pee out of you, huh? Well, goddam, if you ain't a fine one!"

He ordered me into my overalls and led me out of the house, pausing in the kitchen where he picked up a pint cup of whiskey toddy which he always kept warming on the back of the stove. We went out into the back yard and sat down on the boardwalk to the privy. There, after each of us had had a mighty sip of toddy and I had been allowed a few puffs from his Pittsburgh stogie, he delivered himself of a lecture.

I cannot repeat it here, his acidly profane yet somehow hilarious discourse on certain types of religionists and the insanity of taking them seriously. Suffice it to say that, coupled with the toddy, it sent me into muffled gales of giggles. It sent me smiling to sleep, and left me smiling in the morning.

Having suffered the cruelest of childhoods himself, my grandfather believed that anything that contributed to a child's peace of mind was good, and that anything that disturbed that peace was bad. I hold to that same belief. It is one of the very few things I do believe.

Grandfather, or "Pa" as he was known to the entire clan, was an old man from my earliest recollection—just how old even he did not know. Orphaned shortly after birth in a period of indifferent vital statistics, he had been handed around from one family to another, worked always, fed seldom, and beaten frequently. For all that his memory could tell him he had been born big, raw-boned and doing a man's work.

He might have been fifteen when he enlisted as a drummer boy in the Union Army, but he believed he was nearer ten. By the end of the war he was a full-fledged sergeant, an inveterate gambler, a confirmed drinker, and a stout apostle of the philosophy of easy-come easy-go. He didn't know what he wanted to do, but he was certain that it must pay a great deal and have very little physical work attached to it.

There was no such vocation, of course, for a brash young man who could barely read and write. Back in his home state of Iowa, he worked for a few years as a stone mason, the only trade he knew, and usually gambled away his money as fast as he got it. When his luck at last changed for the better, he took the resulting several hundreds and went to St. Louis. There he sat in one of the big games for seventy-two hours straight, leaving at its end with more than ten thousand dollars.

He liked big things, simply for the sake of bigness, and about the intrinsically biggest business in those days, for the small capitalist, was hardware and farm implements. Pa bought out his hometown dealer in those things and set out, to all appearances, on the career of a prosperous and respectable merchant.

These appearances were deceptive. He was not respectable, by many definitions of the term, and any prosperity he may have enjoyed was as brief as it was accidental. He liked to gamble and carouse as much as he ever had. He felt a fatal friendliness for the financially distressed, and as fatal an indifference for the well-heeled. To his way of thinking, the loss of one's money in a poker game was an entirely valid reason for failing to pay a bill, and to such an unfortunate he was prepared to extend credit indefinitely. Fiscally excellent risks, on the other hand, were apt to be dunned ahead of time and to have their bills padded: this on the theory that they had probably stolen their money, anyway, and that he could put it to better use than they could.

But his biggest trouble, perhaps, was his complete unreadiness to settle down. Now "chained," as he thought of it, to a wife, children and business, he grew more impatient with every passing day. He could not bear to haggle. A customer who hesitated over a purchase would first receive a sharp reduction in price, and then, if he still hesitated, the exasperated suggestion that he get the hell out until he made up his mind.

Such shenanigans as these could only end in one way. Very late one summer's night, Pa loaded a covered wagon with his family and such personal chattels as he could get onto it and quietly drove away, leaving his home and his business behind him. The word "his" is used loosely. They were no longer his and the lighter articles he carted away would not have been if his creditors had caught him.

He homesteaded in Nebraska territory, and, for more years than he cared to remember, he did two men's work. He farmed, he ran a dairy, he carried on an extensive masonry contracting business. Finally, as he was nearing the age of fifty, he paused to take inventory.

He owned his own comfortable home and several acres on the edge of town. (And he had set his married son up on a valuable farm.) He owned several small rental properties in the town proper. It was enough, Pa decided. With his Civil War pension, he could get by nicely. For the rest of his life, he would never do another damned lick of work.

He bumped his masonry carts together, loaded them with tools and implements, piled his working clothes on top—and set fire to the lot. Then, donning his "gentleman's" uniform of blue serge suit, large black hat, and Congress gaiters, he set about catching up with his fun.

Alas, times had changed sharply for the worse during his long spell of industry. There were no *real* gambling games any more—only penny-ante skirmishes which were an insult to a spirited man. There were no real two-fisted drinkers any more—only molly-coddles who sipped half-heartedly at their drinks and then went on about their business. There were no *real* men any more. If you "called" a man, the ninny would have you hauled into court instead of making the proper response with fists and feet.

A practical man (by his own admission), Pa drew such satisfaction as he could from his whiskey jug, his boxes of long black stogies, and verbal jousting with his wife. But the first two were only adjuncts to the good life, not the life itself, and my grandmother would not play fairly with him. After a few relatively feeble remarks about how "nasty-mouthed," "filthy," and "no-account" he was, she would simply lock herself in her room, leaving Pa more frustrated than ever.

Surcease came—or, rather, began—with Pa's decision that he needed a horse and buggy to get around in. There are tamer animals in the jungles of Africa than the one he brought home. Not only was it unbroken, as the seller had honestly pointed out, but it declined to be broken. And, slowly, as the terrifying beast kicked to pieces his brand new buggy, Pa's face lit up in a beautiful smile.

That was the beginning. The end did not come until Pa, by breeding and selection, had populated the barnyard with the muliest cow, the fightingest chickens and the fiercest hogs ever assembled by man. The chickens did not lay and were too tough to eat. The hogs were lean, muscle-bound warriors which no stock-buyer would have as a gift. The horse could not be made to perform for more than a few minutes at a time. The cow—the only one I have ever seen do so—gave skimmed milk and very little of that.

Pa loved them all. They gave him what he needed.

Every trip into the barnyard was an adventure. The chickens ran at him, wings beating furiously. The cow butted and tried to crush him against her stall. The hogs were constantly attempting, with occasional success, to knock him down and gnaw on him. The horse kicked, bucked and nipped.

The animals were at some disadvantage in being unable to curse, but otherwise the incessant warfare was carried on on terms as even as Pa could devise. The kicking horse got kicked. The butting cow got butted. The zooming chickens, with their furiously beating wings, were in turn zoomed at, Pa thrashing his arms wildly. The hogs, who used everything they had on him, got considerably better than an even break. Pa met their onslaughts with nothing more than his boots and cane.

Although Pa's bathing was confined to washrag-and-basin dabbling, this should not be interpreted as meaning that he was hygienically careless. He simply had his own ideas about personal hygiene. Nights, mornings, and numerous times in between, he took great draughts of whiskey to "kill the poisons" in his system. To maintain his body at the same even temperature, he wore heavy woolen underwear winter and summer. He ate large quantities of liver, brains and kidneys (to fortify his own). And bedtime found him battening down every window in the house to shut out the noxious night air. Finally, to get back to the subject of animals, he would not sit down in the privy in the normal fashion, but stood up on the seat and hunkered over the hole.

He was in this semi-helpless position one day when the privy door blew open. A huge dominecker rooster, seeing a once-in-a-lifetime chance, dashed in and pecked him severely about the loins. Pa was outraged by this grossly unfair attack, but he did not resort to an axe as a less fair man would have. He simply ignored that particular rooster from then on.

When the fowl flew at him, he would ward it off brusquely or merely step aside, then calmly proceed on his way. After a few days of such rebuffs, the rooster began to stand by himself in lonely corners of the barnyard. His comb wilted; his beak drooped nearer and nearer to the ground. Now and then the other chickens, always quick to spot an outcast, would swoop at him and peck him sharply on the head. But he never fought back.

One day, when he was dreaming no doubt of happier times, he wandered too close to the hog lot. A sow poked her snout through the rails and ended his misery forever. Pa said it served the son-of-a-bitch right, and let that be a lesson to me—why, me, I don't know—but I could see that he was badly upset over the affair. Stamping into the house, he emptied the pint toddy cup without pausing. When my grandmother, anticipating the usual outburst of prandial profanity, remarked that if he didn't like her cooking he knew what he could do, Pa only looked at her moodily. In fact he ate almost a half a pie —"leather and lard," to use his customary appellation—before getting back to normal and hurling the plate into the garden.

All my life I have been the victim of the inhumane and unjust botching of potentially good food. My mother was a woman of indifferent appetite, and thus lacked the basic essential of a good cook. My wife—well, my wife is a wonderful cook, but I usually do the family cooking. I got ptomaine poisoning from the very first restaurant meal I remember eating. Looking back from my present state of antiquity, I can't recall eating more than a few dozen good meals that I did not prepare myself.

If I dine at a friend's house a treasured recipe, handed down in the family for generations, will suddenly go sour. A restaurant with an unimpeachable reputation will blithely risk all for the dubious pleasure, say, of serving me stale eggs fried in goat grease. I have known but one other person to suffer from such a frightful conspiracy. A small con man named Allie Ivers (of whom much more later), he had a way of protesting which only insufficient nerve has kept me from using.

Allie owned an enormous sponge, selected with much care for its unusual powers of absorption. Before dining out he would fill this sponge with dirty water. When his meal was served him, he would slide this sponge under his napkin, hold the napkin to his mouth, and . . . but need I say more? Suffice it to say that the sight of Allie staggering about in apparent agony, a horrible liquid spouting from his napkin, could empty a crowded restaurant in the space of five minutes.

But I was about to speak of Ma's—my grandmother's cooking. And since I cannot use Pa's descriptive terms, and no others are adequate, I am somewhat at a loss as to how to proceed. I must settle, I suppose, for the statement that nowhere—in hobo jungles, soup kitchens, greasy spoons, labor camps—nowhere, I repeat, have I eaten anything as bad.

The good woman was an omnivorous reader of farm-magazine food and health "authorities," and her ideas changed with theirs from day to day. Salt caused hardening of the arteries—so that condiment might be omitted, from a dish which had to have it. Baking powder "had been known to cause digestive disturbances"—so Ma, until she was advised to the contrary, would leave it out of her biscuits. On the other hand, a few drops of vanilla added to baked beans not only gave them an "unusually piquant" flavor but was "a certain safeguard" against pellagra. So you know what went into the bean pot.

It made no difference to Ma that one might prefer unpiqued flavors, pellagra and even death to beans with vanilla in them. You got vanilla. At least you got it until she learned, say, that left-over chocolate custard made a "marvelous addition"—whatever that meant—to Boston's favorite vegetable.

The fact that Ma might not have any leftover chocolate custard was no deterrent to her compounding of such a recipe. She would make some and leave it over. Ma, need I say, had a decidedly literal mind.

Mom, Maxine and I were in no position to complain, although, following

Pa's precepts, I often did to my eventual sorrow. But Pa protested enough for all of us. Insofar as he could, he stuck to a diet of meat, cooked by himself or eaten raw, and he encouraged us to do the same. But every mealtime brought on an outburst of profanity, table pounding and hurled dishes, as furious as it was futile. It was one of my regular after-meal chores to go out into the garden and bring in any dishes which had not been shattered.

I think the fates must have provided Ma with a steel-lined stomach as recompense for depriving her of all sense of taste. In no other way can I account for her ability to eat heartily and healthfully of her own fortunately inimitable cooking. As for the Thompsons, I think we certainly should have died except for Pa's constant dosing of us with whiskey.

Both on arising and retiring, we were required to take generous drinks of toddy. And when school was in session, we kids got another big drink upon our arrival home in the evenings. In winter, the whiskey was a cold preventative, to Pa's notion; in warm weather, it served to "purify the blood." In days to come, I was to regret this early acquired taste for alcohol. But, at the time, I do not believe we could have survived without it.

While Ma could botch a meal quite capably by herself, it cannot be denied that she received considerable inadvertent assistance from Pa. For Pa was the official firebuilder, and he pursued this vocation more as an outlet for his tempestuous temperament than for any utilitarian purpose.

Pa began the chore by opening all the drafts on the kitchen range, and walloping it fore and after with an extra-heavy duty steel poker. This shook the soot out of it, so he said (and judging by the ineradicable carbon-hue of the kitchen there was no reason to doubt him). It also put him in the fine and furious fettle necessary for the task ahead.

Removing every lid from the top of the stove, Pa piled in kindling, corn cobs, coal, newspapers and everything else handy with a wild indiscrimination that was marvelous to behold. Onto this pile, which normally extended a foot or so above the top of the stove, he dropped an incendiarist's handful of burning matches. Then, snatching up a gallon can of kerosene, he emptied the better part of its contents into and over the range.

No fire in the hell which Pa incessantly referred Ma to could have been more awe-inspiring. It didn't just burn; it exploded. It groaned and panted and heaved, snatching at persons and objects ten feet away and leaping clear to the ceiling. By the time it had burned down enough for Pa to replace the stove lids, weird things were happening to its internal structure. Coal was smothering the kindling; half-burned newspapers were clogging the drafts. According to whim, it might go out entirely at the very moment Ma began her alleged cooking. Or, suddenly puffing smoke and sparks through every crevice in the range, it might begin to burn anew and with an intensity that made mock of the original blaze.

Beyond beating it with the poker, which he was ever ready to do, Pa refused to take any responsibility for the stove's fractious actions. It wasn't his fault if Ma didn't know how to keep a good fire going. Anyway, as he pointed out with some truth, nothing short of taking Ma out and shooting her—a course he frequently recommended—could greatly improve the household cookery.

# VII

VERY EARLY ONE morning Pa poked me into wakefulness with his cane and presented the inevitable cup of toddy. I was to get dressed and come quietly out of the house at once. He was going to take me to see what "a bunch of god-damned fools look like."

I obeyed, of course, and as we strode away from the house in the dusky dawn, his calloused hand gripping my small one, Pa jogged my memory with a little jovial profanity.

No revival meeting was complete in those days without a prediction from the preacher as to the date when the world would end. The preacher who had scared the daylights out of me had stated that six calendar weeks from the day of his departure the world would be no more.

Very few of the townspeople had taken this nonsense literally—not sufficiently so, at any rate, to act upon it. But, silently, Pa had marked those few well, and shortly we were standing before the residence of such a family.

Pa, who had known almost exactly what to expect, emitted an amazed and scornful snort, and loudly proclaimed that he would be goddamned. What, he demanded of me, as though I were personally responsible for the sight, were this man and his wife and their three children doing in their nightgowns? And why had they climbed upon the roof of their modest cottage? . . . Well, (having partially answered his own questions) why the nightgowns? Were they going to spend all their time in heaven sleeping? And why stand on the roof? Didn't they think God could lift 'em all the way? Didn't they know He could spot as big damned fools as they were even if they hid in the cellar?

This indirect quizzing of the pious porch-perchers was just getting under way when, from opposite directions of the street, two furious clouds of dust appeared. They came parallel with us simultaneously, and from them there eventually emerged Pa's son and son-in-law, respectively my uncles Newt and Bob. The two men joined us on the walk, and where Pa had left off in his razzing they took up.

When the possibilities of the situation were exhausted, all of us hurried on foot around the town, "before the damned fools (could) come to their senses." But I think I shall drop the curtain on that tour. While I tried to outdo my relatives in laughter that morning, I actually felt a strong sympathy for those we laughed at. I winced for them—and I still do. Perhaps because I have been a bigger fool so many times myself.

Newt—we did not use titles such as "uncle" and "aunt" on my mother's side of the family—was a better-educated version of his father without, however, possessing quite so much of Pa's rough good humor. He had been farming on his own for only a few years when he came off second-best in a battle with a horse, and his left foot had to be amputated. And, possibly because he tried to walk without a crutch or cane (no one was going to make *him* a cripple!), the stump became infected.

Periodically, thereafter, he had to be operated on. He had to submit to the gradual trimming away of his leg and the fitting of a succession of artificial limbs. He was in almost constant pain, and his surgical expenses were enormous. Yet, as he went about the tilling of a large farm and the rearing of a big family, he never complained. There was a surly undertone to his laughter —but he did laugh—and he was apt to be painfully sardonic and sarcastic even in kindness—but he was kind.

An Englishman of noble family, my Uncle Bob had settled in this small Nebraska town for reasons he never revealed. He began his business career there as a storekeeper, branched from that into dealing in land, and wound up as a banker. Although not a modest man in many ways, he took no credit for his success but attributed it all to the invention of the cash register. Except for that splendid device, he could not have trusted his affairs to employees, thus leaving himself free for increasingly larger and profitable ventures.

Bob had an ironclad rule never to touch his capital for living expenses. He also insisted on making an annual and substantial increase in that capital. He was the local agent for dozens of items, ranging from patent flea-soap to gasoline lamps, and persons who borrowed money from him were apt to find themselves loaded with these things as a condition for receiving their loans.

Most practitioners of the sharp deal are close-mouthed. Not so, my Uncle Bob. To anyone he could buttonhole, he bragged about how he had "stung" this person or "skinned" that one.

Actually, as I came to learn in time, Bob's avariciousness was a pose. His schemes and his jeers were simply his way of making small-town life bearable. Like Pa, Bob was far too big a man for his environment. The only way he could endure it was to dwell in a kind of tantrum. Secretly, Bob was one of the most generous men in town.

Although we must have been aware of each other before then, I seem to have made almost no impression on him, nor he on me, until I was almost seven. The occasion was dinner at his house. He was seated at the head of the long table, and I at the foot, and in between were his wife, his six children, his four Persian cats and his two Airedale dogs. There was a long hickory ferrule at his side which he wielded throughout the meal, occasionally correcting a cat or a dog with it, but, more frequently, smacking his children when they erred in etiquette. Betwixt ferocious scowls at me he sent his offspring to the front room, by turns, to rewind the phonograph and replace one classical record with another.

I was greatly awed. When, abruptly, he asked me if I knew what Brann's

*Iconoclast* was, I could scarcely gather my wits sufficiently to stammer out an affirmative.

"Something to eat, isn't it?" He beamed at me falsely. "Something like cornflakes."

"N-no," I said faintly. "It's a magazine."

Bob chortled sarcastically, wagging his head in ironic wonder. A magazine, eh? Oh, that was very good! I would tell him next—he supposed—that Shakespeare was not the name of a fountain pen! I would tell him that, would I? And he bared his teeth in so terrible a grimace that my hair literally stood on end.

Nevertheless, I told him, even as he had prophesied.

Bob snarled at me hideously, then suddenly threw out another question. "Who," he said, "was Scoopchisel?"

"S-scoop . . .? I don't know," I said.

"You—don't—know? You don't know!" His face colored in a spasm of rage and bewilderment, and, for a moment, I thought surely that this was to be my end. But somehow, though the effort was obviously a drain in his innermost resources, Bob managed to bring himself under control. He addressed me at length and with patience, a fond glow coming into his fine gray eyes. And always thereafter, I discovered, I could move him into this benign mood by raising the subject of Scoopchisel. Scoopchisel, the greatest writer of all time, a man robbed of his proper due by his sneaky brother-in-law, Byron.

It was Scoopchisel who had written the immortal lines:

> So get the golden shekels while you're young
> And getting's good.
> And when you're old and feeble
> You won't be chopping wood.

But he was at his best when annotating the work of other poets. To Fitzgerald's inquiry, "I often wonder what the vintner buys, one half so precious as the stuff he sells," Scoopchisel had retorted, "Protection!" Anent Pope's statement, "Hope springs eternal in the human breast," Scoopchisel had said, "Until you're married, than it moves its nest."

I was so impressed with the works of Scoopchisel that even after Pop and the rest of us had reassembled and I was well advanced in grammar school, I quoted him. Which inevitably led, of course, to my inditing a pained and accusing letter to my Uncle Bob. He replied promptly.

He would not advise me—he wrote—to accuse my teachers of ignorance, nor would he confess that Scoopchisel had never existed. He would only say that every man had to believe in something and that he liked to believe in Scoopchisel, and even though the latter had never lived he damned well should have. "In short," Bob concluded, "keep your hat on and your head ducked. The woodpeckers are after you."

Newt and Bob had sons approximately the same age and some eight or ten years older than I was. Two more inventive, mischievous lads would be hard to find, and they stood always ready to supply any devilment which I could not dream up for myself. One of our more successful enterprises was the electrification of certain privy seats around the town. My cousins did the wiring, and supplied the dry cells. I, lying with them in a nearby weedpatch, was allowed to throw the switch at the crucial moment. There are no statistics, I suppose, on the speed with which people leave outdoor johns. But I am certain that if there were, the victims of our rural electrification project would still be holding the record.

I entered the first grade of school in this town, and shortly thereafter I had reason to complain to my two cousins that my teacher was picking on me. The good youths were seriously disturbed—or seemed to be. We retired to the loft of Newt's barn to confer. There, after we had all had a good chew of tobacco and a swig from a purloined bottle of wine, they reached a decision.

My teacher, they advised me, was suffering from a malady known as horniness. She "wanted some but didn't know how to get it." It was their suggestion that I linger in the schoolroom after the class had gone out and jab her "where she lived." This would show her that I was a "pretty gay guy" and my troubles would be well on the way toward their solution.

Well, I had seen just enough of the mating antics of farm animals to accept this scheme as entirely plausible. I became so enthusiastic, in fact, that my cousins began to believe in the stunt. They fell for their own rib as hard as I had. Excitedly—and no longer joking—they repeated their instructions, adding a message for me to pass on to the teacher. I was to tell her that they were rarin' to go, any time and place she suggested, that they would undertake to do their best for her and she would leave the trysting place relaxed and rejoicing.

That was not the exact message, but it conveys the general idea. The words my cousins used, while considerably more graphic, were somewhat less polite.

So I trotted off for school the next morning, silently rehearsing the scene I was about to play—convinced that happier days were just ahead. True to my instructions, I lingered behind at recess time. When I at last started out the door where the teacher was waiting impatiently, I triggered my forefinger and jabbed. Then, having proved I was a "gay guy," I started to deliver my cousins' message.

I didn't get as much as a word of it out before the teacher, an apple-cheeked German girl, affixed her hand to my ear and hauled me squawling toward the principal's office.

I was saved from I don't know what unpleasantness by two circumstances.

First, the teacher's sense of delicacy prevented her from more than hinting at the nature of my crime. The strongest indictment that the principal could evince from her was the statement that I had been "pranking nasty." Secondly, this principal, like many another person in the town, was in the financial clutches of my Uncle Bob and was reluctant to offend him—as he felt he would —by punishing me.

So he gave me a mild talking-to, after the teacher had been sent on her way, plus a pat on the head and the suggestion that I pattern my conduct, in the future, after "that splendid uncle of yours." Then, I was dismissed to the playgrounds. I looked up my two cousins, forthwith, and charged them with giving me some very bad advice. They, having lost much of their previous day's enthusiasm, were vastly relieved to learn that I had not involved them, and they readily acquiesced to my demand that I give each a "swift kick in the arse." Thus, the matter ended.

Whether my teacher was any kinder to me thereafter, I don't remember— probably she had been kind enough in the first place. I do recall that never again did she come within my reach. She was no fool, even if I was.

These cousins of mine operated under a peculiar code of logic which, although it seemed entirely clear and sensible to them, was as maddening as it was incomprehensible to the outside world. Even I, a sympathetic participant in most of their stunts, was baffled and bewildered by them more often than not.

One spring, when the boys had foresworn crime for several months—and there was a growing feeling that they might escape death by hanging, ending their existence with nothing worse, perhaps, than life imprisonment—their delighted families presented each with a handsome bicycle. I was on hand at Newt's farm where the presentation ceremonies were held, and an impressive occasion it was.

As head of the clan, Pa spoke first, punctuating his blood-curdling remarks with wild slashes of his cane which might well have brained less agile youths. Newt and Bob were the next speakers, in that order, brandishing their respective cane and ferrule. Then, with the air sizzling with profane threats, the ladies stepped forth wielding whips and switches. And while their vocabularies were free of curses, their lectures were nonetheless fearsome and awe-inspiring. The general feeling seemed to have been expressed by Pa's declaration that the boys had better, by God, behave themselves and take care of their bikes or they would be nailed to the barn door and skinned alive.

The boys listened with seeming meekness. Then, accompanied by me, they repaired to the interior of the barn where they proceeded to disassemble the bicycles into several hundred odd pieces.

Discovered in this outrage, as they soon were, the two youths pleaded for time. Given a matter of a week, they promised, and they would convert those childish playthings, the bicycles, into a thing of great beauty and utility. Exasperated and exhausted, the adult relatives gave their consent without striking a blow.

The week passed in a hubbub of furious activity. The boys acquired several sheets of stout roofing tin. They got hold of a quantity of hard wood and steel rod and paint, and the basic parts of an old gasoline water pump. Assisted by me, they pounded and sawed, shaped and soldered, painted and sawed and bolted together. And by the eve of the seventh day, so very real—though often misdirected—was their genius, they had created an automobile.

It looked like an automobile—save for the wheels—down to the minutest detail. It ran quite as well as many of the automobiles of that day.

Our adult kin were both dumbfounded and delighted as we made a brief trial run up and down the barn corridor. All unsuspecting of the ultimate and abysmal objectives of the two youths, they made no protest when the latter announced that the first full-scale demonstration would be held on the morrow.

Both my cousins and I spent the night at Newt's house. The following morning, attired in our Sunday's best, we marched haughtily into the barn. We tuned and oiled the motor of our automobile until it purred like a cat. We wiped the gleaming red body free of the last speck of dust. Then, we climbed into the front seat, with me in the middle, and drove grandly out into the yard.

We circled it twice, allowing our beaming relatives and the neighbors they had pridefully summoned to feast their eyes upon us. With this, the promised demonstration taken care of, we suddenly roared full-speed to our previously determined destination—the open door to the food cellar.

The door was flush with the ground and opened into a long steep flight of stairs leading under the house. We went crashing and smashing down them, shedding fenders and other of the automobile's components as well as sizeable bits of our own epidermis. Then, at the bottom, where the steps ended in an upright door, the engine shot from beneath the hood and we shot over it. The whole house shook with the impact of flying bodies and machinery, and the explosions of fruit and vegetable jars.

Bruised, bleeding and besmeared, we managed to claw our way back to daylight and the fearsome reception awaiting us. But the automobile had so wrecked the stairs and jammed into the lower door that no one could get back down into the cellar.

As soon as he could do anything but curse, Newt announced that he was through. "I give up, by God," he stated, and he declared that since the family was cut off from its supply of fruit and vegetables, they could all simply die of scurvy and the sooner the better. "There's a hell of a lot worse ways of dying," he pointed out grimly, and no one could gainsay him.

Fortunately, after a few weeks of meat and gravy and the like, and when scurvy seemed actually imminent, he was persuaded to adopt a more sensible course. The result was a new entrance to the cellar through the kitchen floor, a new door and new stairs—and complete physical exhaustion for my cousins and me. For Newt, naturally, did not lift a finger on the job. He was one of the three foremen—Pa and Bob being the other two. And so well did they handle their duties, we were hardly able to stir from our beds for a week.

The one last piece of orneriness which my cousins and I collaborated in almost got us all killed. It came about after much reading and discussion of the literature of parachuting, an art then in its infancy.

Mom and we kids were preparing to rejoin Pop in Oklahoma, and the various connections of the family had gathered at Newt's house for a farewell Sunday dinner. When the meal was over, my cousins and I slipped out to the barn loft where, earlier, we had concealed three bed sheets and a length of clothesline rope. In no time at all we had parachutes—I don't know what else to call them—tied to our shoulders, and were ascending the sixty-foot tower of the cow lot windmill.

It was a cold, windy fall day. Shivering, I looked at the stock tank adjacent to the mill, studied the four-foot depth of water which was supposed to "break" our fall. Shivering, a little sick at my stomach, I wanted to withdraw. But my colleagues jeered me hideously. At one and the same time, they swore that I was a damned cowardly calf and a mighty brave kiddo. So up the tower I went.

My cousins followed me, goosing and punching one another. Arrived at the top, they ordered me to move around the platform to make room for them. I tried to, but the platform was small. The only way I could hang on was by reaching up and grasping the direction-arm of the windmill fan.

The action coincided with a sudden, sharp gust of wind, and this, with my weight, resulted in disengaging the locking device. Before I knew what was happening, the mill had begun to spin and *I* was swung out into space, jerked and flung first one way then another.

My cousins ducked and cursed frantically as my flailing feet almost knocked them from their perch. Shouting at me to "drop in the tank, dammit," they both tried to scramble down the ladder at the same time. Neither would give way to the other, and they jammed there, tangled in a mass of sheets and clothesline. I continued to swing this way and that, screaming, my eyes clenched tightly.

The back door of the house opened and people streamed out.

Pa, Newt and Bob were in the vanguard—the first two waving their canes, Bob brandishing a long hickory ferrule which he was seldom without and usually found use for. Behind this trio came one of my aunts, carrying a buggy whip, another equipped with a piece of harness strap, and Mom and Ma armed with switches, a plentiful supply of which was always kept around the house.

They might not know how to get us down from the tower, as soon became apparent. But they had plans for us, obviously, when we did get down. All my mother's family were like that, and yet they were warmhearted, children-loving people, too. It was simply second nature with them to attack every situation with acid words on their lips and a weapon in their hands.

Gathered around the base of the tower, around the tank, they shouted up incoherent directions and threats. Mom tried to climb up after me and was dragged back. Pa and Newt gave the wooden uprights a severe caning.

Above the turmoil there suddenly came the sound of splintering wood, and the step to which my cousins were clinging gave way. They went plummeting down into the tank, landing squarely on their backs. The water rose out of the vessel and descended upon the waiting posse. The latter, cursing and screaming according to sex, latched on to the two youths and proceeded, as the saying was, to tan their hides.

This exercise, coupled with the cold water, so calmed my relatives that they at last thought to relatch the lock on the mill. I was able to swing back to the platform, and thence descend to earth where, everything considered, I got off pretty lightly since everyone was exhausted.

# VIII

MY SISTER FREDDIE was born during a severe economic depression. It was a hard winter for the nation in general and for the Thompsons in particular. Pop had begun to dabble in the oil business, and not very profitably. Mom was in the hospital much of the time.

Our house had twelve rooms (Pop had felt that we needed something larger with the advent of Freddie), and the fires of hell couldn't have kept it warm. The plumbing was constantly freezing and bursting. I froze and burst out with cold sores which my schoolmates promptly diagnosed as cancer. Looking back, I find my cold sores to have been the one cheerful facet of that winter. I had but to wave my festered hands and the toughest bully in school fled before me shrieking.

There were repercussions with my recovery, but even these worked out to my advantage. I got a great deal of splendid exercise in racing up alleys and shinnying over back fences. My reflexes became trigger quick. Without losing the look and the feel of it, much of my awkwardness disappeared.

To take Mom's place while she was in the hospital Pop hired a woman who, with undeserved generosity, shall be known herein as Mrs. Cole. A large puffy woman with a ragged topknot of walnut-stained hair, she was the indigent relative of some friend of a friend of Pop. That was all the recommendation he needed.

I came home from school one night and found her lying on the lounge in the front room. She was wearing house slippers and a shapeless mother-hubbard. She waved at me limply and remained prone.

"Let's see, now," she said. "You're Johnnie, ain't you?"

"Huh-uh. I'm Jimmie."

"You hadn't ought to say huh-uh, Johnnie. You ought to say yes ma'am and no ma'am."

"Why?" I said.

Mrs. Cole frowned slightly but made no answer. She intended, apparently, to make friends with me. "I got awful bad rheumatism, Johnnie. I can't do much. You're sure going to help me a lot, ain't you?"

I said I guessed I was. "What you want done?"

"Help me set up, Johnnie."

I took her by the hands and helped her to sit erect. Groaning and panting prodigiously, she got to her feet. With a kind of funny feeling in my throat, I watched her go into Mom's room and close the door.

After a few minutes she came out, smelling strongly of medicine or something, moving much more spryly. Maxine came in and was put through the

315

same rigmarole that I had been. At first Maxine said no, she wasn't going to be a good girl and help a lot. Then she said maybe she would.

"What time does your pappy come home?" Mrs. Cole inquired. And learning that he was due any minute, she went into the kitchen. When Pop arrived she was setting the table, obviously suppressing great pain.

Pop was impressed and alarmed. "You'd better sit down awhile," he suggested. "There's no hurry about supper."

"Oh, no," said Mrs. Cole in a piteous voice.

"But you're sick. Do you want me to get a doctor?"

Mrs. Cole said she was past the point of being aided by doctors. "I'll be all right, Mr. Thompson. I been sufferin' for twenty years and I reckon I can stand a few more. Don't you worry none. I ain't going to be no burden on you."

"Why, of course you won't be," Pop declared warmly. "You just sit down, now, and I'll fix things. Jimmie, run down to the store and get some beans, peas, corn, catsup and . . ."

He and Mrs. Cole ate about a quart each of the "succotash." Maxine and I sopped up a little of the juice with some bread. Afterwards, we went to the store and charged a chocolate pie and a pound of wienies, and ate sitting out on the steps.

Pop had to leave town for a few days early the next morning. He did not disturb Mrs. Cole when he left, and when we arose she was still abed. She was pretty sick, I guess, with a hangover from her "medicine," and declared pitifully that she could not arise.

"Just don't bother me, now," she whined. "Warm you up some of that nice good succotash."

Maxine and I bought some pie, soda pop and potato chips for our breakfast. We had Hershey bars and bologna for lunch. By supper time, Mrs. Cole was getting pretty hungry herself and became active long enough to open a can of chili and fry some hamburger.

Things went on like that for weeks. Pop had to be out of town the greater part of the time, and when he wasn't he spent little time at home. His mind was more than occupied with financial matters. Anyway, he had never been inclined to concern himself with family routine except on the periodic sprees I have mentioned. And those weren't much fun without Mom around.

Once in a while he would ask us how we were feeling or if we shouldn't clean up a little, but I doubt if he heard our answers. We couldn't see Mom often, and then for only a few minutes, and we were made fairly presentable for those visits.

So we went on for weeks, unfed, unwashed and in the main unschooled, for Mrs. Cole never knew whether we went or not, and the attendance laws (if there were any) were unenforced. We slept with our clothes on, a labor-saving and warmth-promoting trick Mrs. Cole had taught us. We ate almost nothing but pie, chili and hamburger. We spent our days in prowling the dime stores, seeing picture shows and loafing.

One noon while we were seated on the porch eating a lunch of pie and pop, Mom came home. She had left the hospital without the doctor's permission. She had had a premonition, she said, that she was needed at home.

Maxine and I dashed out to the taxi, jumping up and down with delight. We asked her if she was going to stay with us, and we tried to take Freddie away from her, and—and then we kind of stood back, shuffling our feet.

"What's the matter, Mom?" I said. "What you crying about?"

"N-nothing," said Mom. "Oh, you poor babies! *Where is that woman?*"

"Mrs. Cole? She's still in bed. She don't get up this early."

Mom's eyes flashed, and she brushed her nose angrily against Freddie's blanket. "Oh, doesn't she?" she said. "Well!"

She was so weak she could hardly walk, but she went up the stairs ahead of us. She laid Freddie down on the lounge and looked around the living room. An angry moan, like that of a spurred horse, broke from her lips. She moaned again as she surveyed the filthy dining room. Glancing into the kitchen, she moaned loudest of all.

Stepping to the door of her bedroom, she drew back her fist. But she lowered it in a gentle knock, and the second knock was no more than firm.

Inside the room the bed creaked, and Mrs. Cole grunted sleepily.

"Now, you just stop botherin' me," she whined. "I told you not to call me till you seen your pappy comin'."

A terrible smile spread over Mom's face. She knocked again.

"You hear me?" called Mrs. Cole. "You want anything to eat, got down to the store an' get it. I got all I can do lookin' after myself."

Mom knocked again.

"Now you better get away from there," Mrs. Cole shouted. "Go to a pitcher show. Go down by the river an' play. Get away from there afore I come out to you!"

Mom began knocking steadily, and Mrs. Cole's warnings grew more dire. At last she arose, lumbered to the door and flung it open.

As I have indicated she was not a fast-thinking woman, and it was fixed in her mind that it was Maxine and I who had been doing the knocking. So, glaring angrily at Mom, she spoke the words that were intended for us.

"Now, you're gonna get it," she declared. "I'll warm your britches for you. You won't be able to set down for a week when—when—when—"

"Go ahead," said Mom. "Cat got your tongue?"

"W-who—who are you?"

"I'm these children's mother," said Mom. "I'm the wife of the man who hired you to look after them. I'm the wife of the man who's been paying you good money to turn my home into a pigsty. I'm the wife of the man who—I'm the—*I could murder you!*" yelled Mom.

And she damned near did.

Shrieking objurations at Mrs. Cole just to look at us kids, just to look at this house, she gave the housekeeper a kind of bearing down shake which brought her heavily to her knees. She boxed her ears, then, until her topknot came undone. And then Mom began kicking her. Mrs. Cole fell to her face and tried to crawl away, and Mom followed, kicking, giving her a crack upon the ears when the opportunity presented. Finally, her strength exhausted, she stumbled and sat down upon her.

Very wisely Mrs. Cole lay still, and Mom was sitting on her, weeping hysterically, when Pop and the doctor arrived. Pop had been out of his office when Mom left the hospital. He had hurried home as soon as he was notified of her unauthorized departure.

Mom was put to bed. The doctor examined Mrs. Cole. He had had a few words with Mom and he was an observant man. So, in Pop's presence, he told Mrs. Cole that he was slighting his duty in not reporting her to the police. Her rheumatism and other ailments were myths, he said. She had better start getting some exercise and lay off whatever she was drinking.

Mrs. Cole departed, swiftly and meekly. But her memory lingered on. It was months before Pop could acquire the nerve to interfere in household matters, and he was pretty diffident about it then.

# IX

ONE SATURDAY MORNING, a few weeks after the Cole affair, Mom, Maxine and I were eating breakfast when a polite knock sounded on our back door. Maxine and I hollered "come in" and Mom shushed us and went to answer the door.

We heard a soft voice inquire, "Begging your pardon, but do you have any work I can do?" And Mom's reply, "Well, I don't know. We can't really afford to hire anyone, right now." Then, following a heavy silence, she said, "But don't you want to come in out of the cold?"

A woman with a little boy of about four came in. Negroes. The woman was about twenty-five, and her eyes looked almost as large as her pinched, starved face. She wore only a shawl around the shoulders of her patched but spotless gingham dress, although the weather was below zero. The boy, a wizened but cheerful-looking little fellow, was little more warmly garbed.

Mom told them to sit down, and went over to the stove and got busy. That was one thing about Mom. She never wasted words when action would do the trick. She cooked them an enormous breakfast and cleared out, shooing us ahead of her. Digging back in the closets, she produced an armful of her and my discarded garments, old and outworn but still serviceable.

"Now, you just put these on before you leave," she said, when she took them into the kitchen. "You'll catch your death of cold running around the way you are!"

"Yes'm," the woman said. "Now what work do you want me to do?"

"That's all right," said Mom.

"No, ma'am. It won't be all right unless I do some work."

"Oh, well," said Mom. "You can wash the dishes if you want to."

Viola—that was the woman's name—washed the dishes. Afterwards, a little mopping-up was indicated so she mopped the floor. In so doing she got water across the threshold of the next room, so naturally that had to be mopped, too —and before it could be mopped it had to be swept, and while one was sweeping one room it was foolish to ignore another. After sweeping, the furniture had to be dusted, and . . .

Viola went to work for us.

Some relative of hers gladly took her son to board for a fraction of her wages, and Viola moved into our house. And while she was an angel, if there ever was one, she was a source of deep confusion—at least to Mom and me.

Mom had always had to be somewhat penurious to offset Pop's generosity. She had become irrevocably sharp in money matters. When she was quoted a price on an object she automatically demanded a lower one, backing the demand with derisive comments on the potential purchase. Salesgirls hid when they saw Mom coming. When a huckster or peddler stopped at our house, he usually left with a bewildered look on his face and bitter curses on his lips.

That was Mom and *that* couldn't be Mom where Viola was concerned. Viola was constantly belittling her own efforts. Mom had to scold her to keep her from working herself to death, and force presents and money upon her with naggings.

Mom became terribly upset. After a session with Viola she was apt to be kind to butchers, her pet abomination. One night when she had been skinned into accepting two pounds of bone and gristle masquerading as stew meat, Mom broke down and cried. She told Viola she was driving her crazy, and if Viola didn't "stop it" she didn't know what she was going to do.

Viola wept right along with her. She said she knew she hadn't been earning her keep, but she would do better from now on. Moreover, she had saved most of her wages, and we could have the money back.

We were a northern family by heritage, but we had lived a big part of our lives in the South, and we—were children, at least—thought southern. Hence, the reason for my puzzlement with Viola.

It was obvious even to me that she was a far superior person to Mrs. Cole. She was, in fact, the mental and moral superior of many white people I knew. But she was black, and everyone knew that Negroes were a shiftless, lazy lot who couldn't be trusted out of sight. Everyone knew that the lowest white was better than the best black.

The only way I could account for Viola's superiority was on the basis that she was part white, but this she would not admit.

"No, sir, Mister Jimmie," she laughed, when I plagued her. "I'm black, all right. All black."

"But how do you know, Viola? You might not be."

"I just know. I know the same way you know you're white."

I could not desist. Once I got some riddle on my mind, preferably one that was foolish or of no possible consequence to me, I could not expel it until it was solved.

So, in the end, I forced Viola to confess her whiteness.

She was peeling potatoes and she had just nicked her thumb with the knife. She held the bleeding digit up for me to see.

"You see there, Mister Jimmie? You don't see any white blood like that. That's all-Negro blood."

"It is not either!" I exclaimed. "That's white people's blood! It's just like mine!"

"You're joking me, Mister Jimmie."

"I am not! You're white, Viola—partly white, anyways. I guess I ought to know what white people's blood looks like!"

"I guess you should," Viola admitted in an awed voice. "Well, what do you know!"

"I knew all the time I was right," I said loftily.

Mom looked upon Viola more as a friend than a servant. But, as she was fond of saying, she didn't want friends around all the time. Thus, as she recovered her health and the economic situation improved, Viola left us for another job. Once a week, however, she returned to us for a day to give the house a good cleaning.

She did not want to take any pay for this work, but Mom always forced her to take something; if not money, some discarded clothes. As for her new employers, Viola had very little to say about them. About all we could get out of her was that they were mighty nice people, but that she'd rather be with us.

It was Pop who finally let the cat out of the bag. Not, naturally, that he'd been trying to keep the truth from us. He just hadn't thought it of any particular consequence.

"Why, she's working for the governor," he revealed. "He gave her some little job in the mansion on my say-so, but the family liked her so well she's running the whole thing now. She—"

"The governor," said Mom, blankly. "Oh, my goodness! I've had her coming over here on her day off to sweep and scrub and—"

When Viola next appeared, Mom rebuked her for the deception, then insisted on treating her as company.

Viola didn't want to be treated as company. She just couldn't bear it, she said. And, since Mom remained firm, her visits became more and more infrequent. Finally, they stopped altogether.

We missed her terribly.

# X

HAVING ACHIEVED CONSIDERABLE success in his dual profession of attorney-accountant, Pop swiftly began to lose interest in it. That was Pop's way. He was forever advising others—notably, me—to choose one line of endeavor and stick to it, but he himself was incapable of such singleness of purpose.

Political friends who learned of his feelings offered to obtain him an appointment as United States marshal. Pop declined. They offered him a Federal judgeship. He declined that, too.

Various lucrative ventures and positions were proffered him, and he consistently turned them down. He was quite capable of making his own way in life, he stiffly averred. And during the next two- or three-odd years he set about earnestly to prove it.

I could not name all the ventures he was active in during that period, but they included the operation of a sawmill, the proprietorship of a hotel, truck farming, running a bush-league ball club, the garbage-hauling contract for a certain Oklahoma metropolis and turkey ranching.

As each business or endeavor failed, we were left with certain mementoes of it: assets—to use the term loosely—which were at once non-liquidatable but yet, for one reason or another, impossible to discard. Thus, by the time of the demise of the turkey ranch, our residence and its environs were so encumbered that one could hardly get into it, or, once in, out.

Zoning laws and health ordinances were unheard of or unenforced in those days, else all of us would certainly have been carted off to institutions—penal or protective. As it was, Mom finally became hysterical. She declared that she herself would see to Pop's commitment if he did not come to his senses.

"G-garbage wagons!" she wept. "G-garbage wagons in the front yard, and —a-and h-horses in the garage, a-and ploughs on the front porch, a-and—"

She went on with her recital, becoming more and more agitated with the mention of each item. The incubators in the bedrooms. The gangsaws in the living room. The cigar showcases in the kitchen. The tomato plants in the bathroom. The dozens of newly hatched young turkeys, which roamed the house from one end to the other. The—

"And that ball player!" yelled Mom. "I swear, Jim Thompson, if you don't get him out of here, I'll—I'll murder both of you!"

This last reference was to the occupant of our sleeping porch, a rheumy old party who combined an affection for chewing tobacco with very poor eyesight. He could not have hit a bull with a bass fiddle, as the saying is. Pop, of course, perversely regarded him as a second Ty Cobb.

322

"You get him out of here!" Mom shouted. "Get all this junk away from here. Either he and it goes or the children and I do!"

Pop gave in, not, naturally, because he could be swayed by threats, but because he was quite as weary of the situation as Mom was. He found some political sinecure for the ball player, and gave away the other animals and items. Good riddance it was—as none knew better than he. But you could never make him admit it.

For years, nay decades, no visitor came to our house without learning that Pop had once owned a very valuable ball player ("another Babe Ruth") or some very valuable horses ("the same blood strain as Man O' War") or several hundred prize turkeys ("their eggs were worth a hundred dollars a dozen"). To hear Pop tell it, he had been on the point of cornering the world market in tomatoes or timber or hotel gaboons ("genuine antiques, mind you"). All the nominal dross which Mom had forced him to get shed of had actually been gold, and only her callous and ignorant interference had prevented his reaping untold wealth.

"Of course," he would sigh bravely, in concluding his recital, "I don't blame Mrs. Thompson in the least. It was my own fault for listening to her."

He would laugh hollowly, then, his face fixed in a stoical mask. And while Mom choked and stammered incoherently, our guests would stare at her open-mouthed, pity and horror mingling in their eyes.

Of necessity, and as much as it irked him, Pop had continued to practice law and accountancy. But he was constantly on the lookout for some new field of activity, and he finally found it, or so he felt, in the booming Oklahoma oil fields.

I mentioned a few pages back that his first dabblings in this business were not too successful. This, on reflection, seems an unfair statement of the case. They were successful enough, but Pop's generosity and trustingness turned them into failures.

On one occasion, after several shrewd deals, he gave a "friend" twenty-five thousand dollars to tie up some leases for him. Instead, the man bought an automobile agency and placed it in his wife's name. There was nothing Pop could do about it. The law regards such an action as a breach of trust, and its attitude briefly is that anyone who suffers it has only himself to blame.

Another time, Pop accepted the word and the handshake of a pipeline executive in lieu of a written contract. As a result, when the pipeline company found it inexpedient to connect with his first oil well, he could only let the torrent of black gold pour into the nearest creek.

It was a few months after this last fiasco, when Pop was again hard at work at his now-detested law-accountancy practice, that he met a man named Jake Hamon. Or, I should say, re-met him. For he had known him casually during his early days in Oklahoma. At that time, Jake, a former roustabout with the Ringling Brothers Circus, had been a six-for-fiver around the pioneer tent and shack towns. That is, he bought wages from workers in advance of their due date, giving the needy borrower five dollars for each six he had coming.

Jake was still in the loan business at the time of his and Pop's later encounter, though on a slightly different level. He owned a string of Oklahoma banks. He also owned a railroad, oil wells, refineries, office buildings—so much, in fact, that he had acquired the sobriquet of "John D. Rockefeller of the Southwest."

He asked Pop to audit his banks and to equip them with a more efficient accounting system. Pop, having nothing better to do, gladly agreed.

"I won't charge you anything, of course," he said, casually. "Just my expenses."

"Why?" Jake demanded.

"Well"—Pop was a little set back. His generous offers were not usually received in this fashion. "Well, after all we're old friends and—"

Jake interrupted him with a rude four-letter ejaculation. "Who the hell says we're friends?" he snarled. "I haven't seen you in years, and if you're as big a dope as you act like I don't want to see you again. Friends, hell! I've heard about some of your friends. Forget that friend crap. Name me a fee for this job, or get the hell out of my office!"

Smarting, Pop named him a fee—one that was outrageously high. And Jake chortled happily.

"You see?" he grinned. "All you need is a tough guy like me to ride herd on you. You stick with me, Jim, and you'll wear diamonds."

So Pop went to work for Jake, and for the first time in his life he held on to a large share of the money he made. The relation of the two men, at first, was that of employer and employee. From that it shifted to a point where Pop was Jake's advisor on various deals, at a percentage of the profits. And in the end they became partners in the deals—usually oil—with Jake providing the lion's share of the money and Pop carrying out the necessary negotiations. Pop became a familiar figure at lease auctions and distress sales. The transactions were frequently cash on the barrelhead. And on at least one occasion Pop's brief case contained a million dollars of Jake's money.

While Pop made and continued to make a great deal of money with Jake, "the Southwest's Rockefeller" himself profited vastly by the association. Even as he watched over Pop, so did Pop watch over him, checking the ugly temper and cynical attitude which, as Jake would surlily admit, had cost him millions and made him a public-relations man's headache.

Unfortunately, no one likes to be reminded of his faults, real and harmful as they may be. And the closer their association became and the greater their familiarity, the more flaws they found with one another. Nothing that the other did was right. Pop was a "softie," Jake an "illiterate boor." Jake was a "slob," Pop a "high-toned dude." So it went.

Since Pop was genuinely fond of Jake, and vice versa, and both had given concrete proof of that liking, it always seemed incredible to me that they could have come to a parting of the ways.

Pop refused to talk about the breakup for a long time. When he finally did explain, I could only sit and gape, for the *casus belli* had been a suit of underwear.

It had happened—the breakup—in the sweltering hotel room of an Oklahoma boom town. They were there, pending the closing of a business deal, and during their stay Jake's mistress had arrived. He got her a room across the hall from theirs, and spent the nights with her. During the day he stayed in his and Pop's room, conferring upon business matters.

It was hot, as I have said. He seldom wore anything but his underwear. And one morning, when he was prowling restlessly about their room, he surprised Pop in a disgusted frown.

"What's the matter with you?" he inquired gruffly.

"I was about to ask you the same thing," Pop retorted.

"What do you mean? What are you staring at, anyway?"

"Since you asked me," said Pop, coldly, "I was looking at your underclothes. When was the last time you changed them?"

"Why, you—" Jake's face turned scarlet. "You two-bit bookkeeper, I ought to—!"

He exploded into a torrent of abuse.

Pop replied similarly.

Before they could see the ridiculousness of the situation and get control of themselves, each had said unforgivable—or at least unforgettable—things and their partnership was ended.

They saw one another after that, but there was a certain stiffness between them. And Pop had reason to suspect—or felt he had—that Jake still bore a grudge against him.

Next, Pop lost almost ten thousand dollars in a poker game with Jake, Gaston B. Means and Warren G. Harding.

The game took place on the Harding presidential campaign train, upon which, as two of the Southwest's most prominent Republicans, Pop and Jake were guests of honor. It began with relatively low stakes which Jake, with much jibing and jeering, managed to steadily increase. Finally, with all the cash available in the pot, Means dropped out, and the contest was between Jake, Harding and Pop. In other words, since Pop was too stiffnecked and proud to demand a table-stakes game, it was no contest.

Jake could write his check for any amount. And certainly the I.O.U. of a future president was good for any amount. Only Pop's betting was restricted.

He tossed in his hand, a club flush. Immediately, although he had anted heavily on the previous round, Jake laid down his hand—the value of which was absolutely nothing. Harding took the pot with three threes.

Pop was considerably, if not justifiably, irritated. He did not see Jake again until some two years later when the latter summoned him to his death bed. Then, with matters past mending, they sadly agreed that the biggest mistake of their lives had been the ending of their association.

Pop, feeling that Oklahoma was not big enough for the two of them, had transferred his activities to Texas. And there he had drilled four oil-less oil wells in a row, at a cost of more than two hundred thousand dollars each.

Jake, sans any friendly restraint or guidance, had become increasingly misanthropic, and, finally, his mistress took a gun to him and he died of the wounds.

# XI

WE MOVED TO Fort Worth, Texas, in the fall of 1919, shortly before the coming of my thirteenth birthday. The city was riding a tidal wave of post-war wealth. New building was months behind the demand, and there were a dozen purchasers for every available house. So, for several weeks, we were forced to live in a hotel suite. The period was one of the most unpleasant in my checkered career.

For the first time in my memory, I was immediately under Pop's eye day in and day out. And Pop, who had taken only a spasmodic interest in me until then, now began to make up for lost time. I was a rich man's son, he pointed out, and some day I would inherit great wealth. I must be made into a proper custodian for it—sane, sober, considerate. I should not be allowed to become one of those ill-mannered, irresponsible wastrels, who behaved as though they had been put on earth solely to enjoy themselves.

No error in my deportment was too tiny for Pop to spot and criticize. No flaw in my appearance was too small. From the time I arose until the time I retired, I was subjected to a steady stream of criticism about the way I dressed, walked, talked, stood, ate, sat, and so on into infinity—all with that most maddening of assurances that it was for my "own good."

We had two cars in the hotel garage. Pop took me there and placed me under the supervision of the foreman mechanic, instructing him to treat me as he would any hired hand. For the ensuing week I assisted in the overhauling of our automobiles. Rather, I did the overhauling with some minor assistance from one of the mechanics. I was too outraged and sullen to discuss the work, so I did not dispute Pop's bland statement that the experience would teach me a great deal. For that matter, it did teach me a great deal—namely, that repairing cars was a lousy way to make a living. And never again, except in the direst emergencies, did I so much as change a tire.

Always in the past, Mom had served as a bulwark against Pop's extremes of family management, but she proved remiss in this emergency, a fact decidedly less puzzling in retrospect than it was at the time. Pop had behaved intelligently—instead of with his sporadic brilliance—throughout his partnership with Jake Hamon, and she was naturally inclined to regard his intense interest in me as a continuation of that intelligent behavior. Moreover, say what you will, it is difficult to dispute the judgment of a man who has made a million dollars.

I was finally impelled to dispute it, in fact to raise holy hell about it, when Pop took me to buy my school clothes, the chief item of which was a blue-serge knickerbocker suit with velvet-braided lapels and pearl buttons. I had not used any profanity in years—and never in front of Pop whose nearest approach to cursing was an occasional darn or gosh. But now I cut loose. Before I could be dragged out of the swank men's clothing store, the swallow-tailed clerks were fleeing for cover, their manicured fingers stoppering their scarlet ears.

I was returned to the hotel and confined to my room. As further punishment, I was advised that I would not be allowed to accompany the family on a tour of the oil fields, but would remain in Fort Worth in the custody of Pa.

I advised the family—at the top of my lungs—that they could all go to hell.

Pa had joined us in Fort Worth with the announced intention of getting us settled, but actually, I am sure, as a way of getting away from Ma. He had given me none of the support I expected in my skirmishes with Pop, and I was thoroughly disgusted with him. Pa—the orphan—said that I was damned lucky to have a smart man like Pop looking after me. He said that it was every man's right to make a damned fool of himself, and that my turn would come later.

I was disgusted with Pa. I felt that he had failed me sorely. Thus, the following morning, when he came into my room after the family's departure, I told him to get the hell out.

"Have a smoke," said Pa, tossing me a foot-long Pittsburgh stogie. "Got a little surprise for you."

The surprise, or part of it, arrived right behind him: a white-jacketed waiter with a pitcher of boiling water, a bowl of lemons and sugar. Pa took a bottle of bootleg corn whiskey from his hip and mixed us two tremendous hot toddies.

"Kind of like old times, ain't it?" he said, slanting his savagely humorous old eyes at me. "You remember that night out by the privy when—Now, what the hell you sniveling about, anyway?"

"I—n-nothing'," I said, choking back a sob.

"Light up, then. Drink up. Stop acting like a goddamned calf. Anything I hate to see it's a fella cryin' in good whiskey."

I lit up and drank up. The steam from the toddies mingled with the clouds of cigar smoke, and the morning sunlight shone through it upon Pa's bald head. It seemed to me he wore a halo.

"I tell you somethin', Jimmie," he said casually, freshening our drinks from the bottle. "We all got our own way of doin' things, an' that's the way we got to do 'em. Ain't no man can do a thing another fella's way. Ain't no use tryin' to make him. He'll just go his own way all the harder, an' he'll be your enemy besides."

I nodded my understanding, although I was far from agreeing with his doctrine. Pa went on to remark that while other people had their ways, he also had his, and it was no more than just and proper that he should pursue that way since I had been left in his charge.

"In other words," he concluded, "anyone that thinks you're going to tag around with me in that outfit your Pop bought you has got another goddamned think coming."

He gave me another stogie and urged me to help myself to a second toddy. Then, he left the room, returning a few minutes later with one of his "uniforms"—complete even to the wide-brimmed black hat and Congress gaiters. All that was missing was the cane, and Pa promised to pick one up for me if I felt too naked without it.

Happily, the stogie lodged in the corner of my mouth, I dressed.

The hat and the gaiters had to be stuffed with paper to be wearable. And since Pa stood six feet to my five and weighed two hundred pounds to my one-ten, the suit was a trifle large. But this difficulty was easily solved—to our satisfaction at least. The pants legs were rolled up and under for a few inches, likewise the coat sleeves. A few pins here and there and the job was done.

True, the seat of the pants bagged to my knees, but the coat reached below them. One hand washed the other, to use Pa's metaphor. I looked fine, he declared, and no one but a damned fool would think otherwise. So, equipped with fresh stogies, we sallied forth.

During my long residence in Fort Worth, I often felt that it was cursed with more than its share of damned fools. But it was a western city, and peculiarities of dress went more unmarked than otherwise. Thus, while I drew a number of startled glances, no one, damned fool or otherwise, said or did anything about me.

Pa and I ate a whopping breakfast of steak, eggs and hot cakes, and only once did he see fit to criticize me. That was when he observed me eating from the sharp edge of my knife, and he pointed out the danger of it, suggesting that I use the reverse edge instead.

After breakfast we went to a pool hall where Pa beat me five games of slop pool and I beat him two. We returned to the hotel, then, for a few before-lunch drinks, and following lunch we went to a penny arcade.

Pa had brought the bottle with him, and he became quite rambunctious when "A Night With A Paris Cutie" did not come up to his expectations. He caned the machine. I think he would have caned the arcade proprietor, but that shrewd gentleman wisely gave him no back talk. Instead, he returned Pa's coins and led him out to the sidewalk. He pointed to a burlesque house across and down the street.

"Why look at pictures," he inquired, "when you can see the real thing?"

"Well, now," said Pa, greatly mollified. "Maybe you got something there, friend."

Fort Worth had a number of burlesque houses at that time, and we were able to obtain choice seats on the front or "baldhead" row. Except for three brief and alternate absences, we stayed there until the house closed at midnight.

Those absences? Well, first I went outside to buy a cane so that I could hook the girls on the ramp as Pa did. Then, Pa went out for a fresh supply of whiskey. Then, I went out for a carton of coffee and sandwiches.

It was a wonderfully satisfying day. Pa had given a bottle to the ushers and sent a couple of others backstage, and in that place he and I could do no wrong. We hooked the girls' garments until they were reduced to near nudity. Pa climbed upon the ramp and chased them backstage. Yet they responded with laughter and joyous shrieks, and occasionally one would stoop swiftly and plant a kiss on Pa's head.

Each of the succeeding three days, at the end of which the family returned, was a reasonable facsimile of that first day. Hot toddies in the morning, then a pool game, then a burlesque house, with drinks and meals being imbibed at strategic intervals. Also much talk from Pa, much advice delivered in his casual back-handed fashion.

I am afraid that most of what he said was wasted upon me. But I was imbued with a little of his wisdom, at least briefly. I gave Pop no further argument about the clothes, and I submitted silently if sullenly to his criticisms. For a time, I was docile.

Then we bought a house and Pa returned to Nebraska and I started to school.

Texas had only eleven grades of school as compared with the twelve in other states. Thus, as an eighth-grade student in the Oklahoma schools, I was technically a first-year high-school student in Texas. Being extremely praise-hungry, and anxious to shine in Pop's eyes, I took advantage of that technicality.

Nowadays, it is no unusual thing for a twelve-year-old—and I was still twelve—to enter high school. But it was unusual at that time. More important, in my case, it was completely unjustifiable.

I had read voraciously and far in advance of my years, and I was a walking compendium of largely unassimilated knowledge drilled into me by Pop. But I was sadly prepared for the inelastic high-school curriculum. In our various moves from place to place, I had been absent from grammar school practically as much as I had attended. Now, I was missing a whole year. I knew nothing of cube and square root and many other things upon which the high-school subjects were predicated.

Despite the sorry state of my elementary schooling, I think I might have done passably in the higher grades if I could have put my heart into it. I have almost always managed to do the things I really cared about doing. Similarly, however, and doubtless regrettably, I can do nothing at all if I do not care. And I become uncaring very quickly if I am prodded or driven, or if the people involved are distasteful to me.

To put the last thing first, the Texans were distasteful—or so I soon convinced myself. I studied their mannerisms and mores, and in my twisted outlook they became Mongoloid monsters. I saw all their bad and no offsetting good.

Texans made boast of their insularism; they bragged about such things as never having been outside the state or the fact that the only book in their house was the Bible. Texans did not need to work to improve their characters as Pop was constantly pressing me to do. All Texans were born with perfect characters, and these became pluperfect as their owners drank the unrivaled Texas waters, breathed the wondrous Texas air and trod the holy Texas soil.

Texas, it appeared, had formed all but a minuscule part of the Confederacy, and as such had slapped the troops of Sherman silly and sent Grant's groaning to their graves. Singlehanded—almost, anyway—it had thrashed the bully, North. Then, as a generous though intrinsically meaningless gesture, it had conceded defeat, thus ending the awful bloodshed and preserving the Union.

Just as all Texas males were omnipotent, invincible and of irreproachable character, so were all Texas women superbly beautiful and utterly virginal. And woe to anyone who hinted the contrary. Being of an open mind (by my own admission), I was willing to concede that the Texas female was probably somewhat more personable than a Ubangi, but I would make no concessions on the second score. I delighted in pointing out the historic incompatibility of virginity with wife- and mother-hood. Mock-innocent, I demanded that the peculiar Texas situation be explained to me. As a rule, my heretical quizzing was rewarded at this point with a punch in the nose; if not, I would extend the questioning into the sacrosanct realm of Texas sweethearts and sisters.

That, invariably, would get me not one punch but a dozen.

Anything that a Texan might be sensitive about or hold sacred, I jeered at. There was no trick too low for me if it would discomfit the Texans.

I recall—and it makes me squirm to do it—the pleased astonishment of the coach when I applied for a place on the high-school track team. How unselfishly delighted he was that I was at last coming out of my shell. I recall his almost tearful joy as I skimmed tirelessly and swiftly around the track—a half mile, mile, mile-and-a-half, two miles. I was a natural-born two-miler, he declared—rangy, wiry, long legged. I was the best two-miler he had ever seen, and he hugged me ecstatically. The two-mile event was in the bag. If only he had a few more lads like me!

It was a damned good thing for him that he didn't have any more like me, for, while I represented our school in the intramural two-mile race, I did not run it.

I trotted up in front of the grandstand, sat down in the middle of the track and lighted a cigarette.

Only my tender years, I suspect, saved me from being lynched.

# XII

I HAD NOT completely plumbed the abyss of ignominy when I came under the influence of a Boy Scout leader, and for a time my descent was checked. Then, suddenly and inexplicably, he became cool and critical, and I resumed my career of making everyone else as miserable as I was.

Years later, when I was shaking out of the grandfather of all hangovers, Pop tried to get at the root of my trouble.

"I just can't understand it," he complained. "I can't see how it started. You were always such a bright, likeable, willing youngster. So well-balanced and adaptable."

"I was, huh?" I laughed hoarsely. "Well, well."

"Of course you were! Why, your scoutmaster made a special trip to my office to tell me about you. He said you were the finest boy in his troop."

"Don't kid me," I said. "That guy got me to liking him, then he turned on me and he never gave me a pleasant word from then on."

"Now, I wonder why he did that." Pop frowned in honest puzzlement. "I believe I did tell him that praise could be very bad for a boy, and that I hoped you wouldn't acquire a swelled head. But surely—"

Well.

I was easily the most unpopular student in school. Also, it goes without saying, I was the poorest student. I had read all the standard historians, Gibbon, Wells, even Herodotus, yet I could not—rather, would not—pass the Texas history courses. I had read a complete twelve-volume botanical encyclopedia, but I failed in botany. I had read Ibanez's *Mare Nostrum* as well as some of Alarcon's shorter plays in their original language, yet I failed in Spanish. I had sold fillers to the pulp periodicals and brief humorous squibs to such magazines as *Judge,* but I failed in English. Most thoroughly, I failed in algebra and geometry, two subjects which struck me as so wholly nonsensical that they were *beneath,* beneath contempt—if you follow my meaning.

In one of my softer moments, I proposed a bargain to my math teacher: if she would prove to me that her chosen subjects were not as stupid as I claimed, then I would study them. She did not take me up on the offer, and she seemed very embittered by it. The good woman gave me what is doubtless the lowest grade ever meted out to a student—not just a zero, but zero-minus.

I was a high-school freshman at twelve. Almost six years later I was still a high-school freshman. From being the youngest I became the oldest, from being a beardless stripling I grew into manhood (junior grade). Strangers to the school often mistook me for a member of the faculty.

I was expelled and suspended so many times for disobedience, refusing to study, cutting classes, playing truant, et cetera, that I lost track of them. So also did the school. Suspensions were piled upon expulsions and expulsions upon suspensions, so that the harried records clerk never knew when I was legitimately present or illegally absent. Along toward the last, just before she gave up the unequal struggle with my status, I overheard the tag end of her plea to one of my teachers, ". . . please do not suspend him until he is reinstated from expulsion so I can suspend him as of last month so I can reinstate him to be expelled, so—s-so—*I'M G-GOING C-CRAAA-ZY!*"

Now and then, sometimes for the better part of a term, I escaped into the upper classes. But inevitably my scholastic record would catch up with me, and I would be returned to the freshman fold. One term, having received so many lectures that I had begun to fear for my hearing, I decided to try to reform. I promoted myself into the senior class. There, where I rightfully should have been had I behaved as I should have, I was polite to the teachers and I studied as I had never studied before. My grades soared higher and higher. As the end of the term neared, I was placed in that select group of students whose marks were so good that they were excused from final examinations.

When finally they were apprised of my status, my teachers were incredulous. They had had no dealings with me before that term, and they could not believe that I was the James Thompson who had established an all-time record for boorishness and boobery. Unfortunately, there was indisputable proof that the onerous and ornery James was one and the same with theirs. So, since I lacked the prerequisite courses, my brilliant term's work availed me nothing. I received no credit hours for it.

I was right back where I had started, still a freshman.

Despite my chagrin and disappointment, I did not feel that my work had been entirely wasted. For one thing, I had rid myself of a worrisome suspicion that I was as stupid as most people thought. For another, I had been made to see the inexorable crux of my problem.

Obviously, mere study and better behavior were not going to get me out of high school. Not, that is, within a reasonable time. No matter how hard I studied nor how well I behaved, I would still have to spend four more years in school on top of the approximately six years I had already served. The records would force me to.

So there was the problem, not in me, as I saw it, but in the records.

Something would have to be done about them.

At this time, and for some time prior to it, I was employed as a night bellboy in a large hotel. The list of my acquaintances extended into places which, in my present pious state, gives me shivers to think about. A Square Sam myself, I was known to be "strictly okay" and a "right kid." In no time at all I was in touch with a burglar, explaining my problem and asking his help on a fee basis.

"I dunno, kid," he said, scratching his head doubtfully. "I'd like to help you out, but—well, I just dunno."

"But it's a cinch," I said. "The stuff isn't in a safe. All you have to do is pick the locks on a couple doors. Then, you get rid of my record card and fill in one of their blanks. I'll tell you just what to put on it, and—"

"I don't know nothing about those things, kid. I'd foul it up for you, sure."

"Don't do anything to it, then. Just get rid of the record and bring me one of the blanks and—"

"Huh-uh. I go into a place once, I'm through with it. I don't go back no more. Anyway, suppose they look for that card and it ain't there. They'd come down on you like a ton of bricks, kid."

"Well"—I hesitated—"how about this? Take someone with you that—"

"Look, kid!" He held up a hand. "You just don't do things that way. A guy's a penman, he don't do nothing else. He wouldn't touch a burglary for love or money. There's only one way to do this job. Get to the party that keeps the records. Put a fix in with her."

"She's not on the take," I said glumly. "I know that dame!"

"Well," he shrugged, "that's the way you'll have to swing it. If you can't do it from the inside, you just ain't gonna get it done."

I left him disconsolately, all the more depressed because I knew he was right. A new record card, filled out in a hand wholly dissimilar to that of the other cards, would be damnably incriminating. Even with a fix in, the crime was certain to be spotted. For as long as school was in session the cards were referred to, and there were certain teachers who knew my record by heart.

I had not one problem, then, but two. To do the job from the inside, and to do it right at the close of the school term. Thus, by the time there was again occasion to refer to that card, I would be safely out of reach, my sins would have become dim in the minds of the authorities, and any long-memoried snoop who sought to make trouble would find his contentions impossible to prove.

It was a large order, one seemingly impossible to fill. Yet fill it I must or become the world's only senile schoolboy.

So fill it I did. And I shall tell you how I did it a little later.

Meanwhile, let us move back in the story, taking its events in as proper a sequence as their general impropriety will permit.

# XIII

POP'S LUCK WENT sour almost from the day he set foot in Texas. The fortune which I was to inherit shrank at the rate of almost four hundred thousand dollars a year. I naturally thought it was a hell of a note to be losing all that dough without so much as a soda to show for it, but I was more concerned with certain issues tangential to the main one. Briefly, as I discussed them with Pop, they were about as follows:

First of all, was a man who had made such a thorough screw-up of his own affairs a suitable mentor for me? (I did not think so.)

Second, with him losing money at the rate of a couple thousand dollars a week, was there any sense in my knocking myself out for a pittance on some part-time job? (I did not think so.)

Finally, since I apparently would have no dough to look after, wasn't all this Spartan training I was undergoing pretty damned stupid? (I thought it was.)

I was not trying to be snide or facetious, and I was irritated and bewildered that Pop should think I was. I pointed out that if I wanted to be smart-alecky or nasty, I could do a heck of a lot better than that. ("Just ask anyone, Pop.") But Pop was as near to being furious as I have ever seen him.

Addressing me as "sirrah," he let it be known that I was pretty poor comfort for a man no longer young whose life's gleanings were slipping through his fingers, never to be grasped again. He said that when he was my age he had done such and such and so and so, and all I could do was get into trouble and sass my betters. He said that I was completely irresponsible and out-of-hand, and that the remedy lay in work and more work. He had been too easy-going with me, he said, but now the old free and easy days were over.

I was to study every night from dinner until bedtime. Also, since I had chosen to quit my part-time job as a soda jerk, I would find "suitable" employment on the weekends.

The first ordinance did not bother me particularly. I was no more popular in the neighborhood than I was elsewhere, and normally remained indoors at night for reasons connected with my health. I did not study, naturally, but the fact was difficult to prove. I was always writing something. I always had a half-dozen books spread in front of me. They never had anything to do with my lessons, but Pop would have been the first to argue the fact. *The Prince*, to his way of thinking, was a splendid and necessary adjunct to the study of civics. So also was there an indisputable relationship between Schopenhauer and sociology, Malthus and mathematics, and Lycurgus and commercial law.

It was easy, then, to meet Pop's "study" requirements. But finding part-time work was something else again. Such employment was difficult to find in that

335

day, and it paid very little when one did find it. It will seem incomprehensible to our contemporary youth, who sneer at offers of a five-dollar fee for mowing a lawn, but my wage as a soda-jerk had been five dollars for an approximate thirty-hour week.

Pop was a firm believer in the adage that there is always work for those who want it, and when I found none in the time allotted me, he supplied it. He bought a ladder, brushes, and a supply of paint and set me to work painting the house.

Now, while I showed little liking for useful employment, it does not necessarily follow that I liked useless work any better. And this was worse than useless. The house was only a few months old. It stood in need of paint much less than I. Disgusted and resentful, I did the job at the rate of a few inches a day, painting over and over the same places. The end effect, naturally, was that of a checker board, and the whole place had to be done over by professional painters.

We lived in an unincorporated suburb of Fort Worth. Like our neighbors —a meat packer, a steel magnate and another oil man—we had bought the lots surrounding ours, and our total land holdings were probably an acre. Pop now caused a barn to be built on this surplus land, and furnished it with two purebred Jerseys. And I, I was advised, was in the dairy business.

Since we were outside the city limits, our neighbors were without legal recourse. Mom, her frugal soul mollified by the prospect of free milk for the household, did no more than hint that Pop had become a hopeless lunatic. I protested, of course, bitterly, profanely and continuously. And knowing something of Pop you will know how little my protests accomplished.

I was to have full charge of the cows—"a free hand," as Pop put it. The family would receive its milk free, the remainder would be distributed through a house-to-house milk route, which would be "no trouble at all" for me to establish. I would be allowed to keep any monies remaining—after the care and feeding of the cows had been paid for.

"It's a wonderful opportunity for you," said Pop. "You should be very grateful."

I said something that sounded like "ship."

Not that I gave a damn really, but there were no profits from the business. Jerseys are not the hardiest breed of cattle, and one visit from a veterinarian consumed the returns from a week's sale of milk. Too, while customers were fairly plentiful in the beginning, they did not continue so. They seemed alarmed by a milkman who lost no opportunity to declare that he would be fried with onions sooner than touch a drop of that "blank blank triple-blank Jersey juice."

I put up with the dairy until summer. Then, being told that I would have to keep the cows staked out during the day—move them around on a tether from one vacant lot to another—I went down to the railroad yards and caught a northbound freight.

I got as far as Kansas before I was apprehended and returned.

I waited a few days, then caught a freight southward.

I was brought back from Houston.

Pop sold the cows.

I was made to feel, of course, that I had behaved very badly. The family had been put to much expense and trouble, on my account, and the only return I would give them was insolence and shiftlessness.

I was bewildered by this attitude, and still am. Even more now than I was at the time.

I have three children, one a fifteen-year-old boy. I think they are pretty good kids, but honesty compels me to say that no one of them has ever made a bed, washed a dish or swept a floor without violent protest. Moreover, they commonly refer to their mother and me as "nuts" or "screwy" and they frequently suggest that we "turn blue" or "stop breathing" or otherwise end our patent misery.

You see, when these children were quite young we had an elderly man living with us. This man would not let the children lift a finger to any task, reproaching us scornfully and speaking darkly of "child slaves." He would not let us reprove them, no matter what their misdeeds. He sternly ruled down the suggestions that treats should be withheld for bad behavior, and that allowances should be earned with household chores. Naturally, the kids got pretty spoiled.

Who was this man, you ask? Who was the man who encouraged our children in insolence, who constantly bawled us out for failing to swallow his dictum that kids were kids and should only be addressed with words of praise?

Who?

Pop.

# XIV

WE SPENT A large part of that summer at the fashionable Spa, in Waukesha, Wisconsin. The family lounged about the place "taking the waters," and I found employment as a plumber's helper. I did not mind it too much.

Jack, the plumber I was assigned to, was a prize goldbrick, a man who saw no virtue in work whatsoever. "I can lay right down aside a job and go to sleep," he would boast. He seldom referred to work as such, apparently hating even the sound of it. He spoke of it rather with a kind of glum obliqueness as "the Killer."

He struck me as being an extremely wise and discerning man, and I treated him with due deference. Under his earnest tutelage, I became almost as expert at stalling and loafing as he.

One morning, the morning after a day we had killed in repairing a leaky toilet trap, the boss plumber confronted Jack with considerable severity.

He said that he had put up with just about all he was going to, and that he would be "forced to take steps" unless Jack improved his ways.

Jack blinked at him stolidly. Then he reached into an inside pocket, took out a notebook and withdrew a sheaf of clippings from it.

"Read those," he commanded.

The boss read them, perforce. They were all obituaries of people who had died while working.

" 'At's what you're up to," Jack would growl, at the conclusion of each clipping. "You tryin' to kill me, maybe?"

There was obviously but one acceptable answer to the question, and the boss made it over and over. In fact, as Jack glowered and glared at him, his huge hands fondling a thirty-six-inch Stillson, our employer began to anticipate the gloomy inquiry. He could not stand it if anything happened to us, he babbled. We must take better care of ourselves and avoid over-exertion in the summer heat.

Jack finally allowed him to escape to his office. Whereupon, of course, my colleague placed his hands on his hips, spread his feet, sucked in his lungs, threw back his head, opened his mouth to its widest, and addressed the ceiling with a bellowed promise to kill that dirty son-of-a-bitch.

Along with obituaries of people who had succumbed to "the Killer," Jack collected French postcards, and many was the hour we whiled away with these in the restfully cool sanctuary of bathrooms, basements and cess-basins.

"Looky at them," Jack would say. "Now, ain't that somethin'?"

"Now, ain't that somethin'!" I would respond.

"Betcha they's plenty o' people'd give a thousand dollars to see somethin' like that."

"Betcha they *is* plenty."

Jack felt there was an unreasonable and foolish prejudice against these "art studies" and that a fortune awaited the person who could overcome it.

"Everyone likes 'em themselves," he said, "but they're afraid to let on. Now, if you could get everyone to lookin' at 'em all at the same time, out in the open like—"

"Yeah," I frowned wisely. "All at the same time. Out in the open like."

Jack was much impressed with the manner in which I held up my end of our discussions. He said I had a way of getting right to the point of a thing, and that I did wonders toward clarifying his own thinking.

We were installing guard rails in a local food-processing plant when the solution to the French-postcard-prejudice problem came to him. Generous man that he was, and grateful for the many times I had gotten to the point of things, he promised me a full half of his potential millions.

"Yes, sir, Jimmie," he said, nodding to a conveyor belt. "That's the way to do it. We hit the nail right on the head."

"Yes, sir," I said, blankly. "That's the way to do it."

"Them packages."

"Them packages."

"We slip 'em in there."

"We slip—Hey!" I said. "What are we waiting for?"

It seemed odd that this triumphant moment should have marked the beginning of the end of a beautiful friendship. But I am forced to report that it did. For now instead of plunging forthright into the cause, and forging ahead to victory and riches, Jack held back in ultra-caution. We had to do the thing right, he said. And they was plenty of things to be worked out before we could do it right.

As the days passed, and two items appeared in the ranks of things-to-be-worked-out for each one I expunged, I became impatient with Jack, then suspicious of him. I declared that he was deliberately delaying operations until I had returned to Texas where I would be unable to reap my just dues as co-owner of the company.

Jack was placatory for a time. But I seemed to detect a certain lack of candor in his manner—a damning sheepishness. So my indictments continued, and finally he was brought to respond with hideous slurs. He said I was an eager beaver, willing and wilful fodder for "the Killer." He would bet money, he said, that I *liked* to work; he had had his doubts about me from the beginning, and my vigorous manner and unseemly impetuosity had now revealed the awful truth to him.

We stopped speaking after that.

We did not speak again until the eve of my departure for Texas, when we shook hands diffidently and exchanged stiff farewells.

More than thirty years have passed since that stilly evening in a Wisconsin plumbing shop. Thirty years, in which I have become the non-inventing inventor of such things as story-book toilet paper, cigarettes with built-in matches, neckties which assume the hue of the gravy dropped on them and a tongue-shaped sponge for licking stamps. So I can understand Jack's attitude now. I can see that the more beautiful a dream, the more hopeless its realization, that we have but to grasp to destroy it.

All I could see at the time, however, was that a venal and crafty man had taken sorry advantage of an innocent and trusting boy. And for months after our return to Texas, I searched for proof of Jack's perfidy.

Every container of food that came into the house was carefully dissected by me—cartons, labels, wrappers, tax stamps. I even took apart the lids of catsup bottles and cracked open the stoppers to sauce carafes. Since I declined to explain this activity, mumbling only of a million dollars and people who thought they could kid me, the family was more than ever convinced that I didn't have a brain in my head.

Which, I imagine, was a pretty fair statement of the case.

# XV

THE SCHOOL I attended was not too far distant from Glen Garden Country Club, so it was only natural that I should gravitate there in search of week-end employment. I found it, as a caddie, and I liked it. At least, I liked it better than the other types of work I had thus far encountered. There was something about receiving pay from play which pleased me very much. And, as a Glen Garden caddie, one had the privilege of playing on the course at certain hours.

You were out at the club at the crack of dawn, you and Ben Hogan and Byron Nelson, and all the other caddies who were ambitious to improve "their game." There wasn't a full set of clubs among the lot of you, but that didn't matter. You formed into foursomes, according to your handicap. You strode down the dew-wet fairway, calling back and forth to one another, diagnosing each other's drives and approaches as competently as any pro. Later in the day, when the jobs were being passed out, you would engage in profane and bloody struggle behind the caddie shack. But now all the niceties of etiquette were observed. All was politeness and consideration.

The game made you that way.

I thought it was pretty swell.

Well, though, caddies were paid sixty-five cents for eighteen holes, and there were more caddies than there were those who wanted them. On a good day, during a tournament for example, you might "get out" twice for a total of thirty-six holes. And if the tips broke right for you, you might make as much as a dollar seventy-five or two dollars. This was darned big money, of course, for a mere twelve or fifteen miles' trudging with a fifty-pound bag on your back. But it was seldom that one enjoyed such great good fortune.

On an average, you were lucky to get out for eighteen. Or maybe a round and nine. And there were days when you waited around from dawn to sunset without ever getting out. Obviously, as Pop pointed out, caddying was neither dependable nor lucrative.

He did not forbid me to continue with it. In fact, although my habit of ellipsis may have made him appear otherwise, Pop very seldom ordered me or forbade me to do anything. Pop believed in "reasoning a thing through," in "looking at a matter from all sides." There were times, as I have indicated, when I preferred being proved an ingrate, idiot and all-around horse's ass to giving in. But these times were infrequent. I didn't particularly mind being an i., i. and h.a., but the process of establishing my status was just too damned wearying to be endured.

Pop spoke amusingly of "grown men, chasing a little white ball around a cow pasture." He looked down his nose as I boasted of "breaking forty." He himself had broken forty at my age, he said, forty acres of virgin land with only a one-horse plough.

I was spending two days a week at the golf course. Two days that once gone were lost to me forever. Two a week, one hundred and four a year—three hundred and twelve in three years.

Pop grew more eloquent with every word, and I grew older. When, at last, I retired to the bathroom for a smoke, it was with bent back and trembling, rheumatic legs. And I had to study myself in the mirror for minutes before I was convinced that I still had teeth and did not have a long gray beard.

Naturally, I retired from Glen Garden.

As I mentioned a while back, I had sold several short squibs to magazines. This activity was not encouraged, since my puny sales were taken as proof that I lacked talent and was frittering away my time, but neither was it actively discouraged. I had ceased to write, except occasionally and in the greatest secrecy, out of fear of publicity. I had taken a dreadful and prolonged razzing as the result of my writing, and I wanted no more of it.

Semaj Nosmot. How mellifluous the name had sounded when I invented it, and how hideous it became to me! Ah, vanity, vanity, what pitfalls dost thou mask. Semaj Nosmot. . . .

I used that pen name only once, but unfortunately that once was on a return envelope. I returned home from school one evening to find myself addressed as Semaj and Nosmot, and I could see nothing at all funny about it—a fact which I was soon stating at the top of my lungs—but I was the only one who couldn't. Mom and Pop soon called a halt, seeing that I was badly hurt and upset, but they could not restrain an occasional snicker and chuckle, nor were they very successful in restraining Maxine and Freddie.

Wherever I went in the house there were whispers of "nosmot" and "snot-pot" and "semaj" and "messy jam." And even as I started to flee the house, a chorus of catcalls drifted in from the street:

> Se-maj-uh Nos-mot
> Fell in uh pisspot

Maxine and Freddie had found the joke too good to keep. It had gotten into the public domain, all of which constituted enemy territory.

The above doggerel comprises but one of the jibes to which I was subjected in the ensuing weeks, and since there is no point in repeating it and the others are largely unprintable, I shall spare you further details of my ordeal. The point is that I had ceased to pursue writing for fear of being pursued by Nosmot.

But the furore had died down by now. The razzers had worn their material threadbare and were as weary of it as I was. It seemed safe enough to resume writing, but with the returns from magazines so small I tackled a new outlet. I gathered up the several invoices from my free-lance checks and exhibited them to the editor of the Fort Worth *Press,* modestly suggesting that in me there was at least the making of a star reporter.

He did not seem to look at me in quite that way. Or, for that matter, in any other way. With the ears beneath my pork-pie hat growing redder and redder, he remained bent over his work for the space of perhaps ten minutes. And he appeared deaf to the jovial patter which poured more and more desperately from my lips.

My skin-tight Valentino pants suddenly seemed six sizes too large for me. There was a terrible lump in the vicinity of my Adam's apple. Somehow, I gathered, I had erred grievously in my approach, but I could not think how it could have been. As a close student of Hollywood movies, I had become an expert on editor-reporter relations.

Reporters always sat down on the editor's desk. They always kept their hats on their heads, and cigarettes in their mouths. They always addressed the editor as "Old Socks" or "Kiddo" and tossed off such bright remarks as, "Don't pump me, Mac, I'm full of beer." I had done all these things. It looked to me like this guy didn't know his stuff.

At last, he looked up. Then he stood up. Silently, he plucked the hat from my head and the cigarette from my mouth. Then, he placed his palms against my shoulder and gently but firmly pushed me from his desk.

"Would you like to sit down?" he asked politely.

"Y-yes, sir," I stuttered.

"Please do," he said, gesturing to a chair.

I sank into it. He asked my age.

"Ffff-fourfifteen," I swallowed. "Almost fifteen."

"Oh?" His face softened. "I'd have said you were older. These checks—they're really yours? You've actually sold to those magazines?"

"Yes, sir."

"That's very good. I've never been able to sell as much as a two-line joke to a magazine. Why don't you just keep on with it? Why do you want a job on a newspaper?"

I explained the situation pretty incoherently, I imagine, but he seemed to understand.

"Well," he said, at last, "I can't offer you a thing. You go to school, you say, until three-thirty in the afternoon?"

"Yes, sir. But—"

"Can't offer you a thing. Nothing at all. Do you use a typewriter?"

"Yes, s—"

"Nope, it's out of the question. Nothing I can do for you. Know the city pretty well?"

"Y—"

"Well," he said casually, "I think we can probably work something out for you. But first—"

This was long before the founding of the American Newspaper Guild. Seasoned reporters drew twenty-five dollars and less for a work week of fifty and sixty hours, and youngsters breaking in frequently worked for no reward but the experience. So, for the times, the terms of my employment were more than generous.

I reported on the job at four in the afternoon (at eight A.M. on Saturdays), and remained as long as I was needed. For my principal duties as copy boy, phone-answerer, coffee-procurer and occasional typist, I was paid four dollars a week. For the unimportant stories I was allowed to cover, I was paid three dollars a column—to the extent that they were used in the paper.

Due to their very nature, my stories were usually left out of the paper or appeared in such boiled-down form that the cash rewards were infinitesimal. About all I could count on was my four dollars' salary—which just about paid my expenses.

This circumstance, coupled with the fact that I was away from home to all hours, soon resulted in a series of conferences between Pop and me. The discussions ended several months later when I ended my employment with the *Press*.

As is apparent, I was a very perverse young man. I customarily headed myself in exactly the opposite of the direction which others tried to head me, and I resented all attempts at reforming me. With this kind of make-up, I had profited about as little personally from my experience on the *Press* as I had in cash. But the seeds of improvement had been sown through the medium of example. I had been shown and allowed to observe, instead of being told. And gradually the seeds sprouted.

I abandoned my Valentino pants and haircut. I ceased to smoke except when I actually wanted a cigarette. I became careful about such things as shined shoes and clean fingernails. I started to become courteous. I was still guarded and terse, ever on the lookout for slights and insults, but I did not ordinarily go out of my way to be offensive. As long as I was treated properly—and my standards in this matter were high—I treated others properly.

I would like to say, in this connection, that good manners and consistent courtesy toward others are the most valuable assets a reporter can have. I know, having worked on metropolitan dailies in various of these United States. In my time, I have interviewed hundreds of people, notorious and notable. Movie stars and murderers, railroad presidents and perjurers, princes, panderers, diplomats, demagogues, the judges and the judged. I have interviewed people who "never gave interviews," who "never saw reporters," who had "no statement for the press."

I once interviewed a West Coast industrialist, the third highest-salaried man in the United States. Because of his morbid fear of kidnappers he had made his home into a virtual fortress, and he was almost hysterical when I, having got hold of his phone number, called him up. He had never given an interview, he had never had his picture taken, and he would not do so now.

I told him I could understand his feelings and we would forget about the story. But would he be kind enough to tálk to me for my own personal benefit? I had made no whopping success of my own life, I said, and I would appreciate a few pointers from a man who had. Grudgingly, and after checking back to see that the call was bona fide, he consented.

I went out to his house in the morning and I stayed on through lunch and into the afternoon. Finally, as I was getting ready to leave, he said that he felt rather uncomfortable about withholding the story. I said he didn't need to feel that way at all. I was in his debt for the privilege of talking to him.

"Oh, hell," he laughed abruptly. "I'm probably a damned fool, but—"

I got the story. Also a picture. Soon after that, since no one tried to rob or kidnap him, the industrialist got rid of his guards and his armament, and began enjoying life and his income.

Only once in my experience as a reporter did courtesy and consideration fail to pay off. That was in the case of a Washington real estate lobbyist, an ill-mannered boor with an inflated head whom all-wise Providence has since removed from circulation.

This man had sent advance notice of his arrival in the city where I was working, and I and the opposition reporters were at the train to meet him. We were there at his invitation, understand. But he looked through us coldly. If we wanted to talk to *him*, he said, we could do it at his hotel. We followed him there, and still he had "no time" for us. Perhaps, after he had had his breakfast.

We waited while he had his breakfast. We waited while he got his haircut. We waited while he kidded interminably with the cigar-stand girl. He then advised us that he was going up to his suite for a nap, and that he would "probably" be able to see us in an hour or so.

The other reporters and I looked at each other. We went to the house phones and conferred with our editors. Their opinion of this character happily coincided with ours—that he was a pea-brain who needed a lesson in manners, and that the pearls of wisdom which he allegedly had for our community should be retained for shoving purposes.

I relayed this message to the lobbyist. He slammed up the phone, threatening to get "all you bastards and your editors, too."

He got in touch with our publishers. He got in touch with our managing editors and our desk men. He threatened and blustered. He pleaded, he begged. He tried to bring outside influence to bear on the newspapers.

He called press conferences, and no reporters showed up. He addressed banquets and meetings, and issued a steady stream of press releases. Not a word of what he said or wrote appeared in the newspapers.

Now, the real estate interests are probably the most powerful bloc in any community. But the potential club they formed, and which our friend had waxed vain in swinging, could swing more than one way. And so he soon found out.

The local realty operators began to look at him askance. What kind of man was it, they wondered, who could so mortally offend three large newspapers? In how many other cities had he incurred similar displeasure? They and other groups around the country were paying for his activities. They were paying him to influence legislation, to make them look good to the public. Was this the way he went about it?

The lobbyist was in complete disfavor with his nominal supporters when, at week's end, he sneaked out of town. But despite the all-around frost he had received, his manners remained virtually as bad as ever.

Back in Washington, he dished out considerably more boorishness than a certain party girl cared to take. She retaliated vigorously and effectively.

Her attack didn't quite kill him, more's the pity. But being concentrated on the area which the Marquis of Queensberry held sacrosanct, it did the next best thing.

Briefly, while the lobbyist may still be interested in women, he has nothing to interest them.

*Noblesse oblige!*

# XVI

AFTER LEAVING THE *Press,* I found brief employment on *Western World,* an oil and mining weekly. I had no regular hours, being summoned for work only during certain rush periods when extra help was needed. Neither did I have any regular duties. I did a little of everything, from addressing envelopes for the subscription department to reading copy to running errands to rewriting brief items. Occasionally, when there was space to fill, I also wrote poems—very bad ones, I fear—of the Robert Service type.

My pay was a magnificent three dollars a day, but I never knew when I would be called to work, having to hold myself in readiness at all times. And the times that I was called seemed constantly to conflict with my family's plans and schedules. Also, or so I imagined, my adult colleagues were not treating me with proper respect but consistently took advantage of their age and my youth to heap me with indignities.

They were all my bosses. All had the privilege of sending "Kid Shakespeare" and "young Pulitzer" after coffee or carbon paper, and they invariably chose to do so at the worst possible moments. As surely as there were visitors in the office, as surely as I was in the throes of epic composition, frowning importantly as I addressed my typewriter, there would be a cry of, "Hey, kid," followed by the suggestion that I wake up or get the lead out and busy myself with some quasi-humiliating errand or task.

This was probably all for my own good. A writer who cannot take it may as well forget about writing. But I had taken and was taking so much elsewhere, actually or in my imagination, that I could take little more. And finally, after a wild scene in which, to my horror, I very nearly bawled, I stormed out of the office and returned no more.

I went into a kind of decline during the next few months. I could not muster the slightest interest in the several part-time jobs I secured—in a grocery store, a bottling plant and on an ice wagon—and was soon severed from them. To all practical intents and purposes, I ceased to look for others. I was not unwilling to work, but I was not going to work for nothing—"nothing," being the standard rate of pay as I saw it. Moreover, I was not going to work at something that "didn't make any sense"—a category as generally standard as the rate of pay.

I played hooky more and more often, spending my school hours in burlesque houses. To finance these expeditions, I put in an occasional day at the golf course.

A photograph of this period reveals me as a thin, neat, solemn-faced young man, surprisingly innocuous-looking at first glance. It is only when you look more closely that you see the watchfully narrowed eyes, the stiffness of the lips, the expression that wavers cautiously between smile and frown. I looked like I hoped for the best, but expected the worst. I looked like I had done just about all I was going to do to get along and others had better start getting along with me.

I found people who met this last requirement at one of the smaller burlesque houses which soon received my entire patronage. It opened around ten in the morning, and except for interludes of cowboy pictures the stage shows were continuous. The performers saw me a dozen times a day, always applauding wildly. They began to wink at me, to nod, and soon we were greeting each other and exchanging brief pleasantries across the footlights.

There was an amplitude of seats during the hours of my attendance, so the manager-owner-bouncer made no objection to my semi-permanent occupancy of one of them. In fact, amiable man that he was, he came to profess pleasure over my patronage and alarm at my absences. He said he felt kind of funny opening the house without me, meanwhile sliding a pack of cigarettes into my pocket or asking if I'd had my coffee yet. He pressed me constantly to come clean with him, to tell him what I honestly thought of his shows. And he seemed never annoyed nor bored with my consistently favorable reviews.

I became a sort of fixture-without-folio around the place, showing up when I could, making myself useful when I chose. I relieved the ticket-taker. I butched Candy (Getcha Sweetie Sweets, gents—a be-ig prize in every pack-age!). I assisted backstage with such widely assorted tasks as firing blank cartridges and hooking brassieres.

I drew no pay, but I was never in want. On the contrary, I ate and smoked much more amply than I had on my salaried jobs. The impression had become prevalent, somehow, that I needed looking after, and everyone took it upon himself to do so. Through the medium of the Friday "amateur shows" I was even provided with substantial amounts of spending money.

Perhaps you remember these shows, three-sided contests between the audi-ence, the amateur and the implacable hook? Some totally talentless but deter-mined wretch would stand stiffly center-stage reciting, say, Dan McGrew or singing Mother Machree. And the louder he talked or sang the louder became the howls and boos of the audience. He would persist, poor devil, even hurling back the squashy vegetables which were hurled at him. But his evil destiny would not be denied. The dreaded hook—a long pole with a shepherd's crook at the end—suddenly fastened around his neck, a stagehand yanked vigorously and the hapless amateur literally soared into the wings.

Lest nasty suspicions arise in the minds of the spectators, I could only appear on the show every two or three weeks. But I did very well at that, usually receiving the five-dollar grand prize, or at least the three-dollar second prize. And, yes, the judging was completely fair. My friend, the manager, held the various prizes over the various participants' heads. The amount of applause one received determined the size of his prize, if any.

I had a half-dozen very corny and completely unoriginal routines worked out with the assistance of the show's regular comics, but my act was usually confined to two which seemed to delight the audience more each time they saw them.

In one I dashed onto the stage with a prop bundle of newspapers under my arm, madly shouting such nonsense as "seven shot in a crap game," "ten found dead in a graveyard," "woman killed—Dick Ramsay's wife," "big disaster at soup factory—vegetables turnip and pea"—and so on for a matter of three or four minutes.

The second act, and the most popular of the two, was somewhat more elaborate. I strolled out of the wings, clad only in a lace baby cap and a diaper, and with a simulated chaw of tobacco in my cheek. Then, taking exaggerated aim at the props about the stage, I spat—the pit drummer providing suitable sound effects. And with every simulated expectoration a chair fell apart, a picture shattered, a milk bottle exploded or a table was shorn of a leg.

That was all there was to it, but the audience loved it. It was almost always the winner of the grand five-dollar prize.

One evening, following my act, when I was lounging backstage in my diaper, a man in puttees and a checkered coat suddenly appeared as from nowhere and virtually hurled himself upon me. I was, of course, guilty of all sorts of crimes, from truancy to smoking on street cars, and I was sure the total had long since equalled a capital offense. Thus I could only believe that this man was a detective and his rapid-fire babble an indictment. I neither heard what he said nor was able to reply. It was left to the performers to interpret to me and respond for me, which they repeatedly and enthusiastically did. But even after he had left, with a savagely jocular slap at my diaper, I remained in a trembling daze.

Me, an actor? A *motion picture* actor?

It just couldn't be.

It was, however, as I found out the following morning when I reported at what had been the office of a one-time lumber yard. The check-coated, putteed man was the director-producer of a brand-new picture company dedicated to the production of two-reel comedies. And I was to act in those comedies, starting as of right now. I had what it took, he assured me. ("Chaplin, kid, that son-of-a-bitch'll have to *swim* back to England.") He had been in the business for years and he was never wrong about these things.

I have since learned enough about picture-making to know that scenes are shot out of sequence, and they appear to be a meaningless jumble to one unfamiliar with the story involved. But knowing nothing of the kind, then, I became as bewildered as I was dazed. I moved in an all-too-apparent stupor, which no amount of shouting from the director-producer could snap me out of. My mind found much to feed its suspicion that I was the butt of a cruel joke.

In rapid order, I was costumed as a cowboy, a baker, a conductor (streetcar), a policeman, a lifeguard and a blind beggar. I was impelled to dive through windows, fall down steps and stumble into mud holes. I was knocked down, walked on, booted and tossed. I was hit with pies, crockery, salami, baseball bats and beer barrels. And once a live bull snake was hurled at me so that it twined around my neck.

The more I went through of this, the less I became accustomed to it. I performed like a zombie of the Piltdown era. Finally, his aggravation having increased by the fact that a blemish on my chin loomed monstrously large in the rushes, the director profanely discharged me.

I was one goddamned thing, he said, that he *had* been wrong about.

Naturally, having put him to so much trouble and expense, I received no pay.

The aforementioned blemish turned out to be the opening salvo in an attack of barber's itch, so for more than three weeks I was confined to the house, brooding over my recent failure and the many failures preceding it.

Actually, as I eventually learned, I had lost nothing. The picture company had begun operations on a shoestring, hoping to obtain financing via stock-selling. Failing to do this, it had been unable to finish even that one first picture. It was never released, and the producer-director skipped town owing everyone.

I recovered from my malady and returned to the burlesque house. But I was no longer happy there as I had been. Everyone was nice to me, and everyone tactfully avoided the mention of motion pictures. Yet I was moody and restless. I felt that I had to do something—I simply *had* to. Something to rid me of the ugly stigmata of failure. Why, good God, I was almost sixteen years old and I had been a success at nothing!

Every night as I brooded wakefully in bed, I swore that I would make the following day different from the one just spent. But the following day found me spending it exactly as I had the previous one. I would be back at the burlesque house relieving the ticket-taker, butching candy, romping backstage with the chorus girls—wasting the golden hours which, once gone, would never come again.

Late one afternoon, a vaguely familiar-looking young man purchased a box of candy from me. He was both casual and brisk about it, first fumbling interminably for the necessary dime, then whipping out a five-dollar bill and impatiently demanding his change.

I counted it out to him. Just as I finished, his hand came out of the pocket with the dime he had been looking for.

"Here," he said, crisply. "Here's your dime. Let's have the five back."

I gave it to him—rather, I allowed him to withdraw it from my hand. I wandered absently on down the aisle, absorbed with the problem of doing *something*. And a full five minutes passed before it dawned on me that I had been done out of four dollars and ninety cents.

It was too late then, of course, to do anything about it. My fives artist would have skipped the show immediately and gone in quest of another sucker.

Nonetheless, I dashed back up the aisle looking for him. And there he was, still in the same seat, grinning at me and holding up the five.

"Just keeping in practice," he said, innocently. "You weren't worried, were you?"

# XVII

I HAD FIRST seen Allie Ivers in police court, where he appeared on a charge of swindling a storekeeper and I appeared in the interests of the Fort Worth *Press*. He was thin, blond and pale, with the most innocent blue eyes I have ever seen. He looked about sixteen years old the first time I saw him. He still looked sixteen, ten years later. Our paths crossed and recrossed during those years, and he often referred to me as his best friend (a reference which I often found debatable). I knew him far better than anyone else. Yet throughout our association, I never knew where he lived, I never learned anything about his background or antecedents, and I was never sure of how he would behave from one day to the next.

About all you could be sure of with Allie was that he would almost always do the unexpected—particularly if it was illegal—and to hell with the consequences.

Once, in an unusual moment of confidence, he gave me a hint of his philosophy. "I'd dive off a thousand-foot cliff," he said, "to get to a drowning man. After that, I don't know. Maybe I'd save him. Maybe I'd hang an anchor around his neck."

"First stealing his shirt," I suggested.

"Well," said Allie reasonably, "What would a drowning man need with a shirt?"

That was as close as I ever got to really knowing Allie. He remains the most imponderable of the strange characters who, throughout my life, have gravitated to me like filings to a magnet.

The judge took one look at him that day in police court and decided that no such demure youth could have "mitted" twenty dollars from the grocer's cash drawer, then shortchanged him with his own money. He rebuked the arresting officer and dismissed Allie. I followed him outside.

Identifying myself as a reporter, I asked him to tell me the truth. Was he guilty or not?

Now, Allie's favorite reading was the penal code and his knowledge of law was something to turn a supreme-court justice green with envy. So, after a momentary start, he widened his wide blue eyes and confessed his guilt.

"That's not all," he said. "I stole a package of peanuts on my way out of the store."

I made a note of this, and Allie went on to recite other crimes. His regular occupation, he said, was stealing fur coats from whores. "They've all got them," he explained. "I don't know why they sock so much dough in coats when they spend nine-tenths of their time in bed."

I asked Allie about his *modus operandi.* He said it was simple. Having gained entry to the whore's room in the guise of a customer, he asked for a complete examination of the merchandise before purchasing. Then, with the deluded woman in the altogether and hence unable to pursue him, he grabbed her coat and fled.

"It's nice clean work," said Allie. "I'm going to get back to it as soon as the market gets better. Right now I've got all the pawnshops overstocked."

Allie said that next to stealing fur coats he liked to steal baggage. And this too was simple, he added modestly, involving little more than the ownership of a red cap and a badge. Also, he went on, he had done very well for himself by dividing the city into districts and assigning them to pickpockets on a percentage basis.

"My big trouble," said Allie, in conclusion, "is that I'm too restless. I keep jumping around from one racket to another. As soon as I get one going good, I move on to something else."

I was as preposterously naive in some ways as I was sophisticated in others. But I would like it made clear, lest I appear a bigger dunce than I was, that I believed Allie's story because it *was* true. Every word of it. This selfish young man had not only stripped whores of their hirsute habiliments and trusting travelers of their luggage, he had also defrauded some supposedly shrewd denizens of the underworld itself. In fact, as he confided to me later, he was never happier than when engaged in taking the takers. They put him on his mettle, added zest to existence in a way that the yokels never could.

In the case of the pickpockets, for example, Allie had visited Houston and Galveston, convincing a coterie of dips that the fix was in in Fort Worth and that, for a percentage of their take, he was prepared to assign them choice districts wherein they might "run wild." They fell for it—a number of them at least—and descended upon Fort Worth Allie began collecting his percentage. The pickpockets began landing in jail.

To the run-of-the-mill operator, the incarceration of the first pickpocket would have been a signal to skip town. But Allie Ivers definitely was not run-of-the-mill. As one after another of the pickpockets was knocked off, Allie went around to the others and explained that the guy had been gypping him on his percentage and had thus lost his license to steal. He sternly advised them to take heed and to make no errors in arithmetic while calculating his due. Understandably alarmed and anxious to retain his good will, the dips gave him his agreed on cut and more besides.

Within a very few days, of course, the true state of affairs became known, i.e., they had been paying for a fix which did not exist. But while there was an intensive search for him for a time, Allie also seemed not to exist. And the eventual opinion in police circles was that the pickpockets had created him, a fictitious fall guy, in the hope of excusing their own misdoings.

Allie spent the winter in Miami. "For my health," he explained, succinctly.

Well, though, to get back to the confession he had made to me, the truth or the falsity of it made not the slightest difference to a libel-conscious newspaper. True or false—and my editor called it a hop-dream on paper—it was a yarn such as to invite mayhem on the reporter who submitted it.

Being a man of exquisite courtesy and kindness, my editor merely folded and refolded it, forming it into a plug which he held in shape with a rubber band. He handed this to me.

"That hole in your head," he said. "Take care of it."

. . . Allie and I met outside the burlesque house, and he insisted on taking me to dinner. He said he had thought about me many times—worried about that story he had given me. He had meant no harm by it and hoped it had played no part in my descent to my present position.

I was pretty short with him, at first, but he seemed so genuinely interested in my welfare that I swiftly thawed. We had dinner in a very good restaurant, and I brought him up-to-date on my activities. He laughed a great deal, but softly and sympathetically. There was the look in his eyes of a bored child who has stumbled upon a strange and intriguing toy.

"We'll have to do something about you," he kept saying. "Yes, we'll certainly have to do something."

"What kind of—uh—work are you doing now?" I asked.

"Bell-hopping," he said. "I'm down at the H—Hotel. It's not quite as good as stealing, but it's a change. I was getting pretty bored with the con."

"That's a pretty swell hotel," I said.

"I've been in worse," Allie shrugged. "They've got very good locks on the doors."

"Could I"—I hesitated—"Do you suppose I could—?"

"Why not? Why don't you ask?"

"Aw, I guess I better not," I said. "I have to go to school. I've been laying out a lot, but I have to go."

"That's all right," said Allie. "You can work at night. They have a hard time keeping boys on the night shift."

"I—I guess not," I said. "I—they wouldn't hire me. My folks wouldn't want me working at night, and—"

"Kind of lost your nerve, huh?" Allie nodded wisely. "Afraid to try anything for fear you won't make it. That won't do. Drink your coffee, and let's get going."

We went, with me lagging behind and protesting that I'd better not. At the side door of the hotel, Allie drew me up to the leaded panes and pointed to a paunchy, pompous-looking man with a carnation in the buttonhole of his black broadcloth coat.

"That's the man you see, the assistant manager on this shift," said Allie. "Now you go in there and tell him he either gives you a job or you'll piss in his hip pockets."

"Aw, for—" I tried to break loose.

"Do it your own way, then. I'm going to stand right here and watch you."

"Huh-uh, Allie," I muttered. "I don't look good enough, and—and I got a pain in my stomach, an' he'll think I'm crazy asking for a job in a place like—"

Allie's hand closed around my forearm in a grip that was surprisingly and painfully strong. "You get in there," he said, firmly. "If you don't, I'll yell for the cops. I'll say you made me an indecent proposal."

Something told me he would do exactly that.

I went in.

The assistant manager glanced at me wearily as I began a jumbled application for a job on nights. Then, while I was still mumbling he murmured a word which sounded like "hate" and which, I was sure, summarized his feelings about me, and strolled away.

Relieved that he had not had me arrested, I turned and tottered toward the door.

I had taken only a few steps when a swarthy, slick-haired young man with CAPTAIN emblazoned across his wine-colored jacket appeared at my side.

"You're going the wrong way, Mac," he said smoothly. "The tailor shop's back this way."

"T-tailor shop?" I said.

He grinned and took me by the elbow. "Couldn't understand Old Mushmouth, huh? You'll get used to him. Now, let's get you fixed up with a uniform."

# XVIII

IT WAS A weird, wild and wonderful world that I had walked into, the luxury hotel life of the Roaring Twenties. It was a world which typified rugged individualism at its best—or worst, a world whose urbane countenance revealed nothing of the seething and sinister turmoil of its innards, a world whose one rule was that you did nothing you could not get away with.

There was no pity in that world. The usual laws governing rewards and punishments did not obtain. It was not what you did that mattered, but how you did it.

Nominally, there were strictly enforced rules against such things as getting drunk on duty, intimacy with lady guests and forcing tips from the stingy. But the management could have knowledge that you were guilty of all those crimes, and as long as you did them in such a way as not to give rise to complaints or disturb the routine of the hotel, nothing would be done. Rather, you would be regarded as a boy who knew his way around and was on his toes.

And this attitude, I suppose, was not nearly so strange as it seems.

It was the bellboy who was always in closest contact with this hurly-burly world, a world always populated by strangers of unknown background and unpredictable behavior. Alone and on his own, with no one to turn to for advice or help, he had to please and appease those strangers: the eccentric, the belligerent, the morbidly depressed. He had to spot the potential suicide and soothe the fighting drunk and satisfy the whims of those who were determined not to be satisfied. And always, no matter how he felt, he had to do those things swiftly and unobtrusively.

Briefly, he had to be nervy and quick-thinking. He had to be adequate to any emergency. And a boy who was inadequate in his own emergencies was also apt to be so in those concerning the hotel. In a word, he wasn't "sharp." He didn't "know his way around," and thus, axiomatically, did not belong around.

In the indictments lodged against bellboys in the hotel "growler," the rough equivalent of a ship's log, one word appeared over and over—*caught*. A boy was fired or fined or turned over to the police because he had been *caught* in an offense, not merely because he had committed one.

There was no day off in the hotel world. The night shift worked seven days a week, from eleven at night until seven in the morning. The day shifts were also on the job seven days, but their hours were adjusted to the then universal long-day, short-day of the hotel world. One of the two shifts came on at seven in the morning, quit at noon, returned at six and worked until eleven at night. The following day it came to work at noon and quit at six P.M., the other shift working the double-watch long-day.

One night, when there was an unexpected flurry of business, a day boy was held over onto the night shift. It was his second holdover of the day, and he had been on duty since seven in the morning. So, after the business had been taken care of, he claimed the "late" boy's privilege of a room, and fell exhausted into bed.

Unfortunately, he had not rid himself of his cigarette before going to sleep. When he awakened a couple of hours later he was on the point of being incinerated and asphyxiated. Almost strangled, he got the windows open. Then he dragged the mattress and bedclothes into the bathroom and put them under the shower.

Scorched, but not seriously harmed, he got the fire out. But the expensive blankets, spread and box-mattress were ruined. Being caught in a mess like this would bring down the direst punishment which the hotel could devise.

The boy considered every angle of the seemingly hopeless situation. Then, he went downstairs, confessed his crime to the night clerk, and proposed a way of extricating himself with honor and profit. All he needed, he said, was the use of the emergency key (used in opening doors locked from the inside) and the assistance of one of the lobby porters.

Being exceeding sharp himself, the night clerk flatly refused. Under no circumstances would he involve himself in the matter.

"I'm going into the coffee shop for a bite to eat," he said. "And I had better not hear of you using the emergency key or the porters while I am gone."

"I understand," the boy nodded. "I see what you mean."

Now, one of the more or less regular residents of the hotel was a more-than-regular drinker, a man who passed out early and stayed passed out. It was his misfortune to be a guest of the hotel on this particular night.

He burst into consciousness from his stupor with his room filled with acrid fumes and his bed and himself literally floating in water. He did not need to ask the assembled company—which included the porter, clerk and bellboy—the cause of his plight. That was all too obvious All he could do was thank them for saving his unworthy life, and offer recompense for the damage.

He tipped everyone handsomely. He distributed additional gratuities (without knowing it) when he paid the clerk's claim for damages. Then, because he had been so tractable in a trying situation, he was transferred to another room at no charge.

"It'll have to be one that's been slept in," the clerk explained. "But I know the former occupant quite well, and I assure you—"

"Not at all," the man protested. "Very kind of you."

So they took him down to the other room and put him to bed on a mattress and under bedclothes that were still warm with his own body.

News of this stunt spread throughout the hotel, and the employee participants were marked as men on their way up. As for their scapegoat, the management's attitude toward his part in the affair was also characteristic.

Here was a man who got so besotted that he could be lifted and moved about without waking. Obviously, anyone who habitually attained such a condition was a menace to himself and the hotel.

So his name was entered on the "heel list"—a catalogue of undesirables—and he ceased to be a guest.

Since practically every hotel man worth his salt had begun his career as a bellhop, the tendency was not to be too severe on a sinner who, on the whole, appeared to be a "good boy." If you didn't "cry" (crying was bothering the management with a problem), if you were, by and large, personable, punctual and perspicacious, if you were an all-around boy—one who could fill in instantly for the valets, food checkers, waiter captains and the operators of elevators, switchboards and Elliott-Fisher machines—if you were all that, you were entitled to consideration no matter what your misdeed.

There was only one elevator operator on the night shift, and he was often too busy with guest traffic to bother with mere bellboys. Thus we were in the habit of opening up one of the driverless cars and transporting ourselves. This fact led to my first experience with the strange ways of hotel discipline, and a singularly terrifying experience it was.

I had been on the job about two months at the time, and was attending a party of vaudevillians in a third-floor suite. I had also been imbibing freely with those vaudevillians, so much so that I was very far from being sharp and on my toes. I left their rooms and trotted back to the elevator banks. I inserted a key in the door of my chosen car, swung the door open and stepped inside.

Inside the shaft, that is. Another boy had come along and taken my car.

I fell five floors in all—the three above-ground and an additional two into the basement and sub-basement. It wasn't an unchecked fall, of course. I was grabbing at cables and gear all the way. But you may take my word for it that even with full catch-as-catch-can privileges and no holds barred, a five-story fall is a hair-raising and painful ordeal.

I lay at the bottom of the pit for a few minutes, too shocked and pain-wracked to move. Then, groaning and mumbling dazedly, I sat up.

The pit door snapped open, and an ashen-faced engineer looked in at me. He helped me out, then ran to inform the room clerk of my accident.

This particular clerk—one of several I was to work with—was the epitome of all room clerks: crisp, cool and cynical. He looked me over, the corners of his mouth quirking strangely.

"Hurt pretty bad, eh?" he said. "Like to take the rest of the night off?"

"N-no, sir." I suppressed a groan. "I feel fine."

"You're drunk. You've got a breath that would knock a horse down."

"I haven't had a thing to drink," I said. "I've been chewing a new kind of cough drop,"

"You're drunk. That's why you fell down the elevator shaft."

"Me?" I laughed shakily. "I didn't fall down the shaft, sir. I was—uh—"

"Go on. And you'd better make it good, understand?"

"I—uh—I save tinfoil, sir. Off of cigarette packages and gum wrappers. I climbed in there to look for some."

The engineer turned suddenly and departed. The clerk was abruptly stricken with a spasm of coughing.

He recovered from the fit, jerked out a pad of fine slips and began to write. "You're going to have to sharpen up," he said curtly. "Get on your toes and stay there. You're a fairly good boy—show quite a lot of promise on some occasions—but you'll have to do a lot better."

"Yes, sir," I said.

"All right." He ripped off the fine slip and handed it to me. "Now get yourself washed up and cleaned up, and get up on that floor! Right away, understand?"

"Yes, sir," I said, and I looked down at what he had written:

> To J. Thompson, bellboy, $1 fine.
> Caught in general untidiness.

My next experience with the peculiar ways of hotel discipline came one morning when I had been held over onto the day shift. I was very tired and had taken a few drinks to pep myself up. Those few set so well with me that I took a few more, after which, as nearly as I could reconstruct events, I sat down in one of the lobby sand jars and went to sleep.

The bell captain promptly spotted me and I was hustled down to the locker room. The assistant manager, the same one who had hired me, followed us, vowing that I ought to be murdered.

"Of all the no-good blank blank blanks," he yelled, "you're the world's worst! You're fired, get me? Fired!"

"Y-yes, sir," I said.

"Another thing," he snarled, turning toward the door. "One more thing. Don't you dare come around here asking for your job back—for at least a week!"

To the best of my recollection, I was fired six times during my several years at the hotel. I was always rehired, sometimes within the same night. Five of my firings were for drinking, the other for smoking in a guest's room—all very serious offenses. Yet the hotel consistently rehired me where it curtly refused jobs to boys discharged for nominally trifling reasons. Failure, it seemed, could only be offset by ability. The "sharp" received every consideration, the dull got nothing.

This was all wrong, I am sure. But as a frequent traveler and diner-out, I often look back with longing on the days when an employee might be discharged on a moment's notice, without severance pay for himself or penalty for his employer—simply on the grounds that he was unsuited to his job.

# XIX

As a bellboy I supposedly drew a salary of fifteen dollars a month, but in practice I seldom saw a penny of it. It was almost always consumed by fines, cleaning and pressing charges, insurance fees and the like. My earnings were in tips which ranged from virtually nothing a night to as much as fifty dollars.

On a bad night, a Sunday say, with no parties going on and few guests arriving, I might make less than a dollar. But on a good Saturday or during a lively convention, it would be no trick at all to knock off twenty-five, thirty-five or fifty or more dollars. Or, I should say, it was easy enough to do after I learned my way around. My first week on the job, I barely earned enough to pay for my cigarettes and carfare.

During normal times, only two bellboys were used on the night shift, and they were often idle except for the hotel's endless untipped "dead work." My first working companion, a "boy" of some forty years, took advantage of my ignorance to the end that I did the lion's share of the dead work and got a very small lamb's share of the profitable "bells."

He would take a call over the bell captain's telephone without letting on that it was a call. It would be a wrong number or a guest inquiring about his mail or something of the kind. Then, having saved up four or five bells, he would take care of them all on one trip. He also sent me on calls to empty rooms, and gave me bells which he knew to be trifling while he took the good ones.

After a week or so of this, I began to get wise to Pelly, or Pelican, as he was called, and I retaliated with the same stunts he had been pulling on me. I tried to reason with him. I pointed out that as surely as he tricked me, I would trick him and that we would both lose money as a result. But Pelican took this as a sign that I was weakening. He told me, in effect, to do my damnedest and that I would find his damnedest considerably better.

We night boys had many duties which took us behind the desk, chores such as cleaning the key rack and sorting mail. So, around three o'clock one morning, I removed a rate slip from the room rack and called Pell from a mezzanine house phone.

I spoke in a high, pseudo-feminine voice. I told him that the window in my room was stuck and asked for a bellboy's assistance in opening it.

Pell promised to take care of the matter, but I could tell he was suspicious. Peering through the rails of the mezzanine, I saw him hurry to the room rack, then nod triumphantly as he saw that there was no rate slip for the number I had given him. Obviously, or so he thought, the room was unrented. Actually, it was occupied by one of the crustiest old dowagers ever to curse a hotel with her patronage.

Pell snatched up the bell captain's phone and rang the room. I crept down the stairs, slipped around behind the key rack and returned the rate slip to its proper place. Then, I sauntered up behind him, listening to him read "me" off.

"I'm comin' after you," he was saying. "You keep up that squeaky-voice crap an' I'll come right up there'n get you. I'll turn you wrong side out. Kick your tail end right out through your teeth. Who I think I'm talkin' to? Why, you goofy pin-headed granny-dodger, I'm—I'm—"

He had turned and seen me. A look of pure horror spread over his face.

"Y-you," he stuttered, pointing a wobbling finger at me. "I t-thought that you—"

"Yeah?" I grinned at him. "As I was saying, Pell, I think we'd better stop rooking each other, don't you?"

He slammed up the receiver, silencing the outraged shrieks that were pouting over the wire. Lifting it again, he gave hasty instructions to the night switchboard operator. She was to say that the call had come in from the outside, from whom she did not know. If she made the story stick, he would buy her a five-pound box of candy.

Well, she made the story stick, and Pell escaped the penalty for his lack of sharpness. But never again did he gyp me on a call. We got along so well together that I felt quite depressed when he was literally chased out of the hotel. I was saddened by the event, but I still think it was one of the most hilarious I have ever witnessed.

Pell and the then room clerk, a Mr. Hebert, detested each other. Pell was constantly stating his intention of quitting or getting a transfer to days. Just as constantly, Hebert announced his intention to fire Pell or have him transferred. Yet neither did either. They chose rather to stay on the same shift, making things tough for each other.

Being in authority, Hebert would appear to have had the advantage of Pell. He could fine him, load him with dead work, bawl him out cruelly before other employees. Having done those things, however, and being unwilling to fire him, there was little else he could do. Pell, a mere bellboy with no authority, could do plenty.

He was a very smooth talker, a wonder at insinuating himself into the good graces of touchy and exacting guests. Having convinced such a person that he was "all for him" and hated to see him mistreated, Pell would reluctantly reveal that the man had been given the worst room in the house and at double the usual rate.

"They call this the dead room," he would say (to repeat one of his lies). "I think there must be some kind of germs in the wallpaper, the way everyone dies that stays here. Now, I know you won't let on that I told you—I just think you're a very nice gentleman, and I don't expect any big tip for tipping you off, but—"

At this juncture, the guest would usually tip Pell handsomely, step to the telephone and sulphurously demand that Hebert switch him to another room. Hebert would want to know why, naturally. The guest, enjoined to secrecy by Pell, would refuse to explain. He simply wanted another room, and he wanted it right now, by God, and he'd better not, by God, be gypped on the price.

Red-faced and bewildered, wondering, aloud, what the hell was getting into people, Hebert would do his best to satisfy the man. But the suspicions of a man who had been placed in the dreaded "dead room" at a double rate were not easy to assuage. By the time he had finished talking to the guest, Hebert was on the point of talking to himself. Sweat was pouring from his face and he was trembling in every joint, and there was a wild look in his eyes.

It was Pell who spread the rumor that Hebert wore no pants behind the high marble counter, a canard which—according to the sex and temperament of the guest—resulted in looks of disgust, scowls, and howls of laughter for the baffled and blushing room clerk. Pell was also responsible for the widespread belief that Hebert maintained a stable of whores in the hotel, renting them out at very low rates to gentlemen who could prove they were "all right."

"He don't care about the money, see," Pell would explain. "He's one of these guys that gets a bang out of it. Now, don't let on that I told you—"

Poor Hebert. He had a strong hunch that Pell was at the bottom of his many and maddening difficulties, but he could not prove it.

If Pell had had as much patience as ingenuity, I think he might have succeeded in his announced intention of driving Hebert nuts. But harassed as he was, Hebert stubbornly refused to crack up. And, annoyed by this perverseness, and emboldened by success, Pell attempted a master stroke.

As I have mentioned, there were two assistant managers. One was a primly urban man who managed to be both exquisitely efficient and completely unimpressive. The other, the "Mr. Mushmouth" who had hired me, was likewise an able hotel man but so turbulent and foible-filled that he seemed to mirror the strange world he worked in.

Essentially kindhearted, he was always a little wary, ready to leap down the throat of anyone who seemed to take advantage of him. Short and paunchy, he was also very vain—vain and sensitive. He was ever ready to interpret a friendly smile as condescension or a helpful gesture as a jibe. And hell had no fury like his when he felt himself slighted.

I got along very well with him, probably, I suppose, because we were much alike.

He would come in at the side door at around six in the morning of his long day, his shoulders hunched like a prize fighter's, his sleep-haggard face set in a deep and watchful scowl. Crossing the lobby at a steady but wary gait, he would pause at the end of the long marble counter, where he liked to find me stationed, and slowly turn sideways to it. Then, he would remove his beautiful Homburg hat and diffidently thrust it at me.

"Mrningjim," he would grunt.

"Mrningsir," I grunted back at him.

"Srningouside."

"Rnedallnightsir."

"Huh."

"Yuhsr."

At this point he would usually turn and scowl at me and I would scowl back at him. But sometimes, when the feeling was upon him, he would continue the "conversation" for several minutes, deliberately speaking with increasing unintelligibility and being replied to similarly, until we made less than no sense at all.

I was the only one he would speak to until he had had his breakfast. Hebert, poor soul, insisted on crying out a cheery "good morning" to him, but all he got in return was a hate-filled glare.

After breakfast, the assistant manager would return to the lobby for a brief report on the night's events from Hebert. Then, he would reclaim his hat and make an outside inspection of the hotel. His routine was always the same. He was always the same. Vain, sensitive, quick tempered. Thus, the raw material of Pell's plot against Hebert.

There was a great deal of paper work on the night shift, and Hebert was supplied with a rubber stamp of his name to use on the countless invoices and charge slips which required his endorsement. Pell obtained an impression of the stamp on a piece of paper. He had a duplicate made and brought it to work with him. Then . . .

The explosive and suspicious little assistant manager was in an even more terrible mood than usual that morning. He barely grunted at me, and he looked like he could have killed Hebert for the latter's insistently cheerful greeting. Shoulders hunched, hands clenched into fists, he disappeared into the coffee shop.

Pell plucked the Homburg from my fingers, and went behind the keyrack. I followed him immediately, but he had already begun his vandalism and nothing was to be gained by interfering with him. I could only stand and watch as, over and over, until the fine silk lining was a mess, he stamped the name *E. J. HEBERT* in the assistant manager's hat.

"Now," he said, "you and I had better get out of here. We don't want to be around when Old Mushmouth comes after his lid."

"You're telling *me,*" I said.

We hid on the mezzanine directly above the cashier's cage where Hebert was working. We waited, listening to the occasional thud as Hebert used his stamp. The assistant manager returned and they conversed briefly. Then, seeing that neither Pell nor I were around, the A.M. asked Hebert to hand him his hat.

"Certainly, sir," said Hebert. And, still carrying his rubber stamp, he went around behind the key rack.

Pell and I returned to the lobby, he by the front stairs, me by the rear. I made myself as inconspicuous as possible, but Pell took up a position on front post, only inches away from the window where the assistant manager was waiting.

Hebert came back with the hat, carrying it tenderly crown-up as he had found it. He passed it through the window.

"Ankyou," grunted the assistant manager, starting to lift it to his head. Then, he paused, eyes popping, and said, "Wottnell!" He looked up, glaring terribly at Hebert, and an almost subhuman growl came from his throat.

Hebert smiled nervously. "Something wrong?" he said.

The assistant manager made no answer. He simply grabbed Hebert by the necktie, hauled him halfway through the window and began beating him with the hat.

The room clerk was taken completely by surprise, but he was not too dazed to see that Pell had somehow inspired the assistant manager's attack. So he grabbed the bellboy by the collar and dragged him into the fray. For every blow he received he gave one to Pell, and Pell, tangled between the two men and helpless with laughter, was powerless to resist.

The assistant manager tried to shove him out of the way, the better to get at Hebert. But the clerk hung onto him. Pell was jerked back and forth, catching the blows intended for Hebert as well as those intended for him. And as the struggle waxed furious, an ink pad flew from his pockets and a rubber stamp with it.

Panting, the assistant manager released his hold on Hebert and made a grab for Pell. "Bstd!" he snarled, flinging himself at the bellboy. But fast as he was, he wasn't quite fast enough.

The last I saw of Pell he was heading for the rear landing, and the assistant manager was right behind him, aiming a kick at his fleeing posterior at every third step.

# XX

A FEW YEARS ago I met one of the boys—by then a man, of course—I formerly hopped bells with. He was the owner of an automobile agency in a large southwestern city, and I also was enjoying some small success. Naturally, we fell to discussing the other boys we had known, those whose later lives were familiar to us.

One had been killed by the FBI while resisting arrest as a suspected kidnapper. One had been hopelessly crippled while attempting to blow up a safe. Two had committed suicide when still very young men. One had overdosed himself with salvarsan, bit his tongue off in a spasm of agony and drowned in his own blood.

Not a very pretty picture, but that was only part of it. Another boy of our acquaintance had become a renowned geologist, another a doctor and another a minister. Two others were managers of large hotels.

"All in all," my friend said, "I suppose about as many of us turned out all right as didn't. About the same percentage you'd find in any other group."

"That's true," I nodded, "the percentage is the same. But I don't think you'll find the division within another group so drastic. Take a bunch of grocery clerks starting out together, or a group of filing clerks or service station attendants. Some will get ahead, some won't. But the spread between them won't be small and gradual. Five of them will die violent deaths while the other five become relative big shots."

My friend frowned, thoughtfully. "Y'know," he hesitated, "it's kind of like it was on the job, isn't it? There wasn't any middle ground. You were either in or you were out."

"That's the way it looks. It did you a lot of good or a lot of harm."

"Which do you think it did you?"

"Well," I said, "I'm here."

In most pursuits, temptation stands on the sidelines. It does not grab but beckons, and once passed it is gone. But it was not thus in the luxury hotel of my day. Temptation followed you, placing herself in your path at every turn. And, paradoxically, succumbing to her often meant a reward, and resistance, punishment.

You worked in the hotel, but you worked for the guests. Your earnings, your very job depended upon their good will. So why offend a wealthy drunk by refusing to drink with him? Why snub a lovely and well-heeled widow when it was so easy to please her? And what about these people, anyway? If they were all wrong—these publicly acclaimed models of success and deportment—then who was right?

There was an unhealthy tendency to acquire complete contempt for the monied and a consuming regard for money. Money was apt to mean far too much and people nothing.

Living in a world of topsy-turvy standards and constant temptation, a boy could easily become involved in serious and long-lasting trouble. To survive in that world he had to be very, very lucky and have a fair degree of intelligence. But more than anything else, he had to be able to "take it," to absorb the not-to-be-avoided abnormal without being absorbed by it. Or, to state the matter simply, he needed a strong sense of humor.

If he had that, he was usually all right. Far from harming him, the hotel life would do him a lot of good.

It was during the big conventions of business and fraternal organizations that, as the saying was, the men were separated from the boys. They descended upon the hotel on an average of twice a month, and I grew to look upon them with a kind of delighted horror. They meant much money, but they also meant wracked nerves and utter physical exhaustion. All the incongruities and inconsistencies of hotel life were multiplied a dozen times over.

A day or so before a convention started, the hot-shots would drift into town. These were the professional bellboys—men—who traveled the country over and made a career of working the conventions. They knew all the angles and they played them all. They had to.

All bellboys paid a daily "tax" or "kick" to the captains for the privilege of working. The convention hot-shots not only paid this, but they also paid for their jobs. During an oil men's convention, for example, a four-day job sold for two hundred dollars plus a daily tax of ten dollars.

Since selling jobs is a federal offense, the question of what happened to all this money is one I consider too delicate to answer. But I will say that no hot-shot ever successfully appealed a bell captain's decision to the management. And one of the captains told me he was "goddamned lucky to hang onto a third of the take."

The hot-shots received nothing for their money but the hotel's permission to go to work. There was no guarantee that they would not be fired or jailed thirty minutes after they stepped on the floor. There was no guarantee that they would be able to get—or hold onto—a uniform to work in. That was their headache, something to be worked out between them and the regular bellboys.

There were never more than twenty-five uniforms—but the number of bellboys during a convention often rose to a total of forty. And while the hot-shots were tough, the regulars were no pantywaists. So every change of shift marked the beginning of a battle with as many as three boys struggling for the same uniform.

Lockers were broken into. Tailor shop employees were threatened and bribed. Boys were tripped up and knocked down and sat on and stripped of their uniforms. One did not enter the locker room unless he was prepared to do battle.

Not all the quarrels arose over uniforms. Gypping on bells was the order of the day, and if a guy didn't like it he knew what he could do about it.

Those fights. They were strange, hideously fascinating affairs.

The combatants-to-be would first remove their uniforms and stow them away for safekeeping. Then, wordlessly and without preliminary, the fight would start. Its one rule was that no blows could be struck to the face. A knee in the groin was all right. A kick in the instep was all right, or a rupturing punch to the kidneys or a paralyzing blow to the heart. But a man's face must never be marked.

The fighters would weave their way through the crowded locker room, here passing in front of a boy who was shaving, there squeezing between a pair who were fastening one another's collars. No one paid any attention to them. No one tried to interfere. Everyone had more than enough to do to take care of himself.

Since all the boys were above average toughness and since one rarely knew a dirty trick unknown to the other, the fights usually ended in some kind of compromise. A no-gyp compact would be sworn to or an agreement would be arrived at whereby a uniform and a working-shift were shared. Often it was that way, but not always. Inevitably, some of the hot-shots were driven on and some of the regulars driven out.

Everyone had it in for everyone else. No matter what he made, no one was satisfied. There were thousands of dollars in cash among the bellboys as the end of a convention approached, and every boy knew it and wanted it. Not just part, but all. This resulted in twenty-four-hour-a-day dice games in the locker room. Some of the biggest games I have ever seen, and I have seen some big ones.

The play would go on and on, with the players dropping out when they lost the dice, hopping bells for an hour or so, then getting back into the game as their turn came again. It was an all-or-nothing contest. No man was allowed to quit winner as long as the others wanted to play. If one was forced to drop out of the game, his winnings were impounded with one of the captains.

They could be maddening things, those "last man takes all" games. With forty boys involved, the odds were forty to one against your being the final victor. Yet I could never keep my money in my pocket where it belonged.

I would come down at night, and lay bets while I dressed. I might be cleaned out immediately, but more often than not I would win. Five hundred, a thousand, fourteen or fifteen hundred. But always the time came when I had to quit—leaving my winnings with the captain, (The captains, I should say, were well-chaperoned during their comings and goings.)

When the end of the convention came, and the final game with it, I sometimes had two or three thousand dollars "riding." And I would envision myself as that lucky last boy, a teenager retired on a modest fortune. Now, however, "piker bets" were disallowed. You faded what the other man wanted to shoot —and what he often chose to shoot was the exact amount of your winnings. The others had come into the game with big bankrolls and added to them. They could double up and triple up on the bets, cleaning you—or I should say, me—out in minutes. And, needless to say, they invariably did.

Still and all, thanks to a confidential talk with Allie Ivers, I did not do too badly in these games. I never got out with my temporarily won thousands. But by the process of "rat-holing"—surreptitiously palming an occasional ten or twenty—I often got away with hundreds.

The cops on the beat were aware of these dice games and frequently came in for a few minutes to watch the play. On the whole, they were like most of the other cops I have known—good, honest fellows doing a hard and thankless job at low pay. But there was an exception in the person of a cop called Red, a husky giant with close-set eyes who had admittedly donned a shield for what he could get out of it.

Red was always gambling and losing, then lying about the sum he had lost and grumbling that the game was crooked. He was always begging for a few dollars to get back into the game—the loan being repayable on a tomorrow that never arrived. The boys sneered at him, insulted him, profanely refused to fade when he was shooting. Still Red hung on, a whining, grumbling, insult-proof sponge.

I had been bell-hopping for something more than a year when Red tried to tap me for ten dollars. I told him to go to hell. More accurately, I told him I wouldn't lend him the sweat from my socks if he paid me Niagara Falls for interest.

"Why, Jesus Christ!" I protested, my voice cracking with irritation. "What's the matter with you, anyway? You're a cop—you're supposed to be someone. How in hell can you hang around here begging money from bellboys?"

"Aw, come on," he insisted, not in the least embarrassed. "What's ten bucks to you? You've got plenty of dough."

"Nothing doing," I said. "You've already four-bitted me out of five or six bucks. Chisel someone else."

"I'll pay it back. First thing tomorrow."

"Nuts."

I went on dressing, trying to ignore him, but he wouldn't give up. He didn't want the money to shoot craps with, he said. He didn't even want it for himself. He needed it for his wife and baby, for some medicine and groceries.

"Wife and baby?" I said. "I didn't know you were married."

"Sure, I am. Been married right along. Come on, Jimmie. I wouldn't ask you for it if I just didn't have to have it."

"Well," I hesitated, "I've got a family of my own to take care of. If I was sure you'd pay the dough back—"

"Tell you what I'll do," he said promptly. "I'll hock my nightstick with you. That's good security. You know I can't get by working very long without it."

"All right," I said. "I think I'm making a mistake, but—"

I gave him the ten and locked his night stick in my locker.

When I came to work the following night, the locker had been broken open and the club was gone.

I was pretty sore, to put it mildly. But the situation appeared to have its bright side. Having done this to me, Red would doubtless steer clear of the hotel for some time to come.

I was starting to change clothes, consoling myself with the thought of Red-free nights sans whining and begging, when the locker-room door opened and in he came. He was grinning broadly. The night stick was dangling from his wrist.

"About that club," he said. "A fellow over at the station house had an extra he wasn't usin'. He gave it to me."

"I see," I said.

"So I guess I'll just let you keep that other one."

"All right," I said.

"You don't mind, do you?" he grinned. "That's all right with you, ain't it?"

"Supposing it wasn't?" I said.

"Yeah?" He chuckled. "Supposin'?"

He went out, laughing openly. I went on dressing. I'd paid ten bucks to get the horse laugh, and I had to like it. I'd been dared not to like it.

Allie Ivers had come onto the night shift with me and knew of my loan to Red. He was as chagrined as I when I told him how Red had repaid the favor.

"You're not going to let him get away with it, are you?" he demanded. "Don't tell me you're just going to grin and take it!"

"What else can I do?"

"Fix the bastard's clock! Make him wish he'd never been born!"

"Yeah? And how am I going to do it?"

"I'll think of something," Allie promised.

He did think of something, and before the night was over. I listened to his scheme incredulously, by no means sure that he wasn't joking.

"You're kidding." I forced a laugh. "We can't do anything like that."

"Sure, we can," said Allie. "I'll get this babe I know to give him a fast play, make a date with him. She'll give him the number of one of the rooms the hotel's blocked off for the summer. When he comes in here—you'll have to slip him upstairs, of course—I'll—"

"But a—a *cop!*" I protested. "My God, Allie—to do that to a cop!"

"He's no cop. Wearing a uniform doesn't make a man a cop. What's the matter with you, anyway? I'm trying to do you a favor."

"Well, I—"

"I thought you trusted me."

"Well, I—"

I was still less than seventeen years old. And seventeen is seventeen, no matter what it has been through or up against. Moreover, despite my patent hardheadedness, I suffered from a deeply rooted feeling of inferiority. I wanted to be liked, and felt impelled to defer to those who gave me liking.

So I consented to Allie's plan. Two days later, at about two-thirty in the morning, Red beckoned to me furtively from the lobby side entrance.

I went out to the walk. He pressed a ten-dollar bill into my hand.

"Just playing a little joke on you," he said, giving me an amiable nudge in the ribs. "Okay? We're friends again?"

"What do you want?" I said.

He told me—although, of course, I already knew. Suddenly, as though it were another's voice speaking, I heard myself refusing.

"You've got no business up there. No one's got any business there. Those rooms are blocked off. They're too hot to stay in this time of year. Why, they haven't even got any bedding in 'em, and the telephones are discon—"

"Oh, yeah?" He grabbed me roughly by the arm. "Don't hand me that stuff! I got plenty of drag around this town. You try to crap me, an I'll make you hard to catch."

"All right," I said. "If that's the way you want it."

He went around to the rear entrance, and I took him upstairs on the service elevator. He followed me down the hall to a small court room. Then, dismissing me with a contemptuous nod, he tapped on the door. It opened, and he stepped into the darkness.

There was a dull thud and a grunt, and the door closed again.

I went back to the rear landing where I waited nervously for Allie. He arrived shortly with Red's pants which he tossed down the incinerator chute. He similarly disposed of the key to the room.

"Everything's fine," he assured me, urging me toward the elevator. "Didn't hurt him a bit."

"But Allie, I—what's going to happen to him?"

"How do I know?" said Allie, cheerfully. "I'd say he'd probably sweat to death if he stays in that room very long. Good riddance, too."

"But—"

"Yes, sir," Allie mused, "it's quite a problem all right. He can't call for help. He can't use the telephone. And if he did manage to get down the fire escape, where would he go from there? What's he going to do without—"

"Allie," I said, "I just remembered something. They've got the water cut off in those rooms. We can't leave him there in this weather without any water."

"He's got plenty," said Allie. "I noticed there was quite a bit in the toilet bowl."

Whatever Red's sufferings were, during the two days he spent in that room, they could have been as nothing compared to mine. I was sick with fear and worry. Finally, on the night of the second day, I insisted on putting an end to Red's imprisonment.

Allie pointed out that Red could gain release from the room any time he chose to. All he had to do was pound on the door until someone heard him.

"But he can't do that! How would he explain—"

"I wonder," said Allie.

He was entirely prepared to leave Red in the room until thirst and heat and hunger drove him to some act of desperation. But seeing that I was on the point of a nervous collapse, he reluctantly gave in to me.

We filched the passkey from the desk, and a pair of porter's pants from the laundry. Early the next morning, some two hours before the end of our shift, we went up to the room.

The door was still locked from the outside. We unlocked it cautiously, looked in and went in.

Red was gone.

Obviously, he had left by the fire escape. But what he did after reaching it, I do not know. He may have crept down to the alley at night and hailed a cab. Or he may have gone up the escape to another room, helped himself to the occupant's clothes and then made his exit. I don't know how he got away from the hotel. Only that he did.

Allie and I learned that he had been fired from the force, presumably for absence without leave. Yet the grins and winks of the other cops hinted that this was not the sole reason for his dismissal. Apparently and literally, Red had been caught without his pants. As a result of this, we gathered, he had not only been fired but also "floated" out of town.

"Like a bum," said Allie. "And what's wrong with that?"

# XXI

PA—MY GRANDFATHER—used to say that being broke wasn't so bad, but going broke was pure hell. Watching Pop's decline, his brief and occasional ups and his long steady downs, I saw the bitter wisdom of Pa's philosophy.

Having drilled four dry wells for himself, Pop began drilling on contract for others, mortgaging his oil field equipment to get the necessary financing. He did very well on the first contract, and almost as well on the second. But the third was a financial failure plus. The drill bit struck granite a few hundred feet down, and this virtually impenetrable rock forced him to take a year to drill a well which should have been completed in a month. He lost all of his earlier profits and all of his drilling equipment and wound up thousands of dollars in debt.

Our cars were sold, our house and furniture mortgaged. He leased a smaller rig, and went into the business of pulling pipe from abandoned wells. But the cycle of mild successes and whopping failures still pursued him. Two jobs made money, the third was a break-even, the fourth put him out of business, his credit ruined and more deeply in debt than ever.

He set himself up as a rig (derrick) building contractor—an enterprise which required only hand tools and labor. And here at last, it seemed, he was on his way back up. He squeezed the last possible penny from every contract. He oversaw his own jobs. He did hard physical labor himself.

But he was getting old, nearing an age when active participation in an exacting business would be impractical. And while he made some money on every job, it was never very much. With little but his time and experience to invest, his income was proportionate. To get into the big money you had to take turnkey contracts—i.e., you supplied all necessary material for a job, as well as the labor. By so doing you profited on dozens of commodities, instead of one, and your overall reward was large, if, of course, you figured correctly and nothing went wrong.

So Pop sunk everything he had and everything he could get into a turnkey contract. And his estimates were so sound that he completed it days ahead of the penalty date. He sent due notice to the contractee. The latter wired his congratulations. He would arrive the following day to inspect and accept the job.

Well, he arrived all right. But by the following day, there was no job to inspect. The first tornado in its history had struck the area. Splintered to smithereens, the rig was scattered over half the county.

With no capital and no credit, Pop became a dealer in leases, or, to use a contemporary and contemptuous term, a lease louse. There were thousands like him in the oil country cities. Middlemen of middlemen—men so far removed from the principals in a deal that they frequently did not know the latters' identities.

One would get hold of a lease on a short-term option. Another would assume the job of getting it drilled (necessary to validation) on a percentage basis. He had no assets of his own, but he knew someone who knew someone with assets, supposedly. And this last person knew someone who knew someone who would do the drilling for part cash and an interest. And the part-cash man knew someone who knew someone who could get workmen on a cash-interest basis. And—

But enough. It was not as funny as it may sound.

Sometimes, at the end of a transaction, there were a few thousands to split up between the dozens of "lice." Rarely, however, was a transaction carried through to a successful culmination. Somewhere along the way, as it moved from one broke broker to another with each snipping away a fragment, it simply disappeared.

One of the choice jokes around Fort Worth concerned a "louse" who turned out to be a dozen other guys. He put a short-time option into the mill. Then, knowing the ramifications through which it must proceed, plunged back into the milieu of someone who knew someone. After weeks of frantic effort the first deal seemed ready to bear fruit. All the principals and sub-principals and sub-sub-principals were to meet in his office. As he waited for them, his one worry was that they might not all be able to crowd into the tiny cubbyhole.

The time of the meeting came and went. Hours passed and it grew dark, and still the louse remained alone. Finally, the tragicomic truth dawned on him. No one was going to show up, because "everyone" was already there.

I could never laugh much over that joke, since Pop was the louse involved. He gave up his cubbyhole and became a curbstone operator. I looked him up one morning and asked him to come to breakfast with me.

He did so, rather coolly. He had been cool and formal with me for some time. At first he had argued sternly against my going to work at the hotel. Then, his affairs went from bad to worse, and my earnings were necessary for the maintenance of the family. Pop's attitude changed. He no longer argued.

It seemed to him, I suppose, that I had usurped his position in the family. I could not help it, perhaps, nor could he, but the fact remained. I was my own man. So be it.

We were like polite strangers to one another, rather than father and son.

So, this morning, we sat across from each other in the restaurant booth, dabbling aimlessly with our food and talking in monosyllables. And, finally, after a number of false starts, I managed to broach the subject that was on my mind.

"It's about one of the guests at the hotel, Pop. He's acted kind of funny ever since he checked in. Always watching me when he thought I wasn't looking, and making up excuses to talk to me. Prying into my background. Well, last night I took some cigarettes up to his room, and he opened up with me. I found out what it was all about."

"I see," Pop murmured absently. "Very interesting."

"Well," I hesitated. "The point I'm getting at—what I wanted to ask you was, did you ever hear of a man named L——?"

"L——?" Pop showed a little more interest. "I knew him fairly well. He was on President Harding's private train with me for a day and a night."

"What became of him?"

"No one knows. He was president of some corporation in Kansas City. He disappeared one night with more than a million and a half dollars of the company's assets—cash and negotiable securities. Why do you—?"

Pop broke off abruptly, his eyes suddenly sharp with interest. I nodded.

"He's here, Pop. It's the same guy I was telling you about. He's still got most of the loot, and he'll give it up if he's promised immunity from prosecution. He trusts you, more than he trusts anyone else, anyway. Can you swing it? I mean can you—c-can we make the bonding company give us a cut for—?"

I was afraid he'd say no, he was always so straitlaced and upright about everything. But he had been a lawyer and knew that such deals were made every day. The proposed transaction was entirely legitimate, he said, and he became almost as excited over it as I was.

"What's his room number? I'll call him right now, and tell him—"

"He's checked out," I said. "He moved out of the hotel as soon as he'd talked to me, and I don't know where he went to. But we made arrangements for us to meet him tonight. How much would we make on the deal, Pop? Five or ten thousand?"

Pop laughed fondly. "Somewhat more than that," he said. "Ten per cent is the usual fee for a negotiator, and I imagine the bonding company would be very happy to pay it. In other words, if L—— has as much as a million and a half left, we should get—"

"A hundred and fifty grand? Wow!"

We talked and talked, becoming really friendly for the first time in months. I confessed that along with being pretty stubborn and hard to handle I had been drinking far too much—that anything at all was too much for a boy my age. Pop confessed that his own behavior left much to be desired, and declared he was turning over a new leaf. Things would be different with us from now on. He'd get into some safe but reasonably profitable branch of the oil business. I'd quit the hotel and concentrate on school—get out of high school some way, and go on to college.

Pop and I agreed that it was best to say nothing to Mom about the impending deal. Not too worldly wise, it would only worry her.

We ran through the arrangements for meeting that night, making sure we had them right. Then, since it was far too late for me to go to school, I went on home.

Mom was pretty cranky with me. Unlike Pop, she did not feel that my financial contributions to the family exempted me from parental dominion. She wanted to know why I hadn't gone to school instead of "loafing around town." And she obviously did not at all care for the evasive answers I gave her.

She scolded and fussed, until at last there was nothing left to say and she was as weary as I. I went to bed, then, telling her to call me at seven as I wished to see a show before going to work.

I was supposed to meet L—— at eight-thirty on the bridge over the North Trinity River. He would pick me up in a car, providing I was alone and he deemed it safe, and we would drive on into the packing-town section of Fort Worth. At nine-thirty, still providing that L—— was given no cause for alarm, we would pick Pop up in an isolated area. They would then exchange commitments, as attorney and client, and the details of the transaction would be worked out.

Well, Mom did not call me at seven, but at nine. She said that if I was too tired to go to school, I was too tired to go to shows. It was ten o'clock before I got to the bridge, an hour and a half late for my appointment with the suspicious, badly frightened L——.

It was too late, of course. I waited for him until it was almost one, making myself seriously late for work, but he never showed up. Where he went to or what became of him, I do not know.

I was sick with disappointment, and the blow was a crushing one for Pop. As for Mom, well, what was the use in telling her the truth—that the two hours of sleep she had forced on me had cost more than one thousand dollars a minute?

# XXII

ON WEEK DAYS I went from work to school and remained in class until three-thirty in the afternoon. It was usually five or six o'clock before I could get to bed, and I had to rise at nine-thirty in order to be at work on time. Obviously, I did not get much sleep. Daytime sleep is apt to be an uneasy thing, achieved in spats and spurts which leave one wakeful but unrested. Frequently, during the dazzlingly hot Texas summer, I went whole days with no sleep at all.

Being of very hardy stock, I seemed little affected by my rigorous near-sleepless life for more than two years. But it was telling on me. I had acquired a persistent and annoying cough. My appetite was almost non-existent. I was drinking more and more, so much so that I was buying pints and quarts instead of depending on free drinks from guests.

Also, although the fact was hard to detect on one with my wiry build, I was losing weight steadily.

As I passed my eighteenth birthday and entered my third year at the hotel, the hitherto concealed signs of illness began to break through to the surface. I was suddenly gaunt instead of merely thin. I had brief but frightening spasms of nervous trembling. My cough had a hollow echoing sound. I was filled with morbid self-doubts, and no amount of whiskey would completely dispel them.

Mom and Pop begged me to quit the job. In our circumstances, the suggestion seemed maddeningly foolish and I refused to discuss it.

Because I was supposed to be a "fairly good boy," the nominally hard-boiled management tried to give me a hand. The word filtered down from somewhere that I should not be fined or disciplined except on higher authority, and I should not be held over except in extreme emergencies. Moreover, if I chose to sleep an hour or so at night in one of the checked-out rooms, no one was to take notice of it. And whatever I wanted to eat within reason was to be provided at no charge by the coffee shop chefs.

I appreciated these favors, both for their intrinsic value and for the good will they reflected. But I enjoyed them no more than a week or two before I was forced to call a halt. They made the other boys too resentful. A man may survive with the disesteem of his employers, but let him be generally disliked by his fellow-workers and he is through.

My friend the assistant manager, he of the sensitive soul and the terrible temper, had shown increasing concern for my obvious illness. He always lingered for a few moments after handing me his hat, mumbling diffident inquiries as to how I was getting along and grumbling suggestions to take it easy.

"Better get off of bells," he suggested one morning. "Try you on something else."

And try me he did.

In succession, I worked as assistant night auditor, valet, food checker, telephone operator, elevator operator, steam presser and assistant maître d'hôtel. But in the end I came back to bell-hopping.

I believe that the challenge of so many jobs was good for me, and I certainly acquired much valuable experience. But I was not improved healthwise, and I could not afford the financial loss which the other positions put me to. They paid well enough, I suppose, but the amounts seemed niggardly compared with my bellboy earnings. So, half regretfully, I returned to my original job.

I dragged through the months, obsessed with a weird feeling that I was slowly falling apart. And though I felt pretty hopeless about it, I attended school faithfully. This was my last chance, I knew—the last year I would be going to school. Either I got out now, with proper scholastic credit, or I never would. My six years of misery and frustration there would be wasted.

Spring came, and suddenly I felt better than I ever had. I was eating and sleeping less than ever, coughing harder and drinking more. But still I felt wonderful. Nothing seemed to bother me. I was never tired, my mind had never been sharper. I was brimming over with good feeling, always smiling, always ready to burst into laughter at the smallest joke.

My extensive reading had not carried me into the fields of psychiatry and morbid psychology; hence, I accepted my feeling of well-being at its face value instead of as the euphrasy—the false elation—which precedes collapse. Persons far advanced in alcoholism know that feeling. So do tuberculosis patients, and those suffering from severe nervous complaints. It is Nature's way of preparing the afflicted for the ordeal of breakdown.

Being triply prepared, for reasons you may probably guess, I felt triply good.

On Friday afternoon of the next-to-the-last week of school, I paused at the doorway of a study hall, called gayly to the girl inside, then—moved by a sudden hunch—went in and joined her.

"How you doing, Gladys?" I said. "Keeping you in after school, are they?"

"N-no." She tittered shyly. "Everyone's so busy getting ready for graduation that they asked me to help with this stuff."

She was a bashful, dowdy girl, one of those helplessly homely drudges who knew everything in the books and little outside of them, and who would go through life in some minor, ill-rewarded capacity. I had known her in several classes, during my periods of self-promotion, and while I was a different type of outcast I sympathized with and felt sorry for her. Because she was shy and obliging, she was constantly being imposed on. The school employees were always dragging her in on jobs which they were paid to do.

"Making out report cards, huh?" I said. "Like to have me read the record cards off to you? You can go a lot faster that way."

"We-el—" She tittered again. "If you're sure you want to."

"There's nothing I want to do more," I said truthfully. And dragging a chair up to the desk, I sat down at her side.

I took charge of the record file, and began calling the names and grades off to her. Coming to my card, I made myself a senior and gave myself passing grades in every subject.

She looked up, a faint frown on her face. "I—uh—I didn't know that—"

"Yes?" I said.

"Nothing. I mean, I was just going to say how funny it is that people can be in the same grade and have different teachers for every subject."

"Well," I shrugged, "it's a big school. Incidentally, some of these record cards are pretty badly worn. I think we'd better make out some new ones."

I pulled a dozen odd cards from the file, sliding my own in among them. Somewhat troubled, she began making out new cards from the information I gave her.

I called out my name. I called out the class—senior, second semester. I started calling off credit hours.

Slowly, she laid down her pen and looked up again.

"J-James, you can't. You're not going to graduate, are you? The diploma list is already made out, and I d-don't believe I saw your name on—"

"No," I said. "I'm not going to graduate, Gladys."

"B-but—"

"I don't have enough credit hours to graduate," I said. "Just enough for college entrance."

"Y-yes, but—"

"That isn't much, is it? I've gone to school here for six years. I've made some of the highest grades ever made by a senior. But I still can't graduate. All I have is enough credits to go to college—if I ever have the chance to go. Does that seem like a lot to you? Do you think it's too much, Gladys?"

She looked at me steadily. Then, slowly, she shook her head.

"No," she said, "I don't think it's too much." And she picked up the pen again.

A new card went into the file, one of more than a dozen. It gave me fourteen and a half credit hours, one and a half short of the number necessary to graduate.

I took all the old cards with me, tearing them up on the way home.

Thus, I finished high school. Just before, figuratively speaking, I was finished.

I hadn't been home an hour when the good feeling rushed from me like water rushing down a drain. Then, after a long moment of absolute emptiness, my heart stuttered and raced, beating faster and faster until one beat over-lapped the other. Blood gushed from my mouth and I fell to the floor in convulsions.

Doctors came, although I was unaware of their presence. They administered to me wonderingly. I was eighteen years old, and I had a complete nervous collapse, pulmonary tuberculosis and delirium tremens.

# XXIII

FROM A PURELY medical standpoint, I should have died. In fact, I should have been dead long before. I seemed to be completely drained of physical resistance. Well over six feet tall, I weighed less than a hundred and ten pounds. And a good part of that weight, in the doctors' estimation, appeared to be scar tissue. My kidneys were bruised. My ribs floated. My skull had been fractured in three places. I had an incipient rupture. My shoulders were sprained so that the arms did not articulate properly in their sockets. My knuckles had been "knocked down," my fingers broken. Nothing about me was as it should be, physically speaking. As the doctors saw it, I had nothing with which to battle the diseases from which I was suffering.

Fortunately for me, I come from very rugged stock. On both sides of the family, my ancestors were a tough stubborn people. Migrating from England to Ireland to Holland and thence to America, they drifted westward from Pennsylvania—after the revolution against King George—and the farther west they went, the tougher and more stubborn they seemed to get. They regarded illness and injury as annoyances, and succumbing to them, weakness. Many had died violent deaths, few of any infirmity but old age.

So, while I was bedfast for several months, I lived. Because the will-to-live was bred into me. Because I was too stubborn to die.

My illness, and the financial crisis it precipitated, was not without its bright side. It forced us to do things which we should have done long before. We gave up our home and its furnishings, and moved into a rented house in a working-class neighborhood. Thus, we were simultaneously freed of oppressive interest payments and the necessity of maintaining "face" among people who had known us when.

We could live on half the amount we had formerly spent. We were free forever from our most avaricious and persistent creditors. Pop worried less and was able to move about more freely. He made several fast lease deals which, though small, were enough to keep us going.

After a convalescence of some four months, I was able to be up and about, taking care of myself instead of being taken care of. But I was still very weak and thin, and the doctors were not at all pleased with the state of my lungs. I would never recover, in their opinion, in the low, damp climate of Fort Worth. I belonged in a high and dry altitude, and the quicker I got to it the better.

So, early one morning, I stood at the edge of the highway on the outskirts of Fort Worth, one arm supporting an upstretched thumb, the other clutching a small bundle. There was a change of clothing in it, toothbrush and razor, a nickel table and pencils. That was about all.

A car stopped. The driver swung the door open, and I climbed in.
"Where you going, kid?"
"West," I said.
"How far?"
"A long ways. I don't know exactly."
"Lookin' for work? What kinda line you in?"
"I'm a writer," I said. And somehow my voice rose. "I'm a writer!"
"Sure, now," he said, amiably. "Sure you are."
We sped down the highway, and the sun rose behind us, warm, friendly, gentle, silvering the long asphalt ribbon to the west.

I spent more than three years in West and Far West Texas. A bum and casual laborer at first, an itinerant but solvent worker later. In the beginning, I thought it one of the most desolate areas in the world, populated by the world's most arrogant and high-handed people. Only harsh necessity kept me there. As time went on, however, I came to love the vast stretches of prairie, rolling emptily toward the horizon. There was peace in the loneliness, calm and reassurance. In this virgin vastness, virtually unchanged by the assaults of a hundred million years, troubles seemed to shrink and hope loomed large. Everything would go on, one knew, and man would go on with it. Disappointment and difficulty were only way stops on the road to a happy destination.

As for the West Texans, I became every bit as fond of them as I was of the land they lived in. They were not quite so much arrogant, I found, as plain-spoken. Their first say-so on a subject was also their last one. They said what they meant—whether painful or pleasant—and they meant what they said. No snub was implied by silence. It meant only that the West Texan concerned had nothing to say.

One day, a few weeks after leaving Fort Worth, I went into a store in the then village of Big Springs to buy a work shirt. The proprietor tossed one on the counter. The price, he said, was two dollars and fifty cents.

"What!" I exclaimed. "Two-fifty for just a plain blue work shirt?"
"You want it?" he asked.
"Well, no. I can't pay—"
"Reckon we're kind of wastin' time, then," he said, casually, and he tossed the shirt back on the shelf.

Red-faced, my ears burning, I turned and walked away.

I had reached the door when he called to me, still in that casually indifferent tone. I hesitated, then I turned around and went back.

"What price shirt was you lookin' for, bub?" he said. "Somethin' about a dollar?"
"About that," I nodded. "But—"
"Think I got one left. Yeah, here it is."
He took it off the shelf—the two-fifty shirt—and began wrapping it up.

"How about some pants?" he said. "That pair you got on is just about the most ragged-assed I ever seen."

I laughed unwillingly. "I guess not. They're pretty bad all right, but—"

"Call it a dollar for the shirt *and* pants," he said. "What size you wear, bub?"

He wrapped the two garments, tossed them to me and raised his hand in an indifferent salute. I thanked him, telling him I would be in to pay what I owed as soon as I could.

"Glad to see you, bub," he nodded. "Don't owe me nothin', though."

"But the shirt alone was—"

"It and the pants was one buck. I set my own prices, bub. Don't need no one to help me."

"Well, I—I see," I said.

"So long," he said, and without another word he slouched back to the rear of the store.

Thus, your typical West Texan—a man who might give you a mile but who would not give in to you an inch. They seldom smiled, those West Texans, and I don't recall ever hearing one laugh. Yet they had a wonderful sense of humor. Their wit was of a dry, back-handed sort, based in anti-exaggeration and understatement—delightful once you understood it, baffling and even a little terrifying to an outsider.

One of my earlier positions was as a "sweater" in an oil field gambling house. A sweater, as you may know, is one grade above a bum—a person tolerated by the management for making himself useful to the customers. He is allowed to sleep on the dice tables at night. Now and then, when he hustles a round of drinks or sandwiches, the players toss him a chip. The job is obviously a precarious one, and the man who holds it is usually the possessor of a large thirst. Hence, he is in a more or less constant state of anxiety. Figuratively, and often literally, he sweats.

This place was about twenty miles out of the county seat of Big Springs, and late one night it was raided by a party of deputy sheriffs. Players and house employees resisted furiously. The lights were shot out, and bullets, bludgeons and bottles crashed and thudded in the darkness. Unable to see who was whom, everyone began an indiscriminate slugging of everyone else.

I crawled behind the bar and eventually made my way out to the roof and down to the ground. Here I was grabbed by an old rancher who was loading his ancient touring car with casualties from the brawl.

"Give me a hand with these fellas, slim boy," he said. "Gotta get 'em in town to a doctor."

I demurred, at first, feeling more than a little shaky. But the rancher had thoughtfully "borried" a quantity of potables from the bar, and being liberally refreshed with these I soon fell to with a will.

We piled the combatants into the car, my companion merrily insisting that there was always room for one more, and roared off toward town.

The road was a former cowpath, now deeply rutted by trucks and filled with sinkholes and washouts. As the car bounced and sailed into the air, landing with bone-breaking violence, groans arose from our cargo.

The rancher frowned with annoyance. He increased his speed, and the groans increased. They became yells, shrieks, curses. Some of the awfullest profanity I have ever heard filled the night.

Grimly, my friend emptied the bottle he had been drinking from and handed it to me. "Bunch o' dirty mouths," he scowled. "Give 'em what for, slim boy. Make 'em quiet down."

"Oh, I don't think I'd better," I said. "After all, they're hurt."

"Fellas that yells that loud ain't hurt much. Give 'em somethin' to fuss about!"

"But they're cops, deputy sheriffs. They'll—"

"*Huh!*" He slammed on the brakes. "I thought they was sportin' fellas!"

Grumbling angrily, he took a shotgun from the floor boards of the car and climbed out. Sternly, he ordered the thoroughly revived deputies to unload.

They did so. He lined them up in front of the headlights of the car, examined them briefly and declared them physically fit.

"Danged ornery coyotes," he said, bitterly. "Buttin' in on a nice friendly game! Takin' advantage of a pore ol' man what can't see good! I'll learn you, by gadfrey. You want to get to town, start walkin'!"

It was ten miles into town, a greater distance perhaps than many of the saddle-born, boot-shod deputies had walked in their entire lives. Moreover, as one of them pointed out, it was almost impossible to see where one was walking.

"Hadn't ought to do this to us, Jeb," he protested. "A dark night like this a fella's liable to step spang onto a rattlesnake."

"Don't give a dang if you do," the rancher retorted. "Never liked rattlesnakes nohow!"

We left them there on the prairie, and drove back for a load of gamblers. More than three hours later, we passed the deputies as they limped into the outskirts of Big Springs.

Fearing repercussions, I was not very conspicuous around the gambling hall for the ensuing week. But my trepidation seemed unwarranted. The deputies dropped in for drinks and a hand of cards, amiably admitting their error in raiding the place. "Just plumb bit off more'n we could chew," they said. "Didn't have no idee they'd be so many o' you fellas around." Their attitude was, generally, that they had perpetrated a joke which had backfired on them.

And exactly two weeks from the date of the first raid, they raided the place again.

One man was killed in attempting to escape. Two others were critically wounded. Then, with the remaining habitués under arrest, the deputies took axes and chopped the gambling hall into kindling. All this quite casually—as politely as circumstances would permit. They had taken the joke that was played on them. Now, they were returning it.

Fortunately, I had stopped "sweating" the night before and was not among those present.

# XXIV

MY NEW JOB was with a salvage contractor, a man who bought abandoned derricks and dismantled them for their lumber. It was quite a profitable business, lumber being a high-priced commodity in the plains areas, and he paid his employees well. But none of them worked for him very long. Those who did not have the good sense to quit when they saw what was required of them inevitably fell victim to the laws of gravity.

I was put next to the job by a character named Strawlegs, a one-time banjo player and an all-time dipsomaniac. He brushed over the nature of the work lightly, emphasizing only the money to be made. But even had I known nothing of the oil fields—and I knew quite a bit—I would have known that the job was dangerous.

"You're dead wrong," Strawlegs insisted, "and I'll prove it to you. Grab ahold of that porch roof, there. That's right, pull your feet up. Now, you're all right, aren't you? You can do it, can't you?"

"But I'm only a few inches off the ground."

"What's the difference, as long as you don't let go? It wouldn't be any harder if you were a few feet up."

"Or a hundred and ten," I suggested sardonically.

Well, I took the job, needing money badly. And Strawlegs, who was then the contractor's only other employee, received fifty dollars for recruiting me.

My survival, during the subsequent several weeks, can only be credited to a miracle.

We would climb to the top of a derrick, lugging tools and ropes with us. Then, perched more than a hundred feet in the air, we would weave ropes through the crown block, and swing off into space. The ropes could not be tied around us, of course. They were wrapped around our waists in a half-hitch which we snubbed with our feet.

We would swing down to the first crosspieces, get a lowering rope around them, and knock and pry them loose at one end. Then, we would swing over to the other end, hang on with one hand and knock and pry with the other, eventually lowering the lumber to the ground.

There are four sides to a derrick, of course. Strawlegs and I each took two, always careful to work opposite each other. In this way, neither side became weaker than the others, and the great tower did not immediately react to the loss of its bracing. It was not until you were about a third of the way down, a mere eighty feet or so above the sagebrush and cactus, that weird and frightening things began to happen.

The giant legs of the derrick would start shivering, first one, then another, until they were all shivering in unison. Then, with ominous gentleness, one side would lean forward and the other backward, swinging you in through the tower or swaying you out of it. And just when you were sure that it was going to topple, carrying you with it, it would straighten again and lean over another way. When it wasn't shivering it was leaning, and when it wasn't leaning it was dancing, shimmying in a crazy cater-cornered way. Finally, as you neared the bottom, it was doing all three. There was virtually nothing to hold the huge beams in place, and they showed their freedom with such a wild swaying and pitching that it was all one could do to hold on.

Usually, we did not take out the last crosspieces. As the contractor put it, there was no use in taking chances.

We slid down past them, scurried out of the tower and cut the guy wires on one side. Then we ran, and the tall timber skeleton collapsed with an earth-shaking crash.

Because the work was always a long ways from town, Strawlegs and I usually lived on the job, setting up batch in the inevitable tool shed. Now and then, however, we had to or felt we had to go into Big Springs. And on one such occasion we got involved in a donnybrook. I can't say how it started, and I doubt that any of the other participants could. It was just one of those things that happen when too many men get too much to drink. Anyway, Strawlegs got a fractured skull out of it and had to be taken to a hospital, and I got knocked through a plate-glass window.

A party of deputies began collaring the miscreants. One of them laid hands on me and hustled me toward his car.

"But I haven't done anything!" I said, not too truthfully. "You think I like getting knocked through windows?"

"Shoulda aimed yourself better," he said. "Ought to been ziggin' when you was zaggin'."

"That's not very damned funny," I said. "I get—"

"And that's a fact," he nodded soberly. "You wanta move or you want me to move you?"

I was fined eighteen dollars for disturbing the peace. Then, much to my amazement, I was given three days to pay up and released without bond.

I passed the deputy on the way out of the courthouse. "See you soon," he said.

"Sure, you'll see me all right," I said.

"I'll see you," he said. "And that's a fact."

The derrick we were working on was forty miles from town. It had been erected more than ten years before, and the trail to it was so overgrown and eroded that it was practically impossible to see, let alone traverse. Even the contractor had lost his way several times, and wound up in another county. It was spring-breaking, low-gear going for a stout truck.

I was sure that the deputy would never find that trail, nor get to the end of it if he did find it.

The morning of the fourth day arrived. The contractor was off scouting another job. Strawlegs was still in the hospital. I was up in the derrick, rigging the ropes and removing shivs from the crown block, when a car came over the horizon. It was listing to one side, steam pluming from the radiator, and it clattered deafeningly.

It stopped fifty yards or so away, and the deputy got out. He waved to me, then sauntered up to the derrick floor, teetering in his high-heeled boots.

"Howdy," he called upward, and waited. "Dropped around to see your buddy yesterday. Said to tell you he was feeling fine."

I stared down at him. Finally, I found my voice. "Have a nice ride?"

"Tol'able. Left town last night."

"Well, here I am," I said. "Come on and get me."

"Ain't in no hurry. Just as soon rest a spell."

"Why don't you shoot me?" I said. "I'm a pretty desperate criminal."

"Ain't got no gun." He grinned up at me lazily. "Never seen much sense in shooting, And that's a fact."

He stretched out on the derrick floor and put his hands under his head. He closed his eyes.

I sat on a crosspiece for a while, smoking. Then I climbed up to the top of the rig and took the hatchet from my belt. I chopped at the edge of the crown block, sending down a shower of grease-soaked splinters.

He brushed them off, lazily, pulling his hat over his face.

I chopped out a small piece of the block, catching it in my hand before it could fall. I took careful aim and let go.

It struck near the side of his head, bounced into the air and landed between his folded hands. He sat up. He looked up at me, then looked at the piece of wood. He took out his pocketknife and began to whittle.

There is always a wind in West Texas. It blows relentlessly, straight off the North Pole in winter, straight out of hell in summer. It was summer now, early summer. The wind rolled through the derrick at a baking, dehydrating one hundred and twenty degrees. There was no protection from it. I had no water. By noon I was getting dizzy, and my throat felt like it had been blistered.

The deputy stood up, looked around and sauntered into the tool shed. Some fifteen minutes later he came out, wiping his mouth with the back of his hand.

"Like to have some chow?" he called. "A little water?"

"You kidding?" I croaked.

"I'll find a pail. You can pull it up on the rope."

He started for the tool shed again. In spite of myself, I laughed.

"Let it go," I said. "I'm coming down."

He was a good-looking guy. His hair was coal-black beneath his pushed-back Stetson, and his black intelligent eyes were set wide apart in a tanned, fine-featured face. He grinned at me as I dropped down in front of him on the derrick floor.

"Now, that wasn't very smart," he said. "And that's—"

"And that's a fact," I snapped. "All right, let's get going."

He went on grinning at me. In fact, his grin broadened a little. But it was fixed, humorless, and a veil seemed to drop over his eyes.

"What makes you so sure," he said, softly, "you're going anywhere?"

"Well, I—" I gulped. "I—I—"

"Awful lonesome out here, ain't it? Ain't another soul for miles around but you and me."

"L-look," I said. "I'm—I wasn't trying to—"

"Lived here all my life," he went on, softly. "Everyone knows me. No one knows you. And we're all alone. What do you make o' that, a smart fella like you? You've been around. You're all full of piss and high spirits. What do you think an ol' stupid country boy might do in a case like this?"

He stared at me, steadily, the grin baring his teeth. I stood paralyzed and wordless, a great cold lump forming in my stomach. The wind whined and moaned through the derrick. He spoke again, as though in answer to a point I had raised.

"Don't need one," he said. "Ain't nothin' you can do with a gun that you can't do a better way. Don't see nothin' around here I'd need a gun for."

He shifted his feet slightly. The muscles in his shoulders bunched. He took a pair of black kid gloves from his pocket, and drew them on, slowly. He smacked his fist into the palm of his other hand.

"I'll tell you something," he said. "Tell you a couple of things. There ain't no way of telling what a man is by looking at him. There ain't no way of knowing what he'll do if he has the chance. You think maybe you can remember that?"

I couldn't speak, but I managed a nod. His grin and his eyes went back to normal.

"Look kind of peaked," he said. "Why'n't you have somethin' to eat an' drink before we leave?"

I paid my fine. I also paid for a bench warrant, the deputy's per diem for two days and his mileage. And you can be sure that I made no fuss about it.

I never saw that deputy again, but I couldn't get him out of my mind. And the longer he remained there the bigger riddle he presented. Had he been bluffing? Had he only meant to throw a good scare into a brash kid? Or was it the other way, the way I was sure it was at the time? Had my meekness saved me from the murder with which he had threatened me?

Suppose I had hit him with that block of wood? Suppose I had razzed him a little more? Suppose I had been frightened into grabbing for my hatchet?

I tried to get him down on paper, to put him into a story, but while he was very real to me I could not make him seem real. Rather, he was too common-place and innocuous—nothing more than another small-town deputy. Put down on paper, he was only solemnly irritated, not murderous.

The riddle, of course, lay not so much in him as me. I tended to see things in black and white, with no intermediate shadings. I was too prone to catego-rize—naturally, using myself as the norm. The deputy had behaved first one way, then another, then the first again. And in my ignorance I saw this as complexity instead of simplicity.

He had gone as far as his background and breeding would allow to be amiable. I hadn't responded to it, so he had taken another tack. It was simple once I saw things through his eyes instead of my own.

I didn't know whether he would have killed me, because he didn't know himself.

Finally, as I matured, I was able to recreate him on paper—the sardonic, likeable murderer of my fourth novel, *The Killer Inside Me*. But I was a long time in doing it—almost thirty years.

And I still haven't got him out of my mind.

# XXV

WHILE THE DERRICK dismantling was dangerous, it was not particularly arduous as oil field jobs went. The contractor didn't hurry us. There was a chance to rest between jobs. We worked a few days, and laid off a few—a situation perfectly suited to a man who was not in the best of health. So, though I swore to quit daily, I stayed on for weeks.

Strawlegs and I were fairly well-heeled when winter came on, and we were forced to quit. Because jobs generally had to be scrounged for in the oil fields and transportation service was nonexistent, we bought an old Model-T touring car.

We odd-jobbed through the boom towns of Chalk and Foursands, then settled down temporarily on a pipeline job between Midland and Big Springs. The pay was fair—four-fifty a day less a dollar deducted for "slop and flop." The bosses were hard men, but they were not slave drivers. Still, I soon had more of the job than I could take, and so had Strawlegs. Neither of us was physically capable of swinging a shovel and pick for nine hours a day, seven days a week.

Winter was with us, however. We had very little money and no other prospects for work. The only thing to do, seemingly, was to stay here without working. So, after many inquiries and a careful study of camp routine, we did that.

The bosses assumed, naturally, that everyone in camp was working. It followed than that everyone would have earnings from which the dollar-a-day could be deducted, and no head-count was made at meal times. Thus, to eat and sleep free, it was only necessary to keep out of sight during working hours.

Immediately after breakfast, Strawlegs and I slipped off into the underbrush, remaining there until lunch time. After lunch we disappeared again, and returned for supper and the night.

Strawlegs was well-educated and had traveled widely and well before booze got the best of him. We both shared a deep interest in the nominally inconsequential, and could spend hours discussing the stamen of a sage bloom or the antics of an ant.

There were four hundred men in the camp—drifters, bums, jailbirds, fugitives from justice. Of necessity, such camps were always isolated and they moved in and out of counties as the work progressed. It was impossible for the local authorities to police them, so the camp bosses did the job. Sometimes they were deputized, sometimes not. In any case they dispensed a pretty fair brand of justice.

Gamblers and bootleggers followed the job, traveling in cars and setting up their own tents on the outskirts of camp. They were allowed to operate freely, as long as they did it at night and behaved themselves. The bootlegger's product had to be good, and his prices reasonable. The consistently "lucky" gambler was quickly spotted and eliminated.

More than once I have seen a boss ("man with the stroke") step up to a crap or blackjack table and order the proprietor to pack and get. There would be no explanation beyond, possibly, "You've got enough," or "knock off while you're able to." And I never knew of but one gambler to object. The words were hardly out of his mouth before a fist landed on it and a boot landed under his table, scattering chips, cards and cash to the wind.

One night two whores drifted into camp and were promptly ordered to leave. The bosses were somewhat more explanatory about this edict than others since "ladies" were involved. They pointed out that the men were generally a rough and ready lot who would certainly look upon the women as fair and free game. The two would get nothing for their trouble but exercise, and much more of that than they wanted.

Well, the women left, but sullenly. And late that night they slipped back into camp. The forty men in the first of the ten tents took charge of them. They got no farther, and they almost didn't get out of it alive.

As their wild shrieks ripped through the night, the "strokes" leaped cursing from their cots. They jerked on their boots, snatched up pick handles and advanced on Number One tent on the run. But there were only ten of them, and many of the men in adjoining tents sided with the occupants of the first one. The onslaught of the bosses was met with clubs, knives, cot legs and razors. As fast as one workman went down, his head split open by a whizzing pick handle, two more sprang forward to take his place.

But the pipeliners didn't have to win, and the strokes did have to. Otherwise, they were through in the oil fields. So, finally, they formed a ring around the mauled and hysterical women and fought their way out of camp.

The camp set an abundant table in the hundred-yard-long dining tent. There were usually three kinds of meat, even at breakfast. In addition to meat, the average lunch and dinner included a half-dozen vegetables, cornbread, biscuits and light bread, coffee and milk, pie, cake and fruit. But preparing twelve hundred huge meals a day under primitive conditions was something to test a saint, and pipeline cooks were very far from sainthood. Thus, despite good raw materials, the end product was not always good. And despite the variety and abundance, one did not always get what he wanted or as much as he wanted.

It was hard to get a dish passed. When it was passed, it was likely to be emptied before it got to the man who requested it. So the moment they sat down at the table, the men started grabbing meat, potatoes and cake—whatever was nearest them. And fearful that they might get nothing more, they dumped the contents of the bowl or platter onto their own plates. One man would have eight or nine pounds of meat in front of him, another a gallon of potatoes, another a whole cake and so on.

The flunkies (waiters) rushed more food to the table, refills of the original dishes. But these likewise were apt to proceed no farther than the men who grabbed them. They would simply throw away the remainder of the uneaten cake, meat or potatoes and empty the second dish onto their plates. Inevitably, much more food went under the table than into the men's stomachs.

The bosses did what they could to correct the situation, but they were never completely successful. The cooks—invariably hard-drinking, short-tempered men—grew murderous. They botched food, deliberately. They threw dirt into it. Sometimes they did worse.

One night we were served great platters of golden brown, "breaded" pork chops. There were so many of them that even the greediest men could see that there was plenty for all, and every man was able to fill his plate. Then, they cut into the chops, and the meat almost dripped with blood. It hadn't been cooked, only browned lightly on the side.

Outraged and profane yells rose from the table. Snatching up handfuls of the bloody pork, the men rushed toward the rear of the tent where the meals were prepared. The cooks stopped their charge temporarily with hurled kettles of boiling food. Then, before their would-be murderers could fully recover, the culinary staff fled the tent as one man, scampering across the prairie in their white uniforms and caps like so many overstuffed, outsize jack-rabbits.

I imagine that they were later picked up and driven into town by some of the bosses. At any rate, they did not return to camp, and a new batch of cooks was brought in in time to cook the morning meal.

## XXVI

By working as a team at the table, Strawlegs and I fared uncommonly well, and the abundance of food combined with the long days of rest did wonders for us. We moved on, when the job ended in mid-winter, very nearly broke but in better health than we had enjoyed for a long time.

We went back to Foursands. There was no work there so, after a few days, we went to the town of Midland.

We found no work here either, not enough to support us. Finally, much against our better judgment, we sold a third interest in the car to a man named Bragg.

I learned two very valuable things from this transaction. First, that when things get so bad they are about to get better; second, that no bargain is better than a bad one. The day after the deal was made we got work on a highline job, but Bragg would not allow us to buy him out. We were stuck with him, and if there was ever an undesirable partner to have in anything he was it.

He was a giant of a man, more than six feet six inches tall, more than two hundred and fifty pounds of almost solid muscle. And every ounce and inch of him was packed with unadulterated meanness.

Bragg publicly addressed us as "turds" and "turdheads." He would talk about revolting subjects at mealtimes, making us sick to our stomachs. He was forever knocking us breathless with slaps on the back or bumping into us in such a way as to send us sprawling. Then, he would insist on shaking hands —crushing our fingers until we were forced to grovel.

I remarked a few pages back that no one is wholly bad, but if Bragg had a single redeeming feature I don't know what it was. The nicest thing I can say about him is that he was a no-good, double-dyed, rotten son-of-a-bitch.

We had to live on the job, sleeping and cooking out when the weather permitted, shacking-up in the nearest tool house when it did not. Bragg bedded down on the cushions of the car, and covered himself with the side curtains. Strawlegs and I had to make do with our blankets. Bragg ate two-thirds of the food or more. He paid for a third or less—and sometimes he would pay for nothing.

It was always our fault whenever anything went wrong with the car. Bragg would neither pay for repairs nor let them go unmade.

About the only work Strawlegs and I could do was with the pick and shovel, digging the holes for the highline towers. Bragg, however, was skilled at several kinds of the work involved. He worked steadily—two days to our one. While we were often too hard up to buy cigarettes, he saved money hand over fist.

He would take the car with him on days when we were not working, returning at nightfall like as not with a broken spring or a blown-out tire which, of course, he blamed on us. Bragg's idea of a hilarious joke was to leave us out on the prairie all day, dozens of miles from town, without food or water.

Knowing of nothing else to do, Strawlegs and I stayed on—hopefully, at first, thinking that things might improve, then, out of pure stubbornness. Obviously, Bragg wanted us to give up and move on, leaving him in possession of the car. So, though it was a losing proposition for us, we stayed.

When the highline job ended in the spring, we suggested selling the car and dividing the proceeds. Bragg flatly refused. He was going on to the town of Rankin, he said, to an impending pipeline job. We could do as we pleased, but he was going in the car, necessarily taking our two-thirds with his third.

Strawlegs and I decided to go to Rankin.

It lay seventy miles to the west, and there was not a filling station nor house throughout the distance. The road was a rutted, red clay trail, stretching through a dry, sparsely grassed desert.

We had two blowouts in the first ten miles. By nightfall we were only halfway to our destination. We had to stop then, since we could not proceed fast enough for the magneto-powered lights to function. Pitching camp at the side of the trail, Strawlegs and I were allowed a little bread and bologna and water. Bragg took charge of the rest.

When morning came, he finished what remained of the food and water, and ensconced himself comfortably in the back seat. With his feet in our necks and nothing in our stomach, we continued on our way.

We didn't continue far before the radiator began to boil, and cursing us for the lack of water, Bragg ordered a stop. We let the engine cool a while, and drove on again. A few more miles and the overheated motor again forced us to stop.

Bragg got out of the car and hauled us out. Perching himself precariously on the front spring, he unscrewed the cap of the radiator and urinated in it. He stepped down, grimly, advising us to emulate his example.

We did, insofar as we were able to. But we had had very little water and the drying wind had taken most of that from us. For all Bragg's cursings and poundings on the back, we could not produce something we did not have.

We drove another ten miles, perhaps, before the red-hot engine again forced a halt. And this time there was another difficulty which called for water. Our joltings and the climate had loosened the spokes of the right rear wheel. Unless they were soaked and allowed to swell, the wheel would soon fall apart.

Bragg cursed us until his throat was hoarse. He grabbed us by the neck and bumped our heads together.

"Smart bastards," he grunted. "Just look what you went and done! Whatcha going to do now?"

"You can have my share in the wreck," I said, for it would cost far more to repair now than it was worth. "I'm going to walk on into town."

"That goes for me, too," said Strawlegs.

"Oh, no you don't," snapped Bragg. "You ain't givin' me your share—not now, anyways—and you ain't goin' off to town after water. We're goin' to carry it in, me and you turds, and you're damned well goin' to carry your share."

*Carry it!* We stared at him incredulously. "Carry the—*it?*"

"Carry the car. Grab onto it!"

Well, we carried it, the right side of it, that is. With Strawlegs and I at the front wheel, elevating the heavier section, and Bragg at the rear, we lugged the car the ten miles into town.

Strawlegs and I were more dead than alive when we got there. But, with Bragg prodding and threatening us, we managed to get the old Ford into a junk yard. The proprietor gave us ten dollars for it, distributing the money himself so that Strawlegs and I got our share.

This was not Bragg's idea of a fair way to divide things, but there was not much he could do about it. There were hundreds of pipeliners in town, men we had known from the last job. He could not get tough with us without becoming painfully involved with them. Moreover, I think he saw that he had pushed us just about as far as he could and that he would either have to kill or be killed if he didn't leave us alone.

So, he parted from us, with many curses and threats, and we never saw him again, neither in town or out of it. The pipeline job was not nearly so imminent as it had been rumored to be, and I imagine he decided not to wait for it.

With no work immediately available in Rankin, Strawlegs and I caught a ride to McCamey. An orchestra was winding up its engagement in the town, and Strawlegs had known the leader in better days. The latter offered him a job as a banjo player, and, at my urging, he took it. It meant the parting of the ways for us, of course, but that parting was not too far off at best. Certainly, I did not intend to tramp through the oil fields any longer than I had to.

Strawlegs was a very good banjo player, as, if you have guessed his right name, you know. He was also a very good little guy. On the last night of the orchestra's engagement in McCamey, he met me outside the dance hall and pressed his earnings to date upon me.

"You'll need this before you find work," he insisted. "Anyway, you've got it coming to you."

He then revealed that he had gotten fifty dollars from the derrick-salvaging contractor for recruiting me. So, seeing him conscience-stricken over the deed and greatly concerned for my welfare, I took the money and we said goodbye.

The hiring office for the projected pipeline was at Rankin, but construction of the line was to begin near the town of Iran, extending from there to the Gulf of Mexico. I went there, finding no work in McCamey and a hundred men for every job in Rankin.

Iran was far Far West Texas—a handful of false front buildings and a few dozen people dropped down in the middle of nowhere. The town had once been the center of a shallow oil field, but now there was almost no drilling activity. It existed largely as a stop on the stage lines west and as a trading post for ranchers.

Obviously, the residents had little for themselves, but what little they had they shared. They were a more sharply drawn version, an emphasized extension of their brethren West Texans. I was so touched by their kindness and reluctant to impose upon it that I stayed outside of town as much as possible.

With a few cans of food, coffee, flour and salt pork, I "jungled up" on a table rock overlooking the Pecos River, cooking in a lard can, sleeping with my back to a low fire. I was safe there from the rattlesnakes and other poisonous creatures which infested the area. Now and then at night I had brief spells of delirium tremens—a recurrent form which sometimes afflicts a person long after he has stopped drinking—but they were never severe. Almost as soon as I started yelling, the illusion of things crawling over me vanished.

I wrote a great deal during the days—vignettes, sketches of people I had met. Most of what I wrote I tore up. I passed the days writing, thinking, swimming in the river, eating and sleeping. So the long summer waned, and fall came.

Construction on the pipeline began. I was given the job of guarding it at night.

I don't know why. There was nothing about me that would have intimidated the most timid malefactor, and I had never fired a gun in my life.

## XXVII

A FEW YEARS ago, before I began to fight back at booze instead of merely fighting it, I was a patient in a West Coast sanitarium for alcoholics. I had become a habitué of such places, as had many of my fellow patients. By way of whiling away the time, we took turns at relating the horrific adventures which alcohol had gotten us into.

One man—an actor—had inadvertently crawled into the Pullman berth occupied by a heavyweight fighter and his wife.

A reporter had bedded down in a garbage wagon and was dumped into a penful of hungry hogs.

A writer, gripped by a fit of vomiting, had become lodged head and shoulders in a toilet seat and had to be extricated with crowbars.

One of the best, or, at least, the funniest stories was told by a Hollywood director, a sad-eyed little man who was given to spells of extreme melancholia.

For years, when he reached a certain stage of saturation, he would telephone the newspapers and announce that he was about to commit suicide. He really meant to when he made the calls, but by the time the reporters arrived he was always out of the notion.

The reporters and photographers became very irritated with him. The least he could do, they declared, was to scratch himself up a little or take a few too many sleeping pills, or do something they could make a story out of.

But the director adamantly resisted their pleadings and cursings and jeerings. Scratch himself? Horrors! He might get an infection. Sleeping pills? Never! They gave him a stomach-ache.

Now, the local reporters always had more than their fill of Hollywood characters, and this guy seemed to be a little too much to bear. They couldn't ignore him. He was an important man, and there was always the chance that he might decide to go through—or partly through—with his threat.

Every newspaper man in town was burned up with him. Along toward the last, the desk men were conversing with him somewhat as follows:

"Now, Bob, you've disappointed us very badly. I'm afraid we can't believe you any more unless you give us at least a little evidence of good faith."

"I will!" the director would sob. "Honestly, I will. I know I haven't done the right thing by you boys, but I'm going to make up for it now."

"Well"—the editor would hesitate fretfully—"I'll give you one more chance to make good."

The director summoned them late one night, deciding as usual, after they arrived, that neither death nor its approaches seemed attractive. But before the first trembling syllables passed his lips, the reporters grabbed him.

Cackling with insane glee, they begged him not to hang himself. "Don't do it, old friend! Please don't hang yourself!" they shouted. And they removed the cord from his robe and knotted it about his neck.

The reporters stood him up on the end of the bed and tied the cord to the chandelier.

They jerked the bed from beneath him.

The chandelier came loose from its moorings. The director landed on the floor and it landed on top of him. Stunned as he was, he retained enough sense to scramble under the bed and stay there.

"Of course, they didn't intend to actually hang me," he explained, relating the story. "But they did want me strung up long enough to get a picture. And I'll bet those heartless, cold-blooded bastards would have torn down every chandelier in the house to get one!"

The newspaper men spent some time in trying to drag him from beneath the bed. But seeing that he remained obdurate and elusive, and in view of the fact that they had accomplished their purpose of teaching him a lesson, they finally left.

The director emerged into the open.

He wasn't really hurt, but in his dazed and drunken condition he saw himself at death's door. He telephoned for an ambulance. The vehicle arrived and he was loaded in. It sped away again, eventually coming to a long hill. About halfway up the incline, the back doors flew open and the director flew out.

He shot down the hill on the wheeled stretcher. ("I was strapped to the goddamned thing.") By the time he neared the bottom, he was traveling at a really awesome speed. The stretcher swerved suddenly and leaped the ditch. It crashed through a barbed wire fence, ploughed through a fruit orchard and came to rest finally more than a hundred yards from the highway.

The director got the straps unloosened and staggered back to the road. His pajamas in tatters, and much of his epidermis as well, he limped back to his house.

"I looked like a walking pile of hamburger," he said. "There wasn't a spot on me that wasn't black and blue or bleeding. Naturally, I called the newspapers to give them the story of my terrifying experience. They told me to drop dead. I called the hospital. I was going to have them verify the story to the newspapers. They told me to drop dead, too. You see, these bastardly ambulance attendants had lied about me. It scared hell out of them when they saw I was missing, so they picked the stretcher up out of that field and told the hospital authorities that I had refused to leave the house.

"It didn't mean a thing that I was virtually cut to ribbons. Drunks are always messing themselves up. So there I was with the biggest story that ever came out of Hollywood, and I couldn't get a damned line in the newspapers. That was the last time I committed suicide. There just wasn't any point to it.

Those suspicious bastards wouldn't give me a write-up if I *did* kill myself!"

I had no adventures which would top that one, but I recounted a couple, anyway. One occurred on the pipeline, as an outgrowth of my recurrent d.t.'s. The other . . .

. . . I had gone north to enroll at the University of Nebraska. I had had to leave Texas very hastily—for reasons I will reveal later—and I needed work immediately. I tried the two newspapers in Lincoln (the site of the university). I tried the university press and the branches of two syndicates. Finally, I tried a farm paper. And here the two young assistant editors, instead of delivering the fast brush-off I had gotten elsewhere, looked upon me as though I were something good to eat. They gave me the best chair in the office. They pressed cigarettes upon me. They beamed and cooed over me, nodding significantly to one another.

I should say that I was very well dressed. The hotel had expected its employees to dress well, and I had never regarded good clothes as a luxury. I had on a hundred and fifty dollar suit and thirty-five dollar shoes. An imported topcoat was slung over my arm, and I had pigskin gloves in one hand and a forty-dollar Borsalino hat in the other.

So the editors looked at me and each other, and they thought it "highly possible" that they could give me a job. Not right at the moment, but—

"You're enrolling in the College of Agriculture, of course?"

"Good God, no," I laughed. "I'm going to go into liberal arts. Why would a guy who wants to be a writer go to—?"

The editors started talking to me. No one, but positively no one, enrolled in liberal arts any more. A. B.A. degree had as little academic standing as a diploma from a barber college. The thing to shoot for was a B.Sc. in agriculture. There was a terrific demand for writers who knew agriculture. The government was snatching them up as fast as they graduated. There were splendid openings on farm periodicals. Why, take their own case, for example. They were ag college seniors, and already they had these excellent jobs.

They insisted that I go out to "the house" for dinner to discuss the matter.

Well, I knew nothing of such things. I supposed that a bunch of them were keeping batch at this "house" they spoke of. It dawned on me, as we went up the walk of the splendid edifice, that I had made a mistake. But I didn't know how to get out of it. I still didn't know, hours later, after I had been wined and dined and talked to so much by so many that my head was swimming.

It was the traditional fraternity "rush" and it rushed me right off my feet. They pledged me to the house. They enrolled me in the College of Agriculture. And that was the beginning of one of the most God-awful periods in my harried and exasperating career.

The students were assumed to have a sound general knowledge of farming which I didn't have. I had been too young during my several years on farms to learn anything. Furthermore, my hatred of cows was so great that I detested practically everything connected with farming.

My "brothers" could get me no jobs, naturally. I had to get my own, and plenty of them, to keep up my fraternity assessments. The brothers had all they could do, and then some, to keep me from flunking out.

They didn't mind losing my company, understand, they could have done very well without that. But the house treasury couldn't afford to lose the income which I represented. They had to keep me in the fraternity, hence they had to keep me from flunking.

Like most fraternities, the house had exhaustive files of examination papers, extending back for decades. There were also files on the various faculty members, complete dossiers of their likes, dislikes and eccentricities. So, while one group of brothers worked on me, another turned the heat on my instructors. Wherever they went, the poor devils were surrounded by earnest young men pleading my cause so persistently and insistently that it was impossible to say no to them.

There was one man, however, who did say no—loudly, emphatically and repeatedly. He was a little Italian, an exchange professor in pathology, and he had been sore at me ever since I had dropped my fountain pen into a sixty-pound churn of butter. He said that since it was impossible to dissect me (which he really wanted to do), the next best thing was to flunk me.

He was a hard guy, but the brothers had dealt with these tough babies before. And when, as promised, he flunked me on the mid-term final, they gave him the works. The entire membership of the fraternity turned the heat on him.

The house was powerful on the campus, and the result of the "works" was nothing less than astounding. The professor's mildest jokes in class were greeted with wildly appreciative laughter. His most inane remarks were applauded as pearls of wisdom. He was literally carried about the campus by a horde of young men whose admiration for him was equalled only by their praise of Italy.

The professor began to weaken. They gave him the "killer punch." He was made the guest of honor at a house dinner, and every brother stood up, one at a time, and sang his praises for a minimum ten minutes.

At midnight they chauffeured him home, so flushed with pleasure that his face looked like a beet. And when the escorting party returned, I was informed that I was "in." I was to be given a new examination on the morrow, and I would be certain to pass it.

The news obviously called for a celebration, and we had one. I had a terrific hangover the next morning when I presented myself to the professor.

He was all smiles and mysterious grimaces. Wiggling his eyebrows significantly, he whispered that we would go downtown for the examination. "A ver' fine place, I know," he giggled. "A frien', he has so kin'ly let me use it. Here, where there ees so mooch pipples—"

I had never been able to understand him well—one of the many reasons he had disliked me—but I thought I saw his point. It was Saturday, and a great many students were around. If anything unorthodox was to be done, it was best to do it elsewhere.

We went downtown to a building largely occupied by governmental agencies. At the tenth floor, we walked down the dark corridor to a door near the end. There was no sign on it except an abbreviation as incomprehensible in my fuzzy state as it was uninteresting, and an arrow indicating that the entrance proper was elsewhere. The professor unlocked the door and waved me inside.

The shades were drawn and the room was quite dark. Judging by the heavy leather chairs and the rows of glass-shelved bookcases it was some kind of law office. He led me into an adjoining room, equipped only with a table and several chairs, and turned on the light.

"Ver' nice, yes?" He raised his eyebrows at me. "Zis way there is no complaint. You pass examination—ver' steef. You do it, I do not'ing."

"Yeah," I said. "I guess that's right."

"I lock doors so ees no distorbance. Two hours, yes, I come back."

He left by the door of the other room. I unlimbered the pint of whiskey in my pocket and had a hair of the dog. Sitting down at the table, I took out the list of examination questions.

And I almost fell out of my chair.

I didn't know what had happened—whether he had over-estimated my abilities or given me the wrong set of questions, or whether he had decided to play a cruel joke on the brothers and me. But I knew I could never pass this examination. I didn't know the answer to a single question.

I took another long drink, trying to think. I took two more drinks. If I could get in touch with the house, put one of the brothers to work on the cram file—

I looked around the room. I glanced into the other one. No telephone and the doors were locked. I paced back and forth fretfully, too worried to give the professor the cursing he deserved.

I raised the shade and the window, and looked out.

The room faced on a court. Cater-cornered to my window, some five feet away, was another. It was glazed and only raised a few inches, so I could not see what it opened into. But it seemed to me it should be a corridor.

I studied it thoughtfully, raising the bottle again. I came to a decision.

I couldn't jump or step across to that window, but it would be an easy fall-over—a trick I had learned in my derrick-salvaging days. If I didn't make it, of course, if I should slip or miss—

But I had done harder fall-overs before and almost as high up, high enough up to be fatal if I had fallen. Height didn't mean anything in itself. A trick could be done as easily at a hundred feet as at ten.

I climbed out on the ledge, crouching. I straightened until I was almost erect. Feet braced, arms outstretched, I let myself fall.

There was a split second when I was holding on with nothing but my heels, staring down into empty space. Then, my hands smacked down on the wooden base of the window and my fingers gripped the inside.

I raised my head and peered in.

It wasn't a corridor but a restroom. I was looking at an angle into one of the stalls. An elderly woman—a char apparently—was seated on the toilet.

She looked at me. I looked at her. She blinked absently and shook her head. She took off her glasses and blew on them.

I eased my hands back out of the window to the brick ledge outside. Suspended in an aching, shaking arc, holding on with my toes and fingertips, I waited.

And waited.

And waited.

I couldn't go back. I couldn't go on. I could, of course, but the old gal might drop dead. She undoubtedly would scream her head off. And how could anyone explain a deal like this—crawling through the tenth-floor window of a women's john?

I think I have never heard a sweeter sound than the flushing of that toilet. Unless, that is, it was the click of the hall door as it closed behind her. She had gone without coming near the window. Apparently, she distrusted her eyes as much as she seemed to.

I gripped the inside of the window again, and pulled myself up on the ledge. But I couldn't go on with my plan. The woman was probably working in the corridor, or I might run into someone else. Anyway, I just didn't have the heart for it.

I repeated my fall-over, returning to the room I had come from. I sank down at the table and killed the rest of the bottle.

I was seated there, half-dozing, when the professor arrived.

"We are all feenished, eh? We are . . . Mis-ter Tomseen, where is . . . You have wreet-en noth-eeng!"

"Not a damned noth-eeng," I nodded surlily. "What'd you expect?"

"What deed I"—he chocked. His eyes began to bulge. "Mister Tom-seen, why do you theenk I—what do you think this ees?" He waved his arms wildly, the gesture encompassing the other room and the abbreviated legend on the door. "What, Mis-ter Tom-seen? You cannot read, no? You have no eyes, yes?"

He glared. I stared. And, slowly, the terrible truth dawned on me. A friend of his . . . A governmental agency . . . And what kind of agency would a friend of his—?

"Oh," I groaned. "Oh, *no!*"

"Yes, Mis-ter Tom-seen. Oh, yes. A babe in arms, no. A drooling idiot, no. They could not do it, too smart they would be. But you—*you*—*!*"

Me, I had done it. I had failed a pathology examination in a pathology *library!*

. . . Now, back to the pipeline.

# XXVIII

STRETCHED OUT ALONG the big ditch, and moving farther and farther into the wilderness as the line progressed, were several hundred thousand dollars' worth of equipment and supplies. There were two ditches, twenty electric generators, a dragline, trucks and tractors. There were gasoline and oil dumps, bins of tires, tubes, spark plugs and a hundred other accessories.

It was my job to guard this stuff.

All night long I tramped up and down the ditch, walking the line above the Pecos at one point. I carried a weather-proof gasoline lantern and a repeating rifle. My instructions were literally to "shoot any son-of-a-bitch that shows his face and ask questions afterward."

I rather liked the job in the beginning. The days were still long, and even at midnight there was a friendly semi-twilight over the prairie. By standing on top of a ditching machine, I could see from one end of the job to the other. Very little walking was necessary, and when I did walk it was with comparative safety. I could see and avoid the rattlesnakes, the tarantulas and the great twelve-inch centipedes who considered this area their own private domain.

These things had been bad enough before the coming of the pipeline, but with its advent they seemed to have gotten ten times worse. They weren't any more numerous, of course, but they were considerably more active. The reverberations of the machinery shook them in their subterranean apartments. Dynamite blasted out great sections of their cities. The ditches scooped them up—there was one nest of a hundred and sixty rattlesnakes—and hurled them out upon the prairie.

Naturally, they didn't like this a damned bit.

The more foolhardy and determined of them gave battle on the spot: this was their home and they did not intend to be dispossessed. The majority, however, preferred to bide their time. They vanished among the sage and rock, waiting until the earth-shaking machinery stilled its clatter and the sun went down. Then, they came swarming back to seek their former dwelling places and to scare hell out of me.

Having no place to hibernate, they became increasingly active and aggravated as the days shortened and cold weather set in. They crept under the canvas jackets of the generators. They hid in the recesses of machinery. They moved endlessly up and down the line, creeping into the joints of pipe, crawling under the curves of the gasoline drums. I was safe from them nowhere, neither on the ground nor up on the machinery.

I had thought I was completely rid of the d.t.'s—the illusions of crawling things. Now, they came back and with increased frequency and intensity.

I fought them in the only way I knew how. I would force myself to walk straight toward the spiders and snakes that loomed in the light of my lantern. Sometimes they would melt away under my boots, and sometimes they would not. Instead of vanishing, a diamond-shaped head would lash out venomously, or a ball of centipedes would explode and swarm up my legs. I would drop my lantern and run, brushing hysterically at myself—run and run, shrieking, until I could run no more.

I gave up fighting. Too often an apparent illusion became reality. I tried to get transferred to a day job, but it was no soap. They could get no one to take my place.

Every morning I told myself that I couldn't take another night. But every night I came back. I had waited all summer for the line to start, and it seemed a shame to quit now. Also, I had invested heavily in winter clothes which would be of no use to me on another job.

So I hung on, night after night, and every night was more agonizing and fearful than its predecessor.

A tarantula bite is not fatal, I understand, only painful. But these evil-looking spiders terrified me more than any of their nightmarish colleagues. They grew to the size of a soup plates, and they were furred like rabbits. They could leap like rabbits, too, a dozen feet or more. And they invariably would leap at anything that showed up in the darkness— the lantern, my face and hands.

I never saw one of them alone. There was always at least a pair of them, marching side by side, and sometimes there were squadrons. I lived in mortal fear of them.

Late one night, I was walking the line across the Pecos, moving cautiously to preserve my balance on the snow-covered pipe. I had reached a point about mid-stream when, looking ahead, I saw a double file of pie-shaped blots—a squadron of tarantulas marching straight toward me.

I knew it was an illusion, but—but nothing If a thing exists in a man's mind, it exists. My heart began to pound wildly. I choked up with terror I turned around and started to head back toward the other bank. There, marching toward me from that direction, was another tarantula squadron.

I let out a wild yell and plunged from the pipe.

I fell thirty feet, smashing through the ice-sheathed river and going all the way to the bottom. Fortunately, it was not wide at that point, and despite my heavy boots and layers of thick clothing I managed to get to shore.

Soaked to the skin, I scrambled up the bank and cranked up a generator. I jumped the spark on a plug, got a fire started and rigged up a makeshift shelter with canvas. I huddled in it, hugging the fire while my clothes dried, shivering, miserable, but thoughtful.

I had gotten over my illness. Now, and for some time, I had been going downhill again. No job was worth that, and certainly this one was not.

It was time to pull out—to get completely out of the oil fields. My destiny wasn't here. I had never intended it to be. The West had been good to me, but it had done all it could. Now, it was my turn to do something, and something much better than what I had been doing.

My clothes dried. Dawn spread over the prairie. I kicked out the fire, walked into camp and quit.

# XXIX

I RETURNED TO Fort Worth in the winter of 1928. Except for the fact that
Maxine had married, everything was about the same or more so. Pop was
earning practically nothing. The family was barely skimping by.

I applied for a job at the hotel and was turned down flatly. The assistant
managers and bell captains I had known were gone. The a.m. I applied to liked
neither my appearance or my record.

"Nothing for you," he said curtly. "You've been in too much trouble around
here. Anyway, you're too big to be hopping bells. A fellow as big as you ought
to be out heaving coal."

"It doesn't have to be bell-hopping," I said, my face turning red. "I can hold
almost any job around a hotel."

"Sorry."

"I'll tell you something," I said. "I think you're too little to be an assistant
manager."

He grinned, coldly, and walked away.

I thought he had acted pretty ornery, but I couldn't greatly disagree with
him on the point of my size. When I first went to work at the hotel, I had been
well under six feet. Now, I was six feet four. While I was still underweight my
broadened shoulders gave me the appearance of massiveness.

I was pretty self-conscious about my size. There were few other hotel jobs
worth having, but I hadn't really wanted to hop bells. I was too big. Being a
menial contrasted unpleasantly with the rugged independence of my recent
years.

But I had to have a job, and quickly. So, unable to find anything else, I went
to work in a chain grocery.

Theoretically, the work week was a mere seventy-four hours. Seven to seven
on weekdays and seven to nine on Saturdays. The actuality, however, was
something else. One had to arrive at six during the week to have the store ready
for its seven o'clock opening, and at least another hour was spent in cleaning
up and closing up at night. On Saturday, the biggest business day, one came
to work at five and was lucky to get away in the early hours of Sunday
morning. Sunday, or what remained of it, was usually spent at sales meetings,
refurbishing the store or in taking inventory.

My salary was eighteen dollars a week.

I learned a very valuable lesson from this outfit, i.e., the longer the application blank, the worse the employer. This company insisted on knowing everything even remotely concerned with a prospective employee—everything from
the size of his shoes to the religious and political preferences of his relatives.

407

In fact, the only thing it was not interested in was how he could exist on a virtually non-existent wage.

Although it was obviously a losing proposition, I held onto the job, looking around for another whenever I had the opportunity. This finally led me to a meeting with Allie Ivers, who, since I knew what his attitude would be, I had hitherto avoided.

Allie had been permanently discharged from the hotel for dropping the baggage of a non-tipping guest out of a window. He was now the manager of a wildcat taxi service, a calling well suited to his superb gall and larcenous nature.

"You," he exclaimed, starting at me incredulously. "You are putting in a hundred hours a week for a lousy eighteen bucks? I'm ashamed of you, Jimmie! You can go back to the hotel."

"They won't take me," I said. "I'm too big."

"Keep on working in that store," said Allie, grimly, "and you won't be. They'll have you down in worse shape than you were before you went west. You can't feed yourself, let alone your family. You're about to be kicked out of your house and you all need clothes and medical attention. I'll tell you what's too big about you—your head. You think you're too good to hop bells."

"That's not it," I mumbled, although it was just about it. "Maybe I could have gone back, but I sort of told this assistant manager off."

"So what? You know how hotel men are. He probably laughed about it when he got off by himself. Anyway, there's two assistant managers and one sticks strictly out of the other's business."

"Well," I said, evasively, "how would I go about it?"

"How would you go about it," Allie mocked. "You stand there acting dumb and asking me. Get out of here! Get over there and get you a job."

I got out. I went over to the hotel.

I talked with the coffee shop manager and the maître d. I talked with a room clerk, a couple of the auditors, the chief engineer and the steward. I knew all these people, and had done favors for them. They all agreed to put in a strong word in my behalf.

Now, an assistant manager is held responsible for anything that goes wrong on his shift, and a great many things can go wrong if his key personnel so choose. Insofar as his position will permit, he must be obliging with them.

It was Sunday afternoon when I talked with my various friends at the hotel. Having been unable to install a telephone at home, I waited around the lobby for the results.

The assistant manager on duty was the same one who had turned me down. He saw me and started toward me several times. Each time his phone rang, calling him back to his desk. After the last call, he motioned for me to come to him.

"Been studying you," he said, his mouth twitching. "You don't look nearly as big to me as you did."

"Yes, sir," I said. "You look a lot bigger to me."

He grinned good naturedly. "Well, like to come to work tonight?"

"Very much. If I can get a uniform altered to fit me."

"You will," he said firmly.

And I did.

Out of the great mass of stuff I had written in the oil fields, I had placed two short pieces with a locally published magazine of regional literature. The rate of pay had been low, but, because of its high standards, it was considered an honor to appear in it. I responded promptly when the editor, having learned that I was back in town, asked me to drop in for a visit.

I spent the larger part of an afternoon with him. He was a kindly man but a frank one, and I was able to accept his estimate of me without resentment. I had talent, he said, and also that dogged persistence without which talent was worthless. But that was just about all I had. Whatever my skill, I was writing from motives which were basically childish. I was trying to "get even" with people—to show 'em I wasn't so dumb as they thought I was, and to make them sorry for the many slights, real and fancied, which I had suffered. I lived too much inside myself. I needed to write more—much more—of what I saw, and less—much less—of what I wanted to see.

I was not well read, as I had thought myself. Here again I had tried to "show people," to prove that I knew more than they did. I had read something of everything but never everything of anything.

The editor thought it would help me immeasurably to go to college. College would bring some order to my chaotic efforts at self-improvement. It would help to bring me out of myself. I would be placed in an environment where writing was not looked upon as effete or slightly ridiculous.

He, himself, was an alumnus of the University of Nebraska. If I could see my way clear to enrolling, it was just possible that he could arrange a student loan for the tuition, or, perhaps, a small scholarship.

I thanked him and promised to think about it, but the project was obviously impossible. Financially speaking, we were just beginning to see daylight at home. And summer was coming on—always a bad time for hotel business.

I told Mom and Pop about it, and they insisted that I should go, by any and all means. Pop could find some way of maintaining himself. Mom and Freddie could stay with my grandparents who, as you will remember, lived in a small Nebraska town. But I just couldn't see it. All we had was each other, and I would be almost twenty-three years old when the fall school term started. It was crazy to think about it.

But, I did think about it, of course. And very unwisely I mentioned it to Allie.

"Hmmm," he mused. "I think you should go, Jimmie. How much dough would you have to have?"

"A lot more than I'll ever get," I said.

"Maybe not. I think I may be able to think of something."

I met him the following night, and he had indeed thought of something. In fact, he had done a great deal more than think about it. I listened to his proposition, and told him flatly to go to hell.

"But what's wrong with it?" he inquired, putting on an air of great puzzlement. "There's big dough in it, and you don't have to invest any. What's wrong with selling whiskey?"

"It's against the law, for one thing!"

"So what? It won't be very long. Everyone knows prohibition's on the way out. Hell, you can clean up, Jimmie! You can get away with it where no one else could. You stand in good all over the hotel. The management trusts you, and—"

"They're going to keep right on trusting me, too!"

"You can wholesale—push the stuff with all the service employees. We'll see that they don't buy from anyone else, and you can hold the price up."

"Who's we?"

"Some of Al's boys. They're taking over here on the booze."

"Al? You mean—?"

"Uh-huh. That one. Incidentally, Jimmie, I don't think they'll like it if you turn this proposition down."

"They can lump it then," I scoffed. "Al Capone's boys! You mean Allie's, don't you? Get someone else to hustle your booze."

"It's not mine, honest." Allie held up a hand. "I'm not making a nickel on it. I was just trying to help you out."

"You'd better go back to stealing baggage," I said. "You're no good at lying any more."

I went on to work.

About one o'clock that morning, Mom called me. She sounded frightened.

"J-Jimmie. Two men—t-two men in a big Cadillac were j-just here."

"Yes?" I said. "What's the matter? What did they want, Mom?"

"I t-tried to stop them, but they came right on in. They left four cases of whiskey for you."

# XXX

I MET THEM the next morning, or, rather, they met me as I came out of the hotel's service entrance. Soft-spoken, modishly dressed young men, not a great deal older than I, they were not at all like the creatures which my study of gangster movies had led me to expect. We had breakfast together, and I felt encouraged to explain why I could not sell whiskey for them.

They listened quietly, without interruption. I finished my explanation, and still they sat waiting, staring at me steadily.

"Well"—I laughed nervously—"that's . . . you see how it is. I've never done anything like that, and—"

"What you going to do with the stuff, then?" One of them interrupted casually. "You can't sell it, what you going to do? How you going to pay for it?"

"Well, I—I—"

"You owe for four cases, ninety-eight a case. Call it three hundred and ninety dollars. You got the dough?"

"Look," I snapped, "I didn't order that stuff. You can come out to the house and pick it up, or I'll have it brought back to you. Any place you say. But—"

"You got the dough?" he repeated. "How you going to pay for it, then?"

"But I just finished telling—All right," I said. "All right. I'll sell this, but—"

"Good. You got a nice set-up there. Be good for ten, fifteen cases a week when you get organized."

It was like talking to a stone wall. They didn't argue. Their attitude was simply that there was nothing to argue about.

To be honest, I think I could have been firm at this point without serious danger to myself. I wasn't involved with them yet. They had too much to lose to risk trouble with someone who could appeal to the authorities with figuratively clean hands. They were paying off, of course, but no fix is ever solid. The purchaser is supposed to use it with discretion, to do nothing which will seriously embarrass the seller.

So, I had only to say no and keep saying it, and, I believe, the matter would have been ended. But despite a lifetime of pushing around, I had never developed a tolerance for it. And this latest instance, which had seriously frightened my mother, was particularly distasteful to me. It seemed to me that these characters needed to be taught a lesson, and that I was just the lad to do it.

"All right," I shrugged. "How much time do I have to pay up?"

"How much do you need?"

411

"Well, just getting started this way, it'll probably take me a week to sell it —all of it. Of course, I can pay you off a case at a time if—"

They didn't want to do that, as I was sure they would not. It would be too much trouble. Also, it bespoke a distrust which could be very unhealthy for the enterprise.

"We won't crowd you any. You have to run over a day or two sometime, why just say so. You play with us, we play with you. Later on, maybe, you can make it cash on the line."

"I couldn't do that for quite a while," I said. "Well, I could I guess, but—"

But they understood. I'd just been squeezing by. I and my family needed all sorts of things, and I was to go right ahead and take care of those needs. Naturally. That was as it should be. What was the sense in a guy working if he didn't have any dough to spend?

We'd wait awhile before going on a cash basis. Say, a couple of months from now.

We worked out the arrangements for delivery and payment. I went on home.

Pop was out of town for a few days, and was thus unaware of the previous night's happenings. Much against her will, I persuaded Mom to keep mum.

"I don't know why," she sighed. "I just don't know why it is you're always getting mixed up in something."

"I didn't mix up in it," I said. "I was mixed up."

"You certainly are! You're really mixed up if you think you can cheat those fellows. Honest to goodness, Jimmie, do you actually believe you can?"

"You wait and see," I promised. "I'll take those birds like Grant took Richmond."

The hotel was what was known in the trade as a "tight" or "clean" house. Bellboys returning from errands outside the hotel were always subjected to close scrutiny by the house detectives. If their uniforms bulged suspiciously, or if they were carrying a package of a certain size, they were almost certain to be searched. Whiskey was bootlegged, of course, in spite of all the hotel's precautions. But to carry out an operation of the size I contemplated was impossible by the usual pint-at-a-time methods. My base of operations, as I saw it, would have to be on the inside.

I have mentioned that a number of the lower-floor rooms were blocked off in hot weather. Since it was hot now, I purloined the key to one, using it as a storage room for whiskey which I brought in in inexpensive suitcases.

A supposed "guest" drove up at the side door and tapped his horn for a bellboy. I trotted out, removed his "baggage" and carried it up to my room. This same thing took place a dozen times a day with bona fide guests and baggage, so my comings and goings went unmarked, apparently, and while other boys had been caught and discharged and sometimes jailed for bringing in a pint, I brought in case after case. There was no trouble at all for quite a while.

I paid for the four cases promptly at the end of the week. The following week, having obtained a transfer to days, I sold six, and the week after that I sold seven. Each week I brought in a little more, paying up on the dot when the week was ended. In a very few weeks, I was handling and paying for upwards of ten cases.

Now, regardless of what my wholesalers thought, this was an enormous amount of whiskey to move in any hotel, even one that ran wide open. I had to re-wholesale of the bulk of it to other bellboys and service employees, taking a very short profit or no profit. And along toward the last, in order to get rid of the stuff, I sold several cases at a loss. On the overall transactions, of course, I made money—several times the sum I would have made at legitimate bell-hopping. But this was nothing like the amount which I might reasonably have been expected to make.

The money was spent almost as fast as I get it on clothes, on medical and dental attention, on a car which I had Mom buy and leave on the sales lot. These things and our day-to-day living expenses left me with very little surplus cash. "Al's boys" were scheduled to supply that—a quantity sufficient to travel on and to live on indefinitely and comfortably afterward.

The "boys" were just a little hesitant when, at the beginning of the week I meant to be my last, I ordered twenty cases. I had always paid off, hitherto, and I had an excellent reason for wanting so much, but still . . .

"This convention—you say it's going to be a big one?"

"You read the papers," I shrugged.

"How come you want all the stuff at once? Why don't you take part of it at the beginning of the week and part in the middle?"

"I always have got it all in at one time," I said.

"Yeah, but twenty cases. That's two grand."

"Well, let's let it go," I said, easily. "We'll have thirty-five bellboys working, and there's a chance I might be able to turn the whole twenty the first day or so. But give me five or ten or whatever you want to."

I got the twenty, but not without some uneasiness on the part of the boys. They hinted strongly that a substantial cash down payment would be welcome, and when I pleaded a shortage of money a partial pay-off for the mid-week was arranged.

That was fine with me. I wasn't going to be around by the middle of the week. If things went as I planned, I would work two days of the five-day convention and skip town.

I figured that I should at least be able to dump the whiskey at its wholesale price. Probably, with the house packed and so many boys working, I would do considerably better than that. With only a little luck, I should turn it for three thousand, or—if the breaks really fell my way—four or five thousand.

Anyway, it would be a very nice piece of change. Enough to give Pop a stake. Enough so that Mom and Freddie could live with me, when I entered the University of Nebraska, instead of staying with my grandparents.

The opening day of the convention was one of my long days—seven until noon, six until ten. As always, during the first shifts of a convention, there was very little fast money. The guests weren't limbered up yet. They were interested only in getting registered and cleaned up.

I sold two pints of whiskey at retail, and the remainder of a case—less one pint—at wholesale. That was every nickel I had in the world, a little more than a hundred dollars, when I knocked off at noon. I went home and to bed, intending to store up rest for the long hard grind I had ahead of me.

The whiskey would be reasonably safe from theft during these first two shifts, but it would not be safe after that. As soon as they got themselves orientated, and the booze market began to boom, every hot-shot bellboy in the hotel would be after the stuff. They would try to steal it from me, just as I was stealing it from my wholesalers. They would steal it, dump it and skip—exactly as I planned to do.

When I went back to the hotel tonight I would have to stay there—sleeping in the whiskey-storage room and never getting too far away from it—until I was ready to pull out. It would be tough, nerve-wracking. Almost thirty-six hours of staving off a three-sided peril. The wholesalers were suspicious of me and might become more than that at any minute. The hot-shots were out to rob me, the hotel detectives to catch me. The federal prohibition agents . . .

I had seen no signs of the prohibs so far, but that didn't mean they weren't on to me. Bushels of empty bottles were being carted out of the hotel every week. The management was getting alarmed. If the prohibition agents were on their toes at all . . .

It was too much to worry about. I closed my eyes and went to sleep.

About three that afternoon, Mom shook me awake.

"Jimmie! They found your whiskey. Prohibition officers!"

"Huh? What?" I sat up drowsily. "How do you know?"

"It just came over the radio. They got five cases, they said, and they're looking for the person it belongs to."

# XXXI

I WAS STILL half asleep, too drowsy for the moment to comprehend the true and terrible nature of my plight. As I recall it, I even laughed a little sleepily. Only five cases, huh? Well, that wasn't so bad. And as long as they didn't know who—

Then, it hit me, and suddenly I was wide awake and shivering. Five cases! Hell, if they had found five cases they had found it all! It had all been there in the one room. They'd only *reported* five cases, but they'd gotten every damned last bottle. Those prohibs—yes, and doubtless the assistant managers and house detectives—would be drinking my booze for the next six months.

They knew who the stuff belonged to all right. They'd just been waiting for me to get the cache built up good. Now, they'd knocked it over, and it was my cue to stay away from the hotel and keep my mouth shut. Otherwise—

But my wholesalers! I couldn't skip town now. I didn't have the money. And if I stayed here and couldn't pay them . . .! For all I knew, they might have gotten the news already. They'd think I'd sold fifteen cases, and they'd want their dough. Probably, since I could no longer work at the hotel, they'd demand a settlement for the full amount. The loss of an alleged five cases to the prohibs would be my headache.

I pushed Mom out of the way and snatched up the telephone. I called Allie Ivers.

He had just heard the news himself, and his alarm was every bit as great as mine.

"I'm sorry as hell I got you into this, Jimmie. I just thought you could play it safe and easy, and—"

"I know, I know," I said. "I laid myself wide open. What had I better do?"

"Beat it. Get out of town as fast as you can."

"But I can't! I'll have less than a hundred bucks by the time I gas up the car. I've got a thousand miles to travel, and I have to take my mother and sister with me and—"

"You won't have a head left on your shoulders if you hang around here. I'm not kidding you, Jimmie. If I thought it was safe for you to wait until tomorrow I'd have you do it. I could scrape up some dough for you and—"

"Forget it," I said. "I'll-I guess we'll manage some way."

I hung up the telephone and began flinging on my clothes. I told Mom to start packing.

"Packing!" she stared at me incredulously. "*Packing!* Are you completely out of your—?"

"Don't pack, then. Just get ready to travel. Pop can take care of the other things later."

Mom grumbled, but she didn't argue much. Without understanding all the details, she knew I was taking the only way out of a very serious mess.

She called Freddie from the schoolgrounds where she was playing with some other children. The two of them began to pack, and I called a taxicab.

I sped into town and got the car from the sales lot.

I had never seen it before, except from a distance. But Mom had always been a shrewd bargainer, and she seemed to have surpassed herself in this case. The body, the tires, the upholstery—all looked first-class. The motor seemed to be a little tight and sluggish, but that was only natural in a car which had been standing idle for several months.

Pop was at home when I returned. He was obviously displeased with the news of my bootlegging, but more concerned for my safety. I had to leave. The family was breaking up. It was no time for the reproaches which he must have felt like handing me.

We got the car loaded and made our farewells. Hardly more than an hour from the time of the radio news flash, Mom and Freddie and I were on our way out of town.

It was a scorching hot afternoon. We had gotten about five miles out on the highway when smoke began to rise from the hood. Before I could get to a filling station, some five miles farther, the motor was pounding ominously.

I got out and looked it over.

The radiator was full of water. The fan belt was okay, and the oil gauge stood at the full mark. I let the car cool awhile, then I drove on again.

The motor grew hotter, the pounding louder. Mom looked at me, frowning.

"What's the matter, Jimmie? Why does it do that?"

"We've got a flat crankshaft," I said. "It's been packed with sawdust and tractor oil. Now, it's working loose."

"Is it—will it cost much to fix?"

"It will. And it won't stay fixed. The bearings will work right loose again."

"But how . . . what in the world will we do?"

"Go as far as we can, then—well, we'll have to see when the time comes."

We rode on, and smoke and fumes poured up through the floor boards. The whole car shook with the pounding of the motor. Freddie stoppered her ears with her fingers and hung her head out the window. Mom snatched her back inside, turned on me furiously.

"Honest to goodness, Jimmie! What *is* the matter with you? This car's about to fall apart and we're practically broke and we've got to travel halfway across the United States and—and—and you sit there laughing! What's the matter with you, anyway? How can you do it?"

"I don't know," I said. "I guess I just don't know of anything else to do."